"only the
<u>super-Rich</u> |"
Can save us."

"only the super-Rich can save us!"

To Katherine!

Ralph Nader

Imagine to Envision!

[signature: Ralph Nader]

SEVEN STORIES PRESS

NEW YORK

A Seven Stories Press First Edition

"Only the Super-Rich Can Save Us!" is a work of the imagination. None of the real-life individuals whose names appear in these pages participated in or bear any responsibility for their actions as portrayed in this book. But we hope that they would approve.

Seven Stories Press
140 Watts Street
New York, NY 10013
www.sevenstories.com

In Canada: Publishers Group Canada, 559 College Street, Suite 402, Toronto, ON M6G 1A9

In the UK: Turnaround Publisher Services Ltd., Unit 3, Olympia Trading Estate, Coburg Road, Wood Green, London N22 6TZ

In Australia: Palgrave Macmillan, 15–19 Claremont Street, South Yarra, VIC 3141

College professors may order examination copies of Seven Stories Press titles for a free six-month trial period. To order, visit www.sevenstories.com/textbook or send a fax on school letterhead to (212) 226-1411.

Frontis art © Robert Grossman

Book design by Jon Gilbert

Library of Congress Cataloging-in-Publication Data

Nader, Ralph.
"Only the super-rich can save us!" / Ralph Nader. -- A Seven Stories Press 1st ed.
    p. cm.
ISBN 978-1-58322-903-3 (cloth)
  1. Philanthropists--United States. 2. Rich people--United States. I. Title.
HV27.N33 2009
361.7'40973--dc22
                            2009021712
Printed in the USA

9 8 7 6 5 4 3 2 1

This book is not a novel. Nor is it nonfiction. In the literary world, it might be described as "a practical utopia." I call it a fictional vision that could become a new reality. Some known and not-well-known people appear in fictional roles. I invite your imaginative engagement.

—Ralph Nader
Washington, DC
July 2009

To the Meliorists, their advocates, beneficiaries and all those who follow to broaden and deepen their pioneering footsteps in reality.

ACKNOWLEDGMENTS

The three pillars who helped in similar and different ways to bring this "practical utopia" to the readers are (1) Dr. Claire Nader for her acute observations and suggestions; (2) Joy Johannessen for her joyful and engrossing editorial contributions; and (3) John Richard for his surehanded review and production finesse. Stalwarts all.

Warren Buffett
Bill Cosby
Barry Diller
Phil Donahue
William Gates Sr.
Joe Jamail
Peter Lewis
Paul Newman
Yoko Ono
Max Palevsky
Jeno Paulucci
Ross Perot
Sol Price
Bernard Rapoport
Leonard Riggio
George Soros
Ted Turner

I n the cozy den of the large but modest house in Omaha where he had lived since he started on his first billion, Warren Buffett watched the horrors of Hurricane Katrina unfold on television in early September 2005. He saw the furious winds and the avaricious waters breach the levees to cover three quarters of the historic city of New Orleans. He saw helicopter video crews surveying tens of thousands of residents lost, marooned, or fleeing the devastation of the roiling waters. He saw terrified people isolated from their would-be rescuers, too distant and too few.

Deeply affected, he stayed home the next day to watch the nonstop coverage of floating corpses, people stranded on housetops crying for help with outstretched arms, chaos and collapse inside convention and sports arenas overflowing with human despair, human kindness, and human depravity. He saw the exodus of thousands fleeing along the roads to anywhere, mothers and fathers clutching their children's hands, sometimes whole extended families, all of them looking for water, food, medicine, any kind of shelter.

On the fourth day, he beheld in disbelief the paralysis of local, state, and federal authorities unable to commence basic operations of rescue and sustenance, not just in New Orleans, but in towns and villages all along the Gulf Coast.

How could this be happening in the world's wealthiest country, with all the tools of modern engineering and meteorology at its disposal? Where was the Louisiana National Guard? Deployed to Iraq? How could bureaucracies so contagiously prevent each other from performing the tasks for which they existed? Why were the rescuers mostly ad hoc volunteers, propelled to action by care for their neighbors?

Warren was shaken to his core, so much so that he postponed closings on two large corporate acquisitions. He hadn't had a clue about the ineptitude or recklessness or rottenness of the people in power, who couldn't seem to respond to a vast natural disaster after years of assurances that they were ready for any calamity. Even the poorest of countries buried their dead quickly. What must the world think of a supposedly advanced country that left bodies bobbing in swollen waters or rotting in the post-Katrina sunshine?

Warren felt a wave of shame that bored through to his gut, his soul. He had to do something personally, immediately, at least for the refugees on the roadsides. For now, the hardest-hit place of all, the Ninth Ward, was inaccessible. He summoned two assistants, one to drive him nonstop down to New Orleans, the other to arrange for truckloads of food, water, blankets, portable toilets, basic medicines, sturdy tents, and sleeping bags, all to be accompanied by as many public health workers as they could muster.

Twenty-six hours later, he and his convoy arrived at a scene from Goya or Hieronymus Bosch. Some two thousand people lined the roads—babies, children, parents, grandparents, stunned or crying or dozing fitfully, hungry and homeless and hopeless. Warren's relief workers quickly took charge. The physicians and medics erected temporary structures where they could mend the injured and treat the sick. Life-sustaining supplies were distributed on the spot. Canvas shelters were soon in place.

In the midst of all the activity, Warren was supervising and helping in the distribution up and down the roadside and into the adjoining fields. Word began to spread to the astonished families who thought the world had abandoned them. A megabillionaire from Nebraska had arrived with critical resources and personnel. The refugees watched in wonder as the renowned septuagenarian, in jeans and rolled-up sleeves, moved along the road, clearly in command.

Coming upon a family of a dozen or so adults and children huddled about a crude campfire, Warren reassured them and consoled them. He took their hands, hugged their trembling children, and looked into their eyes. The old-timers noticed that there were no reporters, no photographers, no television crews. A composed elderly grandmother cupped his hands in hers and cried out, "Only the super-rich can save us!"

Three days later, on the drive back to Omaha, straight north, the grandmother's words kept reverberating through Warren's head like a series of thunderclaps, each time eliciting outrage and flooding shame. But by the time the town car turned into his driveway behind the tall shrubbery, the dominant occupation of his mind was a deep, cool resolve.

He knew exactly what he had to do—now, fast, fundamentally, and unyieldingly!

I n a high mountain redoubt above the Alenuihaha Channel, seventeen megamillionaires and billionaires sat on a wide balcony overlooking the lush green island of Maui and the far Pacific Ocean. They were alike in only three ways: they were old, very rich, and very unrepresentative of humanity, which they intended to save from itself. The man behind the gathering, the richest of them all, was Warren Buffet, who had rented the entire premises of a small luxury hotel for that January 2006 weekend. All the participants either knew each other or knew of each other, and the canny Warren had made sure that any gaps were filled in by distributing professional and personal biographies beforehand.

As his guests watched the sun set, talking quietly and sipping their drinks of choice, Warren rose. "I hate to take you away from this splendid view, but we have work to do," he said, and led them downstairs to a spacious atrium, inviting them to take their seats at a perfectly sized round table.

Warren's owlish visage assumed a solemn cast as he commenced. "My friends, what brings us here is a common foreboding—a closing circle of global doom. The world is not doing well. It is spinning out of control. Its inhabitants have allowed greed, power, ignorance, wealth, science, technology, and religion to depreciate reality and deny potential. With our capitalist backgrounds, it's easy for us not to be beguiled by the plutocracy's self-serving manipulation of economic indicators. We know how wealth is being accumulated, defined, concentrated, and stratified. Why, four hundred and fifty of us have wealth equivalent to the combined wealth of the bottom three billion impoverished people on Earth.

"We know of the portentous and manifold risks we face, both now and in the future. The global environment is fragile, under severe assault. It is toxic, eroded, warming, and it's vulnerable to genetic engineering for short-term profit. Viruses and bacteria are subjected to increasing stress that yields deadly mutations, and weapons of all kinds are more widely and easily available than ever. Artificial intelligence is on a fast track to dehumanizing us. As a species, we are learning more and more but are less and less able to keep up with what's happening to us as human beings, and to our world, its land, water, and air. Many solutions have been proposed, yet even at the basic level of abolishing massive poverty and advancing public health, they are applied too slowly and haphazardly to achieve any real human betterment. And this at a time when we have more powerful global tools than ever before, because of the amassing of flexible capital and the proliferation of facilitating technologies. Never in history has there been a greater opportunity to effect change.

"For my own part, I must tell you that I am not the person I was a year ago. I've been thinking hard about what I want to do with my remaining years, with my capital, credibility, and hopes for coming generations. I have been described as the investment world's 'big bang,' and I do not want to go out with a whimper, if you'll pardon the cliché. I had planned to go on increasing the value of my estate and use it to establish a huge posthumous charitable foundation, but now I realize that's just a rationalization for continuing to do what I do best while escaping responsibility for what's done by others. Besides, why rely on the smug foundation world, which has brought forth so few innovations while spending trillions of dollars? Why bequeath to unimaginative people? I want to go out having advanced and implemented a grand design, and I want to do it now with the best talent available. I suspect that similar feelings are stirring in your minds and souls as well, and that's why I put out the call to you."

Warren paused, looked around the table, and raised his glass of Cherry Coke. "It's the beginning of a new year, my friends, and this gathering, I hope, is the beginning of a new direction for our planet. Here's to you all. The floor is open."

"Here's to you too, Warren. It's about damn time!" It was no surprise to anyone that Ted Turner, the "Mouth of the South," was the first to speak. "The world is going to hell in a poverty handbasket," he declared. "For years I've been trying to alert people to environmental disasters and overpopulation and the need to raise awareness of the peril so that nations will rise above their disputes and come together against these impersonal common enemies. Nuclear weapons did some of that between Russia and America in the recent past, and now inspectors on both sides are overseeing the dismantling of thousands of warheads. Maybe on epidemics, famine, natural disasters, and other frightful developments that trample national boundaries, we can overcome the lesser local hostilities that keep countries from cooperating. Lord knows I'm ready to do what I can. I've got plenty of time on my hands now that I don't have Time Warner on my hands," he finished with a grin.

Amidst the laughter that swept the table, Paul Newman lifted his glass of Old Fashioned Roadside Virgin Lemonade to second Ted's toast. "Warren, your call last month gave me a jolt of adrenaline the likes of which I haven't had since I quit racing last year. And I couldn't agree with you more about the whole foundation thing. Newman's Own is doing well, and the money's actually helping kids and their families, but only in the thousands. It doesn't cross the charity-to-justice line—the old palliative versus systematic divide. So I'm with you all the way on that, but I wonder if you and Ted aren't biting off a little more than all of us can chew—"

"Or gum," grumbled Sol Price, the acerbic mass-merchandising pioneer, who at ninety was the oldest of the group. He was once called the father of the retail model later imitated by Sam's Club, prompting him to reply, "I wish I'd worn a condom."

Paul flashed his famous smile. "Oh, come on, Sol, you've got more on the ball than most men half your age. But listen, what I was going to say was that Warren and Ted were talking about massive problems on a global scale. I'm all for new directions, but the planet is an awfully big place, Warren. Shouldn't we get our own house in order before we talk about projecting globally?"

"I was thinking the same thing," said Bill Cosby, "but national and international distinctions aren't all that clear anymore, whether we're talking about peace or arms control or my tormented ancestral home of Africa or WTO globalization and our loss of sovereignty. Whatever strategies we come up with, we have to remember that some of them may have global consequences, but on the whole I agree with Paul that we ought to focus our efforts here at home. Think global, revolutionize local."

Warren took a sip of his Coke. "Well put, Bill." It was the conclusion he had reached himself, but he wanted his colleagues to come to it on their own. "What does everyone else think? Is it the consensus that we frame our—what shall I call it?—our Redirections project to address the vast political and economic inequities of our own country?"

There were nods of assent all around.

"All right, good. Let's move on to the general principles and goals that should guide our enterprise."

"Here's a principle for you," said George Soros, who was a natural for Warren's group as an inveterate exhorter of his wealthy colleagues to be more socially conscious. "Whatever assets we assemble, whatever approaches and structures we decide on, we must advance them within open societies so that they can be deliberated, applied, or revised with the consent of those whom they are meant to aid. History has taught us that well-meaning impositions grafted onto the body politic or the political culture do not take readily and sometimes backfire ferociously. Believe me, as someone who's contributed nearly three billion dollars to further a global vision of open societies, I know what I'm talking about. For every successful movement like Solidarity, there are countless grassroots groups working their hearts out all over the world, but in the end they're crushed by the power of supreme global capitalism allied with subordinate government."

"As we saw for ourselves during the last election, George," said Peter Lewis, progressive founder of Progressive Insurance. "Between us, we gave something like thirty-five million to political

groups working for change, and what did we get? Nothing. Whatever we put forward must have a multiplier mechanism attached.
In this room we represent a net worth somewhere short of eighty
billion dollars. We'll have to multiply ourselves, as we'll have to multiply what George called the assets, approaches, and structures we
intend to advance. Otherwise, it will just be more of the same."

"Déjà vu all over again," Warren said.

"Oy, you with your baseball references," said Bernard Rapoport,
the effervescent "capitalist with a conscience," known to friends and
associates simply as B. "I agree with Peter, as may be natural since
we both made our fortunes in the insurance game. But I would add
a caution: we must challenge bigness wherever we find it, and avoid
it in our own efforts. Bigness is a curse. It is too bureaucratic, too
autocratic, too top-heavy in making decisions, too remote from the
ground, and too ubiquitous in our present state of corporate
socialism or state capitalism, as my friend Seymour Melman used
to say. Bigness is also too addicted to concentrating power, and too
inimical to competition and democratic processes. Our economy is
being crippled by all these companies that are 'too big to fail.' Bigness all over the world spells omnicide over time, to my way of
thinking."

"Mine too," Phil Donahue joined in. "And not only that, but we
mustn't come on as messianic. We need to find the common touch,
to be able to go with the flow as we change and redirect the flow.
People have to view what we're doing as an opportunity for better
days, as alleviation of their pain, anxiety, worry, and fear."

"You are so right, Phil. We must be seen as offering ways of nurturing happiness, children, dreams, peace, fairness, honesty, and
public morality. We don't want to be seen as nags." Yoko Ono
paused to take a sip of tea. "I have to say that I was very surprised to
get your call, Warren. I don't consider myself a power player, and I
really couldn't see myself hanging out with a bunch of super-rich
old men, but then I got to thinking. For decades I've been preaching
peace and the importance of spiritual and artistic values, and what
good has it done? Maybe you remember that a couple of years ago

I bought a full page in the *New York Times* and left it blank except for the word 'peace' in the center in small type. I didn't receive a single response. It cost me fifty thousand dollars, but I didn't care about the money. It was the silence that got to me. Really, the *New York Times* and not one response. So I guess I'm ready for something new, which is why I decided that a bunch of super-rich old men wasn't such a bad idea after all."

"How honored we are," Sol muttered.

Paul cleared his throat. "Speaking of artistic values, let's remember that a little drama and mystique can't harm our efforts. Color, sound, light, excitement, humor, fun, joy, comfort, a sense of striving, the right metaphors from daily life, paradoxes to pique interest, success stories that people can relate to within their own frames so that these frames can then be stretched."

"I'd like to pick up on Yoko's mention of children." The unmistakable voice came from Ross Perot. "My own boy is running my business now, so I have plenty of time for our efforts, and I'd like to suggest a major motivating approach. People tend to care more about their children than themselves, and will often sacrifice anything for them. Children draw out our better instincts and make us take a longer view of matters. Our country is mortgaging its future in many ways, not just with huge debts and deficits on the economic front. The deficits are piling up environmentally too. We are short-changing our children through the grotesque distortion of public budgets and wasted tax dollars, through the militarization of just about everything that relates to other countries and other peoples."

"As Ross says, we do need to take the long view, but we don't have a long time to take it." This from Max Palevsky, who had made a fortune as a corporate pioneer of the computer age and multiplied it during the dot-com revolution. "It is one rocky voyage on turbulent seas that we're embarking on. We were drawn here by multiple magnets of determined solidarity and purpose, and now we need a hard-core sense of urgency that must prevail over our other commitments. 'There is a continual dying of possible futures,' Juvenal said, and we can't afford any more such deaths. I suggest that we assume a one-year life expectancy for all of us—that is, we need to do what we're going to do as if there were only one year left on Earth."

A smile flitted across Sol's face. "The world runs: have fun running with it—that's always been my motto. We won't buy any green bananas, Max."

"I cotton to the idea of speed too," Ross said. "Some people believe in an incremental approach, building support over the years. We don't have that luxury anymore. The country needs a justice jolt! Now! It's in a deepening rut, with lousy leaders. Besides, the faster we move, the less likely we are to lose our momentum and burn out."

"True," said Barry Diller, multimedia dynamo. "I like the one-year timeline. It means a one-year sabbatical from my many business interests, but that fits perfectly with my inclinations right now. It's a move from success to significance. Never was I prouder than when I wrote an op-ed for the *Times* urging the FCC and Congress to make telecommunications policy as if the people owned the public airwaves—which they do. If we're looking for assets, the commonwealth assets owned by the American people are a great start. The people own the public lands—one third of America—the public airwaves, the trillions in worker pension trusts, the vast research and development budgets the government doles out, yet corporations control what the people own against the people's interests. If we're looking for Redirections, this is one giant Redirection of existing assets toward the common good. It's a matter of what is fundamentally right and fair."

"And when the super-rich emphasize fairness, people stop what they're doing and listen. They begin to trust, to believe in what could be," said Jeno Paulucci, founder of Chun King and other highly successful frozen-food lines. Jeno had started out as a fruit peddler, and knew a lot about fairness and what could be. "One place to start is taxation, where it's for damn sure that those inside and outside Congress who write the tax laws avoid fairness like the plague. Who around this table doesn't know that their net worth would be less than half of what it is today if it weren't for tax inequity?"

Sol roused himself. "That's right! For years I've been trying to get someone in Congress to introduce a small tax on wealth that would raise significant tens of billions every year from people like us. I have yet to succeed in getting such a bill introduced, even though I'm obviously not pushing my own financial self-interest. So to hell with Congress. Let's take matters into our own hands. What we need now are grand visions that are practical to achieve, such as the abolition of the raw poverty that afflicts tens of millions of our fellow Americans. It's not as if we don't know what to do. A living wage is the most immediate step, along with health insurance, technical training, decent housing, a reverse income tax, and good public facilities. A longer-range goal is capital ownership for the masses to supplement their wage income. These are all approaches that can in no way be dismissed as utopian schemes."

"On the subject of taxes," said noted attorney William Gates Sr., who was getting just a little tired of hearing himself referred to as the father of the world's richest man, "I'm sure you all remember my drive to preserve the estate tax. I learned a lot from that struggle, and I came away from it with a lesson that applies to all of us here. We can't stay behind the scenes. We've got to project ourselves and what we stand for in public, as public personalities, not through spokespersons or proxies or PR firms. If we're going to communicate our authenticity, we've got to be willing to speak and write, to debate and testify, to be questioned and cross-examined and challenged. An open society cannot be generated by a small 'secret society' meeting in private and pulling strings. If we're to be seen as educators, as possessing moral suasion, we can't cling to anonymity, as much as some of us would like to. To be sure, our affluent peers, in their myopia, may view our venture like they did the estate tax, as conflicting with their interests and our own, but that is part of our strength and credibility."

"I'd like to go back to Barry's notion of commonwealth assets for a minute," Bill Cosby said. "There is another commonwealth—the family, the neighborhood, the community, the service clubs. They all provide the critical support and reaffirmation of values that get people though their days. They've been hammered by our rampant commercialism—undermined, displaced, depleted—yet they're the building blocks for Redirection, already in place but in need of revivification. People find their identification, their comfort level, their rhythm in communities. That's what made my show so successful."

"You know, the DVD of your first season is still a big seller at Barnes and Noble," said Leonard Riggio, chairman of the chain, "and your new book is flying off the shelves. But if you'll allow me a slight redirection of the conversation, let's remember that we're business people striving to plumb new depths, scale new heights, and push new frontiers, and we need something that no one has mentioned yet, something we're all very familiar with—a capital budget and an operating budget. How much seed corn are we offering before our genius for leverage kicks into action? Obviously we want to be lean—no bureaucracy, no bigness, as B says—but we'll need emissaries directly accountable to us, and we'll need to 'project wealth' at the outset in order to secure the mass media when we want it. It was the projection of wealth that brought Ross much of his early and well-deserved attention. Appearances rooted in good causes and strategies do count, after all."

"They do indeed, especially the appearance of material success in this culture. It gives you the benefit of the doubt, it opens ears and eyes." It was unusually sedate language from Joe Jamail, virtuoso lawyer, known far and wide for his bold courtroom style.

"I've been wondering when we'd hear from you," Ted drawled. "Ever since we started, I've been expecting you to light into one of us about one thing or another. What's got into you? And the rest of us, for that matter. Let's face it, we've all got egos the size of Turner Field, but we've been agreeing with each other like Quakers at the meetinghouse. What gives?"

Warren permitted himself a slight self-satisfied smile. "It's true that you're a prize collection of strong-willed, nonconforming successfulists," he said, "but I invited the sixteen of you here for this first Maui roundtable out of hundreds of possible candidates. The choices were anything but random. My staff conducted exhaustive background investigations to determine intangibles such as temperament, ego control, knowledge, experience, determination, willingness to risk, circles of influence, degree of independence from curtailing loyalties and obligations, capacity to take heat, backlash, ostracism and rejection, absorptive capacity for new directions and subjects outside your range of understanding, track record in keeping confidences, and above all, moral courage. All of you have also expressed sadness, anger, disgust, fear, and hope for our country. With this kind of preparation, I was confident that our meetings would be characterized by a high degree of harmony and a—" Warren broke off, startled by what might or might not have been a loud snore.

"Yes, Sol, what is it?"

"Jet lag. Warren, please, a man needs his beauty sleep."

Warren consulted his watch, a Timex he'd had since starting on his second billion. "Thanks for the heads-up, Sol. I was so absorbed in our discussion that I lost track of the hour. We've put a lot on the table tonight for thought, response, and decision. If you'll indulge me just a little longer, I'd like to ask that we remain here for another hour in total silence, thinking about what we've heard and said and jotting down any additional reflections and ideas. It's a technique I've learned from some of my business partners in Asia and, like the prospect of hanging, it concentrates the mind wonderfully. I've used it with my executives to great effect, so give it a try, my friends, and then we'll retire for the evening."

Although a period of silence was an alien concept to many in the room, they all had too much respect for Warren to object. Every one of them had been at the edge of despair over the state of their country before his clarion call to action, but now they were galvanized, even Sol, who had been about to scoff and take himself off to bed when he remembered that in 1986 he'd bought stock in Warren's company at $5,000 a share that was now worth close to $100,000 a share. If it was good enough for Warren, it was good enough for Sol.

The next morning, after a breakfast of tropical fruits, the collaborators rejoined the dialogue.

"I trust you all had a good rest and are ready to take matters to the next stage, my friends," Warren said. "First, let me ask what reflections and ideas came to you during the period of silence last night. Shall we start with our resident curmudgeon and skeptic? Sol?"

"I'm telling you, Warren, I would never have believed how efficient and productive silence can be. I've got more ideas than I've got candles on my birthday cake, and that's saying something."

"Same here," said Max, "and you know, I think it's sitting together elbow to elbow that makes it work. It's a little like that Buddha-within-you type of group meditation, with one crucial difference. This group has an elaborate secular mission, no ifs, ahs, or oms." He chuckled at his own joke, provoking an impenetrable gaze from Bill Cosby.

Warren popped open a Cherry Coke. "Okay, Sol, let's hear those ideas of yours."

"Well, for starters, it came to me that we can create an entire sub-economy that builds markets and employs solutions kept on the shelf by vested interests. With our circles of influence and persuasion, we have the resources to start or acquire companies that break through in renewable energy, nutritious food, cooperative closed-loop pollution cycling systems, alternatives to toxic materials, housing for the homeless, health co-ops, zero-polluting motor vehicles, recycling, and even television-radio-internet programming to arouse the public and displace bad marketing that depletes family budgets. All this would be driven by a broad strategy for a self-reliant community-based economy sustained by civic and occupational training, capital ownership, and the expansion of commonwealth control of commonwealth property such as public lands and pensions, as Ted was saying yesterday. The various parts of this sub-economy would support each other, convert positive human values into economic delivery systems, and enlarge perceived possibilities for a better, happier life.

"Of course, opponents of the sub-economy will attempt to block it through predatory practices, media freeze-outs, and legislated restrictions of the kind we've seen in our history all too often, but we have the clout to repulse them until the success of the sub-economy drives them out of business or into mimicry. We are business people, we know what leverage and promotion are all about, we know the distortions the giant multinationals use to paint gross waste and destructiveness with a gloss of capitalist efficiency. We have lived in the eye of the lie for decades. Which is why we are ready, more than ready."

Sol's impassioned delivery, coming from a visionary entrepreneur with a compassion for the downtrodden, visibly moved the others, as if they too had taken their particular flights into this imaginative sub-economy. Warren, sitting on $46 billion, found himself physically agitated, but that was nothing compared to the whirring of his neurons alighting on the possibilities. There were a few moments of silence before an animated conversation picked up and one voice, George's, emerged.

"In working for open societies, I've learned a few things that are relevant to Sol's sub-economy and whatever other initiatives we choose to fund. Money can seed democratic institutions that can then fall from their vulnerability to autocratic forces or implode from poor selection of leaders and staff. Open society seeding is not like sowing seeds that turn themselves into sturdy trees with the help of sun, water, and soil. There are too many hurricanes trying to bring these fledgling institutions down. That's why we need a closed-loop strategy in everything we do. Look at efforts to combat global infectious diseases like TB, malaria, and AIDS. Bill's son is trying to do just that with his vast foundation grants, and he's probably feeling frustrated by the lack of delivery systems even for simple vaccination programs or other preventive measures. The science is in place, the material resources are in place, but not the end-point delivery. The US foreign aid program, where it is actually foreign aid, has suffered from this same sequential vacuum down to the community level. How to close the loop? The loop is closed by people on the ground where the needs are to be met, people operating in their own culture with their own local talent. Failure is a high probability without a closed-loop approach."

"That's right," said Peter. "We have to dig the roots deep by promoting the establishment of a whole variety of national and local grassroots groups focused on a range of consumer, taxpayer, community, and labor issues. I'm thinking here of the Citizens' Utility Board model. CUBs represent the largely unrepresented. They're instruments for reducing the enormous disparity of power between big companies and ordinary people. Consumer Advocates have proposed that the government require utilities, industries, the postal service, and so on, to include in their bills and mailings inserts allowing recipients to join such groups by checking off their membership and paying modest dues, an objective vigorously opposed by the companies concerned. But we can do it directly ourselves—after all, it's only a matter of money, message, medium, and graphics—and then these groups can start up quickly, with total membership in the tens of millions. Just consider the number of people who for twenty or thirty or fifty dollars will join a group espousing universal healthcare or a living wage or fair taxation or a clean environment or preservation of Social Security or pensions, or whatever priorities arise over the long run. These groups become our base."

"And they can be tremendously effective," Bill Gates said. "A mere thousand or so of us rich folks got together to fight the repeal of the estate tax, and when the Republicans tried to make repeal permanent, I think we made the difference, shoring up the Democrats, educating the public, and puncturing the propaganda that this repeal was intended to save small farmers' inheritances—a total falsehood. It was actually for the benefit of the top fraction of one percent of estates, including our own."

George nodded. "It's what Richard Parker at Harvard talks about in *"Here, the People Rule"*: facilitating the civic and political energies of the people—and, I might add, in a deliberate democratic manner, learning from the feedback of an open society."

"Well, as long as we're talking basics," said Max, "let us dig deeper still. Will the people be sufficiently motivated to join these groups, and if so, will they participate? They may join if they're interested in the group's mission, but look at credit unions and food co-ops—most of the members barely participate at all. Taxpayers don't show up at town meetings even though they know they'll have to pay more or endure more waste without their say. So we have to address the problem of motivating people, since our schools and our culture don't prepare them for active citizen roles, do they?"

"I've got it!" Ted exclaimed, slapping the table. "We need a mascot. How about a hawk?"

"That's fine for a certain basketball team, Ted," Warren observed wryly, "but not for a political initiative like ours. Everyone will be thinking hawks versus doves, and we don't want that."

"Yeah, you've got a point there. Okay then, maybe a . . . a . . . hell, I don't know, some critter, something with universal appeal, something that gets people laughing and talking to each other at the diner or the water cooler the next day."

"Great idea, Ted. Maybe you and I can brainstorm on it later," Phil said.

"You know," said Paul, "this reminds me of William James's phrase 'the moral equivalent of war.' He meant something nonmilitaristic that would motivate the citizenry to action as powerfully as war does. Waging peace doesn't quite cut it, does it? Because it's not visceral, it's cranial. Visceral can refer to many levels of the human psyche, though these days it rarely rises to neck level, much less higher, because the cultural marketplace consistently downplays imagination as it tries to confine the visceral to the gonadal. But visceral can also mean savoring debates and contests or absorbing different dimensions of beauty, of aesthetics. It can mean the idea of the heroic, where both physical and moral courage roam. Visceral can mean the arts that take a civilization to new peaks of appreciation and reward. We have to disseminate our ideas viscerally, in a way that embraces all these positive meanings and reaches wide national audiences, something that can be facilitated by . . . hmm, let's see. By Barry," he said with a wink.

"Sure, Paul, I'll do some thinking about media strategies. And while I'm at it, why don't I arrange some leveraged buyouts of TV and radio stations so we can establish our own network covering the entire country? I've done so many mergers and acquisitions that it's a matter of routine in my law firm. Piece of cake."

"I second Paul and Barry heartily," said Phil. "Access to mass media outlets is crucial. To take just one random example, if I may, TV talk shows can raise possibilities, what ifs, and prospects of the good life for viewers and their progeny. We have to give people the sense that we're not talking about some utopia but about long-overdue improvements. If we can get people thinking, 'Why not?' and 'Who says we can't?' and 'Let's work together for love of our troubled country,' the launching of our concrete programs and initiatives will fall on more fertile soil."

Yoko looked up from doodling furiously on her notepad. "Along similar lines, I think we should have a symbol of some sort, a design of strength and beauty. We can't underestimate the immense power of the aesthetic impulse. Short of the survival impulse, no other exceeds its depth—not greed, not lust, not envy, not gluttony. People can do without all these for long periods of time, or even forever. People cannot do without aesthetics. Just ask anyone how much money it would take to get them to agree to a permanent four-inch nose elongation or a threefold enlargement of their ears, even with no loss of function. It's no accident that the words 'truth' and 'beauty' have been joined together in the arts and literature of all cultures."

"One thing's for sure," said Bill Cosby. "We'll need every tool and idea we can muster to reach, inform, and organize the people. And we'll need all the power of the media and arts to immunize them against the anticipated pack of lies and smears and manipulative propaganda from the plutocrats. This is essential, to head off the master foolers who can command large audiences in every medium."

Leonard laughed. "I like that, heading them off at the pass. It reminds me of my father. He was a boxer, you know, loved the sport. He always said his idea of boxing was not getting hit. And speaking of master foolers—or should I say master fools?—won't we have to enlist Congress in our efforts at some point, and won't that bring us up against the big campaign contributors? So why not raise the

entire net sum spent on congressional elections and make it available to candidates with no strings attached if they forgo all other
fundraising, or if they only accept contributions under fifty dollars,
or some such formula? That would free the Congress, or a majority
of them anyway, to do what's right, short term and long term. Great
investment, maybe two billion dollars a cycle."

"An excellent proposal," said Bernard. "I am so tired of writing
checks to these cowards in the Democratic Party who keep frittering
and flattering their way to political failure. Even when they agree
with me on topic after topic, they vote the wrong way or they don't
stand and fight for what they truly believe. It's all about money up
there on the Hill, more so than at any time in my experience over
the past fifty years, and it's getting worse. Just one big ongoing
bazaar. But to guarantee campaign funds leaves open the question
of how to apportion them among incumbents and challengers, and
that's going to be thorny."

"Yes," Warren said, "but let's not get ahead of ourselves. The idea
is sterling, and that's enough for now. Are there other general areas
we haven't touched on yet, other thoughts you may have had during
our period of reflection last night?"

Peter spoke up. "As to my 'silence dividend,' I guess you won't be
surprised to hear that it concerns insurance. The industry is all about
managing risk, though too often it interprets managing risk as managing liability, which are two different if related phenomena. In our
redirections mission, we'll be confronting risks that either materialize by the hour or are looming on the horizon. Already, some
European reinsurance companies like Swiss Re have drawn the connection between their profitability and climate change. They want to
do something about global warming, a concern that obviously goes
beyond conventional actuarial determinations of premiums and loss
ratios. It requires a much longer time scale—let's call it the corporate responsibility time zone. It's a concept we can use in terms of
aggregating assets and identifying new approaches. We can expand
the insurance function to help redirect markets."

"I agree," said Ross, "and one of the assets we'll have to aggregate to decisive intensity is our credibility. We need to search our nation for people whose performance, image, and strength of numbers enlarge our credibility instantly—and I emphasize the importance of the word 'instantly.' Momentum is the wheelbase for comprehensive, careful planning. So where do we look? Let's start with the veterans' groups. I know these people and they know me. I know that the American Legion and the Veterans of Foreign Wars keep electing leaders who are absorbed with two issues—protecting veterans' benefits and maintaining a strong military. Have you ever seen a presidential election where the two major candidates aren't clamoring to speak to the Legion and VFW conventions? That gives you an idea of the bipartisan pull of these organizations. It should also give us other ideas, no? I'm sure there are other groups that have the same broad credibility with millions of people and can be persuaded of the need for redirection. And let me add that redirection has to be viewed in patriotic terms, whether through traditional notions or by redefining patriotism acceptably. To me, patriotism is love of country, which means love of its people and its children and its land. It does not mean love of war."

"There's another form of patriotism not much recognized except in courts of law," said Joe, buttoning his suit jacket reflexively. "I mean the jurors. When you give jurors an opportunity to exercise their lawful power to do justice after absorbing detailed arguments and cross-examinations on both sides, and after being instructed by the judge, ordinary people rise to the occasion and take their duties as citizens very seriously. Jurors get a taste of democratic power legitimately exercised in the name of justice, something rarer than a raw steak for most people. Is there a lesson here outside the courtroom arena? You bet. You can bet your house on it. That deep sense of civic responsibility is a tremendous resource we can tap into, especially if we contrast it with the deep civic irresponsibility of our political and economic system as currently constituted. Every day millions of Americans feel that they're being pushed around, underpaid, excluded, uninsured, penalized, disrespected, ignored, and generally put on hold or told to get in line and shut up. We have to start with people's perceived injustices, not just with our ideas of their injustices, because that's how we get their attention so we can move toward causes and remedies, and onward to liberty and justice for all, as we like to say."

"When the truth is that liberty and justice are only available to some of us," Bill Gates observed sadly.

Joe took a long sip of his scotch. "Say that again, Bill."

"Say what? Liberty and justice for some?"

"Hell, yes, that's it!" Joe snapped his fingers. "We'll start a drive to change the end of the Pledge of Allegiance to 'with liberty and justice for some.' We'll get a member of Congress to introduce a Pledge the Truth amendment, like that guy did in the 1950s to get 'under God' inserted, and then we'll stand back and watch the fireworks. Just you wait, especially when the bill receives the kind of grassroots defense that we can generate. We can make sure this will be more than a one-day story about a bizarre bill in the congressional hopper."

"That's brilliant, Joe," said Bill Gates. "The trick will be to connect the uproar intricately with everything else we're doing, to give it legs that will get people thinking, if not marching, to mangle a metaphor or two. The possibilities here are many. For example, hard-pressed teachers in inner-city schools who can't get the most basic supplies can start having their students say the 'for some' Pledge every morning. That ought to rub some nerves raw."

Joe let out a hoot. "Beautiful! Let's run this one past some of our imaginative friends, people who would be geniuses on Madison Avenue if they could stand the place, people who are the right kind of troublemakers. They shouldn't be too hard to find."

"I believe I've got some of them working for me," Ted said. "I'll check and get back with you. Meanwhile, we've been talking about civic approaches to tipping the balance of power to help the have-nots and the powerless, but let's get back to the economic arena and the marketplace for a minute. The Internet lets buying power and blog power form fast, though it's still pretty crudely organized. You can shop around for the best price, but there's not much collective negotiation or bargaining. Even with sophisticated software and operating systems like Linux, the awesome world of the Internet hasn't shifted much power from sellers to buyers, or from the political parties to the voters, for that matter. We should discuss ways to mobilize constituencies in virtual reality as well as everyday reality, because in both realities, financial companies, service firms, and credit organizations are tilting things more and more in favor of the sellers. Just look at credit scores and all those damn penalties and surcharges that are now simply debited so there's no need for the consumer to make out a check. Some of these charges are way out of line, like the ones for bouncing a check or even depositing a bounced check. Loss of control over our money breeds greedy debit rip-offs and fraud. And don't get me started on the gigantic fraud and billing abuse in healthcare. Our economic system is way, way off balance and getting worse. Look at the genetic testing that discriminates against certain workers—"

"And don't forget the diminishing freedom to sue the bastards, a freedom curtailed under the guise of controlling a phony 'litigation explosion,'" Joe interrupted, sounding more like himself. "Hell, the explosion is the sound of the big companies suing each other's asses. For everyone else, the courtroom doors are slammed shut in all kinds of ways—loss of rights, costs, caps, delays, compulsory arbitration, et cetera. So if you're going to latch onto redressing imbalances, keep the doors to our courts open."

"I've always believed that the tort system is an excellent form of quality control for my industry," Peter said. "There are abuses on both sides, but the overriding issue here is who can and cannot use the courts or the law itself to redress grievances and keep the big boys honest."

"Is that the sun I see setting in the west over the shimmering Pacific Ocean?" inquired Sol pointedly. "It's not enough we skipped lunch?"

"You have only yourself to blame," Warren said. "You're the one who got us going with your eloquent oration on the sub-economy. However, at this juncture, let us adjourn to an early dinner, a dazzling buffet you can eradicate at your own pace. Then we'll have our period of silence to think about what we've said and heard around this table."

At the sumptuous dinner, in a wraparound glass-encased dining room, the vistas were breathtaking. If this group was seeking new horizons, they'd come to the right place. The Pacific was well named, stretching serenely into an infinite distance—a perfect metaphor, in both quantity and quality, for the foresight they were striving to achieve.

As they sat down to their repast, Warren wondered what they would choose to discuss. He was used to the chitchat at exclusive dinners for the rich and powerful. He knew that the small talk during breaks in important business meetings usually signified relief from the tension of the meeting or from the participants' sheer concentration on making sure they were at the top of their game. To his pleasant surprise, the conversations that broke out in clusters of two or three around the large dining table extended the topics and concerns of the previous working meetings. There was no rupture, no change of pace, no step down from the significance of why they were there. The diners continued with what they'd had on their minds but hadn't had an opportunity to say.

During the serving of a gigantic Hawaiian dessert, the kind you rationalize eating because of its presumed fruity nutrition, Warren tapped his spoon on his glass. "My friends, I am greatly encouraged by the level of commitment and the vibrancy of the ideas I heard from you during our dinner conversations. With each of you making your contribution, the whole effort begins to take shape, tactical, strategic, philosophical, and anticipatory. There is plenty of material to think over during our silence period, or shall I say, plenty to be silent over."

With that, the collaborators repaired to the conference room and took their places around the table for an hour of silence, after which they wished each other good night and retired.

In the morning, at the final session of this first chapter of their momentous journey, Warren opened the proceedings with his customary directness. "My friends, during our engagement with a hearty breakfast, I want to say a few words by way of a send-off and lay out a series of charges for the next month, before we return here for our second gathering.

"First, you will all receive a transcript of our conversations through a secured system, since we want to keep our work in confidence. Next, I want to reiterate that we are not out to meticulously plan the future, as if we could, but to press for a redirection of major aspects of our political economy, new paths that are life-sustaining, productive, and peaceful in a constantly changing environment. The more we can focus people on positive and creative redirections, the more they will move voluntarily and rationally toward their better futures.

"Now, as to our next meeting here. To summarize and crystalize our deliberations, here's what I believe we must each do on our own during the next month. Our first task is to consolidate our epicenters, by which I mean reaching out to people we trust, people who are on the same wavelength and can do one or more of the following: contribute money and financial leverage, deliver other groups for various tasks, such as unions and veterans' organizations, give intellectual rigor to our proposed redirections, and broaden our access to and acquisition of media. Consolidating the epicenter also means finding unentangling alliances, with no quid pro quos or deals, locating natural economic allies, like the sustainable technology people, enlisting others among the super-rich who are up to our demanding criteria and may be willing to pitch in, thinking deeply about replication dynamics and how to increase the velocity of the events we put in motion, and doing all of the above with the urgency dictated by our presumed one-year life expectancy.

"We'll be in touch during the month, of course, to review progress and roadblocks. Meanwhile, keep in mind that we go public only when we are ready. Our priority at our next gathering should be to prepare a spreadsheet for action in well-meshed sequences that anticipate both serendipities and opposition. Rolling out our initiatives in the right sequence is critical, not just so that each stage furthers the next, but to maintain our own solidarity and cohesion, to stay on the same page, if you will. Dynamics are also key here. At present, the 'bad guys' are forcing the 'good guys' to play defense and fall back on their heels all the time. We intend to reverse that dynamic. In my experience in business, the crucial dynamic is staying on the offensive, setting the agenda, making things happen rather than reacting to them. The energy that flows from being on the offensive is incredible. And we also need an early alert system to pick up signs of a counteroffensive so that we can react accordingly. Your respective successes tell me that in your own areas of activity you have done this well, even intuitively, but clearly we're entering a much bigger game, and we have to scale up and extend our radar."

Warren paused and looked around the table. "Finally, may I propose a toast?"

As one, the assembly raised their mimosas.

"To our own evolution and to our posterity's future on our beloved and only planet Earth as we reach for the stars."

"Hear, hear," said one and all. There was not a smile in the room.

The next day, back in Omaha, Warren established a Secretariat headed by four of his most trusted associates, who set up a closed-circuit teleconferencing system for regular communication among the members of the core group. His first message was an afterthought that he wished had occurred to him in Maui, but on the other hand, it was a good opportunity to make sure that the lines were reliable and secure. He suggested to his confreres that they each undertake an initiative with public visibility as a way of probing the country's mood, and perhaps with some coordination, as long as nothing could be traced back to the Maui group. His only stipulation was that the Secretariat be notified of any activity forty-eight hours in advance. He told his colleagues that the purpose of his proposal was to quicken the pace and get some early feedback so they'd have a better idea of what lay in store. Privately, he added to himself that it would give him the measure of each of them.

CHAPTER 2

Nurse Jane Harper came home from a hard day in the respiratory unit at St. Vincent's, kicked off her thick-soled white shoes, and sank into her favorite armchair. Reaching for the remote, she turned the TV on and tuned to CNN to catch the news. Wolf Blitzer was in the middle of a story about the trial of those two Enron guys, Lay and Skilling. Jane hoped the judge would throw the book at them. She was on her way to the kitchen to make herself a Lean Cuisine when a loud squawk stopped her in her tracks.

There on the screen was a parrot, the most gorgeous bird she'd ever seen, all iridescent reds and blues and yellows, cocking its head and fixing her with its bright eye as it said with uncannily perfect diction, "Get up! Don't let America down!" Under the parrot's feet was a running banner urging viewers to call or e-mail about an improvement they'd like to see in the country, nationally or locally, something they'd be willing to work toward. "Get up! Don't let America down!" the parrot squawked again.

Jane thought about Lucinda Jackson, a single mother who'd come in today with her two small children, all of them suffering from shortness of breath. Like many of Jane's patients, Lucinda and her kids lived near a bus stop and had to breathe in the acrid pollution the buses spewed every seven minutes or so. Jane knew that some cities were converting to cleaner natural-gas fuels, but not Birmingham, where the bus fleet was aging and poorly maintained for emissions control. She saw the effects firsthand every day. It was a terrible situation, and she'd been angry about it for a long time, especially on behalf of Birmingham's children, but when she'd gone to the mayor's office last year to lodge a complaint, she was told there was no money for conversion.

"Get up! Don't let America down!"

Nurse Jane Harper grabbed her telephone and dialed the toll-free number at the bottom of her screen.

Stan Yablonsky pushed open the heavy wooden door of Clancy's Cave, shrugged off his Buffalo Bills jacket, and sat down at the bar next to his friend Mike O'Malley.

"Gimme a double Jack neat, Ernie," he said to the bartender.

"Hard day at the plant?" Mike asked.

"Hell, yeah, with all the layoffs there's half the people doing the same amount of work." Stan sighed. "Could be worse, though. Least I got a job."

Ernie slapped a cardboard coaster down on the bar and set Stan's bourbon on it.

"Thanks, Ernie." Stan turned to Mike. "So how 'bout you, buddy? Those little tweakers leave gum on your chair again or steal all the chalk?"

Mike laughed. "Those kids are a handful, all right, but you know, I feel for them. They're in the sixth grade and half of them still can't read, not that there's enough books to go around. And it's a tough neighborhood, high unemployment, shitty housing, drugs—"

"Hey, lighten up, man. I'm not in the mood for one of your lectures. How 'bout I buy you a beer?" Stan knocked back his bourbon. "Another round over here, Ernie, and turn on ESPN, wouldya?"

"What do you care? The Bills've been out of contention since December," Ernie said, but he reached up and flicked the TV on. As he was about to change the channel, the screen filled with the familiar faces of Paul Newman and Bill Cosby.

"Liberty and justice for all?" Newman was saying. "Don't make me laugh, Bill."

"That's my job, Paul," Cosby replied, "but this is no laughing matter."

"Hang on, Ernie," Mike said. "Let's watch this for a minute."

"Aw, c'mon," Stan grumbled, "put on SportsCenter."

"[T]o expose the lie we tell every time we recite our Pledge of Allegiance. What we have in this country, Bill, is liberty and justice for some."

"Damn right, and the 'some' doesn't include the kids in our crumbling inner-city schools, the retirees defrauded of their pensions by corrupt corporations, the folks in New Orleans' Ninth Ward, the vets who come home to inadequate medical care and no jobs . . ."

As Cosby continued his catalogue of the manifold injustices afflicting American society, the camera closed in on his face—that reassuring, genial face welcomed into millions of homes for so many years, now grim with anger—and then panned back to reveal a huge blowup of the Pledge of Allegiance with "for all" crossed out and replaced by "for some."

By now, Stan and Ernie were staring at the TV along with Mike.

"And so we urge you today"—close-up on Newman now, with steel in those blue eyes—"to take the Pledge pledge, to bring our Pledge of Allegiance in line with reality by saying 'with liberty and justice for some' until the day when we can all truly say 'with liberty and justice for all.'"

"Jesus, Mary, and Joseph," Mike O'Malley said. He had a long night ahead, still had to grade papers and do his lesson plan on the Underground Railroad, but at least he knew how he was going to start his class tomorrow morning.

Arlene Jones set a cup of coffee and a slice of apple pie in front of the lone customer in the corner booth of the Treezewood Diner, a truck stop just off I-70 in central Pennsylvania.

"Give a holler if you need anything else, hon," she said as she went back behind the counter.

Normally the Treezewood was packed at all hours, even during the graveyard shift, but tonight there was a blessed lull. Arlene turned on the news to see the latest on that big snowstorm they'd been predicting, but what she saw instead was a shock of silver hair over a puckish face. Was she in a time warp? Hadn't Phil Donahue been off the air for a decade or more? She turned up the sound.

"The always controversial talk-show host has stirred up fresh controversy with his op-ed piece in yesterday's *New York Times*," the anchorman said. "The piece was titled 'Who Is Denying America Its Future? A Wake-up Call.'"

Arlene didn't know who was denying America's future. She didn't know who was denying her own future. All she knew was that she'd spent thirty years working for tips and what she managed to make on the side mending clothes. According to the anchorman, Phil had said something in his op-ed about vested interests depriving people of their collective power and stripping them of their rights.

Arlene blushed, remembering those male strippers on Phil's show. She'd loved that show, and not just for the beefcake. She'd loved it for the way Phil raised issues no one else was willing to raise, for the way he'd given voice to his vast audience, mostly women who were home to watch him because they were caring for their children or their aged parents, or getting ready for the afternoon shift at some dull, low-paying job.

"Rather mysteriously," the anchorman said, "Mr. Donahue ended his piece with the words 'Stay tuned.'"

Arlene nodded. Yes, she would. She would definitely stay tuned.

On the outskirts of Oklahoma City, Jack Soaring Eagle walked slowly down the long, dusty drive that led from his trailer to his mailbox. He was hoping his unemployment check would come today. Up until last year, he'd been making pretty good money as a foreman in a kitchen appliance factory, but then the owners shut the place down and moved to China. Things had been tight ever since.

Jack opened the battered tin box, took out a handful of letters, and shuffled through them, scanning the return addresses as he walked back to the trailer. No check, just junk mail, a couple of bills, something from the local Cherokee council, and—what was this? He stopped, arrested by a striking image in the upper left corner of the last letter. It was a simple, elegant line drawing of an eye that seemed to be looking far into the future. Under the eye were seven human figures, each extending a hand to the next, and beside it was a name: Yoko Ono.

Jack went inside and sat down at his kitchen table, studying the envelope. A letter from Yoko Ono? Must be some kind of joke. He'd never cared much for the Beatles, didn't like most of their music—that "yeah, yeah, yeah" was like fingernails on a chalkboard as far as he was concerned—but he remembered reading about John and Yoko's "Bed-in for Peace" back in '69 when he was stationed in Saigon. He and a lot of his buddies had already turned against the war in Vietnam, sickened by horrors like the My Lai massacre and by the politicians' lies about body counts, and he'd appreciated what John and Yoko were trying to do. Jack opened the envelope.

There was the eye again, at the top, followed by a letter from Yoko explaining its symbolism. She called it "the Seventh-Generation Eye," representing the principle that leaders must weigh all their decisions in terms of their impact on the future as far as the seventh generation to come. Jack didn't have to read on to learn that it was a principle derived from the Great Law of Peace of the Iroquois Confederacy; it was an integral part of the American Indian belief system, and one that guided his own tribe's deliberations.

Yoko went on to say that she wanted to do her part for the seventh generation by sending an energy-saving compact fluorescent lightbulb (CFL) free of charge to any household requesting one. All the recipients had to do was provide name and address, along with one sentence explaining why they wanted such a bulb and specifying wattage. "I know a lot of you will think I'm off in the ether again and this is just another one of my wacky ideas," Yoko wrote, "but when you stop to consider that a single CFL can save two thousand times its own weight in greenhouse gases, maybe you'll decide it's not so wacky. Multiply that by millions of people using these bulbs, and it's enough energy to replace dozens of fossil fuel and nuclear power plants. Please join me in this simple act that will help insure the future of our planet. With thanks in advance from myself and your great-great-great-great-great-great-great grandchildren."

Jack sat drumming his fingers on the tabletop for a minute. Then he stood up and got the pad and pen he kept by the phone. "Dear Yoko Ono," he wrote. "I would like one seventy-five watt CFL to read by, and because it will brighten my life just like your letter has." He paused, then added "Gratefully yours" and signed his name with a flourish.

In the weeks following the Maui meeting, the activities of Warren's colleagues in the core group had exceeded his wildest expectations. He couldn't turn on the news or read the paper without hearing about an initiative one of them had launched or some controversy they'd stirred up.

As promised, Ted Turner and Phil Donahue had put their heads together to brainstorm about a mascot for the group's efforts. Ted's thoughts naturally ran along avian lines, and it wasn't long before they hit on the idea of a parrot. Phil called a friend of his in the highly regarded veterinary program at the State University of New York in Delhi, and was able to procure a splendid scarlet macaw, along with the services of linguistic trainer Clifton Chirp. Chirp rolled up his sleeves and went to work.

Patriotic Polly hit the airwaves in fifteen-second spots shown on thousands of stations, and was an immediate smash. She would have won an Academy Award in her category, if there were such a category. Amazing what an animal could communicate to humans, Warren thought. Fully 13 million viewers had e-mailed or called in their choice of a change they were willing to work for in their country or state or town, and Patriotic Polly was the talk of the nation for days. Late-night TV comedians joked about what else she might say, and Letterman offered a year's worth of crackers as a prize for the best submission. One unintended side effect was that the price of Amazonian parrots skyrocketed.

Hot on Polly's heels had come the Cosby/Newman telethon, a live three-hour event carried by all the major networks thanks to the behind-the-scenes exertions of Barry Diller. When the three men told the rest of the core group about their plan for the show at the first post-Maui closed-circuit conference, Joe Jamail and Bill Gates Sr. had suggested that the Pledge of Allegiance be one of the segments, which was why Mike O'Malley's class and hundreds of other classes around the country were now starting off the day with "liberty and justice for some." And that was only the first half-hour of the telethon. The rest of it was devoted to demonstrating how the media uses public property—the airwaves—to foster complacency, serve power, sell junk, and trivialize or distort or cover up the news. Cosby demanded a giveback of daily hours on the broadcast spectrum to citizens who wished to join together and create their own networks, to be funded by license fees imposed on the airtime that TV and radio had been using for free since their industries began. Newman showed clips from his own collection of independently produced films and documentaries to illustrate the kind of programming that the people, with well-funded studios, producers, and reporters, would put on the air. Then both of them announced an instant poll to be conducted via the toll-free number flashing on the screen, and over the next hour the audience registered an overwhelming desire for such a people's voice. Finally, Cosby and Newman urged viewers to flood the FCC and Congress with demands for legislative and regulatory hearings on such matters as children's television, coverage of civic action, and whatever ideas of their own they wanted to advance.

The next day, the headlines read, to paraphrase, "What the hell were Cosby and Newman doing? Trying to wreck their careers? Are they nuts?" The editors of the *Wall Street Journal* had a follow-up observation in an editorial titled "Possessed by Marx," wherein they dutifully accused the two men of being closet communists seemingly headed toward senility. Cosby and Newman wrote a letter to the editor in response. Unabridged and printed in full, it read, "Stay tuned."

On the flight home from Maui, Phil Donahue had composed the dazzling op-ed that was published a few days later in the *New York*

Times and covered on some of the nightly news broadcasts, even on small local stations like Arlene Jones's. In his "wake-up call," he didn't beat around the bush about who was denying America its future. He pointed squarely to commercial interests that said no to the well-being of the people, and then he gave a rousing rundown of how the people's power, if awakened, could effect change. The response was tremendous. Not all of it was positive, but to judge by the letters that poured into his office, about 85 percent reacted as if they'd just overcome a long period of constipation: "What can we do?" they wrote, or "Here's what we're doing in our area that should be disseminated," or "Note to rulers: lead or get out of the way!" NBC was bombarded with letters demanding the return of Phil's talk show. Then there were the calls from friends who seemed to have come alive. Two of the wealthiest of them wanted to meet with him in Manhattan "to see how we can get things moving in this country." With his down-to-earth language, Phil had obviously hit a nerve. Lots of people were willing to jump out of the cake for him.

Yoko Ono had returned from Maui and gone straight to her New York studio. She'd been deeply affected by everything she'd heard at Warren's gathering, and particularly by an impassioned conversation she'd had with Bernard Rapoport over dinner, about the universal human obligation to posterity. Dear old B. Yoko fervently believed that the future could be made beautiful. Most people didn't see it, but art could put it right in front of them, give them an unmediated awareness, what she liked to call "a somersault of the mind." It was strange how people could tolerate injustice, brutality, fraudulence, and a host of other wrongs without being moved to act. Maybe they were bored, or maybe just defeated by a combination of the complexity of the world's problems and their own sense of powerlessness. But they did care about their children and grandchildren's future, a future they viewed with anxiety and uncertainty in this fast-changing, perilous world over which they had so little control, except to strive for a modicum of financial security. Art could cut through all that. Art could move them toward action.

Hour after hour, in silence and solitude, Yoko searched for the tao, the way, the path to the image that would crystalize the Maui mission. Finally it came to her, in her own somersault of the mind: the Seventh-Generation Eye. Quickly she sketched it, and then the seven linked generations, a symbol representing the connection between present and future through the most expressive organ of the human body, the window of the soul.

Yoko sat up at her drawing board and stretched. Astonishing how she'd seen it all at once, as if the proverbial lightbulb had dropped down over her head to signal a sudden idea or inspiration. She laughed at the cliché, and was still laughing as she moved to her computer and began typing a letter about lightbulbs. Oh, art was grand!

Over the next few days, Yoko mobilized her extensive network of friends and contacts to help her send out a million letters like the one Jack Soaring Eagle received, and close to 20 million e-mails, all from lists properly rented. She went personally to the main manufacturer of compact fluorescent bulbs and cut a deal to buy them at a wholesale price of $2.50 each, a considerable reduction from the usual wholesale price of $7.50 or more. Attached to each bulb she sent out would be a message estimating the amount of coal, oil, gas, and nuclear fuel wasted because General Electric, through its near monopoly well into the seventies, sold incandescent lightbulbs that burned out quickly and had to be replaced often.

As for Bernard, he'd also been thinking about his conversation with Yoko when he returned home to Texas. Bernard had always had a dream, ever since his father told him that if a society takes care of its children, it will also be taking care of itself. Part of what Papa meant was that people who would otherwise resist change could be persuaded to support it if they thought it was for the benefit of children.

Bernard placed ads on select cable channels saying that he would establish after-school Egalitarian Clubs to teach children civic skills and democratic values like equality of opportunity and the importance of a decent standard of living. Then he unloaded the provocation that brought a torrent of attention and criticism in the following days. He said that the big corporations were on an omnicidal track in the world—destroying our democracy and the environment, to give just two examples—and that a new generation of Americans had to learn to control, replace, or displace corporate power, especially since the schools were now instruments of corporate propaganda, both directly and indirectly. He spent hours giving interviews, drawing on his impressive historical knowledge of corporate crimes, abuses, tricks, and treasonous behavior toward the masses. It was as if he had prepared for these interviews all his adult life. A CEO himself, he was accused darkly of being a traitor to his class by at least one prominent business commentator, but Oprah Winfrey had him on her show for an hour with six seventh-graders from the Chicago public schools. It was an interaction for the ages.

Like Bernard, Jeno Paulucci had a long-cherished dream, that of establishing an alternative national chamber of commerce with local and regional chapters. He had had his fill of existing chambers that put corporations ahead of people in what amounted to a master-servant relationship. Jeno was the most naturally gregarious of the core group members. When he called himself "just a peddler from the Iron Range," this Republican wasn't kidding. Starting dirt poor in northern Minnesota as the son of immigrants, he'd built and sold some fifty companies, having a ball all the way. He loved his workers and treated them so well that he welcomed unions. He loved competition so much that he once proposed a price war to a larger competitor, until his lawyers admonished him about the antitrust laws. If there was one thing he knew, it was that commerce had to serve people, not the other way around. He had recently made just that point in his boisterous autobiography, *Jeno: The Power of the Peddler*.

Jeno drafted a two-page proclamation of the People's Chamber of Commerce, barnstormed with news conferences in ten cities at the rate of two cities a day, and took out ads on business cable channels, all of which led to extensive television and radio interviews. He always sounded the same note, inviting businesses of all sizes to join up by paying initial dues of $50 and signing the declaration of people's business principles and practices that a business ethics friend of his had written back in 1978. Once this first stage was completed, a more comprehensive founding convention would be held to create a chaordic organizational structure on the model originated by Visa founder Dee Hock. Hock coined the term, a blend of "chaos" and "order," in a book published in 2000, *Birth of the Chaordic Age*—"chaos" being defined in the context of current chaos theory as elaborated by the Santa Fe group, not in its more familiar dictionary meaning. In accordance with Hock's principles, the People's Chamber of Commerce would feature maximum autonomy on the periphery (the local chapters), which would be loosely linked to a small core group that set obligatory minimum standards. The PCC would be chaordic for optimum creativity.

To the astonishment of everyone but Jeno, 78,000 businesses signed up in two weeks. As he had anticipated, many of them were franchises, large and small, which promised to bring in thousands more members. The PCC, Jeno said, was the beginning of the end for the giant trade associations—drug, auto, mining, food, energy, banking, insurance, defense, real estate—that monopolized the voices of business.

This incipient challenge to the sodden hegemony of the Washington-based trade associations became the news and then the speculation of the hour. "Where is it all heading?" one trade group president asked. "How can the people speak for business?" remarked another in a CNN interview, unaware how much he was communicating. After the first round of press, Jeno would only say to the legions of interview requests, "Stay tuned," a comment that was tantalizing to reporters almost beyond their endurance. The news media knew Jeno well from his days as a grand networker with a Rolodex the size of a Ferris wheel, and they knew something big was coming—but what?

The uproar over the PCC was matched by the uproar Peter Lewis created in the insurance industry. Peter had forged his tumultuous, iconoclastic career in this industry, and he owed his massive, still-growing wealth to it, but he had long wondered about its central hypocrisy. Insurance companies talked about risk management as if it meant the best way for their computers to get the most profit out of existing risks. To Peter, that was not risk management. To Peter, risk management meant risk reduction or loss prevention. The insurance companies' dirty little secret was that they would accept more losses as long as they could collect more premiums. Why? So they'd have more dollars to invest. Today investment income was central to the swollen profitability of insurers, in contrast to the situation decades ago, when insurance underwriters were more like engineering firms, scrutinizing risks and trying to make it on premium income. In the nineteenth century, insurance companies would refuse to insure a factory without improvements in boilers to avert then-frequent explosions, but the insurance companies didn't operate that focused way anymore.

Peter took out a full-page ad in the *Wall Street Journal*, disclosing for starters that the fire insurance industry didn't do much about fire prevention because fewer fires would mean less business. Despite lip service to prevention, these companies went out of their way to overlook weak fire codes, lax enforcement, and substandard materials. At the bottom of the ad was Peter's signature and the line "Interviews by the media are invited." Minutes after the paper hit the stands, the phones in his office started ringing off the hook. The fireworks, so to speak, began exploding all over as Peter extended his criticism to health, life, worker's compensation, and auto insurers, and then to gigantic reinsurers like Munich Re and Lloyd's of London. He had an easy time with the reporters, who knew little about the subject, and the insurance executives were afraid to debate him. "Human and property tragedies have become the near exclusive inventory of the insurance companies," he declared, "when these companies should be the sentinels of health and safety in every area, from the local hospital operating room to the global environment."

Cascades of controversy erupted in every sector of the society and economy touched by the insurers. The story broke on a Monday, and by Saturday, Peter was satisfied that the dynamics he had generated were multiplying on their own. He settled back in his favorite chair at his Park Avenue duplex and inhaled deeply. Tomorrow he would digest the week. Today it was time for sweet serenity.

Having slept the entire way home from Maui to San Diego, Sol

Price awakened the next morning refreshed and rejuvenated, or at least alive, and immediately took out full-page ads in the *New York Times*, the *Wall Street Journal*, the *Washington Post*, the *Boston Globe*, the *Los Angeles Times*, and the *St. Louis Post-Dispatch*. He also bought a minute to run the ad on *Meet the Press*. Under a big, bold head-line—"IS THIS THE WAY WE, THE SO-CALLED OLDER HIGH AND MIGHTY, WANT TO LEAVE OUR COUNTRY?"—was a series of short phrases describing the decay and decline of our nation, all the worsening trends and tragedies. In large type at the bottom was the message "O Rich and Powerful, arise, you have nothing to lose but your country, your world, and your descendants' respect! Let's go to the heights and exit not with a whimper, wallowing in luxurious boredom, despair, and discouragement, but with a bang!"

The ad was a grand slam. Sol couldn't believe the response. He heard from hundreds of influential people in retirement who had been silent for years. Some wrote letters. Others called him or just showed up at his home or office in their chauffeured Rolls and Mercedes, some with canes, all with fire in their eyes. Sol knew what to say, having thought for years about national Redirections and priority reversals. One by one he met with them, communicating, motivating, taking their addresses, and ending the meetings with, "I'll be back for you. Get ready."

Within days of returning from Maui, Ross Perot bought thirty minutes' worth of time on the networks coast-to-coast and appeared with charts showing how the American people had lost control of their federal budget. He showed where their taxes were going and how the self-styled tax cutters were just cutting taxes on wealthy people like himself, producing mega-deficits and thereby taxing babies who would be responsible for the huge interest payments on the treasury debt when they grew up. He gave graphic examples of waste and corruption. He said that the Iraq war was "an economic sinkhole" and "a graveyard surrounded by quicksand," and that "we'd better bring our boys home pronto." He took calls from viewers and encouraged e-mails and letters of support. They came in the millions, heartening him with messages like "Great to see

you back!" and "You're telling the truth again, Ross!" He was especially gratified by the response from veterans regarding their
treatment when they came home from the wars. Many of them
agreed with him about Iraq. Among the strongest endorsements he
received was a letter from the Boston chapter of Veterans for Peace,
which called itself the Smedley Butler Brigade in honor of the highly
decorated Marine general (two Congressional Medals of Honor,
among many other awards for bravery) who retired in 1935 and then
wrote a book asserting that he'd been "a racketeer for capitalism,"
sent in to make various countries "safe" for US banks, oil companies, and other corporations.

Leonard Riggio came home and took it to the streets. Ever since
he was a boy in Brooklyn, he'd had a visceral reaction to the way the
working stiffs and the poor were treated on a day-to-day basis. Contacting neighborhood groups and labor leaders he knew, he quickly
put together a rally of 25,000 people of little means in front of the
New York Stock Exchange. They carried placards bearing slogans
like "The Poor Will Be Heard From—From Now On," "Stay Tuned,
Paper Pushers and Speculators, This Is Just the Beginning," and
"Tear Down That Wall Street!" Leonard marshaled some great
speakers whom no one had heard of, determined as he was to bring
out energetic new people who believed in movements, not just rhetoric. From the ghettos and barrios and slums of New York City came
fire and brimstone about deeply felt injustices. Leonard supplied
sandwiches for lunch and gave out posters, placards, and bumper
stickers to the crowd to help spread the word. Exactly what "the
word" was he didn't say, heightening the anticipation of dumbfounded reporters by intimating that today's rally was only the tip
of the iceberg. When pressed, he pointed to a group of ralliers, each
of whom held up a letter to spell out "Abolish poverty! Give us what
we've worked for! No ifs, ands, or buts!" Coverage that evening and
in the next morning's newspapers was tinged with puzzlement over
what this rally foreshadowed. Pictures of wide-eyed stockbrokers
gazing from their office windows bespoke trepidation.

A few days after Leonard's rally, Ted Turner uncorked an idea he'd had for years. Quickly he assembled a group of thirty irreverent older billionaires—Barry, Peter, and George from the core group, the rest from the top of the Forbes 400 list, together representing nearly every line of industry and commerce—and christened them Billionaires Against Bullshit. They were his friends, people who enjoyed his hospitality and showmanship, two of them fellow yachtsmen from his America's Cup days. As a longtime media master, Ted knew that the best way to confront lies was not with the truth. The truth must be accessible, always on the shelf, so to speak, but lies were best confronted with marching feet or easily understood symbols. He was always amazed at how little awareness of this historically rooted point there was among activists bent on improving the human condition. Ever the flamboyant entrepreneur, he staged a huge media extravaganza with a series of giant screens portraying the deceptions and dissembling of those at the top in Washington and Wall Street. One by one, after the lies were sonorously announced, Ted's billionaires splashed a slurpy bucket of bull manure on the prevarication screens. The reporters, nibbling on their canapés, gave up on maintaining their objectivity. They laughed and nodded and wondered to themselves why they couldn't throw tough questions at the bullshitters they had to cover day after day.

The solons and moguls named on the screens were not amused upon learning how they'd been demeaned. Time Warner received several angry and threatening calls from the White House. When one exasperated special assistant was told that Ted was no longer on the board but was merely a large shareholder, he sputtered, "Well then, sell his shares!" The cool Time Warner executive replied, "Capitalist principles would have us leave that decision to Ted."

After the visual event came the news conference, where a crusty veteran reporter asked, "Okay, Ted, you've given us some kicks, but what's to say that Billionaires Against Bullshit isn't bullshit itself?" Ted absorbed this sonic blast and instantly wished that the press would treat the current occupant of the White House with similar forcefulness. Recovering, he replied simply, "Stay tuned."

Joe Jamail was savoring Ted's televised antics in his Houston office when he decided what his initiative would be. This "King of Torts" was always taking on big cases with millions or billions of dollars at stake, and as a result he was always postponing doing something close to his heart, something that would allow regular people to use the justice system and actually get some justice out of it. He believed that the intangible benefits of public confidence in the justice system went way beyond getting people refunds or bringing the big corporations to account.

Joe unveiled his brainchild proposal with fanfare at a well-prepared news conference with live TV hookups, including C-SPAN from Houston. With his well-known talent for the dramatic, he announced that he was putting $15 million of his own money behind the formation of the People's Court Society, a network of law students and law professors who would advise, gratis, any person wanting to use any small claims court case that passed a basic standard of credibility. Existing legal aid services and public defenders did very good work under hampering conditions, he said, but they couldn't begin to reach a majority of the excluded. The PCS would rent space at or near all 174 law schools in the country, and on Main Streets everywhere, so that working people and consumers, tenants and patients, could drop in and receive either representation or clear advice about how to represent themselves if they so wished.

Joe also gave notice that companies guilty of fraud or harm would no longer get off scot-free simply because their victims couldn't afford attorneys and expensive legal proceedings. Judge Judy was an amazing ratings success because people cared about small injustices between individuals. Now, through the accessible PCS, they'd be able to take on the big boys as well, in hundreds of small claims courts all over the country. "For too long," Joe said, "small claims courts have been used as collection agencies by commercial creditors and landlords. Now these courts will be used for the little guy. The corporate crooks have sliced up the class action rights of the people and made it more difficult to file for bankruptcy because of job loss or health expenses. Now they're going to have to face those they've fleeced." Behind him as he spoke was Judge Learned Hand's famous dictum, "If we are to keep our democracy, there must be one commandment: Thou shalt not ration justice." The letters were two feet high to make the point.

The next day, the tortfeasors' lobby went berserk. "Joe Jamail is promoting a flood of frivolous litigation," declared the US Chamber of Commerce. "The PCS will undermine our global competitive edge, cost American jobs, raise taxes, and burden the business community unsupportably," roared the National Federation of Independent Businesses. Joe was denounced for his effrontery in hundreds of press releases, business editorials, and tirades by pompous talk show hosts, chief among them Bush Bimbaugh. Laughing all the way, Joe replied, "Access to the law is part of a just society. They're used to having it all to themselves. No more. The floodgates of justice are about to open."

Bill Gates Sr. also made a big splash in the weeks after Maui. In notices placed in labor, consumer, and taxpayer publications, he offered to pay for the Delaware incorporation of anyone who applied over the following twenty-one days. His aim was an egalitarian one, he said, since corporations had just about all the constitutional rights of human beings but enjoyed privileges and immunities far beyond those of lone individuals. Corporations had more freedom to sue, to go bankrupt, to pay lower taxes, to receive welfare; they could create overseas subsidiaries and holding companies, and they could avoid being jailed because they were artificial entities. In dozens of ways they were superior and unequal, under laws largely of their own making. "So if you can't beat 'em, join 'em and receive the blessings of limited liability," Bill's notice concluded. His motto, a twist on Huey Long's "Every man a king," was "Everybody a corporation."

Bill further announced that he was forming a committee to run five corporations for federal and state elective office in the next couple of years. Since corporations were legally deemed to be "persons" and could avail themselves of the equal protection of the law under the Fourteenth Amendment, there was no reason they shouldn't be able to run for senator, governor, state legislator, etc., as long as they met age and residency requirements. "Corporations are people too," Bill said at a news conference before befuddled reporters. He added that a six-person advisory committee on constitutional, corporate, and electoral law would be formed to combat challenges to this equality movement, and he pledged a vigorous defense against any lawsuits blocking his project to give more "voices and choices" to American voters.

Max Palevsky came back from Maui with an idea. He was not in the best of health but had a dynamo of a brain and knew more than most denizens of the planet about the enormity of the challenges facing it. Max had been in a funk for years, particularly after funding several important California electoral initiatives, including some on campaign finance reform, all of which lost. Even after some spirited female-gazing during country club lunches with his friend Warren Beatty, his resurgent libido did not put him in any persistently creative civic mood. Until Maui, he couldn't see a breakthrough for himself.

Max's obsession had always been civic anomie—the failure of so many citizens to exert even minor efforts to combat or diminish injustices that they themselves perceived as harming them. When he was a child, his family had lived in New England, in three different towns, and his parents would sometimes take him to town meetings. There were always lots of empty seats in the small school auditoriums or the rooms at Town Hall. Over the years, in conversations with liberal activists, Max brandished this memory at them and taunted them about all the union members who voted Republican, directly against their own interests as working families. War, religion, guns, the flag—whatever—distracted them from essential matters like pay, pensions, safety, health insurance, public services, and the way big business used government against them. The same held true for poor voters; a quarter or more voted Republican. All this led Max to an iconoclastic thesis: that even if all obstacles to democracy were removed and there was a perfect playing field, most people would not play, would not show up or speak out.

Now he decided to experiment to prove his point. Renting out a six-thousand-seat convention hall in Los Angeles, he offered free tickets to anyone who would agree to attend two presentations on two consecutive nights. He left the content of the presentations deliberately vague, saying only that they were designed to test a sociopolitical hypothesis and that the results would be sent to all attendees within a month. But the real draw was the promise of entertainment by a hot new band, the Cool Drool, plus a surprise celebrity appearance and free fruit, soft drinks, and snacks.

The first night, a Monday, the hall was almost full and anticipation was high. After a sensational performance by the Drool, the lights dimmed and Max gave the signal to start the slideshow he'd commissioned, which used visuals, sound, and light to brilliant effect. On a huge screen, as a familiar-sounding voice provided running commentary, images of injustice appeared one after another: children in Los Angeles, chronically hungry, ill-housed, and deprived of the medical treatment they needed; shrunken workers dying from asbestos-induced mesothelioma; US soldiers dying in Iraq for lack of simple body and vehicle armor while members of the Halliburton board clicked champagne glasses over huge Iraq war contracts; executives sitting in their lavish offices as that familiar voice intoned, "They make an average of $10,000 an hour, while their workers average $9.00 an hour"; young blacks with no prior record, imprisoned at five times the rate of young whites with no record; a powerful montage of the president giving his reasons for invading Iraq, causing more than 650,000 civilian deaths, and the headlines showing that he was lying. On they came—pictures of children abused in juvenile detention camps, of low-income people cheated by economic predators, of young fathers killed on construction sites because of dangerous working conditions, of loyal factory workers brought down by toxin-induced cancers—with imagery, statistics, and human tragedy all working to engage the minds and emotions of the audience. Then the lights came up and Warren Beatty, the slideshow's narrator, walked on stage. He asked what kind of world we would be leaving our children and grandchildren if we didn't get serious, wake up, and take back our country. He urged his listeners to get involved in organizations working for change—ushers were passing out flyers listing a hundred of these, along with mission statements and contact information—and then he thanked the audience for their attention and opened the floor to questions.

For several long minutes, no one spoke. Finally a few people asked questions about the accuracy of this or that part of the presentation. No one asked, "Well, what can we do, when can we start?" Remarkably little anger was expressed, except by an injured carpenter who was cheated by his worker's compensation carrier. No one proposed a future meeting, rally, or march for the environment or against the war or for any other cause. Afterward, as the audience streamed out of the hall, Max's people stationed at the exits reported that only about 10 percent were talking about the presentation. The other ninety were already into small talk about where they were going or who they were meeting. However, many mentioned how good the food was or how terrific the band was.

The next evening, a slightly smaller crowd showed up. Again the food and music were outstanding. After the opening performance, a silver-haired orator took the stage and unfurled a string of calmly delivered racist, sexist, homophobic, and ethnic slurs. By the third minute, the audience was shouting and throwing fruit and rolled-up newspapers at the stage, but the speaker continued, advantaged by a loudspeaker system that gave him sonic supremacy. Some people jumped up and stormed out of the hall. At no point did the speaker advocate acts of violence or suggest that the objects of his derision should be harassed or run out of the country. He simply unleashed a flurry of bigotry, citing bogus studies and fictitious history as foundations for his opinions. Within thirty minutes the hall was empty. Max's people at the exits reported that nearly everyone had expressed outrage and disgust. The event was page one in the next morning's LA papers, and the second story on the local evening news, right after a hot police pursuit. The sparse media coverage of the first event had focused on the Cool Drool and Warren Beatty.

Max waited three days before presenting his analysis in a full-page ad in the *LA Times*. He described the two presentations briefly and concluded, "The real deeds of government and business that kill, sicken, deprive, and defraud are far less upsetting to Americans than some nobody's bigoted words. Unless, that is, the deeds happen to touch on a personal injustice inflicted on an individual, in which case it's a horse race as to whether the personal bad deed or the terrible bad word provokes the most anger. A society that can't act to redress bad deeds in a motivated manner is on a downhill race to decay. A society that goes berserk over verbal slurs, however false and offensive, is a society that will distract itself in an escalating war over words." At the bottom of the page was the thought-provoking line "Pick Your Poison."

Max left town early the day the ad appeared, hoping to keep the focus on the issue he'd raised rather than on himself. Initially the outrage and vitriol poured forth as he'd expected, but then the reaction became more thoughtful as some of the talk shows, letters to the editor, and opinion pages began delving beneath the knee-jerk, politically correct rejoinders. Of course Max knew his little experiment was oversimplified, but it did provoke a lot of lively debate and a little introspection—a key result he'd hoped for. He hired an anthropologist and a psychologist to analyze the whole hubbub before the next meeting in Maui. He had more such tests in mind, much more refined. "Stay tuned," he told one of his editor friends. "Stay tuned."

Among the more interested readers of Max's ad was George Soros, who had been taking in the exploits of his Maui colleagues with no little amazement. A man who had long believed in fundamental change within an open society—his motto was "It is not a revolution until it succeeds"—George walked his talk, but his unflagging moral and financial support of democratic movements and institutions in authoritarian countries, and lately in the United States, had left him feeling a bit wearied by how difficult change was, how much more powerful the forces of disintegration, habit, and greed seemed to be than the forces of integration, tolerance, and justice. At first, it had been difficult for him to envision what he could do post-Maui that he hadn't done pre-Maui, but he banished the thought. He would do something bold, something out of character for his fairly retiring, almost academic personality ("Soros" would be the antonym for "Trump" if there were ever a celebrity dictionary of antonyms). He would challenge the editorial page editor of the *Wall Street Journal* to a debate at historic Cooper Union in New York City, site of many famous debates over issues like slavery, suffrage, labor, war, and civil rights. The debate resolution would be as follows: "Resolved that the principal threat to democracy in America and around the world is the large multinational corporation." As if that weren't bold enough, George called in some favors from high-ranking contacts at the World Bank and the International Monetary Fund, and the two institutions were persuaded to sponsor the debate. This decision was so discordant with the image of the Bank and the IMF—both had long been accused of being imperious, antidemocratic, insensitive to the impoverished, and wedded to ruling oligarchies—that the announcement created a frisson of disbelief in the airy upper circles of global finance and industry. The ruling classes most definitely took notice.

The editor of the *Wall Street Journal*'s editorial page was a man by the name of Reginald Sedgwick. He hated George Soros, who had been slammed by the paper in more than thirty-five editorials. To Sedgwick, Soros was a traitor to his class for making big money out of big money, especially in currency speculation. To have the ultimate successful global capitalist espouse progressive policies, oppose Republicans in elections, and support higher taxes on corporations and the rich was the ultimate apostasy. Unfortunately, no one could call Soros a communist or socialist—two of the *Journal*'s favorite epithets—nor could he be dismissed as an armchair philosopher who knew nothing about the real business world. George Soros had played the business game for the highest stakes and had won again and again, for himself and his legions of loyal investors. He would be a formidable opponent, and Sedgwick was tempted to decline the challenge—he had a bully's cowardliness when it came to someone of his own size—but the business press and the right-wing commentators and talk show hosts were touting him as their champion, licking their chops and rising as one to proclaim that he was the man to slay the forked-tongued dragon. He had no choice but to accept.

The day of the great debate—besieged by every media outlet from *The Onion* to *Vanity Fair*—came and went. And so did Sedgwick. He resigned his post the following month. In devastating detail, George demonstrated how hierarchical, monetarily fanatical megacorporations crushed dissent, civic values, and open societies while cozying up to their autocratic or dictatorial counterparts in government. He argued convincingly that the world's hopes and dreams, and even its continued existence, were at stake in the global collision between democracy and myopic corporatism, with its control of capital, labor, technology, media, and government. The great debate left the halls of Cooper Union and started around the country as if the self-censoring media had finally seen the light. When asked what he could possibly do for an encore after such a triumph, George replied, "Stay tuned."

For his own part, Warren Buffett hadn't exactly been twiddling his thumbs in the weeks since Maui. He and his people had been assembling the all-important brain trust that would respond with alacrity in specialized fields, from drafting legislation to assessing the feasibility of solar energy conversion on a wide scale. Among those enlisted were first-class wordsmiths and communications experts, specialists in friendly ultimatums and local mobilization, talented recruiters, and a whole array of people well versed in matters relating to budgets, billings, contracts, science, engineering, public works, healthcare, access to justice, corporate governance—the list went on. Without disclosing the existence and mission of the core group, Warren told these people that he was in the preliminary stage of launching a project for broad reform and wanted them on board. They responded with a sense of hunger for new directions.

Warren had also been refining the operations of the Secretariat and orchestrating the weekly closed-circuit TV conferences that enabled the core group to keep abreast of each other's initiatives and report on their efforts to consolidate their epicenters. Many of them had gone home and started with selected members of their bemused extended families, who were so astonished by their overachieving older relatives' sudden energy after returning "from some trip" that they immediately agreed to contribute to the cause, again without being told the full dimensions of the cause. Core group members had similar positive results with many of the other billionaires they approached, and they also secured commitments of support from groups that were longtime recipients of their donations or had been galvanized by one of their exuberant initiatives. Warren was impressed by the range of these organizations, which included taxpayer groups worried about huge deficits and wasteful spending—was it a coincidence that such groups first received national attention on the *Phil Donahue Show?*—sustainable economy institutes, local veterans' associations, antipoverty groups, neighborhood associations, several trade unions, media reform and access organizations, consumer groups and consumer cooperatives, nongovernmental organizations representing defrauded patients, tenants, debtors, insurance holders, and car buyers, educational and civic entities, small investor clubs, local environmental leagues, artistic groups responding to Yoko, and groups of wealthy retirees bored out of their minds playing golf or bridge.

As Maui Two approached, Warren felt a growing admiration for the achievements of his colleagues in so short a time, and marveled again at the creativity of their initiatives. As a major owner of a giant reinsurer, he'd had a rough moment when Peter took the industry on, but he told himself that he was being tested, and he met his inner conflict with silence and valorous inaction. The rest of the initiatives filled him with joy, and he was so taken with Patriotic Polly that he'd carved out some time to answer calls to the toll-free number advertised during her spots. His first call was from a respiratory nurse in Birmingham, Alabama, who told a heartfelt story. She said she was ready to act but didn't know what to do. Without revealing his identity, he promised to look into the matter and call her back in a couple of days.

Warren went to his newly formed brain trust—officially named the Analysis Department—which was able to provide details and prices for bus conversions to natural gas: overall reduction in pollution tonnage, reduction in illnesses and property damage over time, and so forth. Then he had a hunch. Was the City of Birmingham demanding competitive broker bids for its municipal bond sales? It turned out that the answer was no. Warren called on the Analysis economists, who estimated that if the city insisted on competitive bids, it would save $45 million in bond dealer fees every two years on average. Presto. More than enough to pay for the bus conversions and even purchase some new energy-efficient buses. A call to Ted located two Alabama members of Billionaires Against Bullshit who swung into action. The rest was history. The city government didn't know what hit it—there was a furor in the papers and on television—and quickly announced a competitive bidding policy and a natural-gas conversion program. The nonplussed Jane Harper was interviewed so often she became a civic celebrity and received a promotion at her hospital.

Warren smiled to himself at the recollection and popped open a celebratory can of Cherry Coke.

A Sunday evening toward the end of January found the eminent political columnist for the *Washington Post* poring over a pile of clippings. David Roader prided himself on being a modest forecaster, in between covering what he tiredly called "the humdrum of cyclical political nothing campaigns." In his pile he spied a series of developments that suggested a fledgling phenomenon. There was certainly enough there to warrant attention in his twice-weekly syndicated column. He sat down to write, his glasses perched well below the bridge of his nose:

> Maybe I'm seeing more than meets the eye, but have you noticed some unusual activity by some unusually rich people in the last month or so? One billionaire starts a fast-growing populist business association to take on the business behemoths in town; another organizes a big demonstration by the working poor in front of the New York Stock Exchange; yet another has

taken on the entire insurance industry, of which he is a leading executive. One has placed full-page ads in major newspapers calling on his affluent peers to exercise a higher order of social conscience. Maybe it is to be expected that a cable industry pioneer noted for his maverick views would take it upon himself to launch Billionaires Against Bullshit, and maybe it's not so remarkable that a very rich plaintiffs' attorney has established a litigation network to file zillions of small claims against big companies, and maybe the wizard from Waco wants to climax his career by using his wealth to form after-school civic youth clubs, but it's all happening at once. And that's not all. An erstwhile computer software entrepreneur is sponsoring bizarre back-to-back hoedowns to show that people care more about bigoted words than about harmful deeds. At the same time, according to my sources, the Chief Business Investment Guru of the United States, a major investor in this newspaper, is making calls at a furious pace to round up more billionaires in an effort, as he puts it, "to turn this country around." And remember Soros v. Sedgwick? To top it all off, the well-to-do father of the world's richest man is busily incorporating thousands of individuals in the state of Delaware, and intends to run some corporations for elective office—all in the name of egalitarianism!

I may have missed other similar eruptions, but I know enough to draw an interim conclusion. All these men are billionaires, most of them are in their seventies, eighties, or early nineties, and many of them end their interviews and press conferences with the same two words, "Stay tuned," all of which points to some sort of connection between them.

Something is bubbling here. Whether that something is heading for a seismic upheaval it is far too early to say, but in my fifty-one years of political journalism, I have never seen such stirrings from the very gut of the plutocracy. And the Internet traffic regarding the rich guys' activities leaves Britney and Paris in the dust.

No one who has read the newspapers for the past six years can have failed to notice the corporate crime wave, the contempt for prudent and self-restrained business behavior, the buying of political favors, and the lack of corporate patriotism in our country. Even leading business publications that rely on corporate advertising revenue—among them *Fortune* and *Business Week*—have been so taken aback by these unsavory trends that they have run cover stories and editorials denouncing corporate outlaws and their limitless greed. At present it is impossible to tell whether the activist billionaires represent this same resurgence of corporate ethics or something much more revolutionary. I guess we'll just have to stay tuned.

Monday morning, in his comfortable home in the nation's capital, Brovar Dortwist was sipping hot black coffee with his young Arab-American wife, Halima, as he checked the major newspapers on his laptop. Brovar was a conservative lobbyist—or rather, *the* conservative lobbyist. Every Wednesday at 10:00 a.m., in his office on K Street, he brought together more than a hundred of the most aggressive, no-holds-barred lobbyists and greasers in the corporate-occupied territory known as Washington, DC. Sitting at the head of a large table with standing room only around it, Brovar was the commander in chief, using his direct pipeline to the White House and his rapid-fire style to bark the craven missions of the week and send his troops forth to carry the banner of the almighty buck.

To call these sessions corporate pep rallies would be to underestimate the intense preparation and the vast resources in place. Brovar streamed out directives concerning the White House, Congress, the federal agencies, and the courts, all with the objective of consolidating the control of government by private economic power—what President Franklin Delano Roosevelt called "fascism" in a 1938 message to Congress urging the creation of a Temporary National Economic Committee to investigate the abuses of economic concentration. Most of Brovar's directives were part of a concerted offensive to secure more tax havens, tax reductions, and deregulation; to expand corporate control over the public's commonwealth assets; to weaken the government's enforcement capability; to restrict the right to sue the corporate predators in court; and in general to strengthen the power, privilege, and immunity of the corporations vis-à-vis the multitude of regular people who did the work and paid the bills. There was so little defense to play these days. In the sixties and seventies, those pesky citizen advocacy groups and their congressional allies made life so trying, until the great corporate counterattack launched by the Business Roundtable began harvesting its rewards during the later Carter years and the two terms of Ronald Reagan.

Sinking his teeth slowly into a petite Middle Eastern pastry, Brovar came to Roader's piece and paused in his swift scanning. He read every word and sat frowning at the polished mahogany surface of the dining table for a good five minutes. Then he packed up his laptop, gave his wife a distracted peck on the cheek, and strode off to work.

CHAPTER 3

A month after their first Maui gathering, the members of the core group journeyed to the mountaintop hotel once again. Warren had arranged for a light supper, during which he suggested that they all retire early to be fresh for an intensive day's work tomorrow. Not a chance. The dining room was abuzz with lively exchanges about the events of the previous month, the diners too engrossed in their conversations to think of sleep.

"Warren, please, a man needs to shmooze," said Sol, and returned his attention to Bernard and Yoko, who were discussing ways of popularizing the Seventh-Generation Eye symbol.

Warren threw up his hands in mock despair and went over to see what Max was talking to Bill Gates about so intently.

At a corner table, Cosby and Newman were deep in thought over nearly untouched plates of lomi salad. They'd been stunned by the response to their telethon, which had been a huge success even though it flew in the face of what an adoring public expected of them. Now the need to take the next step was gnawing at them, but they still hadn't hit on an idea.

Paul speared a chunk of salmon. "Dead money," he said.

"Come again?"

"Don't you play poker, Bill? It's what's in the pot from the guys who fold. Just think of all the vast fortunes lying around in some trust, or in stocks, bonds, money markets. They're dead, inert, going nowhere in terms of the needs of the world, or even worse, passively serving oppression. Dead money is just money making money, instead of making things people need or making things happen. We've got to find a strategy for jolting dead money into live money,

65

something that goes beyond simple charity or donations to political campaigns that get seedier by the year. We've got to resurrect dead money!" Paul finished with a plate-rattling bang on the table.

Bill, a chronic philanthropist who'd put his own money to work funding educational projects and outreach to inner-city youth, had been listening to all this with mounting excitement. "Amen, brother!" he said. "I hear you, I'm with you now. Dead money is like a stagnant pool breeding mosquitoes. Live money is like a gurgling brook full of marine life and on its way to join a river. But you're right, charity isn't enough. Remember those 'I Have a Dream' commitments where wealthy folks pledged to pay for the college educations of seventh graders if they hung in and made it through high school? Okay, that turned dead money into live money for those kids and their futures, but against the needs of millions of children, it was a drop in the bucket, just like the money the two of us give to this or that cause."

"Yes, there's no doubt that live money can make a real difference to individuals, but the challenge is to direct it toward fundamental change. There are some good development models out there, like one I saw from the UN Development Program on the enormous jump-start effect of some forty-five billion dollars on health, nutrition, and drinking water in impoverished areas of Asia, Africa, and Latin America. That's live money on the scale we're going to need here if we're going to succeed. For starters, consider how much it would take to follow through just on Leonard's idea from our last meeting about funding congressional elections."

Across the room, Warren stood up and yawned loudly. "I don't know about the rest of you Maui mastodons, but I'm turning in."

Paul and Bill exchanged a look. "Wait a minute," Paul called as they pulled their guitars from under the table, tuned up, and broke into "This Land Is Your Land." All joined in on the chorus.

"Great way to end the evening," Warren said. "I only wish I'd brought my ukulele. Good night, everyone. Sleep well so we can get started catapult-style at eight after the best breakfast you'll have had in a month."

With that, they all repaired to their rooms, and the star-studded Maui night descended on the slumbering future earthshakers.

The next morning, Joe was awakened by a commotion in the hall. "What the hell?" he said as he jumped out of bed and flung open his door to see Ted grinning like a maniac and shouting, "Get up! Don't let America down."

Sol's door opened. He stood there in his pajamas for a moment, taking in the scene with a scowl. "Everybody's a comedian," he said, slamming the door.

After a buffet breakfast that exceeded Warren's prediction, the group assembled around the table in the conference room.

"Good morning, all," Warren said, "and special thanks to Ted for rendering our alarm clocks unnecessary. I want to begin by saying how impressed I was by the energy and ingenuity each of you displayed during the month between our last Maui meeting and Punxsutawney Phil's unfortunate sighting of his shadow the other day. Our first order of business is a status report on your initiatives so that we're all up to speed on the latest developments. Ross, will you start us off?"

"Sure, Warren, happy to oblige. My TV presentation brought in just over five million calls, letters, and e-mails from old Perotistas—I have to admit that I always kind of liked people calling themselves that—and from whistle-blowers and folks with all sorts of utopian schemes, personal complaints, and good solid ideas. I've opened a small office to process them and distill the serious from the whimsical. And I'm glad I denounced the Iraq war and went to bat for POWs and MIAs, because now the veterans' groups, at least most of the ones I've heard from, will go to bat for us." Ross went on to tell his colleagues how his growing distaste for the war had drawn him closer to the Smedley Butler Brigade and their still very timely analysis. "Which reminds me," he said. "Should we consider bringing a military man into our deliberations, for credibility on issues of defense and national security?"

"I've been wondering about that too," said Paul, who'd served as a Navy gunner during World War II.

"Yes, might be a good idea," Warren said. "Someone like Anthony Zinni would be perfect. He's a retired four-star Marine general and an outspoken critic of the war, with a service record and a chestful of medals that make his patriotism unassailable. But let's table this matter for now and take it up when we've all had a chance to think it over. Meanwhile, who's next?"

Phil pulled a letter from his jacket pocket. "This is an offer from the head of NBC. He wants to give me a national talk show, and get this—he specifically wants me to deal with injustice, hard solutions to the nation's problems, bold doings among ordinary people, and the plight of millions of Americans who get pushed around or shut out while they do the essential, grimy, everyday work that keeps the rich and famous sitting pretty on top. He says NBC wants 'a new Dr. Phil for the new burgeoning civil society.'" Phil smiled as he neatly folded the letter into a paper airplane and sailed it toward Warren. "Too late, big suit. The train has left the station. We've got much bigger fish to fry, including him. Right, Barry?"

"You bet, Phil. I had to pull some strings to get Paul and Bill's telethon on the major networks, but pretty soon we won't need them at all. Remember what A. J. Liebling said? He said the only way to have a free press is to own one. My corporation already owns a bunch of TV, cable, and radio outlets, and my staff is working on buyouts that will give us a national network of stations with strong local and regional loyalties, like WTIC in Hartford and WCCO in Minneapolis. Not that I'm buying these particular stations, but you get the idea."

Sol cleared his throat. "Me, I still prefer a good newspaper, and that ad I took out in the big dailies really paid off. For a while there, my office looked like we were running a bingo tournament," he said, and described the parade of mega-wealthy oldsters who had descended on him in San Diego, earnest men and women who were bored, depressed, resigned to leaving this Earth in an ungodly mess, until they read his message and respected the messenger. Sol was no dot-com tycoon in his forties appealing to the cane-and-wheelchair set to give back. "I've asked my staff to collate their names according to likely areas of action, geographical location, and amount pledged."

"Did you know—"

"Did I know what, Mr. Squawk-Like-a-Parrot-at-the-Crack-of-Dawn?"

"Did you know," Ted said over the laughter that erupted around the table, "that a dozen of your guys joined Billionaires Against Bullshit? We started out with thirty, and now we've got fifty-five. There'd be more, but we screened all the applicants to get rid of the ones who were too compromised by bullshit investments or just wanted to join as an ego trip. We also turned away a few foreign billionaires because they're not US citizens, but we told them to stay tuned."

"It's extraordinary, isn't it," said Bill Gates, "this desire of the older rich to make a difference in the world? I think we're really on to something here. In my own fundraising during the past month, I drew heavily on my longstanding group of wealthy men and women opposed to the repeal of the estate tax. I selected the most likely large contributors, met with them or made a personal call, and explained our undertaking in general terms, indicating that specifics are coming. Then I declared my donation and asked them to do likewise as a pledge. I was pleasantly surprised by their impatience with the stagnation of our country and by their agreement with our judgment that purposeful upheavals and realignments are long overdue. One of them, a very successful retired investment banker, and a prominent advocate of public campaign financing, even said, 'Only if the effort is full throttle, Bill, only if it's full throttle. I'm not interested in due diligence.'"

"I got some good results from friends and associates too," Yoko said, "but I also got some chronic poor-mouthing from very rich people who keep discounting their acquired wealth every year as if they're starting from scratch."

Bill Cosby was nodding in assent. "That's just what Paul and I were talking about at dinner," he said, and recounted their conversation about dead money. "We think it's a vital concept, and we're going to commission an economist to give us some hard numbers."

"Speaking of hard numbers, let's see where we stand with our finances." Warren passed a stack of cards around the table. "Over the last month, the Secretariat has collected the names of the super-rich you contacted and the amounts they agreed to contribute contingent on what you yourselves offered to put up. Those contingent pledges, I'm pleased to report, total six billion dollars. Now if you'll all indicate your own contributions on these cards and pass them back, I'll do the math."

Warren collected the cards, jotted some figures on a notepad, and looked up with a broad smile. "Nine billion dollars. That gives us a total of fifteen billion for our first operating budget. Not bad," he said, thinking to himself that if his own contribution was the largest, he was also the richest, and that these people were dead serious. He'd chosen well.

"As to the nuts and bolts," he continued, "all funds donated will be forwarded to a trust escrow account within seven days. The trust will then establish two accounts under proper IRS rules, one for charitable purposes and one for lobbying and political purposes, the former deductible and the latter definitely not. Allocations from the escrow account will be based on the priorities we set as we proceed. So shall we proceed?"

"Let's," said Leonard, self-designated street person. "As you know, twenty-five thousand strong turned out for the Wall Street rally. We had sign-up tables all over for those interested in further action, and we collected about three thousand names. Of those, we've identified a hundred or so born or seasoned organizers for future events. We've analyzed in detail all the feedback from the rally—the impressions of our people on the ground, the overheard talk in the crowd, the water-cooler reaction of the stockbrokers in their offices, the press coverage and commentary—and I can tell you that you haven't seen anything yet. We've planted the seeds of mass rolling demonstrations, marches, and rallies across and up and down our country."

"The People's Court Society is on the move too," Joe said. "There's a wonderful flood of litigation underway, and the law schools have really gotten on board. I'd originally thought of this as a nice extracurricular activity for the students, but deans and professors have embraced it as a welcome addition to their for-credit clinical programs. As just a taste of what's in store, two hundred small claims suits have already been filed against major corporations. The law students were already trying to advise their poor clients in other clinical programs, so it was a quick shift from begging to litigation. The legal press has yet to take much notice of the coming shockwaves, but it won't be long."

"Hey, people are corporations too!" Bill Gates said to another wave of laughter. "They've been flooding my office to incorporate themselves under Delaware's generous laws, and in the process, they've learned firsthand about the double standard between corporate status and citizen status. Corporations have all kinds of privileges and immunities. For starters, as nonvoters, they can deduct their expenses when they sue and when they lobby. Citizens who are voters cannot. More on this later. For the time being, thousands of people are having fun naming their corporate selves, and the local press is having a field day covering this 'corporate explosion' in their midst. As for the other project, the one to run five corporations for public office, it's still in the planning stage, with the advisory committee preparing for their third intensive meeting. We've had inquiries about potential candidacies from a number of small corporations, but we haven't yet filtered them to see if they're just practical jokers. Initial commentary on my news conference was rich with satire and ridicule on the issue of 'personhood,' but the media braying has since abated."

"If I can jump in here," Bernard said, "there's been considerable interest from parents and teachers in my Egalitarian Clubs, but what's really engaged people is the whole issue of the public schools as instruments of corporate propaganda and commercialism. That's touched a much more sensitive nerve than corporate abuses involving consumer harms or environmental damage. We've got big companies refusing to pay their fair share of property taxes, demanding and getting abatements, and starving the local school budget; big companies advertising in the schools themselves during the twelve-minute Channel One period, pushing sugar, fat, soda, and junk food; big companies pouring garbage entertainment and violence into the minds of kids after school. There's lots of repressed rage coming from beleaguered parents who realize more and more that big companies are raising their children while they, the fathers and mothers, are at work, putting in longer and longer hours."

"But there are still plenty of kids who haven't been brainwashed," Yoko said. "Some of my favorite letters asking for CFLs were from kids who said that they knew how hard their parents worked and wanted to help them save money, or that they wanted to save energy so there'd be more for kids in other parts of the world, or that they thought the Eye was 'way cool' and loved what it stands for."

"So all in all, Yoko, how many Americans will it take to screw in your lightbulbs?" asked Ted with a Turnerian twinkle.

Yoko smiled. "All in all, Ted, my office has subcontracted for the shipment of more than three million energy-efficient bulbs, and we've got the names and addresses of everyone who requested them. That's a good list to have in terms of our other initiatives, especially those concerning energy and sustainability."

"I hope you've all seen the letter Yoko sent out," Warren said. "Even apart from the brilliance of the Eye design, it's a masterpiece. And so is your letter, Jeno."

"Thanks, Warren. For those who haven't had a chance to read it, I'll try to summarize. I wrote to the tens of thousand of businesses that signed up for the People's Chamber of Commerce, and began by cataloguing one grievance or dissatisfaction after another that many businesses have with their Washington-based trade associations. These associations have a bureaucratic drive of their own. They inflate all the terrible things the government will inflict on the industry if the money doesn't keep flowing into their coffers. They concoct outrageous demands for privileges, subsidies, and tax loopholes from Congress to justify larger budgets. They manufacture hinterland fear and frenzy, as they did with the right to sue in court, despite having no factual basis for their hype. And these trade lobbies never support national interest agendas. Shouldn't they be using their muscle to get the energy industry and the auto companies to refine their products for greater efficiency? Isn't that in their own economic interest? My letter cited example after example of how narrow, craven, and self-seeking these trade associations are, when the interests of the people of the United States should come first and foremost. But in the long run, our history demonstrates that displaying foresight and espousing principles of fairness, justice, and democracy, as the PCC intends to do, lifts all boats."

Peter raised his mug of coffee. "Hear, hear! I read your letter, Jeno, and it's a knockout. With your permission, I'd like to send a copy out to some business associates."

"Same here," came a chorus of voices, Ross describing the letter as "a clarion call," Max as "a prospectus for the future," Sol as "a challenge to the conscience of the merchant class, perfectly tuned to the audience."

"You're a hard act to follow, Jeno," Max said, "especially since I haven't had the time to expand on my experiments with civic arousal, other than to review all the popular and scholarly commentary. The anthropologist and the psychologist aren't getting along because they differ radically on the explanation for the behavior of the two audiences in Los Angeles. I told them to stop arguing and finish their reports ASAP, and then I'll decide on my next move."

Warren turned to Peter. "And what about those verbal thunderbolts you hurled at the insurance industry's tepidness or deliberate inaction on protecting lives, property, and health through loss prevention?"

"Well, after their PR flacks got done denouncing me from pillar to post, a low roar was heard, and now it's beginning to sound like an approaching typhoon of outrage from policyholders, firefighters, employees in the workplace, people all throughout the insured economy. I think I gave them a way to articulate their concerns, and I think they trusted what I said because I criticized my own golden goose. And miracle of miracles, the Senate Commerce Committee has perked up from its well-compensated slumber and announced five days of public hearings, to begin in a month. Maybe it's because the chairman is facing a rare closely contested election this year, but in any case, they've asked me to be the lead witness, and they've assured me that the committee is prepared to use its subpoena powers in abundance. That could lead to a real shake-up, especially if our group takes advantage of the coming thunder and lightning."

"Bravo, Peter." Warren consulted his notepad. "I think we've heard from everyone now, except for you, George. You got global coverage for your debate with Sedgwick, and I'm still seeing clips of it on the news. Had any takers for another debate?"

"Not a one," George said with an expressive arch of his eyebrows. "No news here, except that I'm told Sedgwick bought a spread in New Mexico and is raising ostriches."

"Good, he can put his head in the sand with them," Warren said, "and on that note we'll adjourn for lunch. There's a cornucopia of fruit, banana bread, and coconut pudding awaiting you in the dining room."

"I'll have the pastrami on rye," Sol said.

After lunch, as everyone was settling in for the afternoon meeting, a tall, dapper man in a suit and bow tie strode into the conference room.

"My friends," Warren said, "allow me to introduce Patrick Drummond, director of our Secretariat, a managerial wizard and one of my closest associates for the last twenty-five years. It's Patrick who deserves the credit for the smooth workings of our closed-circuit conferences, and it's Patrick who's been receiving all your communications for the last month. I've asked him to join us this afternoon to take notes on our discussion and collate the results."

After a cordial exchange of greetings, the group got down to hard tacks to set an agenda for action during the coming month. Hour after hour, the roundtablers worked at a furious pace, refining goals, setting priorities, allocating the human and material assets assembled during the past month's work, and deciding who would take primary responsibility in which areas. They interacted like smoothly meshing gears, expressing strong views without acrimony. They had checked their egos at Warren Buffet's door. Already predisposed to action, knowing what they wanted, drawing on their boundless entrepreneurial energy, realizing that collectively they had an unprecedented capacity to effect change, they were determined to get moving, to get the job done—at least their part of it—within a year. They knew that if it took longer, the opposition would have more time to mobilize and their chances of success would diminish.

A powerful new human force was being unleashed in that conference room, contrary to all cultural and psychological expectations about the rich, famous, and successful, contrary to the conventional view of human nature as greedy and self-serving. On top of that wondrously endowed mountain in the middle of the Pacific Ocean, Warren's warriors felt giddy with hard-headed hope. They worked on into the evening, until Warren stood to adjourn the meeting. "I thank you all for your labors, my friends," he said. "And now, supper, silence, and sleep."

In the morning the group rose without help from Ted and gathered around the familiar round table for a working breakfast. Warren opened the meeting by passing out agenda sheets that he and Patrick had prepared overnight.

"What you see here," he said, holding up his own sheet, "is a list of the major Redirections distilled from all our previous discussions and exchanges. I continue to use the word 'Redirections' because it connotes flexibility and a sense of learning as we go. It also connotes, however unexciting, the absence of dogma, rigidity, and isms. The excitement will come in other ways, you can be sure. Your names appear next to the Redirections for which you volunteered to assume either primary or secondary responsibility during yesterday's meeting.

"These ten Redirections were chosen with an eye to their potential for amassing additional human and material assets, arousing the downtrodden, securing positive media attention, provoking reaction from the vested interests, motivating the young, highlighting solutions, cracking the mind-suppressing paradigms of the intellectual classes, enhancing countervailing challenges to the power structure, redefining patriotism in terms of civic duty, and fast-tracking some long overdue practical improvements in the lot of millions of Americans. As we move on to implementation, let's all remember the importance of replication dynamics and leveraged velocity, as discussed during Maui One."

While Warren was speaking, his colleagues had been studying their agenda sheets with evident approval.

REDIRECTIONS ACTION AGENDA

1. First-Stage Improvements (economic inequality, health, energy, food, housing—a just society and fair economy): Max, with Jeno, Sol, and Bill C.
2. Congress: Bernard, with Leonard and Peter.
3. Electoral Reform (voters, candidates, parties, shaking up incumbents): Warren, with Bernard and Max.
4. Posterity (children, school budgets, youth clubs): Bernard and Yoko, with Ross, Paul, Bill C., and Warren.
5. Promotions (media buyouts, people's networks, staged events, theater, spectacle): Barry, Ted, and Phil, with Paul, Yoko, Bill C., and Bill G.
6. Credibility Groups (veterans, civic organizations, women's clubs, etc.): Ross, with Paul, Bill C., and Peter.
7. Sustainable Sub-economy (breakthrough companies, progressive business organizations): Sol and Jeno.
8. Access to Justice: Joe and Bill G.
9. Mass Demonstrations (rallies, marches, teach-ins, etc.): Leonard and Barry.
10. Citizens' Utility Boards (massive expansion of dues-paying civic advocacy groups): George, with Jeno and Max.

"I think each Redirection is largely self-explanatory," Warren went on, "but perhaps I should say a few words about two of them. Unlike existing Citizens' Utility Boards, our CUBs won't restrict themselves to the big power companies, but will address a broad range of consumer and public concerns. We're using 'CUB' generically, since these groups will certainly be of utility to our citizens. The Promotions Redirection represents what Patrick and I heard from all you media and performance types who kept harping on the need to dramatize our efforts in ways that will appeal to mass audiences.

"Now let me suggest a few organizational principles. First, each Redirection project will have one manager and one clerk—that is all. Their function will be to keep things moving, locate glitches, and report any crucial logjams or opposition to the Secretariat for higher-level action. Keeping the staff slim accords with a managerial philosophy of devolution, which means always pushing the work and energy down to the community or to the best real-life platform. Otherwise we'll end up building a top-heavy apparatus, and we all know where that leads. As for support services, our Secretariat will work out budgets with your single manager and single clerk, and will arrange for task-specific teams to gather data and prepare reports as needed. The Secretariat remains the back-and-forth communications hub.

"Obviously there will be much experimentation in the coming month. Let's hope that exuberance doesn't breed too many blunders. The Redirections are designed for minimal error, with no catechism, no doctrine, just an open source philosophy with intermediate and goal-targeted compasses. Remember too, over the next month, to make waves, not tsunamis. Be very attentive to feedback and subsequent refinements. You won't have much time for this, but you ignore it at your peril. Reflexivity, right, George?

"I see that I'm making a speech here, but I can tell from your faces that you're all satisfied with our Redirections agenda. I think you'll agree that our work here is done, so with your indulgence, I'll go on with my closing remarks.

"Some of these Redirections are bucking broncos, others are slam dunks, and still others are just plain fun. They should all eventually become sheer joy. Some of them are tools for building power, while others are forms of direct pressure for substantive change like a living wage.

"Speaking of joy, I've talked to each of you privately about bringing on board Bill Joy, formerly of Sun Microsystems, which he cofounded. He's the most imaginative technical futurist thinking and writing today, and yet he's completely grounded in reality. He is not an elder like most of us, but he's wealthy enough, and without objection I'll call him to make the invitation. He is the great antidote to these techno-twits who are imperiling us with their contempt for the ethical and legal framework necessary to contain future Frankensteins. We have many skills around this table, but science and technology—with apologies to computer wiz Max, who now calls himself a Luddite—are not among them. That is what Joy brings to us, along with impressive foresight and an alert energy.

"One last reminder. I'm sure you all saw David Roader's column in the *Post* speculating about a possible connection between the recent activities of certain billionaire oldsters. Well, if that's all the astute, well-connected Mr. Roader knows, then I think our secret is safe for now, but be careful. It's fine if people make connections between us as individuals—in fact, we want them to—but please safeguard our acting as an entity for the time being. Public disclosure of this group would galvanize our opposition. The time will come when the opposition builds to such a point that we'll step forward in our strength and unity and enter the fray for the showdown. By then we will not be alone."

Whereupon they all drank a toast to their mighty endeavor, took leave of each other, and boarded two business jets supplied by Warren and Ted for the journey back to the mainland. The next day, a short paragraph in the *Hollywood Reporter* noted a sighting of Paul Newman and Bill Cosby at the Maui airport.

Monday morning in New York City, George Soros summoned his three-person action team, which he'd put on high alert well before he landed at JFK. He wanted a meeting within twenty-four hours with the prime advocates of the CUB model, Robert Fellmeth, a dynamic, prolific law professor from San Diego who'd written a report on the subject a few years back, and John Richard, a longtime CUB proponent who knew intimately the kinds of arguments used against them. By noon,

George's team had made the invitations and put together a memo on the two main existing CUBs, in Illinois and San Diego, as well as all the CUBs that had been proposed but rejected. They'd also compiled a list of CUB sectors to be rapidly developed: banking, investment, and brokerage; auto, health, home, and life insurance; postal services and utilities; Social Security and income taxation; consumer, tenant, and voter rights; and anticonsumer (as in credit and software) standard form contracts. Attached was a description of the CUB structure: membership, dues, elected boards of directors, staffs of organizers, publicists, attorneys, economists, and other technically skilled people. Those solicited for voluntary participation would be reached through selected mailing lists and demographically targeted mass media, in keeping with the principle of closing the loop on the ground.

George devoured this information and waited impatiently for the four o'clock deadline for his team's report on available mailing lists and the best estimates on costs and rates of return. That's what successful, self-made people of wealth are like—big on detail while keeping the big picture in mind. They are chronically averse to procrastination—one definition of an entrepreneur is someone who never does anything today that could have been done yesterday—and that trait alone gives them a major advantage over their competent but slower-paced peers.

George's team also prepared a report on how the existing CUBs had adjusted to the Supreme Court's split 1986 decision prohibiting laws or regulations that required companies to place invitational inserts in their billing envelopes. At the time, Justice Rehnquist delivered a blistering dissent in defense of the California regulation requiring such inserts, and rejected the narrow majority's ruling that the regulation violated the electric utility monopoly's First Amendment rights, specifically its right to remain silent! The tortured logic here is that if the inserts were allowed, the utility would have to rebut their consumer-oriented content. After the decision, the San Diego CUB had to go to less rewarding cold mailings, but the Illinois CUB secured passage of a law requiring state government mailings above a certain number to enclose such inserts.

On Tuesday morning, Robert and John arrived at George's office promptly at nine. George told them what he needed, fast. First, a draft invitational letter containing the basic message; he'd have his writing experts add the flash. Second, all possible leads for recruiting the best possible directors and staff for each CUB, these positions to pay good upper-middle-class salaries with benefits. Third, a plan to get the CUBs underway immediately, for an interim period of eight months, to allow the structure to get on track before the members took over to elect a board and assume other governance duties as befitted a grassroots association. Fourth, liaison with the tiny existing citizen organizations that had been working for years against various companies' abuses. All these tasks would be budgeted immediately, George said. Both men agreed to take them on.

John foresaw logistical needs that required immediate attention—offices, legal and promotional services, a whole infrastructure for establishing enduring institutions. George, already on this, said that a three-hundred-room Washington hotel was available to house the national CUB offices. The hotel wasn't doing well, and he knew the CEO of the chain, who would sell for a reasonable price. The rooms would become offices, each with a bath. There were several conference rooms, as well as cooking and exercise facilities for the staff. Perfect. Modest renovation could be accomplished within a month.

On his flight across the country, Robert's encyclopedic mind had outlined a substantive agenda for each of the CUBs, with starting times for the items staggered and backup strategies attached. George was impressed. It wasn't even noon. He ordered lunch and champagne. The material assembled by his team of three the day before now had to be digested in detail.

Working outward, the group discussed the five-year budget line, the websites, the preliminary announcements, the estimated paid memberships over five years, the initial actions—petitions, lawsuits, agency interventions, public hearings, reports, articles, conferences, rallies, and other kickoff activities—and the short- and longer-range objectives, hammering out the details with precision. Robert proposed a two-year average membership objective of 1.5 million for each of the fifteen different CUBs—some would be larger, some smaller—with average dues coming in at $50 a year. John proposed a central service organization to handle media, accounting, Internet facilities, legal advice, etc., and to be lodged in the hotel so that the CUBs could concentrate on their substantive missions, especially intensifying member activism back home. George said to himself, "These fellows are the kind of talent and experience lying in wait that we can expect to find everywhere—mature, experienced, short on funds, but hanging in there year after year."

The last question to be resolved was when liftoff should be and whether all the CUBs should launch at once. Everyone agreed that each CUB should have its day, with the announcements spaced two days apart to allow time for media coverage and for the opposition to get their licks in and help make even more news. The millions of letters mailed out for each CUB would be timed so that the bulk of them arrived in the middle of the national news focus and the launch of the website. George expressed hope for a 5 percent return, an unusually good number. As for liftoff, it would be in thirty days sharp, meaning right after Maui Three, though of course George didn't mention that.

Over at the Congress Project, the agenda was nowhere near as self-executing. In their initial huddle, Bernard, Leonard, and Peter tried to reduce this enormously indentured institution to human scale. The 535 men and women of Congress all had offices in DC and in their home districts or states. They had dozens of staffers enabling, scheduling, and shielding them with varying degrees of sycophancy and sincerity. Bernard and his colleagues had many years of contact with members of Congress and their top staff. Not much of it was useful for the task at hand, except to underline the importance of the multibillion-dollar buyout to replace the money of the lobbyists.

But before getting to that blockbuster foray into the real political wars, the three men attended to the infrastructure necessary to change such a mired behemoth. Money is the lubricant of incumbency, in that it helps sitting members to ward off challengers in both primary and general elections, but votes, not money, get politicians to Washington, DC, so it starts with the people back home. What do they need to know in order to elevate their expectations of congressional performance and take matters into their own hands to make it happen? Make what happen? The three agreed on this one: replace all who do not meet a minimum standard of heeding the interests of the people. Bernard estimated that fewer than 15 percent of those in Congress would survive such a cut. But what standard? That started them down a line of thought about standards of performance: standards of empowering the people back home; standards of informing the people back home through studies, website information, oversight hearings on the executive branch, and scores for voting records; standards for judicial confirmation; standards of accessibility. If, for example, more than a third of a legislator's time was spent raising campaign money during an election year, that would fall beneath the standard of accessibility. Admittedly, such standards could not be mathematically quantified, but at least they would shine a nonpartisan and institutionally focused light on Capitol Hill. The men knew that these standards, once written, would be fodder for the numerous citizen groups in Washington that were information sinks. The Congress Project would need special budgetary support for a crash effort. They called the Secretariat. Done.

Next, they would hire two hundred full-time organizers, assign them proportionately to the fifty states, and send them out with major advance publicity to each congressional district with an approximate population of 600,000, to find residents who in turn would be willing to find two thousand voters in each congressional district serious about establishing a Congress Watchdog group. Each group would have a full-time staff and office, with a budget for part-time workers. Their immediate tasks would be public evaluation of incumbents and public accountability sessions. In each district they would distribute cards allowing voters to declare their positions on various issues on one side, and showing how their senators and representatives voted on those issues on the other. That way the voters would be able to see at a glance how their views compared with the deeds of the lawmakers, not the rhetoric. Local media and relevant websites would receive regular dispatches about deeds versus rhetoric, and Barry's democracy networks of TV and radio stations would be sure to publicize these extensively.

With adequate financial resources and organizers, two thousand serious voters in each congressional district was a realistic goal. For one thing, almost every district had one or more universities, colleges, or community colleges. For another, letters to the editor in local newspapers and magazines could be scoured for names, and the lists of millions who'd responded to the various core group initiatives after Maui One could be broken down by zip code. The organizers could drive a Congressional Action Bus through cities and towns to bring out people willing to make time for turning Congress around. After all, it was an institution that spent some 22 percent of the people's income and could send their children off to war, raise their taxes, give their commonwealth property away to corporations, and leave them defenseless against rapacious lobbies that kept wages down, drug and fuel prices up, and big business happy.

A vital part of the organizers' work would be to screen admission to the Watchdog groups through interviews and questionnaires designed to establish common ground at the outset. Potential members would be expected to devote a minimum of twenty hours a month to monitoring their representatives' positions on a livable wage, universal cost-effective health insurance, and the rest of the First-Stage goals for a greater and better America. They would also have be reasonably well-informed on these issues so they could impress the media and their friends and neighbors with their commitment. Such preconditions would assure a high degree of unity and minimize bickering and indecisiveness.

Now for the Blockbuster Challenge. The project staff began by preparing a preliminary estimate of the amount spent by members of Congress in the prior election. Subtracting resignations or departures from office, the total for the House and Senate came in at about $2 billion, just as Leonard had predicted at Maui One. This 2 billion would come from the core group's operating budget and would be administered by twelve trustees, distinguished men and women who had completed their careers and had no further ambitions for power, status, or lucre. The trust would match each incumbent's net fundraising in a giant buyout of the special interests that normally funded them. The slogan would be "Buy Back Your Congress: The Best Bargain in America." Any incumbent who resisted this no-strings buyout, other than by rejecting all private contributions, would be on the A-list for defeat by the Congress Watchdogs and their allies. Just that simple. Until the passage of a fair public campaign finance law, a similar amount of money would be raised every two years, preferably through small contributions from the aroused citizenry, to continue the Great Buyout.

Having developed the Congress Project to this point, Bernard, Leonard, and Peter put in a call to the Promotions Project and got Barry, who was eager to discuss synergy and to work with them as an early real-life test of his networks and media strategies. He promised to have a plan ready in three days and suggested that they all meet soon afterward.

At the Promotions Project, deliberations tended to have a certain combustible quality, given the temperaments involved: Barry, the bone-crushing, mercurial boss; Ted, the iconoclastic, impulsive, daring visionary with his feet on the ground; and Phil, the vernacular imagery king whose show served as America's Town Meeting on public taboos every morning for nearly thirty years. To these three gentlemen, selling the core group's mission to the American people was a priority that could scarcely be overstated. They knew better than most the kind of big-money multimedia counterattack that was awaiting them, and they wanted to anticipate every weakness and come back strong against every smear, deception, and lie. They knew a titanic battle lay ahead.

Barry had been acquiring radio, TV, and satellite outlets ever since Maui One, through the magic of leveraged buyouts. He had a law firm that spit them out like extruded plastic. It was all a matter of financing. Buying good income-producing assets solved that problem, though Promotions would need a modest budget from the core group for restaffing and some reprogramming of station content, which had to be serious and irresistible, like *60 Minutes*. As for newspapers, there was no need to buy one; it would be cheaper to buy space for ads that made news themselves, in the style of Bill Hillsman, the iconoclastic adman. As for movies, Barry would contact the Dreamworks duo and others he'd brought into the business, to discuss some imaginative assignments that would intrigue the video-doused younger generation.

They approached the next subject gingerly. The media, even the mass media, was only as good as the message, the presentation of the message, and the timing. When the counterattack came, they'd be ready for the big boys, with their Madison Avenue skillsters and their endless treasuries, but meanwhile, they needed a smash hit out of the box. They mulled over the slate of Redirections for visual, symbolic, and emotional intensity. Of course they would coordinate with the Congress Project and all the other Redirections—that was a big part of their job—but as an opening salvo, Congress just didn't cut it, no matter how hard they tried to personalize Capitol Hill, or more accurately, Withering Heights. They all racked their brains. The hopelessly competitive Ted was determined to come up with something that would surpass the rousing success of his and Phil's brainchild, Patriotic Polly, but in the end it was Barry's idea that won the day. They would start in California, the trendsetting state, with what pool players called a bank shot.

With Ted and Phil on speakerphone, Barry placed a call to his close friend Warren Beatty, the progressive but indecisive Hollywood actor who had been making noises about going into politics for a long time. California's current governor was a former grade-B actor whose political decisions were daily irritations to Beatty. Twice he had publicly chided "my old friend Arnold," who chose not to reply. California had a large deficit that could be erased with one piece of legislation that the Democratically controlled legislature would be pleased to pass: a return to the level of taxation of the very wealthy before the tax cuts drowned state revenues in a sea of red ink. Governor Schwarzenegger was adamantly opposed to such legislation, probably because he had so many super-wealthy friends and contributors. To meet the state's expenses, he kept floating huge bond issues and cutting programs for those on the lower rungs of the income ladder. This would be the heart of Barry's pitch to get Beatty off the fence.

"Hello, Warren, Barry Diller here," he said when the actor picked up.

"Hi, Barry, got a good script for me for a change?"

"You bet, but not the kind of script you mean. I have a two-stage plan that will put you in the governor's mansion."

"Are you kidding? Really, Barry, what's the scoop?"

"Simple. You get your ass out of Mulholland Drive and hit the road, contacting all your wealthy friends and their friends up and down the California Gold Coast. Your message: you are going to donate what the tax cut awarded you to the public treasury, and you want them to do the same as part of a reverse revolt of the rich. Then you all go to Sacramento, demand that the megamillionaire governor follow suit, and lean on the legislature to repeal the tax cut. We will provide you with staff and media backup, two press people, and a list of the California super-rich."

"Who's 'we'?" Warren asked.

"Me, Ted Turner, Phil Donahue, and your pal Max Palevsky."

Warren whistled. "Quite a group. You know, I just did a thing with Max last month."

"Yeah, I heard, quite a thing. Anyway, like I was saying, we'll get behind you all the way, with whatever you need. By next week, I'll have four billionaires, give or take, lined up to announce their own tax-cut givebacks and accompany you on your swing up the state. Two of them have real star power. The resultant uproar and the media saturation on your historic bus trek will get you to ninety-nine percent name recognition, if you don't have it already, and after you take Sacramento by storm, you announce for governor. When millions of Californians see what you've done outside the governorship, they'll be ready to believe what you say you're going to do inside it once you evacuate the corporate cyborg who's there now. So, what do you say?"

"Tempting, but I don't know. Why don't we have dinner at the club and talk it over?"

"Look, you've already thought about running and weighed the pros and cons. It's time to make a decision, Warren. It's time to fish or cut bait. I'll call you back tomorrow morning for your answer—unless you have any more questions?"

"No, I guess not. Okay, Barry, call me at ten."

"Well, fingers crossed," Phil said as Barry hung up.

At ten the next morning, Barry called back, and Warren said yes. Three times. At long last, his demons of indecision were exorcised, and he was ready to put his ideas and convictions into practice. Barry was ecstatic. He told Warren that the aforementioned support team would arrive at his home in seventy-two hours. "Then we'll have a conference call for the rollout no more than two days later. Ciao."

Barry sat back in his desk chair and contemplated the coming campaign. "The Reverse Revolt of the Rich," he kept repeating to himself. "Something's not quite right. Aha. The People's Revolt of the Rich, that's it! The perfect oxymoron to pique interest." He pulled out his famous electronic Rolodex, and within hours he had commitments from the four billionaires he'd promised Warren, and from a dozen more who agreed to come on board, partly persuaded on the merits and partly flattered by Barry's call. Like others in the core group, Barry was discovering that he could call in an enormous number of IOUs because he'd almost never asked his affluent peers for anything, except maybe to buy some tickets to a charity ball or make the tiny allowable contribution to a political candidate. There were golden assets in them thar hills!

When the core group members were informed of the Beatty initiative, they were all for it. Max didn't mind that Barry had dropped his name without talking to him first; he'd been Warren's close friend for thirty years, and they'd had many a bachelor adventure together. Bill Cosby loved "the imposition of responsibility on the rich by the rich but for the people," as he put it. Bill Gates offered to tap his estate tax group for more billionaires to join Beatty, and Ted said he would canvass his Billionaires Against Bullshit.

Meanwhile, the Mass Demonstrations Project was in active collaboration with the First-Stage Improvements Project. Together, Leonard and Max launched what they called the lunchtime rebellion—rallies in the main squares of the older cities, like Pittsburgh, Chicago, Detroit, San Francisco, Los Angeles, Atlanta, and Boston. The rallies started small on a Monday, but the colorful speakers and the distribution of nutritious lunches soon attracted larger and larger crowds. The topic was economic inequality, with dozens of vivid examples that resonated with the daily experience of the lunchtimers. Leonard and Max drew on the work of Bill Gates's coauthor on the keep-the-estate-tax book, Chuck Collins, whose collection of inequalities was unsurpassed in the nation. They had their organizers distribute material filled with data, personal stories, angering comparisons between CEO pay and grunt worker pay— $10,000 per hour compared to $9.00 per hour—accompanied by an explanation of how continued inequality would destroy both our worker economy and our democracy.

Halfway across the country, in a quiet office in Omaha, Warren and Bernard began the arduous work of marshaling the best proposals for electoral reform. They considered the rights of voters, candidates, and parties, with the objective of a competitive, diverse spectrum of choices. Their working premise was that the electoral system is fixed, not just by the corrupt political machines that have marked our history, but by a 217-year-old Electoral College and an exclusive, winner-take-all, commercially funded two-party system that effectively results in an elected dictatorship. In the economy, such domination would be in violation of the antitrust laws. In the electoral arena, it was politics as usual. But as a federal judge once said, "Democracy dies behind closed doors." Smaller parties and candidates who might have affected the content and sometimes the margins in two-party races had the doors closed on them by a bewildering, arbitrary, capricious, and sometimes venal array of local, state, and federal election laws that prevented them from competing and having a chance at the voters. No other western country had as few candidates on each ballot line and as many obstacles to both voters and candidates as the United States. Not even close.

As businessmen who started out small against the big boys, Warren and Bernard knew how crucial it was to keep the doors open to new blood, new proposals, new energies, budding movements— even if or precisely because their preferred party was on top. They were tired of lesser-evil choices for voters. They also knew that dozens of blue-ribbon commission reports on electoral reform were gathering the proverbial dust, pathetic victims of politics as usual.

How, then, to get the show on the road? They arrived at three approaches. First, a big-time shakeup of the system through a massive media campaign and mobilization rallies under the umbrella of "Bring Back the Sovereignty of the Voters." These would emphasize the usual ingredients of electoral reform: public financing of campaigns, eradication of obstacles to voting and running for office, open access to debates, varieties of instant runoff voting, proportional representation, same-day voter registration—and, Bernard insisted, binding none-of-the-above (NOTA) choices on all ballot lines. NOTA would give voters what they did not have—the opportunity to vote no confidence in all the candidates. Should NOTA win, that ballot-line election would be nullified and a new election with new candidates would be scheduled within thirty days.

To head Operation Shakeup, Warren had his eye on an old friend of his, Jerome Kohlberg, a retired billionaire investment banker with a proven passion for electoral reform. One call from Omaha to his Hamptons residence and he agreed immediately, asking if he could start yesterday. Warren said he would be contacted within a week with the comprehensive plan and resources; in the meantime he should study the reform proposals and make his own contacts to expand the clout behind the operation.

Approach number two they called the Trojan Horse Strategy: mobilize all the former members of Congress who had been driven away by the stench of the system. Warren called Cecil Zeftel, a former member of the House from Hawaii, who had written a searing book about the putrid lobbying and cash-register politics dominating our national legislature. Bernard called James Zabouresk, ex-senator from South Dakota, who'd retired with a similar public blast. The two men agreed to lead the effort and said they would start rounding up their former colleagues right away. Zabouresk wanted to stress the human costs of not having electoral reform, such as no health insurance for millions of people.

The other hoof of the Trojan Horse Strategy would be to infiltrate congressional staff with new staff committed to electoral reform. Bernard had marveled over the years at the influence of perhaps two dozen key staffers in either body who were the trim tabs that turned the ship around. Although there were predisposed "ships" among the lawmakers, they were often demoralized, but the flame was still there. The staffing initiative would have to extend to congressional offices back home to track emerging grassroots pressures for change and convey them up the line.

The third approach was the most audacious: create a one-issue political party with an electoral reform platform at all three levels of government. Upon formation, the Clean Elections Party would announce that it would go out of business once the platform was enacted into law. It would have no other ambitions, no other agendas. Starting a new party was an uphill task, but if the money was available, the forlorn longtime advocates of reform would swing into action all over the country. The very simplicity of the party's purpose—to show the way to clean elections so that the people had a fighting chance to address the widely perceived needs and injustices they encountered in their daily lives—would have an undeniable appeal.

Warren got himself another Cherry Coke and poured a glass of red wine for Bernard. It was time for a break before they composed a memo to the Congress Project, with which they would coordinate their activities closely. Bernard wondered how the Access to Justice Project was doing, since there would also be some overlap there. They put in a call to Bill Gates's resort home in the San Juan Islands and got an update from him and Joe.

No two lawyers could have been more different physically, temperamentally, and in outward demeanor than Bill, tall and measured with words, and Joe, shorter and given to bombast, not to mention bursts of profanity. Bill liked to joke about the time Joe was on *This Week* and Sam Donaldson asked how much he made from the Pennzoil case. On national TV, Joe shot back, "That's none of your business. That's between me and the IRS." (Later it was reported that his fee was $450 million.) But on the myriad issues involving access to justice, there was an iron bond between them. Equal justice for all was their professional passion, and Bill had even persuaded the Washington State Supreme Court to establish an Access to Justice Board. "Nobody makes it alone," he said repeatedly, noting that poverty or privilege are dealt to human beings from birth and that a just society tries to level the playing field.

With the People's Court Society in full swing, Joe and Bill set out to broaden its base of operations by bringing in the bar associations and judges' organizations. At the same time, they realized that "access to justice" had to be defined more concretely. The phrase begged for detail, for human interest, for a portrait of the kind of society that real access to justice would bring. But as Joe pointed out, quoting one of his heroes, philosopher of jurisprudence Edmund Cahn, "You cannot understand justice unless you understand injustice." To that end, they would commission a report that would be called "The State of Justice in America: Supply and Demand" and would break the access issue down state by state as well as at the federal level, providing a taxonomy of different injustices, estimating the tangible and intangible costs to society, and reviewing the inadequacies of the law and the justice system, as presently constituted, to cope with demands for justice—in short, demonstrating conclusively the serious gap between the demand for justice and the supply.

From their own contacts and from Analysis in Omaha, they collected a list of names and systematically worked through it to put together a group that could prepare such a report on an eight-week deadline. Over three days, the response from law school deans, professors, and students, from leaders of the bar and mavericks alike, from neighborhood activists and moonlighting reporters, was more than sufficient to signal the Secretariat that it was a go. Bill thought that some state attorneys general could be convinced to announce annual State of Justice Reports that would begin to frame statewide standards and workable measurements of justice and injustice. That would give the project important backing. Calls from Bill, Joe, and key friends to the attorneys general of the fifty states and the Commonwealth of Puerto Rico brought forth six definites and twelve maybes; the rest were noncommittal or opposed. One of the latter said that such a report was "impossible to conceive, politically suicidal to put out, and hopelessly expensive to implement."

"All the more reason to do it, right, Bill?" Joe said.

For all they had accomplished, both men were still casting about for a big idea, something that would build on the momentum of the "for some" Pledge, which was still a subject of hot debate in the media and the schools. They couldn't very well expect Newman and Cosby to have a telethon every month, so they pondered in silence for the better part of an hour. They were getting a little frustrated, and Bill knew it was almost 5:30 p.m., when Joe started on his daily scotch, *de rigueur* for years. They needed something that would sow widespread outrage at injustice, but what? Interesting that an ethnic or racial slur from some cabinet secretary or sports coach was national news, provoking demands for resignation, but real injustice seldom aroused such intensity, even when exemplified. Max's cultural conundrum.

Suddenly a light went on in Bill's mind. Why not hold two national essay contests on the questions "Which state is the most unjust in the nation?" and "Which state is the least unjust in the nation?" Essays would be limited to ten thousand words and would be judged by an impartial panel of retired judges, prosecutors, defense attorneys, and civic leaders. Winners, runners-up, and second runners-up would receive respectively prizes of $100,000, $50,000, and $25,000, plus a complete bound set of the decisions of the United States Supreme Court.

Joe responded with enthusiasm but added that they would need an infrastructure for the nationally announced contests, to generate controversy in the media and among politicians and jurists. Some of Ross's credibility groups might be useful here. They also decided to ask Barry to start an Injustice of the Day segment on the television and radio networks he was developing. And maybe Leonard could organize justice marathons, with the proceeds going to a legal aid fund for the indigent. These marathons could be occasions for media-smart street displays showcasing the runners and local celebrities.

When Ross was told about the essay contests, he was thrilled. His Credibility Project had been stalled. It was hard to get veterans' groups, scout troops, women's clubs, and service clubs like the Elks and Rotary excited when they couldn't be told much about what was going to happen. After poring over profiles of dozens of national groups with local chapters, Ross decided that his project would start by contacting them with offers of help, charitable contributions, and free professional advice, and expressing a genuine interest in their programs and objectives. Ross would cultivate his relationships with the American Legion, the VFW, and several smaller organizations of wartime vets. Paul and Bill Cosby each had their own niches with the many charities to which they had donated generously, like the Hole in the Wall camps, the United Negro College Fund, and the NAACP, and Paul had a huge following among auto racing fans as the oldest successful racer in NASCAR history. Bill Gates could furnish a list of health and medical charities that the Gates Foundation had been working with for several years in the increasingly prominent drive against global infectious diseases. And Ted was highly thought of in environmental and peace circles, not to mention among the ranks of carnivorous Americans who liked bison meat. Now, with the essay contests, Ross and company could approach these various groups with something solid, inviting their memberships to enter and compete for the not inconsiderable prize money.

At the First-Stage Improvements Project, which was responsible for hands-on solutions to the injustices that were being catalogued, quantified, and publicized by the other projects, Max and his cohorts chose the mantra "Make America Number One as a Humanitarian Superpower." They began with a discussion of fundamental principles.

"Whether our leaders choose to acknowledge it or not," Max said, "our democracy rests on a compact among the American people. I call it the Basic Livelihood Compact. Few would dispute that everyone should have adequate food, shelter, healthcare, and education. The paralysis in our country arises over how to achieve these goals. Some argue for the marketplace, some for the government, some for a combination of delivery systems, and feelings run high on all sides. We can't avoid this gridlock, but we must overcome it. Our goal is the double circle of material happiness—self-starting, self-reliance, and self-preservation in the inner circle, and community self-starting, community self-reliance, and community self-preservation in the outer circle. My study of history convinces me of the value of strengthening local community, particularly in its economic and environmental dimensions. Some sage once said, 'Without community there is crisis.' Just look at our inner-city neighborhoods and our rural poor."

"Very well put," said Jeno. "But if we're proposing a livable wage, full Medicare for everyone with cost control and quality control, basic nutrition for the poor, low-income housing programs, good public transit, strong environmental protection, acceleration of renewable energy output, public control of commonwealth assets— you know the list—well, it all sounds pretty federal to me. It doesn't sound like building a grassroots movement for Redirection."

"True," Sol said, "but there's no real contradiction. To advocate action on the federal level is simply to recognize where the power and money to reduce widespread inequality presently lie. As the Redirections gain momentum, power will be devolved to the self-reliance circles. But in our federal system the protector of last resort—I'm speaking of national security, natural disasters, pandemics, R and D, and so forth—will be the federal government. As far as Redirections go, our core group will put the movement on the tracks, but only the organized populace can get to the destination."

Max was nodding impatiently. "So let's get started in a high-profile way that will bring all these issues down to earth. I propose that on five successive days, commencing next week, two billionaires a day demand that Wal-Mart change its business model, allow unionization, and pay its workers no less than $11 an hour, with full health insurance. If

Costco can treat its workers fairly and remain a successful discount giant, Wal-Mart can too. With Ted's billionaires, Bill's pro-estate-tax group, and our own contacts, we have a treasure trove of names to call on. They should come from retailing, banking, real estate, manufacturing, and communications for maximum impact. Some of them will be speaking as large shareholders in Wal-Mart."

"That's a hell of an idea," Jeno said. "Let's connect with Promotions on it ASAP."

"Right," Max said. "And we'll have our project manager prepare a Wal-Mart strategy memorandum for the billionaires to digest so that they can speak for themselves and not through spokespersons. The memorandum should outline a uniform demand, followed by a list of points that can be varied to build the story for the country and the media. Promotions can work with the billionaires so that they all reinforce the central demand, but with distinctive touches that reflect their business experience and different facts about Wal-Mart and its competitors. Two unions and a number of community groups have some very up-to-date websites that will be useful to the manager."

Before they adjourned for the day, Jeno suggested that Sol should be the first to make the demand because he knew plenty about the Costco model, having helped create it, and would be preaching what he once practiced in the same line of commerce. Sol agreed to lead the charge. As head of the Sustainable Sub-economy Project, he didn't exactly have time on his hands, but there it was largely a matter of putting together the pieces. So much work had been done by so many around the world, from concept to operating models, that it was primarily a gathering exercise. Meanwhile, Jeno, who was the sub-economy liaison with the People's Chamber of Commerce, reported that within a week the PCC would be operating out of its sustainable building headquarters in Washington, DC, just vacated by a leading environmental organization. The staff was planning a blowout of an announcement and opening day festivities.

After two days of reviewing the material assembled by the project manager, Sol and Jeno decided to lead with the sustainable practices whose benefits would radiate most widely: first, solar energy, which came close to being the universal solvent of many environmental devastations and perils; second, the expansion of a carbohydrate economy to replace the present hydrocarbon economy; third, preservation of species and their ecologies; and fourth, the displacement by sustainable technologies of toxic and destructive technologies like the gasoline-powered internal combustion engine, atomic power, and synthetic petrochemicals. It was understood that all four were interrelated and mutually supportive objectives.

Sol gave a world-weary sigh. "Which is all well and good, Jeno, but blah blah blah. How do we get people where they live? There've been so many studies, scientific warnings, exposés, and documentaries, but somehow, even with frightening visuals, the public isn't moved to action. We need something new, something outrageous."

"If it's outrageous we want, I think we know where to find it," Jeno said, reaching for the phone to call Ted.

The next day, during a conference call with Ted and the rest of the Promotions team, Sol and Jeno laid out their priorities. "We know what we want to do," Sol said, "but how do we get people behind us? How do we jolt them?"

"Jolts," Ted said, his eyes lighting up. "Let's see—"

"Hemp," said Yoko.

"Hemp?" said Jeno.

"Hemp. Brilliant," said Sol, who turned out to be a fount of information on the subject. "Hemp is five thousand years old, a tough, long-fibered, and most versatile carbohydrate. Industrial hemp is legally imported, but our US farmers can't grow it because it's on the DEA banned list as being too similar to marijuana. But it's not psychotropic because it is only a third of a percent THC—the substance that induces a high in marijuana smokers. In other countries industrial hemp has been used for clothing, fuel, food, chlorine-free paper, lubricants, and thousands of other products. George Washington and Thomas Jefferson grew it. Henry Ford built a car from industrial hemp, and auto companies now use it to make parts for interior passenger compartments. During World War II, growing hemp to make strong rope was encouraged as part of the war effort, but if you grow it in the US today, you're arrested and your crop is confiscated. A coalition of hemp supporters, including the International Paper Company, farmers' organizations, state agriculture commissions, state legislators, and environmental and consumer groups, has petitioned twice to get it off the DEA list, once under Clinton and again more recently. Both times the petition was denied in bipartisan decisions. There's been no movement on the issue, except that one member of the House, Don Saul of Texas, has finally introduced a bill to legalize the domestic growing of industrial hemp, with four co-sponsors. Unfortunately, House leaders have yet to schedule hearings."

"Thank you, Professor Price," said Bill Cosby.

"Not at all," said Sol.

"Hey, didn't Woody Harrelson get arrested years back for publicly planting a few hemp seeds in Kentucky?" asked Phil.

"Yes, and a jury acquitted him," Sol said. "He lives in Maui now."

"There's your jolt," said Barry. "I'll call Woody and ask if he'd be willing to come to DC and stand in front of the White House with fifty farmers and activists, each holding a flowerpot, and all simultaneously planting industrial hemp seeds in their pots. The visuals will fly across the nation when the police descend to wrench away the pots and haul the fifty offenders off in their paddy wagons. We'll call it the Pot Revolution, an ironic twist on the word 'pot' that's sure to generate more controversy. We'll need advice of counsel to avoid a conspiracy charge, and of course Joe's team will give the demonstrators free legal representation. I know that Peter and some others in our core group support the legalization of marijuana, but with apologies to them, we'll have to be careful to distinguish clearly between marijuana and industrial hemp and to downplay any involvement of marijuana users and their advocates. They'll only distract from what will become a mass-media educational campaign that shows how the carbohydrate economy can strengthen national security by reducing dependence on foreign oil and promoting many additional environmental benefits. Two generations of absurdity are enough."

"The Pot Revolution—that's wonderful," said Bill Gates. "Let's try to come up with something just as good for solar energy. It drives me crazy the way solar has so often been relegated to articles in the real estate section about some house or small building partially solarized, and then it's back to ho-hum. Amazing, isn't it, that planet Earth's greatest free lunch from its birth to this day is a subject seen as unexciting. Imagine how exciting it would be if the sun stopped shining."

Bill went on to relate a story about a visit years ago to the Hanford Nuclear Reservation in eastern Washington State. He was talking to some nuclear engineers about the complex systems they were creating to store and treat radioactive wastes and keep them from leaking into the groundwater that feeds the mighty Columbia River. Shaking his head at the convoluted engineering details, he asked them why they didn't just retrain themselves as solar engineers because solar was the future and they must know it. To which one older engineer replied, "The atom is endlessly fascinating, a limitless intellectual challenge. Why, solar energy is just sophisticated plumbing. Not very interesting." "Only crucial to the planet's future," Bill found himself retorting as he strolled out the door.

Ted had been listening to all this with a furrowed brow. "Got it," he said suddenly. "Girls. Girls, girls, girls!"

Yoko rolled her eyes.

"We'll find hundreds of beautiful women and dress them up as solar commandos or whatever, and we'll use them in a series of Aztec-type festivals dedicated to the Sun God. Without the human sacrifice, of course."

"Not so fast," Sol said. "I can think of a few good candidates."

Ted was too revved up to laugh. "These festivals will be so graphic that the media won't be able to resist them. They'll be marvels of sound and light. We'll commission Mesoamerican historians and anthropologists to make them as authentic as possible within the confines of demonstrating modern solar technology in dramatic ways that rebut all the myths and lies about solar energy conversion. You know how nuclear physicists keep saying that solar isn't practical because it's too diffuse? We'll put a giant magnifying glass over a giant vat of eggplants and tomatoes, and then we'll give out bowls of delicious stew. Solar engineering is all about concentrating and transmitting solar energy—elementary, my dear Watson, but still not enough for these nuke naysayers."

"I'd add some onions," Yoko remarked dryly.

Ted ignored her. "Naturally, the festivals themselves will be solar-powered to the fullest extent possible. We'll make a big deal out of the Sun God—his mythology, his rituals, his powers. The religious right will jump all over this as sacrilegious, but their sermons will only help us reach wider audiences. The more thoughtful clergy will remind parishioners that the world may have been made in seven days but millions of years later the sun that sustains it still isn't its energy source of choice. The Sun God festivals will launch a national mission to go to the sun the way we went to the moon."

"Not a bad jolt," observed Sol. "How long will it take to get the festivals off the ground and organize the pot people?"

"Not long if we put a couple of teams on it twenty-four/seven," Barry said.

"All right, let's have our project managers do that," Sol said.

Yoko had been unusually quiet during the conference call because she was preoccupied with thoughts about the Posterity Project, which still hadn't met because the members had been so busy with the other Redirections. They were having their first session tomorrow, in Omaha, and when the call was finished, she headed straight for the airport.

When she arrived at Warren's home by taxi, he welcomed her warmly and ushered her into the dining room, where the rest of the group was just sitting down to a late lunch. As they ate, Yoko told her colleagues about the discussion with Sol et al. and the plans for the Pot-In and the Sun God festivals. "And you know," she said, "jolts are fine, I'm all for them, but what I've been thinking about is guilt and shame. Our generation is using posterity as a dumping ground for its failures, leaving them a ravaged Earth, a debt-ridden government and economy, and a war-racked world. We are woefully irresponsible toward our posterity. Even the word 'posterity' isn't used anymore as it was in speech after speech, declaration after declaration, by our eighteenth-century forebears. To me, the neglect of certain words is a telling sign of where we are as a people. We love to talk about the future, but that word doesn't convey the same personal obligation to those yet to be," she said solemnly, and went on to describe a poster she was working on, a stark representation of knives being hurled at a group of children, with "Pollution," "War," etc., in black letters on each knife in midair, to symbolize all the ills this generation was leaving behind. "The subtlety of modern art is of little use here," she added.

Warren, who had intended to leave his entire fortune to a foundation before his Maui conversion, had a somewhat different take on the Posterity Project. "First," he declared, "trust is the antidote to feelings of guilt and shame. We must articulate a relationship of trust between the generations, rooted in the kind of individual trust that exists between parent and child. Parents feel guilty or shamed when they don't give their all to their children because they know they've violated that relationship of trust. Our task is to elevate the parental trust commitment to the level of a generational commitment. I suggest the formation of a National Trust for Posterity to advance this trust commitment as a yardstick for today's policies, programs, and practices, much as environmental impact statements or historic preservation covenants do in their particular spheres. With this one overriding concept of intergenerational trust, the NTP will consolidate the many, many insufficient efforts in civil society to protect and nurture posterity and enable future generations to 'fulfill their human possibilities,' in John Gardner's apt words. It's really just a matter of putting your Seventh-Generation Eye into practice, Yoko, and it has to be as dynamic in action as the Eye is as a symbol. It has to have both steak and sizzle. It has to be sound and tough, with a directional dynamic worthy of Maui."

Ross, who had been busily taking notes, spoke up. "Easier said than done."

"Yes, so let's get going!" said Bernard, half rising from his chair in excitement. "Let's put some substance on this scaffolding. Give it outstretched arms, give it Yoko's brilliant logo, give it schools that teach students to tell truth to power, give it Youth Clubs for Civic

Experience after school, give it neonatal care, caring daycare, nutrition care, give it ways to tap into youth ingenuity, youth questioning of our generation's stagnation, give it a Youth Political Party, give it network television programs by and for college students, high school students, and elementary school students, sit them in circles around hip adults who'll pepper them with questions and guide them out of the cultural cocoons that have devalued their imaginations and expectations for themselves. So many kids are growing up in stultifying, violent, pornographic environments—we have to change that. We have to give them new, enticing experiences and horizons."

Ross summoned the project manager, and together the group hammered out a detailed plan for the NTP. They'd been working for several hours when Warren stood and stretched. "Time for a break. Let's see what's going on in the world," he said, turning on the evening news.

The lead story was the amazing journey of Warren Beatty up the coast of California in a natural-gas-powered bus with a big sign on both sides, "The People's Revolt of the Rich," surrounded by contrasting pictures of how the rich and the poor live in the Golden State. On top of the bus was a giant picture of Governor Schwarzenegger with the words "Hasta La Vista, He Won't Be Back!" During the interview segment, the reporter asked Beatty just what he was doing. "Getting very rich people to reject their tax cut and pay what they were paying ten years ago so that California can get out of debt and have the funds to meet its vital public responsibilities," he replied. "And how is that going?" she asked. "Well," he said, "I'm getting a little mansionitis, but these billionaires are opening their doors. About half of them are coming on board for the trip to Sacramento. This has to be the richest bunch of bus passengers in human history." The reporter laughed. "Do you think you'll succeed?" she asked. "Of course. With the people and the super-rich on the same side, how can we fail?" Beatty said, flashing his famous wink-smile as he stepped through the high gates of another mega-mansion.

"Well, it does take your breath away," said Bernard.

"Get ready to lose more breath," Yoko said quietly.

CHAPTER 4

Monday morning, after a light breakfast, Warren and his guests from the Posterity Project gathered in his office for the weekly closed-circuit TV conference with the whole core group. When all the screens were up, Warren began.

"It's hard to believe that little more than a week has passed since we last met in Maui. So much is happening, with people all over the country receiving assignments, preparing action plans, contacting affinity groups, and building the infrastructure, that it's been hard for the Redirection projects to keep up with each other. For that reason, I've cautiously doubled the size of the Secretariat staff to eight, and Patrick has established a Recruitment Department to stay on top of our staffing needs. That should help, and I'm counting on you to let me know what else the Secretariat can do to keep things running smoothly. Now, down to business. What's going on with Wal-Mart, Sol?"

"Just a second, Warren," Jeno said. "I'm as eager as everyone else to hear from Sol, but I've been thinking about that Roader column. I'm worried about it. There must be dozens of eager-beaver reporters out there trying to follow up on his suggestion of connections between us, and they may blow our cover. And you know all the corporate honchos and lobbyists read him, so what if they start thinking about a counterattack sooner than we anticipated? I've got two ideas for preemptive strikes, self-extending collateral drives to divert and distract the business lobbies.

"First, taking off from Sol's earlier concept, we buy some retail franchises and small businesses in just about every line of commerce and manufacturing around the country. I'm talking about local insurance agencies, finance companies, fabrication and assembly shops, auto dealerships, real estate brokers, stockbrokers, gasoline stations and oil dealers, small banks, pharmacies, cinemas, restaurants, grocery stores, beauty salons, mortgage companies, small radio stations, law practices, physician practices, plumbing and electrical businesses. You can always find these outfits for sale in the trade press classifieds, sometimes at bargain prices. Call this collection our attack sub-economy that will get inside each of these large commercial industries, inside their trade associations, inside their conventions, where our business managers can raise hell about bad practices and blow the whistle on marketing and product abuses. It never ceases to amaze me how much incriminating information pours out of these conventioneers' mouths with the drinks flowing. These inside units of ours can cause serious embarrassments and even force better practices, especially if they're joined by other long-exploited small businesses boiling with suppressed anger. Taken together, their efforts will expose the dirty linen and throw the powers that be on the defensive.

"My other idea is to establish a lecture forum for retired business executives who'll be induced to give their speech of a lifetime, their valedictory assertion of truths that they were either unable or unwilling to express during their active careers. Those who *know* finally *say*. Well-publicized and positioned at highly visible places like the National Press Club, these speeches will be literally sensational. Finally, the top insiders speak out. Free at last. Free at last! They'll name names and tell the untold stories. Week after week they'll keep big business distracted as it scrambles to rebut one of its prominent own and keep the lid on its internal Pandora's boxes. Like the attack sub-economy, the speeches will further our overall mission, and may also help us recruit new men and women for our efforts. Obviously this lecture series has to be handled with sensitivity and professionalism. We should extend the invitations personally, peer to peer."

There was silence for a moment as the group digested the wisdom and urgency of Jeno's proposals.

"What a way to start off a Monday morning!" Peter finally said. "A brilliant response to a provocation—the best invigorator of the mind."

Warren looked around at the closed-circuit screens and at his guests from the Posterity Project. Everyone was nodding energetically. With their backgrounds, they were under no illusions about the looming counterattack from the Goliaths of industry and commerce once they were awakened to what was heading straight for them.

"As you can see, Jeno," Warren said, "your ideas are receiving unanimous acclamation. I'll have the Secretariat establish an implementation team to cost out both projects and enlist the necessary staff. There's no time to lose, especially with our assault on Wal-Mart coming up. Over to you, Sol."

"I'm making the first call to the CEO this afternoon, along with our fellow billionaire Raul Escalante, who's known for treating his workers superbly while making a fortune." Then, like an NFL coach planning an offensive drive, Sol laid out the next moves. "Assuming Wal-Mart has no comment or declines our demands as none of our business, we contact five members of the company's board of directors who've had dealings with some of us in the core group. Here's our message: Do you have any idea of the gravity of what's coming next? Please don't confuse what is about to confront Wal-Mart with the ineffectual maundering of the unions, which haven't managed to organize a single store after eight years of effort, even with a great case to bring to the workers. Wal-Mart is spreading a low-wage business economy, and its large regional competitors are pressing for worker cutbacks and givebacks to compete with the arriving behemoth, as in southern California. Wal-Mart employees make so little that they have to avail themselves of taxpayer-funded welfare services—and Wal-Mart shows them how! Many can't afford the co-payments on their lousy health insurance. Wal-Mart is a union-buster like the nation has never seen in the retail business, rushing SWAT teams to any store where there's a glimmer of pro-union activity.

"For the workers and taxpayers and communities of America, Wal-Mart spells going backward into the future, reversing the very trajectory of economic progress in America—higher wages, higher consumer demand, better livelihoods. Wal-Mart's extremely well-paid executives are presiding over a spreading pull-down economy, going to dictatorships like China for suppliers who pay their serf labor thirty to fifty cents an hour, and demanding that its remaining US suppliers pull up stakes and move to China if they can't meet the China price here. All this has got to stop. That's what we tell the five directors, who'll be given seventy-two hours to get a response from management. Meanwhile, two more billionaires will be calling the CEO every day for the next four days. Those conversations should get more and more interesting—or shorter and shorter—as pressure builds from the directors.

"If the deadline passes and the response remains negative—I don't know why I bother to say 'if'—then we roll out a two-pronged action plan. First, our organizers will select five Wal-Marts around the country to unionize. Workers will be invited to a secured auditorium and given ironclad guarantees. For being pioneers in unionizing Wal-Mart's more than one million nonmanagerial employees, they'll get full legal support for free, media backup in their communities, and a waiver of their union dues for the first three years. If they're illegally fired, we find them better-paying jobs in the same community. If they like, they can take jobs in one of the storefronts we're going to open, with names like Wal-Fart or Wal-Part. Wal-Mart is likely to sue, charging trademark violation, which plays right into our hands, since we already have any number of attorneys itching to defend the cases and find out more about Wal-Mart's internal operations in the process.

"The storefronts will also carry out multiple exposés of Wal-Mart, from the way they hire illegals and mistreat them—remember that notorious case where they locked workers in overnight, fire exits and all?—right down to the fact that many of its products aren't actually the cheapest, as they claim. The Wal-Mart SWAT teams will sweep down the minute they find out about the unionizing drive, as they're bound to, and through our worker intelligence system their maneuvers will be chronicled daily for an equally quick response. Things will really be heating up by the middle of next week. The ten billionaires will be available for national media interviews and will be well prepared to parry the obvious Wal-Mart counterattack that billionaires don't need Wal-Mart, do they? To spread the message in a more personal way, we'll have peaceful picketers in front of some two hundred Wal-Mart stores, including former employees. They won't be hard to find since the turnover is up to fifty percent a year."

Another hush greeted Sol's masterful presentation. Again Peter broke it.

"Well escalated! There's nothing a large corporation fears more than sustained second- and third-strike capabilities."

"I didn't think it was possible to be any more energized than I already am," Leonard said, "but I was wrong."

After briefer reports from the other Redirections, Warren urged everyone to make institution-building a priority in the coming weeks. He pointed out that when the assault on the citadels of corporate power began in earnest with the implementation of each project's substantive agenda, the resultant controversy and uproar might compromise the establishment of the necessary organizations, and that the substantive agendas would go nowhere without the infrastructure to support them. "It's tedious, detailed work, to be sure," he said, "but no harder than building a business from scratch!"

And with that he brought the closed-circuit briefing to an end and dispatched his troops to battle.

Out in Santa Cruz, it was 6:00 a.m., and the other Warren was already showered and dressed. He'd spent the night at the nineteenth-century mansion of an old friend who'd bought real estate in Hollywood and Beverly Hills in the fifties and made a killing. Not wanting to wake his host, he fixed himself some coffee and strolled through the manicured grounds until he came to his friend's sculpture garden of ribald Roman statuary. He sat down on a cement bench next to a fountain in the form of a satyr gleefully taking a leak. Normally he would have laughed, but he was absorbed by thoughts of the coming week. The People's Revolt of the Rich bus was steadily filling up with billionaires. They were four days away from Sacramento, and the rest of the seats had already been reserved by the additional super-rich they would collect as they completed their itinerary through Monterey, the Bay Area, and Silicon Valley, with deliberate detours through poor neighborhoods.

Warren gave the satyr a rueful salute and returned to the house. After leaving his friend a note of thanks, he packed his bag and rejoined his compatriots on the bus. A caravan of five hundred reporters and their gear was now following the billionaires' every move up the California Gold Coast, ensuring headlines all over the country and worldwide. Warren's years of Don Juanism with rich and famous women made him everlastingly fascinating to the media. At the state legislature, the air of expectation was so electric it could have powered a turbine, and it wasn't long before leaders of the Senate and Assembly invited Warren to address a joint session of both houses on Friday.

Warren wanted to see Arnold first, to give him a chance to join the movement, but his repeated calls were received by Arnold's secretary with a polite "I will give the governor your message." Falling back on a venerable Hollywood trick, he had another bus rider put in a call in the name of Arnold's former agent, and of course Arnold got right on the phone. Warren confessed his little practical joke and asked, "Can we meet Friday morning before the joint session?" Arnold knew he had to think fast, faster than in his most desperate movie scenes, and this time with no one to program him. He was on his own. He couldn't ride and he couldn't hide, so he decided to play. "Sure, Warren, how about breakfast at my home around seven thirty? Just you and me for some frank talk in confidence. I don't think bringing your bus friends would serve our mutual purposes." Warren agreed, and after some small talk about old times, they said goodbye.

Warren gazed out the bus window at the crowds lining the roadside mile after mile. It was like the Tour de France. People were holding signs cheering the bus on and thanking this or that billionaire known to be aboard. Many of the signs read, "You are not alone!"—a message that touched the bus riders deeply. Imagine ordinary people telling them, with all their wealth and friends in high places, that they were not alone. Rolling through Monterey and San Francisco, the bus brimmed with animated talk, not about yachts and vintage wines, but about how to answer the barrage of questions the billionaires would face at their press conference in the state capital. Some of them were giving Warren suggestions about his speech to the joint session, which was sure to be carried live on cable television.

Outwardly Warren was the picture of calm, but inside he was feeling butterflies. He decided to put in a call to Richard Goodwin, one of President John F. Kennedy's most masterful speechwriters.

"Dick," he said, "it's been too long since you were at my place twisting the tail of the cosmos. Listen, I need your help, and I need it fast. After you get my notes and suggested tone, I want you to write my address before the California state legislature. You'll have to hit the Internet to beef up on current conditions out here, but I want the speech to close with my announcement that I'm going to run for governor on the Democratic ticket. I want vision, eloquence, uplift, policy seriousness, and a case for my ability to perform in this august office, all with dramatic pace—and that means you."

"You're right, Warren, it's been too long," Dick replied. "I'd be delighted to dust off whatever modest skills I have and get you a draft in two days, but I'll need one more lengthy conversation to capture your voice. I don't recollect that you've given many political speeches that may have been taped, but if you have any, zip them out to me."

"Fine, done. Talk with you soon, Dick."

The bus rolled on into Berkeley, where students were massed in support—"UC-Berkeley for THESE Billionaires!"—and hop-skipped through Silicon Valley. By the time it reached Mountain View the last seat was taken, stranding some big dot-com investors, and a second bus was quickly commissioned to join the steadily lengthening caravan. To turn metaphor into reality, some joker rented a camel to trudge alongside the slow procession.

Among the spectators lining the road were two old friends, day workers on their lunch break from a construction job on a half-finished McMansion. Arnie Johnson and Alfonso Garcia, both in their mid-thirties, married, and with a couple of kids apiece, loved to argue politics and sports, especially sports. Where politics was concerned, they were died-in-the-wool cynics.

"People's Revolt of the Rich?" Arnie said as they watched the lead bus go by. "What the hell is that supposed to mean?"

"Beats me," said Alfonso. "Probably just some stunt by folks with too much time on their hands."

"Yeah, like the rich ever done anything good for my black ass. Or your Mexican culo," Arnie added with a jab to Alfonso's arm. "C'mon, amigo, we'd best get back to the plantation."

Hours later, as the caravan headed down into the Sacramento Valley, graced by a beautiful sunset, Warren called Barry to thank him for showing the way and jarring him out of his interminable inertia. "My wife has found a new reason to love me," he declared. "What are friends for," said Barry, who'd been following the bus trek closely and thinking about which Redirections Warren should speak out for. He suggested that the address to the legislature be titled "New Directions for the Good Life" and focus on the daily needs of Californians, with clear reference to poverty—almost half of all children are classified as "poor" or "near poor" by the state's economists. "The bigger your message, the smaller Arnold looks," he concluded. Snapping his phone shut to turn to the media acquisition work, Barry thought to himself that there must be many more such repressed celebrities languishing in corners of self-inflicted futility, just waiting to be roused.

Monday afternoon, not long after the first wave of lunchtime rallies was breaking up, Sol placed his call to Leighton Clott, the CEO of Wal-Mart.

"Good afternoon, Mr. Clott, Sol Price here, with Raul Escalante on the line. We've been reading about your travails with your critics, the lawsuits, and the media coverage of your every slip-up, and we've got some advice for you, advice steeped in our own business experience and subsequent reflection."

"Well, this is a pleasant surprise," said Clott, "especially from the two of you. We're open to any advice offered in good faith these days."

"As ours most certainly is," Sol said. "We strongly urge you to announce your willingness to let workers in your stores, offices, and transport facilities form unions by cardcheck. If a majority in each workplace sign up, the union is certified and you begin bargaining in good faith. It will be good for Wal-Mart's workers, for wage levels in general, for consumer demand, and for all you folks in Bentonville sleeping at night. What do you say?"

There was stunned silence at the other end of the line. All the warmth had left Clott's voice when he spoke again. "I assure you that we have thoroughly and repeatedly considered every aspect of unionism with our top executives, our legal advisers, and our board of directors. The answer is a definite no, never. Gentlemen, kindly mind your own business, and good—"

"Just a minute," said Raul Escalante. "Wal-Mart is so big, so pervasive, that it's everybody's business. You're driving down wages inside the country, pushing your suppliers to China, replacing American workers with exploited Chinese workers, all to an extent unequaled by any other company in American history. From now on, what's good for Wal-Mart better be good for the United States, and not the reverse."

"Good day, gentlemen!"

As Leighton Clott hung up on Sol and Raul, the opening day of the People's Chamber of Commerce was getting underway in front of the Green Building in the embassy section of the nation's capital. A blue-on-white banner stretched across the façade, emblazoned with Alfred North Whitehead's sagacious words: "A great society is a society in which its men of business think greatly of their functions." Jeno was master of ceremonies, flanked by Ted Turner and Oprah Winfrey on one side, Andy Grove and Peter Drucker on the other. Winfrey, Grove, and Drucker had been persuaded to present themselves by specific appeals based on their writings and public statements—a case of words generating deeds, such as showing up. What also drew them was the PCC manifesto, which used phrases and formulations new to these seasoned luminaries, things like "the corporate destruction of capitalism," "crime in the suites," "high-status slavery," "corporate fascism," "constitutionalizing the corporation," "quo warranto," "dechartering with probation," "environmental bankruptcy," "chaordic restructuring," "the enforceable corporate covenant with society," "the foresight to foresee and forestall," "tort law as protector of the physical integrity of human beings, their property, and the natural environment," "solarizing technology," "the carbohydrate economy," "from greed to need to seed," "respect for taxpayer assets," "the commonwealth economy," "the seizure of leisures," "the commercialization of childhood," "the pornography of style versus the engineering of substance,"and "We are the fauna!" Profoundly intrigued were the corporation philosopher of the century, the cofounder of Intel, and the talk show queen. So were several dozen scions of industry and commerce who during their tenure had displayed signs of compassion, vision, and reflectiveness about the human condition. Their attendance, together with that of Robert Monks, trenchant shareholder critic of "corpocracy," enraged the US Chamber of Commerce and the National Association of Manufacturers, which both sent cameramen to record the proceedings.

Jeno minced no words in his opening remarks. He said that with few luminous exceptions, big business was myopic, inflexible, averse to quality competition, intolerant of strong democratic movements and unions, disdainful of democratic procedures, and lustful for political power. He said that its leaders were narcissists, stalwart in their mission to expand the corporate culture of greed, ferocious in their suppression of the rights of investors to control the companies they legally own, and single-minded in their determination to enrich themselves to the detriment of the corporations they were supposed to manage. They were more interested in buying customers through mergers than in attracting customers through superior goods and services. They were too friendly to accommodating dictatorships, and terminally shortsighted because of quarterly yardsticks of earnings and performance.

"All these traits," Jeno declared, "have ramifying destructive consequences for the innocent, for the environment, for representative government. In the long run they spell the ruin of these vast corporate empires themselves, as we've already seen with the Enrons and the WorldComs. Believe me, as a man who's spent a lifetime confronting corporate giants in a variety of business endeavors, I know whereof I speak. By contrast, the People's Chamber of Commerce will be known for doing just the opposite of what big business and its manipulative trade associations have been doing. As of today, we have more than eighty thousand members who are already practicing what the PCC is preaching. They're treating their workers well, pursuing sustainable environmental practices, holding their suppliers to these standards, and selling products or services backed by warranties guaranteeing automatic returns or refunds. Most of our businesses are small, with less than a hundred million in revenue per year, but some are reaching toward a billion in annual sales. Many sell innovative new products or services that empower consumers and laborers in accordance with progressive business standards. Dozens of them are in evidence here on this launching day, with exhibits and free samples that I urge you to try for yourselves."

Jeno was followed by Ted, who documented what he called "the omnicidal trajectory of unbridled corporatism." In one area after another, he detailed the global travesties attributed to or condoned by giant multinational corporations. "The world was never meant to be run according to one overriding and narrowly conceived standard of profit that smothers the values of a humane, sensitive civilization," he said in conclusion. "Not a single religion has approved of such a perverse channeling of people's lives. Indeed, every major religion has warned its adherents to limit the power of the merchant classes because their singularly obsessed drive for profit is so inimical to spiritual and civic values." Ted's speech, delivered in what one reporter described as "a resounding drawl," mesmerized the audience and even provoked scattered applause from the press corps.

Jeno was about to conclude the official ceremony when George Soros showed up unscheduled and was given a few minutes to speak. He used his time simply to ask whether there were any CEOs or trade association heads in the crowd who wanted to make a brief statement or debate him or his associates at a later date. There was a long silence. Nobody came forward. George had made his point. Now it was the reporters' turn, and the hands flew up.

"James Drew, *Washington Post*. How big are your budget and staff, Jeno?"

"Big enough to do the job. The budget is in the millions of dollars annually, and the staff is smart enough to scare the hide off the corporate fossils who've taken over our nation's capital."

"Is this another one of your Roman candles, Ted?" asked Sam Sniffen of the *Atlanta Journal-Constitution*. "Are you really going to give it your time?"

"A lot more time than I ever gave the Braves," Ted said, drawing a laugh, since everyone knew he'd been the most actively involved owner in the team's history. "Giving business a new face and a conscience beats winning the World Series any day."

"Reginald Sesko, *Business Week*, question for Mr. Drucker. Why are you here, sir? What do you expect from the PCC?"

"I expect great things from them. At last there's a national organization that will vigorously pursue some of my longtime urgings to top management, such as reducing CEO compensation to no more than twenty-five times the entry-level wage in their public companies. You can't imagine how many tangible and intangible problems that one move of self-restraint would resolve. For one thing, it would curb the incentive to inflate profits, offload debt, and in general cook the books to increase the value of executive stock options. Great for employee morale as well. Look at Southwest Airlines."

"Oprah, you don't seem the type to be up in arms about big business," said Laurie Newsome of ABC. "Why are you here?"

"The type? And what type would that be? Day in and day out on my show I see the sad results of big business as usual—parents with no time for their children because they have longer and longer commutes to dead-end jobs that don't pay them enough to have a decent life, people rushing around trying to keep body and soul together, turning to tranquilizers or worse. Family life is being disrupted by an unforgiving economy dominated by big business. Too many of these big companies have no respect for parental authority and are directly exploiting millions of kids with junk food, mindless games, and violent entertainment. Too many of them use spin, phoniness, dissembling, and fraud to push dubious products and services. Oh yes, I'm the type. Every one of us should be the type."

Cries of "Tell it, Oprah!" and "Right on!" rose from the crowd, and it was a minute or two before Tamika Slater of the *Nation* could make herself heard.

"Mr. Grove, your company is a huge recipient of corporate subsidies like tax credits, tax holidays in various communities, and free R-and-D transfers from Washington. The PCC is solidly opposed to corporate welfare. How do you reconcile your support for this organization with its stand against so much that makes Intel more profitable?"

"I'm no longer active with Intel in any executive capacity. I am, shall we say, emeritus, and a mere consultant. That means you're seeing a new Andy Grove, one who's no longer burdened by responsibilities to Intel and its shareholders. I'm free to speak my mind."

"Follow-up, Mr. Grove. You didn't answer my question. Are you for or against these government subsidies and tax abatements?"

"In most instances, I'm against them, and most certainly against the kinds benefiting Intel—which I am still proud to say is one of the most profitable companies in the world."

"Jeno!" shouted a stringer for the *New York Post*. "What's your first attack on the corporate establishment going to be, and when can we expect it?"

"Attack? We prefer to call it competitive market discipline. Within a month or so, we'll release a major report on the plethora of tax-funded corporate subsidies and all the legislative loopholes that amount to backdoor corporate welfare. We'll enlist a coalition of liberal and conservative think tanks that have already come out against various business giveaways but have never been able to put political muscle behind their stance. I'm referring to Public Citizen, the Heritage Foundation, the Progressive Institute, the Cato Institute, and Taxpayers for Common Sense, to name the more prominent ones. There will be other compelling ways of communicating our message about the corporate raid on the taxpayers, so stay tuned. Meanwhile, I thank you all for coming and invite you to join us under the tent out back, where an array of food and drink from local producers awaits you."

A few blocks away, at the Congress Project suite, Bernard, Leonard, and Peter gathered to ponder their next move. The first order of business was to find qualified people to coordinate the fifty-plus-one Congress Watchdog Groups and administer the Blockbuster Challenge. From the now burgeoning talent bank, the project manager had come up with two names so prominent that there was no need to look further. The first, for the Watchdog Groups, was Donald Ross, founder of a large public relations firm for nonprofits. Before that, he was known for his exceptional talents as a student-citizen organizer. Huge rallies against nuclear power, organized with giant attention to detail and at lightning speed, bore his imprint. Now about sixty years old, he was wiry and tightly wound, sometimes cynical but always forward-looking. At the moment, he just happened to be out in the field organizing a few congressional districts against their terrible incumbents.

For the Blockbuster Challenge, the clear choice was Joan Claybrook, president of Public Citizen and longtime partisan Democrat, also in her sixties. She'd spent a great deal of time lobbying on Capitol Hill and knew the twists and turns, the woes and whims, the gravity and the greed of the place. Her biggest issue? Campaign finance reform. She'd need very little convincing as to the Blockbuster's merits.

Two hurdles. Both candidates would have to be interviewed and vetted. And both would have to be willing to resign their present jobs and start their new ones right away. "We'll need assurances," said Bernard, "that they still have the energy and drive for their tasks, and that they'll keep our project in confidence despite their close ties to the Democratic Party. We'll send their dossiers over to Recruitment and tell them we want feedback in seventy-two hours, and then I'll call the two of them personally, if there's no objection."

The project manager reported that the paper on congressional accountability standards would be done by the end of the week. The talent bank was being scanned for the two hundred field organizers for the Watchdog mobilization. All feedback databases from the first month's initiatives were being culled for likely prospects to comprise the blocs of two thousand voters in each congressional district. At the same time, teams were preparing recruitment materials and interview instructions for the organizers. Once on board, the two thousand would attend training seminars and be equipped with timely information about their representatives in the House and Senate. This information would be available both on paper and online, at each Watchdog website.

"That reminds me," said Peter. "It is truly the acme of arrogance in this day and age that most voters cannot tap into their computers for data on their representatives' voting records. I suggest that we round up a dozen prominent citizens, perhaps including a few of us from the core group, to make an immediate public demand that every member of Congress join Representative Frank Wolf of Virginia and the other nine who've already put their voting records on their websites in clear, easily retrievable fashion. They'll be given a one-month deadline, and if they refuse, they'll be excoriated throughout their districts and states. The punishment process will be called Getting to Know You, and will expose all their bad votes along with any other facts damaging to their political reputations. An initiative like this will break their collective intransigence on disclosure, which is favored by an overwhelming percentage of voters."

"Getting to Know You. I love it," Leonard said, whistling a few notes from the song. "Go with it, Peter. Once it gets moving, we'll work it into the themes of the lunchtime rebellion. We've had modest turnouts for our first few rallies this week, but I'm confident that they'll grow and spread to more and more cities. All these people voting with their feet on their lunch hour give us another pool of possibilities for the Watchdog Groups, beginning with the rally speakers and volunteer organizers. For obvious reasons, we'll be making a special effort to draw out the veterans in these crowds and send their names over to Perot's Credibility Project. And let's remember that the two thousand voters should include people of local influence across a representative spectrum of the American public. Replication dynamics and leveraged velocity require careful attention to the composition of each Watchdog Group. We should also think about developing adjuncts to backstop the two thousand, like a youth auxiliary for door-to-door canvassing. Refinement, refinement, refinement." Leonard turned to the project manager. "Okay, give us the ASAP timetable for the big move-out. When can we get this show on the road?"

After summarizing proposals and progress to date, the manager estimated that once Donald Ross and Joan Claybrook were brought on board, it would take one month to consolidate organizing efforts in the districts and prepare for the public unveiling of the Blockbuster Challenge.

"A month?" said Peter. "Isn't that pushing it a little?"

"It's pushing it a lot," Leonard said. "And that's what we're going to do!"

Back in New York City, George was deeply absorbed in digesting the current abuses and lobbying issues attached to each of the business sectors that the CUBs would soon be challenging and countervailing. He was no stranger to business chicanery, but he found himself repeatedly taken aback by all the scandals in banking, insurance, and finance, and by the regulators who did nothing about embedded patterns of outlawry. A quick study, he saw that the regulatory laws were essentially no-law laws, dead-letter laws whose principal function was to deceive ordinary people into thinking that the government cops on the corporate beat were looking out for them. Then there were the utilities with their cost-plus pricing power, equivalent to a government's taxing power. Their coded monthly bills were inscrutable, and even if you could understand them, there was no way to challenge the accuracy of their meters. The patsy regulators had no way either, and in any case were too busy biding their time until the companies offered them lucrative positions.

As for the millions of direct or mutual fund small investors, forget it. They got whatever was dealt them, and they couldn't even take the broker boys or mutual fund moguls to court. The fine-print contracts all stipulated compulsory arbitration of disputes with no possibility of appeal. Privatized law dictated by the most powerful party in a dispute violated George's very notion of an open society under the rule of law. He was getting angrier by the hour. His own business career was all about taking speculative risks on the British pound or the Japanese yen—basically, high-level gambling. It was hard to be attuned to abuses when you were rolling the dice, and he hadn't realized the extent to which manufacturers and vendors of goods and services could harm or defraud consumers. When he got to the food industry, his mouth went dry with astonishment over what was done to food and what was put into it these days. The countless cases of landlords pushing poor tenants up against the wall by failing to comply with building codes or maintain essential services made him wonder again—where were the police, the prosecutors, and the judges? All the shenanigans before, during, and after elections weren't news to him. But the imaginative political drive displayed by both parties toward superficially differentiating each other and obstructing any smaller competitors made him feel a pang of self-reproach, inasmuch as he was a heavy financier of that stagnant system of least-worst candidates. True to his belief in an open society, George never allowed himself to be jaded about wrong-doing.

It was when he came to the memoranda on taxation that he really wanted to take a shower. He was only too familiar with the sleights of hand that allowed the wealthy to shirk their taxpaying responsibilities.

His own attorneys and accountants had used some of these maneuvers to swell his fortune; after all, they were "perfectly legal," in the phrase used by New York Times tax reporter David Cay Johnston for the title of his book on the mastication of the tax code by the lobbies of the rich. What particularly caught his eye were the opportunity costs detailed in the memos—the critical unmet needs of children, the disabled, the homeless, the sick, and every American who relied on public services, from good mass transit to clean drinking water.

Pondering all these harms, George had an idea that had somehow been overlooked in the previous week's head-to-head deliberations and planning for the CUBs launch. He put in a conference call to his consultants, Robert Fellmeth and John Richard.

"Gentlemen, for at least a week before each mail drop, we should use the local and national media to highlight the most serious abuses in each business sector. Pronto, we need a clipping service to gather stories on hot spots in towns and cities where these scams are creating controversy or inviting prosecution or civil lawsuits. Then we'll place some hard-hitting ads, and between those and the coordinated efforts of the Promotions Project, along with the coverage we're bound to get on talk shows and news programs, we'll bring immediate and high visibility to the issues the CUBs will be taking on."

In their private conversations, Robert and John had been waiting to see if George would arrive at this conclusion, because coming from him, the effort would get underway more authoritatively. They vigorously seconded his idea and offered their services to this Promotions Project they hadn't heard of before. Instantly recognizing his slip of the tongue, George said, "Oh, it's just my nickname for some of the ad guys around the office who've been giving me feedback on our CUBs endeavor, but it's the two of you I want in charge of this new media strategy. The budget is there already. What do you say?"

"Consider it done," said Robert, and they signed off.

Out in Malibu, Max had been brooding about what to do as a follow-up to his words/deeds experiments. He'd had a number of ideas, most of them contemplations that visited him at bedtime, but he'd dismissed them all as banal—he was very demanding of himself, brutally so, one of the traits that had endeared him to his Maui colleagues. He was about to throw up his hands when it came to him late one night in a mad flash.

The next morning, with the help of his computer-savvy assistant, he prepared two full-page ads and arranged for them to run in the *South Bend Tribune* on consecutive days. Initially he'd thought of going to the *Observer*, Notre Dame's student newspaper, but he didn't want the politically correct hassle and probable rejection. He called the Secretariat to give them forty-eight hours' notice, as agreed at Maui One, and then, as a courtesy, he called Phil, a staunch Notre Dame alum.

"I take your point," Phil said with a sigh after Max explained his plan. "I wish I didn't, but I do. Go for it with my blessings."

Two days later, the first ad appeared. It showed photos of Notre Dame's varsity football team over the past four years, rows of headshots of the starting lineup with their names and positions underneath. A majority of the players were black. The headline read, "Funny, They Don't Look Irish!!!"

The next day's ad ran the photos again, this time under the headline "Why Aren't They Called the Fighting Zulus???" The body of the ad marshaled data reinforcing the visual point that very few of Notre Dame's football players were Irish Americans anymore, as was no doubt apparent to fans and alumni. In years past, many of the players and coaching staff were indeed Irish Americans, with names like Ryan, Leahy, Hart, Doyle, O'Malley, and Shanahan. Those days were gone. White players were now a distinct minority—except, interestingly, in the positions of quarterback and center. So why promote the fiction? Why the soft racism that described African Americans as "the Fighting Irish"? "It is time for fairness, for contemporary relevance, for color to matter in the words of description," the text concluded, inviting responses to the newspaper's letters column or to the website of the ad's signer, a group calling itself the Out of Africa Jocks Lodge.

The subsequent uproar was beyond astounding, and it wasn't confined to South Bend. It erupted everywhere. Seldom had there been such outrage (sprinkled with gleeful support in certain quarters), not over the NCAA's exclusion of minorities from executive positions, not over the subordination of academics to football, not over the NCAA's gross negligence in failing to police the use of performance-enhancing drugs or the constant illegal gambling on games, not over the wholesale commercialization of amateur sports, with the players sweating for nothing on hard artificial turf while the NCAA, the coaches, the universities, and the advertisers raked in the bucks. But "the Fighting Zulus"? Historic bellowing from the sports media, the right-wing radio talk shows, and literally millions of opinionated Americans. In two weeks, Max would try to drive his point home in another full-page ad, this one delineating the NCAA's chronic greed and malfeasance, but he knew the words/deeds duality was going to be a hard nut to crack. It would require different kinds of nutcrackers down the road.

Up in her New York studio, Yoko was reflecting on the core group's mission and the progress of the various Redirections. They were all moving along, but she still didn't see the sizzle. To her, art was the sizzle, the catalyst. "We're all in the same boat," she reasoned, "us and the opposition. We have to act in ways that invite trust. The natural state of life and the mind is complexity. Art can do an end run around complexity by offering an unmediated experience of complete relaxation of mind and body. Art can put people in touch with their higher feelings and predispose them to think about peace—in their households, in their nation, in their world."

Yoko liked art that made people say, "What's that about?" And then the conversation began. She loved to ask questions predicated on the power of aesthetics. For instance: What if the government required the infusion of a harmless red dye in all airborne emissions from factories and vehicles? How long would the regulators and the public tolerate air pollution if it turned everything it settled on red—clothing, cars, homes, planes, ships, tanks, buildings, lawns, skin, hair? That one regulation alone, she believed, would stop polluters of the air. "We should be against pollution, if only because it is ugly," she had once heard a philosopher-scientist say, and now she had a plan for embodying his words.

Another somersault of the mind came to her. Without mentioning the Redirections per se, she would issue a broad call to artists in all fields—visual, musical, poetic, and literary—to submit work that would represent the core group's goals, work that would make justice beautiful in all its particulars and practicalities, and give the process of achieving it an aesthetic appeal in itself, though with one caveat stemming from her experience in the tumultuous 1960s. Artistic creations could be so overwhelming in their emotional impact as to distract from the practical work they were meant to inspire. In the context of social justice, aesthetics had to be means to just ends, not ends in themselves.

Working late into the night, Yoko shaped a scaffolding for the graphic and musical arts teams that she would assemble from the response to her call. A movement for the future that was not only powerful but beautiful would earn posterity's respect and gratitude, just as the great art and architecture of past centuries were cherished today. John Ruskin had known this feeling of grandeur, the liberation of the human spirit through art, and Yoko knew it now, tinged with poignancy, for she sensed her own John in loving communion with her thoughts.

On Thursday, Maui Month Two, Week Two, the People's Revolt of the Rich closed in on Sacramento. The city had never seen such a media crush. The two busloads of billionaires rolled into the center of the state capital trailed by hordes of reporters representing sixty different countries and every branch of the media, commercial, independent, and nonprofit. It didn't hurt that some of the billionaires had followings of their own, or that Warren had cultivated the leading anchors, columnists, and feature writers of the news business for years, some of them quite intimately before his marriage.

Arriving on the grounds of the imposing state capitol, the passengers disembarked for a reception hosted by the majority Democratic Party, which was eager to embrace Warren as a media-centric counterpoise to their arch-adversary, Governor Schwarzenegger. The party leaders assured Warren that the votes were there to pass the restoration of the tax on the super-rich, but added that they wanted the governor on board first. Puzzled, Warren asked whether the votes were sufficient to override a veto. "Theoretically, yes," replied the Senate majority leader, "but who knows once Arnold unleashes a media barrage accusing us of drying up investment money and creating a hostile business climate."

Warren quietly responded by describing the bus trip through some of the most devastatingly poor areas of the Golden State. He'd directed his drivers to go through these communities so that his wealthy friends, looking out the windows, could see for themselves what the gross maldistribution of income did to people's lives, to their families, to their immediate surroundings. The eyes of the children, stopping their play to stare at the sleek buses and the pursuing press vans, were haunting. It was clear that if the ruling classes did not restrain their greed, these kids were going nowhere, except to lives of drudgery, poverty, addiction, incarceration, or other varieties of desperation.

The reception hall grew still as Warren, with the actor's descriptive skill, enveloped his listeners in the gravity of purpose that had suddenly possessed him a fortnight ago. Then one of the billionaires told of his horror and disgust and shame at what he'd seen on the road in between mansion stops. A real estate magnate did the same, and then a billionaire with a shipping fortune, and another who had founded banks, and yet another who'd made it big in the insurance industry—which itself was given preferential tax treatment right in the California constitution. The lawmakers simply were not used to encounters with people of massive means who wanted to give, not take. They felt cleansed somehow, as if the legislative halls had been fumigated.

The next morning, when Warren presented himself at the governor's mansion, Arnold personally flung open the door. Outwardly he was Mr. Universe, inwardly he was a calculating cyborg. Over fruit bowls, fair-trade coffee, ham, eggs, and seven-grain toast, he listened as Warren ardently made the case that Arnold should send a tax restoration bill to the legislature and set an example by giving up his own tax cut. Such a move would electrify the state, even the country. It would assure Arnold a place in history, outrage the slimy New York bond dealers, and focus political attention on the needs of the many Californians who were not among the fortunate. Warren rested his case and hungrily dug into his breakfast.

Arnold chewed ruminatively on a bite of toast, as if pondering the complexity of it all. He took a sip of coffee. "Warren, in many ways we are quite alike, not in terms of background or style or movies, but both of us like to win, and neither of us is satisfied with being a successful actor. We both believe there's more to life than fiction, than the set, than the accolades, than the swarms of beautiful, willing women and the big bucks. We are at that age, you know, when we want to go nonfiction. When I ran for governor, the most solemn promise I made was that under no circumstances would I raise taxes. Given my polls and my troubles with the legislature, I have little left but my dynamic personality, Maria, and my sacred word. Besides, I really dislike taxes philosophically—I meant what I said on the campaign trail. You wouldn't want me to break my word, would you?"

Warren put down his fork. "More like two percent of your word. The revocation of a notorious ten-year-old tax cut for the rich is hardly what the people will consider a tax increase. With the massive debt saddling the state, you shouldn't have made that pledge in the first place, certainly not to the wealthier residents here."

"I will never go back on my promise to Caddyfawnyuns," said Arnold, stonily gritting his teeth.

"Aren't you going to ask me if I'm going to run against you?"

"Well, are you?"

"It would be utterly gauche of me to make that decision over ham and eggs in su casa," Warren replied, "and I've got to get over to the Assembly now anyway. Thanks for the grub, Arnold, and for letting me know where you stand. Whatever happens next, remember that it's all part of the price of politics, the agony of the arena, so to speak." And with that he took his leave.

The atmosphere at the joint session that morning was charged. Enthusiasm had replaced demoralization. The governor was going to get his comeuppance after three years of browbeating and ridiculing the lawmakers and having his way on issue after issue and bill after bill. In this heightened air of expectation, the off-again, on-again screen god soon had the audience eating out of his hand. Dick Goodwin had delivered a superb speech that needed just a few touches to make it vintage Beatty. It was direct, clear, eloquent, factual, and full of equity. It was an expression of irony with heart, of justice with logic.

Nearing the end of his remarks, Warren paused for dramatic effect. The legislators hung on his next words. "This morning I breakfasted with my friend the governor. I begged him to introduce the tax restoration bill and put an end to the indenturing of California to New York City's giant bond creditors. I told him that millions of Californians, young and old, would find their lives improved, and in some cases saved, by this reallocation of monies to those who should have received them before raw power prevailed for the benefit of avarice. He refused to budge, saying his word was his bond and he would never break his promise. But promise to whom? To the top two percent who already have more money than they can spend? He made a promise to be the governor of all the people of California, and that promise supercedes his pandering. After serious thought, I am now prepared to announce my candidacy for the governorship of this misgoverned state of California and to pledge—"

The roar that rose in the Assembly and, from the spillover crowd of staff and guests in the corridors, drowned out the rest of his sentence. Three years of pent-up frustration exploded like fireworks, and the bright light of optimism lit up the capitol. As the deafening applause continued, Warren decided to develop his pledge paragraphs into a major address to be delivered on the day he filed for his candidacy. He knew when to stop, took a bow, and left the podium with a triumphant wave.

Before the day was over, the joint session of the legislature had passed the tax restoration bill and sent it to Governor Schwarzenegger, who promptly vetoed it with the curt message "I will keep my word." A few hours later, the Senate and Assembly overrode the veto with 70-percent majorities in both houses. The Democrats joined by a substantial number of Republicans who already sensed a budding rebellion in the lunchtime rallies that were growing by the day in five California cities, not to mention the spectacle of Warren's billionaire bus buddies giving back their tax cuts, speaking out for social justice, and turning their backs on the grand old policies of the party of the rich.

By the Friday of Warren's speech, the first phase of Sol's offensive against the Wal-Martians was nearly complete, with the last two of the ten billionaires having bent the ear of CEO Clott. To keep the pressure on, Sol asked Bernard and Jeno to make the conference call to five of the company's board of directors.

The conversation began cordially enough, with everyone reminiscing about their past business dealings with each other, but it soon became apparent that the directors did not want to hear the pro-worker message their callers delivered once the pleasantries were over. Evidently they'd been well chosen and well programmed by the hard-bitten management. Gerald Taft, one of the newer directors, made the mistake of patronizing the callers as simply uninformed and too removed from the brutal competitive market that Wal-Mart had to face. "You all retired so long ago," he said. "It's a different world out there." Jeno ignored the slight and calmly said that this would not be the last attempt to get the board to adopt a cardcheck policy nationwide. Longtime director Joseph Cobbler stiffened. "Even if the whole world is against us, we will never abandon our opposition to unions, their work rules, their exorbitant demands, and their inflexibility on matters concerning our suppliers. We have a highly successful business model, you know," he finished in a huff. "Very well," said Bernard, "very well, but we urge you to stay tuned." When the call was finished, Cobbler sat staring at the phone. "Stay tuned? What the hell do they mean by that?" he said to his empty office.

So far Wal-Mart was playing right to Sol's script. He had his organizing teams on standby, and that afternoon they flew out to the five targeted Wal-Marts, in Arkansas, Connecticut, Illinois, Missouri, and Arizona. They began by calling workers at home and inviting them and their families to a dinner the next evening, no obligations, just good food and drink followed by a discussion of how they might improve their economic prospects. The dinner, they were told, was being sponsored by Sol Price, retired founder of Price Club. Most of the workers were too scared or suspicious to accept; the minority who did in effect preselected themselves as more venturesome.

After drinks, appetizers, entrees, and dessert, each of the five lead organizers presented a proposal for a workers' union to bargain collectively with Wal-Mart management. The plan was put forth in detail, in the knowledge that one or more of the guests in the dining room would almost certainly leak it to the bosses the next day. The organizers passed out copies of an agreement guaranteeing the workers free legal representation, media support, and better-paying jobs if they were fired. For their part, the workers were to start meeting with the organizers right away to prepare their demands to management and gird themselves for the arrival of the notorious Wal-Mart SWAT teams. They were assured they would have support on this front too.

Of the forty or so workers attending each dinner, about half, give or take, signed the binding guarantee and declared themselves ready for the struggle to come. When those who declined to sign had left, the diners broke up into informal clusters of workers and organizers talking goals and strategy. Sol's people were on high alert because they knew that Wal-Mart had a network of informers who were given additional incentives to attend union organizing meetings and sign up. Sometimes these informers were known to their coworkers because they also operated inside the Wal-Marts, ferreting out disgruntled "associates," union sympathizers, or spies sent in by big-box competitors, but employee turnover was so rapid that new snitches popped up all the time. One way to spot them at union meetings was to see who was particularly gung-ho and who was simply prepared to do what needed to be done. Informers tended to volunteer for extra duty because it would get them into the more confidential meetings. Accordingly, at the close of the evening, the organizers took the most enthusiastic of the workers aside for intensive conversations in an effort to determine which of them were company plants.

Sure enough, the next afternoon, all Wal-Mart "associates" in the selected stores were summoned to a meeting with an outside team of "inspirational motivators"—otherwise known as a Wal-Mart SWAT team. These worthies began by showing a film about the evildoing of corrupt union bosses who enriched themselves from the members' pensions and hefty monthly dues, dining at posh restaurants and vacationing at luxury resorts on cushy expense accounts. The film ended with a montage of union leaders under interrogation by congressional investigating committees or being led off to jail in handcuffs. In the hush that followed, the teams proceeded to paint a bleak picture of life under the unions, with their rigid work rules that would prevent "associates" from "exploring their full potential" by shifting from one job experience to another to see which promotional ladder fit them best. Regretfully, the teams implied that higher union labor costs might portend a reduction in the number of "associates," and predicted other thunderstorms likely to disrupt "the present harmonious relationship" between Wal-Mart and its employees, all the while skirting the line beyond which even the National Labor Relations Board, with its pro-company bias, would have to declare an unfair labor practice. And of course the SWAT teams knew that Wal-Mart's lawyers could tie up NLRB proceedings for months or years, and that even if the company eventually lost, the sanctions were soft, just a matter of reinstatement and back pay.

At the conclusion of their presentation, the inspirational motivators invited questions and discussion, confident that they'd dissuaded most of their audience from even thinking union. From past experience, they knew that only two kinds of "associates" would pipe up—the intrepid and the ones who were about to quit anyway.

"Can we be fired if we go to organizing meetings and participate in their activities?" asked a young woman at the Missouri store.

"It is against the labor laws to fire someone for union organizing activity," the team leader replied smoothly, "but our experience is that associates who engage in such activity may not have the energy and attitude to do their jobs up to Wal-Mart's standards. So let's say that not meeting company standards can relieve you of your associate's position."

"Which union is behind this drive?" asked a middle-aged man with thinning hair. "Or are you just giving us an 'orientation' about the bad behavior of union bosses generally?"

"We have not determined at this time whether any particular union is activating. You must know that the unions are always swarming around our great company like gnats." The team leader wasn't lying here—Wal-Mart really didn't know who was behind this latest agitation. "Now if there are no further questions, let's get back to work. And remember that no union activity is allowed on Wal-Mart premises or parking lots."

By the time the SWAT teams finished their sessions, Sol's organizers had rented empty stores near each of the five Wal-Marts selected for the cardcheck drive, and were busy draping the windows with banners provocatively proclaiming the opening of a Wal-Fart, Wal-Dart, Wal-Cart, Wal-Part, and Wal-Hart, in lettering that bore an ostentatious resemblance to the company's trademarked name. The next day, two hundred Wal-Mart stores around the country would each be picketed by groups of a hundred or more people, some of them former Wal-Mart employees, so designated by bright buttons on their shirts and caps. Barry's Promotions

Project and Leonard's Mass Demonstrations Project had both been assisting for more than a week to lay the groundwork for these events.

Friday was a red-letter day. The pickets dominated the evening news in the communities where the two hundred Wal-Mart stores were situated. The ten billionaires who had called Wal-Mart's CEO held a joint press conference and made themselves available for interviews that were not just critiques of Wal-Mart and arguments for enlightened labor relations, but exposé machines. All kinds of internal Wal-Mart e-mails, documents, and propaganda directed to "associates" were cited or released. One telling item was the company health plan, which had such high co-payments and was ridden with so many deductibles and exclusions that many of the workers didn't qualify or couldn't afford it on their paltry pay and shortened hours.

The billionaires had a field day with the overblown pay packages of the top Wal-Mart executives and the tens of billions of dollars amassed by the Walton family on the backs of workers who could scarcely afford rent in some cities, never mind food, fuel, transportation, clothing, and other necessities of life. Another hot disclosure was a recent memo to Wal-Mart suppliers declaring that global competitive pressures required them to meet the China price either by reducing costs (i.e., cutting wages and benefits) or by actually moving to China, which accounted for more than $15 billion in Wal-Mart orders annually, and was now Wal-Mart's official world headquarters outside the United States. The billionaires' press release, featured on most of the network news shows, included all this information and more, along with a state-by-state list of Wal-Mart suppliers, thus assuring follow-up stories in the local press: "Is it true? Are you closing down and going to China?"

On two other business fronts, waves were threatening to inundate Wal-Mart's vaunted PR machine. Mobilized by the core group, large stockholders, both individual and institutional, began demanding that Wal-Mart adopt the Henry Ford approach of raising wages in order to increase consumer purchasing power. These investors also pressured their brokerage firms to put the heat on Wal-Mart, hoping through their combined efforts to prompt a downgrade of Wal-Mart stock. But the other wave was the real stunner, never anticipated in any of Wal-Mart's worst-case scenarios. In the five target communities, dozens of small retail operations that had been hanging on by a thread took out full-page ads in the local papers to announce that they would beat Wal-Mart's prices on an abundant range of inventories, commencing in two weeks. The ads, adroitly designed and phrased by the anonymous wordsmiths at Promotions, offered huge savings on Wal-Mart's top forty hottest-selling products.

In Bentonville, Arkansas, the National Wal-Mart War Room went into 24/7 overdrive. The Wal-Mart SWAT teams had plenty of experience in thwarting union organizing, but they'd never encountered anything like this onslaught of small-competitor fire sales. Management turned to in-house corporate counsel for advice.

Wal-Mart's lawyers studied their options. Should they recommend trademark infringement lawsuits against the five storefront Wal-Mart knockoffs, which were openly disparaging the company in every conceivable manner, using satire and ridicule and attacking the veracity of the Wal-Mart pledge to meet any price, no matter how low? What about those fire sale ads, which did not mention any termination date? The company attorneys smelled rich angels backing all these stores; if they were right, they might succeed in a tort action for willful interference in Wal-Mart's economically advantageous relationships, without actually having to document a conspiracy, though it was a long shot. Wal-Mart could not just go on a fishing expedition hoping that discovery following a lawsuit would turn up the evidence. They also had to anticipate public opposition to this kind of bullying of the little guy, especially after the pummeling small businesses had taken for years at Wal-Mart's giant hands.

What Wal-Mart had not anticipated was that even as they scrambled to come up with an effective strategy, Sol was deploying SWAT teams of his own to bust the union busters. Each team had six members: a field-tested attorney; two people savvy about the media and publicity generally, especially at the community level; one experienced negotiator; an engineer skilled in staging and logistics; and an economist with expertise in the psychological impact on the managerial and executives classes of declines in the bottom line. In the course of his career, Sol had relied on such teams for a variety of purposes and had found their services invaluable. His lead team had worked together for five years and had ironed out all abrasions, leaving a smoothly functioning force in place. Its vital statistics: average age, forty-six; four men, two women; one African American, one Mexican American, one Jewish American, two Anglo Americans, and a Mongolian American. They'd been chosen on merit, not for diversity, and that was how it turned out.

Sol sent the lead team to the Arkansas site to coordinate the operation from Wal-Mart's backyard. By the Friday of the billionaires' press conference, comparable teams had arrived in the other four locations and were quickly at full throttle, operating in close contact with the lead team but two days behind in order to reduce error and false starts. The first order of business was to reassure the rebel "associates" backing the union drive and to bolster their efforts. The next was to convey to the store managers—and thereby to the bosses in Bentonville—that what was happening in these five communities was just the opening salvo in a well-funded, tightly orchestrated national assault to be unleashed on Wal-Mart in the coming weeks. Projecting a credible penumbra of threat over the vast rest of Wal-Mart's terrain was a key to success.

The secret strategy of the Sol-SWATs was to let the opposition in on the secret. With the lead team setting the tempo, they contrived a series of "leaks" to the overenthusiastic volunteers already identified by the union organizers as company moles. It was too obvious to leave "confidential" documents lying around for the moles to find, so the teams announced "deep background sessions" to give the workers a detailed rundown on the massive national campaign that would soon be backing the individual guarantees they had already received. Thoughtfully, the teams announced these sessions days in advance so that the moles would have time to equip themselves with hidden recorders.

With the union drive, the picketing, the investor revolt, the fire sales, and the widespread stirrings of anti-corporate sentiment, Sol's Wal-Mart offensive was now on track for victory, but the drama would be intense. Would Wal-Mart take any of the face-saving opportunities they were offered, or would they only respond to overwhelming force? In either case, ongoing pressure from deep resources would lead Wal-Mart, the largest of the giant corporations, to fissure. Being an inherently expedient and opportunistic institution, it would come around once it evaluated the more costly alternatives—simple arithmetic, little to do with morality. That was the hope.

Sol crossed his fingers.

By the third week of February, the press was all over the lunchtime rebellion. It had taken a while, but now reporters were tallying additional cities and daily crowd increases as if they were covering major league baseball. The message was out: economic inequality broke down into non-livable wages, nearly 50 million Americans without health insurance, corporations and the rich not paying their fair share of taxes, big money counting more than votes, the poor paying more and absorbing more toxic pollution—and that was just the beginning. In every city there were local illustrations of these gross inequalities, such as which neighborhoods got good police and fire services and which did not. Before long, the crowds were joining in with "Tell 'em about Ballard Avenue Dump!" and "What about our schools crumbling while our taxes pay for that big stadium over there?" and indignantly on and on.

Soon there was a spate of editorials wondering who was behind these lunchtime rallies. Editors set their investigative reporters on the money trail and found that it dead-ended with local billionaires. "Why?" they asked, nonplussed. "Why not?" said the billionaires. All over the country, Ted's boys were coming through. The *Wall Street Journal* editorial gang took notice with a lead screed titled "The 'Why Not?' Billionaires." It called them old fogeys with nothing

better to do than play at being latter-day rabble-rousers. A quick
letter to the editor from one of the billionaires asked simply,
"Rabble? Is that what you call hardworking Americans who choose
to exercise their right of free assembly on their lunch break?"

Just as Leonard had hoped, the rallies took on a life of their own,
with spellbinding speakers, local musicians, poets, sketch artists,
even dancers. Advance preparation by his teams of organizers
assured that all this cultural excitement, important as it was, did not
distract from the main themes: a living wage; high-quality cost-con-
trolled universal health insurance; tax reform to shift the burden
upward on the income scale and onto the speculators and polluters;
and the immediate improvement of public services across the board.
Schools, transit, libraries, parks, recreational facilities, public procurement, public works, and public administration (police, fire, child
welfare, upkeep of the streets, enforcement of building codes) needed
major upgrades. Since each city had its front-page urgencies in these
areas, the rally speakers were never short of material.

But there was also room for the unexpected. In Fountain Square
in Cincinnati, five thousand demonstrators turned their rally into a
spontaneous protest against the Iraq War and occupation. In concert with Leonard's team, local organizers decided to make Iraq the
theme of the week, which ended with a Friday rally that drew the
biggest crowd yet. And what a rally it was—the lunchtime regulars,
their ranks swelled by thousands of citizens from all walks of life,
and at the center the soldiers back from Iraq, some on crutches or
in wheelchairs, defiant, articulate, passionate, hugging older veterans from past wars, challenging their smug, cloistered
commander in chief, redefining the patriotic course of action as
withdrawal from a war based on lies and soaked in blood, a war
whose multiplying effect was the recruitment and training of more
and more terrorists from more and more countries, as the White
House's handpicked director of the CIA himself had told a Senate
committee. Behind the speakers' platform was a huge screen, courtesy of the Mass Demonstrations budget, for live video appearances
by Ohio's governor, senators, and representatives, who had been

called days earlier and asked to reply to the ralliers' demand for a way out of Iraq. To the accompaniment of martial drumbeats, each politician's name was called out, and if said politician didn't come onscreen within a minute or so, the crowd roared its disapproval. Only one face appeared. "Although I cannot be with you in body, I'm with you in spirit," intoned a state congressman from Cleveland. "When can we have your body?" the ralliers roared back. Blushing, he replied, "As soon as my schedule permits." "Not good enough!" a leather-lunged Marine bellowed. "God bless you, and God bless America," said the congressman as his frozen smile faded from the screen.

It was an altogether different scene in Orlando, Florida, where fifteen thousand workers showed up from the Disney dens, the farm fields, the fast food restaurants, the lawn care companies, and other low-paying sectors. A majority of them were Latinos and African Americans, but a solid minority were the "poor whites" whose plight was often overshadowed by the routine exploitation of minorities. Many of the workers were holding aloft signs showing their hourly wages: Wal-Mart, $6.75 before payroll deductions; McDonald's, $6.15; Superior Tomatoes, $5.50; Spick and Span Janitorial Services, $7.00. On wages like those, they couldn't afford even the basics of a decent life, much less frills like healthcare.

None of these workers were unionized, but many of the speakers were active in union locals whose members were passing out organizing literature that announced several upcoming meetings and guaranteed privacy in bold print. Leonard's people were also circulating through the crowd, some of them giving out submarine sandwiches and fruit drinks, others collecting signatures on clipboards. Few workers signed; most recoiled slightly, as if afraid of having their concerns recognized. They had come to the rally, yes, but they weren't about to jeopardize the little they had by doing anything to suggest that they might cause trouble. Even as they heard speaker after speaker deliver a powerful pro-labor message, they couldn't shake the atmosphere of intimidation that hovered over them at their jobs and in their neighborhoods. Every day they had to contend with abusive or absentee landlords, price gouging, shoddy merchandise (especially the contaminated meat and spoiled food regularly dumped into low-income markets), payday loans with interest rates as high as 400 percent, furniture purchased under usurious installment loan agreements, and a host of other predatory lending practices. No voice. No remedy. No political representation. Just plenty of police making sure they didn't stand an inch beyond the area approved in the rally permit.

Reporters at the scene noticed that the demonstrators didn't seem angry, unlike the California farmworkers under César Chávez during the grape boycott decades earlier. Those campesinos had fire in their eyes as they shouted, "La huelga! Justicia!" These workers seemed resigned to their fate and just plain tired, as was also noted by the employer infiltrators wending their way through the crowd. However robust the speakers were, the reaction was subdued—until the police grabbed two young women who were shouting slogans and pushed them into the street. One of them, discernibly pregnant, lost her balance and fell hard. Her husband charged the cops, and then it all unraveled—more pushing and shoving, more police wading into the crowd with billy clubs, demonstrators fighting back, people screaming and falling, sirens wailing, bullhorns blaring threats of arrest. The rally speakers pleaded for calm, and the flaring tempers finally died down, but that evening all the national news programs showed the "disturbance," as they called it, and because it was tied to the demand for a living wage, the business pages gave the story play too, noting darkly that dozens of other big demonstrations for economic justice had taken place that day all over the country.

Watching the coverage at home in Waco, Bernard thought to himself that Orlando was a shot across the bow, just the thing to show that the proletariat, long considered moribund by the plutocracy, still had a cutting edge. Decades ago his father had immigrated to America from Russia and become a pushcart peddler, selling blankets and clothing door to door. Sometimes little Bernard would accompany him. When they finished their rounds, Papa would shake his finger with anger over the miseries of those downtrodden people and argue passionately for a major social upheaval on their behalf. Bernard never forgot his father's intensity at those moments.

Barry was also watching the televised coverage, which was generally above his expectations, apart from the usual yellow journalism of a few cable networks. But he knew that once the novelty wore off and the rallies and other Redirections showed seriousness of purpose—in demanding public control of the public airwaves, for instance—the big media would either try to ignore what was going on or caricature such initiatives as dangerous revolutionary ideologies. Talk radio—the hound dogs of the commercial media—and the heavily right-wing cable news and opinion shows would lead the charge, in part through the technique of personal destruction, singling out vulnerable individuals and portraying them as ogres or deranged radicals.

Barry resolved to redouble his already accelerated schedule of leveraged buyouts for a radio and television network covering the entire country. His law firm could produce the boilerplate purchase contracts at a moment's notice, and bankers were always standing by for him, such was his sterling track record. By his estimate, the deals for the network would be cut by the end of February, and the actual takeover of the stations would be complete by the end of March—and not a day too soon, given the huge coverage of the Redirections and the coming battles. There would be twenty-five television stations, two cable channels, thirty AM radio stations, ten FM radio stations, one satellite radio station, and links to associated websites. That should do it for audience saturation. The programming work had to start immediately, with the task of creating lively and controversial shows that would draw high ratings, after the *60 Minutes* model, and the additional challenge of parrying the anticipated propaganda and smear campaigns from the opposition. That meant enlisting on-air talent and off-air investigative experts with dispatch.

Barry reached for his Rolodex.

CHAPTER 5

W hile Sol was stepping up the campaign against Wal-Mart, the company's normally cool and calculating top executives were scurrying around like mice in a maze. They could hardly believe the reports coming in from the field. Dismayed by their disarray, their hands-on CEO assembled them for a briefing. He commenced soberly.

"Our great company is under a domestic attack that could have global repercussions, and we must deal with it now. In little more than a week, the balance of power has begun to tilt toward our enemies. There are picketers at two hundred of our stores, and though they can't get close to the doors because of private property restrictions, they're sufficiently intrusive that sales are suffering. Customers just don't want to endure the hassle of the chanting, the police presence, and the surveillance cameras.

"We have indications that the picket organizers are planning similar obstructions in front of more stores shortly. In the five areas most under assault, those despicably named storefronts—Wal-Fart, Wal-Part, etc.—are spreading the usual union slander about our company and picking up additional numbers of ex-associates who will no doubt feed them more grist for their noxious mills. Our SWAT teams in these five areas, including the one right here in Bentonville, where our revered Sam Walton started his first low-priced store, report that they can't get a handle on what's happening. Because no existing unions appear to be involved, all our teams can do is to try to infiltrate the meetings of the shadow opposition and the traitorous associates who've gone over to them.

"As you know, some important shareholders have been calling to demand that we raise wages and improve benefits. The timing of these calls indicates coordination, particularly since institutional shareholders—mutual funds and pension funds—have also transmitted their demands in writing. One retired billionaire after another has taken out an ad or given a news conference to brag about how successful his business was even with—or because of—high wages and good benefits for the workers, and to showcase ex-associates with tear-jerking personal stories that come across as very believable.

"Small stores in the vicinity of our discount havens are announcing forthcoming sales on our best-selling products at prices lower than ours, which also suggests close coordination in those five locations. The mom-and-pop businesses we replaced when we located in their backyard are coming back to bite us. Don't underestimate their local political power, especially given their backing. Yes, we have identified the ringleader. He is the patron-saint-turned-devil of the wholesale-retail discount store movement. Sol Price knows our vulnerable points along the whole chain of supply. He knows our margins, our spoilage. He knows how we think. He knows we're so big that we have few influential allies except for the politicians we take care of. He knows all we have are millions of satisfied customers. When he called me urging a cardcheck, he didn't say that he was the force behind this disruptive drive, but the trail leads directly back to him, even though we don't know the details."

"Sol Price?" exclaimed the executives around the table in a chorus of alarm.

"That man is a legend for his shrewdness and tenacity," said an executive vice-president. "And he can't be dismissed as a radical or a union boss."

CEO Clott tried to calm the increasingly distressed executives. He announced a week of intensive intelligence gathering, along with the destruction of sensitive documents and e-mails on advice of counsel, under his daily direction. "Then we'll be in a position to present the board of directors with a comprehensive plan of action," he said authoritatively. "Meanwhile, let's pay a visit to the Bentonville store to see what we can find out for ourselves. I'll also commission a poll to gauge the effect of this unprecedented campaign on public opinion and on Wal-Mart customers themselves. It's essential to know where we stand."

In the midst of all the core group activity, Warren was doing a superb job running the Secretariat and was also taking an active role in various Redirections, but he wanted to do more. He decided to deliver a blistering denunciation of the excessive pay of the CEOs and executives of the Fortune 500. He had spoken out before in measured terms, asserting that these huge compensation packages blinded executives to what was best for shareholders and the business in general, created a moral authority gap with workers, and produced incentives to engage in creative accounting that inflated profits and misled investors. Stock options for the bosses were particular tools of mischief. And they all knew that their pay packages were self-determined and would be rubber-stamped by their board members, who in turn were rewarded with large per diems and other payola. Year after year executive pay kept outstripping worker wages, economic growth, company growth, or any other indicator under the mother sun. A *Fortune* magazine cover story declared that nothing could stop this escalation, though the editors deeply deplored the greed at the top.

Warren begged to differ with *Fortune*'s prediction, and he did so in an address before the National Cattlemen's Convention in Omaha's cavernous public arena. After laying out the red meat of his argument with calm precision and logic, he concluded with a stirring peroration. "We're not waiting for Washington or the White House or the Securities and Exchange Commission to do the job, because they are under the influence, and I'm not talking about booze. We're going to mobilize the mutual funds, the pension trusts, and the individual investors who own these corporations. They're going to demand shareholder approval of pay packages and accountability from the executives who are supposed to be working for them, not the other way around. Together, we've got the financial muscle to make it happen, and happen fast, you hear?"

They heard. Cattlemen are conservative people from conservative states working in a conservative business that puts steaks on dining room tables, but they had always felt manipulated by the "suits" in the pricing pits of Chicago and the skyscrapers of New York, by the giant middlemen and the giant supermarkets with their huge markups, by all the rich white-collar guys who never had to endure the grit and grime of raising livestock. Now the richest man in America was proposing a plan to put wheels on the wheels and "steer" to victory—not just words, action! They roared their approval in a ten-minute standing ovation. The press was dumbfounded by the reaction.

As he left the convention, even the supremely confident Warren wondered if he had bitten off more than he could chew. He rarely, if ever, forecast his moves or predicted victory, but in this case he felt he had to put himself on the spot to provoke the burst of adrenaline that would be required of him and his colleagues. He also knew that with all the debate and excitement generated by the Redirections, executives were likely to be on the defensive, and that the vast majority of investors, including the institutions, would be supportive. Still, what had to be done had never been done before.

In his methodical way, Warren laid out his design for action. As CEO of a major holding company, he had already set the example with his annual salary of $350,000 and no stock options or bonuses. His company was the marvel of the investment world, with stock valued at $5,000 per share in 1986 now soaring to nearly $100,000 per share—the highest by far on the New York Stock Exchange. From this pedestal, Warren served on the boards of several large companies, including the Washington Post/Newsweek corporation. He knew he could swing these companies, although he'd have to persuade the *Post*'s dominant family, which controlled the voting shares on such matters. Then he'd marshal his own vast contacts and the relevant people from the core group's epicenters; set up high-level meetings with the heads of the large mutual and pension funds, the NYSE, and NASDAQ; ask Leonard to organize a demonstration of investors on Wall Street; and coordinate it all with Barry and his media network. As one big company after another fell into the fold and officially ceded investor control over executive pay, heavy publicity was likely to follow. Interlocking directorates would further the spread of investor control. The Fortune 500 would be holding their annual shareholder meetings soon, and Warren would stoke up all those securities attorneys from the pro bono talent bank to prepare resolutions calling for investor control over the pay packages of each company's top four executives. Major investors would be lined up to register their support either by signing the resolution or issuing a statement. The shareholder meetings, no matter how remote their sites, would be packed with supporters who would have good media backup from Barry as well as on-the-scene publicists. To send a political message, a resolution of support would be circulated in Congress and the larger state legislatures. State securities regulators, state attorneys general, and the White House would also be solicited for support. To implement all these objectives, Warren hired a skilled ten-person staff that he wryly referred to as "the Boiler Room."

When the plan was circulated to the core group, the first call came from Leonard. "Good news, Warren," he said with a laugh. "The CEO of the company at the top of your list is my younger brother, and I'm the major shareholder." But what really tickled Leonard's funny bone was the prospect of two hundred thousand investors surrounding the New York Stock Exchange and the major investment and brokerage houses. Warren was impressed, but not so much that he didn't ask, "How in the world are you going to get two hundred thousand investors?"

"Well, they'll be mostly small investors, of course, but with Barry's media and Ross's credibility groups, especially retired veterans and business clubs like Rotary and Kiwanis, we can do it. I'd say it'll take about two months—a couple of weeks after Maui Four."

"I'm relying on you, Leonard," said an amazed Warren.

Out in California, a rejuvenated Warren Beatty was reviewing the latest draft of his formal announcement speech for governor. Once again, Dick Goodwin showed that he hadn't lost his touch. The

address was magisterial, studded with historical allusions that legit-
imized the fundamental changes in power, wealth, income, and
priorities so logically and factually laid out in scintillating paragraph
after paragraph. Fundamental democratic values undergirded every
sentence and idea as proof against distortions, red-baiting, and
right-wing casuistry. Goodwin deployed quotations from America's
best political leaders of the past, and from revered conservative economists like Adam Smith, Herbert Simon, Friedrich Hayek, and
Milton Friedman, to deflect anticipated attacks from the corporatists.
He made the beauties of California's geography the focus of the
announcement and wove otherwise dry facts about devastating and
cruel conditions into vibrant and sonorous rhetoric. But what most
enthralled Warren about the speech was its seamless portrayal of
his transition from movie heartthrob to actor/writer/director of
political movies like *Reds* and *Bulworth* to passionate spokesman on
crucial issues facing the country, and finally to crusading politician.
As he sent back his edits and comments, he reflected that this was
his best script yet. How on earth could the Democrats have failed to
enlist Dick Goodwin in their battle for the White House in 2004?
Did anyone remember any of John Kerry's speeches or campaign
themes that year, except possibly his silencing of John Edwards'
"two Americas" presentation on poverty and moral obligation,
which had galvanized audiences during the primary season?

The next question was where and how to deliver his speech.
Advised by the canny public interest lawyer Harvey Rosenfield, he
decided to give it in four locations in one day, starting out in Los
Angeles with his family on the steps of a decrepit branch library in
South Central, going on alone to San Diego State University and
then the Imperial Valley, where he'd be surrounded by farmworkers
who harvested a large portion of the country's fruits and vegetables,
and ending up at the Presidio on San Francisco Bay. He'd have to
use a private jet and spend some of his own money, but for once it
was worth it. He'd have a primary fight with three other Democratic
candidates, but he was confident that the voting public would relish
a showdown between him and Arnold. As launch time approached,

Warren felt a great load lifting from his shoulders. Years of doubt, years of playing surrogate politician, years of hesitation about himself were washing away.

Ever since his speech to the Assembly, he'd been boning up on conditions in the state, not just the usual ones the press asked about, but all the needs government was meant to address and was ignoring. He'd consulted with specialists on children and schools; on sustainability and local economic development; on poverty, healthcare, immigration, tax equity, and corporate welfare; on land, water, and air utilization; on slums and sprawl; on law enforcement from the streets to the business suites; on the responsibilities of the wealthy to the people of California. When announcement day came, he exceeded the expectations of the media with his spectacular address, his refusal to pander, and his demonstration of resolve. His former days of womanizing were alluded to, of course, but what else was new—and compared to Arnold the Stud? With the billionaire buses and the reinstatement of the old tax on the wealthy fresh in everyone's mind, Warren came across as both a man of action and a man of his word. Initial polls registered a 63-percent approval rating for the speech, and one columnist wrote that the race was Warren's to lose. Back home with Annette and the children, a tired but happy man planned his next move.

In weeks three and four of Maui Month Two, the rumble against the corporate supremacists and their political allies grew louder by the day, like the approaching hoofbeats of a cavalry charge. The mass media knew that something was afoot, but they couldn't figure out whether it was just some eccentric rich guys on a justice lark or a bigger, more coordinated movement. The People's Chamber of Commerce was challenging its reactionary larger counterparts to specific debates at the National Press Club, and in the process defining what progressive businesses stood for—unheard of in Washington, DC, where trade associations were supposed to collude, not debate. The lunchtime demonstrations continued to grow in number and spread to new locations. Two prominent retired CEOs gave tell-all valedictory speeches at the Press Club, leaving the real estate and agribusiness industries reeling. Even the business-friendly Justice Department bestirred itself to announce that it would investigate the charges, and several members of Congress urged the attorney general to do so with dispatch.

Jerome Kohlberg, Warren's retired billionaire investment banker from the Hamptons, launched Operation Shakeup with a press conference on electoral reform, releasing a white paper naming the one hundred worst abusers in the area of campaign financing, and singling out a number of donations he claimed were illegal under federal law. He tied these sleazy contributions to the quid pro quo politicians who accepted them, raising intimations of bribery. An uproar ensued, but what could you do to a retired billionaire who'd preceded the press conference with fact-filled ads on radio and television and in the major New York newspapers? He concluded by saying that all campaign television ads under five minutes should be banned, citing the views of advertising guru John O'Toole, former president and chairman of Foote, Cone and Belding, who once worked for Richard Nixon's campaign and had written a book called *The Trouble with Advertising*. This blast caused Madison Avenue to go ape and unleash a volley of slashing attack ads in response. Kohlberg promptly fired back.

Bernard hit more media pay dirt with his own press conference on corporate commercialism in our schools. As a prelude to his project to establish after-school Egalitarian Clubs, he read out his roll call of the worst offenders, who replied with a chorus of indignant protestations of innocence, claiming they were just giving the kids what they wanted. "Yes," rejoined Bernard, "like junk food, junk television programming in the classroom, censored teachers, and an excessively narrow vocational curriculum."

Meanwhile, in the old Progressive tradition of the late nineteenth century, the Promotions Project began sending lecturers around the country to speak to civic groups and local chapters of the PCC.

These were all people with experience in matters of social and economic justice, and with reputations sufficient to draw interested audiences. Promotions advertised their appearances well and made sure they were featured prominently in the local media. Their topics were diverse, but they generally started with some hot local issue and then linked it to broader themes of government of, by, and for the people, equal justice under the law, and the other concerns being addressed by one or more of the Redirections.

The radio attack dogs were baffled by the white-hot controversies erupting everywhere over real abuses of power. Their big advertisers kept calling to egg them on—but on to what, or whom? They were like drooling bloodhounds straining at the leash to hunt down their quarry, but they'd lost their sense of smell. Sure, they spewed their daily denunciations of the lunchtime rallies, had a field day with the "Fighting Zulus" caper, tore into Joe's small claims litigation, snickered over Warren Beatty's alleged dalliances, and rushed to defend Wal-Mart, calling the giant retailer "the best anti-poverty program in American history." But they couldn't make any ism stick, couldn't cry conspiracy, couldn't plausibly tar the assorted billionaire elders with the usual labels: fags, atheists, child killers, flag desecrators, feminazis, socialists, communists, anarchists, French, national nannies, cop-haters, peaceniks, disarmers (gun controllers), traitors, the blame-America-first crowd. Epithet-starved, they turned to management for advice.

The media barons who syndicated their programs had noticed a pattern of mergers and acquisitions by Barry Diller—unusual activity, and unusually fast, even for him. They'd also noticed that the strange goings-on of the past month were getting more than customary airtime on his existing brace of radio and TV stations. Of more concern was the steady daily decline in audience ratings for their bombastic right-wing loudmouths, and the slow but steady rise in ratings for Diller's stations. But there was no hard evidence that anything more was involved than the man's notorious idiosyncrasies, and all they could do was urge the talk show yappers to stay hot on the trail and ask their listeners for leads. "Something's starting to happen," said one CEO in an e-mail to Bush Bimbaugh, "and we damn well better find out what it is before it gets done happening."

On the morning of the hastily scheduled meeting of the Wal-Mart board of directors, the company's top six executives gathered over an early breakfast in their war room. On the long wall was an elaborate mural of the Wal-Mart Colossus bestriding the globe, but the Big Six were not admiring the artwork. They'd done their best to digest the huge volume of intelligence and anecdotal reports they'd received from their operatives, and they'd crafted their presentation carefully, but they were still nervous. They had two plans, one if the board simply went along with the CEO's recommendations, and the other if there was a board rebellion. Either way, they all knew events were accelerating so fast that a decision had to be made by the end of the day. The company had been in hot water before, over local dustups that were sometimes widely publicized but could be easily defused by an apology and a little cosmetic corrective action. This was drastically different. With stiff upper lips, they raised and clicked their customary glasses of fresh-squeezed orange juice, chugalugged, and walked down to the board conference room for pre-meeting pleasantries.

The board members seemed unusually subdued. A few of them were conversing quietly, but there was none of the standard small talk about golf and grandchildren. For a week or more, they had all been under unprecedented pressure from shareholders, mutual funds, billionaire friends, and badgering reporters inquiring about their stance on Wal-Mart's labor practices, and even about their own personal pay and perks. Some of them had seen their names on placards at the lunchtime rallies in the cities where they worked. And then there were the websites, those awful blogs with no sense of propriety and no barriers to rudeness.

CEO Clott brought the meeting to order at 9:00 a.m. sharp. He asked everyone to turn off their cell phones and said that the room had recently been debugged and that no staff would be allowed to enter until lunch. Then he began.

"Ladies and gentlemen, I wish to preface my remarks by assuring you that our intelligence capabilities are close to total. Little of what our shadowy adversary is doing escapes us. We have a direct line into its moves in the five targeted stores and around the country. What you are about to hear is not supposition and rumor. What you are about to hear is fact, reality, the adversary's forward plan of attack. True, we do not have the whole story, but we know enough to go toe to toe with this adversary on the ground.

"We are entering a period of grave uncertainty. Already our company's stock has lost ten percent of its value. That translates into billions of dollars and does not augur well for our management incentive program. Of course, stock can go back up after a company weathers a crisis, and more than a few large corporations have done just that. But what we are confronting is not just a major crisis, and not a steady-state one at that, such as a major product recall with known parameters. We are facing the most sophisticated assault on a company's wage and benefits policy ever. Our in-house Wal-Mart historian finds nothing comparable, nothing remotely on this scale, in any of our prior unionization confrontations, or indeed in any such confrontations in our nation's past.

"Many of us have been on the receiving end of calls from Sol Price. You know what a formidable adversary he can be, with his knowledge, his labor relations record, and his bull terrier personality. He knows the nerve points of our business and the nature of our customer base. Already the storefronts are spreading lies about the indirect costs Wal-Mart passes on to the taxpayers, small businesses, workers whose wages are depressed by our policies, workers who lose their jobs as a result of the China price, and on and on. His people are even delving into alleged differences between our shelf prices and our register prices. Moreover, given our labor turnover, there are a lot of grievances and allegations of wrongdoing circulating, and the storefronts are collecting all of them. The picketing at two hundred Supercenters is depressing sales because of the noise and ruckus. Sol Price has agitated a substantial part of our shareholder base, which has alarmed the investment advisory fellows in New York. And his very rich cohorts are all over us with squeeze plays that few besides people like us can understand. Particularly worrisome is that all these initiatives are being developed as models to be applied in every corner of the country that our stores service.

"At the five targeted stores, the number of our associates signing up to be the nucleus of the union organizing drive is reaching a critical mass. Imagine, Price's people are offering free union membership for three years, no dues at all, zero! Unlike past feeble and ultimately futile attempts by a few unions, this invasion has limitless resources, talent, and business acumen at its disposal. Price's SWAT teams, though not impenetrable, are producing more than a little anxiety among our Wal-Mart SWAT teams in the five localities. Our teams know how to quash budding union drives led by two or three local organizers who don't have the backing or the experience to thwart us, but they aren't trained to deal with guys their own size, so to speak.

"As if all that weren't bad enough, there are new blasts in the chute. Next week a national advertising buy will sharply compare how we're required to treat our associates across the Atlantic under various European labor laws—decent wages, paid vacations, unionizing rights, pensions, childcare, family medical leave—to how our stateside workers are faring. We have advance copies of these ads, and they are simply devastating, making our wonderful company look downright unpatriotic. We also have advance notice of a video campaign showing how our Chinese suppliers mistreat their workers, and how we allegedly coerce our domestic suppliers to close down and move to China at the expense of their loyal US workers, some of them military veterans. Both campaigns are pitched to the mass media, the investment community, the Congress, and the state legislatures. For the time being, they've written off the White House, but probably not for long.

"I don't want to sound too downbeat, but we have to face the bad news. On the other hand, we are not without resources and talent of our own. Over the last several years we have waged a successful fight against the unions. Not one Wal-Mart has been unionized, nor has there even been a majority sign-up of our associates, with the exception of one meat department that has since, shall we say, been discontinued. So permit your management to put before you, for your close consideration, several possible strategies of counterattack.

"First, we can simply hunker down and wait them out. Sure, they may cut into our sales, depress our stock a bit more, even unionize a few stores, but we can bargain in apparent good faith for a long, long time before we arrive at any labor agreements. You know what the hoops under the NLRB can be like in contested proceedings.

"Our attorneys have advised us that we can sue the storefronts and their backers for intentional interference with our economic right to conduct business, given their clear vindictiveness. However, we are a little large to gain much sympathy from the courts, not to mention the public out there—Sprawl-Mart versus Main Street and all that—and proving direct causation would be difficult, according to the attorneys. We might find out more through discovery, but we have good intelligence now, and besides, our opponents seem to have little to hide.

"Our economists are prepared to produce an analysis of cost increases resulting from any successful cardcheck effort, to show how many employees would have to be laid off to maintain our profit margin. If we disseminate this information widely among our workforce, our opponents may have difficulty getting a majority to sign on, even with the cardcheck.

"There is another possibility, something we haven't done very extensively to date, and that is to organize our customers into consumer associations opposed to higher prices. Our outreach department believes that with the proper inducements such associations would attract a large membership, but not a dynamic and driven one, given their ostensible purpose.

"Finally, we could go after Sol Price. Even though he appears clean, his discount stores, first out of the big box, were soon challenged by our estimable founder with his Sam's Club chain, built on Price's model but with bigger expansion resources. We could paint Sol Price as having a grudge match in his retirement. So what? most people would say, if they weren't yawning. This one has no legs. Everyone would marvel at his energy. We'd end up turning him into a sex symbol and watching him promote Viagra on TV.

"To summarize, then, with some combination of the strategies I've outlined, we can bring the onslaught against us to a protracted standstill. While our adversaries have deep pockets and can offer fired employees better jobs, free legal representation, sympathetic media, and so forth, we believe they are working within a limited time frame. To the best of our knowledge, they have not planned for the long haul. Assuming that's the case, the unanswered question is whether the resources and energies they've put into play will become self-replicating and self-sustaining. If so, waiting them out becomes a weaker option. Our company will be embroiled in constant struggle and under constant media scrutiny, a particularly troubling projection since we are not going to win all the battles at our thirty-eight hundred stores. It will become a war of attrition. It will be draining and distracting, win or lose.

"Well, ladies and gentlemen, I think that's about it, short of calling in the Marines, but maybe we should take over their PXs first." CEO Clott paused for a laugh, which was not forthcoming. "The floor is now open for your reactions and suggestions," he said, coughing into his hand.

"What would it do to Wal-Mart to pay its workers more?" asked Alicia Del Toro, a recent addition to the board. "Say at the level of Costco, which seems to be making a pretty good profit. I know Costco isn't Wal-Mart, but they're a substantial big-box discount chain."

"You're right. Costco isn't Wal-Mart and does not share our business model. When reporters ask us this question, we say that if we increased our average pay by $2.90 an hour and reduced health insurance co-payments, the cost would be equivalent to our annual profits. Next question, please."

"Excuse me, Leighton, but do you take me for a reporter? First, the extra pay is deductible, and so are the added health insurance costs.

Second, a reduction in executive compensation packages would go a long way toward making up the difference, not to mention improving the morale of over a million workers. Third, you're not taking into account your constant productivity increases from having fewer and fewer associates operating ever larger Supercenters. Fourth, you're ignoring the fact that higher pay reduces employee turnover, which is astronomical—it's as if you're running a temp agency! Fifth, have you calculated how many sales you'd lose by raising prices enough to compensate for raising wages? Not many, I suspect, but I'm sure your experts can arrive at a very precise understanding of what consequences flow from what variables. Finally, please don't talk down to us. We're not rubber stamps, you know."

More than slightly taken aback, Clott coughed into his hand again. "Forgive me if I conveyed that impression. I certainly didn't intend to. I'll have a thorough analysis done for the board within a week, also taking into account any concerns others of you may have."

"With due respect, Leighton," said Frederick Buck, an emeritus professor of economics, "Alicia has a point, and there are other productivities to consider too, such as going to just-in-time inventory, factoring in your China price savings, and who knows what else. But why in the world didn't you have all this data in our briefing books in comprehensible fashion?"

Clott stuck his damp hand under the table. "Well, quite frankly, I didn't think we'd have to go there. I assumed that the board had the requisite confidence in management to take our recommendations. Is it the general feeling of the board that you want further information, and if so, does that mean you're reconsidering our absolute opposition to unions and cardchecks? May I see a show of hands?"

"Time out!" said Sam Sale, retired CEO of the country's largest sporting goods chain. "The question is too ambiguous. It's not, at least for me, that I want to reconsider our opposition to unions, but I do want the information as a broader basis to assess our options."

"May I have a show of hands on the rephrasing of the question?" Clott said.

All but three of the seventeen board members raised their hands, throwing the executives off script. Had Sol gotten to the board? After what seemed an interminable silence in the large conference room, the CEO composed himself. Time for plan B.

"All right, if Wal-Mart changes its present labor policies, what can we do to take the steam out of the opposition? Basically, we'll have to adopt a new business model, but in such a way as to avoid the impression that we're capitulating. We adjust price schedules to allow for across-the-board increases in wages and benefits, from starting pay up to middle management. Top management takes a small cut in compensation, and officers take a slightly larger but still modest cut, which gives us some moral stature. Instead of capping the average work week at twenty-nine hours to squeeze savings out of the payroll, we give our associates a forty-hour week. We increase the company's share of health insurance premiums, eliminate the most restrictive deductibles and exclusions, and offer normal pensions or 401(k) retirement plans. This is essentially what we're doing by law in Europe, where we're still making good profits, and it will deflect the criticism that we enjoy a taxpayer subsidy because we refer our associates to federal or state welfare services, particularly Medicaid. Then we plan a major media campaign explaining that our kinder and gentler business model will necessitate somewhat higher prices for our loyal consumers—which isn't the case because of our productivity and China savings, though of course we can't say that.

"In presenting this alternative business model to you, I am aware that I'm proposing the most revolutionary makeover of Wal-Mart since Sam Walton launched this great company. Even to think of this kind of change is humbling, to say the least, but your votes on the last question suggest that you're prepared to contemplate it. I and my fellow executives make no recommendation. We await your response."

"Here's my question, and it's simple," said a tight-lipped Joseph Cobbler. "What would Sam do?"

"He'd get the facts," said Ken Keystone, chairman of the board. "He'd want to know."

"I agree," said Gerald Taft. "I think I speak for all of us when I say that we board members in our individual capacities have been catching hell for the past couple of weeks. Reporters, shareholders, disgruntled employees, the New York investment crowd, cranks, Wal-Mart scholars, unionists—you name them—are all over us. Speaking just for myself, I am a banker, and in that capacity I believe I've contributed to the board's oversight of the company and its deliberations. But I did not sign on to the board last year to be viewed as an ogre and hounded by some of my own wealthy peers, no less. Sol Price doesn't play dirty, I know, but he does play relentless. He doesn't go personal, but he puts the pressure on and turns the screws. I simply do not see light at the end of the tunnel. Does anybody here?"

"What tunnel?" objected Robert Shear, former president of Wal-Mart. "I thought we only see horizons here in Bentonville. Are we starting to lose our cool? Let's not panic. We're still the number one company in the world. We're still the greatest retail innovator in the world. Our satisfied customers vastly outnumber the forces arrayed against us, and these forces do not include prosecutors, grand juries, or judges. In my view, management should continue to monitor the situation, gather intelligence, keep the opposition off balance in this intensifying game of chess, and think anew about this novel challenge. All of us board members must go on high mental alert, and perhaps try to meet with Sol Price. You never know what you'll find out."

"What I just heard sounds to me like a modified motion to table, adjourn, and meet again soon," Clott said. Alicia Del Toro frowned, but there were nods of relief from most of the board members. "I'll see to it that you receive the requested information promptly, ladies and gentlemen, and I assure you that we'll stay in the closest touch."

On the last Monday of February, Warren devoted most of the closed-circuit teleconference—now a daily event—to a review of the critical mundane details of the core group's work. He reported that he'd hired Seymour Depth, longtime director of the Peace Corps, now retired, to head the Recruitment Department, which was up to speed with its staffing tasks for the CUBs, the Congress Watchdogs, the volunteer and paid talent banks, and the lecturers, organizers, interviewers, and media specialists. Applications were far in excess of the growing needs, but once qualifications were addressed, the number dropped. Many good-hearted people were applying mainly as an outlet for their personal discouragement or alienation, and some were intensely idealistic but out of touch with the practical demands of the assignments, so Recruitment was engaged in a very large but kind winnowing process. "We're keeping all their names, which now number over two million, because there will be other ways to invite their contributions at more modest levels," Warren concluded, turning to his colleagues for updates on their projects.

George, Jeno, and Max reported that the CUB mailings were on schedule and would reach more than 150 million households by the time they were complete, though with some duplication given all the different kinds of CUBs. They were optimistic about a good rate of return and would try to improve it with follow-up resolicitations. Barry reported that the websites he'd set up for the various Redirections were receiving millions of visits and that many people were leaving their e-mail addresses. He noted that in anticipation of the Pot-In at the White House this Thursday, the industrial hemp website was particularly hot. "Mine too!" Ted chimed in. "That Sun God site is hotter than a nun's dream, and the festivals have really caught on, as you'll see for yourselves on Friday when the first two blow your minds." Barry suppressed a smirk and added that the number of volunteers for both events was way beyond expectations, in part thanks to the mailing list of 3 million recipients of Yoko's bulbs.

Bernard's Egalitarian Clubs were off to a slower start. Parents were too busy working, commuting, or ferrying their children around to competing after-school activities like sports or music lessons. Middle-class mothers were virtually nonstop chauffeurs. Children from poorer families were left alone watching television—the latchkey kids. "It looks like I'll have to hire field organizers to set up a few dozen clubs as models," Bernard said with a sigh. "Not all excellent ideas are received with immediate acclamation. I am heartened, though, by the rising clamor from parents in response to the commercialism-in-the-schools campaign. School districts are starting to review conditions and promising to report to parents soon."

After brief remarks from Ross Perot on the Credibility Project, from Peter on his forthcoming testimony before the Senate Commerce Committee, and from Sol on Wal-Mart ("Enough already! Read the papers!"), Leonard said that the Congress Project was on track and that Donald Ross and Joan Claybrook had been hired, subject to strict cautions against Democratic partisanship coloring their work. They agreed to the terms and would commence the week after Maui Three. Bill Gates reported that every day hundreds of people were registering with his project to incorporate themselves. "As yet," he said, "no suitable corporations have presented themselves as candidates for political office, but I'm sure this counterintuitive tactic will bear fruit in plenty of time to make a blazing statement about the unequal treatment of 'persons' under the law. Oh, and by the way, after consulting with Newman and Cosby, Joe and I have decided to kick-start our State of Justice drive with the Pledge of Allegiance. We're holding a press conference tomorrow morning at ten—apologies for the short notice—and we hope you'll all tune in. I know these various projects will take a while to incubate, but when they do, Katy bar the door!"

"Katy?" Warren said with a chuckle. "Katy who? Has she been vetted by Recruitment?"

Early Tuesday morning, Joe and Bill met to go over their plans for the press conference. The previous week, they'd incorporated a small nonprofit in Washington, DC, with the single objective of legislating a change in the Pledge of Allegiance from "with liberty and justice for all" to "with liberty and justice for some." They'd rented a room at the National Press Club, and their staff was now festooning it with American flags and erecting a huge blowup of the

Pledge with "all" crossed out and replaced by "some." The reputations of William Gates Sr. and Joe Jamail assured a respectable turnout of reporters and columnists, but those two gentlemen were taking no chances. The day before, they'd issued a press release announcing the two essay contests and the prize money, the support of the six state attorneys general for annual State of Justice reports, and the forthcoming introduction of the Pledge legislation in Congress by two representatives from largely African American and Latino districts, as well as two senators from states with great inequalities of wealth and income. Late in the afternoon, they'd briefed the most vocal right-wing members of Congress and invited them to respond, as they surely would. In an hour, an excellent sit-down breakfast would be served to the men and women of the fourth estate to put them in a receptive frame of mind.

Come 10:00 a.m., not a square inch of the large Press Club room was unoccupied. Bill Gates strode to the podium with no notes or script. He swept the room with a steady gaze and began.

"The law in our country is living a lie. When it isn't actually written by and for the abusers of power and the corporate crooks, it is applied very selectively, coming down hardest on lower-income people and with a feather touch on the affluent and well-connected. There are even many cases in which the authorities use the law as an instrument of direct oppression. You all know about our proposed change in the Pledge of Allegiance. We advance it with thanks to Bill Cosby and Paul Newman, who first suggested it in their telethon last month. Over the coming days we will back it up with studies and in debates all over the nation. Daniel Webster once said, 'Justice is the great work of man on Earth.' We will be devoting our utmost efforts to insuring access to justice for every man, woman, and child in America." He paused and looked out over the audience again. "And now I'd like to introduce Joe Jamail for a few remarks before we take your questions."

"Thank you, Bill. Societies that live by hypocrisy will decay in hypocrisy. On the battlefield of Gettysburg, Abraham Lincoln declared that our nation was 'conceived in Liberty, and dedicated to the proposition that all men are created equal.' That is an eloquent way of saying that our nation is one in which the people are afforded equal justice under law. Lincoln knew that his words expressed an ideal and that Americans would have to dedicate themselves to making it more of a reality. Our legal institutions must represent that 'inner air, an inner light in which freedom lives and in which a man can draw the breath of self-respect,' in the words of Adlai Stevenson. As a nation, as a society, we are far, far from that destination. 'With liberty and justice for all,' our Pledge of Allegiance tells us. Millions of Americans take that pledge every day. Tens of millions take it every year. And what happens after we stand and solemnly utter these words with our hands over our hearts? Words are not efforts. Words are not deeds. Words are not, ipso facto, truths. Untruthful words should not disgrace our Pledge of Allegiance when neither efforts nor deeds follow from the exercise of our vocal cords.

"We must not allow our recital of the Pledge to lull us into false complacency and patriotic self-praise. Americans progress when they face reality, not when they succumb to illusion. It is for that reason and no other that we're launching a national initiative to change the final words of the Pledge to 'with liberty and justice for some.' Already more than three hundred inner-city schools have adopted the change in the wake of the telethon, and we have provided them with handsome posters of the revised Pledge. We expect the movement to spread across the land. We also expect vigorous discussion and robust debate to spread, particularly when our supporters in Congress introduce legislation mandating the change later today. The more concrete these discussions and debates, the closer we'll get to the grim realities we must change. Liberty—call it freedom—does not exist without power. As Marcus Cicero said more than two thousand years ago in Rome, 'Freedom is participation in power.' We need both freedom from abuses and freedom to fulfill our dreams. We need a Pledge of Allegiance that helps us make good on Ralph Waldo Emerson's succinct definition of our country: 'America means opportunity, freedom, power.'" Joe paused for a moment. "For all."

A reporter from the *Washington Times* jumped out of his seat brandishing his notepad. "Isn't this just one gigantic gimmick, Mr. Jamail?"

"No. Next question."

"Are the two of you colluding with Bill Cosby and Paul Newman?" asked a young woman from Fox News.

"Of course not. We're just indebted to them for raising the issue so publicly. They really started us thinking, and we know we're not the only ones," Joe said smoothly as he turned to call on Jim Drew of the *Washington Post*.

"What reaction do you expect from the American Legion and the Veterans of Foreign Wars?"

"I don't know. What I do know is that many of these veterans are living examples of the situation our revised words are meant to describe. I'm a veteran of World War II myself, and so is Bill, if that's anything to go by."

"Mr. Gates," said Basil Brubaker, the Washington correspondent for the *New York Times*, "Senator Thurston Thinkalot has just released a statement that reads in part, 'Two ambulance chasers trying to change our sacred Pledge of Allegiance to our sacred flag speak for themselves, don't they? All red-blooded Americans will give them a curled lip when they hear about this gross desecration.' What is your reaction?"

"Well, first of all, neither Joe nor I have ever chased any ambulances, but if we had, we probably would have found them full of people injured or sick as a direct or indirect result of the opposition of Senator Thinkalot and his conservative cohorts to health and safety standards. Second, we'll see in the coming days whether or not we speak only for ourselves. Third, anytime Senator Thinkalot wants to debate us, Joe and I will relish the showdown."

That was enough for the reporters. They had their lead, and off they went. From the back of the room, two older men who had been watching the proceedings intently approached the podium and introduced themselves to Joe and Bill as retired attorneys who had spent years in corporate law firms. One of them, John Tucker, said he was now a writer of novels and nonfiction books about miscarriages of justice. The other, Kenly Webster, said that they both wanted to volunteer their services to the State of Justice project. Delighted by the offer, Joe and Bill chatted with them for several minutes and referred them to the project manager for a set of immediate assignments on Capitol Hill.

As they were exiting the Press Club, Kenly said, "You know, for some reason your Pledge proposal reminds me of Patriotic Polly. Did you fellows have anything to do with that?"

Joe and Bill exchanged a quick glance. "I wish," Joe said. "Isn't she great? What a hoot!"

"Don't you mean squawk?" Bill said with a playful jab to Joe's shoulder. "She's a parrot, not an owl."

Kenly and John were still laughing as Joe and Bill climbed into a cab and went off to argue their case for changing the Pledge at the first joint meeting of the Progressive, Black, and Hispanic congressional caucuses.

On Tuesday afternoon, resolved to get the Clean Elections Party underway before Maui Three, Warren and Bernard sat down at a roundtable with a small group of scholars and practitioners knowledgeable about political party formation, historically, organizationally, and legally. Experienced and worldly wise as the two core group members were, they soon got an education about the barriers facing a new political party in a two-party political arena.

A professor of political science began by sketching the fifty different state laws, sometimes with county differences, that governed what a party had to do simply to qualify *as* a party, even before it started climbing the mountain to appear on the ballot. "And in some states," she added, "even if you do get on the ballot, it's likely to be in a spot nearly impossible for voters to find."

"Good grief," Warren said. "What ever happened to letting the little guy, the newcomer on the block, compete with the giants on a level playing field? Sounds like a rigged system, despite all our boasting about the world's greatest democracy—or I guess we should call it the world's greatest duopoly."

"Suppose money was no problem. Wouldn't that make it possible to surmount all these obstacles?" Bernard asked.

"It's not that simple," the professor said. "True, plenty of money gets you the legal counsel and other assistance you need to get the requisite number of verified signatures under different state laws. But a new party with a lot of money will attract the attention of one or both of the major parties, which will see you as a threat to their cushy arrangements in each electoral district. Then the claws will come out of the big cats' paws, and your Clean Elections Party will be up against all the trap doors and litigable ambiguities built into the election laws and regulations by the two parties. And because of tight filing deadlines, time is on the side of the delayers."

"You're also fighting history," said a second political science professor. "The winner-take-all system, controlled either by the two parties (or as is more frequently the case at the state and congressional district levels, by one dominant incumbent party, whether Republican or Democratic) has instilled in voters a 'can't win' dismissal of third parties. Voters want to feel that they're backing a winner. Then there's the hereditary voter syndrome, which comes from a long family tradition of unswerving support for one of the two parties. All in all, you have a very discouraging prospect for newcomers, innovators, reform energies. Even if your new party has a charismatic set of candidates or a great agenda that polls superbly, the voters will desert you in droves when they enter the booth on Election Day. That is the lesson of American congressional history since the days of Teddy Roosevelt's break with Taft in 1912."

"Just hold it there," said a political organizer. "The assumption behind your gloom and doom is electoral victory for the new party. Leaving aside the fixed presidential elections propelled by the Electoral College dinosaur, it's my understanding that while our hosts wouldn't object to winning a race here and there, what they really want is to carry their issue of clean elections. That means, among other things, affecting elections at the margin where there are two closely

contested major-party slates. In such circumstances, small third parties can swing the election in favor of their issue if they convince one
of the major parties that adopting it is the way to win key votes."

"I'm sorry," the professor said, "but I can't agree. Even without
knowing what our hosts' ancillary resources are, such as supportive
networks, mobilized groups, media access, pro bono professional
advice, and so on, I'd say their chances of affecting the margins are
slim because of the overwhelming number of one-party districts in
our country. In the 2002 election, and again in 2004, only five
members of the House of Representatives were defeated, out of four
hundred and thirty-five seats—the fewest in American history. State
races aren't much better. Almost half of incumbent legislators face
no challenger at all from the other major party. They run unopposed, more a coronation than an election. Besides—"

"Listen," another political organizer said, "there are plenty of
things you can do with money. For example, you can target key congressional leaders whose near-automatic reelection has led to
complacency and long absences from their home districts. They are
unprepared for a well-organized opposition candidate. Of course,
you'd have to drop your single-issue party approach if you did that."

"We prefer to remain at arm's length," Warren said crisply.

"Well, in that case, I've got a few things to say," interjected Bill
Hillsman, a fiftyish man whose clothing and facial hair suggested
a maverick mind and a touch of mad genius. "I run a political advertising firm in Minneapolis. All I do is win trophies from my peer
group of much wealthier East and West Coast political consultants
and advertisers, who hate my guts for what I keep saying about
them: that they're dull and unimaginative. Why do I win these trophies? Because my ads are designed to be so eye-opening or
controversial that they produce reams of free news coverage, which
tremendously multiplies the number of eyeballs that see them. It
gets people talking, and word spreads along the grapevine. Result?
My candidates, often unknown and not all that well-funded, either
win or do much better than expected."

"Then you're our man. What do you propose?" asked a half-convinced, half-skeptical Bernard, who had been hearing pompous pitches from political promoters for half a century.

"Here's what you do. Forget the conventional wisdom. Forget history. You have enough money, you run to win in every conceivable race you can enter, from dog catcher to city council to board of education to state legislator to attorney general to governor to Congress and the White House. Every race with a gripping message helps the other races. Every candidate generates epicenters of friends, relatives, coworkers, and people attracted to the issues. They create the proverbial buzz, the excitement that feeds on itself. There are two and a half million electoral offices at the level of local government alone. Many are filled by smug incumbents who wouldn't feel a new breeze unless it blew them over. Often, there's literally no one running for a position until a desperate call at the last minute produces some guy wanting to puff his résumé.

"It's now almost March, so you're up against some petitioning deadlines, mostly from June to September, and you've got to find candidates who are fluent and believe in a clean elections agenda. Fortunately, you can ignore all the other issues because of your single-issue charter from the get-go. I don't know what kind of mailing lists you have, or how many organizers, or whether you've got a brain trust, whether you can expect any business support, whether you can stage rallies, whether you have dynamic people who'll come out for you, whether you've lined up respected retired politicians to help you, whether, apart from advertising, the mass media will be interested enough in reporting your party's doings, whether you have some attractive, high-profile candidates, or whether you can achieve a civic presence in electoral districts—sorry for the tedious list. I don't know any of this, and I'm not probing to find out. All I'm saying is that the more you have of these assets, the more likely it is that I can help you win and win and win until the politicos cry uncle and dutifully march off to vote for clean elections legislation. End of speech."

In the silence that overtook the room, the professors and the other two practitioners smiled patronizingly at what they took to be the rantings of a sincere simpleton who'd hit a few advertising jack-pots for a few clients. But Bernard and Warren weren't smiling; they were stunned. Either this man had penetrated the core group's secure communications, or he was clairvoyant, or it was a case of great minds thinking alike. Preferring to believe the latter, the hosts politely invited comment from the rest of the attendees and then brought the meeting to a close. The moment they were alone, they rushed for the phones to have Recruitment check out Bill Hillsman down to the color of his jagers.

"This guy seems too good to be true," Warren said. "We have to find out fast if he isn't."

Bernard nodded. "He's a regular Energizer Bunny. It's amazing how his go-for-broke attitude changed the entire atmosphere when our learned friends were telling us about the insurmountable gauntlet of hurdles we'd face. We have to investigate thoroughly what he's done in practice, because if we take him on, there is no margin for error."

"No, none," Warren agreed, making a note to himself to ask around discreetly among his Minnesota business associates.

At ten o'clock on Thursday morning, fifty farmers and activists lined up shoulder to shoulder in front of the White House, holding flow-erpots. Woody Harrelson let out a native Hawaiian yell, and all fifty dropped to their knees and started planting industrial hemp seeds. On the advice of DEA attorneys, the police waited until their act was accomplished, then moved in to arrest them all. As one, the demon-strators sat down Buddha-like, cradling their flowerpots between their knees. With reporters speaking furiously into their mikes and photographers taking digital pictures instantly transmitted around the world, two policemen grabbed Woody's arms to drag him away. Just at that instant, as if they had been rehearsing for months, the demonstrators began chanting in unison: "Energy independence! Great food! Tough clothing! Degradable auto parts! Clean paper! More farmer income, fewer farm subsidies! More trees! More jobs!

Less cancer! Less lung disease! A healthy environment!" Some of the police paused, as if contemplating why they were taking all these good things to jail. Their captain, sensing hesitation, barked them back to reality.

A reporter for a leading Hollywood daily rushed up to Woody. "How does it feel to be dragged off to prison?" she asked. "Not bad," he said. "Do you want to have dinner tonight?" Woody knew that experienced attorneys were on site and at the district jail to bail the demonstrators out. Sure enough, they were all out within two hours, on bail of $50,000 each. En masse, they headed toward a downtown club where they feasted on Hemp Cheese Sticks, Hempnut-Crusted Catfish, Lemon Hemparoons, and other delicacies prepared by a New York restaurant owner who'd authored a hemp cookbook. Woody passed out autographed copies of his own book, *How to Go Further: A Guide to Simple Organic Living.*

That same afternoon, hundreds of flowerpots holding tiny hemp plants were mailed to members of Congress in boxes labeled, "Fragile, this package contains domestically grown industrial hemp." Even as the US Postal Service impounded the boxes, six American Indian reservations held hemp-planting rituals featuring traditional religious dances. This presented a touchy public relations challenge for the DEA, which had been given advance notice of the events. Nonetheless, the blunderhead agency accommodated the wildest dreams of partisans by sending black helicopters, parachuting DEA agents, and DEA trucks to the reservations to break up the ceremonies and confiscate the hemp seedlings.

Pictures of the Pot-In were all over television that night. In one clip from an Oklahoma reservation, a reporter thrust a microphone at an older man who gave his name as Jack Soaring Eagle of the Cherokee Nation as he was led off in handcuffs. Another clip showed a demonstrator holding a Department of Agriculture poster from World War II that urged the growing of hemp for the war effort. The celebrity-obsessed media naturally highlighted Woody Harrelson's role, but the bulk of the coverage was devoted to the DEA's shocking invasion of American Indian lands, which was too much even for the *Wall Street Journal*. The next morning, the paper ran a slamming editorial on the front page under the headline "The Freedom to Plant is Primordial, Pre-Constitutional, and Inviolate."

The uproar over the Pot-In was still in full swing when the first two of Ted's Sun God extravaganzas went live on Friday. He'd chosen Phoenix and Seattle as the sites, Phoenix because it had so many sunny days, and Seattle because it was so cloudy and drizzly much of the time. He thought Seattle would serve as an object lesson that solar thermal and electric power could be stored and transmitted anywhere, just as technology had enabled the transmission of energy from the coal mines and the oil fields. He also wanted to challenge the creative energies of the Sea-Tac region's can-do computer visionaries, and contrast them with the inertia surrounding the fearfully radioactive and seeping Hanford Reservation in the rural eastern part of the state.

The festivals were modeled on the old carnivals. They were planned to stretch over two days and built to be taken on the road. A 150-foot golden statue of the Sun God greeted visitors at the entrance to a huge tent with a main arena and smaller sections for various exhibits and demonstrations. The area behind the statue was covered with prayer rugs so that any worshipers who so wished could express their fealty. On one side of the tent was a platform where "the fossil fuelers and nuke boys," as Ted put it, could debate any of his legion of solar specialists. The rules of debate, the choice of moderators, and the process of polling the audience for its verdict were designed for high entertainment value. Another platform on the opposite side of the tent was reserved to give prominent place to local, state, and federal officials so that everyone could see them and convey solar messages of desired action. Not many showed up in Phoenix and Seattle on this first round, but Ted was confident that once the various Redirections were fully underway, especially the Congress Project, it would be hard to keep the politicians away.

Not surprisingly, Ted's formula for maximum exposure in the

media was maximum exposure of hundreds of beautiful young women. These Sun Goddesses had to have companions, of course, so he paired form with function. With very little arm-twisting, he enlisted male solar engineers, architects, and physicists to be their consorts, and christened the duos "Beauties and the Brains." The idea was for the Brains to pay homage to the Sun Goddesses by offering them solar artifacts with all kinds of household, office, vehicular, agricultural, and factory uses. Then the Goddesses would demonstrate these uses to the accompaniment of sensual background music and sound-light shows depicting fossil fuels and atomic power as forces of darkness and destruction, and solar energy as the force of light and life. One such demonstration featured a tall, lithe Goddess training an oversized magnifying glass on the wooden logo of one of the big energy companies until the concentrated power of the sun burned it to a crisp. "Who says solar is too diffuse to be practical?" she asked the audience sweetly. Other shows and exhibits provided equally graphic refutation of one canard after another that had been circulating about solar energy for years: that it was too irrevocably costly, that solar photovoltaic took way too much land surface, that it would be decades, if ever, before solar could make a significant contribution to rising energy demands, that wind power (another form of solar) had limited potential.

With all their elements of spectacle, the Sun God festivals were tailor-made for television, and the coverage was massive. Flipping from CNN to MSNBC to some of Barry's stations, Ted couldn't resist a grin of satisfaction. So far, things had gone off without a hitch, and the press response was largely positive, though some commentators sniped at Ted for excessive flashiness and unabashed sexism.

"Yeah, right, like the media would have blanketed a conference of very distinguished solar experts," Ted muttered to himself as he packed his bag for Maui.

CHAPTER 6

H igh atop the mountain in Maui, overlooking the serene sun-soaked waters of the Pacific Ocean, the core group gathered once again. They arrived brimming with energies they had never felt before in all their active, productive, profitable lives. Some who got there early relaxed with hors d'oeuvres and wine and waited for their colleagues to join them. When all were assembled in the atrium conference room, surrounded by tall windows giving breathtaking views, Warren convened the meeting.

"Colleagues in justice," he began, "as our first order of business, it is my distinct pleasure to introduce our newest and youngest colleague, the farseeing Bill Joy, formerly of signal repute with Sun Microsystems. He is an independent thinker about the practical and ethical import of present and future technology. You will recall our discussion about the critical need to have someone with his expertise in matters of science and technology, and his knowledge of how corporations are proceeding to put these portentous innovations into play. We welcome you, Bill"—applause broke out around the table—"and we reaffirm the confidentiality of our common venture, about which you have been briefed by each of our core members. We invite you to say whatever is on your mind."

"Thank you all for your extraordinary undertaking. On the one hand, it is an unprecedented feat; on the other, its genius is such that I found myself wondering why something like it hadn't happened a long time ago. It should have been so obvious, inasmuch as it takes only a tiny fraction of a percent of very wealthy and openhanded protagonists to get major change underway. Yet there's a culture lock here. The sense of adventure sits all too lightly on the shoulders of those endowed with society's wealth and power.

"I've studied what you've accomplished since your launch, and I applaud your revolutionary thrusts. Like you, I believe that a revolution is only a revolution when it works, not when it's announced or fired up. At present, as you follow through on your initiatives, I see my role as advising you on the technology you're using or could use, along with the technology that may soon be used against you. At Warren's request, my first step will be to set up a secure website for you, to serve as a kind of cyber bulletin board for posting timely information, and to stream video from the various rallies and so forth. Meanwhile, I've got a lot of listening, asking, digesting, and thinking to do before we see if my participation should be broader. After all, you've got a few years on me. Meanwhile, it's good to be here, and good to be one of you."

More applause followed.

"Thank you, Bill. Next, I've asked the very able director of our Secretariat to report on the progress of our various projects and the backup capabilities we've put in place to make them run smartly and smoothly."

At that moment, as if summoned telepathically, the bow-tied Patrick Drummond came in, was introduced to Bill Joy, and proceeded with a comprehensive update on the core group's work thus far. His presentation was videotaped so that parts could be played back if necessary during subsequent meetings.

"When do we eat, Warren?" Paul asked when Patrick had concluded.

"Right now. In the dining room is a light dinner buffet that should be just right given your long travel here and the lateness of the hour. Afterward, we'll have a one-hour silence period around this table, in keeping with our valued custom, and then off to slumber. Tomorrow is what we've all been waiting for—an intensive first take on the nature of the counterattack, its probable sequence and timing. We're all bursting with thoughts and intuitions that must be analyzed and synthesized so that we can anticipate and stop the looming reaction to two amazing months of Redirectional breakouts. We have to be ready, we have to have the institutions on the ground and the pillar assets in place so they can't be undermined, smeared, or coopted."

"Exactly," said Sol, "but tomorrow is another day. Let's eat already."

Which they proceeded to do, with gusto, all the while talking, shrugging, nodding, affirming, challenging, doubting, querying, and galvanizing one another at such a pace that the reflective hour of silence was a godsend.

When everyone else had retired, Bill Joy took a moonlit walk around the lush grounds. He knew that Warren had reserved the entire hotel and that no other guests were on the premises. The management and staff presumably had no idea what was going on, and the waiters and maids loved the generous gratuities. But he also knew that the hotel was defenseless against a deliberate attempt at surveillance. And why not? A small, expensive hotel catering to wealthy honeymooners and retirees should have such worries? After a thorough inspection, his misgivings were somewhat allayed, since he found nothing in the way of gadgets or bugs. Still, he wondered how long this critical privacy could last. During dinner he'd heard Paul Newman and Bill Cosby talking about the wardrobe precautions they'd taken to avoid being sighted at the airport, as a gossip column had reported after Maui Two. Bill Joy resolved to prepare for the worst during future Mauis.

Bright, early, and effusive at breakfast, the core group reconvened in the conference room in good spirits and with heightened perceptions. Sol was reminded of the old saying back in New York City during the labor protests of the thirties: "You can't be tired out if you're fired up."

As always, Warren opened the meeting. "I thought the best procedure this morning would be to go around the table as we did at Maui One and hear what each of us has to say on the question

'Where and when will the counterattack come, and in what form?'
Then we'll discuss what maneuvers of ours will be most effective.
Who'd like to start us off?"

"Well, I'll go first," Barry said, "because I'm not retired and may
have a more current sense of the latest modes and methods likely
to be used against us. There will of course be stages in our opponents' response: first, ignorance of what we're doing, other than
what they've seen of us through our ads and statements in the mass
media and our other public actions; next, initial dismissal and
denial; then the third stage, rebuttal and denunciation; and finally
the stage of realization, fear, rage, and a search-and-destroy counteroffensive. Remember, they start from the position of having a
power lock on all potential challenge points in the political, economic, legal, and media arenas. They're complacent in their sense
of control, but the control is real—just look at what they're doing to
organized labor, the publicly owned commonwealth, and the government itself.

"Their complacency will work to our advantage because it gives
us more time. Still, they do have an early alert system, in the form
of their funded think tanks, whose mission and budgets are based
on spreading alarm through exaggeration and sometimes outright
fabrication. They are very good at this. Look at their drumbeating
before the invasion of Iraq, or their devilish inflation of the regulatory agencies as ogres, when in fact those agencies, if they're not
asleep, perform as consulting firms to the very industries they're
supposed to regulate. To head off these 'pimp tanks,' as one friend
of mine describes them, means feinting and decoying them,
because they're always looking for fancied threats to the 'free enterprise system' and to their corporate donors. I'm getting ahead of
myself, but I do urge you all to think about feints and decoys as part
of our response.

"Now, whom are we talking about in any counterattack? Obviously—"

"Maybe Wal-Mart?" Sol interjected. "Just a wild guess."

Barry smiled. "Right, Wal-Mart, and the other companies and

specific industries we've targeted, along with their law firms and public relations firms, their captive politicians, their own credibility organizations, such as some evangelical churches, veterans' groups and service clubs, their incorporated commercial media, their in-house media, and many of their branch dealers and agents and franchisees in every community. Also fortifying them are the ingrained historic and contemporary myths about free-market fundamentalism that George has written about, and that are difficult to counter precisely because they aren't based in reality. The commercialization of patriotism and charity during disasters further depletes the critical faculties of the human mind. In our monitoring capacity, we would do well to lay all these forces out on clear spreadsheets so we can visualize them."

"There's one sure mode of attack that we don't have to visualize figuratively," said Bill Cosby. "They'll go after each of us. They'll try to compromise our integrity and deflect attention to us rather than what we're doing. The media is attracted to the personalization of conflicts like chickens to grain. The Mexicans have the word for it—*personalismo*. The corporations will employ private detective firms to dig up dirt. They'll try to show that the things we're accusing the business powers of doing are things we did years ago ourselves. They'll unearth people from the past who will try to slander and libel us. They'll have a hard time succeeding with most of us, but you never really know, do you?"

"No, you don't," George said thoughtfully. "I've lived through this kind of assault for years now. My business enemies have gone to the far reaches of the Earth to look for any technical regulations they can accuse me of violating, any palms they can grease to enmesh me in a frame-up. All of us have been so active for so many years, the bases we've touched and the balls we've hit are so numerous, that any probe will uncover plenty of opportunities to twist, distort, and allege. Our very business successes have meant that there were lots of losers, and some of them carry grudges or out-of-context memories of what we may have said. Unscrupulous investigators can easily generate fake composite photographs and remarks and digitalize them all over the world before we find out what they've done. Bill Joy, take this under advisement and help us ponder the response."

The newest member of the core group nodded. "I'll do that."

Next around the table was Sol. "One of the standard corporatist lines of attack over the years is what can be called the 'ism' attack—trotting out foreign, subversive ideologies that they have predisposed the public to recoil against. They did this for years with socialists, anarchists, and communists, and the latest buzzword is 'terrorists.' There are no rebels, resisters, freedom fighters, or agrarian reformers anymore—they're all terrorists now. Well, our enemies certainly can't use those labels against us, but trust the hidebound *Wall Street Journal* editorialists to come up with some new ism, and then the commercial media will run with it. I haven't the slightest idea what it will be, but they'll desperately need a label, a stereotype, and we have to be ready to nip it in the bud, using satire and ridicule and whatever else it takes."

"When I consider this whole question of the counterattack," Jeno said, "I ask myself, How are they thinking? They'll say they need better intelligence, human intelligence. To me that means they'll make a major effort to infiltrate everything we build, right down to our inner groups, whether through disguised informants or spies, or by bribing waiters, bellboys, even taxi drivers. And you better believe they'll be using the latest widgets that Bill Joy can enlighten us about. Infiltration done cleverly can sow discord, acrimony, distrust, and disintegration. In our response, we have to avoid the extremes—paranoia at one end, repression at the other."

Joe spoke up. "Well, you shouldn't be surprised to hear me raise the possibility of frivolous or trumped-up litigation designed to break our concentration, flood us with discovery motions, subpoena our files, and in general tie us up. Having said that, I don't know what their causes of action could be, short of contrived defamation suits or claims that we're messing with their economic relationships. But they'll figure something out, with their white-shoe law firms and endless deductible budgets. And if they don't, they'll file anyhow, trying to survive motions to dismiss in order to bog us down in depositions. As allowed by statutes of limitation, they'll even dig up accusations from past business or employee relationships and file groundless lawsuits to consume our time. Our response to these forays will have to be shots across the bow to convince them that such litigation is a two-edged sword. Still, they may think they can wear us down because of our age and our presumed desire for leisure and time with the grandkids—they'll profile us for certain, Cosby's right on the money about that."

"Yes," Peter agreed, "and it's not just a matter of our reputations. We all have assets, lines of credit, property—they'll go after them. They may use subtle, hidden boycotts against businesses or executives allied with or sympathetic to us. I can see it now. They'll go after the customers and shareholders of my prospering insurance company, stop doing business with us, stereotype us and move to dry us up—a corporate campaign in reverse by the corporatists. They'll depress my stock, our stocks, if they can manage to quarantine them so as to avoid a boomerang bite on their own assets."

"As one who has endured character assassination more than once," Ross put in, "let me tell you that they are going to play dirty—not all of them, but there is always a rogue element doing these things to give cover to the rest who quietly support and sometimes fund the dirty-tricks crowd. They start conventionally enough, sometimes by charging that we are directly profiting from our efforts or have secret profitable designs. Then they may hint darkly at a covert world conspiracy by sticking us with a name like 'the Bilderbergs,' something that will get the all-night-radio UFO types agitated. They may even try to intimidate our children or grandchildren or other family members. Whatever they do, we have to remain cool but calculating. Paranoia can expose us to ridicule from the pundits and cartoonists. Believe me, I know."

"To shift the focus for a minute," said Bill Gates, "I know the defense fellows at Boeing, and one obvious way to put us on the defensive is to charge that we're sponsoring policies and changes that will undermine our national security. Our opponents will try to paint a picture in which the enemies of the American people abroad are in some way aided and abetted by our activities. They'll borrow Lenin's term 'useful idiots' to describe how we're helping the enemy's psychological war against America, even if unintentionally. Sounds farfetched, but we're laying everything on the table before we discuss our counter-strategy."

"It doesn't sound so farfetched to me," Bernard said. "Remember the red scare and Attorney General Palmer's witch-hunts right after World War I, or the McCarthyite smear of some of the best Foreign Service officers ever as 'comsymps' or 'fellow travelers' who 'lost China'? Let's not think it can't happen again. Forewarned is forearmed."

"And that's not the only way of smearing us, B," Yoko said. "I suspect some of our smarter opponents will try to turn some portions of 'the people' against us. They'll look over our agenda and ask who the losers will be among ordinary folks, and then they'll target those folks vigorously to make us out as enemies of the people. I've seen this kind of thing in the music and entertainment world—turning the fans into haters. The Wal-Mart unionizing project presents just such an opportunity to portray us as opposing cheap prices for poor shoppers. It's a tactic that predicts phony consequences of our actions and then hurls them against us. The upper classes have used this tactic throughout history, as in the hiring of mercenaries from the lower classes to oppress the very people they came from. Today they can hire people to go to rallies or marches and disrupt them. We know they have big-time money, and given what's at stake, they'll spend it freely. There are plenty of desperate 'scabs' out there," Yoko finished, turning to Max, who was sitting on her right.

"My first thought was that maybe the big boys will try to lure us into compromising situations while hidden cameras record the lascivious scenes. Then I remembered our ages. Who would believe them? We are beyond the reach of Viagra's wildest Loreleis. Dirty old men we can no longer be."

"Speak for yourself, Max," Ted shot back.

Max ignored him and continued. "I think we're going to get a lot of wildcatting. We're pinching lots of toes, and they're everywhere, right down to Main Street. It's hard even to list the categories of where opposition will erupt. But while I'm at it, let me toss another possibility into the cauldron. I think the multinationals will try to enlist the public and the politicians against us by using the 'adverse business climate' ruse and threatening to pull out of the country, or giving that as an excuse for the factories and businesses they're already sending to China and elsewhere. 'Bad business climate' scorecards terrify politicians. Given the abandonment of our country that goes on every day, it's entirely plausible that the corporations will use the business climate and us as a scapegoat. It will take the heat off the president, Congress, and the states for doing nothing to stop the flight from America, because it's all the fault of 'those guys.'"

Leonard was drumming his fingers on the table. "On the other hand, they could just do nothing. Going from analysis to paralysis to psychoanalysis, they could find it profitable to live with us and what we're doing. Never underestimate their adaptability as long as they can still ring their registers and send out their bills. Sure, some will groan like gored oxen, and some will fail, but as long as others see the advantages and profit opportunities in a 'no more business as usual' climate, they'll step over the whiners in a New York minute. However, if I may propose the greatest of all understatements today, it'll be very hard to predict.'"

Still smarting from Max's remark, Ted went macho. "I've heard it all except one option. What about direct physical action, like taking some of us hostage to stop the rest of us or to smoke us out? Be like bounty hunting. Ransom. The press would love it. TV would be ecstatic—CNN's ratings would skyrocket. But hey, think of what they could do by pulling ads from CNN, which will always be associated with yours truly." He paused, frowning. "Well, anyway, there's my two cents. That leaves you, Warren, our sagacious owl. What do you foresee?"

"Well, you've all covered a lot of ground, so the pickings are pretty slim from my perch. If there's anything we neglected on this first go-round, maybe it's refining Barry's stages of reaction by breaking down categories of reactors who will respond differently from one another in time, intensity, and strategy. I think we should be more attuned to corporate surrogates. Giant businesses do not like to strike directly. That's why even in normal circumstances they have spokespeople, attorneys, academies, spun-off subsidiaries, media intermediaries, and publicly elected allies in Congress who carry water for them, as in some of the savings and loan collapses. Given the perturbations hammering them, they'll be looking to create new surrogates with minimal vulnerabilities and very little to lose, much as we ourselves have used shell corporations in some of our past deals. I also think Yoko's point about our opponents turning some of 'the people' against us is right on. Who knows? The more we succeed in taking away their power, the more desperate they may become, unless the phenomenon Leonard alluded to—stepping over each other to get to the profits—kicks in to give us the gift of divide and conquer. Sometimes we can think too hard here, though I know being prepared for all potential counterattacks is crucial to our success and our personal equanimity. But there are times when I feel, a little recklessly, like saying, 'I don't give a hoot! Let the rats scamper as they may!'

"In any case," Warren continued over the cheers of his colleagues, "it's time for lunch—all native Hawaiian cuisine, so be a little adventuresome."

"I'll have the brisket," Sol said.

In the lunchroom, which was designed to facilitate informality, the core group members strolled to the buffet, sat chatting at small circular tables in twos and threes, relaxed in reclining chairs for a bit of solitude, sought each other out for clarification of a point or to discuss a Redirections problem, or simply, perish the thought, engaged in a little small talk. Bill Joy was taking it all in, moving from one cluster to another, getting a sense of the mood, the determination, the level of human energy or anxiety. As had been explained to him when he signed on, there was no Redirection project dealing with the onrush of science and technology because none of the core group knew enough even to delegate reliably and maintain some semblance of control over such a bucking bronco. But these were no fainthearted oldsters, as he'd seen for himself all morning. With him on board, maybe they'd be ready to hear a presentation during Maui Four without being too shaken up by the doomsday scenario that had to be confronted if it was to be avoided.

His thoughts were interrupted by the arrival of a massive dessert that seemed to contain every fruit that ever grew on the islands and every flavor and shade of sherbet ever concocted. Strong Kona coffee was served as a tasty brake on devouring the delicious dessert too fast.

Back in the conference room, Warren directed his colleagues' attention to the agenda, on which he'd listed Quality Managers and Organizers as the next topic for discussion. He wanted to give them time to digest the morning's speculations on the coming counter-attack before they discussed their response, and besides, the nuts and bolts were paramount. As champion managers themselves, they all knew that the proper choice and oversight of management and organizers was their number one challenge. No matter how well conceived and specific their action plans, they would go no further than management's execution.

Warren circulated a report from Seymour Depth, head of Recruitment, showing that progress was better than expected at this point on the calendar. There truly was plenty of talent out there eager to get on board. Recruitment had been going almost around the clock, receiving résumés, sifting, checking, and interviewing applicants, and recently candidates for the Clean Elections Party. There were now nearly nine hundred lecturers, and some of them were proving to be natural leaders in other capacities. Most of those hired, experienced as they were in such areas as rallies, lobbying, and institution building, had to be further trained for duties and expectations new to them. Moreover, none of the managers, organizers, lobbyists, or candidates could be given the "big picture," for fear of prematurely disclosing the entire network, but they were dealt a big enough piece of their own projects to keep them satisfied.

The progress report summarized numbers already recruited and numbers left to recruit, and appended a preliminary evaluation of the key dozen top managers so far. Jeno raved about the executive director of the People's Chamber of Commerce, a thirty-two-year-old phenom named Luke Skyhi, who had a recall capacity of business history that left Jeno breathless. Luke confessed to having read scores of books on the subject in his early teens. He went on to finish business school and law school in four years, and then he systematically took seven year-long positions in different lines of industry and commerce. When Jeno interviewed him, it was love at first sight, and so far, in his few days on the job, he was building a crackerjack staff and firing off press releases that made the National Association of Manufacturers, the US Chamber of Commerce, and the National Federation of Independent Businesses apoplectic.

George sounded a cautionary note when he came to the line in the report noting that all managers currently on the job were amazed that they did not have to raise money, beg for money, apply for money, or write proposals for money—a completely unique experience for them. "The same applies in my line of work, and it can cause problems. Money that's easy to come by may not be spent frugally or wisely or even ethically. It does liberate the managers to focus exclusively on their missions, but it removes a discipline that is not to be dismissed as useless. The rub is to find a substitute discipline, short of close auditing from the outside, though that's something we probably ought to institute too. But the real substitute discipline has to come from the quality of the budget the managers are operating under and from their own character. After all, large sums are involved here, and speed is of the essence—a potentially wasteful combination."

"Point taken, George," Warren said. "And now that we've refreshed ourselves on this central topic, let's turn to the status of our epicenters. Are they growing, consolidating, meshing, moving, replicating?"

What a response! The red thread running through the reports of every one of the core group members was their amazement at how many people they felt they could call upon without hesitation—the old Rolodex may have been languishing for a while, but once dusted off, it came alive—coupled with their astonishment at the positive reaction. They were uniformly invigorated. Some remarked on how many outstanding IOUs they had and how often these were graciously acknowledged. They had all had sour or sad conversations with people who were bitter, or who were merely sticks-in-the-mud, or who harbored secret sorrows, or who were deeply depressed because of illness or the loss of a spouse, or who had simply given up on the troubled world they were about to leave, but even this negative feedback energized them, such were their personalities, thank you, Warren.

Always looking ahead to the next step, Warren acknowledged the generally good epicenter reports and asked how everyone was managing what appeared to be an overflow of potential joiners. His colleagues replied that mostly they were not. There was no time. These were people who would be insulted if they were contacted by an underling, yet personal treatment in every case wasn't possible.

Bill Cosby proposed a way out, based on comparable situations where prominent entertainers were trying to raise major money for charitable causes. "You select five or six of your best epicentrists with some prominence in their own fields, and you deputize them to call on your behalf, excusing you for being a mere mortal confined by a twenty-four-hour day. A little humor will melt any initial ice. You bond even more with your dazzling half-dozen comrades, and the job gets done more quickly." The idea was well received.

"Is there such a thing as a too big, too busy epicenter?" Paul asked. "Right now, mine is neither, and it's flowing nicely into the desired channels, but I've imposed certain hurdles on my epicenter entrants, and I wonder if I should be doing that."

"That depends entirely on your temperament and theirs," Max said, "and on the assignments you set them, from easy entry to more ambitious kinds of work. Remember, there are never enough worker bees, and without those noble souls the achievements on the ground do not occur, no matter what excellence reigns at the top. And by worker bees I mean detail people striving to implement, implement, implement—probably the toughest of jobs, the dearest of skills."

Bernard sat up in his chair. "Exactly, exactly! That's my biggest problem in getting these Egalitarian Clubs underway. Everybody thinks it's a great idea, but far fewer are willing to do the gritty work to transform it into reality in their own communities, for their own children."

The pads in front of the core members were filling up as they jotted down comments and reminders, with not a single doodle to be seen. No frivolity for this bunch, and no gizmos. After all, most of them had grown up using Underwood typewriters and pre-ballpoint pens. They also agreed that manual note-taking was more secure, especially given shaky handwriting and cryptic abbreviations.

"Speaking of gritty work," Warren said, "the time has come to discuss the nature of our strategy to head off, delay, dissipate, diminish, or defeat our adversaries. Over lunch I asked George to provide us with a synthesis of their probable lines of action and a profile of our reaction. The floor is yours, George."

"Well, it's all a little like a chess game. What will my opponent do if I make this move? It's also similar to speculation in the financial markets. Let me begin by summarizing your premonitions: libel and slander, old grudges reasserting themselves, attempts to tar us with isms and ideologies, infiltration, baseless personal litigation, accusations of profiteering, attacks on our assets and companies, efforts to turn some of 'the people' against us, claims that we are undermining national security and worsening the business climate, hostage-taking or kidnapping, and finally the possibility that they'll adjust to our demands, at least some of them, and in effect do nothing.

"Our planning of the Redirections and their strategies thus far has been very well suited to defense. As decided at our first gathering, we have eschewed all matters relating to foreign policy, military policy, and corporate globalization movements, except in the case of

Wal-Mart's China price. By focusing strictly on domestic conditions and changes, we disarm our adversaries and strip them of many of their attack options, like raising issues of loyalty, or that old grab bag of twisting patriotism in such a way as to secure the allegiance of veterans' and business organizations. We force them to contend on domestic injustice, domestic needs and fairness—an arena where their propaganda is not so effective because it clashes with people's daily experience. This also makes it difficult for them to employ their friends in the government's security services to infiltrate our operations. Are they going to use the CIA and the FBI to infiltrate groups devoted to clean elections, good health insurance, a living wage, affordable housing, consumer protection, and energy conversion to make our country more self-reliant? Are these isms and foreign ideologies? By sticking to domestic issues, we can turn the appeal to patriotism and national sovereignty to our own objectives."

"If I can interrupt for a moment," Warren said, "that reminds me of my earlier suggestion that we bring a reflective retired general like Anthony Zinni into our core group. I think we can now agree that this is inadvisable, inasmuch as it would becloud the clarity of our domestic focus when we emerge more publicly as an entity. However, I'm pleased to report that General Zinni and others in his circle are willing to extend their advice informally."

There were murmurs of approval as George resumed. "Another of our defensive assets is our dedication to building institutions and recruiting the best leaders. Rationally charismatic people like Luke Skyhi will be magnets for the mass media and take the spotlight away from us when our opponents eventually discover that there *is* an 'us.' As these wonderful people assume a high profile, they too will be subjected to libel and slander by the rabid, baying packs on talk radio and cable shows, but as they say, that goes with the territory. And because our recruits have impeccable credentials in their various arenas of social justice, attacks on them may even backfire on the right-wing market fundamentalists. Creating a more viable customer base as poverty recedes, rebuilding public works, applying technology tailored to the people's circumstances, providing voice and access to justice for millions of Americans—none of this represents much of a cause of action even for frivolous litigation. Nonetheless, we should signal in the proper legal publications that any such suits will be met both with countersuits for abuse of process, as well as investigations of the corporate law firms involved and formal complaints to the grievance committees of bar associations or licensing boards. That will really cool them off, unless these business bozos want to proceed in court pro se.

"As for turning 'the people' against us, our opponents may succeed to some degree through cleverness, money, and selective demographics, but remember once again how well we're preparing the groundwork to thwart such maneuvers. Our well-publicized rallies and unionization drives, the CUBs, the People's Court Society, the collaborative credibility groups we're building, the audiences reached by the lecturers, Barry's media focus on justice, the First-Stage Improvements Project centering on widely perceived economic inequalities, the Beatty campaign in California, the solar festivals, the vibrant small business constituency of the PCC—all these and their daily expansion will outrun anything but the most blatant fomenting on our opponents' part. Alert we must remain, however; these opponents may be smug, but they still know how to hire smart operators looking for fat retainers.

"The 'business climate' rant will be a problem, but a little way down the pike. We can prepare for it with a massive media campaign showing that stronger democracies and greater justice have always led to growing economies and larger markets. Just look at two countries comparable in natural resources and size, Brazil and the United States. With one fifth of the population of Brazil, California alone has a substantially larger GDP than that South American giant. The American people need a repeated education that it is democracy, justice, and the rule of law that make capitalism produce a better material life for more people, not capitalism in itself. There was plenty of unfettered capitalism in Brazil, but it was concentrated and cruel and unproductive because there was very little democracy, justice, or rule of law in the course of centuries of domination by plantation barons, monarchies, juntas, and oligarchs.

"We have not given much thought to a move against our investments, assets, and associated firms, which is a real peril, in my judgment. I suggest that a cluster of us versed in analogous techniques during our most aggressive years prepare an investment-asset-affinity corporate protection plan, one that will also address the profiteering charge, and see about the possibility of acquiring a unique insurance coverage. Is there any objection if Warren, Peter, Bill Gates, and Max join with me to work on a plan that we'll share with you during Maui Four?"

"Excellent idea," said Sol. "You can call it the It Takes One to Know One Plan." Those whom George had not named smiled, relieved not to be taking on such a weighty responsibility, while the chosen squared their shoulders with a sober sense of duty.

George acknowledged them with a nod and continued. "From a defensive standpoint, that leaves hostage-taking or some direct physical assault. I consider this highly unlikely, but it cannot be discounted. All of us should start with the studied avoidance of excessive rhetoric, slashing personal attacks, or any verbal or physical expression of vindictiveness that can be conveyed over the media. Remember Max's brilliant experiment showing the power of words over deeds in getting people riled up? Our public utterances, and those of everyone associated with us, must be positive in tone, offering optimism, motivation, and concrete solutions to real problems.

"Bill Joy has some security concerns about our meetings here in Maui and is already working on safeguards. Beyond that, take the normal precautions that I'm sure you've been taking since you became public figures. Wealthy people are always alert to the kidnaping threat.

"Above all, take it easy in the saddle—this is America, after all, and we are well insulated by the nature of our projects, all of which call for overdue reforms, and by their rapid devolution and replicative design. The more the work, the success, and the glory devolve downward, the more the spotlight stays on the ground, where people can see the Redirections in action instead of wallowing in *personalismo* at the so-called top. The emerging open society that undergirds our efforts will in itself be a strong defense.

"Now, to turn to offense, recall first what Barry said about feints and decoys. Joe and Bill Gates are showing us the way with their Pledge the Truth campaign, which is not only substantively significant but also a decoy absorbing the right-wing fundamentalists and the Bush Bimbaugh types on talk radio. I'm sure we can think of many other ways to feint out the more rabid of our opponents and in the process advance our agenda. For example, let's come up with a new role for Patriotic Polly. Or imagine if a large landowner in Wyoming could be persuaded to rent huge advertising billboards blocking the view of the Grand Tetons along scenic highways heavily traveled by tourists. I'm talking about two miles of closely situated billboards pushing whiskey, cigarettes, junk food, porn videos, and the like. The obvious litigation would pit private property rights against the use of public property—that is, the public highways—and throw open the question of whether such use has any legal status. Imagine the publicity. Imagine the roars of the 'wise use' fundamentalists. No end to feints and decoys like this.

"As for the corporate think tanks, we have to make them defend the 'business judgment rule,' that SEC-recognized catchall allowing top management to shut the shareholders out by claiming that virtually any decision executives care to make is necessary in their business judgment. Mergers, acquisitions, voluntary decisions to go bankrupt and vaporize shareholder value—all have been justified on grounds of business judgment, the perennial fig leaf of corporate governance hypocrisy. Get lost, shareholders, you only own the company. It's a stark matter of executive hegemony versus true capitalist ownership. Put the think tanks in that cul-de-sac and they'll work on a hundred policy papers to fight this mortal peril to the closed enterprise system. Jeno's valedictory speeches, the PCC, and the attack sub-economy are inherently offensive instruments that will keep our adversaries scrambling for a response. Remember too that there are many executives who could care less about the business judgment rule and other decoys as long as they maintain their dominance. That's where the united front of business may start to crack, with some companies seeing economic opportunity in our reforms, as will surely be the case at last with solar energy and energy conservation.

"As a final generalization, the more dynamism we put behind showing the contradictions of our political economy and juxtaposing its self-professed ideals with American realities, the better our offense. Hypocrisy is always the Achilles' heels of the charlatans. Holding big business to its highest acknowledged standards is the best offense and the best defense."

"Well reasoned for a speculator, George," Warren laughed. "With that analytic mind of yours, have you ever thought of going into value investing? Never mind, just an inside joke between us. Let me throw open the discussion to anyone who wishes to add to, modify, or multiply what George has laid on the table."

Yoko put down her pen. "I'd like to hear more about Leonard's observation that the business establishment may adjust to the coming changes, as it did a century ago when it was obliged to start complying with safety regulations, labor laws, higher taxation, the ban on child labor, and the like. After all, as I keep saying, from the global perspective we're all in the same boat. The real victory is to get the opposition to see the writing on the wall and make some very major accommodations. For instance, environmental crises are going to do a lot of damage to businesses, not just to ordinary people. The viral and bacterial dangers we see bubbling up in Africa and East Asia are going to disrupt their operations, their sales, their workforce, and even their own operations at the top. These bugs don't recognize Fortune 500 rankings."

"Yoko, you make our ultimate quest clear," Bernard said, "but unless the business bosses see irresistible force and virtual encir-clement, they won't think of complying or adjusting. They have to see on their own that the ball game as they have played it is over. So what you're really asking, as our Redirectional transformation proceeds, is how do we help their better selves or help a different leadership emerge, how do we let them save face, how do we make them live up to their professed standards and jettison their pernicious practices?

"I expect as the months go by that there will be more and more voluntary resignations of CEOs who would rather retire gracefully on their unconscionable pensions than face what's coming at them from all points of the compass, and from their own investor-owners. As for the criminal or grievously greedy among the corporatists, they will fight to the finish. That's where the rule of law and strong law enforcement come in, as well as the purging influence of more corporate democracy. Let's not overgeneralize our opponents. They are a mosaic up and down and sideways, with little in common except their worship of the bottom line."

Ted cleared his throat. "You know, listening to you and Yoko makes me think that we'll have to go global after all before we end our Redirections quest. I'm not talking about the danger of the multinationals abandoning our country and outsourcing themselves, not just their jobs. That's a debatable proposition, if only because of the size and profitability of our markets and the ease with which domestic businesses will move in. I'm talking about Yoko's idea that we're all in the same boat. That seems to imply a planetary imperative from which there's no real escape, doesn't it?"

"On a timeline of decades or centuries, you're certainly right," Bill Joy said, "but for now a year is probably horizon enough for us mortals."

"Well, just a thought," said Ted. "No point in getting ahead of ourselves."

"Especially at our age," said Bill Gates wryly. "But to return to our counteroffensive, from my perspective as a corporate lawyer, I'd say that our legions of billionaires carry a quiet but heavy stick. One determined, driven heavyweight can exert leverage far out of proportion to the influence of the passive wealth on the other side. We have the more motivated among the wealthy, not they, and the right phone call or face-to-face meeting can pull a lot of weight with the top fellows. Also, don't discount the big mutual funds and pension trusts, which on certain subjects can become key allies. That's why it's important to get advance commitments from all our potential supporters on the Redirections we know will be most controversial."

"Here's another note of encouragement," Peter said. "Suppose they huff and puff and roar and rage. So what? We can still continue on our way. It's only when they actually obstruct us that we have to fight back. Let's not assume that what they do will automatically block our path. In my experience, ignoring the opposition knowledgeably is as important as fighting it knowledgeably."

"With that valuable observation, is their anything further on countering the counterattack?" Warren asked. "If not, I suggest we move on to our expected accomplishments for the coming month and deal with any glitches. Is anybody in need of help?"

"Yes!" cried Newman and Cosby simultaneously.

"This idea of massive amounts of dead money and what to do about it has hit a stone wall," Bill said. "We got a thirty-page report from our economics professor—a Nobel laureate, by the way—who estimated that there's a staggering eighteen trillion dollars' worth of dead money in the US alone. More important, he formulated a brilliant definition of what dead money is, identified different kinds of dead money, showed why it remains comatose, who benefits from this status, and who rewards it, and outlined the general conditions necessary to turn dead money into various kinds of live money. In a postscript to his report, his Eminence thanked us for introducing him to the distinction between dead and live money, but while buttressing our sense of what an important distinction it is, he couldn't propose a systematic strategy to move forward."

"I've been giving your excellent distinction some thought, since we were all pretty much sitting on dead money until a couple of months ago," Phil said. "Let's break this line of thinking down a bit. First, the reason most wealth is dead money is that people believe that's what gets them the maximum monetary return. Dead money isn't sentimental; it's in the hands of hardheaded investment types with dollar signs on their brains. That mindset limits the options to socially responsible mutual funds that offer equally good or better returns. There are funds, for example, that invest in affordable housing to take advantage of tax breaks. In Chicago, when my TV program originated there, I knew wealthy people who put some of their savings into South Shore Bank, which uses the money to back very successful mortgages in lower-income neighborhoods, at competitive interest rates. There are all kinds of good causes soliciting large investors to put modest sums into their activities through annuities and trusts. Who among us has not been asked to do this by our alma maters? Notre Dame never stops with me.

"But I don't think this is quite what Bill and Paul have in mind. I understand their live money to mean investments that break open the capital faucet for a great invention or innovation—say, a dimmer switch that saves electricity, or a highly accurate way for a general practitioner to feed a patient's symptoms into a program on the Internet and get a diagnosis from a nephrologist or cardiologist or whatever the relevant specialty. That's a valuable kind of venture capital, and we should be more cognizant of such opportunities, but Paul and Bill seem to be going for more—shuck the yardstick of direct monetary return and invest in life, invest in justice, invest in peace, invest in preserving oceans and forests, invest in the future, and by all means invest smartly and concretely and daringly. Isn't that just what we're doing now? The question is how to turn the bond market and the moribund mutual funds more in this direction, how to redirect the pension money so often invested with corporations that work against labor, outsource jobs, bash unions, and fuel the arms buildup by investing in the military-industrial complex.

"As Paul and Bill discovered, it's hard to find anyone who has any answers beyond their dreams and the outlets I've briefly summarized. I do have one answer. Next year, let's single out some of our notable Redirectional successes and form a vigorous little group to replicate these kinds of investments in an institutionalized manner that will start a tradition, much as Andrew Carnegie started the modern philanthropic tradition, most prominently with his libraries. Historically, many philanthropists turned their dead money into live money by establishing local hospitals, schools, museums, libraries, parks, arboretums, and other lasting institutions. We can do something similar, but something that goes way beyond philanthropy, by taking a proven reform in one state and diffusing it to all the states that have the same problem. For instance, there's a case out of the California courts to increase custody payments from deadbeat dads that could produce many billions of dollars for spouses and children nationwide. Or what about all the uncollected deposits and insurance monies that escheat to the states, or the money that's awarded by the courts in cases involving a particular abuse but not distributed for lack of recipients or claimants? Under the cy-près doctrine, that money could be placed in advocacy trust funds to tackle similar abuses in perpetuity—"

"The cypress doctrine?" Sol interrupted. "Trust funds for trees? What's next?"

"I know, I know, I'd never heard of it either, but when I recently called some of my favorite public law charities, they told me all about cy-près and other ways of putting unclaimed funds into permanent institutions that go after the very injustices that led to the monies being recovered in the first place. Looking back at tapes of my show, I see how many of these injustices were brought to my televised attention in the most poignant of ways, and how few remedies or means of deterrence there were. With the dead money/live money distinction as a catapult, there's great work to be done here."

"Well, you've given us plenty to ponder, Phil," said Bill Cosby.

"That's for sure," Paul agreed. "To get from charity to justice, we've got to keep thinking about ways to tap into the greatest pool of capital the world has ever seen. If even a tiny fraction of one percent of it was diverted into live money, the beneficial consequences could be enormous. Thoreau once said that the mass of men lead lives of quiet desperation. So do the mass of investors, in their own uninspired way."

"Nicely put," Warren said. "Okay, gentlemen, I'll have the Secretariat take up these ideas of yours for processing in the usual expeditious manner."

"By the way," Barry said, "Warren Beatty called up the other day asking for suggestions about a theme for his campaign, something along the lines of the New Deal or the Great Society of past campaigns. That got me thinking about what we should call ourselves once we go public. 'Core Group' just doesn't cut it. Ted and I were talking about this at lunch."

"We need an accurate but bland name," Max said, "something that won't lend itself to conspiratorial innuendo—shades of the Trilateral Commission."

"You mean something like the Fabian Society?"

"Yes, something like that, but clearly very distant from that group's approach."

Bernard sat up in his chair. "Here's what I propose: the Patriotic Meliorist Society."

"The what?" Joe said.

"Huh?" echoed Ted.

"Exactly the desired response," Bernard said. "Meliorists are people who believe in and work toward bettering society. Let our enemies try to distort or caricature that one. Historically, it's a term that was common in old England and in the works of American pragmatists like William James and John Dewey. For some reason, it's slipped out of usage, but you'll find it in every dictionary."

Yoko stifled a giggle. "Really, B, the Patriotic Meliorist Society? The PMS? I don't think so."

There was a moment of embarrassed silence before Bernard laughed. "All right, then, just the Patriotic Meliorists."

"You know," Warren said, "I like it."

"Well, why don't you all mull it over for a while," Bernard suggested. "It does have the virtue of making people ask what it means, and the definition is very straightforward. I think in time it will catch the ear."

"We'll do that, B," Warren said. "Before we go on to our slated goals for the next month, it is my frugal pleasure to report that we have not yet spent a billion dollars. You're all holding to your specific budgets. The pace of spending will increase when we unfurl the Blockbuster Challenge, among other larger expenses. A total of fifteen billion has been received or reliably pledged, with about ten billion in hand. The money has been invested in safe overnight government bonds and triple-A corporate bonds for rapid liquidity. And now, on to March. George?"

"We've got a first wave of fifty million letters in the mail to form ten different CUBs. Projected dues-paying membership for each of them should average a million and a half by the time we've finished soliciting. The mailings are backed by a brace of news features and websites, print, TV, and radio advertisements, plus staggered exposés of the power abuses, industry by industry, that the CUBs are designed to monitor and countervail. Recruitment is busy finding top-flight directors and staff for each CUB, and I've also been fortunate in receiving the expert advice of John Richard and Robert Fellmeth. Each of you should be as blessed in your initiatives. Under their direction, our Service CUB has been established to help the advocacy CUBs with media, fundraising, promotion and sale of reports on consumer abuses, and any miscellaneous brush fires that may break out. The pace is quickening, and by mid-month the exposés will doubtless come under attack from the *Wall Street Journal* types whose revenues come heavily from just those companies the CUBs are intended to watchdog. The various CUB actions are being designed to mesh well with the other Redirections, and will start flowing shortly. Finally, renovations on the hotel I bought in Washington are complete—it's now an office building with a record number of bathrooms."

"How we envy you," Sol said.

"Especially at our age," Bill Gates repeated to general amusement, and went on to report on the Access to Justice Project. "Joe's idea of changing the Pledge of Allegiance has become a master stroke to jolt the country into thinking about both the quality and the quantity of justice. From the moment the Pledge the Truth amendment was introduced in the House and Senate, people have been arguing about it in cafés, bars, and barbershops, on street corners and around the water cooler. Everyone has a strong opinion, from Rotarians and Scout leaders to smokers standing outside their offices in the cold, and of course there have been the expected howls of outrage from the expected quarters. On a more orderly level, law schools are scheduling debates on the state of justice in America, and colleges and universities are planning symposia. The controversy has raced into the mass talk media, and Joe and I have become either poster children or devils incarnate. More and more schools, especially in poorer areas, are adopting our proposed change of language and explaining it to the students. Jeno, do you think your vaunted People's Chamber of Commerce will suggest that its members use the revised Pledge at their business luncheons and other functions?"

"Remember devolution?" Jeno retorted. "That'll be up to Luke Skyhi and his associates at the PCC."

"Simmer down, Jeno, I was just kidding, but we do want to find additional venues for the revised Pledge, so if any of you have suggestions, please send them over to Joe and me. Meanwhile, our immediate task is to get more members of Congress to sign on—we're up to about three dozen—so that the bill will be taken more seriously. The closer it gets to passage, the hotter and more widespread the debate will be, and the more attorneys general will decide to issue State of Justice reports. That will be good for the other Redirections too. It will help fuel the lunchtime rallies, it's integral to the First-Stage Improvements drive for a fair economy, it will make our credibility groups more alert to injustice, and it will swell the sense of urgency washing over Congress and the state legislatures. Precisely because the Pledge of Allegiance has been drilled into all of us since kindergarten, it's a sure way of reaching people who ordinarily wouldn't get involved."

"Thank you, Bill," Warren said. "Bernard, will you do the honors for both of us on our Electoral Reform Project?"

"Gladly. As we told you all a few days ago, we're in the planning stage of forming a new single-issue political party devoted to campaign reform. To bring you up to date, we've thoroughly investigated Bill Hillsman, and he's the real McCoy. We didn't get the color of his jagers, though. Our background check discovered that he doesn't wear underwear.

"This is an election year. Deadlines for candidates and party formation are rapidly approaching. We've put in an all-points request to Recruitment and Promotions for managers, organizers, candidates, and assistance. We've decided only to challenge the most powerful ten percent of legislators in the Congress, given the pressure of time, and to go after a few easier seats where we have a chance of coming in second or maybe even winning, in order to influence voter expectations for future elections. Moving so fast with a new party would ordinarily be seen as crazy, but we have the funds, the legal bulldozers, and the crisp issue of clean elections— the name of the party. And when we announce that it's going out of business once the reforms are implemented, that will really grab people. Finally, electoral reform has a good track record in the state initiatives that have embraced it, and it polls exceedingly well.

"We're working on lining up a slew of endorsements by ordinary people expressing their own legitimate interests in reform in their own words. Then it's off to Promotions and intense news coverage. Many of the credibility groups will be supportive, because while they may be full of partisan Republicans or Democrats, they know in their hearts that adopting the clean elections agenda is something both major parties should and can do. The expanding rallies can start incorporating the clean elections message, which has to be cast in terms that show concretely how it can produce a politics that responds to people's daily needs—your medicines will be cheaper and safer, your air and water will be cleaner and your take-home pay more decent, the corporate criminals ripping you off will be prosecuted, your health will be tended to regardless of your ability to pay, and so on. Otherwise electoral reform is too abstract and too vulnerable to distortion by its enemies."

"Maybe the Clean Elections Party could use some attention from Promotions' theater wing," Warren put in. "After all, look what a splendid job they've done with solar energy and hemp."

Ted was about to second Warren's suggestion when Patrick

Drummond glided into the conference room, handed Warren a sheet of paper, and glided out again.

Warren studied the sheet and looked up with a grin. "It's an e-mail from Leonard's project manager, reporting that the first rally to hit the hundred-thousand mark took place in Los Angeles today."

"Fabulous," Barry said. "Our actor friend must really be tearing up the turf in the Golden State."

"This seems like a perfect time to break for an hour of silence, and then dinner," Warren said. "Afterward we should spend a few minutes discussing our interview policies, since the e-mail also mentions a *Time* magazine cover story titled 'What's Happening in America?' with pictures from six of the rallies in a montage surrounding a photo of Warren Beatty. The magazine won't be available in the distribution chain until late tomorrow afternoon, so we don't know what they've written, but cover stories usually go for five pages or more. Can't wait to see what pieces they've picked up to weave into what kind of speculation. Did *Time* call any of you?"

"They called Bill and me about the Pledge," Joe said, "but we didn't call back."

"No one else?" Warren looked around the table. "Great. That means they're probably not on the trail yet. So far, so good."

While his colleagues stood and stretched their legs, Warren went to a phone in the corner of the conference room, and a few minutes later the hotel's energetic cook, Ailani, came in with a hearty "Aloha, honored guests!" and a tray of refreshments. They all thanked her, chose one of the colorful umbrellaed drinks, and resumed their seats for the hour of silence. What were they thinking during that hour? Were they beginning to feel the pressure from the torrent of Redirectional activity and the steadily expanding corps of people that had to be kept on track? Were they still hewing to their principle of keeping their projects as simple as possible even as they laid the firm foundations for the assault on the corporate citadel? Warren's Secretariat was doing a magnificent job, but even the greatest of rodeo riders gets thrown sometimes. How soon must the victories start coming to keep the momentum going strong? They all had their private misgivings—they were only human, after all—but they told themselves to stay as cool as their drinks. After a few minutes of silence, the beauty and tranquility of their surroundings cleared their heads for a calm consideration of the tasks that lay ahead. By the time they broke for dinner, they were marvelously relaxed, trading ideas and jokes and stories, and simply enjoying the food.

When they reassembled in the conference room, Barry led off with a few media-savvy points about interview requests.

"With the *Time* story about to break, I want to stress that you're all fair game for interviews. If you turn them down, that becomes the media focus instead of the issues you're pressing. And besides, you're the best advocates of your own causes, as Bill Gates argued at Maui One, and as you showed with your subsequent initiatives. Just remember that in no case should you say anything that might reveal your connection to the core group. Our approach should be to make them report on us in micro, not in macro. With each passing week, media attention will increasingly focus on what our opponents are saying as they awaken to their overdue comeuppance. Watch their reaction to Peter's Senate testimony next week or to the unfolding CUB challenges. Their bellowing will take up far more column inches and airtime than our forays against them. At the same time, the principle of accelerating devolution means that more and more of our managers, organizers, and candidates will be taking center stage. Promotions will be there to help them."

"Thank you, Barry," Warren said. "Now let's take up the Block-buster Challenge, which we'll publicize with the slogan 'Buy Back Your Congress: The Best Bargain in America.' No matter how great the idea and its consequences for our democracy, it'll be a bust if it's not handled well—or worse, as the French say, a blunder. So over to you, Bernard."

"Well, first the data. The project staff is still analyzing the gross and net data regarding expenditures in every House and Senate race in the last election. The gross data comes from the FEC, but it's insufficient without the data on how much was spent to raise the money. Separating fundraising expenses from campaign expenses can be daunting, even with the FEC reporting formats, but we need this information because we don't want to be cheated by any legislator who takes us up on our offer, and because it will give us a better understanding of the entire industry of raising and spending campaign money. Once these data are all in and analyzed, we'll come up with an average net for congressional campaigns and mark it up twenty percent to sweeten the offer, but before we can do that, there are a number of questions we need to address. As you know, Joan Claybrook will soon be on board as our Blockbuster manager, and I sent her a list of these questions and asked her to review them. Her response is before you." Leonard gestured to the stapled handouts that had been placed around the table during the dinner break. "Naturally I didn't tell her anything about our core group, so I deleted question nine from my e-mail to her, the one about how to connect the Blockbuster Challenge with the other Redirection projects when it comes to cranking up the heat on members back in their districts and states. Let's take a few minutes to read over what she said."

There was a rustling of paper as everyone picked up Joan's memo.

1. *Who should make the offer?*
The offer is best made by a committee of perhaps a dozen highly respected John Gardner types, retired people of unquestioned integrity and worldly experience—a professor emeritus like Jacques Barzun, a former federal judge, university president, foundation president, diplomat, etc. A nonpartisan ex-president would be the cherry on the sundae.

2. *Where do we say the money is coming from? What options do we have?*
I'm told the money is there, to the tune of $2 billion or more, so yes, everyone will ask where this huge sum is coming from. If you say it's coming from a number of well-intentioned billionaires, you'll be asked who they are,

and very rich people are rarely squeaky-clean, no matter how noble their lives. Here's a thought: you could use some of your $2 billion to raise smaller contributions from ordinary people—say, no more than a hundred dollars—and set up receiving groups in trust in the name of each incumbent. The details would have to be worked out, but these could be PACs in escrow, so to speak, conditional on the incumbent's accepting the clean elections agenda. That way the offer becomes very real because the money is for the asking once the condition is met. Given the contribution cap, there would have to be many such PACs in each district, but they could be given colorful, meaningful names that would help convey the clean elections message. This is a touchy issue, and many minds should be consulted on its best resolution.

3. How do we convince Congress and the public that we're credible, that we can actually produce the money?
If you answer question 2, then you answer question 3.

4. How do we convince Congress and the public that there are no strings attached other than electoral reforms?
If you answer question 3, then you basically answer question 4, though there are some fairly conventional credibility factors you can add, like shifting the burden of proof to anyone who can show otherwise, or getting members of Congress themselves to vouch for you, or inviting reporters to investigate vigorously, or making it clear that even incumbents with the most odious records can receive the funding if they commit to clean elections.

5. How do we proceed if only 10 or 15 percent of the Congress responds affirmatively?
I think you need to set a minimum percentage. I'd say you need 25 percent of the members, in both the Senate

and the House, to make going to all this trouble worth-while.

6. *How can we make sure our offer is lawsuit-proof under the cap limits, as for PACs, and cannot be seen as a bribe either legally or in public perception?*
You get the best five attorneys specializing in campaign finance legalities—including one or two who've worked in the FEC and the Justice Department—to advise you and write clearance memoranda. This you need to do right off, first thing. I highly recommend Theresa Tieknots of Chicago, an expert in federal election and campaign finance law.

7. *Can we move fast enough here, given the tight schedule between now and Election Day in November?*
The schedule is very tight, but with plenty of money I estimate you can get in under the wire. And you have to insist that any monies already collected by the incumbents be returned or given to charity if they accept your offer.

8. *What do we do about challengers to the incumbents and the additional imbalance we may be inadvertently gener-ating against them?*
This is the most nettlesome question if we believe in a level playing field for the candidates, including those from minor parties. I dealt with something roughly similar years ago as director of a project that involved preparing magazine-length profiles of all congressional office-holders running for reelection in 1972—never done before in American history, a thousand volunteers, scores of paid writer-researchers, etc. More than a few members of Congress, fearing a critical report, demanded that we do the same reports on their challengers. "Why just us?"

they asked. "Unfair!" We argued that we were only profiling legislators, politicians with real power and a real
record. Most challengers didn't fit these criteria. Power
has its privileges, we said, but it also has its responsibilities. Challengers have no formal power. In your case, the
concern is reversed. Most incumbents will not demand
that the same offer be made to their challengers—where
there are any. It's the challengers who are going to
demand the offer because they have a harder time raising
money and for them the clean elections pledge is a no-
brainer. In this disparity lies our argument—we tell the
challengers that most incumbents won't take the pledge
and will thereby incur your project's active opposition,
which will invariably help the opposing candidates. In
addition, we tell them that if an incumbent doesn't take
the pledge—which has to involve more than just a verbal
acceptance, as my staff will work out soon—then the project's money will go to the challenger in some pro rata
fashion. That's my first take on this question. I'll try to
ask around among my colleagues discreetly, and when I
come on board, I hope to get the project launchers'
thoughts as well.

"Well, what do you think?" Bernard asked when his colleagues
had finished reading.

"Not bad for starters," Max said, "but that eighth question is a
tough one."

Leonard and Peter, who were Bernard's seconds on the Congress
Project, pointed out that their data on expenditures for every race
during the last election included the challengers. "So their spending
has already been taken into account," Peter said. "We just have to
find the right formula for our disbursements. Everyone who credibly adopts the clean elections agenda should receive funds."

"I agree," Warren said. "A project to buy back the Congress can
hardly stand to be accused of making challengers beg, kneel, and

prostitute themselves because they aren't yet incumbents. Is that the consensus?"

There were nods all around. Bill Cosby added that if candidates had to give back any money they'd already raised, that would be a pretty good indication that their commitment went beyond words. "Their donors will be furious with them," he observed.

"We also have to bear in mind that the Clean Elections Party will be part of the mix and will be running candidates —a further asymmetry if all are not included in the Blockbuster offer. Ironically, our new party won't be able to accept any of the money ladled out by the Blockbuster campaign, because whatever the pro rata formula is, it won't be nearly enough. The Clean Elections Party is the hammer. The hammer has to be bigger than the nails. The new party has to be funded amply as the battering ram for the Blockbuster pledges."

Bernard frowned. "Isn't that an insurmountable problem? I, for one, would want to avoid the spectacle of the Clean Elections Party candidates refusing to take the clean elections pledge."

"Well, it's a problem, all right," Warren said. "Whether it's insurmountable or not remains to be seen. Both projects will have to stay in the closest contact as they unfold over the coming months. Maybe the solution is to have some billionaire announce that he's personally funding the Clean Elections Party, and that the party is rejecting the Blockbuster offer precisely because it supports the Blockbuster objectives, which can't be realized in practice without a one-time resort to unlimited expenditures. One of us can always take this on if need be, but I think it would be best to find a billionaire outside our core group."

"That shouldn't be too hard," Ted said. "One of the billionaires we already have on board may be willing to step in. They've all been a huge help to us so far, and some are taking the lead in their own right. I'm telling you, releasing the energy built up in retirement has been like splitting the atom, and I want more of it. There are plenty more billionaires than you'll find in the Forbes 400, but a lot of them are completely unknown, like the ones who've quietly inherited their wealth or become instant billionaires after the sale of some dot-com or some other hotshot company, or all the millionaires turned billion-aires just from their investments soaring in recent years. I know a guy who founded a nutrition company and watched his stock go from a dollar a share to twenty dollars a share in a year, and another guy who got the same results with his defense company after he invented some detection system for national security. There are billionaires every-where, in the most unlikely places—the Ozarks, Catalina Island, a half-deserted farm town in Nebraska, country club prisons. I even know one from the remote Mesabi Iron Range in Minnesota." Here Ted flashed Jeno a wicked smile. "The thing is, I can't quite figure out how to net the next crop, so it's time to rope you fellows into this pitch for the rich. Any ideas?" He turned to Warren.

"Some of us are rapidly disqualifying ourselves, wouldn't you say? I've already gone out on various limbs, none more alienating to many wealthy people than my stance on investor control of execu-tive compensation. Why don't you get the names of the billionaires that *your* billionaires play with—cards, golf, shuffleboard, yachting, whatever—and ask them to start recruiting."

"I've already done that, Warren. I've taken it as far as I can."

"Well, how about organizing a billionaires' convention?" Joe sug-gested. "Call it the Just Billionaires Convention, something like that, something with class. Maybe that will smoke out the ones put off by Billionaires Against Bullshit."

"Here's an idea," Yoko said. "Propose a number of great causes that billionaires can be proud of attaching themselves to. I know a tycoon who's providing cheap wheelchairs to people in developing countries with severe disabilities—and the tax laws actually allow him to make money from the scheme, would you believe."

"Here's another idea," Phil said. "Research the existing lists of the wealthiest people in the country to see what suppressed passions for justice they may have had years ago that can be reawakened in the much more auspicious climate created by what Ted and the rest of us are in the process of doing. After all, the massive media cov-erage we've received so far has got to be sinking into some of their heads—you know, that 'Why not me?' feeling."

"Listen to this," Yoko said. "At a dinner with a potential epicenter billionaire last month, I broached the subject of doing something dramatic to alleviate poverty, something that would be both fast and ongoing. The billionaire thought for a while, imbibed some Grand Marnier, chewed a handful of walnuts, and said, "My friend, there are at least a million people in this country who wouldn't even notice if their monthly Social Security checks were assigned to a well-organized assistance program for poor families in our blessed land.' Then he laid out an entire plan. With a million donors of checks averaging seventeen hundred dollars a month, you could divide that sum in half and augment the meager incomes of two million families in need by more than ten thousand dollars a year. Two million families on a surer footing means about eight million people all told. The donors could be given the names of the families if they wished, and even meet with the parents and children from time to time. Think of the sensitization to the daily struggles of people who are usually out of sight and out of mind. I'll bet Oprah would be interested. 'I'd be happy to make this my personal endeavor and enlist others similarly endowed,' the billionaire told me. 'There are intangibles here that are quite consequential for the more humane tone of our society, and there is a potential emulation factor for other such endeavors in other arenas.'

"Naturally, I was impressed, though I cautioned him to beware of the enemies of Social Security, who might jump on his idea to promote a means test and chip away at the system's universality. Then I encouraged him to contact Patrick Drummond at the Secretariat for the proper referrals to our burgeoning networks—without, of course, mentioning the Secretariat or the networks."

"That's a great story, Yoko," Bernard said, "but don't we have to face the fact that there are scores of billionaires who are simply too immersed in luxury to bestir themselves? They have worn the garb of greed for too long. I'm reminded of the words of Khalil Gibran, the mystical Lebanese poet and artist who lived in America early in the last century, and who spoke of 'the lust for comfort, that stealthy thing that enters the house a guest, and then becomes a host, and then a master.'"

"Kind of brings it home, doesn't it?" Phil said.

Jeno looked up from jotting the Gibran quotation on his pad. "You know, maybe all they need is a little gradual socialization in the corps of active billionaires or in the midst of an exciting bunch of progressive business people. I think I'll ask Luke Skyhi to form a billionaires' auxiliary of the People's Chamber of Commerce. It's almost comical, sounds like a contradiction in terms, but that in itself ought to draw some of them in, just out of curiosity, and then we'll make the meetings lively and stimulating and fill their minds with prospects of true grandeur. What do you call those places between prison and going free?"

Ted gave Jeno a puzzled look. "You mean halfway houses?"

"Right, that's it. The Billionaires' Auxiliary of the PCC will be a halfway house for the wealthy."

"Ted, what's your assessment of how many billionaires are truly beyond reach?" Peter asked. "By now you must have spoken to more of them than the rest of us put together."

"Well, I get down to brass tacks with them right away—no beating around the bush with bullshit words of evasion, no howdy-doing— and I can tell pretty fast how they're going to break down. About one in five jump on board. They get it. They usually have their own peeves, some of them so relatively trivial that I have a hard time keeping my trap shut—but when don't I? Others are interested in problems that are significant but largely symptomatic of deeper inequalities and distortions of power. A few are dead-on in their analysis.

"Of the remaining eighty percent, about half of them are interested enough to want to meet, seems like they're looking to take on some important challenge so that the future will remember them and their descendants will respect them. Grandparents and great-grandparents don't impress their little ones just by being billionaires. So I meet with them, run some of our initiatives by them to gauge their response, and sign them up if I think they're ready. That's how we got some of the billionaires against Wal-Mart, for example.

"About another twenty percent are clueless—into selling their mega-mansions for fifteen times what they paid thirty years ago, or worrying about their investment returns, their wayward trophy wives, their gout and their livers, their heirs, what have you. I call these the 'Huh?' folks and cast them aside. The last twenty percent are downright hostile, people with the most closed minds and snuffed-out imaginations you'll ever come across. They are defenders of the ruling class, sometimes offensively so. To them I say, 'To each his own. Hope to see you around before the global high watermarks obstruct our vision.'

"As for the emulation effect Yoko's billionaire mentioned, it's hard to gauge. When the guys who are hesitating start reading about their peers, some of them will see how empty their lives have become and will want to get in on the action. If they're the thick-skinned type, they'll think it's a good way to have some fun and do some good. Others will say to themselves, 'Who wants to wade into that firestorm? I want peace, quiet, and comfort.' Rest assured that we'll be stoking the emulation effect in every way possible. My manager is first-rate in that regard."

"All very interesting, Ted," Peter said. "The comparably few calls I've made left me with the impression that the semi-responsive ones are willing to get together and hear more but aren't in any rush. Last week I talked to a fellow Princetonian whom I'm going to meet at the Yale game this fall. But I do have to say that I got considerably better results and a perverse tickle from one of my calls. There I am, speaking to a guy who's loaded from what Henry George called the 'unearned increment'—otherwise known as very valuable real estate—and I'm trying to sell him on certain aspects of our Redirections that he can't quibble over, like energy independence, healthcare, and clean, efficient government, and he's backing and filling about 'cash flow' and being 'heavily leveraged.' I've got his net-worth details on my desk, and they show he's lying through his teeth. He's so liquid he's hired specialists to find outlets for his masses of money.

"So I'm saying, 'Bruce, what about fifty million?' And he keeps thinking he's talking to someone from the Democratic Party or something. I say, 'Bruce, I was born at night but not last night.' He squirms. We've known each other for thirty-five years, so he can't pull the old 'Let's have lunch sometime' on me. I let him squirm. I say, 'Bruce, last year you gave five million just to encourage Jews to marry Jews. What kind of country do you want their children to grow up in? Since then, you've had a bang-up year in commercial real estate, flat out and nonstop.' So he says, 'Peter, how about twenty-five million.' I pause, as if to convey disappointment. Then I say, 'Well, okay, for starters. You'll never regret this contribution, Bruce, nor will your descendants. Now, when do you want to have lunch?'"

"Brilliant!" Bill Gates exclaimed. "We should all try Peter's approach. When I call billionaire lawyers, I always have a wealth biography in front of me too. Lawyers my age are preoccupied by their declining annual income as their younger partners deliberately phase them out, so they cry poor even though they made it big over their productive years, and bigger still with their investments. I use every tool from peer emulation to their long-suppressed professional ideals about the proper functioning of the law in a just society. I know a lot about the issues that upset them, which makes for more targeted discussions. I've set a floor of five million dollars, and I've had considerable success, but I've found that many of them are hungry for some kind of recognition beyond plaques or testimonials or building wings named for them. Somewhere in our expanding talent bank, can we find a person to come up with more substantive ways of acknowledging their gifts?"

"Done," Warren said, jotting a note on his pad.

"Here's my favorite bullshit response to my calls. 'Joe, I think what you're doing is so admirable, but I've been giving my charitable dollars to the Kill the Tapeworms and Lice Children's Association. It does such wonderful work.' Or, 'You know, Joe, my lifelong passion has been supporting the Hospital for Orthopedically Damaged Low-Income Persons. It takes up all my spare time and fortune.' To which I silently say, 'Buddy, I've got your financials and the filings for your charity, and what's there is not what you say is there. You're rolling in dough, and your bullshit is just a cover and an excuse.' What I actually say is, 'I'm not asking you for charitable dollars. We all give charitable dollars. I'm asking you for survival dollars for your children and grandchildren and their children and grandchildren. I'm asking you to take some of that dead money and turn it into live money that breathes life, freedom, health, and possibilities for all human beings to thrive. Give me a call when you're ready to join the greatest cause of them all, peace and justice on Earth, beginning right here at home.'"

Bill Cosby raised his water glass. "Dead money, live money—hear, hear, Joe! Thank you."

"Okay, Ted, you've got your answers, and one of them you won't have to implement yourself, if I heard Jeno right," Warren said. "The rest are in your capable southern hands. Now it's time to break for refreshments and an hour of silent reflection, and after that I suggest you go out on the upper balcony, do some aerobics and look at the stars and the moon shining down on Haleakala Crater on the clearest night you've ever seen. Gives you perspective on space, time, mortality."

"Just what we need," Sol said.

If nature could ever trump nurture, it had to be in a place like Maui. How could anyone, even Sol, start the day less than optimistic in such a scene from paradise? The nation-shakers filtered into the conference room Sunday morning fully restored by their stargazing, an excellent night's sleep, and a delectable breakfast. The topic for discussion was the Wal-Mart unionizing drive.

"My dear friends," Sol said warmly, "may I ask for your views on the possibility suggested by our delightful colleague Yoko that our enemies—in this case, Wal-Mart—will try to turn a portion of 'the people' against us? My SWAT teams have confirmed that Wal-Mart is mobilizing its low-income 'satisfied customers,' and we must counter their populist ploy lest it taint the unionizing effort, and by extension our other Redirectional projects." Despite the gravity of his words, Sol was beaming.

"Well, for sure they're going to concentrate on the five stores under assault," Bill Cosby said, "but they won't be able to muster counter-demonstrations of poor customers without offering lots of goodies and freebies. You know how hard it is to get people out these days. The more Wal-Mart oils their rallies with free food, coupons, toys, et cetera, the less credible their crowds will be, and you can strike at their perceived strength of offering the lowest prices anywhere by organizing your own rallies of consumers who've been ripped off by Wal-Mart, which has had a free ride on this claim so far. But you'll need to know more about Wal-Mart's national effort against you, Sol. Don't you have a mole on their board of directors?"

"What we know is that the board, while publicly putting up a brave united front, is in a state of turmoil. Our billionaires have been working their old friends over. Major economic pressure is being brought to bear. One of the directors, while refusing to turn state's evidence or divulge proprietary information, is keeping us informed of their discussions at what are now weekly meetings of the board. The circle is tightening around Wal-Mart, what with rallies, pickets, SWAT teams, storefronts, fire sales, and we're just getting started. But watch out for the tail of the giant dragon. We can't rule out the possibility that Wal-Mart will start putting two and two together from the press clips and go to groups like the Business Roundtable for assistance."

Warren glanced at his Timex. "We'd better think about wrapping things up, my friends. I'd like us to close with a free-for-all discussion of what's on your mind for the coming months, especially next month. My own view is that each month is going to see an exponential increase in just about everything—our activity, media, counterattacks, serendipities. You can almost feel the growing rumble in the country. My revolution of the investor class against tyrannical and greedy top management is rising like healthy yeast. The coming month is the month that will give roots to our Redirections of power from the few to the many. Soon *Time*'s cover story will be 'Volcanic Rebellion Inside Big Business,' or 'When Business Rebels Shrug.'"

There ensued a vigorous and rigorous review of all the initiatives, full of lively repartee, and leading to refinements and accelerated schedules, especially for getting the Clean Elections Party and its candidates on the ballot before the approaching deadlines. At noon Ailani served lunch without interrupting the flow of conversation, and by one o'clock the core members were on their way home. Maui Month Three was underway.

CHAPTER 7

On the first day of March, a damp, cloudy Wednesday, Brovar Dortwist sat in his K Street office reading the *Time* story. When he finished, he flung the magazine on his desk with a mixture of outrage and apprehension. As a Julius Caesar buff, he was well aware that the Ides of March were rapidly approaching. He scowled at the handsome visage of Warren Beatty, which seemed to wink at him from *Time*'s cover.

Big business was under serious attack, and it wasn't General Smedley Butler of the US Marines coming back from the dead for revenge. It was what Brovar feared most from his knowledge of economic history—a revolt from within, a business rebellion against big business orchestrated by people who knew all the tricks of the commercial trades, all the vulnerabilities and fragilities, all the means big business employed to crush or coopt its adversaries. He could feel the danger, almost smell it. Most of his brethren discounted the signals coming from all points of the compass and thought the People's Chamber of Commerce was an object of mockery garnished with futility, but Brovar disagreed. That was precisely the mistake the liberals made back when they were dominant in the nation's capital.

Brovar was not used to playing defense, to put it mildly. He hated defense down to the core of his being. Although he had some grasp of what he was about to fight, he didn't know whom he was fighting, other than a few wealthy and mostly retired executives. To complicate matters, he didn't entirely disagree with what they were doing, and this nuanced side of him was likely to get him in trouble, not only with his brethren, but with his paymasters and the White

House. Still, he believed without immodesty that no one was better suited to lead the counteroffensive than he.

At ten o'clock on the dot, Brovar entered the Wednesday war room and nodded curtly to his pack of lobbyists and politicos. Dispensing with the usual assignments quickly, he said that he had a major presentation to make, and that it would be uncharacteristically tentative and vague, for reasons they would soon understand.

"You've all been reading the same papers and watching the same newscasts I have these last few weeks. Something is happening, something I haven't witnessed in my adult lifetime. The growing rallies in more and more cities, all the small claims litigation against big companies, the new militance of workers, the assertiveness of the renegade businesses that have joined the PCC, the arrogance of the anti-capitalist sustainable economy types, the resistance of social service groups that we used to mobilize so easily, the increase in anti-business reporting on some networks, the outspokenness of retired executives at the National Press Club, the brazenness of dozens of billionaires, their sudden attentiveness to electoral and corporate reforms, the huge publicity for Sol Price's attack on Wal-Mart and Peter Lewis's across-the-board charges against our many clients, the sense that the atmosphere in Congress is changing, the Patriotic Polly ads and the crude attempt to change the Pledge of Allegiance—well, I'm sure you can add your own examples.

"The problem is that there seems to be no head, no ideology, no overall organization to it all. Yet it definitely seems to be more than the sum of its visible parts, and the visible parts seem to be perched on resources and determination far vaster than we've ever seen before. Maybe I'm making too much of all this. We've become so accustomed to weak or nonexistent opposition in recent years that I may be overestimating what's simply one of the cyclical populist revivals that mark our country's history. So far, at least, there has been little discernible change in our control levels, though the forces arrayed against us appear to be gathering. I hope you're watching the Beatty gubernatorial campaign in California. He seems to be bringing the Reagan Democrats back into the left-wing fold, though it's a little early to tell.

Arnold still has a few muscles to flex. In any case, I'd like to get some reaction from you on what I've been describing."

"My reaction is not to overreact," said a Chamber of Commerce lobbyist. "We have a full plate to get though Congress—the extension of the tax cuts on capital gains and dividends, the repeal of the death tax once and for all, more business incentives, more opportunity zones that waive regulations and taxes, the drive to put Social Security on a business footing, the elimination of the more onerous federal regulations. Let us not be distracted by a few over-the-hill blowhards. Really, Sol Price, Jeno Paulucci, and Bernard Who? Give me a break!"

"I agree," said a representative of the Defense Industries Association. "Our antennae have picked up no movement against the defense budget or our military policies. We haven't applied our latest infrared technology to the rumblings you described, but none of the rhetoric, except for the Cincinnati rally of veterans, has even touched on our domain, which as you all know is pretty extensive in the economic, military, and budgetary spheres. So lighten up, Brovar. We respect your early-warning record, but maybe you're too early for our own good on this one, with due respect."

Ripples of laughter filled the room.

"Our number one priority ought to be tort reform, guys," a pharmaceuticals lobbyist said. "I think I speak for the drug companies, the medical device manufacturers, the doctors, the hospitals, and many of you in allied fields. The trial lawyers and the consumer, health, and environmental groups are all over us on Capitol Hill. We have to concentrate. At last we have the Republicans in charge of the Congress and the White House, and we have to seize the hour. Brovar, unless you're just giving us a heads-up before we resume our usual business this morning, your early alert may be a costly distraction. Which is it?"

Brovar's jaw clenched imperceptibly. "Remember the relentless growth of the conservative movement following our low point after the lopsided 1964 Goldwater defeat? The liberals kept themselves in sneering denial, calling us tools of business, saying we were not only wrong but stupid and dull. That smugness became their undoing. They kept ignoring the signs or interpreting them as aberrations or inconsequential flukes. They're now our doormat. I learn from history. I am cautious and anticipatory, and I have a sixth sense as to when the tides are turning." Here the pixie in Brovar toyed with saying, "The tides turn on the Ides," but he thought better of it. Very few of them would understand the literary allusion. "However, is it the consensus that enough has been said to put us on guard? Let me see a show of hands."

All but a few of the impatient horde raised their hands. Brovar sighed imperceptibly. "Okay, then it's back to business as usual, but keep your ears and eyes open in the coming days and report back next Wednesday about what you think needs discussion."

Whereupon the Wednesday Club commenced discussing high-level government positions that were open and that they wanted to fill with a prepared list of available corporate executives—something that was indeed business as usual.

As the corporate lobbies were breezily failing to bestir themselves, Peter Lewis was preparing to testify before the Senate Commerce Committee. The scene in the large Senate hearing room was chaotic. More tables had to be brought in to accommodate the press corps. The seats in the audience were filled with early birds hired at $20 an hour by insurance lobbyists who would turn up to replace them at more leisurely morning arrival times. Representatives of consumer groups and interested policyholders, expecting first-come, first-served seating and not a payola racket, were outraged. Jostling and cries of protest attracted the Capitol Police, who instituted a rotation system like the one for the Senate visitors' gallery to accommodate the long lines waiting in the corridors. This upset the lobbyists to no end, but they had no choice.

Peter was the lead witness, with no time limitation. He had told the committee chairman, Senator Martin Merchant, that he had a lengthy case to make. He had also assured the committee that he would answer any questions the members cared to put to him. Senator Merchant was in an unaccustomedly tight reelection race and wanted headlines that would make him look like a champion of the insurance consumer, even though he had a reputation as the lobbyists' "business agent" in the Senate. Knowing this, Peter had informed him that the point of the hearings was to enact reform legislation and that he expected the chairman to demand the attendance, under threat of subpoena, of the CEOs of the top ten insurance companies in the health, life, auto, homeowners, medical malpractice, product liability, and workers' compensation sectors. Senator Merchant got the message and delivered the CEOs, who were now sitting not a little nervously in the front row behind Peter. He commenced his testimony after taking the oath to tell the truth.

"Mr. Chairman, distinguished members of the Senate Commerce Committee, I am here today to perform a responsibility that has been shirked for decades by executives of the insurance industry, including myself. I ask permission to insert in the record of these hearings the voluminous evidence and the internal reports and memoranda I've gathered to document my testimony."

"So ordered," intoned the chairman.

"Let me come straight to the point. The dirty secret of the insurers and their imperious reinsurers is their need for stable and slowly growing rates of death, injury, and property destruction, in order to scare tens of billions of premium dollars out of consumers, businesses, and nonprofits. Casualties are their inventory, and they like to keep their inventory growing as long as they can keep their premiums rising. Perhaps the dirtiest part of the secret, all the advertising about their concern for health and safety notwithstanding, is that they not only do little to reduce casualties but at times have actively discouraged efforts to save life and limb. In a few cases—Allstate with air bags, Liberty Mutual with rehabilitating injured workers—the concern goes beyond propaganda and is actually translated into action, but these are lights in an ocean of darkness.

"Before I elaborate on this tragedy of tragedies, a short history of the ugly mutation of the property and casualty insurance industry is necessary. In the early industrial evolution of our country, boiler explosions and the ensuing fires were major perils in factories. They were terrible events. They were frequent. The industrialists were persuaded to take out insurance policies to cover the destruction—hence the Hartford Boiler Insurance Company, among others. These early insurers derived their profits from premiums minus expenses, so it made obvious sense to demand safer boilers and inspect them regularly. The insurers did not wait upon the factories; they actually spent money on research to improve the boilers and develop more stringent safety specifications—that is, they took an engineering approach to loss prevention. Ah, that sacred mantra of today's forked tongues—loss prevention. For most of the nineteenth century, whatever less desirable sales tactics may have been employed, the coming of the insurance man meant the coming of a safety sentinel. You may wonder why our industry doesn't brag about this part of its past, doesn't publish books and encourage movies about some of the more heroic actions the early insurers took to reduce risks. The answer isn't far to seek. Today the transformation of insurers from essentially engineering-driven companies to financially driven companies is almost total, and the industry has suffered a convenient case of amnesia with regard to its own history.

"Let me illustrate current practice with a simple example. If a contemporary insurance executive were offered a choice between a $500 premium with a $250 payout or a $1,000 premium with a $500 payout, which do you think he would take? No question that he'd take the $1,000 premium, because then he'd have $500 to invest instead of a mere $250. Investment income is the honeypot of the insurance industry. They reserve not just for a rainy day but for a permanently expanding investment fund. Their dream is to have such a large reserve that it functions like an endowment and they can pay claims with the investment income on the reserve. And of course, the more they reserve, the more they can deduct from current income, which is why insurance companies have paid so little in federal taxes over the decades.

"A word about the federal tax code as it relates to insurance companies. The insurance section of the IRS code is more complex and inscrutable than any other section, so much so that an IRS commissioner once agreed with the proposition that fewer people understand it than understand Einstein's Theory of Relativity. When tax codes are inscrutable, they are not likely to be enforced, as the same IRS commissioner acknowledged. Where is the IRS going to find experts to explain the code in a court of law? The few who can already work for the industry. Besides, determining noncompliance is an exhausting task that the IRS doesn't begin to have the resources to pursue. Over the years, the industry's formidable phalanx of specialized attorneys, accountants, and actuaries has deterred the IRS from so much as peeping in their direction.

"The relevance of the tax code to the subject of this hearing is clear. By its very impotence, it facilitates all kinds of mechanisms the industry uses to swell investment returns from reserve funds that are greatly in excess of any actuarial necessity. The result is that people are overpaying for diminished protection while the pathetic state insurance 'regulators' fiddle and faddle until they receive job offers to work in the very industry they're overseeing—that is, if they don't come from the industry in the first place. And state legislators with committee jurisdiction over the industry haven't just been coopted, they've been organized by the insurance lobby to protect the industry's interests actively and even defiantly, in what amounts to a form of corporate statism.

"Moving from the infrastructure of avarice and myopia to the business of sustaining a sufficient level of lethality, I direct your attention to an important case study in my appendixes relating to fires. Fire insurers need fires. Without a sufficient number of fires they can't sell as much insurance or charge as much for it. Per capita deaths by fire in this country are three times greater than in Japan and many Western European countries. Fire prevention is a well-established series of applied technologies and rules, from building codes to fire detectors to the location and equipping of fire stations. If we know that fires can be sharply reduced or at least limited in their damage through these means, why does our country lag so far behind?

"In the 1960s, the people at the US Bureau of Standards in the

Maryland suburbs were astonished to notice the dampening stance of the insurance companies toward initiatives underway within the bureau to expand fire prevention research and development. The bureau's staff was disappointed but understood the motivation behind the resistance. Name any area of preventable death, injury, or disease, any economic activity involving risks that have not yet materialized fully or significantly, and you will not see a serious loss prevention presence from the insurance industry.

"Take the last century's death toll from motor vehicle crashes. There were two serious efforts at loss prevention in the postwar period. In the early sixties, a Liberty Mutual engineering vice president named Crandall rebuilt a conventional American four-door sedan with numerous safety features that we now take for granted, such as seat belts, padded dashboards, and stronger door latches. In the seventies, Allstate got a lot of good publicity for pressing the auto companies to install air bags as standard equipment. But such enlightened examples from within their own industry did not persuade the other insurance companies to match the efforts of these two safety-conscious firms. Think of the lives that could have been saved. That noble objective was not enough to make the insurers back their occasional verbal salutes to loss prevention with deeds. Or take motorcycle helmets, proven to reduce fatal head injuries in crashes. State laws requiring helmets—laws that prevent some two thousand deaths and many injuries a year, often among younger Americans—are being repealed with no real opposition from the insurers, except for two small industry-funded groups with grossly inadequate budgets.

"Whether it's hazardous household products, faulty truck brakes, phony vehicle bumpers, unsafe railroad bridges, pharmaceuticals with devastating side effects, toxic chemicals in the workplace or in consumer products, dangerous working conditions in factories, farms, and mines, or a host of aviation perils—like thirty-plus neglectful years of penetrable cockpit doors and latches, from the spate of Cuban hijackings in the late sixties and early seventies to the easy cockpit break-ins by the 9/11 hijackers—the same pattern repeats itself. Why, just insisting on simple roll-bars for tractors would have saved the lives of tens of thousands of farmers in the twentieth century. But when small, budget-squeezed consumer, environmental, and labor organizations were on the front lines exposing these perils, demanding federal and state action, and insisting on corporate responsibility, the giant insurance companies and their foundations and PR machines and lobbying associations stayed home.

"As if the abandonment of loss prevention weren't bad enough, there are junctures where the industry turns to active and vicious assaults on victims and their rights to legal remedies. Insurers have comfortable periods when claims are stable and premiums ample and investment returns robust, but every ten years or so, when interest rates and stock prices decline appreciably, the insurance companies find their returns falling and dust off the 'crisis con job.' They threaten skyrocketing premiums or withdraw coverage from selective markets, and then they point the businesses and professions they're gouging toward the legislatures. 'That's where the solutions are,' they tell their frightened and frantic customers, 'go there for relief, demand a rollback of tort law and restrictions on the amount of compensation that can be awarded for serious injuries in the courts of law.' Yes, get the money-greased absentee legislators to tie the hands of juries and judges, the only ones who see, hear, and evaluate these cases before an open court of law. With every passing decade, tort law, a historic form of quality control for our industry, has steadily been tipped in favor of big companies accused of harm. Even our ancient right of trial by jury isn't sacred in this financially driven crusade to shred judicial protections by legislative fiat. J. Robert Hunter, a former Texas insurance commissioner and federal insurance administrator, has reported on this callous pattern of attack on the innocent injured, when even the investment business has learned to live with cyclical stock downturns since the 1970s. His studies are in my appendixes for the record.

"It is well known how inimical insurance companies are to government regulation of any kind, even though without it they would have flirted with insolvency many a time by overextending themselves. What is not well known, apart from a mandated antitrust exemption, is the industry's lust for government regulation to eliminate, reduce, or subsidize the financial risks nominally underwritten by the insurers. This alliance with government produces a further mockery of their presumed loss prevention function.

"A good example is atomic power. In the fifties, no company would insure a nuclear power plant because there was no actuarial history, and because the little that was known sent chills up the insurers' spines. One radioactive scenario from the industry-friendly Atomic Energy Commission suggested that a meltdown at a nuclear plant would contaminate an area the size of Pennsylvania. So what did the industry agree to? The Price-Anderson Act, which severely limited the liability of utilities owning nuclear plants against claims from the devastated areas, and which is still the law of the land. Now, there are times when an activity or a technology is so risky that it is prudent for insurance companies to deny coverage. Denial of coverage can be an incentive to reduce risks to an acceptable level—another form of loss prevention. Limiting liability by law does just the opposite, but Price-Anderson is what the industry chose to support.

"Another good example is medical incompetence, a silent epidemic that produces countless injuries and nearly a hundred thousand deaths a year, excluding the two hundred fifty or so people who die each day from hospital-acquired infections, as estimated by the Centers for Disease Control. So how do the medical malpractice insurers behave? They refuse to implement experience-loss ratings that would raise premiums for bad physicians and lower premiums for good ones. They also hike premiums by reclassifying medical specialties—from three in the 1950s to more than twenty today—to reduce the insurable pool per specialty per state. You've heard the outraged cries of physicians blaming their off-the-chart annual premiums on trial lawyers, juries, and the tort system. Don't believe it. There are some nutty verdicts, often overturned, but either way it's all a seedy cover to get you and the states to reduce liability and make it harder for plaintiffs to have their day in court than it already is, with ninety percent of medical malpractice victims not even filing claims. I'm reminded of what the famous architect Frank Lloyd

Wright once told a convention of doctors: 'Unlike you, my friends, we cannot bury our mistakes.'

"Mr. Chairman and members of the Committee, I have only sketched in the briefest manner an industry that has turned grotesquely on its own history, its own mission as the nation's safety and health sentinel, and its own vested interest in reducing claims. Its unchallenged power has turned this former incentive into a perverse incentive for inaction, surrender, cowardliness, the cover-up of known safety defects, and an aggressive attack on deterrence and on the laws that protect millions of innocent Americans.

"The insurance business has rarely attracted the best and the brightest of executive talent. It is, after all, a fairly simple business, a business of large numbers—money in, money making more money, less money out. Why couldn't the government engage in this type of routine transaction without the duplication, the massive overhead and executive salaries—look at the chiefs of the big HMOs—and the profitable waste built into such sectors as health insurance? It could. That's for you to decide." At this point, the ten CEOs sitting behind Peter blanched, all the arrogant composure of their exalted corporate status seeming to drain from them. "After all, you make flood insurance possible by guaranteeing it with the full faith and credit of the US government. You make crop insurance possible in the same way. More and more, the insurance lobbies are putting you in the position of reinsurance, making big profits while they lay the ultimate risk on Uncle Sam's shoulders. Best of all possible worlds, no? Uncle Sam, the all-purpose guarantor for more and more of the insurance economy. And that doesn't include the Washington bailouts.

"Another little-noticed aspect of the industry is the inbuilt conflict of interest between its big customers and its small customers. When insurers write policies for large industrial companies in, say, directors' and officers' liability, product liability, or workers' compensation, they knowingly place themselves in potential conflict with individuals they've insured, as in the case of an auto insurance customer injured on the highway because of a tire defect the manufacturer is responsible for. If you, the Congress, were in possession of all the files of the insurance underwriters regarding hazardous conditions, toxic exposures, product defects, reckless professionals, et cetera, almost none of which are being reported to safety and public health authorities, I'm certain that you would be outraged enough to take legislative action.

"In summary, the capitalist incentive that used to drive the insurance companies to reduce their costs by actively assuring safer conditions has been turned on its head. On its head! As long as they can increase their premiums and reduce their liability through legislative action, they will continue to ignore their health and safety responsibilities. Sure, they'll take out some ads to the contrary, their insurance agents will take part in community safety efforts—say, safer crosswalks for schoolchildren—but these are pittances relative to what this trillion-dollar industry could do for our economy and for the well-being of millions of people. By returning to their historic role of loss prevention, insurers could incur the gratitude of everyone except the funeral and hospital industries. They could reduce the immense costs of property damage. Merely by working for more protective vehicle bumpers instead of the chrome eyebrows used now, they could save lives and dollars. Three hundred people die every year in rear-end collisions with big trucks. In dense fog and on slippery highways, bumpers can stop cars from being submarined under the backs of trucks. Even though bumpers have been proven effective in the prevention of these cases, trucks are not required by law to have them. Billions of dollars in avoidable repair bills would be saved with seven-mile-an-hour bumpers on all vehicles. The industry knows this but by and large could care less.

"Thank you, Mr. Chairman, for your patience and interest in a situation that affects your constituents every day of their lives. They will be most pleased that you have taken this bold initiative. I look forward to your questioning and that of the committee, and I particularly look forward to your subsequent examination of my colleagues just behind me who have graced us with their presence here today. For the reporters in this hearing room, I recommend that you immerse yourselves in the specifics of the appendixes I've placed in the record, which will keep your investigative talents working overtime Thank you again, Mr. Chairman."

"And thank you, Mr. Lewis, for making visible that tip of the insurance iceberg and the industry's perverse incentive, as you call it," Senator Merchant said. "My first question relates to you. In your long career building your own insurance company, have you been doing the same things you accuse your competitors of doing?"

"Yes, with a few notable exceptions here and there."

"Then with all due respect, why should we listen to you?"

"Because I have now chosen to do the right thing, which is to blow the whistle that could prevent the untold casualties and costs continually inflicted on the American people. To quote Martin Luther King, 'I am free at last, free at last.'"

"Is this new role you've fashioned for yourself going to be an advantage to your company?" the chairman asked.

"I hope it will be an advantage to all companies in all insurance lines. I hope we'll all be hiring more engineers and health specialists and fewer financial analysts."

"Thank you, Mr. Lewis. I have no further questions at this time. My colleagues will now commence their questioning."

"These advertisements you've been running in the newspapers and on television—who is paying for them?"asked Senator Prune.

"I'm paying for them, Senator. You see, I'm a very rich man."

"If you had one bit of advice for your ten CEO friends sitting here, what would it be?" asked Senator Catskill.

"Reverse the perverse incentive. If you feel you can't, then ask the government to provide uniform requirements for the entire industry. If you won't, then quit."

"Very succinct, Mr. Lewis," said Senator Foxer. "Do you have proposed legislation to 'reverse the perverse incentive'?"

"Yes indeed. A comprehensive analysis, together with a proposed statute and a section-by-section analysis, is in the appendixes for your consideration. It foresees a new day for America in terms of health, safety, economic and taxpayer efficiencies, and the innovations prompted thereby. This is big, Senator, really big. I would be delighted were you and your colleagues to take the time to absorb the practicality of my proposals and their long-term beneficial consequences, including insurance industry leadership against global warming and other effects of fossil fuel technology that could have calamitous consequences at a period in our nation's future when you and I are pushing up daisies."

Senator Sunup raised his eyebrows. "Global warming? Mr. Lewis, aren't you going rather far afield? Aren't you really proposing an insurance industry that will be a health and safety Nazi vis-à-vis its customers? Isn't this just a new tyranny of a new bottom line?"

"Hardly, Senator. Already some European insurers and reinsurers are taking global warming very seriously and lobbying their governments for energy efficiency and energy conservation policies. A great economy adjusts to save itself as well as others."

"Well, Mr. Lewis," drawled Senator Bitter, "we've got a saying down where I come from in Louisiana, and after listening to you go on and on, I'll say it. This dog don't hunt. Are you going through an end-life crisis?"

"Our world is going through an end-life crisis, Senator. I want to use what time I have left to improve my country, to make it an example for other nations to emulate, to give all the world cause to say, 'God bless America.' Congress can help mightily to make that happen."

As Peter's words rang out in the hearing room, the audience sat mesmerized. The proceedings had reached an emotional pitch seldom seen on Capitol Hill. Some of the CEOs were wiping their brows with their monogrammed handkerchiefs, and not because the room was warm. In the press section, the reporters were licking their chops in expectation of the CEOs' imminent hari-kari performance. Peter's charges were humming on the wire services and over radio and cable TV even before the questioning got underway. The story was clearly going to lead the evening network news, barring some major tragedy.

At the back of the hearing room, the attorneys for the ten CEOs were huddling in great agitation. Fortunately for them, Chairman

Merchant announced a ninety-minute lunch break, whereupon they hustled their clients into limousines and drove to a nearby corporate law firm on Pennsylvania Avenue. In a secure twelfth-floor suite, they ordered in sandwiches, soup, and drinks, and then the hoariest of the lawyers, a celebrated adviser to presidents, stood to address the CEOs.

"Gentlemen, this hearing is more than an embarrassment, more than a media riot," he declared in stentorian tones. "It is a grave danger to each of you personally. Without knowing the exact nature of Lewis's accusations, without having digested his hundreds of pages of appendixes that name names, places, and dates, we are able to counsel you only for your own legal protection, not for that of your companies."

"That's certainly an unusual statement by legal counsel," said the CEO of the country's largest health insurer. "I always like to think that the CEO and his company are the same for purposes of policy positions. To divide us from our companies is to open a huge can of worms that might lead to our compensation packages."

"Ordinarily you would be quite correct," said the hoary lead counsel, "but this isn't an ordinary situation. First, Lewis's charges are essentially unrebuttable in the setting of a congressional hearing. You can of course allude to some of the positive steps you've taken, but he has already anticipated and belittled them. Years ago, the auto company chieftains tried that before a Senate hearing in attempting to rebut a young critic who charged that they had done little to make their cars safer. The Senate committee handed them their heads. It was disastrous. Coercive legislation followed very quickly."

"There are times when the only advice is the least worst advice," said one of the younger lawyers.

"There are times when you have to be prepared for the worst by avoiding it," said another.

"The worst, gentlemen, is prosecution for perjury and imprisonment," said a third.

"What did you say?" chorused the ten CEOs.

"I am afraid, gentlemen," the hoary lead counsel intoned, "that this is the time for *you* to be afraid. You are about to enter an arena in which you are highly vulnerable. The chairman is going to play to the crowd. Our sources tell us that his questions are going to be CEO-spe-cific and company-specific, and that three other senators are prepared to follow up. There are no time limits to this hearing. Once you are up there, there is little we can do to help you. We can confer with you at the witness table, but that irritates the committee and breeds sus-picion among the reporters. It makes it seem that we have something to hide. As your attorneys, we have consulted among ourselves and come to the same conclusion as to what we must advise you to do."

"And what is that?" asked the CEO of one of the auto insurance giants.

"You must take the Fifth Amendment."

Cries of outrage filled the room: "What? You can't be serious!" "The Fifth Amendment? Are you crazy?" "We aren't criminals, sir!"

"Gentlemen," said the hoary lead counsel, "if you do not take the Fifth, you are asking for trouble. Permit me to explain. You will be under oath. The chairman doesn't want this to be a one-day hearing, so you may find yourselves testifying for days. The questions that will come at you are designed to make you perjure yourselves. We can show you some sequences if you like, but there is little time and this is our unanimous advice—the best of a bad range of options. During the uproar after the hearing concludes, your counsel will address the press and explain that the hearing was booby-trapped and that you were not given the nature of the charges so you could prepare yourselves in due time. We'll play you as the victims of a witch-hunt by a chairman desperate to save his political career. In the coming days, we'll advise you about how to reach other mem-bers of the committee through lobbying and campaign contributions so as to abort further hearings requiring your pres-ence. For now, you just have to keep a stiff upper lip. We'll provide you cover with the media as you're whisked out of the building to your limos.

"Now, here is exactly how you are to proceed when the hearing resumes this afternoon. You will make no opening statements. My associates are passing out copies of the script we've prepared for you once the questioning begins. Do not try to embellish, or you'll be deemed to have waived your right to take the Fifth. We have prefaced the actual plea with courteous remarks of a general nature, to convey your respect for the committee and your solemn obligation to your shareholders and employees. Please rehearse these words in the few minutes we have left so that you can declare them at the hearing with executive strength and forthrightness, *on advice of counsel.* This will shift the spotlight to us, and we know how to talk to the press in such situations. Some of us have represented organized crime figures before congressional committees, so we are not without experience. We are of course drawing no parallels here, merely reassuring you of our professional abilities."

It was fortunate that the CEOs had downed their lunch by this time, though to judge by the whiteness of their faces, there was no guarantee it would stay down.

Promptly at 2:00 p.m., Senator Merchant brought the hearing to order again. The CEOs were asked to take their seats at the long witness table, shoulder to shoulder. They were asked to stand. Then, with a dozen photographers clicking away, they all raised their hands and took the oath. You could have cut the suspense and tension in the room with a knife.

"Please be seated and commence with your opening statements, gentlemen," Senator Merchant said, "from left to right if you will."

"I have no opening statement, Mr. Chairman," said the first CEO.

"I have no opening statement, Mr. Chairman," said the second.

"I have no opening statement, Mr. Chairman," said the next.

By this time murmurs were coursing through the audience. Expressions of wonderment adorned the faces of the more seasoned reporters and guests, who knew just how unusual this scene was. As each of the remaining CEOs declined to make an opening statement, Chairman Merchant began to suspect that something was fishy. Business executives always had opening statements crafted to put their best feet forward, establish cordial relations with the committee, and anticipate the overall pattern of questioning.

"Very well, gentlemen," he said. "In that case, we can proceed to the questioning all the more quickly."

It took three or four questions per CEO, but inside fifteen minutes they had all taken the Fifth.

"Very well, gentlemen," the chairman repeated. "You've made your choice. You refuse to respond to charges from one of your industry's most successful executives. You'll have to live with the consequences. This hearing is adjourned!"

The audience was dumbfounded. The press raced to file the stunning story. For once, Peter was all but speechless, telling a clutch of reporters in the hallway, "I have no idea what they're up to. All I have are suspicions, which I can't share with you for just that reason. I guess we'll just have to wait and see."

And what of the chairman? He was basking in the sun of being the white hat, the good guy who launched this wave of criticism of the widely disliked insurance companies. Immediately after adjourning the hearing, he issued a statement to the effect that his staff would continue the investigation, but everyone who knew him understood that his words were pro forma. He'd milked the cow, and he had enough to last him until November, given the legs this controversy was sure to have and all the interviews he would be asked to give.

That evening the late-edition tabloids had a lot to scream about: "Top Whistle-blower's Barrage Provokes Insurance CEOs into Taking the Fifth," "New Merchants of Death, Charges Top Insurance Tycoon," "Insurance Industry Lets People Die for Profits." All three network newscasts led with the story. No one who saw the coverage that night would ever forget the spectacle of the ten CEOs standing to take the oath and then taking the Fifth. It was as indelible a visual as when the tobacco executives swore before Congress that they did not believe that smoking cigarettes causes lung cancer.

Over the next few days, the specialized insurance press bored deeper. Since most of these publications were essentially house organs, they had no trouble contacting inside sources that would level with them about what was going on. What they were told was that the only way for the industry to keep this story from exploding was to ignore it and take the brickbats. An editorial in the *Insurance Gazette* argued that turning away from the controversy was a mistake, that the industry was underestimating Peter, just as it had when he was a small auto insurer. Hadn't he already spent big bucks saturating the country with his charges before the hearing? What made them think he would stop now because ten CEOs stonewalled a Senate committee?

True to the *Gazette*'s prediction, Peter unleashed another torrent of ads filled with juicy tidbits from his appendixes and calls for further investigation. The PCC and the newly launched Insurance CUB ran with the incriminating evidence. The lecturers had fresh material. The aborning Congress Watchdog Groups demanded action from their senators and representatives. Some of the credibility groups saw how they had been betrayed. The lunchtime rallies made Peter's testimony their main theme and struck new nerves in the white-collar crowd. The sustainable sub-economy people took up the matter of cooperative self-insurance entities to break the dependency on the perversely incentivized insurance industry. Promotions took off with the hearings, and Barry decided to devote his Injustice of the Day segment to insurance abuses for the next two weeks, soliciting audience reaction in follow-up call-in shows.

It wasn't long before whistle-blowers began emerging to confirm Peter's charges in abundant detail. Files were leaked, putting a goodly portion of manufacturers and corporations on the defensive. As they tried to cope with outraged victims, trial attorneys, and hospitals, deceived professional societies and regulatory agencies, one sector after another sought to evade responsibility. It wasn't us, said the manufacturers. It wasn't us, said their wholesalers and dealers. It wasn't us, said their insurance agents when greeted with skepticism at Rotary and Kiwanis luncheons. Ministers and rabbis started sprinkling their sermons with citations from Leviticus on the subject of knowing thy neighbor to be endangered and not speaking out. Day after day, the press mined the now fabled appendixes and upped the ante, vying to deliver the most dramatic stories of the impact of the perverse incentive on regular people and their deceased or injured kin. Imagine the plight of hundreds of thousand of insurance agents inundated by millions of calls from customers who sounded like White Sox fans in 1919 pleading with Shoeless Joe Jackson to "say it ain't so."

By the end of the second week after the hearing, product liability suits were being filed right and left, and public demands for product recalls rose sharply. Manufacturers quickly scheduled expensive seminars at large urban hotels to train insurance specialists in quality control, inspections, and the wide array of safety standards and specifications in various areas. Some companies got the message and quietly began hiring more engineers and chemists and biologists. The auto insurers gave the Insurance Institute for Highway Safety an adequate contribution for a change, targeted to its crash-testing of vehicles for operating safety and bumper integrity. Long-recalcitrant insurers joined formally with their corporate compadres to expand the work of Advocates for Highway and Auto Safety. Some state insurance regulators, prodded by their attorneys general, even opened investigations.

Peter watched it all with relish and no little wonder. Global warming might be causing problems here on Earth, but apparently Hell was freezing over.

Meanwhile, back at the Redirections Ranch, the Secretariat was hard-pressed to keep up with the breakneck pace of developments and the torrent of media attention. Coverage of the Sun God festivals had peaked while the core group was meeting in Maui, with articles in the business pages, the real estate pages, the science pages, the religion pages, and even analyses by two prominent architectural critics. Ted was especially gratified by the religious furor the Sun God provoked in the televangelical world, with its hundreds of radio and TV outlets, magazines, and newsletters. Fire-and-brimstone Sunday sermons denounced such idolatry, such heresy, but viewers, listeners, and readers all over the country were getting the solar message one way or another as the media followed up with stories on the practical uses and benefits of solar energy for this generation and those to come. From the responses on Ted's Sunrise website, it was clear that people everywhere were talking about the solar festivals and touting their own solar energy uses, from heating water to powering highway signs and remote naval installations.

The Pot-In had also continued to generate headlines, and within a week of the demonstration and subsequent arrests, fifty-three members of the House and seventeen senators had signed on to Congressman Don Saul's legislation "to free industrial hemp from the Dark Ages of ignorance," as he put it. The lawmakers were angry enough at the manhandling on the reservations to get the facts, and then they got angrier. "It is remarkable what organized street action can produce when it combines facts with passion," said Congressman Saul in a CBS clip replayed during one of the core group's daily closed-circuit updates, prompting Yoko to pronounce, "This is the dawn of the Carbohydrate Revolution."

The *Time* magazine cover story had turned out to be little more than a summary in typical Timese of what the press had reported in bits and pieces during the previous two months. Nothing new, except for bringing it all together under the *Time* banner. "The business rebellion against big business is gaining unprecedented momentum and appears not to be haphazard or random. The rebels seem to be aware of each other, though to what extent is not yet known," the story concluded. The magazine flew off the newsstands, and letters to the editor poured in, many of them suggesting injustices that would invite further rebellion, some saying that the business rebels were destroying the free enterprise system, others urging the rebels to go international so as not to undermine the global competitiveness of US companies.

In the wake of the *Time* piece, *Newsweek* began preparing its own cover story. *Business Week* came out with a short article and a long editorial supporting the rebels, citing many of its past stories about corporate malfeasance, "now under challenge from within the business community itself." The *Wall Street Journal*'s editorialist begged to dissent, sniffing at the rebels as "modern-day Trojan horses bringing subversive forces into the market system under false pretenses," and urging the business community to wake up and face the tumultuous reality sweeping America. He did not specify what facing the reality meant.

As for the right-wing corporatists on talk radio, they didn't know what to make of it all, and tried to discount their increasing numbers of antagonistic callers as "first-timers on the radical fringe." Pawn Vanity sharply attacked a caller who charged that he was using the public airwaves to make millions for himself while paying nothing in return. "Possession is ninety percent of the law, and I've got possession," Pawn scoffed. "Maybe not for long, you freeloader," replied the caller before Pawn pulled the plug on him with a disgusted snicker.

Such was the pompous old order, which did not have a clue what was coming over the horizon as Barry, Phil, and Bill Cosby put the finishing touches on their plan to take back the airwaves. The corporate talking heads had no idea that they were about to be labeled Welfare Kings who fed at the trough in Washington, DC, and sponged off the public while shutting out the voices of freethinking people and showcasing their dittoheads.

Barry outlined the overall strategy, which was to use the Redirections projects to educate as many millions of people as possible as quickly as possible. On the last Wednesday in March, the lunchtime rallies would surround major television stations in fourteen cities and then watch the quandary. Would these stations report this extraordinary protest against their theft of the public airwaves, or would they ignore it and become grist for the rest of the media's holier-than-thou ridicule? The largest rally would take place at the headquarters of the Federal Communications Commission in Washington, to highlight where the authority rested to do something about the heist that had been going on since the 1927 Radio Act and the 1934 Communications Act—billions and billions of dollars owed to the people via their government but never paid because the laws allowing free use of the spectrum were written under the giant lobbying eye of the nascent radio industry. "What self-respecting business would ever give away its property?" the ralliers would demand—an argument impossible for any self-respecting capitalist to refute.

Barry and his colleagues agreed that at this point they would restrict their attack to the broadcasters' free use of the public's property and show how the rents owed could fund wholesome entertainment and educational programming. The Audience Network idea and other proposals for the sharing of daily spectrum time were deferred until an aroused public could provide an independent force—a media CUB—to counter the powerful National Association of Broadcasters lobby. Meanwhile, they would rely on the rallies, the lecturers, the new Cable CUB, and the other Redirections for a relentless buildup of public anger at being cheated. The PCC would urge Congress to hold hearings and act. Promotions would line up prominent media people and honest brokers like former FCC commissioner Nick Johnson for interviews.

Once the Congress Watchdog Groups got underway, payment for use of the public airwaves would be one of the first issues out of the box for them. They would draft legislation starting with a preamble of findings on the broadcast industry's emphasis on trivia, sports, constant weather forecasts, fluff, chitchat, and eight to nine minutes of advertising in a thirty-minute news program, at the expense of hard reporting, stories presenting different sides of controversial issues, and the news needs of the local community as ascertained from community input. The key to defeating the media powers—and they almost never lost in the nation's capital—was to pressure them and the Congress from all sides simultaneously.

The two hundred field organizers carefully recruited to enlist the two thousand core citizens for the Congress Watchdogs in each district were filing daily e-mail diaries with their nerve center in Washington. From their dispatches, it was increasingly apparent that they were finding both their feet and their voice as they moved though town and countryside looking for gathering places where people actually talked to one another—not as easy a task as it would have been fifty or a hundred years ago. These days people were glued to TV screens in public places like airports and waiting rooms, or were rushing through their sandwiches in fast-food outlets. It was too early for Little League and softball games, and bowling leagues were not very conducive to talk. For the most part, the union halls were shrouded in an air of depression, no longer home to expansive hopes. But bars were still bars, even with their ubiquitous TVs. The Elks, the VFW, the American Legion, the Shriners and Knights of Columbus still believed in person-to-person conversation. And beer. It was mostly men who frequented these places. Better bets for women were Grange meetings, potluck suppers, church functions, garden clubs, book clubs, daycare facilities, and senior centers. There were lunch counters and family-owned restaurants, and people were always chatting in barbershops and beauty salons, though jokes and gossip tended to predominate.

Adjusting to the individuation of American society, the organizers started striking up conversations with people waiting for buses and subways, construction workers on their lunch break, office workers getting some air in urban parks. People walking their dogs in these small green oases turned out to be good prospects, even if the conversation was frequently interrupted by yelps and wayward canines. The dynamic two hundred learned to seize every one-on-one opportunity while continuing to mine the group gatherings.

One chilly March evening in Buffalo, New York, an organizer named Kyle Corey went into Clancy's Cave, ordered a Bud, and sat down at a corner table. As he nursed his beer, he couldn't help overhearing an unusually animated conversation at the adjacent table, where five or six friends just happened to be spouting off on their working-class grievances and all the media coverage they'd seen on "those retired super-rich guys."

"I think some of these billionaires got grudges from years back and mean to get even by getting mean," said a guy in a Bills jacket. "I don't trust 'em as far as I could throw the Prudential Building, but it's great for us working folks while it lasts."

"You can bet it won't last, Stan," said a pale middle-aged woman with a pencil stuck behind her ear. "For twenty years I've been keeping the books for one corporation or another, and I can tell you that whenever anyone on the inside starts a dustup, they always end up cutting a deal."

"Don't jump to conclusions, Jackie. What about the Pledge the

Truth drive? It could have been just a flashy issue on that celebrity telethon a while back, but now it's a bill before Congress. And my students have learned more from a month of saying 'with liberty and justice for some' than they'd get from their textbooks in a year. Or how about those big lunchtime rallies? A friend of mine went to a lecture at his Rotary club the other night and met some people who are planning to get one going here."

"So what, Mike?" Jackie said. "It won't come to anything."

Mike pointed at the TV over the bar, where the evening news was showing footage from the day's rallies. "Just look at them, will you? These are people like us. They're talking like us. They're hard-working stiffs who want better wages, health insurance, pension protection, the whole ball of wax. They want a voice that's heard!"

"All I know," a young man in an army jacket said quietly, "is that I got my money back from an insurance company that ripped me off when I was in Iraq, because some law students helped me win in small claims court for free. They told me some billionaire lawyer from Texas was funding them. Okay, maybe it's not such a big deal, but it shows a feeling for the little guy, and that's not a feeling we get from the politicians. They love us when we're heading out to war and forget us when we come back."

The woman sitting next to him put a muscled arm around his shoulder. "Honey, that's the god's truth. But listen, maybe it *is* a big deal. You know why I think something's going on? I keep the radio on low on my bus routes, and the Bush Bimbaugh types are having kittens. They're going nuts over these rich old guys, calling them senile, traitors to capitalism, threats to their beloved Wal-Mart. I don't know, there are lots of pieces here, but I'm watching the news and reading the paper every day. It's almost exciting."

"Hey, Ernie, how about another round over here," Mike called to the bartender.

"Hell, yes," Stan said, "and it's on me this time. We'll drink to the revolution of the super-rich, as my union boss calls it. May they blow the whole rotten system to hell."

Kyle picked up his beer and went over to the group. "Mind if I join you?" An hour later, Mike O'Malley found himself signing on for the New York State Twenty-seventh District Congress Watchdog Group, and the Iraq vet was giving it serious thought. When Kyle got home that night, he described his visit to Clancy's Cave in his e-mail diary and sent it off to the nerve center, where other organizers read it and reported that they were hearing similar spontaneous conversations more and more, often vehement and studded with four-letter words, including the name of the president.

When these reports were conveyed to the core group at the next day's closed-circuit conference, there was cautious optimism. If ordinary people were talking about the Pledge and the PCS and so on, the Redirections were starting to get through. "The revolt of the masses," said Bernard, recalling his radical father's words, "always starts in the bars and cafés, where people can think freely without the big bosses looking over their shoulders. What we need now is a Tom Paine-type pamphlet to get into millions of hands. What about going to Dick Goodwin on this? He did a great job on the Beatty campaign. He knows how to bring home what the working classes and the dispossessed are going through, with just the right mix of outrage, historical allusions, patriotism, and appeals to enlightened self-interest, all in marvelously inspirational language." Bernard's proposal met with immediate support, and Barry said he would call Dick right away.

Throughout March, Warren devoted the bulk of the closed-circuit updates to the Clean Elections Party and the looming state deadlines. This project would be the sternest test so far of Recruitment and Promotions. Getting the word out for petitioners, organizers, and candidates in the selected districts meant relentless media exposure and website action. As the résumés flowed in, Recruitment had to process, reject, or accept for almost immediate deployment. Attorneys were standing by, ready to move the moment they received word from one state after another.

Electoral Reform put out a special call for someone to serve as titular head and public face of the Clean Elections Party. Recruitment proposed five good prospects, and Leonard interviewed them, deciding for reasons of credibility to choose two individuals from opposite ends of the political spectrum: Phyllis Schlafly, outspoken social conservative and longtime critic of "dirty-money elections," in her phrase, and John Bonifaz, a Harvard-trained lawyer who had written widely that the "wealth primary," as he called it, was unconstitutional. Each agreed to curtail their other commitments and devote half their time to the CEP for the next eight months.

By the end of the third week of March, Congress was beginning to feel the Redirectional heat. According to the *Corporate Crime Reporter (CCR)*, the House and Senate Appropriations Committees were beefing up budgets for enforcing the laws against corporate crime, some by as much as 50 percent, after years of stagnation or actual decline in funding for the various regulatory agencies and the Justice Department. It was a sign, said the *CCR*, that key politicians had put their fingers to the wind and sensed an approaching gale.

Congressional eyebrows were further raised by reports from their home offices that local service clubs—Kiwanis, Rotary, Lions, League of Women Voters, etc.—were inviting a new breed of organizers and lecturers to their weekly meetings, perhaps at the urging of maverick members, perhaps out of sheer boredom with the usual fare, or perhaps because of the admirable comportment, cogent observations, and common sense of the speakers. Whatever the reason, the reception accorded these visitors was thoughtful and largely positive. The audiences seemed to feel that change was long overdue and that the greed of the big boys was out of control, as no one understood better than the small businessmen and businesswomen who made up much of the membership of these groups. At the close of their presentations, the lecturers took questions, and the first was usually "Who's paying you to do what you're doing?" To which they truthfully replied, "Some billionaires who love their country, by which they mean loving the people of their country. They want nothing more than to give back. That's all I know about them."

Over at First-Stage Improvements, Max, Sol, and Jeno were deliberately keeping things under the media radar, in part to give the wide and deep infrastructure time to become established and operational, and in part because their experts from Analysis couldn't agree on how and when to go forward with each improvement. They were all champions of justice, they all had a record of working to "make human beings more human," in Benjamin Franklin's words, but they were used to puffing on their pipes and pondering for hours in their armchairs. Mark Green, a veteran mobilizer of policy wonks, was brought in to expedite their deliberations, and they soon found themselves on a fast assembly line. Max, Sol, and Jeno were hard taskmasters with a shortened concept of time. For now, though, until the groundwork was firmly in place and the fire they'd lit under their eggheads produced some heat, they agreed that the Wal-Mart campaign would be their project's standard-bearer.

On the last Monday in March, Lob Corsage sat in the comfortable dining room of the Cato Institute's fine new building on Massachusetts Avenue, reviewing his notes for the speech he was about to give to a luncheon meeting of Institute fellows and guests. A libertarian-conservative think tank heavily funded by business types, the Cato Institute was so active in its various convocations that it seemed to be a fixture on C-SPAN. Today the dining room was crowded, as Corsage was a well-known analyst who had sponsored many a conference of his own, bringing together liberals of various stripes to ponder the current and the coming. His speech was titled "A Progressive Look at the Progressive Revival."

As the diners were finishing their excellent meals, Corsage rose to acknowledge the spicy but kind introduction by Cato's president, and then he commenced.

"Ladies and gentlemen, my words today flow from my hope for a progressive revival in this great land of ours. I venture to call it a hope, and not an illusion or delusion, because of encouraging signs from many quarters over the last few months. Allow me to enumerate them.

"First, the polls. In part because of the recent rash of corporate scandals, the public is demanding stronger regulation and expressing a lack of confidence in business. More and more, this response is cutting across party lines, reflecting the hits taken by workers, pension funds, and small investors in all geographic regions—red and blue states alike, if you will.

"Second, there is growing anti-corporate activity on the campuses—always a bellwether. The students are increasingly critical of the outsourcing of health insurance and the high cost of student loans, textbooks, and housing. Since the protest is proceeding significantly from economic insecurity, it isn't as ideological as it was in the sixties or as it still is in the environmental area.

"Third, there are more bestsellers among populist books criticizing plutocrats, oligarchs, and runaway executives with their outrageous self-determined overcompensation. Sales still don't match those of conservative tomes, but they're climbing. In a similar vein, progressive documentaries are breaking attendance records and reaching larger audiences through DVD sales. Your kind of documentaries hardly exist. We dominate in the marketplace of comedy and satire as well. And just look at the growth of Air America, which is taking on more and more radio stations to compete with the right-wing shows.

"Fourth, organized labor has split into two camps. I interpret this as a sign of determination on the progressive side to put more muscle and money behind organizing workers in low-paying, nonoutsourceable sectors like fast food, healthcare, and maintenance. Wal-Mart is feeling more heat about its low wage policies, its pressure on domestic suppliers to move to China, and its hollowing out of Main Street, USA.

"Fifth, for a long time now, progressives have been able to put people on the streets by the tens of thousands, in Seattle, New York, San Francisco, right here in Washington, on the big issues of civil rights, women's rights, gay rights, arms control, globalization, and war. The lunchtime rallies taking place all over the country even as I speak are only the latest instance.

"In summary, things are getting better for progressives every day. The tides are turning. I'll leave it there so we can move to what for me is always the most enlightening part of the program, your questions. Thank you."

"Mr. Corsage, you have a wide-ranging knowledge of liberal programs and have written extensively about the current liberal agenda," said a woman from the Heritage Foundation. "At the federal level, what three bills, what three regulations, and what three cases do you expect to win over the next two years?"

"I'm afraid that's too detailed a prognostication for me, ma'am. I'm not clairvoyant. All I know is that liberal groups file regulatory petitions and lawsuits and get their friends in Congress to introduce bills all the time. Which ones will prevail, I can't tell you."

"Well then, can you tell us which three pending bills, petitions, and lawsuits you consider most important?" the woman persisted.

"I'm sorry, but I don't want to be specific. If I were, you'd all laugh because you wouldn't think any of them had a snowball's chance in hell. Rest assured, however, that the seeds are there and will someday bear fruit."

"A bitter fruit, no doubt," she sniffed.

A fellow of the American Enterprise Institute raised his hand. "Mr. Corsage, this 'revival' you speak of—have you seen any tangible changes coming out of Washington with regard to progressive objectives, or do your remarks simply refer to a growing political capacity?"

"I was speaking of the latter. You have to have political capacity, as you put it, to bring about these changes."

"Now that we are speaking primarily about capacity, do you have any firm indicators, like increased union membership, that would make your claims about a coming progressive revival more concrete?" asked a lobbyist for the National Association of Manufacturers.

"As far as I'm aware, union membership is still declining, but there is a growing emergence of ethical business organizations like the Social Venture Network and the recently established People's Chamber of Commerce. More and more consumer cooperatives and organic farms are selling their produce profitably in urban and suburban markets. A lively group called Progressive Democrats of America is pressing the regular Democratic Party to take more progressive positions on a living wage, universal health insurance, and a crackdown on corporate crime, fraud, abuse, and privilege."

All eyes turned to a man who stood up at the front of the room. "Listening to you, Mr. Corsage, I'm surprised that you haven't mentioned the recent surge of antibusiness attacks by certain retired chief executives—the subject of a *Time* magazine cover. I trust you are familiar with the wide range of assaults reported in the press. Is all that part of your 'progressive revival'?"

"Mr. Dortwist, I've been reading the same reports you have, and I'm absolutely astonished and delighted by what these gentlemen are doing, but I have no idea where all this activity is coming from, how enduring it's likely to be, or what the big picture may be. That's why I omitted most of these recent agitations from my remarks today. I can tell you that the liberal advocacy groups I'm close to have never been contacted by these people in any way."

Brovar sat down and instantly e-mailed this bit of information to his list, noting that the lack of contact between the business rebels and the usual liberal suspects could not be accidental, and that it suggested a wholly new force with an ambitious and confident mind of its own.

The question period concluded. Waiters served dessert and coffee as conversations sprang up at each of the tables for ten. No one was talking about Lob Corsage's remarks, not even at his own table near the podium. Clearly, the guests were neither interested in nor worried about the prospect of any "progressive revival." The talk was all about their own work, the agendas they were moving through Congress, upcoming publications on deregulation, possibilities for raising more business donations, their own side business ventures, and their junkets to Bermuda, Hawaii, and Baja, all expenses paid by a variety of trade associations. The corporate think tank business was alive and well and convinced that the future could only be more bullish.

Lob Corsage finished his coffee, gathered his notes together, and looked around at his tablemates. The way their conversations veered away from the luncheon topic had not escaped him. He left crestfallen, wondering whether his candor in front of an adversarial crowd was a mistake. After all, the nation's capital was above all the place where perception was reality.

As March drew to a close, the Secretariat kept methodical tabs on the accelerating pace of the Redirections. The CUB groups in particular were moving along with commendable speed, and much of the credit was due to the backup dynamos, Recruitment and Promotions. Recruitment completed the daunting task of culling the 13 million responses to Patriotic Polly for likely prospects. George called Warren and asked to borrow Bill Hillsman, who created a clever advertising campaign that helped produce a rate of return for the CUB mailings in excess of 5 percent—even better than George had hoped. The renovated hotel was filling up with new and seasoned public advocates for workers, consumers, investors, policyholders, and other key groups that had gone unrepresented because of the absence of grassroots power in Washington, DC.

Thanks largely to Recruitment, the quality of the project personnel at all levels was impressive. In the weeks since Maui Three, Seymour Depth had assembled a staff of eight hundred interviewers—themselves carefully recruited—and assigned them to the core members on an as-needed basis after training them intensively in a multi-stage screening system that was a wonder to behold. Not every applicant for the thousands of open project positions was expected to go through the entire sequence. Some were so well known to the core group or by general reputation that their selection was a foregone conclusion. What they had done spoke for itself.

As for the rest, when the résumés and videotapes came in to Recruitment headquarters—and they came by the ton, from word of mouth, advertisements, websites, and the like, forwarded by project staff to safeguard the core group's collective identity—the first task was to apply the basic criteria established for all hires, then those tailored to specific jobs. For example, field organizers had to meet different second-level criteria than did attorneys or analysts or promoters. Equipped with these yardsticks, Seymour's staff weeded out the obvious rejectees and then called the references of those who remained—a tiny minority, fewer than one in twenty. Although applicants obviously listed references from whom they expected strong recommendations, such people could usually be counted on for candor under questioning—"You wouldn't want her to be employed in a job she doesn't like or isn't suited for, would you?"—and it was fairly easy to draw them out if they seemed reticent at any point. Recruitment found that the most sterling of the applicants usually had recommendations from top-flight people—it took one to know one. It was hoped that more and more positions would be filled through referrals from those already working on the various Redirections projects.

The next step was to check out the applicant's background and the veracity of the résumé. If that cleared, the interview process commenced. It was a six-hour process, with forty-five minutes for lunch with one or more of the interviewers. The first interview was a one-on-one, followed by a two-on-one, then a three-on-one. Rare were the individuals who could fake it when the interviewers pushed them politely but hard. There were telltale signs. If an applicant was asked, "How do you take criticism?" and answered, "Okay, if it's con- structive," there was a good chance that he or she was excessively sensitive to criticism and rough-and-tumble work pressures. The preferred response was something like, "I appreciate criticism because it helps me improve and keeps me on my toes."

Other questions: What do you read regularly? What books have you read in the last year? What do you watch on television? Who has had the greatest influence on your development up to this point? What would you like to be doing ten years from now, twenty years from now? What would you most like to be remembered for? Do you have a temper? (Few said yes, but their answers invited follow-up questions that could be illuminating: You mean you're never moody? You mean nothing gets you angry about what's going on in this world?) Do you ever get discouraged, and what do you do about it? Do you ever expe- rience stress that might affect your work? What are your strengths for this job, and what are your weaknesses? What is most important in doing this job— integrity, character, personality, experience, or skill?" If the reply was "All five," the applicants were asked to rank them in importance and explain what they understood to be the difference between character and personality. Finally, they were asked what they had done to advance social justice, on issues large or small.

All the interviewers were skilled interpreters of body language— calmness, anxiety, nervous tics, blushing, eye movements, clammy hands—but they also understood that many highly proficient people might have any or all of these apparent negatives. It went without saying that applicants with disabilities enjoyed equal protection under the law and were considered strictly on merit. Privacy require- ments forbade inquiries about family obligations that might impede the most capable of applicants simply because they were caring for a sick parent or child out of loyalty and love. Often they volunteered such information, and if they were deemed otherwise qualified and the job permitted, they were hired to work from home or allowed to set their own hours. No one had to explain to Seymour Depth that justice required flexibility.

For those who survived the interview process, Recruitment arranged social occasions—barbecues, picnics, volleyball games, con- certs—where they were likely to let down their hair and reveal more about their attitudes and personalities. The culminating event was an evening of good food and drink followed by a freewheeling discussion and debate among the applicants on the signal issues of the contem- porary economy, the purpose being to assess their curiosity, their thirst to learn, their openmindedness, and their willingness to correct their mistakes without hesitation or defensiveness. At the end of the evening, each applicant was handed a sheet of paper with a sentence at the top that read, "The maldistribution of wealth, power, and influ- ence in the United States stems from ____ having too much power and ____ having too little." They were asked to fill in the blanks with their top three choices and write a short essay on their recommenda- tions for a fairer redistribution, as a way of finding out whether or to what extent they were grounded in a political philosophy.

By this stage there had been dropouts, leaving a hard core who had demonstrated their qualifications and commitment. Before making the job offer, the interviewers bluntly put one final question to each applicant: "Did anyone ask you to infiltrate this organization, and if so, what did you say to them?" The theory was that the very directness of the question, while not a foolproof screen, would elicit responses—hesitancy, facial expressions, body language—that could be closely evaluated through the intuition and judgment of the interviewers. Thus far, in all the hirings, Recruitment had received no feedback on any infiltration, but Seymour Depth knew that the likelihood would increase with each passing week.

The superb job that Recruitment was doing daily was a testament to the core group's conviction that it all started and ended with the quality of the people on board, something they had learned over and over in their many years of running their own organizations and companies. Nothing was more important during these building days when a fresh new power was being released and taking institutional root all over the country. The days were filled with meticulous preparation and energizing controversy. As more and more inner-city schools adopted the revised Pledge of Allegiance, the communities around each school exploded with debates. The press had a field day covering the story and editorializing about it pro and con—no advertising money at stake, raw emotion on display day after day, and plenty of graphics illustrating the harsh reality of "with liberty and justice for some." It was an amazing innovation in social provocation—with more to come, if Bill Gates Sr. and Joe Jamail had anything to say about it.

At the same time, the fiercely energetic Bill Gates was hitting critical mass with his project to run corporations for elective office as "persons." He had located seven companies that met the legal requirements for age, background, residency, and US citizenship. His staff attorneys began preparing for the inevitable attempts by state election officials to block these candidacies. A group of artists who had responded to Yoko's call was brainstorming on memorable names for the corporate candidates and working on a theatrical format for the news conference that would introduce them to the public next month.

The personal incorporation movement was also going like gang-busters. Already, six hundred thousand employed and self-employed people had filled out Delaware Incorporation Papers, negotiating their conversion either with the help of free counsel or with a simple soft-ware program announcing their "business purpose."

Not to be outdone, Joe was overseeing the geometric increase in small claims court litigation against the nation's largest corpora-tions, 250 of them at last count. The suits numbered in the tens of thousands as complainants' grievances poured in and the PCS went into high gear. The formerly obscure small claims courts themselves were astounded, not just by their expanded dockets but by all the media attention and the flood of calls from the big corporate law firms. The fat-cat attorneys were asking questions like "What is your procedure for removing these cases to the county superior courts?"—much more costly to the plaintiffs—and "Can motions to dismiss be transmitted by fax, or is a personal appearance required?" All over the country, the local press was making small claims court a regular beat.

The more intricate Joe's spider web became, the more he liked the challenge—he was a born scrapper. His web was beginning to catch one systematic fraud after another perpetrated by banks, insurance companies, HMOs, car dealers, payday loaners, rent-to-own gougers, mortgage scammers, unscrupulous landlords, and greedy credit card companies, with all their one-sided contracts full of charges, penal-ties, and deceptions. The companies began to present dismissal motions based on fine-print binding arbitration clauses, and the small claims court judges did not like this maneuver one bit. More and more default judgments were issued against corporate defen-dants who failed to appear. Big business was learning what justice meant when the fleeced, the injured, the excluded, and the penniless had access to it. Joe even filed half a dozen small claims of his own to get a better feel for the process, and of course to get more press.

The spider kept spinning his strands, and the web kept growing. Sixteen other spiders were busily at work adding to webs of their own. It was time for Maui Four.

CHAPTER 8

Bill Joy arrived at the hotel two days early to scout out the premises with the latest technology and his own sixth sense. There were no overt signs of intrusion, but he wasn't taking any chances. He swept the entire place with the most advanced debugger yet developed, one that could even detect parabolic microphones. He chatted up the management and staff on homespun topics, casually delving into the personal lives of the waiters, housekeepers, and gardeners. Luckily it was a small hotel. He fancied himself an excellent cook and easily struck up conversations with Ailani and the kitchen staff.

At his urging, the core group took additional precautions to get through the Maui airport unrecognized. Newman and Cosby wore the same camouflage that had worked for them last time. Phil wore a fake mustache and a broad-brimmed hat. Ross wore sunglasses and a mohair skullcap. Yoko wore a Stetson, and Ted wore a Celtics sweatshirt. Warren wore his unassuming, folksy persona and disarming smile.

Assembling in the dining room during a glorious evening sunset, the core group exchanged hugs and greetings in jet-lagged delight. Bernard made a toast, presenting them with another pearl of wisdom from his collection of quotations, this one from Reinhold Niebuhr: "Man's capacity for justice makes democracy possible, but man's inclination to injustice makes democracy necessary." They all clinked glasses and sat down to a working dinner to follow up on the naming of the core group. Conversation flowed easily over the usual delicious Hawaiian fare. Bernard said that on reflection he thought they should drop the "Patriotic" and just call themselves "The Meliorists' Society." Max felt that the possessive plural had undesirable connotations of ownership. He suggested that "The Society of Meliorists" might be a more mellifluous arrangement of the words. Bill Cosby agreed it sounded smoother that way but was afraid it conveyed more a sense of some secret society than of the betterment of society. In the end, the consensus was to use "Meliorist" in the singular as an adjective: the Meliorist Society. Barry would have Promotions complete a publicity plan in April but hold it in abeyance until the core group decided to go public, or was exposed and made to go public.

After dinner, they repaired to the conference room and commenced a one-hour period of silence. By this time they were all enthusiastic converts to this ingenious idea of sitting elbow to elbow in disciplined contemplation. It was strangely competitive and trusting at the same time. It gave them a sense of mental order and a focused overview of recent activities. No one wandered or doodled. Everyone was absorbed in intense concentration, occasionally jotting down notes and reminders. Now more than ever, they needed intellectual rigor and clarity of vision and purpose. After all, in less than thirteen weeks, they had set the country on fire in the best sense. They had laid the groundwork for a whole array of new populist institutions. Above all, they had set in motion a momentous redirection of their country's inverted priorities and started it on the path to becoming a sane, elevating society. But that was the easy part. Now that the established rule of the few was being challenged on so many fronts, the dynamics would accelerate and grow more hazardous and complicated. At Maui Four they were nearing the transition from seeding the tools and institutions of democratic power to effecting fundamental change across the board in an epic confrontation with the powers that be.

When the hour was up, Warren exhaled deeply and looked around the table at his silent colleagues. "Time for all good Meliorists to hit the hay," he said with a wink.

In the morning Warren called the meeting to order promptly at eight. The first item on the agenda was whether the Redirection projects should lock in with existing citizen groups that had been working on many of these same objectives for years.

Joe was quick to oppose the idea. "I say no to allying ourselves with groups that would surely start sticking their noses into our plans, thus jeopardizing our security and the all-important factor of surprise. They'd also want to participate in our decisions, thus compromising our essential independence and speed of action. Most of these groups aren't remotely on the same wavelength or accelerated timetable that we are. And besides, by not hooking up with them, we give them truthful deniability, which will convey to the media that totally new energies are in play here. The media loves new energies, or even the mere perception of them. Remember when the right-wing evangelicals came out to defeat a sitting congressman from the South in a primary contest back in 1980? Man, did the media balloon their power after that. But the biggest argument against any lock-in is that there's not much in the way of assistance or influence that these groups, even without their baggage, can add to our efforts. Actually, they may help us more by being on the outside and jumping on the bandwagon later. I rest my case."

"I think it's an airtight one, Joe," said Ted to nods all around the table. "As usual, the King of Torts carries the day."

"All right, then," Warren said, "let's move on to another subject. I've asked Bill Joy, who has been listening and observing for a month now, to make a few remarks."

"Thank you, Warren. Let me start with a question. Have any of you read an article of mine that was published in *Wired* magazine in 2000, with the somewhat presumptuous title 'Why the Future Doesn't Need Us'?" Only Ted raised his hand. "I see. Well, I'll get to it in a minute, but first I'd like you to consider the omnibus Redirection you've called First-Stage Improvements. I emphasize 'First-Stage,' which includes economic equality, healthcare, energy, food, housing—in short, the basics of a decent livelihood and material dignity. No doubt you've contemplated many further improvements, but I understand that to win the people's support and give them a secure base, the First Stage is not only critical but a precondition for any Second Stage.

"Now, to my article. Developing faster than anticipated in most quarters are three technologies that I call GNR—genetics, nanotechnology, and robotics. Through genetic engineering, it is now possible to change the very nature of nature. Nanotechnology, or the technology of matter at the molecular or atomic level, is sure to have unintended consequences that we can't begin to foresee. Robots and computers are able to reprogram and replicate themselves to a degree that suggests they will one day sever their dependence on human control. These technologies threaten the survival of the human species, if not the planet's organisms and ecosystems in their entirety. All I ask of you in these overwhelmingly busy times is to read the article, which should take about an hour, and archive it in your minds. If nothing else, it may heighten your sense of urgency about accomplishing the objectives of the First Stage. It should also give you a sense of the vast scope of the stateless multinational corporations that are the main progenitors of GNR research, development, and application. GNR is bereft of legal and ethical constraints, and there is no countervailing power to restrain it, as was the case with the doomsday weapons of the Soviet Union and the United States in the days of Mutually Assured Destruction. With GNR, the commercial motivation rules—and God help us. I recede to listen further."

A chill descended on the room, though the sun was shining brightly through the huge windows. "Frightening," Max said finally. "I'll make your article a priority as soon as I get home."

Warren nodded soberly. "We all will, and we thank you for the wake-up call, Bill. I won't even attempt a smooth transition from doomsday back to our agenda. We'll just go on to the next item. Our epicenter billionaires have been busy thinking up proposals, and of the several dozen that have been forwarded to the Secretariat, three appear to be particularly promising.

"My old friend Jerome Kohlberg suggests that we organize a buyout of General Motors, whose stock is approaching a thirteen-year low, with a valuation a fraction that of young Google. His argument goes like this. GM is a company mired in technological stagnation. Its obsession with quarterly returns leads it into short-sighted production strategies, so that it gets caught with large inventories of gas-guzzling SUVs, for example, at a time of high gasoline prices. Its top executives are mediocre and unable to rationalize the company's multilayered bureaucracy or change its tradition of subordinating engineering and scientific talent to the powertrain and marketing departments. Yet with all that, GM is close to number one in sales in China, the fastest-growing vehicle market in the world, and is still about the largest motor vehicle manufacturer worldwide. As such, it has major potential to lead the global auto industry and turn it in the direction of an Earth-friendly motor vehicle fleet—clean engines and clean fuel, new safety and energy efficiency standards, materials that are degradable at the end of a vehicle's life cycle. It could also foster the mass transit market aggressively, since it has long had manufacturing and conversion capability in this area.

"Jerome believes that taking GM over and turning it around would be the greatest environmental, geopolitical, economic, and health and safety advance in American history. When I called him about his proposal, he volunteered to head the buyout effort—after all, his firm pioneered the whole takeover business and still leads the field—but he added that GM is a big fish with a powerful tail and he would never consider going after it without the full backing of what he senses is our entire group. He's been reading the newspapers and watching television just like everyone else. 'Think of it, Warren,' he said. 'No more begging this company to change. No more futile attempts to regulate it or sue it. It would be *ours to direct.* What's good for GM *would* be good for the country!'"

Warren paused and shuffled through some papers until he found the one he wanted. "Jerome's proposal contains a postscript that I'm going to read to you because it dovetails so intriguingly with an earlier idea of Sol's. 'For a relatively achievable sum of capital, either through private equity acquisitions or leveraged buyouts, we could create our own sub-economy of companies in each sector of industry and commerce and then make these growing concerns models of the kind of business practices we want, unleash them as prototypes of innovation, foresight, and responsibility. Good PR and marketing backup would attract the finest business talents in the land, and colorful branding would attract consumers. Again, no more begging, no more trying to regulate, no more shareholders or outside reformers engaging in protracted and pointless litigation. These companies will be ours to direct, in manufacturing, banking, insurance, energy, timber, housing, tourism, food, drugs, healthcare, retail chains, finance, transportation, agribusiness, real estate—an entire sub-economy! Talk about leverage!'"

"Talk about thinking outside the box!" Ted exclaimed.

"Brilliant but redundant," Sol grumped.

"A note of caution," interjected Barry. "I thought we were confining ourselves to initiatives that we can get up and running on their own in a year's time. Wouldn't you say that the GM proposal is unlikely to reach that stage by the end of 2006?"

"Maybe we'll want to extend the year for important projects like this one," Yoko suggested. "After all, we didn't know what we were getting into when we started, and developments have already exceeded our expectations."

"Let's review the other two proposals before discussing time frames," Warren said. "The next one came separately from four billionaires who all wanted to do something about the price of gasoline, heating oil, and natural gas. Americans are in an uproar over what they believe to be gouging, collusion, and governmental indifference greased by oil industry types around the president and the vice-president. Businesses small and large are wondering what adjustments they'll have to make and what moves they'll have to forgo. There are reports that people might freeze to death this winter because the low-income energy assistance program is so woefully underfunded. Hundreds of billions of dollars are pouring into the coffers of the oil industry. Record hyper-profits are being reported each quarter. To add insolence to injury, the president is pushing to liquidate and privatize Amtrak. The common rallying cry from our four epicentrists is 'Go after the oil companies and the American people will be forever in your debt.'

"The third and last proposal is to put out an old-fashioned four-page newspaper with big headlines and lots of pictures, to be distributed at thousands of busy intersections between four p.m. and six thirty, by paperboys and papergirls shouting, 'Extra, extra, read all about it!'just like in the good old days." Warren glanced around the table. As he had anticipated, this idea struck a chord and brought nostalgic smiles to the faces of his graybeards.

Phil snapped his fingers. "Why not connect 'Read all about it!' with taking on the oil companies' greedy adventurism at the expense of the working people of our country, not to mention the poor and unemployed? The media will go nuts. Maybe the Posterity Project can recruit these street-corner gangs. What do you say, Bernard? For starters, I bet you'll find plenty of interested kids at the Pledge schools, and this could be a great way of stirring up some enthusiasm for your Egalitarian Clubs too. The Congress Watch-dogs will also come in handy here, as will the energy CUBs. It's all beginning to fit together, isn't it? The pieces of the democracy puzzle are falling into place. Yes!"

"It looks like there's a consensus on 'Read all about it!' and the oil companies," Warren said. "As for how long it will take to get the General Motors project to a point of self-sustaining momentum, that's open to discussion, but before I get back to Jerome, I think we need our own report from Analysis on objectives, cost, timeline, and consequences."

"Clearly this project will long outlast the year just in its conception and initiation," Max said, "so the prior question is what we can do at this early stage to put a foray into General Motors on a secure financial and managerial foundation that will allow it to mature and achieve results. I agree with Warren that we need an analysis before we can answer this question, and that in itself will take some time. For example, there are two corporate raiders who already have sizable positions in GM and are pressing the company to take steps that they believe will increase share value—but what steps, and what impact would they have on Jerome's takeover plan? This is one of the host of things we have to know even to make a preliminary judgment."

Warren was about to follow up on Max's remarks when Patrick Drummond glided into the conference room, passed him a note, and glided out again. Warren scanned it and then read it aloud. "'The Secretariat has received word that the *Washington Post* is assigning its regional reporters to a story on "the average person's response to the growing upheaval against big business." The *Post*'s editors are trying to get a feel for what has changed on the ground for regular people. Do they get a better hearing when they complain about a product or service, or when they contact their members of Congress, or when they have a dispute with their HMOs? If not, or if none of those situations pertain, do they expect to get a better shake in the foreseeable future because of this upheaval, or do they think it's just a high-level struggle between two business philosophies? The *Post* expects to publish a long front-page story a week from Sunday.'"

"It seems a bit early for a story like that," Leonard observed. "Our ground game is just getting underway, and apart from Joe's small claims extravaganza, our initiatives haven't produced many concrete results for individuals as yet. I wonder what criteria they're using to define 'the average person.' Let's hope for a representative sample of the millions of people who support us, because the story will help shape public perceptions of what we're doing, and may speed the pace of our opponents' response. Not to mention that we can expect lots more such articles at the local and regional level once the *Post* inaugurates the genre."

"Maybe we should collect this kind of anecdotal information for ourselves and use it on our new democracy networks," Ross suggested. "It would be a rich source for features, news segments, documentaries, and magazine shows. What do you think, Barry?"

"Of course, great idea. It should be an ongoing adjunct to our entire Redirectional drive. And let's not forget the print media."

"We know you won't, Barry," Warren said. "I'm going to open up the floor to general discussion shortly, but first I want to review the budget situation with you. And remember that full details are always available to you on demand. Assuming a fifteen-billion-dollar budget for the year—and it looks very likely to be available, since most of it is already in—we're on track and in good shape to cover the rising curve of expenditures we expect in coming months. In the three months that have passed since Maui One, we've expended two billion dollars, which includes salaries, rents, advertising, some prepaid television and radio time, the costs of setting up the Congress Watchdogs and the like, and the cost of the CUB mailings that are inundating the postal system as we speak, and will continue to inundate it for the next two months. Our in-house auditors are well trained and motivated to keep track not just of how much we spend but of what we're receiving in return. So far that's been relatively easy because the returns are largely quantitative—the number of people and buildings and other resources that comprise our various projects. Soon the evaluation will become qualitative as well— results, impact, changes.

"Okay, my friends, your turn. What's on your formidable minds?"

"I wish to inform my sister and brothers," George announced sonorously, "that on April seventeenth—which happens to be tax day this year, since the fifteenth falls on a weekend—I shall be delivering a major address before the American Society of Newspaper Editors convention in Washington, DC, on the topic of chronic inefficiencies in corporate capitalism as compared with efficiencies in governmental programs. Once and for all, I shall puncture the hubris that has fostered one of the most entrenched myths in the world, and a very dangerous one at that. C-SPAN will certainly cover the event, but I trust that Barry will bring it to tens of millions of people here and abroad through his networks and other media outlets."

"With the greatest journalistic pleasure, George. Just get me a copy of your speech forty-eight hours in advance and we'll wake the world."

"I have an announcement too," said Bill Gates. "Next week, the first People Are Corporations jamborees will take place in cities all over the nation. The gatherings will be boisterous with a spirit of liberation. Hundreds of people will be freed by incorporation to enjoy the same evasive powers as the big boys, the same lax tax laws, the same ease of escape into bankruptcy, the same privilege to use parents and children—holding companies and subsidiaries—to protect and enlarge their profits, bolster their immunities, and avoid accountability. These new corporate people will be demanding corporate welfare, from which there is much to choose. They'll take tax-deductible trips to the Bahamas or other havens where they can rent postbox cubbyholes to reduce their federal income taxes. Since they have eternal life, they can't be subjected to an estate tax, they'll argue. They'll start deducting any expenses incurred while lobbying their elected representatives or suing other corporations. They'll clamor for corporate 'incentives' to remain in the state where they're working, and they'll threaten to move en masse to another state if they don't get them. They'll have standing to sue in cases where standing is denied mere mortals. And that's just the tip of the legal and political double standard that applies to corporations as compared to real people.

"Thanks to Yoko, I've got a team of terrific artists and playwrights collaborating on skits that will dramatize all this at the jamborees. I swear we're going to turn American corporate jurisprudence on its head. If we can't force the corporations to clear out of the category of persons, then we'll turn persons into corporations, with all the special privileges and immunities that in effect make a mockery of the preamble to the Constitution. It's not 'We the People' who call the shots in the United States, it's 'We the Corporations'—yes, including Microsoft, but don't tell Bill Jr. I said so."

Jeno laughed. "Well, it's not as if all of us haven't been involved in corporations in one way or another, but as we know, there's a right way and a wrong way to run them. Which reminds me to say that the report on corporate welfare I promised during the launch of the PCC has been delayed. Sorry, but it's been more difficult than I expected to collect data on scores of little-known but very costly programs and abatements."

"I'll bet it has," Bill Gates said. "Take all the time you need to make your report exhaustive, Jeno. Meanwhile, there's no shortage of corporate shenanigans for us to examine."

"To come at the subject of corporate shenanigans in a slightly different way," Bernard said, "I've been noticing that more and more people are coming forward as ethical whistle-blowers. I realize that we have a network of pro bono attorneys to represent them if they're fired or sued, but that's defense. Since all our off-spring groups are encouraging people to stand tall and speak out, we need some positive reinforcement for those courageous Americans who do. I've long believed that moral courage is rarer than physical courage. For one thing, physical courage is often instantaneous—not always, of course, witness Officer Serpico of the NYPD—with no time to think of all the pros or cons before the act of bravery occurs. General George Patton once described battlefield courage as 'fear plus five minutes.' With moral courage, you have time to think of the harmful consequences to yourself, your employment, your family, your standing with less courageous peers, the loneliness and ostracism of it all as the headlines, if there are any, ebb. And still people of moral courage step forward with information known to dozens or hundreds of others who stay put and remain silent.

"I propose that we establish a moral courage award for the many deserving persons—perhaps thousands a year—who exhibit bravery in situations arising out of our Redirectional efforts. There would be public ceremonies in the appropriate localities, institutionalizing recognition of these fine Americans and putting the corporate world on notice that they're not alone, that they're backed by a powerful network that will protect them and help them find better jobs than they had before. It will be a way of saying very clearly, 'Let the harassers beware.' Moreover, an award for people who bring their conscience to work will produce more whistle-blowers, which will make organizations that abuse power think twice about continuing their abuses or engaging in new ones. What say you all?"

Yoko, who was sitting next to Bernard, put an arm around his shoulder. "Beautifully put, B, a cry for the liberation of conscience in stifling and cruel bureaucracies. What good is freedom of speech if it doesn't follow you to the workplace when terrible crimes are being committed? I hope there'll be a museum someday honoring the pantheon of these glorious people."

"In my view," said Bill Gates, "moral courage is the highest expression of humanity, and not only because of what it exposes and deters but because it's contagious. It spreads to people possessed of less fortitude and helps them do the right thing instead of standing by and watching as the seeds of evil sprout before their very eyes. In an era when performance reviews are the only compass and newly perilous technologies are rising amongst us—as Bill Joy has just pointed out so chillingly—we need to shine a spotlight on people who are guided by a moral compass."

"I take it there's unanimity here?" Warren asked to more nods all around. "B, will you and Yoko work on a design for the award and a format for presentation?"

"Gladly," Bernard said.

Yoko was already sketching ideas for a medal on her notepad. "Of course."

"I've been wondering why the bunch of us, well known to our families and colleagues as cantankerous old cusses, almost always agree unanimously," Joe said. "I know you addressed this at our first meeting, Warren, but it's still pretty amazing. Maybe it's because we have a common public philosophy of a just and open society and at this stage in our lives"—he rose from his seat—"we mean business! But not for ourselves. We have nothing to lose, they can't do anything to us, posterity is our sunlight, and we don't have time to dicker and posture.

"When people ask me where I get the information that fuels my sense of injustice, I tell them from the business media, starting with the *Wall Street Journal*. The concentrated economic powers are so entrenched that they've come to believe that regular exposés of business crimes, fraud, and political manipulation go nowhere, produce no consequence or action. They understand that the media moguls deem such reporting important because it attracts readers, raises audience ratings, and increases profits. They know they can endure a day or two of modest criticism and then watch it all blow over. The Food and Drug Administration recently required three companies selling asthma medications to warn patients that these medications themselves can produce severe asthma attacks. Amazing story. Hardly a ripple. That's why the People's Court Society will never run out of causes of action, and why its efforts are crucial in redirecting our society to the proposition that the law will rule, even in the case of small injustices that corrode the quality of daily life, especially among the impoverished."

"At the risk of more unanimity," Max said, "spot on, Joe."

"At the risk of spoiling the unanimity, I'm not sure Joe's right that they can't do anything to us," Bill Joy said. "He's taken a lot of brickbats, but a word of caution here—be wary."

"Hey, I negotiated with the Teamsters for years," Jeno laughed. "Say, Peter, you've been very quiet today. Is it all those brickbats you've been dodging lately yourself ?"

"After a month like the one I've had, I'm just relaxing and listening."

Joe picked up his water glass. "I propose a toast to Peter, whose performance under fire during the month of March displayed true moral courage. The attacks hurled at him by his lifelong peers and the baying pack of reactionary commentators presaged what we'll all soon experience, perhaps even more intensely. May we come through it as he did, with flying colors of character, personality, veracity, and sagacity."

"Hear, hear!" Glasses clinked.

"With such an extended toast, it's a good thing there isn't booze in these tumblers," Paul joked.

"Especially on an empty stomach," Sol said.

After lunch, the meeting resumed with another bulletin from the Secretariat. Warren read it out. "'Media critic Harold Mertz has written in his weekend column that four publications—*Time* magazine, the *Wall Street Journal*, the *New York Times*, and his own *Washington Post*—have assigned full-time reporters to what he called the "business rebels beat." His sources say that these reporters will be backed up by investigative teams and the regional offices of the publications. One editor is quoted as saying, "Never in my thirty years of journalism has our country experienced such a rapid and widespread upheaval within conventional business. Who is behind it? We know the names of some of these provocative actors, but I suspect there's more to the story. We have some good leads, and we aim to rectify the lack of information as fast as possible.'" Warren paused. "Well, here we go, my friends."

"It was only a matter of time," Phil said, "but let's hope the time won't come for another month or so. Once the ball of yarn starts to unravel, there may be significant distractions from our work. Our challenge is to stay out of the limelight for as long as possible while our new infrastructures put down roots, and once we're in it, to take control and turn it to our advantage. For what it's worth, that's my media advice."

"I couldn't have put it better myself," Barry said. "Just one caveat. It can't be stressed often enough that we have to remember to speak only about the projects with which we're already identified and say nothing that might tip the press off to Maui. We've got to focus the reporters, not let them refocus us. Most of us are old hands at this in our business careers, but this is a different cup of tea. We can't hide behind trade secrets, proprietary information, and all the other balderdash about competitive advantage we business executives use to dodge questions that have nothing to do with competition."

"We ought to be able to gauge how far the reporters are getting from which of us they call and what questions they ask," said Max. "Let's be sure to trade notes on this during our closed-circuit briefing. In the meantime, full speed ahead with the infrastructure, especially the Congress Watchdogs, the CUBs, the PCC, the rallies, the lecturers, and the Clean Elections Party. The faster and better these instruments of democracy develop, the more likely we are to get some of the First-Stage Improvements through Congress before the November elections. Democratic agitation produces the enabling ambience, but the moving train is in the results."

"It's all about staying fast and furious on the offensive, as I emphasized during Maui One," Warren said. "We have to be very sensitive to any tipping of the scales in the other direction. That's why I think George's coming address to the editors' convention is so important. It's a foursquare attack on the central dogma of corporate capitalism—the myth of its continuing efficiencies. As such, with the help of the PCC and our own network of executives and billionaires, it will generate a creative and far-reaching debate that puts the multinationals on the defensive and advances our goals. Ideas matter, as they say."

"By the way, Max, what do you think of all the democratic agitation around the Pledge of Allegiance?" Bill Gates asked. "Only an asteroid heading for Earth could do more to shake up all these people who are so outraged by a word change that simply describes reality."

"Yes, I've been fascinated by the action-reaction here. It shows the anger that results when reality goes up against mythology through words alone. Imagine what's going to happen when deeds move into the fray. I've been too busy to do anything more with the Fighting Zulu ads, but you've extended my hobbyhorse very well. Keep pushing things to a conclusion, whether victory or defeat. As the pressure intensifies, we obtain more data."

Joe cleared his throat and burst into off-key song. "'O! say, can you see, by the dawn's early light, what so proudly we hail'd at the twilight's last gleaming?'"

Everyone stared at him with a mixture of surprise and dismay, except for Bill Gates. "What Joe means," he said, "is that Max doesn't have to worry about obtaining more data. Right after we get home, Joe and I are going to turn up the heat on the already red-hot controversy over the Pledge by starting a drive to make 'America the Beautiful' our National Anthem. It's much more consonant with democratic values, and besides, as Joe just demonstrated, 'The Star-Spangled Banner' is notoriously difficult to sing."

"Wow!" Ted exclaimed. "That's dynamite. Do you think Patriotic Polly could sing 'America the Beautiful' in another round of ads?"

"Better than Joe could," Warren said. "Lest he decide to treat us to more of his vocal stylings, let's take a break. I recommend a brisk walk around the grounds to loosen the limbs and breathe in the ocean breezes. We'll eat at seven and then have two hours of silence to stay with our thoughts about our respective and collective missions. As Isaac Newton said when asked why he towered above his fellow scientists in brilliance, and I paraphrase, 'It's not that I'm so much more brilliant, it's that I can concentrate and think through a problem longer than my peers.'"

At supper, circulating around the dining room as was his custom, Bill Joy detected a common thread in the conversations. The Meliorists were sounding each other out as to how they were taking the growing pressure of their work. It was clearly on all their minds. They were probing, however subtly and graciously, to see how their own pressures compared with those besetting the others, how their colleagues were coping, and whether anyone was showing early signs of cracking. What about their families? Was there any strain? Did any of their spouses know about the core group? Not as far as they could tell, they said, and their children and grandchildren continued to be dazzled by the energetic activities of their elders. So far so good. It looked like Warren's team was as stable, steadfast, and farsighted as ever, and above all, marvelously into the details.

After dessert—a spectacular mirage of sweetness surrounding a reality of fruity nutrition—they reassembled in the conference room. When the silence period was over, Warren invited impromptu comment on any topic of interest or concern.

Ted started things off. "I want to thank you all for your feedback at our last meeting. Your suggestions helped me round up eighty-eight more billionaires in the categories of on board or tempted. I got two calls from Russian billionaires who wanted in—you know the kind—but I told them we were keeping things strictly native for now. Between my gang and your epicenters, we have plenty of committed billionaires who are willing to reach out and socialize their wealthy friends, so Jeno and I decided that a Billionaires' Auxiliary of the People's Chamber of Commerce would be superfluous."

"It's still a great idea, though," Jeno added with a note of regret. "Just for the name alone."

Sol weighed in. "The fire sales at the mom-and-pops near the five Wal-Marts started last week, and customers are flocking to them. The Wal-Martians are beside themselves because their Supercenters are like ghost towns."

"What I can't get over," Ross said, "is the nearly uniform excellence of the managers and directors of all the various projects and initiatives, and especially those otherworldly superstars running Recruitment. Seymour Depth is aptly named."

"And Barry's shop isn't far behind," Peter said. "Their motto should be, 'Great undertakings without promotion are like candles in a sea of darkness.'" His colleagues applauded.

"Max, I want to take issue with you about words versus deeds," Bernard said. "It's been on my mind. Words are not harmless. They can incite, spread hatred, generate riots or stampedes. Remember Justice Holmes—no one has a right to falsely shout fire in a crowded theater. Words can slander, coarsen public dialogue, frighten the public. I concede that harmful deeds have the first claim on our attention, but we can't ignore our responsibility to condemn harmful words as well. That is our free speech right and obligation."

"Bernard, free speech, of course. All I'm trying to do is give sharp relief to the disproportionate emphasis on the condemning of words over deeds—the boo factor versus the do factor, you might say—and to expose the politically correct syndrome that makes those who boo feel satisfied with themselves and keeps us from searching for a deeper understanding of why people say such things. On this point, I defer to brother Phil, who has noted on more than one occasion that the more exposure you give these bigots, the more they're unmasked and deflated. He made a career out of doing that on television."

"Well, part of a career, anyway," Phil said.

"Some unknown cleric slams Phil in a uniquely ignorant manner and gets some media for his snarling," Bernard went on, "and before you know it, Phil sends an invite to his show and the fellow looks like a fool in front of a national audience. It's when we try to shout down the bigots and they return to their den of like-minded conspirators that the real trouble starts. As Justice Brandeis said in another context, 'Sunlight is the best disinfectant.' We must do everything we can to drive home the awareness that saying is not doing. An old Chinese proverb puts it well: 'To know and not to do is not to know.'"

"Words to ponder," Warren said. "Thank you, Mr. Bartlett. Anything else for further discussion?"

"I see from the financials that media buys are a big-ticket item in our expenditures so far. Is this going to slack off?" Leonard asked.

"Yes," Barry said. "We had to pour it on at the outset to show the media and the public that our projects have a credible capacity to reach millions and counter any media buys against us. As we go on, I'm sure our activities will generate more and more free media, almost automatic media, because the press respects power and nervy topics. To keep building the institutions, we'll still need ads and mass mailings, but they'll be more targeted and therefore cheaper. On our networks, on the stations under our corporate umbrella, we're not permitting any media buys from the Redirections projects. The new radio, TV, and cable outlets, via my leveraged buyouts, are being established under independent corporate frameworks so there'll be no conflict of interest."

Sol tried and failed not to yawn.

"Okay, let's call it a day," Warren said. "It's been a long one, and we've got a lot to pack in tomorrow morning before we return to the mainland."

Whereupon, in twos and threes, the Meliorists drifted to their rooms under a moonlit sky, a steady Pacific trade wind ruffling what was left of their hair. Even Bill Joy slept soundly.

Morning found the early risers strolling through the hotel's lush gardens, which were alive with colorful bird life. Then it was off to a light breakfast and over to the atrium conference room.

"I suggest a more philosophical bent to our discussion today," Warren began. "By now you must all have a backlog of ruminations on the underpinnings of our enterprise, and I'd like to hear them. Of course, as always, if there are details you want to hash out, by all means do so. God is in the details."

"You always set the right tone, Warren," said Bernard. "In my opinion, we haven't spent enough time grounding our activities in a sound moral philosophy. After all, much of what we're doing represents the age-old struggle between greed and need, between fairness and fraud, between—all right, I'll come straight out and say it—between good and evil. We're trying to give truth to equality, liberty, inalienable rights, all the best instincts that animated our Founding Fathers. The moral foundations of our society are not propositions to be intoned but spiritual energies to be released for the betterment of the people. There's so much pain and despair out there. As Yoko said at our first meeting, we can't come across as lecturing, but societies are moved by great beliefs as well as concrete actions—probably more by beliefs. You can bet that the counterattack, when it comes, will put much more effort into devising specious versions of reality and abstract, emotional assaults than into contending with our movement on the ground. I'm not suggesting any ideology here—we've had that discussion. What I do stress is a spiritual dimension rooted in the best of the past, the cultural norms of the present, and the bright prospects for the future. Man does not live by facts alone—perhaps unfortunately, but that is the case."

"Won't Dick Goodwin be addressing that dimension in the Tom Paine pamphlet he's working on?" Yoko asked.

"I expect he will," Bernard said. "His style over the years has been to use the best from our past to provide a moral and ethical basis for today's politics."

"Maybe he can run some training sessions for our lecturers to help them bring more philosophical depth to their presentations," Paul suggested. "And Promotions can use the pamphlet as the basis for a new series of ads. Yoko, what about your artists, musicians, poets?"

"That's where we start from, Paul. I've always believed that there's a huge overlap between the aesthetic, the moral, and the spiritual. Our teams are working up some wonderful expressions, but they won't be gospel singing. They'll be new conveyances of the old—the bold new. And the strictly secular."

"I guess this is more along the lines of a detail," Sol said, "but what's been bothering me is that not enough work has gone into galvanizing and organizing the pioneers of the sustainable subeconomy. Jeno and I were talking about this last night. Luke Skyhi of the PCC has been calling us to urge a weekend of events staged in major urban arenas to bring visibility to these businesses, perhaps a series of trade shows where a few of us might appear along with CEOs who've proven the profitability of conservation, renewable resources, and so on, people like Yvon Chouinard of Patagonia and Ray Anderson of Interface Corporation."

"Many such companies are members of the Social Venture Network, once a very promising and effervescent organization," Jeno said. "Unfortunately, it's become a little moribund lately, and seems devoid of any larger purpose than to exchange information about sustainable and marketable techniques. We can provide these companies with a much larger platform and enthusiastic audiences ready to be roused. Great fit, I think."

"There are already plenty of sustainable business fairs with displays on solar technologies, hydrogen vehicles, and the like," Ross pointed out. "Luke's arena shows will have to be different. To my way of thinking, they'll have to demonstrate by example the bankruptcy of the vested technologies of waste and harm. He'll have to stage a frontal assault, a technical and political confrontation that makes a clear case for the displacement of these technologies of yore, which must also be on display so that their destructiveness isn't merely described but vividly dramatized—another job for Yoko's artists. The one compelling word that needs to stay in the minds of the attendees and the media is *displacement*."

"Exactly!" Jeno said. "An excellent refinement. That will be our watchword from coast to coast. Without displacement, the shows will only play to feelings of curiosity and hope. We're all beyond that now."

"Yes," Paul agreed, "way beyond it. You know, I've been thinking about why this group has been able to get so many currents flowing so quickly in the past three months. As an actor, I spend a lot of time reading scripts, and few make my cut. What I'm looking for is a screenwriter with an intricate imagination that comes across in a clear and gripping way. A sage once said, 'The rut in which our mind descends is the prison in which our brain lies stagnant.' Our minds have liberated our brains, and the great sword that has struck our chains is that of a sublime imagination, a moral imagination, an expectant imagination, an experience-driven imagination, a resourceful and resilient imagination, and yes, even a combative imagination."

Bill Cosby applauded. "Keep it up, Paul, and you'll win another Oscar."

"Well, isn't it imagination that pioneers, that innovates, that perseveres?" Paul asked. "Sure, emotions, resources, and knowledge come into play, but imagination is the lubricant. It's been said that the only true aging is the erosion of our ideals. How true. But ideals are inert without imagination. Look what's happening and multiplying in our country with just a small portion of the fifteen billion we've raised. Pardon the sermon, but I think it's vital that we keep the imagination level high in ourselves and among our key project staff. It's not just budgets, programs, agendas, goals, and results. The brewer's yeast is imagination, fermenting in our society and our world to free our brains from our constricted minds."

Joe raised his glass of papaya juice high. "To imagination forevermore."

The Meliorists toasted with gusto.

"It's hard to imagine a better note on which to head home," Warren said. "Please be sure to make yourselves available for the daily closed-circuit briefing, since the news will be coming in thick and fast. By the way, the memo on how to protect your assets, promised last month, is on the side table for you to pick up as you leave."

As the gathering broke up, Bill Joy sauntered over to Warren and asked, "What makes you think your circuit is so closed?" The two men had an intense ten-minute conversation in the corner of the atrium before they too headed for the airport.

CHAPTER 9

Monday afternoon, Bill Gates Sr. and Joe Jamail announced their drive to make "America the Beautiful" the National Anthem of the United States. It would take an act of Congress. Bill Hillsman had created an ad comparing the beauty of the American countryside—amber waves of grain—with the martial flag symbolism of "The Star-Spangled Banner," written during the War of 1812 against the British, who were now our allies.

The right-wing media took the bait at comedic speed. "Our Anthem was born in blood and guts," thundered Bush Bimbaugh, "and that is what America stands for. America is not a tourist attraction, not a languid landscape. Our Anthem is masculinity, 'America the Beautiful' is femininity. Which do our enemies and adversaries abroad fear the most, I ask all you feminazis?" Joe and Bill knew that Bimbaugh and his ilk would use up their air time and print space ranting about the Anthem for weeks to come while overlooking the real power shifts taking place right under their noses. A perfect feint and decoy. For Bill Hillsman, it was his chance to prove that the right ad pays for itself many times over when it generates a cascade of free reporting, media commentary, and person-to-person conversation. So vituperative were the denunciations by the nationally syndicated right-wingers that the network television news devoted a minute or two to the ruckus and played part of the Hillsman ad. Joe left a message for Bill Gates saying simply, "I think we got the baying pack's number."

On Tuesday, the valedictory at the National Press Club was delivered to a packed luncheon ballroom by a retired Wal-Mart vice-president who came loaded for bear with copies of internal memos. One proved that the company's top executives were well aware of the hiring and mistreatment of illegal aliens. Another dealt with the more than accidental divergence between the posted prices of the products on Wal-Mart's shelves and the higher prices rung up on the computerized checkout registers, justifying it on the grounds that the customer was given an itemized receipt and could always return the merchandise before leaving the premises. "Pennies by the billions add up," as some irreverent "associates" liked to say. The former VP pointed to a big chart mounted behind him, comparing the pay of top Wal-Mart executives—about $10,000 an hour, forty hours a week, plus perks and benefits—with the median worker wage of less than $8.00 an hour, not the $9.58 claimed by management and swallowed uncritically by the media. He explained how Wal-Mart cranked the figure up by averaging in higher-paid supervisory workers and truck drivers, and then he took questions from the press with precision and aplomb. His presentation dominated the wire services and cable news channels all day, and Wal-Mart's stock dropped by 3 percent. So popular were these Press Club events, which were now almost thrice weekly, that tickets were sold out a month in advance. Tomorrow a retired credit card executive would disclose the secrets of overcharging in his former industry.

On Wednesday, Luke Skyhi of the PCC completed his plans for the sustainable economy arena shows in ten cities. The events were designed to close the loop between means and ends by demonstrating exactly how sustainable companies would improve the living standards of ordinary people. Having received the approving nod from Jeno and Sol, Luke decided to move fast, scheduling the ten shows for the Friday-to-Sunday weekend of what would be Maui Five, unbeknownst to him. The Secretariat touched base with the core group, and after much consultation they decided to skip Maui Five, further consolidate the infrastructure, give themselves a breather to allay their slightly suspicious families, and participate in the shows whenever they could. Luke and his best and brightest team gave themselves one month to pull off this historic visual and economic breakthrough. Fortunately there were timely cancellations at two of the biggest arenas, Madison Square Garden in New York City and the Target Center in Minneapolis.

The Thursday after Maui Four became known nationwide as the day when four hundred thousand Americans announced their incorporation at Bill Gates Sr.'s jamborees. People from all walks of life flocked to parks and stadiums across the country sporting their corporate charters around their necks, and wearing caps and T-shirts printed with the slogan "People Are Corporations Too." To roars of approval, accompanied by the famous Roman Army drumbeats—boom! boom! boom-boom-boom-boom!—speakers extolled one privilege and immunity after another that now accrued to these converts to corporate status. "People are fed up being people," declared leading corporate analyst Robert Weissman, at the Pittsburgh jamboree. "They desire upward mobility and power, the power to evade, escape, disappear, reappear, to be in many places at once, to deduct their entertainment and lobbying expenditures and delight in the loopholes and amenities of the tax code and the corporate bankruptcy laws." Charles Cray, a speaker at the Las Vegas event, particularized the benefits unique to Nevada-chartered versus Delaware-chartered corporations. Delicious buffets half a football field long provided free food under banners that read, "Corporations Are Eaters Too."

For the reporters in attendance, the whole scene was so far outside their normal frame of reference that they ran around with their cameras, mikes, and pens as if lost in a labyrinth. "Is this some kind of gag? April Fool's Day has come and gone, you know," said one of them to a woman in a nurse's uniform at the Birmingham jamboree. "I'll thank you to show some respect when addressing Birmingham Can, Unlimited," replied Jane Harper tartly. "You manufacture cans?" asked the bewildered reporter. "I manufacture can-do's," said Jane. Eventually, toward the end of the daylong jamborees, the press began to absorb the message. If the double standard in American law favored corporations over people, then why not have the people become corporations? This wasn't a giant gag, it was a giant demonstration of seriousness about a fundamental inequity.

On Friday, Bill Gates made it a double whammy with a press conference announcing the candidacies of five corporations for five state governorships. The corporations all met state requirements for elective office. They would be running under new names that signified the principal issue for each campaign, and that had been duly filed with the relevant secretaries of state: the Clean Up the Corrupt Texas Legislature Corporation, the Dethrone Corporate Welfare Kings Corporation, the Outsource CEOs Corporation, the Living Wage Corporation, and the Stamp Out Corporate Crime Corporation. Volunteer petitioners, identified by colorful headbands reading "Corporations Are People Too," were already on the streets collecting qualified signatures and were meeting with an enthusiastic response. The first wave of political advertisements for each corporation candidate would roll out over the weekend. When Bill Gates was finished with the formal announcements, the press corps was treated to a hilarious skit depicting the five corporations on the stump and in debates with perplexed opponents.

Over the weekend, the Meliorists took a well-earned rest from their exertions and relaxed with their families. On Sunday they read with interest the *Washington Post* story about the average citizen's response to the extraordinary activities of certain older individuals whom the paper called "the Three R's—respected, resolute, and rich." The story confirmed the reports from Kyle Corey and other field organizers for the Congress Watchdog Groups. Like the conversation in Clancy's Cave, the responses of those interviewed by the *Post* revealed a mix of skepticism and support, though the balance seemed to be tipping in the direction of support.

On the second Monday in April, Warren Buffett's poll of investors came out. Buffett was always news, but this was big. Among its more significant findings, the poll showed that 88 percent of individual investors and 91 percent of institutional investors believed in investor control over executive compensation packages. A large majority also believed that after passing a reasonable ownership or petition threshold, they should be given printouts of the names of all the shareholders in their companies so that they could propose competitive slates for the boards of directors and mount credible campaigns on their behalf. By a margin of four to one, they supported cumulative voting and their right to approve any merger that totaled more than 5 percent of the larger merging partner by revenues or employees. The full poll was posted on Warren's website, along with links to related articles in the press.

On Tuesday, Barry Diller and Bill Cosby awaited the first television airing of the "Pay Back, Pay Up!" advertisement exposing the broadcast industry's fleecing of the public through its free use of the airwaves. Once again, Bill Hillsman came through with a knockout ad. A full minute long, it showed a representative cross-section of Americans with hundred-dollar bills flying out of their pockets and purses into the coffers of suitably jowled media moguls. "Who says there's no such thing as a free lunch?" asked the voice-over. "There is, when it's on all of us. You own the public airwaves. Like any landlord, you should make sure you receive your rent. Contact the FCC and demand that it collect the millions you're owed. Then you'll have the money to put on the kind of programming that will make you proud, engaged, stimulated, and happy to have your children watching television. Call your members of Congress at 202-224-3121, or write them. They can't resist two hundred million landlords." The narrator was none other than the esteemed former CBS anchor Walter Cronkite.

Channel 7 (ABC) in Washington, DC, was scheduled to run the ad first, before it went national. At the last minute, the station pulled it on instructions from the higher-ups. No surprise. Promotions had anticipated censorship and was ready. It sent the ad out to the electronic and print media with a sharply worded statement pointing to a historic pattern among broadcasters of suppressing news about their privileged and subsidized status. From congressional hearings to critical conferences and reports, these FCC-licensed companies had long been deciding what was not in their commercial interest to tell the people, using the people's own property.

The print media and Barry's networks went to town on the Channel 7 blackout. Some broadcasting conglomerates that also owned newspapers and magazines did not report the story, but the *New York Times* and the *Washington Post* front-paged it and ran editorials strongly taking Channel 7 to task. They also printed the entire text of the ad, which was replayed all over the Internet and discussed endlessly in Blogland. The debate was on. Demands that Congress and the FCC act came from all quarters as liberals and conservatives joined hands on this simple matter of fairness. What a buildup for the huge rallies planned for the end of the month!

As the second week of April went on, these latest provocations of the Meliorists gathered force. The whole idea of the corporation candidates struck a chord among more and more people, especially those with a mischievous streak. The press was fascinated and started profiling the directors and officers of the five corporations, who had all educated themselves on the issues described by their corporate names and were highly articulate. Business reporters fell over each other covering this maverick phenomenon, which they recognized as something fresh and a little zany, but backed by money and influence. Almost breathlessly they ignited a public debate over corporations as "persons" and what that meant if the consequences were pursued. Could corporations be imprisoned if convicted of a felony? If so, how? By blockading the headquarters and padlocking the door? What about capital punishment? How would the state carry out the corporate death penalty? By pulling the corporation's charter? Forcing it into bankruptcy, firing all the directors and officers? John Stewart of *The Daily Show* had a field day with the material.

There arose such a clamor from Oregon, stimulated in part by Greg Kafoury and Mark MacDougal, two hyperactive trial lawyers, that Bill Gates located a sixth corporation willing to run for that state's governorship as the Draft Corporations Yes Corporation. Veterans comprised the board of directors, and peace advocates were the officers. Meanwhile, citizen groups began circulating petitions demanding that corporations pay their income taxes at the higher federal rate that applied to individuals—after all, corporations were people too. Right-wingers insisted in screeds to the nonplussed letters editor of the *Wall Street Journal* that corporations, as "persons," should have the right to vote, as should their independent corporate subsidiaries and holding companies, as long as they were eighteen years old.

Warren's investor poll also continued to attract attention in the business and political press. Opinion was divided, with slightly more than half of the commentators endorsing the changes in corporate governance favored by most of the polled investors. The rest said that such changes would hamper management, make executives less venturesome, and prove unworkable in practice. Another rollicking debate was underway, in the course of which there were additional disclosures, such as company ruses to hide higher executive pay by covering the tax obligation on the already lavish compensation packages. A pro-investor advertising campaign designed by the indefatigable Bill Hillsman fueled the controversy further. His theme was that corporate executives were destroying capitalism, whose principles included control by owners and excluded government bailouts that would nullify or circumvent the discipline of the free market. "The ads make a fair point and are historically accurate," the *Wall Street Journal* was forced to admit, but went on to discount Warren's poll as stemming from "the dubious motivations of a disgruntled aging executive." Right, Bill Hillsman thought to himself. Warren Buffett, the second-richest man in America, and getting richer by the year. Extremely disgruntled.

On the first day of the congressional spring recess, seventy-year-old Billy Beauchamp, chairman of the powerful House Rules Committee, headed home to southwest Oklahoma in a corporate jet owned by the Viscous Petroleum Corporation. A thirty-eight-year House veteran, he had had no opponent for the last thirty of them, except for the occasional accountant or attorney looking for free publicity on a campaign budget of $20,000 or less. Politically, life was so easy for Congressman Beauchamp that he had grown more and more portly and courtly over the years, and more and more powerful. All House bills had to go through his Rules Committee before getting to the floor, and he was one tough gatekeeper, quick to block any legislation he didn't like, or to attach rules barring amendments and restricting the time for debate. Part of his power stemmed from the fact that there was nothing he needed, neither legislation nor favors. Campaign funds and PAC money for his loyalists came to him in boatloads from corporate interests as a matter of course, and he had no burning causes of his own, other than to maintain the power of business. He regularly entertained lobbyists who came to his office bearing their road maps for congressional action—or inaction—and served a special brandy when the oilmen and gasmen dropped in.

But on the flight home, Billy Beauchamp was not reminiscing about his triumphant legislative career. He had other things on his mind. His long-slumbering rural district was bursting with political agitation, and he wanted to get a reading from some of his old friends, the farmers and ranchers and small businessmen who were the backbone of his past reelection coronations. There was no better place to do that than Fran and Freddy's Feed, a family-owned restaurant in Lawton, the Comanche County seat. Despite his worries, the congressman was looking forward to the house specialty, chicken-fried steak with cheese grits.

That evening, seated in a big booth with his friends after much hearty backslapping, Billy asked them what they thought was going on lately. To a man, they expressed their loyalty to him, and to a man they conveyed warnings about what was looming on the horizon.

"This year is different, Billy," said Ernest Jones, a Lawton banker. "It's as if everything's turned on its head. None of us have seen anything like it. Folks here are putting together the pieces of what's been troubling them for a long time."

"I've been getting that feeling for a while now," Billy said as a gum-chewing waitress shuffled over to take their orders—house specials all around. "Look at her," he went on as the waitress ambled back to the kitchen. "Everyone in this restaurant used to treat me with deference and respect, but now what I see in their eyes is that I'm history. And what the hell is that weirdo button they're all wearing? Is this some kooky anti-establishment mood like in the sixties, or is it a real movement?"

"Might could be," said farmer Gil Groundwork. "I got me one of them buttons myself. Came with the lightbulb I sent for when that Yoko Ono letter came around. It's the Seventh-Generation Eye."

"Say what? You going hippie on me?" Billy looked at Gil in disbelief.

Gil pointed at a busboy clearing a nearby table. "See that T-shirt? What does it say?"

Billy squinted at the busboy as the waitress arrived with five large platters. "'Sooners Rather Than Later.' Very funny. I take it they're losing their patience."

"I reckon they've just about kicked it into the ditch," Gil said. "This kid is probably making five-fifty an hour before deductions. He can't pay his way with that, and lots of people are telling him he doesn't have to if he just takes up with all these marchers and organizers."

"And the old-timers are talking to the kids, showing them their calluses and their poverty after a lifetime of working their asses off for rich guys." Hal Horsefeathers looked down at his work-roughened hands. "We're telling them not to let the same thing happen to them."

"Hey, let's call a spade a spade," said John Henry. "It's all about greed and power, Billy, greed and power that won't let up. For greed and power, nothing is ever enough. It's time for the populist posse to ride again. Myself, I'm sick of my own repossession shop—too many people in debt, can't pay their monthly charges, the interest and penalties pile up, and my guys move in. It's a nice living, but it stinks. Wasn't going to do anything different, but then along come these rich old guys, and by God, they make sense."

Congressman Billy Beauchamp frowned and looked down at his

plate for consolation, cutting himself a big bite of chicken-fried steak. It wasn't as good as it used to be.

April 17 was not only tax day. It was also a very taxing day for big business. In Washington, DC, George Soros was about to give his seismic speech on the inefficiencies of corporate—he emphasized *corporate*—capitalism. In New York, the mother of all Wall Street rallies, whether labor, civil rights, environmental, or antiwar, was surrounding the New York Stock Exchange. It was an unprecedented gathering, a rally of nearly two hundred thousand investor-owners—Leonard had delivered on his promise to Warren—demanding that their ownership guarantee control. The first speaker was a law professor who had served on the SEC. "Ownership *means* control. It's been said that trying to organize the sixty million individual investors in this country is like herding cats, but don't you believe it," he declared, and went on to lay out a step-by-step action plan.

Other speakers detailed the corporate crimes responsible for the loss of trillions of pension and trust dollars supposedly held by Wall Street brokers, investment bankers, and bank trust departments. African American investors spoke of the backbreaking toil of the slaves who built so much of the Financial District, including the wall that gave Wall Street its name; they called slavery and its aftermath "centuries of affirmative action for white males." Authors of books about "corporate lying, cheating, and stealing," as one prosecutor phrased it, raised bullhorns to the crowded windows of the surrounding office buildings and bellowed appeals for more whistle-blowers. The ralliers roared their anger and shouted in unison, "Down with the tyranny of self-enriching bosses!" Working off sets of photo cards passed out by Leonard's organizers, they called out the names of the Fortune 100 companies and their CEOs one by one in earsplitting decibels. Representatives of some of the multibillion-dollar institutional investors spoke out in support, as did managers of university endowments. The big mutual funds were reserving judgment—and small wonder, since they had ownership-without-control problems and investor-gouging traditions of their own.

Toward the end of the rally, a retired CEO of a brokerage firm took the podium to announce that the head of the New York Stock Exchange had been invited to speak and had turned the invitation down flat. A deafening chorus of boos arose from the crowd, which surged forward toward the steps of the Stock Exchange. Startled police panicked and began pushing the demonstrators back with billy clubs or dragging them off to paddy wagons. The scuffles and arrests, the handcuffing of some unresisting demonstrators trained in passive civil disobedience, the spectacle of police force trained on a gathering of small investors—all made great visuals for the print photographers and television cameras. Once again the Meliorists had conceived an event that bridged the conservative-liberal divide.

Every April, the American Society of Newspaper Editors descended on Washington, DC, for its annual convention. Over the years the convention had been a command performance for the prominent political, business, and academic personages chosen as speakers. In most cases, the speeches were soporific, routine, predictable anthems of self-promotion, but every now and then an electrifying presentation came along, like the now largely forgotten Cross of Iron speech delivered by newly inaugurated president Dwight D. Eisenhower in April 1953. In powerful language, Eisenhower delineated the folly of the US-Soviet arms race and the inhumane opportunity costs borne by the civilian populations of both nations, especially the children.

Today, anticipation was running high in the giant ballroom of the Washington Hilton. The advance buzz was that George Soros's speech was going to be one for the capitalist ages, a sort of "Move over, Adam Smith—what you forewarned in 1776 in your *Wealth of Nations* has come to seamy maturity beyond your wildest nightmares." George had laid down two stipulations when he accepted the invitation. One was that the speech be carried live, at least on C-SPAN, and that there be full media access. The other was that he speak before lunch, not after. Something of a gourmet, he had seen many a stomach full of food and drink dull the brain and wilt the attention span. Mild hunger had the opposite effect, producing almost undivided attention.

At high noon, the society's president, James R. Rant III, introduced the speaker briskly. "The highly successful financial speculator and philanthropist George Soros needs no introduction. Therefore, I give you George Soros." More than polite applause greeted George as he took the podium, and then utter quiet fell over the room.

For a few seconds, he looked out over the audience. Meeting heightened expectations always made him nervous. He preferred to exceed lowered expectations. Earlier, he had waved away the teleprompter, saying that he was going to extemporize from his notes. That way he could give an impression of informality without sacrificing the precision of his remarks. He could not afford to wander. The last thing he wanted to read in the press reports was, "In a rambling speech today, George Soros said that . . ."

In spite of himself, he began stiffly. "O editors of large, medium, and small newspapers, lend me your open minds. For I will not pander to you with sonorous platitudes. Nay, I will respect you by asking you to join me in a journey toward reality. The free mind engages realities; the indentured mind is enslaved by myths. Concentrated power sustains its hegemony with myths that pacify its subjects. Systems of intolerable control fueled by limitless greed have to justify their domination. Myths serve that purpose.

"Today, the dominant institution in our country is the global corporation. Never have corporations been larger, with revenues comparable to or exceeding the gross domestic product of entire nations, with a grip on government that is scarcely challenged, with technologies of unprecedented reach, with workers who are theirs to hire or jettison at will, with a limitless mobility and capacity to evade the jurisdiction of our laws while continuing to profit from their presence in this land of ours.

"The global corporation's principal claim to legitimacy is its efficiency and productivity. The cold hearts and monetized minds of these corporate behemoths rationalize their autocratic decisions on grounds of superior efficiencies and increased productivities. They will admit of only one master they cannot challenge—the market. The market made me do it, the market is all-wise. They espouse this market fundamentalism shamelessly when in fact they spend their days trying to insure that *they* are the market. They labor to make government and its laws dutiful servants who keep them ensconced as the market powers. With their immense capital they can turn the governments of smaller nations into debtor putty, and when matters become shaky they can download their risks to national and international governmental institutions.

"The global corporation completes its occupation of our minds—and many sharp, learned minds are no exception—by controlling the definitions of efficiency and productivity. Under these definitions, slavery can be and has been justified on the grounds that well-treated slaves enhance the efficiency of any given enterprise. But the time came in our nation's history when it was no longer the market that controlled the outcome. A war was fought and laws were passed to make slavery a grave crime, notwithstanding the fact that it reduced labor costs. How often must we return to the verity that those who define our terms and our yardsticks of economic progress control our dialogue, our very thought processes? That is why so many of us are unable to see that these yardsticks, determined entirely within the corporate sphere, are short-term, shortsighted, and only further reinforced by the stock market, quarterly returns, and executive stock options, barring external intrusions such as effective regulation, litigation, or a civil war. When corporations so overwhelmingly control the premises of the discussion that they are part of the daily catechism in our schools, is it surprising that we all bow to their conclusions?

George paused to take a sip of water. He was hitting his stride. "With your indulgence, let me take you down the abstraction ladder. Let me pose some organizing questions that are based on some of your own finest reporting, your finest hours in journalism, which I choose to take very seriously.

"Is it efficient and productive to dump toxic pollutants into the air, water, soil, food, and property used by millions of innocent women, children, and men? By the corporate definition—reducing costs by using the environment as a free private sewer—the answer is yes. By any reasonable societal definition of efficiency and productivity—where costs have to include the damage to health, safety, and property values—the answer must be no.

"Is it efficient to produce energy-guzzling consumer products such as motor vehicles and household appliances so that the electric and gas utilities and the oil and coal companies can sell more of their products? For Exxon Mobil, Peabody Coal, El Paso Natural Gas, and General Motors, the corporate efficiency answer is yes. For the population as a whole, for the country as a whole, for consumers as a whole, the inbuilt waste of stagnant technologies requires that the answer be no.

"In the context of the growing peril of global warming, is it efficient to keep expanding the use of fossil fuels, to oppose renewable fuels, and to resist enforceable standards for greater energy efficiency? Within the frame of planet Earth and its peoples *and* its economy over time, the answer is a resounding no.

"Is it efficient for the corporations to protect their entrenched wasteful technologies by actively opposing alternative technologies that are better for the human race in the long run? No. It's a case of a powerful inefficiency, so to speak, repressing a powerless efficiency. But the corporation answers yes in all its destructive myopia and continues mortgaging the future while the general public pays the bills.

"Is it efficient for the timber companies to twist the arm of the Forest Service so that they can clear-cut more of the people's land while using totally subsidized roads and paying Uncle Sam absurdly low prices for the logs? And to do it at the expense of protecting the national forests from serious damage and expanding their recreational use for generations to come? For the timber companies, it's efficient to take every last tree standing in our national forests, which supply less than five percent of the country's total timber harvest. For posterity—may we resurrect that word so oft employed by our forebears—it is distinctly inefficient. One only has to look at the denuded upper Midwest and other regions where forests disappeared in the nineteenth century to anticipate the wasteful long-term economic consequences. There was once a thriving lumber business in the upper Midwest; there is none today.

"How efficient was it, in the thirties and forties, for General Motors to conspire with a tire company and an oil company to buy up trolley systems—their remaining competitors—in twenty-eight metropolitan areas, including the world's largest electrified mass transit network in the Los Angeles area, and then proceed to tear up the tracks and lobby government for more highways? Clearly, neither the Justice Department, which moved the indictment against the three companies for criminal violation of the antitrust laws, nor the federal district court, which convicted them, thought it was efficient for the country, but the damage was done. The economic inefficiency of the failure to create a more balanced surface transportation system can be seen today in the daily bumper-to-bumper traffic at commuter hours—more fuel wasted, more time wasted, more air pollution in our lungs, and more accidents on our roads. The work done by innovative transit engineers and at such universities as Northwestern in Evanston, Illinois, gives us a glimmer of the modern, flexible mass transit systems that could have graced those once valuable rights of way.

"Is it efficient for the defense industry to lobby for larger and larger military budgets and unneeded weapons systems when those wasteful and inefficiently contracted tax dollars could be spent on the people's needs instead? Standing before this convention in 1953, President Eisenhower itemized the number of schools and hospitals and public transit systems that could be funded if the United States and the Soviet Union would only lift 'the cross of iron' from their citizenry's shoulders. And yet the industry's top executives have the nerve to complain about all the uneducated workers coming their way. I suppose it's too much to hope that the 'military-industrial complex,' as Eisenhower called it in his farewell address in January 1961, would ever miss a chance to raise the military budget even higher than the one half of the entire federal operating budget it represents today. To the Lockheed-Martins, enough is never enough. To be on the receiving end of tax dollars from Uncle Sam is an efficient result for these companies' bottom lines and executive compensation packages. It is not an efficient result for a country that should have been reaping an annual peace dividend since 1991, following the internal collapse of our major military adversary.

"Is it efficient that the healthcare industry rakes in an annual two-hundred-billion-dollar bonanza through gross billing fraud for services rendered—or not rendered—as documented by the Government Accountability Office of the Congress? Is it efficient for the patients? The taxpayers?

"Is it efficient that the corporate health insurance industry uses about twenty-five percent of every premium dollar for administrative, executive, and bureaucratic expenses when the government's health insurance program, Medicare, only uses three percent on such expenses before paying out? Aren't company efficiencies supposed to advance consumer efficiencies rather than enter into a zero-sum relationship with them? Yet the latter is exactly what the wheelchair manufacturing monopoly and the virtual GE lightbulb monopoly and the automakers with their fragile vehicles did to their customers for many years before consumer advocacy groups and competitive forces finally came to the rescue.

"The Great Lakes once had a thriving commercial fishing industry. No more. Apparently the lakeshore chemical and petro-chemical industry found it efficient to dump mercury and other poisons into these wondrous natural creations.

"Of late the outcry from corporations demanding that government activities be turned over to them through the outsourcing of procurement programs has become thunderously loud. The grotesque increase in taxpayer costs from this commercialization of so many military and civilian services has been camouflaged by the corporate ideology that companies are more efficient than government. Tell that to the Pentagon's civil service procurement officers, who, like Admiral Hyman Rickover before them, can point to one case study after another detailing the massive cost overruns they have had to endure and absorb. Tell it to the auditors of the Hurricane Katrina contracts. Tell it to the Seabees and the Salvation Army, who know a thing or two about efficiency.

"Very few people, even in the Pentagon, know that deep inside that department, at the Walter Reed army research complex, the government maintains its own 'drug company.' For nearly four decades it has been discovering and testing crucial drugs at less than five percent of the development costs that the big pharmaceutical companies claim to justify the exorbitant prices patients pay for drugs. The astonishing expediency of the corporations emerges here as well. The pharmaceutical industry has managed to shape federal policy in such a way that the medicines researched and developed by the government are given free to one or another of the big drug companies under what are essentially monopoly marketing agreements. That is to say, no royalties to the government from profits, and no price controls to keep the companies from gouging their patients, many of whom are the taxpayers whose dollars funded the research to begin with. To add to the windfall, the pharmaceutical firms are always hiring away the government's medical officers and other scientists, with their taxpayer-funded years of experience. These companies obviously think the whole arrangement is a model of efficiency. They're wrong.

"There is no end to the elaborations of the myth of corporate efficiencies, which in fact arise from the imposition of inefficiencies on consumers, workers, and taxpayers. I was just reading a new book by the eminent John Bogle, one of the pioneers of the mutual fund industry, and the founder of the low-fee Vanguard series of funds. His sad and angry conclusion was that the aggregate take in fees charged to the average mutual fund investor over time amounts to one third of investment gains. That, I suppose, is an efficient figure from the viewpoint of the mutual funds' management. I doubt that investors would agree if they were aware of the vigorish.

"You may note that I have scarcely touched upon what economists call the diseconomies of the business corporation. Consider if you will the well-documented human damage from the overprescribing or misprescribing of drugs peddled to the public through massive television advertising and other industry promotions. The adverse effects of these drugs claim more than one hundred thousand American lives a year and produce far larger numbers of serious problems such as gastrointestinal bleeding. When you factor in the warnings of leading medical scientists that the reckless promotion and prescribing of antibiotics overloads patients and generates resistant strains of bacteria, the casualty toll just keeps rising.

"Or what about the epidemic of corporate crime that your publications have been reporting day after day? Trillions of dollars have been drained or looted from workers, pensioners, and 401(k) holders in the past half dozen years. That is some externality! As are the sixty-five thousand people who die every year from air pollution, according to the EPA, or the fifty-eight thousand workplace-related deaths from disease and trauma every year, according to OSHA, or the nearly one hundred thousand people who die annually as a result of medical negligence or incompetence in hospitals, according to the Harvard School of Public Health.

"These diseconomies and many more reported in the press led Ralph Estes, a prominent professor of social cost accounting, now emeritus, to conclude that corporations have done more harm than good. 'What?' you say. 'Has George Soros gone off the deep end?' Open minds, please. Consider that many of these external costs are reflected in suffering and destruction that escapes marketplace feedback—for example, the loss of a loved one without recompense where recompense is due, or the depletion of natural resources through land erosion, deforestation, mountaintop destruction, and so on—or are shifted to future generations. Moreover, and importantly, the very costs transform themselves into many forms of economic demand that fuel business, profits, and jobs.

"Let's take a mundane example—the ridiculously flimsy bumpers on your motor vehicles, which essentially protect nothing but themselves, and that very poorly. The Insurance Institute for Highway Safety estimates annual repair costs model by model. A five-mile-per-hour collision can run you anywhere from five hundred to four thousand dollars, or even more, either directly or in higher insurance premiums. And the other side of cost is sales. The collision repair industry, starting with the original equipment manufacturers and ending with the body shops, takes in billions of dollars a year from the business of fixing preventable damage. It's not as if the auto company engineers don't know how to build simple bumpers that protect other parts of the car in low-level collisions, certainly up to ten miles an hour.

"But, you say, the US economy is the wealthiest and mightiest in the world, despite its huge consumer, corporate, and governmental debt burdens. You're right, as long as we don't ask tough questions about the quality of life it produces. And for whom? And at what expense to posterity? To the global environment? To vulnerable people overseas? At what expense to consumers, workers, and tax-payers, to public services and hollowed-out communities and depleted natural resources? At what expense to distributive justice for the working people of America, to their living standard, their time, their tranquility?

"Let's turn our open minds back to the early 1900s, a period of widespread poverty, insufficient affordable housing, low wages, hungry children. Well, our mighty, wealthy economy roared through the century, stimulated by several wars, and here we are the beginning of the twenty-first century, with an economy twenty to twenty-five times more 'productive' per worker, inflation-adjusted, than in the horse-and-buggy days. So what do the newspapers tell us, sometimes in the most graphic and heart-rending of terms? That we live in a period of widespread poverty, insufficient affordable housing, low wages, and hungry children, that tens of millions of American families are deeply in debt, that disparities of income and wealth in our nation are huge and steadily growing.

"'So why hasn't the capitalist economy collapsed?' you may wonder. Setting aside the fact that it did, during the Great Depression, the answer is simple. Because it is not a capitalist economy, with companies both large and small having an unfettered freedom to fail. Rather, it is a predominantly corporate capitalist economy, with Washington, DC, serving a backstop function of bailing out, guaranteeing, subsidizing, and overcontracting to big business. As the astute restaurateur Nathra Nader once said, 'Capitalism will always survive because socialism will always be there to save it.' Corporate capitalism is in charge, but it is inundating us with manufactured wants and whims instead of delivering the necessities and allowing public budgets to reflect the priorities of a sane and just society.

"Ladies and gentlemen, the task that lies before us is abundantly clear. We must redefine efficiency and productivity as if what matters most is the well-being of our people and their descendants. As if corporations adjust to be our servants, not our masters. Toward this end, we must stop letting the big corporations and their apologists think for us and start thinking for ourselves. We need open minds for an open society. We have nothing to lose but our myths. We have everything to gain by thinking anew about how to create real prosperity for all our citizens, how to protect the environment they live in, and how to insure the peaceful sustainability of our planet.

"Thank you for inviting me to address you this afternoon. May you pursue these inquiries further here at your convention and on returning to your work of opening more minds."

At first, a stunned silence greeted the conclusion of George's speech—five seconds, ten seconds, fifteen. Then a single clap was heard, then two, three, four, a dozen, building to a crescendo of applause from a roomful of standing editors, though the ovation didn't quite drown out some loud booing. Maybe a dozen mossbacks, George thought as he took in the reaction. When the audience quieted, a panel of editors chosen for the occasion asked a few unusually thoughtful questions arising from George's points. It was clear that the editors had listened to his remarks and discarded their prepared questions about the IMF, globalization, and the like.

The reporters in the room rushed to file their stories. The *Washington Post* led with "Global financier George Soros told the American Society of Newspaper Editors today that large corporations are engines of inefficiency and that they get away with it because they hide it in their profit-and-loss statements." The *New York Times* headline read, "Financier-Philanthropist Says Large Corporations Weave a Web of Myths." The *Wall Street Journal* ran with "George Soros Attacks Corporate Efficiency Myth, Asks for Open Minds."

"Not bad," George said, reading the clippings back in his office with his project manager. "We went after the central dogma, and maybe others will follow. How was the television?"

"Thirty-five seconds—a clip of one or two of your pithier lines," replied the manager. "It's not a one-day story. There'll be commentary and editorials, calls and e-mails, and plenty of outrage from the expected quarters to keep it going."

"We'll see," George said. "It certainly was the best possible audience. Before a Chamber of Commerce crowd, the speech would have gone in one ear and out the other, and they'd have jeered me out of the hall. Which is fine, because it wasn't designed for the closed-minded business community, but for market-brainwashed citizens and students around the country. Once the myth starts to collapse, the multinationals will know what it's like when an entombed mummy hits air."

By the third week of April, Sol's campaign against Wal-Mart was putting tremendous pressure on the company. Sales were down in the two hundred stores subjected to regular and very effective picketing, but not nearly as steeply as in the five stores beset by dozens of small businesses that were undercutting Wal-Mart's prices on its forty leading sellers. These fire sales struck at the heart of the slogan seen on Wal-Mart trucks as they traveled the nation's highways 24/7: "Always the Lowest Price. Always." At the same five stores, the Sol-SWATs were completing their work on the union organizing drive.

Company attorneys, Wal-SWATs, and representatives of the National Labor Relations Board were all on location tensely performing their respective roles. As if all that weren't bad enough, Wal-Mart was losing lawsuits unrelated to Sol's crew and all the media attention they were garnering. Denial of lunch breaks caused one judge to rule in favor of thousands of Wal-Mart workers in the West. Women charging discrimination in both pay and promotions won their case. Week after week, Wal-Mart was getting an overdose of bad news.

In response, the company organized demonstrations of satisfied low-income shoppers and loyal workers, but so many Wal-Mart free-bies were handed out that the press discounted the turnouts. Meanwhile, the Sol-SWATs organized counter-demonstrations of exploited workers, small family businesses that had been pillars of their communities until Wal-Mart crushed them, and shoppers who felt ripped off by the company's sales practices. Speakers made sure to cover all the bases. Again and again, they compared the hourly Wal-Mart worker wage with the $10,000 an hour or more paid to top executives, and stressed the company's mandatory better treatment of its Western European workers. Again and again, they explained how local property taxpayers were subsidizing Wal-Mart's privileged presence in their communities, and how federal taxes were subsidizing Wal-Mart's low-wage business model. The speeches were sprinkled with contrived leaks about what was coming Wal-Mart's way on an even larger scale. Sol's partial mole on the board of directors told him that it was this credible threat of a sustained and expanded campaign that most frightened the board and the CEO.

Wal-Mart's standing on Wall Street continued to suffer. Controversy and uncertainty were never good for a company's stock. The number of "market underperforms" recommended by the stock analysts was on the rise, and there were no "buys," only "holds" and even a few "sells." One analyst for a major investment banking firm issued a report warning that Wal-Mart's very business model was in jeopardy. He noted that of the model's two underpinnings—a spectacularly hard-bitten supply chain ending with just-in-time inventory, and low wages and benefits—it was the latter that was particularly in jeopardy. Wal-Mart's stock continued to slide, not precipitously, but at that gradual pace that drives brokerage firms crazy. As one broker put it, "The China price is one thing, but this is more like Chinese water torture."

The last weekend in April—what would have been near Maui Five—saw the opening of Luke Skyhi's ten-city arena extravaganzas showcasing the sustainable economy in a way that dispelled the Goody Two-Shoes aura of so many environmental rallies. The displays, which included some props and visuals borrowed from the Sun God festivals, were emotionally and intellectually stunning. There were no corporate-sponsored greenwashing exhibits like the ones that had usurped the annual Earth Day celebration. Just the opposite. The destructive corporate economy was the focus. The sustainable economy, with its here-at-home jobs, was the solution. The contrast between the two—the portrayal of life under the sustainable economy as compared with the rat race, the disrupted families, the declining living standard of the majority of Americans under the Fortune 500 economy—was stark and dramatic, just the kind of vivid contrast that works to raise expectations and motivate people to act, to shift their buying habits, to refuse to take no for an answer.

No one was more amazed at the impact on the attendees and the media than the established groups and cooperatives that had been working for a sustainable economy for years, crying tediously in the wilderness, for the most part objects of curiosity or derision to all but their tiny cadre of adherents and practitioners. "All steak, no sizzle," wrote one columnist years ago. Laboring in the vineyards largely in vain, they nonetheless represented the future survival path for the planet. For decades their idealism sustained them in the face of their disappointment in a corporate-saturated public that kept looking the other omnicidal way. But these arena shows were something different. They represented idealism backed by power and driven by a strategy of wholesale displacement of the destructive corporate economy. Even the rhythms of the music exuded power. So did the art, the speeches, the technologies. So did the presence of so many politicians and spotters for the big corporations, who showed up uninvited but were more than welcome to attend. Luke Skyhi wanted the political and corporate scions to feel the power, see the power, taste the power, and be in shock and awe of the power. The large arena shows were not only designed to be powerful in themselves; the PCC made sure they signaled that the drive for a sustainable economy was about to move into other arenas, into the legislatures, courts, executive branches, and executive suites of the soon-to-be powers that were. No more Mr. Nice Guy!

Luke Skyhi was beginning to put the pieces of the Redirections network together all by himself. Emboldened by his sense that there were mighty forces at his back, he told the media, in his keynote address, just how the rubber was going to hit the road. His words conveyed a mood of conviction and determination. "No more excuses! The train has left the station, and the track is branching out in all directions, so stay tuned," he said as a quartet of jazz vocalists broke into the theme song Yoko had composed for the glorious weekend, "If It Takes Forever, I Will Wait for You, but the Polar Bears Won't."

Out in California, Warren Beatty's campaign took full advantage of the weekend's arena events in Los Angeles and San Francisco–Oakland, just as it had been taking full advantage of the Sun God festivals and the increasingly vociferous and media-savvy lunchtime rallies in those cities, as well as San Jose and San Diego.

In recent weeks, the campaign had almost been sidetracked by charges of womanizing against both candidates. A salivating press and blogosphere pounced on a flurry of accusations and visuals from jilted husbands and tearful women relaying their stories— often poignant, whether true or not—over and over until the public felt like it was watching an X-rated soap opera. Salaciousness fatigue set in. It turned out that Mutually Assured Promiscuity was as effective a deterrent in the California gubernatorial campaign as

Mutually Assured Destruction is claimed to have been during the Cold War. After a fortnight of TV, radio, and tabloid frenzy, the sexcapades of the two Lotharios became a sideshow, and Warren knew how to keep them a sideshow. He was a different man now, a faithful husband to his adored wife, Annette, and a proud father of their four children. He suavely advised all current rakes in the state to try married life. The reporters ate it up, and the cockhound dustup died down to barroom chuckles and website jokes.

More important political business took center stage. The problems of the state were immense, and perceived as such by most Californians. In ever greater numbers, they felt that their governor had blown the opportunity presented by his initial sky-high poll numbers when he characterized picketing nurses as "special interests" and said he was "kicking their butt." Thus commenced his Waterloo. He had alienated not only the nurses, but teachers, police, and firefighters, with both his style and his policies of protecting the wealthy at their expense. Moreover, with the restoration of the tax on the super-rich over the governor's veto, Warren had staked his claim to the debt and deficit issues that had given the former celluloid action hero some policy credibility.

Barry Diller continued to be Warren's political lifeguard. Quietly he synergized the pertinent initiatives of the Meliorists with his friend's campaign to keep it varied, exciting, fresh, and substantive. It wasn't so much that the agenda was particularly new—it covered pensions, tax reform, water purity and availability, long overdue public works projects to employ the unemployed, a living wage, universal quality healthcare, modernization of public transport to contain sprawl, safe and clean streets, revamped schools that taught civic skills and literacy from the earliest grades, a crackdown on corporate crime and abuse of power, etc.—it was the decisive, unambiguous manner in which Warren argued for it, drawing on all his actor's skills. He made reform seem unstoppable. His campaign left Arnold frittering and the Democratic Party dumbfounded—that is, reviewing his agenda, they found out how dumb they'd been in past election cycles.

Other would-be progressive politicians and candidates all over the country began to take heed. The cliché that as California goes, so goes the nation, seemed less a cliché with every passing week. Nobody took greater heed than the members of Congress—heed mixed with more than a few flutters of fear.

Warren's caravan of the super-rich had grown to four buses that traveled all over California, from the northern mountains to the southern deserts and beaches, from the inner cities and sprawling suburbs to the valleys where migrant farmworkers toiled. The election was his to lose, but he refused to play it safe. He crisscrossed the state tirelessly, his days of chronic indecision long behind him. A transplanted Californian from Virginia, he was on a journey of public self-discovery as much as a quest for the public interest, and Californians were responding in droves.

In Omaha, Warren and the Secretariat spent the Maui Five weekend on a comprehensive ingathering of all the assets and strategies for the coming invasion of the Congress by the people. According to the profiles the Congress Project was compiling, about 15 percent of the members of Congress were as close to first-rate as the voters were likely to get under the present corrupt political-electoral system. The advancement of the First-Stage Improvements would begin with them as the various Redirectional projects sought the most suitable sponsors for the different parts of the overall legislative agenda. But the growing populist fervor would ignore no one on Capitol Hill, not the newly arrived nor the veteran Bulls who commanded the committees. Every member would see just how decisive the stakes were for their ambitions, their parties, and of course their reelection prospects. So entrenched and complacent were the incumbents—the lifers—in their one-party districts or states that they would be completely off guard when the tornado hit the Capitol Dome. They would be flabbergasted, not so much by the legislation, but by the blitzkrieg of people power all around them— especially the people back home who they thought were loyal or simply ignorant or apathetic. The Meliorist legislation that would soon be introduced represented a politically relentless surprise attack on injustices well known to both the solons and the public. The politics of the almighty dollar and the almighty corporation had kept such legislation off the dockets and out of congressional sight for most of America's modern political history.

Which was about to be history, Warren thought to himself as he reviewed the weekend's hard work with weary satisfaction.

CHAPTER 10

D uring the month of May, gas prices continued their upward spiral. Politicians were feeling the heat from the voters back home, but not enough to overcome their fear of and feeding by the oil and gas industry, with its omnipresent, accommodating lobbyists. Although winter was more than six months away, it would take time to get the oil companies to disgorge some of the ill-gotten gains from their profiteering—say, through a windfall tax or a $10 billion charitable contribution to help the poor pay their fuel and heating bills, for starters. Whatever pressure might be brought to bear on the oil giants—and Analysis was preparing a devastating report on their collusion in the form of joint ventures with the overseas cartels and strange, well-timed domestic refinery shortages—the focus had to be on arousing the public to pressure Congress and the oil-marinated White House.

Enter "Read all about it!" and Phil's idea at Maui Four of using it against the oil companies. Through his work on the Egalitarian Clubs, Bernard had located two dynamic people in their late twenties, one working with minority children to put out a community newspaper in South Central Los Angeles, and the other helping youngsters in East New York to create their own radio programs. Ray Ramirez and Nicole Joyner were more than enthusiastic when Bernard approached them about the *Daily Bugle*, as the new paper would be called. They passed their Recruitment interviews with flying colors and started in right away.

Ray and Nicole were tailor-made for the job of finding a battalion of young people to distribute the *Bugle* during the afternoon rush hour at a thousand intersections in scores of cities—Connecticut Avenue and K Street in Washington, corners around Times Square and Union Square in New York, the Boston Commons, Chicago's Loop, Fountain Square in Cincinnati, and so on. It would be a nice paying task for youngsters in need, and would also draw out promising young leaders who were gregarious and assertive—traits they had to have to reach out to millions of passersby. The *Bugle* would be a four-page tabloid with big headlines and arresting pictures. Bernard called Barry and lined up a team of four journalists from Promotions to write the crackling copy. Yoko set him up with a graphic artist who would design the paper so that even the typeface and layout expressed indignation. With their staff in place, Ray and Nicole set a target date of one month to get the project up and running.

Meanwhile, the consolidation and deployment of the Clean Elections Party was proceeding at a furious pace. All kinds of deadlines were looming, and the finest talent was recruited to move this eagle forward fast and flawlessly. What continued to amaze Warren and his organizers was the sheer electoral and managerial talent that came out of the woodwork. It seemed that over the years the country had accumulated a stockpile of frustrated candidates, fundraisers, strategists, logistical specialists, street-level neighborhood organizers, and get-out-the vote geniuses, all waiting with fading hope for a new burst of political freedom. At once professional and refreshingly driven by ideals, they were just the sort of people the CEP needed as field organizers and for the all-important teams of administrators, compliance officers, and volunteer coordinators.

Bill Hillsman agreed to take on the promotional work for the party, from posters, lawn signs, bumper stickers, and conversation-generating buttons to TV and radio spots that would take full advantage of the sharply divergent political views of the CEP's two spokespeople, Phyllis Schlafly and John Bonifaz, to make the case for clean elections. He also planned to produce a series of demographically targeted DVDs that would be distributed by the hundreds of thousands to challenge and inspire voters and enlist their support for the clean elections agenda. That agenda was in the process of being refined by Warren's Electoral Reform project staff, along with a concise fact sheet showing specifically how clean elections would translate into a positive political climate and an improved standard of living—decent wages, affordable housing, universal Medicare, experienced-based education, and all the rest.

The drive to meet the deadlines was going well, in part because of the talent and resources applied to the endeavor, in part because of Recruitment's usual brilliance—in this case, in finding good candidates—and in part because of conventional political thinking on the part of the two major parties. The Democrats and Republicans were in possession of polls telling them that "electoral reform," "campaign finance reform," and the like bored the public and wouldn't change any votes on Election Day. They therefore made no effort to use obstructionist state laws or phony litigation to deny the Clean Elections Party ballot access or force it to miss deadlines. This major party inertia augured well for the project of cutting the Gordian knot that tied elections to the yoke of big money. And it didn't hurt that the new party had the backing to focus on Congress, where there was no atavistic Electoral College standing in the way.

The speed with which developments were coalescing was a tribute to the way Warren and his project manager had structured the CEP. It was not organized from the top down but as a broad tract of parallel pathways, each with district-specific goals. That enabled the state parties to make sure the operational tasks were completed competently and in time to beat the calendar, which was no mean feat. Warren also wanted the CEP campaigns to mesh with the reform initiatives that would be coming from the Blockbuster Challenge and the Congress Watchdogs, but that was a dicey area because strict election laws prohibited any coordination between political parties and nonprofit citizen action groups. He just had to hope that all those bright, energetic CEP staffers would pick up the ball on their own.

The day after the filing deadlines, forty-seven House incumbents and ten Senate incumbents found themselves in the teeth of a robust wind from the Clean Elections Party and its flotilla of candidates with all sails unfurled. These incumbents, who included the congressional leadership and key committee and subcommittee chairs, were soon to realize what a competitive election was all about. For the first time, they would be facing sterling candidates who were not dialing for the same corporate dollars or taking their cues from the same stale crowd of political consultants. They were about to be caught in the act of selling the voters down the river once again, and the Capitol was reverberating with the tremors. The incumbents suspected that the Clean Elections Party would be very successful at raising funds from "the little people" and raising Cain to bring media attention to its "new day" politics, and they were right. Leonard was full of ideas about how to get small contributions from large numbers of people—they were not trade secrets—but to succeed, the party needed integrity, authenticity, and the communications ability to reach these people. Fortunately, all the activities of the Redirections projects would work to the advantage of the CEP as long as there was no organizational coordination between them. Theresa Tieknots and her staff of top-flight attorneys were standing by to advise and monitor full compliance with FEC regulations.

Among the incumbents who awoke to the new day was Congressman Billy Beauchamp, who was shocked to discover that he had an opponent from the Clean Elections Party, a forty-seven-year-old dirt farmer by the name of Willy Champ. An ex-marine, tall, muscular, and outspoken, Willy had received some television coverage two years earlier for his spectacular rescue of a two-year-old girl who had been abandoned by a terrified teenage babysitter fleeing a raging fire. The footage of Willy emerging from the collapsing house carrying the little child with his jacket on fire was played again and again on the local news. Unforgettable!

But Willy Champ was more than a brave man. He was deeply steeped in the progressive history of Texas and Oklahoma, birthplaces of the great populist movement that swept much of the country between 1887 and 1912. Not far from his farm was Elk City, where Dr. Michael Shadid started the first prepaid cooperative hospital in the nation in 1928 and launched the prepaid medical care movement that led to Kaiser Permanente and the famous Puget Sound Health Care Cooperative. As Willy sat in the local library reading books, articles, and newspaper clippings about the farmers' revolt against the giant railroads and banks that were squeezing them, he could hardly believe the Oklahoma of today. It was dominated by big business from one end to the other, and its politicians were mostly on the take and on the double for their corporate overlords.

The Clean Elections Party organizer for Oklahoma's Fourth District had spent days going to one town after another in search of a candidate to run against Billy Beauchamp. The trail led to Willy, not surprisingly, for he was a talker, a joiner, and a helper to hundreds of people. During the talking, joining, and helping, he loved to expand on his favorite topic of returning the political process to the people it was designed to serve. After several conversations with his wife, Felicity, while their three teenage children were asleep in their rooms, Willy decided to take Billy Beauchamp on.

His first act as a candidate was to issue a public invitation to Congressman Beauchamp to join him in the auditorium on the campus of Southwestern Oklahoma Community College for an informal discussion about politics in America and the need for change. His tone was polite and low-key but did not conceal a note of authentic urgency. "Impudent whippersnapper!" Billy Beauchamp expostulated to his chief of staff. "I'll be damned if I'm going to dignify his candidacy by appearing on the same stage with him. Turn him down. Now!" He hoped his bluster concealed the nervous agitation he was feeling as he contemplated the upcoming campaign and recalled the unsettling conversation at Fran and Freddy's Feed.

Over at *Regulation* magazine, published under the auspices of the American Enterprise Institute, the editors were noticing a disturbing trend. Petitions submitted to the whole array of governmental regulatory agencies by "interested parties," as the statutes called them, were sharply on the rise, even in hitherto dormant areas involving corporate subsidy and contracting programs at the Departments of

Agriculture, Interior, and Commerce. There was no apparent pattern among the petitions. Some came from academics, others from environmental and consumer groups, some from businesses, others from parents who had lost a child to an unsafe medication or household product or toxic chemical. The Occupational Safety and Health Administration and the Department of Labor had received a raft of petitions from labor unions, the SEC and the bank regulatory agencies from investors and depositors.

The editor in chief of *Regulation*, Tom Topfield, called a special breakfast meeting of the editorial board to discuss the matter. As they sliced into their cantaloupe, crunched their cereal, and scraped through their scrambled eggs, they agreed that they had never seen so many petitions come into the agencies and departments in such a short time and over such a staggering range of issues—nothing remotely comparable. The one trait the petitions had in common was legal competence. The editors surmised that some top-notch regulatory and contract attorneys must be vetting them for legal and factual accuracy. Sleepy-time "regulatory Washington"—an oxymoron for years—was about to get a big wake-up call, they foresaw with a sense of foreboding, but also a perverse elation because of the heightened importance their business contributors would accord the AEI's labors. Raising his tall skinny latte, Tom Topfield exclaimed, "Gentlemen, hold on to your hats!"

The *Regulation* deregulators were not exaggerating. A huge backlog of petitions that had built up in a climate hostile to regulation was now moving front and center. It was as if a dam holding back thwarted reformers had burst and was flooding the valley of business crime, fraud, abuse, and freeloading. Little did the editors know that even as they were breakfasting, some of these petitions were being redrafted as bills that would shortly be submitted to Congress for action, and would form part of the explanation for why the Clean Elections Party was on the ballot.

To beat its competitor deregulatory think tanks and be first at the trough for prestige and corporate contributions, the AEI put its swarm of analysts into high gear to process the *Federal Register* and the public dockets at all the agencies. It took them just over a week to produce an exhaustive document with specific recommendations and alerts to a vast network of trade associations, law firms, accounting firms, and dealer and agency associations at the state and local level nationwide.

The document broke the petitions down by type. One cluster of them simply sought to update existing health and safety regulations for motor vehicles, railroads, aviation, drugs, food, and hospitals. These were the hardest to oppose, since the necessity of the regulations had been institutionalized and their obsolescence was beyond argument. They were so much out of date by years or decades that companies were able to boast in their advertising that their products "exceed federal standards."

A second cluster had never before touched the desks of the regulators and policymakers. These petitions "of first impression," as the lawyers say, called for the regulation of nanotechnology, artificial intelligence, and biotechnology, including the labeling of supermarket foodstuffs made with genetically modified crops. Bill Joy's astute advice had not been lost on the Meliorists.

Another group of petitions dealt with fraud in Medicare and other federal health payment programs, claiming that billions of dollars a year could be saved through tighter reporting, auditing, and enforcement standards. The agencies regulating credit card companies and bank transactions were asked to declare certain fine-print clauses invalid per se in standard sign-on-the-dotted-line contracts—for example, binding arbitration provisions that stripped consumers or employees of their right to go to court, or provisions stipulating that the vendors could unilaterally change the contract in any way at any time. A group of home economics teachers presented the Federal Trade Commission with a petition sure to shake the advertising world to its foundations. All claims asserted in ads would have to be substantiated in electronic files accessible to both consumers and the FTC. The teachers included vivid details about bogus advertising claims for cars, cosmetics, drugs, food, and assorted other products from light bulbs to tires.

A coalition of taxpayer associations from around the nation petitioned the Office of Management and Budget to require all agencies and departments to provide a cost-benefit analysis for existing corporate subsidy programs, including cash payments, loan guarantees, bailouts, and government giveaways of research and development or natural resources like hard rock metals—gold, silver, molybdenum, etc. The petitioners called upon the OMB to prepare taxpayer impact statements on the steady flow of government assets and resources to corporations, and to publish these statements in the *Federal Register* each year for comment. They indicated that legislation might be necessary if the OMB chose not to act on the petition.

Investor groups, organized in part through Warren's work, asked the Securities and Exchange Commission to rule that any publicly held corporation receiving federal subsidies, as carefully defined in the lengthy petition, must issue bylaws giving shareholders approval over the compensation packages of top executives, again precisely defined. The roars of rage from Wall Street would be heard all the way to Houston.

Comparable decibels were likely to issue from the gigantic government contracting industry, with its tens of thousands of vendors partaking annually in over $500 billion in government business and grants. A petition filed before the OMB by several radio and television stations, no less, sought to require that the full texts of all government contracts and grants of more than $100,000, whether to companies, partnerships, or individual recipients, be posted online for full public review and improved competitive bidding, though there was an allowance for redactions in cases involving national security, legitimate trade secrets, and individual privacy rights. A whole universe of government-business-university relationships would suddenly become visible to anyone interested in them. Timber, coal, oil, gas, and other leaseholds, overseas business promotional grants, agreements with the ubiquitous consulting firms that performed all kinds of governmental functions, including writing speeches for cabinet secretaries, would see the light of day as a matter of routine.

The think-tankers paused to remark on the sheer audacity of what they were surveying. In their wildest exaggerations of the regulatory mind-set of their adversaries, they could never have conceived of the phenomenon they were now analyzing for their various clients. The breadth, depth, speed, quality, and radiating cascades of these petitions took their breath away. What central brain was orchestrating all this, they wondered, and to what end? And why had the safety nuts and the home ec teachers and the investors and all the rest of them filed their petitions so stealthily in the past few weeks rather than publicizing them immediately?

With their document completed and duly dispatched, the AEI strategists continued to ponder these questions. Recalling Harold Mertz's column last month on the four major publications that were assigning full-time reporters to the rich guys' rebellion, they decided to have Tom Topfield get together with the reporters individually to share information. It was high time to get to the bottom of this surging upheaval.

Over four consecutive days, Topfield met with each reporter for a dutch lunch in a private dining room at the Jefferson Hotel. These were meetings of convenience, with the two parties serving as informal sources for one another. There were things that one side could do but not the other. The veteran reporter for the *New York Times*, Basil Brubaker, hinted at sources indicating that the rich guys communicated regularly over a secure closed-circuit TV system. Alas, the *Times* was prohibited by its ethical standards from retaining a firm that might attempt to crack the system. With equal subtlety, Topfield told Brubaker about the wave of petitions and bewailed his probable lack of access to the petitioners, who would no doubt refuse to answer his questions about what they were doing and who put them up to it, because they saw the AEI as too close to business. Happily, such a taint did not apply to an enterprising newspaperman, he observed as Brubaker jotted a note on his pad. And so it went, back and forth, with no real breakthroughs on either side. Brubaker returned to the office and wrote a short piece on the AEI's exhaustive analysis of the petitions and its intense interest in the business rebels. His article prodded the other corporate think tanks to take a closer look at who was behind these recent "assaults on the free enterprise system," as they characterized the burgeoning challenge.

Topfield's lunches with the other three investigative reporters were of small consequence. None of them had any solid leads except what the Meliorists were already going public with day after day, which served as an effective cover because of the scope and pace of the projects. Not only that, but there was no money trail because of the way the Meliorists had set up the funding. What the press saw was what it got—a unique form of camouflage.

In the higher echelons of the business world, frustration was building. The Meliorists were dominating the news daily. A CEO would hold a press conference to announce a merger that would be "a perfect fit," or to tout a new product, or to express support for a tax cut or a proposed trade treaty, and all the reporters wanted to talk about was "the retired rich guys' revolt." Enough already! A group of eleven powerful CEOs put a full-page ad in the *Wall Street Journal* inviting applications for a strong leader who would mobilize the business community to blunt, block, and finally defeat "this nefarious attack on the business of America." The ad stipulated the necessary qualifications—knowledge, experience, a proven track record, stamina, a clean background—and offered a salary of $10 million a year plus a ladder of bonuses pegged to successes. "Urgent! Time Sensitive!" read the headline. The ad stated at the bottom that applications had to be received within five days.

So stringent were the qualifications for this pressure-cooker position, whose occupant would have to report to these undoubtedly imperious CEOs, that many self-starters decided to take a pass. Only fourteen serious résumés came in. The CEOs met in the penthouse boardroom of the Leviathan Corporation to select the winner.

Their choice was unanimous: Lancelot Lobo, forty-eight years old, of Anglo-Saxon descent, graduate of Yale Law School and Harvard Business School, winner of his class prize for the best thesis in philosophy, and widely known as a beyond-the-pale corporate raider in the mold of Carl Icahn. In the background briefing materials was a story about Lobo's father that caught the eye of Jasper Cumbersome III, Leviathan's CEO. Vinegar Joe Stillwell of the Burma-China front during World War II was Lobo père's hero. He wanted his son to grow up, join the army, and rise to the top tough as nails. He named Lancelot after the legendary Camelot knight and expected him to achieve great exploits with the strength and stealth of a timber wolf—a lobo. One problem. Lancelot had other ideas. He wanted to be a tough hombre, all right, but he wanted to do it by taking stock positions in corporations and forcing them to restructure, spin off divisions, whatever was necessary to raise the price of their stock. One advantage to hiring Lobo was that the nation's leading pain in the ass of corporate management would be otherwise occupied. Some of the CEOs in the room had been stung, bullied, or foiled by his hardball tactics, his lawsuits, and his posturing in the press. All had to recognize that Lobo in charge of the counterattack and backed by ample resources was the ideal weapon of mass destruction. They almost began to feel sorry for the retired billionaires.

A call to Lobo to tell him of his selection and invite him to a meeting the following week elicited a loud response on speakerphone. "A week? Are you kidding? I'll be right over. I'm only twenty minutes away by limo." How could the CEOs say no to such haughty enthusiasm? They waited.

Jasper Cumbersome's secretary buzzed the boardroom. "Mr. Lobo is here to see you," she said. "Show him in," Cumbersome replied. The door opened and Lobo appeared. The CEOs gasped. In his muscular arms he held a young pit bull whose lunging was barely restrained.

Cumbersome recovered himself. "Kindly leave your friend leashed in the outer vestibule, Mr. Lobo. This is serious business."

Lobo grinned. "First impressions are everything." He pivoted, parked the pit bull as requested, and returned to take a seat at the large conference table. Without waiting for an introduction, he brashly asked his first and most important question. "Okay, you're the bosses, so exactly what is it that you do not want me to do in the process of destroying this growing cancer in our midst? I don't need you to tell me what to do. That's why you hired me. What do you not want me to do, I repeat?"

"We do not want you to seduce these rich old guys with young maidens, because no one would believe you," said Hubert Bump sarcastically. "What the hell kind of question is that to lead off with? Are you trying to convey that there's nothing you don't know? This is a far tougher job than shaking down a corporation, Lobo."

"It is clear to me, at least, Mr. Lobo, that you must be joking," said Samuel Slick, who was known as the group's diplomat. "Do you mind if we get down to business? There are many details and directions to go over, as I'm sure you'll agree."

"Just a moment," interrupted Wardman Wise, whose reputation was true to his surname. "Mr. Lobo, I trust you understand that you cannot turn the tide against this spreading force, whatever it is, with intimidation. These retired executives are not unknown quantities. They are very experienced, very well-connected, and very strong-willed, witness their entrepreneurial success against the odds. They've all been through the rough-and-tumble of business. If you do not understand this critical point, you will be less than useless to us; you will be making a bad situation worse by playing right into their hands. We admire your relentless energy, but I'm going to recommend that you return to your office, cool off, and come back next week, same time, with a coherent proposal for fulfilling the mission we selected you for today. Otherwise we will regretfully have to unselect you."

The other CEOs exchanged approving looks. It was just the right suggestion, made in just the right tone, they felt.

With a slightly chastened "As you wish," Lobo loped out the door, picked up his pit bull, and disappeared into the elevator.

Back in the boardroom, a heated discussion broke out among the CEOs. "Do we really want such a loose cannon?" asked Sal Belligerante rhetorically. "It's not like these rich oldsters are a gang of terrorists, you know." Most of the others added similar observations. The pit bull caper had truly turned them off.

Again, Wardman Wise brought them together. "We are here not because we're old friends but because we sense something powerful coming on fast, something we do not relish. In that respect we are ahead of our peers. Nor do we believe that the established trade associations, think tanks, corporate advocacy groups, and corporate law firms are up to this new and altogether unprecedented confrontation. All these groups have their routines. They can be expected to put out some criticism in print and television ads, file some opposition regulatory responses, and urge their friends in Congress to stay the course, but that will be the extent of it. The only exception that comes to mind is Brovar Dortwist, whom we've all heard so much about from our lobbyists. It was his thinking, you will recall, that led us to look for someone bold and imaginative, someone who breaks the paradigms.

"Many in the corporate world secretly admire Lancelot Lobo's brass, strategic and tactical creativity, and sheer energy in going after what he believes to be undervalued companies run by stale management. He has brought about many a merger, many a breakup, and many, many a resignation in executive suites. He has made hundreds of millions of dollars, so he is not angling for our paltry ten-million-dollar compensation package. He apparently believes, as we do, that the forces gathering against us must be exposed and stopped. Just why, I don't know, and that does make me a little suspicious. After all, Warren Buffett's drive for investor control isn't all that alien to Lobo's life work, though I doubt he's lost any sleep over the powerlessness of small investors. So let's see what he comes up with next week. Meanwhile, I'll make sure that a more thorough investigation of his motivations is conducted promptly.

"Lest we panic, let's remember that the courts are still largely our courts. Our president and his executive branch are definitely ours. And so far Congress is just fidgety, though a close continuing scrutiny, member by member, is warranted. All things considered, we're in tight at the top, regardless of the stirrings of the masses.

As for the Clean Elections Party, it has chosen the dullest, most abstruse issue imaginable. It will go nowhere, other than to excite some left-wing magazines and a few reform-minded professors and good-government types."

"Words to the wise, gentlemen, from the Wise." Hubert Bump chuckled at his clever wordplay. "It is now the eighteenth of May. Soon Congress will break for the Memorial Day weekend. People will be preoccupied with school graduations and vacation preparations. We can afford to err on the side of caution in selecting a fighting first responder who will not boomerang on us. And by the way, why don't we try to set up some informal meetings with the retired old guys, one on one." He paused and chuckled again. "For the sake of convenience, let's call them the SROs, for Super-Rich Oldsters," he said, thinking of seedy Single Room Occupancy hotels. No one stopped to consider that the acronym also stood for Standing Room Only.

"Good suggestion, Hubert," said Wardman Wise. "We have nothing to lose and everything to gain by talking to the SROs personally in a relaxed setting."

The eleven CEOs vowed to do just that in the coming fortnight.

Throughout May, the Meliorists kept each other informed through their daily closed-circuit conferences and the information streaming on the secure website. Toward the end of the month, in preparation for Maui Six, Patrick Drummond posted a memo on the website summarizing the more salient developments as follows.

> ❯ The PCC has started establishing state chapters. Luke Skyhi is consulting with Dee Hock about structuring the organization chaordically so that the chapters adhere to core values and message, and at the same time have maximum freedom to operate creatively and adapt to local conditions. Luke is also soliciting ideas on how to sharpen the fighting spirit of the PCC's natural allies in the sustainable arena for the mission of displacing the

ecocidal multinational economy. He complains that they behave "like people in the cooperative movement—nice, but without the edge that makes the difference."

❯ Bill C. and Paul request that the dead money/live money discussion resume at Maui Six. They are grappling with the transformation of assets on such a large scale, but believe they are making some progress. Analysis is assisting.

❯ Bernard's Egalitarian Clubs have hit the final exams/ summer vacation hiatus. There are several clubs underway, and many promising prospects for the fall. He's been working on the *Daily Bugle* project with Ray Ramirez and Nicole Joyner, who have now enlisted almost three hundred youngsters to distribute the paper. He reports that the kids are giving him some great ideas about what the clubs should do and how to increase their appeal.

❯ Ted has hired two experienced writers to put out an instant book titled *Billionaires on Bullshit*. He thinks it will be a raging success, taking off on the recent bestseller *On Bullshit*, by Harry G. Frankfurt, emeritus professor of philosophy at Princeton. Ted also reports that one of his billionaires wants to endow a foundation foundation— that is, one that will encourage the super-wealthy to start family foundations along systematic justice lines and will show them exactly how to do it. Ted says he was impressed by this billionaire's sophistication in recognizing the need to sow seeds for basic shifts of power to the citizenry. He referred the gentleman to Bernard, and the two immediately fell into impassioned conversation about injustice. They're now working out the nuts and bolts of getting the new foundation off the ground.

❭ Yoko has completed and sent to her publisher a beautifully rendered art book dealing with "questions your children and grandchildren are likely to ask you." She has tentatively titled it *No Pox on Posterity*, but wonders if a shorter, catchier title is needed. She invites suggestions.

❭ Bill G. and Joe report that their project's monograph, "The State of Justice in America: Supply and Demand," published in early May, has prompted the attorneys general of New York and California to announce that they will issue their own State of Justice reports by Labor Day. Bill and Joe think that other state AGs are bound to follow suit, because of all the publicity about the monograph, and because the essay contests on the most and least just states are attracting so much attention to longstanding inequities and problems.

❭ Leonard is sending each of you a copy of *Economic Apartheid in America*, just updated and out in paperback. He asks you to read it closely in preparation for Maui Six. He particularly directs your attention to page 67, where the authors describe the power shift since the 1970s: "On the Rise have been big campaign contributors, corporate lobbyists, corporations, big asset owners, CEOs, and Wall Street. In Decline have been their opposites—popular political movements, voters, labor unions, wage earners, employees and Main Street." Leonard points out that this is an oversimplification of the sixties and prior decades. Power was concentrated then too, but at least there were battles pitting the people against the corporate bosses. Washington awoke once in a while to recognize why it was there. On some important policies, the Democrats and Republicans actually fought each other. Big Business was well entrenched in the Washington scene, but at crucial junctures it was on the defensive or simply busy holding on to its power. In the mid-seventies the dam broke, and a dazzling corporate offensive on all fronts began to lay the foundations of the present almighty corporate state. The book is a clear-eyed, graphic "primer on economic inequality and insecurity," as the subtitle has it. Leonard thinks it will be invaluable in formulating the action plan for the First-Stage Improvements. He has also cut a deal with the publisher to buy millions of copies at a little above cost and distribute them at the lunchtime rallies.

❯ Peter reports that the number of members of Congress who have placed their voting records on their websites or credibly committed to do so ASAP has now reached 187. Critical mass has been achieved. How much longer will the other members be able to resist such an obvious service to voters without paying a political price? For those who do resist, the Congress Watchdogs will make sure they regret it through the Getting to Know You exposés. The 187 legislators all put out press releases that were favorably received back home by both their constituents and the media. One editorial said of the online records, "Now it's up to the voters to use them."

❯ Warren reports that a team of analysts from Electoral Reform and the Congress Project are putting the finishing touches on a compendium of materials about the careers and affiliations of all the members of Congress. The compendium establishes four categories of senators and representatives: the already convinced, the persuadables, the chronic corporatists, and the rigid ideologues. For each category, it lays out a calibrated series of steps to win them over or to neutralize their opposition by shining the spotlight on them in various forums—in their respective committees, floor debates, and through the media at all applicable levels, back home in their congressional offices, at their citizen meetings during recesses, among their campaign finance patrons and circles of friends, and through feedback from the voters themselves. According to Warren, who has seen the penultimate draft, the analysts have drawn on the finest work of practitioners and scholars of Congress, and have condensed the insights, the history, the customs and sensibilities of that institution into a menu of action for legislating the First-Stage Improvements. "It's as if they were designing an outlet for an electrical plug and achieved a perfect fit," he says. The document will be sent to you shortly. He asks that you digest it before Maui Six so you can add your observations at the meeting.

❯ As General Motors stock continues to fall, feelers about Jerome Kohlberg's takeover proposal are tapping into greater interest. It's no longer pie in the sky, though the company's large unfunded liabilities remain the obvious sticking point.

❯ Progress continues on the Credibility Project, but it is inherently amorphous. Goodwill efforts tend to be just that, Ross says, but they pay dividends in the most unexpected ways. He predicts that the benefits will emerge when conflicts sharpen. The project also meshes well with the continuing expansion and maturation of the epicenters around the core members.

❯ Bill Joy requests to be told immediately of any security breaches or any surveillance of the Redirection projects and of course the core members. He is preparing for all contingencies, including attempts to penetrate the closed-circuit briefings and the website. He urges the core members to continue their high media visibility on their various public initiatives. The more publicity there is now, the bigger the news if any snooping is discovered later.

❯ Wal-Mart's poll of consumers is out, showing high favorables to carefully choreographed questions. Questions that would have produced unfavorables were not used. Publicity was national but light—six-inch-squib level.

❯ Plans for the mass media branding of the Meliorists, due in late April, require more time and have been rescheduled for mid-June. Suggested release date: the Fourth of July. It will be hard to keep the Meliorists as a group under wraps beyond then, nor is it tactically advisable to do so, says Barry. Warren suggests that the Seventh-Generation Eye be adopted as the Meliorist symbol.

❯ Last week George delivered another major address, this time before the annual convention of the American Conservative Union. His theme was that when big business exercises great political power in a society, it seriously distorts and diminishes the efficiency of the market writ large. Too often big firms use their political power to insulate themselves from marketplace discipline, to the detriment of the public good, their politically weaker competitors, and basic conservative doctrines. He said that political power can be an irresistible narcotic for corporatists masquerading as conservatives, but not for genuine conservatives. He peppered his speech with telling illustrations, from bailouts to the stifling of innovation by political forces indentured to stagnant big business. He got a five-minute standing ovation. Those in attendance fully understood his distinction between corporatists and conservatives. Their frustration with Wall Street and with the Republican Party, which steadily expands big government whenever it is in power, was evident in their response to George's trenchant remarks.

❯ The lead team that will be acquiring firms in multiple lines of industry and commerce for the Sub-economy Redirection has been certified by Recruitment and is on the job, Jeno reports. Their budget will reflect a detailed acquisition plan for using leveraged buyouts, drawing on credit instead of cash, and making cash purchases as a last resort. The plan will be completed and on the agenda for review at Maui Six. Barry has designated five of his top people at Promotions to focus exclusively on insuring maximum public and trade understanding of these comprehensive moves. The sub-economy that is emerging out of Luke Skyhi's sustainability shows and other Redirectional initiatives, bolstered by the acquisition of a regular sub-economy, will make for wondrous dynamics and transitions, Jeno predicts, not to mention convulsions of the business status quo. The acquisitions team is talented, experienced, and motivated. They make no effort to hide their excitement.

After reviewing Patrick's memo, the Meliorists began devoting the daily closed-circuit updates to the agenda for Maui Six. Their conversations revealed a rising impatience for action on the First-Stage Improvements. By now the infrastructure for a just, fair, and functional democracy was largely in place. The people were aroused as never before—some 40 million of them, by one Redirection or another, according to the estimates of Leonard's manager at the Mass Demonstrations Project. The CUBs and Congress Watchdogs were ramping up furiously. The organizers and lecturers were making thousands of contacts in the communities and neighborhoods, enlisting active support and creating vital reservoirs of passive support that worked to neutralize potential opposition among the credibility groups. Barry's network acquisitions were in place and soon began to join with his existing media outlets in highlighting the genuinely newsworthy. Ted's Billionaires Against Bullshit were becoming a juggernaut as they increasingly felt the power of their underutilized human and material capital. Warren Beatty's California tidal wave was washing over Arnold and rippling across the nation. Sol's assault on Wal-Mart was lifting the spirits of thousands of despondent people trying to support their families on a pittance. The PCC had sent the hitherto unchallenged trade associations backpedaling into an almost incoherent defensive posture. The steadily spreading lunchtime rallies were waking up urban business districts and politically sleepy suburbs. The theatrics of events like Bill Gates's corporation jamborees, Luke Skyhi's arena shows, the Sun God festivals, and the Pot-In had given the Redirections an aesthetic, satirical, and humorous dimension that tempered the aura of indignation often surrounding the other initiatives. The courageous valedictories, George's addresses, and Peter's congressional testimony got the chattering classes thinking, and not always along conformist lines. Sure, there were glitches—a few interviewees got their incompetence past Recruitment and had to be fired, a few deadlines were missed—but overall, every category of Redirectional effort was going strong.

In addition, the replication and emulation effects so often discussed at Maui were taking hold with a vengeance. The sparks generated by Patriotic Polly, Yoko's bulbs, and Bill and Joe's unorthodox probes of the Pledge of Allegiance and the National Anthem had reached millions who were usually detached from public debate. Weeks of eye-popping events around the country, portrayed on television and reported on the radio, in magazines, newspapers, and blogs, were raising the morale of people of all ages and backgrounds. The signs were everywhere—in impassioned letters to the editor, in the higher quality of call-ins on talk radio, in greater turnouts for local municipal meetings and hearings, in the huge numbers of students seeking summer internships with citizen action groups and local, state, and federal regulatory agencies. Capitol Hill was flooded with résumés from accomplished high school and college students with impressive know-how, instead of the usual on-the-make budding politicians with know-who. The CUBs, the Congress Watchdogs, and even the labor unions were receiving piles of résumés from young Americans wanting in on the action. The new sustainable economy models were quickening the imaginations of millions of young people and prompting them to look beyond the tried and tired avenues of conventional business careers. They were thinking solar, organic farming, appropriate technology, new forms of equitable financing, carbohydrate efficiencies, an end to staggering economic disparities—entirely new ways of meeting human needs, motivated by something other than bottomless greed. More and more citizens could find the often awful voting records of their members of Congress online. The Clean Elections Party was forging a hammer within the electoral system. The Blockbuster Challenge was nearing its unveiling and was sure to attract overflow media attention with its sensible shocker, "Buy Back Your Congress."

All these pincer movements were closing in on the 535 members of Congress, who were about to experience the vivifying of the innate sense of fairness possessed by a majority of the people. Once the First-Stage Improvements legislation was drafted, the Meliorists would move with surprise and alacrity. They were not going to wait for some miraculous change in government personnel. They had realized long ago that with the right mobilization of strong converging pressures, all that was necessary was for elected officials to know how to read and want to keep their jobs.

There was great enthusiasm for the Fourth of July as a rollout date. Paul proposed that they refer to it in their public statements as "Independence Day for the Sovereignty of the People." Barring an unforeseen leak, the Meliorists would go public immediately after the celebration of the Fourth, giving the whole Redirectional phenomenon the personal drama, the unprecedented drama, of the elder super-rich revolting against the reigning super-rich on behalf of the people of these United States.

The Fourth of July had other advantages. Congress would be in session all month, so the multiple First-Stage bills could be introduced right after the Fourth and begin working their way through the House and Senate, all the while generating intense discussion and debate. Meanwhile, parallel legislative drives would be launched in selected state legislatures both as an insurance policy and to put additional pressure on Capitol Hill and the White House. In August, Congress would recess, and the members would be back home where the folks could get at them. When they returned in September, it would be off to the races to enact the legislation before Election Day in November. The idea was to make incumbents campaign for reelection by legislating, not with slogans or by spending big money on vapid television testimonials to their greatness. Their words would be separated from and held up to their deeds, as Max pointed out.

Sol reported that his eggheads had gotten their act together and were almost finished drafting the various First-Stage bills. They had drawn on the best work of public interest lawyers and law professors in past efforts at reform. Mark Green was staying on top of them and making sure that the quality of the legislation was first-rate; nothing would submarine the hopes of sponsors like sloppily or ambiguously drafted bills that left loopholes opponents could use to delay or block their implementation even after they were enacted. Jeno stressed that the First-Stage Improvements had to be presented in such a way that the people viewed them as long-overdue, commonsense measures that were achievable and would displace existing wasteful and disruptive policies. It was supremely important that tens of millions of Americans felt relief was on the way in recognition of their years of unrequited hard work, their squandered taxes, and their frustrated hopes for their children. It would be Promotions' job to make sure that the bills were justified to the public in clear language rooted in the vernacular, not in Senatese or bureaucratese. The Congress Project was drawing up a list of potential sponsors in the House and Senate for review at Maui Six. Every attempt would be made to introduce the bills with no overlapping of committee jurisdictions that would delay action. If there were several willing sponsors for a given bill, the most senior would be chosen; the rest could cosponsor. The Congress Project was also busy choosing, weighing, and sorting influence groups for specific bills. Capitol Hill was about relationships, not just money and power. Lobbyists connected differently with different members of Congress, who all had long memories. Outside constituency groups would play a role as well. The First-Stage legislation would give them an opportunity to flower once again, independent of the Meliorists but working in the same direction. There was no dearth of willing and experienced talent here—after all, it had been a long drought for such groups.

Bernard had been in touch with ex-congressman Cecil Zeftel and ex-senator James Zabouresk, who had ten more former members of Congress, all with sterling, even historic records of progressive contributions to their country, waiting in the wings to lend their support. The Trojan Horse project of infiltrating congressional staff with new hires committed to reform had hit a wall because of extremely low turnover in such positions, so Bernard told Zeftel and Zabouresk about the forthcoming First-Stage legislation, in suitably guarded terms, and asked if they could try to augment their group in readiness for it. Within a week they had lined up a dozen of their ablest former senior staffers, who were delighted by the prospect of resurrecting some of their favorite unfinished business. They were especially keen on a living wage, universal healthcare, an end to raids on the taxpayers, and a crackdown on outlaw corporations (the antitrust subcommittees used to have large staffs).

As May drew to a close, the Meliorists focused all their energies on making the most of this brief window in history before the November elections. They had to weave all the strands of the Redirections into a complex but not overly elaborate tapestry. They had to focus a laser on Congress, shine the light of justice for all over the entire country, and issue a clarion call that rang right through all the entrenched obstacles to success. To that end, the Secretariat had assigned its best talent the task of preparing a comprehensive sequential strategy paper for discussion at Maui Six. The passion at previous Mauis was about horizon, vision, groundwork. Maui Six was the operational plan for D-Day—Democracy Day. America's long slide into the jaws of corporate domination was about to be arrested and reversed.

The week was up. Lancelot Lobo returned to the penthouse board-room with his proposal. Silent skepticism greeted him as he prepared to give his presentation. Wardman Wise's inquiries into Lobo's motivations had turned up something of interest. It seemed that Lobo despised Jeno Paulucci, who years ago had beat him in a merger conflict, and disliked the amiable Warren Buffet, who had snatched two choice acquisition targets out from under him and merged them into his own conglomerate. Lobo hated to lose, espe-cially to people who were so much older than he was. He carried grudges. Not the noblest of motivations for this mission, the CEOs agreed, but it laid to rest any suspicion that Lobo was a Trojan horse or a superficial convert. What troubled them was the possibility that he had taken the job just to grind his personal axes.

"Mr. Lobo, you may proceed," said CEO Cumbersome. "Take as long as you like in outlining your strategy against the Super-Rich Oldsters, as we have christened them, and then we will have an exchange of thoughts."

Lobo inwardly rolled his eyes. "Much obliged, gentlemen. New endeavors are necessarily entered into with the assets and baggage of previous experience. In the past, I have always begun by clearly delineating the territory of the battlefield. It is relatively easy for a corporate raider to locate the battlefield. In the case of the SROs, there is no battlefield on which to engage, or rather, there are so many battlefields that it's impossible to engage on all of them. Even-tually, the SROs will give us a core battlefield, because they seem to want results, not just to stir up trouble. I see all their provocations as means to their end of effecting change by getting to those who hold the real power in our society. Which is a long way of saying that we do not know enough. They haven't shown enough of their hand for us to direct our counterattack effectively.

"I don't believe for a minute that they're just a bunch of lone wolves—if you'll indulge me in the metaphor—who started acting up randomly in January. There are too many clues to the contrary, starting with the 'Stay tuned' mantra. So let's assume that they're acting in concert. So what? Normally we want to know whether our opponents are formally organized, because if they are, we can trace who's funding the enterprise. Well, when we're dealing with billionaires on top of billionaires, we know where the money's coming from, don't we? I mean, one of them is the second-richest man in the world. Instead of getting hung up on whether they're acting in what we might ironically call a corporate manner, let's simply state what we know about what we don't know.

"We don't know their stamina. We don't know how much money they've spent or are willing to spend. We don't know whether collectively they're the source of the recent surge of regulatory petitions, or of the Clean Elections Party, or of the Warren Beatty phenomenon. We know only what they've chosen to have us know—Sol Price's move on Wal-Mart, Joe Jamail's small claims court litigation, Bill Gates Sr.'s incorporation stunts, and on and on. Consequently, what we are left with is a series of investigative probes to flush our enemies out, to find out where the battlefield will be and what cracks they have in their armor.

"The first priority is to penetrate their communication systems and their face-to-face meetings. Given everything they've put in motion, it's a safe assumption that both the systems and the meetings have been operating in overdrive. The second front is to infiltrate their full-time staff and volunteers. We need ears and eyes inside the Beast on a daily basis. I've been told that their interviewers are very good, alert and appropriately suspicious, but like all of us, they're not perfect. And the wider the net they cast, the more vulnerable they are to infiltration.

"Apart from gathering information, what else should our infiltrators do? Should they throw a monkey wrench into the works, sowing discord, sabotaging plans, using all the tricks our own snoops employ routinely? I can see to it that they do. Our people are experienced in corporate infiltration campaigns that don't quite cross the line of the law, in keeping with our avowed policy. Alternatively, we can use the information we glean to mount a public corporate campaign against them. The choice is up to you, but I don't recommend the monkey wrench, because once we unleash the monkeys, there's no guarantee we can control them. Far better to have a big donnybrook right out in the open, an approach that has the added advantage of not responding to the SROs in ways that confirm what they've been saying about big business.

"On a third front, we should muster our troops to engage in skirmishes that will tie them up and draw them into wars of attrition. And who knows how to do this better than corporate lobbyists and lawyers? They are geniuses at the craft. They can stretch the calendar like it was Plastic Man, and let's remember that the SROs aren't spring chickens. Sure, we'll be up against pockets as deep as ours. We won't be able to break them financially, as we do with injured or sick claimants or small businesses or lone investors, but that's not the point. When I was in law school, one of my professors told a story about Bruce Bromley, a top partner at Cravath, Swaine and Moore, who once bragged to an assemblage at Stanford Law School, 'I was born, I think, to be a protractor. . . . I could take the simplest antitrust case and protract the defense almost to infinity. One case lasted fourteen years. . . . Despite fifty thousand pages of testimony, there really wasn't any dispute about the facts.' That's what can be done in the judicial arena alone. Similar trespasses on eternity can be extended to the legislative and executive branches as well.

"Fourth, we should attack their legitimacy, their motives, and their credibility. So far they've had it pretty easy. The blasts from Bush Bimbaugh and our think tanks, the miscellaneous cries of outrage and ridicule just don't pass muster. They're anemic, amnesiac, humdrum, and expected, all noise, no effect. Our ripostes have to come from fresh sources. They have to provoke mass fears, insecurities, passions, and anxieties that can be brought to bear on the SROs. The talent for this job is around and can be retained readily. However, in reviewing our material on the SROs, I noticed one glaring omission. None of them have attacked the military-industrial complex or the intelligence agencies or our country's foreign and military policies. I don't believe that's inadvertent. It's a shrewd choice enabling them to sidestep accusations of being unpatriotic, not supporting our soldiers, and imperiling our national security. They obviously don't want these distractions. They are strictly domestic in focus, which makes our job that much harder—fewer labeling opportunities, so to speak, once the battle is joined.

"Fifth, it goes without saying that all of our corporate assets across the entire spectrum of power, from Madison Avenue to Wall Street to our university friends to the 'corporate government,' as the SROs say, must be mobilized and plunged into action. Because of the unconventional nature of our opponents, we cannot rely on a business-as-usual exercise of corporate muscle. We have to be nimble, imaginative, and willing to revise tactics and strategies in the face of a changing situation, unlike our Michigan friends in the auto industry.

"Finally, perhaps the greatest unknown of all—yourselves and your comparably concerned peers. What are you willing to do, to say, and to risk? You can't just outsource this endeavor and write the checks for it. The SROs have put themselves on the line, and while I realize they're mostly retired, most people of their vintage would not want such tumult in their golden years. They are risking something more than their liquid assets and, for all I know, their investments.

"Before you respond, two points. First, none of this can be accomplished in a week. I estimate that it will take more like four or five weeks. Second, I want you to reduce the annual compensation of ten million dollars plus bonuses you've offered to one dollar. Our opponents are people of conviction, however wrongheaded. They have to be countered by conviction. The credibility that will accrue to whomever you choose to lead this undertaking is an essential component of winning the battle for public opinion. The principle holds even more for someone like me, since my national image is one of maximum self-enrichment, one that paints me as in it only for the money and not for any purpose of making companies more efficient and giving shareholders more value and more rights. Well, not on this watch, should you decide to select me."

CEO Bradford Knowles looked around the conference table at his colleagues. "Mr. Lobo, I think I speak for all of us when I say that your proposal has exceeded my expectations. We asked you to describe your strategy, and you certainly did. Quite impressive, sober, and fundable. Your instincts are finely honed, as evidenced throughout your presentation, and especially in your extraordinary offer to work for a year as a volunteer. That certainly frames our response more personally. Thank you."

"Consider yourself selected, Mr. Lobo," said Wardman Wise. "Our group will commence discussion among ourselves and with our friends in high places with all dispatch. We will provide a budget suitable for the implementation of your plan and will be in regular contact with you as you work out the details. We understand that this is a complex initiative, but we hope you can actualize it in four weeks, five at the outside. Send us your requirements for your executive staff and whatever other resources and facilities you need right away. Keep us informed as often as you believe necessary. And remember, at this stage you are preparing a plan. There are to be no operations whatsoever until we open that gate explicitly in the latter part of June, assuming your work goes smoothly.

"As for the 'greatest unknown of all,' the nature and scope of our own commitment, we'll be hard at work in our private meetings to make sure that it becomes known, to us and to you. I'm sure we'll have a plethora of questions for you in the coming days, but for now we are adjourned. Your clarity and sense of purpose are admirable, Mr. Lobo. Get to work."

Immediately after Lobo took his leave, the self-chosen task force of concerned CEOs moved to schedule one-on-one meetings with the most publicly visible of the Meliorists. They framed their invitations forthrightly and had their secretaries make the calls. The first one was to Joe Jamail's office: "Good morning, this is Janet Kelly at Monolith Steel. Our CEO, Bradford Knowles, has read about Mr.

Jamail's small claims project and would be most pleased to be able to have a few moments with him at his convenience, inasmuch as they both reside in Houston." Out of curiosity, Joe agreed to a meeting. "Sure, why not?" he said to his staff, "but no way in hell is Bradford Knowles going to give a dime to anything that smacks of justice for the little guy." Knowles, both courtly and cruel to the workers who sweated over his blast furnaces, had repeatedly seen his factories cited by OSHA as dangerous workplaces.

Four days later at the Petroleum Club for lunch, the conversation between the two began with inane pleasantries and extravagant flattery from Knowles. Joe cut him off with a blunt question. "So why did you want to get together, Brad? I'm not suing you. Not yet, anyway."

"Well, Joe, I've been reading the papers and watching the news like many of us business executives these past few months, and I just wanted to get your take on things. What are you and the other retired billionaires up to, revving the populace up the way you are?"

Joe was expecting this little maneuver and didn't bite. "Are you referring to the People's Court Society and my efforts with Bill Gates Sr. to change the Pledge of Allegiance and replace the National Anthem?"

"Yes, and a lot more," Knowles said, listing half a dozen of the core group's initiatives. "There seems to be a pattern coming from a central organization, no?"

"These fellows have organized their own enterprises their whole successful business lives. They don't need organizing by anyone. You know what self-starters are like, Brad."

Knowles laid on a thick drawl. "I guess so, Joe, but I'm not very sophisticated. I grew up in Okalona, Mississippi, and psychologically I'm still there. Educate me. Is there an intelligent design here?"

"Absolutely," Joe said. "The rich guys are trying to do what the Almighty told them to do—you know, the Golden Rule and the Ten Commandments. It's not much more sophisticated than that. Your hometown preacher would understand."

"But where are they going with all this reformist zealotry? I mean, do they have a plan to fundamentally change this glorious system of ours, or do they just want to tweak it and make it work a little better?"

Joe saw his chance to turn the tables on Knowles. "To me, making it better *means* changing it. Don't you think it needs to be changed, since the majority of the people are losing ground?" he asked affably, and proceeded to conduct a masterful lunchtime cross-examination on the failures of the power brokers and big corporations to deliver an economy and government that genuinely served the people. Fortunately for Knowles, a former business competitor dining at a nearby table came over and inadvertently rescued him from Joe's cordial offensive. Knowles excused himself and went off to the bar for drinks with his newfound friend.

The CEOs' one-on-one meetings with the other Meliorists were variations on the theme played out by Joe and Knowles. The Meliorists got to know their leading CEO adversaries far better than they could have by reading memos from the informants they'd cultivated ever since the *Wall Street Journal* ad came out. For their part, the CEOs went away feeling that crazy as the SROs were, their eruptions were individual in nature, and that there was no collaboration beyond their taking encouragement from each other's exploits.

Without doubt the most humorous meeting was between Wardman Wise and Leonard Riggio regarding the lunchtime rallies. Leonard toyed with the overly serious CEO. "Hey, just some old-fashioned American protest festivities with a nutritious lunch, Wardman. It's important to let fellows like you know that the working people are still around and can find one another face to face, away from the ocean of screens and machines you've got them glued to every day. That is, assuming they have a job at all, or one that's not on its way to China or India."

Wise kept probing and Leonard kept joshing. He asked his luncheon companion innocently how anyone could have any trouble with what the lunchtime crowds wanted. Then he pounced. "How much do you make an hour, Wardman?"

Wise choked on a bite of watercress. "Well, it's not figured by the hour."

"But you can divide, can't you? You've made an average of, what is it, sixteen million dollars a year over the past five years? That works out to about nine thousand dollars an hour, not counting benefits and perks. What's the average hourly wage in your home healthcare chain?"

Realizing that he had more to lose than to gain, Wardman Wise clumsily changed the subject to some ongoing governmental boon-doggle in post-Katrina New Orleans. The principal upshot of the luncheon meetings was that the Secretariat worked up exhaustive profiles of the eleven CEOs, their past business dealings, their present positions, and their views on public policies and economic philosophy. Just in case.

It took Ray Ramirez and Nicole Joyner less than a month to get the *Daily Bugle* off the ground. True, they had a superlative infrastructure at their beck and call, but the planning, the organizing, the selection of cities and suburbs were all their own. With three hundred newsgirls and newsboys on board, they were confident of hitting the thousand mark over the next couple of weeks as one youngster found another.

The first three hundred hit the streets at 4:00 p.m. on the Friday of the Memorial Day weekend. Their smart uniforms and the stylish design of the *Bugle* caught the eyes of passersby who normally avoided anyone handing out anything. Even more effective were the cries of "Read all about it!" There was a clarity to them, an irresistible nostalgia, a melody of urgency and authenticity in a communications world of virtual reality screens. The three-hour audio training sessions for the kids really paid off.

Wherever possible, the headlines on the *Bugle*'s debut issue focused on the oil and gas industry, as in Dallas: "Extra, extra! Read all about it! Eron Oil pays no property taxes, but you do. Read all about it!" The Cincinnati edition ran with a hot local topic: "Toxic dirt used for landscaping at 4,200 homes. Campaign contributions to look-the-other way officials in City Hall involved. Read all about it!" In Birmingham it was, "Three local schools to be built on toxic brownfields. Children in danger, physicians declare. Prosecution of companies involved in cover-up urged. Read all about it!"

Some of the headlines were national in scope: "Fifty-three large corporations to unload worker pensions on Feds. Millions of workers affected. Local impact devastating. Read all about it!" Or, "White House blocks CDC physicians from warning 250,000 workers exposed daily to dangerous chemicals in hundreds of factories, foundries, and mines. Local industries named. Read all about it!" Or, "Half of all US corporations paid no income tax this year. Read all about it!"

Once the project reached its full complement, it would build on the lunchtime rallies in growing numbers of cities and towns— again the synergy, always the synergy. Already the criers were drawing media attention to themselves, being interviewed by mobile television units and radio reporters. Websites were streaming them to large audiences. They were more articulate than most adults and had studied the issues they were shouting about, so they came across to the press as a new generation of reformers, not as kids parroting headlines for pay.

The criers' project did have an unintended consequence. It was one thing for top executives to read memos and news stories about the doings of the upstart billionaires. It was quite another for them to look out the window of the executive suite and watch young people below excoriating the corporate world to throngs of pedestrians, some of whom might even be their own employees, their own personal staff. Day by day, more and more of them began to feel a visceral sense of urgency about mobilizing a counterreaction. The tastefully furnished metropolitan clubs where they met for lunch began to simmer with a mix of alarm and anger. Their e-mail chatter flew thick and fast as the newly aroused executives sought each other out and put their heads together.

In the congressional dining rooms, secluded nook bars, and gymnasiums, the legislators kept asking each other, "What the hell is going on?" A few were delighted by recent developments, more were alarmed, but even more believed that whatever it was, it would blow over. These were mostly incumbents who had been in Congress for twelve years or more and had a jaundiced view of the public's attention span. Besides, any move to upset their comfortable apple cart would butt up squarely against the obscure and labyrinthine rules they had installed to turn Congress into a procedural obstacle course. The congressional power brokers had learned that substantive opposition to, say, a living wage made for bad press and ugly imagery, especially when they annually raised their own salaries, pensions, and perks, so they fell back on procedural straitjackets that bottled up such legislation for the duration. As one senior senator complacently said to a worried young colleague as they swam together in the Senate pool, "Have you ever heard of a revolution against procedures?" The young senator, finishing a lap, replied, "Yeah, the one you guys started. You pulled off a revolution against open procedures inside the Congress, and nobody reported it. Too dull and complex. So I guess in a sense you're right." He would shortly have occasion to remember this conversation.

On the last day of May, a Dartford warbler, known to be a denizen of the European side of the Atlantic, was sighted in a New Jersey marsh by an avid bird watcher. Astonished and exhilarated, she put the word out. Within hours, droves of bird watchers were heading to the marsh from all points of the compass to catch a glimpse of a species never before seen in America. The bird, a young male, must have sensed the onrush, because it flew off due south. The bird-watchers' network swung into action, reporting sightings of the little transatlantic explorer in South Jersey, then Delaware, then Maryland, until finally hundreds saw it alight on the Capitol Dome of the United States Congress! The hundreds became thousands, and the thousands became tens of thousands, their numbers swelled by a media frenzy. Even the usually sedate European press was enthralled.

The Capitol Police took a dim view of the hordes of onlookers equipped with binoculars, gloves, cameras, and notebooks. Senators, representatives, and staffers looked out their windows in astonishment. Washington was used to big crowds demonstrating on controversial issues, but a bird? Some of the legislators came out and started shaking hands. The warbler appeared to like the Dome, with its pilasters and crannies. There was rainwater. Someone gave it bird food on the sly. It settled in.

Standing outside the Capitol, the bird watchers suddenly realized that they were in the immediate proximity of politicians who could do something about grievances they had harbored for years. Soon clusters of them were organizing themselves around common complaints, such as developers draining wetlands and getting fat off tax breaks to boot. They decided to go inside to visit their elected representatives, who had been assiduously sending out form letters touting their great labors on behalf of their constituents. Happily for the bird watchers, it was Wednesday, usually the day of lowest absenteeism in the Congress.

The absorptive capacity of the congressional corridors was limited, barely adequate for the daily influx of lobbyists in tailored suits and Gucci loafers. The denim-clad bird watchers caused a pedestrian traffic jam as more and more of them poured into the Senate and House office buildings, into the cafeterias and restrooms, adding to their lists of complaints as friends and relatives called them on their cell phones: "While you're there, ask Senator Frisk about that business-sponsored bill to sell off public lands," or "Tell Congressman Carefree that making it harder for workers to get fair compensation for workplace injuries is going to cost him the election," or "Dammit, Maud, make sure Senator Crabgrass understands that he has to support the mandatory labeling of genetically engineered food."

The bird watchers just kept coming and coming. The House and Senate campaign committees of both parties were advised to treat them with courtesy. "There are about fifteen million of them in the country," said one consultant, "and they're a hardy lot, getting up at dawn to slog through chilly estuaries, swamps, bogs, and marshes. They can cause trouble. Polls show that they turn out to vote in high numbers. Don't offend them."

As long as the bird stayed, the bird watchers stayed. Consternation spread through the congressional leadership. They wanted to give the warbler the pigeon-spray treatment, but a move like that could be a disastrous tipping point in the November elections. On Friday afternoon they called an emergency meeting on the single topic of how to get the bird out of town so the bird watchers would get out of town. For reasons of national security, the meeting was held in the Senate Intelligence Committee room. Leaks had to be avoided at all costs!

The party leaders entered the room grim-faced, and not because they were missing their golf games. This was grim business. The entire apparatus of Congress was on overload—the Capitol Police, the kitchen and janitorial staff, the secretaries and receptionists, and especially the security screeners. Worse, the bird watchers were threatening to disrupt the smooth and mutually beneficial business arrangements between lawmakers and lobbyists. And what if a female warbler showed up and decided it liked life on the Dome too? The burgeoning crowds would bring the government to a halt.

Senator Thurston Thinkalot, a stalwart on the Intelligence Committee, led off with a suggestion. "Let's get the naval sonar warfare people over here on the double to drive the bird away with a high-frequency whine. No one, not the press or the birders, would be the wiser."

"I like it," said Senator Crabgrass.

"But what if they damage the bird's neurological system or kill it?" asked Senate Majority Leader Tillman Frisk.

"That would be catastrophic," said Congressman Beauchamp. "For one thing, we'd have the animal rights people all over us. Just remember what happened to a certain California governor who tangled with the medfly. And that was a pest damaging to farmers, not a cute little ball of feathers heroically crossing an ocean to the delight of millions of adults and children watching the daily television coverage."

"Not to mention the websites and blogs devoted to round-the-clock accounts of the bird's every move," added Senator Paul Pessimismo.

There were a few moments of silence as the legislators stroked their chins and furrowed their brows, desperately seeking a solution. Suddenly, a security-cleared staffer rushed into the room to announce that the bird had flown away—"right into the wild blue yonder!" he yelled triumphantly. There was an outburst of hoorays around the table and throughout the Capitol in the offices of the nation's legislators. Outside, like a veering herd of cattle, the bird watchers took off after the warbler, calling ahead with their cell phones to alert the network and the spotter planes that were hovering ten miles away, sweeping the sky with microcameras.

Breaking out the champagne in the committee room, Billy Beauchamp raised his glass in a toast. "God bless bird watchers. They don't stay put long enough to become Congress watchers!"

"Hear, hear!" chorused his colleagues bipartisanly. "Hear, hear!"

CHAPTER 11

As the Dartford warbler was winging its way home—it had had enough of Capitol Hill—the Meliorists were winging their way to Maui. They had taken appropriate precautions, wearing their disguises as necessary, but they were feeling a little jumpy as they gathered in the familiar atrium conference room. All of them had been getting more and more calls from the press asking about links between them. All were having their offices and telecommunications systems swept regularly for bugs. Warren asked Bill Joy to open the meeting with a security update.

"Well, so far so good, according to my latest scans," Bill said. "There have been some attempts to hack into the secure website, but as far as I can tell, it's just a matter of the usual random hackers, maybe teenagers like the ones who broke into some of the Pentagon's sites three years ago. That will undoubtedly change now that the covey of CEOs who placed that *WSJ* ad have found a leader for their counterattack squad—none other than Lancelot Lobo."

A ripple of surprise swept around the table. "Well, well, well," Jeno said gleefully. "So Lobo has crossed the aisle and chosen fame over fortune. Well, I licked him once, and I relish a return engagement."

"As for the hotel," Bill Joy went on, "it's clean, but once you go public, all bets are off. The probability of penetration will soar. All I can promise you is regular surveillance with the latest technology."

"Thank you, Bill. We know we're in good hands," Warren said. "Now let's turn to the major subject of our gathering, Invasion Congress. Patrick Drummond of our now properly fabled Secretariat has prepared an overall strategy, which I've asked him to present to us before we have supper. Patrick, the floor is yours."

"Thank you, Warren." Patrick rose and passed a document around the table. "What you see before you is a synopsis of the work of the finest minds in the field, men and women who have spent their careers striving to understand the interactions between Congress in all its parts and the people in all their parts and of course the corporations. I'm just the messenger and editor. For our guidance over the months to come, I've distilled a number of general operating principles for the drive to pass the First-Stage legislation, otherwise known as the Agenda, and I ask you to take the next few minutes to read them."

As one, the Meliorists directed their attention to the strategy paper.

1. The members of Congress must be made to feel a heightened level of public expectation about prompt improvements in our country—something similar to FDR's Hundred Days, only it won't be the president announcing this Agenda.

2. This heightened public expectation must then be transformed into high personal expectations of each representative and senator. The attitude bearing down on them from all quarters should be something like "Of course we know you'll do the right thing for the people, for our country." No threats of retaliation, electoral defeat, or other combative tactics. The carrot sings along the silent pendency of the stick—the carrot in this case being not power or money but simply the deep approbation of their constituents. In the sixties, senior senators who were knee-jerk apologists for business suddenly turned into civil rights advocates and consumer champions. Why? Because the climate back home had changed.

3. The legislative Agenda should not come to Congress from a central source—the eggs-in-one-basket mis-

take. The bills must come separately from separate sources. The core group's backup support is just that—backup.

4. Public indignation should be directed at the greedy and callous in the corporate power structure, not at members of Congress, at least until further notice. This approach serves to divide the members from the corporatists and undermine the bonding between them. It may not be the approach adopted by angry constituents who have grievances far deeper than ours, but we can help set the tone. Insistence short of indignation leaves indignation at the ready, just over the horizon, just enough that they feel it gathering.

5. Except for the Blockbuster offer, the core group should eschew all campaign fundraising. If it becomes necessary to replace funds cut off by angry commercialists, your extensive epicenters can be urged to make up the difference. You do not want to be viewed as the "heavies" here. It is advised that the Blockbuster offer come directly from the National Trust for Posterity and its luminous board of trustees.

6. The more the flow of persuasions directed at the legislators comes from back home, the better the prospects for victory. The media will be looking for a central source of the initiatives. We have to be very aware of this penchant in the press.

7. The bills of the Agenda need to be ranked in terms of ease of passage, with an eye toward building momentum with each success, and also in terms of constituencies inside and outside Congress.

8. Although the Agenda has been framed to be easily understandable, it still needs symbols, slogans, even artistic and musical elaborations. We need concise

emblems that will evoke our whole enterprise. For example, we can do an advertising blitz centered on a sentence like "This is the year when Americans will lift their country up to new heights of liberty and justice for all." Through constant repetition in the media and by word of mouth, the sentence is reduced to "This is the year," and everyone instantly knows what it means. What we're after here is team spirit on a grand scale. To the plutocrats: "Invest in the people— it's the patriotic thing to do." A powerful message, and all the more so when it comes from mega-millionaires and billionaires.

9. The opposition must be distracted and fractured with decoys and feints. Bill G. and Joe are showing the way here with the Pledge of Allegiance and the National Anthem. We need many more such distractions, specifically conceived to deflect the energies of the lobbyists and special interests from the legislative Agenda on Capitol Hill. One suggestion is that the core group dramatize and personalize the issues by challenging the self-selected corporate team—the CEOs you've met with—to a series of television debates. People love contests and conflicts. Among the highest-rated TV programs are court shows, game shows, and sports shows. Flush the CEOs out in a battle royal, a political Super Bowl. They won't want to accept the challenge, but perhaps Lancelot Lobo will make sure that they do. There's a reason people remember David and Goliath, Robin Hood and the Sheriff of Nottingham, all the heroes and villains of literature: dramatis personae.

10. Surprise and alacrity are key in catching the congressional opposition off guard and moving the Agenda through. Historians of Congress observe that breakthrough legislation—good or bad—more often than

not happens quickly, before a strike-back capability can get underway. This is not a hard and fast rule—it took Senator George Norris, the main protagonist, more than a decade of intense campaigning to pass the law creating the Tennessee Valley Authority—but in general, the faster the better, especially when there is a vocal constituency demanding action on a glaring injustice. The quality of the drafting will help greatly to speed things along. Each bill will be close to letter-perfect when it is introduced.

11. Real-life stories, heartrending or hopeful, are essential to give life to the Agenda. Stories generate empathy, human interest, authenticity, and identification among people in similar circumstances. Promotions will need to set up a new team to be in charge of this. Barry's networks fit in beautifully here and will play a large role.

12. We must marshal all our skills of anticipation to prepare for setbacks and crises. They are bound to occur, particularly if the opposition takes the low road. Think of agitators infiltrating our rallies to sow disruption, or even violence and mayhem. The oligarchy may try a strategy of deniability by using rogue elements to do the dirty work.

When everyone had finished reading, Patrick said, "Well, that's it in a nutshell. A challenge, but doable, I hope you'll agree. I would just add that we should be alert to any changes that come along without legislation or regulation. For instance, the Coca-Cola board of directors is giving shareholders approval rights over severance packages that exceed 2.9 times the previous year's compensation. A very small step by a very large company, but it's got Wall Street quaking with fear that it will start a trend. Credit goes to your tireless efforts, Warren."

"Thank you, Patrick, but the credit goes to you for yet another superlative contribution. Let's break now to digest what we've read while we digest our supper. Then we'll reconvene at nine for an hour of silence. In the morning we'll have a freewheeling discussion driven by our shared sense of urgency about the magnitude of what we must accomplish in the five short months before the elections. We could all use a good night's sleep before we go at it."

And did they ever go at it. The morning discussion began with a review of the Congress Project's compendium. "I've seen plenty of strategy sheets on members of Congress in my time, but this far surpasses any of them," Bernard said. "The first two categories of legislators it identifies, the already convinced and the persuadables, will form the hard core, who are ready, willing, and able to carry the Agenda banner inside Congress. As we can see from the compendium's breakdown, these core legislators are a motley bunch, which is just what we want. They come from both parties, have diverse geographical, ethnic, religious, and occupational backgrounds, and sit on a variety of congressional committees, including the Appropriations Committees and the all-important Rules Committees. It would be nice if they also turn out to have higher-than-average energy levels, a sense of history, an impatience for change, and a reserve of courage for the coming battles. We shall see.

"For all its excellence, there is one exceptionally important category that doesn't receive enough attention in the compendium, in my view. I refer to the legislators' congressional peer groups. Warren, can I ask that your project manager give us a matrix for each member showing circles of influence—say, a dozen of the member's closest colleagues, and the colleagues they respect or fear the most politically whether they're close to them or not? When the chips are down and outside pressure is bearing in on Congress from all sides, the peer groups will be the last stand of the corporatists. And believe me, they know everything there is to know about these groups' personal relationships."

"I have the project manager standing by for our feedback," Warren said. "I'll get him on it right away."

Paul gestured around the conference table. "If I say so myself, we've got a pretty good circle of influence right here. Should we try to meet personally with key legislators? If so, when and where? We'd probably make a big splash if we showed up at their offices back in their districts instead of in Washington. Can we get a heads-up on which members would be most receptive to meeting with us, aside from our own senators and representatives?"

"My take is that we should be selective and respond to the advice of our spotters on Capitol Hill so that our meetings will have the maximum effect at the most crucial juncture," Ross said. "We don't want to fritter away our personal capital too early. We should use it as the final push on any wavering lawmakers."

"Right," Phil agreed. "That's our maximum leverage time, when we know the most about why they're wavering."

Joe held up his copy of the compendium. "This can never see the light of day, you know, not beyond our trusted circle. If it falls into the hands of the press or the opposition, it will be seen as manipulative and cause a backlash among the legislators. The Secretariat and each one of us must exercise the utmost caution here, and the same with Patrick's strategy document."

"Point taken," said Peter to nods all around. "I'd like to go back to the core legislators for a minute. A lot of them will select themselves for the tasks of the Agenda once they sense the support and power behind them and see the feasibility of passage. Inch by inch in the past few months they've been bestirring themselves, reaching out to kindred souls inside and outside Congress, moving from a defensive mentality to an offensive readiness.

"The members of Congress are a bundle of emotions and calculations, sniffing the air, fingers to the wind, wondering about the new forces stirring in the country and moving in on Capitol Hill for a showdown. From this cauldron of imponderables will rise leaders, some of them unexpected, to drive the Agenda home. These leaders are critical, especially in a short campaign, and there can never be too many of them. They're the ones who will drive the schedule, refine the tactics, soothe the irritable, prod the procrastinators, and above all convey a felt sense in Congress of the inevitability of victory, a bandwagon effect. Members of Congress are like the voters in one respect—they want to go with the winners."

"Yes," Bernard said, "and many of them also have an unfulfilled appetite to achieve something in this corporate Congress, which is widely perceived as having done very little for the people for a very long time. This, along with the Congress Watchdogs, the Zabouresk-Zeftel group of retired lawmakers and staffers, and perhaps some personal attention from us with the media in tow, will help to forge the inner congressional corps, while all the other Redirectional forces, including the PCC and the Clean Elections Party, will serve as the outside drivers of the Agenda. Then wave after wave of populist power, driven by a knowledge of all the abuses, by pain, anguish, and outrage, and by a sense of destiny for future generations, will roll over Congress, the White House, and the corporate lobbying establishment. Congress isn't used to wave after wave of populist power. In the past, most reformers have thrown everything they've got into their congressional battles all at once, and when attrition starts with the counterattack, there are no reserves left. Then offense turns into defense, and retreat turns into rout. Fortunately, the depth of our resources and the number and quality of our people permit us serial momentum."

"Well, okay, but it's not just that," Ted said fervidly. "Look at Genghis Khan and his mounted warriors. The military precision of his tactics overwhelmed and routed much larger armies as the Mongols conquered and united more of the world in forty years than the Roman Army did in four hundred, and with remarkable exchanges of trade and technology. Naturally I bring up this military analogy only because of its vibrant imagery for our campaign to pass the Agenda."

Yoko sighed. "Naturally, but you'll forgive me if I don't pursue it. What concerns me is that 'Agenda' sounds so dry and impersonal. Surely we can do better. I move that we call it 'Agenda for the Common Good' when it goes public."

There was a moment of startled silence. It was such an obvious point. Warren looked around the table. "Make it so, Patrick," he said, "and thank you, Yoko."

"You're welcome," she said, and went on to deliver her detailed plan for graphics, posters, billboards, theater, music, all the artistic expressions that would help people connect viscerally with the Agenda for the Common Good and see it as rooted in the best of America's past.

Bill Cosby volunteered a heresy. "But spare us the hip-hop MTV-generation hokum. We have to treat the young seriously, and therefore respectfully, which means no pandering. They're an important constituency. If we can get even a small percentage of them involved in, say, becoming lecturers on their campuses, think how much discussion and debate would be aroused in the high schools, colleges, and universities. From such ferments rise great social movements. Turn off the TV, the computer, the CDs and DVDs—and I'm not just talking about the kids. Get together face to face, put your arms around each other's shoulders, fill the sidewalks, the cafés, the parks, the veterans' and union halls, the senior citizen centers. Refurbish the commons! We've got to galvanize the credibility groups around specific legislation. We've got to use all the dynamics that have been building since January to the utmost for the final drive behind the Agenda."

"You know, that reminds me of how the students at Yale came out in support of the custodial workers a few years back," Paul said. "There was a ton of coverage on it in the Connecticut papers, and I followed the whole thing closely. Remember that movie *Death Takes a Holiday*? Imagine what would happen in our country if the lower third of the workforce took a holiday. Start with the super-rich in Greenwich, Belmont, Beverly Hills, Scarsdale, or any affluent suburb in the USA. There would be no one to care for the aging wealthy—their relatives would have to perform all those unpleasant healthcare duties like emptying bedpans, instead of sipping their martinis in the drawing room while pondering what bequests they were likely to receive from the afflicted. Who would serve the food, ring up sales in the malls and shopping centers and convenience stores, provide daycare for our little ones, sweat to harvest our crops, work for pitiful wages in nonunion factories? And of course, who would do the cleaning and picking up after us? I'm talking about the people whose eyes we avoid when we get off planes or walk past their carts in hotel corridors, the people we tiptoe around while they're mopping our public bathrooms, the people we ignore while they're clearing our tables or washing our dishes or mowing our lawns or hosing down our cars or wiping our butts in hospitals—who would do their work?" Normally the essence of cool, Paul was turning red as he spoke. "I'll tell you who! The same people, only once we pass the Agenda, they'll be paid twice as much, with full benefits, so they can have a decent life for themselves and their families."

Listening in silence, Bill Gates remembered his own speech at Maui One about the importance of the core group shedding their anonymity and standing up publicly to convey the felt emotions behind their initiatives. Well, they had done that, successfully projecting an image of loners on a justice kick, idiosyncratic do-gooders on an adventure. All that would change on the fifth of July, when the Meliorists stepped forth together as a linked force.

Most of the afternoon session was taken up with the catapult on the Fourth of July and the critical uses of the hot month of August, when Congress closed down and its members were off junketing or politicking or on vacation. "The entrenched powers won't know what hit them, and even if some do, there will be so many decoys and distractions that they won't be able to react in time," Barry said. "The distraction campaign will have a second- and third-strike capability because of investigations now underway, courtesy of one of my epicenter billionaires. He's got graft hunters on the trail of suspected wrongdoers at high levels, including two White House special assistants to the president."

The Meliorists pored over a memorandum from their informants titled "The Lingering Atmosphere of Overconfident Greed and

Power in the Corporate Trade Associations and Law Firms." Just what they suspected and desired. The big boys still thought their center would hold. The conversation moved to the specifics of the strategy of diversion, decoy, and distraction. As so often happened in their conversations, one voice emerged. This time it was Joe's.

"In the final analysis, our corporate adversaries are all about themselves, not about the monies and assets they're entrusted with managing. You have to hit them where they live—what I call their petty gut—and that goes for their buddies and defenders in Congress too. That's the most immediately felt and decisive way to distract them. So we get one of those core legislators we were talking about this morning to introduce a bill setting the salaries of members of Congress at the level of average household income, which amounts to a pay cut of about sixty-five percent. The bill will also strip them of their health insurance and their pensions until all Americans have those same benefits. Or Warren gets together with Peter Drucker on a national drive to restrict the compensation of CEOs and top executives to no more than twenty-five times the entry-level wage in their companies, to require full disclosure of the often intricate compensation deals, and to give shareholders full voting authority as owners. Or the PCC mounts a movement to cut off all corporate welfare so that companies have to rely entirely on consumer revenue from their products and services—no more taxpayer subsidies and bailouts.

"Two more ideas, not to the petty gut, just to the gut. First, resurrect the federal chartering proposal of Republican presidents Theodore Roosevelt and William Howard Taft. Back then the slogan was 'National charters for national corporations.' It was a big debate in the Gilded Age—the first Gilded Age, that is. But the company bosses liked the state charters, especially Delaware's, and the states liked the revenues they raked in from the perks they offered the corporations. It was a big deal for little Delaware—at the time, about a third of its state income came from these chartering fees as businesses all over the country flocked to this corporate Reno. The courts were patsies. It was a cushy arrangement for the corporations throughout the twentieth century. Let's put a stop to it. Today's slogan should be 'Federal charters for global corporations.' Let's rewrite the charters for a just compact between these artificial corporate giants and real people. Let's have real regulators, real courts, a real level playing field.

"Secondly, stop the Washington regulatory merry-go-round by establishing a consumer and taxpayer watchdog within the government. In the seventies, a bill creating a Consumer Protection Agency almost made it through Congress several times, but it was blocked by the biggest combined lobbying effort ever. Why? Under the legislation, all the CPA was empowered to do was take the regulatory agencies to court if they were failing to enforce the law or otherwise evading their regulatory duties. Well, the very thought of this agency with its tiny budget of fifteen million dollars going after the FCC, the FDA, the FAA, the FTC, and the whole alphabet soup drove the business lobbyists to many secret meetings in their lair at the Madison Hotel. Just about every industry and line of commerce was represented. They finally got Congress to scuttle the CPA for good in 1979, but its specter is such that whenever any progressive member of Congress even thinks of reintroducing it, staffers send up alarums of political disaster and campaign bankruptcy. Well, that just tells us how terrified the corporate boys are of the CPA coming back. They've won by intimidating Congress, but hell, they'll be bear meat for us.

"So there are some decoys for you—a one-two punch to the petty gut and the corporate gut. They're all understandable to the public, they'll poll well, and many will come with built-in human interest stories about life-destroying neglect, basic principles of fairness, and so on. Also, if we back them knowledgeably in public, the press we get will help create an aura of legislative likelihood."

"Great ideas, Joe, just great," Barry said, "but for now I think we should float them visibly and leave it at that. We don't want them distracting *us*. We've already got enough on our plates with the Fourth. Speaking of which, Promotions is having thirty million copies of the Declaration of Independence printed. On one side will be a facsimile of the original document, on the other a typeset reprint for ease of reading. In the middle of June we'll send them out in shipping tubes to the mailing list the Secretariat has compiled from all the Redirections. Bill Hillsman is preparing an ad campaign that will bring Patriotic Polly back to announce the mailing and urge citizens to substitute in their minds, each time the Declaration refers to King George III, the name of the current George or of a multinational corporation."

"Wonderful," Warren said. "It'll be great to see Polly back in action. And on Joe's decoy concerning obscene executive compensation packages and investor control, I'm happy to report that it's already in the works. What could be more fun than hoisting these overpaid critters by their own ideological petards? Hey, big shot CEO, you believe in capitalism? Then surrender to the authority of your company's owners, who will henceforth decide what you, their hired hands at the rarefied top, will be paid. No more of this monumental hypocrisy that lets you have your cake and eat it too. An investor control petition is on its way to the Securities and Exchange Commission even as we speak. The Investor CUB is all over this with me, and they are really beginning to flex their newfound muscles. Joining with them are John Bogle, the preeminent reformer of mutual funds, and two former SEC chairmen who were prominent Wall Street businessmen before going to Washington. These three have thousands of followers who have bought their books or listened to their lectures on investor rights and remedies, and I'll try to get Peter Drucker on board too, Joe. I anticipate that within two months, the momentum for investor control will reach the point of self-replication and move forward on its own steam, as we envision many of our projects will do. But let's get back to the Agenda now. Anything else?"

"Yes," Barry said over a round of applause for Warren. "Promotions is preparing a list of poll questions on the issues covered in the Agenda legislation. This is essential so the media will have numbers to plug into their stories. We'll send you the list early next week. If you have any suggestions about additional topics or the wording of the questions, relay them to my project manager. The polls will be done in about six weeks, and Promotions will time their release. The pollsters have been chosen for their sterling reputations and will make the polling methodology available to any inquiring reporter or legislator."

Ross spoke up. "I think we should canvass the blocked legislative proposals of the citizen groups for modest amendments or riders to be added to bills that will go through anyway, either in the ordinary course of business or because of our efforts. That would certainly build goodwill and morale among these long-besieged groups, without our having to enter into a close alliance with them and deal with their baggage. Include the simple, fair measures allowing workers to use the labor laws to protect themselves and we may arouse organized labor's demoralized rank and file. One of our goals should be to swell the turnout for Labor Day parades. Even in a union town like Detroit, the Labor Day parade is down to a couple of thousand people. Taking that number up by a factor of ten would catch the attention of legislators, both pro and con, who are sensitive to momentum. Let's set that as a minimum goal and have Mass Demonstrations work on stepping up the intensity and theatrics of the parades. Labor Day will be crucial to our kickoff when Congress returns from the August recess."

"Yes," Warren agreed, "after the Fourth, Labor Day will be the next milestone as we head toward a final congressional showdown, but allow me a few more words about June and July. We'll all have to move our own projects and initiatives along as rapidly as possible in June, because after the Fourth our time and energy will be focused on the Agenda. Joe and Bill's Pledge of Allegiance and 'America the Beautiful' feints are going to be the subject of congressional hearings in June. That should keep the radio and TV talking heads sputtering for the rest of the summer. Don Saul's bill legalizing industrial hemp, in addition to its various virtues in terms of the national interest, has become another distraction for the yahoos of the right. More and more lawmakers and agricultural establishment types are lining up behind it, and even some national security people are supportive because of industrial hemp's potential to reduce the importation of oil.

"Bill Cosby and Paul are still working on how to institutionalize the transformation of dead money into live money, but it's already clear that dead money is coming to life all over the place. Our epicenter billionaires are using their wealth to fund preteen civic training classes during the summer break; to lay the groundwork for new regional colleges whose principal major will be civic skills and analysis; to establish local awards for civic valor as Bernard suggested at Maui Four; to form a taxpayers' investigative organization that will expose wasteful federal and state budgets and their arcane systems of deferrals; to set up thousands of micro radio stations so that citizens can literally use their voices to build better neighborhoods and communities right there; to start a drive against teenage silliness and masochism and show the kids how commercialism is controlling their minds and their lives; and to launch a national veterans' movement to reclaim patriotism from its present misuse as a tool of censorship and conformity in the service of the oligarchs and the military-industrial complex.

"What is most amazing about this veritable blizzard of activity involving tens of millions of Americans is the way it has brought out their manifold talents and their best natures, which we all knew was the factor that would make or break our year's work. And the blizzard goes on. For instance, the next phase of the 'Pay the Rent!' drive against the broadcasters is scheduled for next weekend. Bill and Barry, will you give us a few words on this?"

"Happy to," Bill Cosby said. "We've planned demonstrations in front of the major television stations in the fifty largest media markets. The signs, banners, and props will meet every criteria for graphic TV footage. We expect a minimum of five hundred well-briefed and motivated demonstrators who will move from one station to another during the six o'clock news hour so that the stations will have an opportunity to report live on what's happening right outside their windows. Most of them won't, which will prove to the community that they're willing to censor anything that affects their longtime freeloading on the public. Leading the demonstrations will be some well-known members of the community, though you can imagine how many others declined when they were approached to confront big media in their hometown. The ones who accepted were those who've been shut out for so long that they have nothing to lose—labor leaders, neighborhood activists, community reformers. It's almost certain that the local newspapers will find all this newsworthy—that is, unless they're owned by the companies that own the stations. In either case, we'll collect valuable data on which stations did or did not cover the events and why. There's also going to be a big demonstration in Washington, but I'll let Barry tell you about that."

"Well, barring rain, we'll have five thousand people demanding their rent in front of the National Association of Broadcasters headquarters off Connecticut Avenue. There isn't much room to assemble, but by the same token the surrounding streets will be packed for the photographers and cameras. All requisite demonstration permits in DC and around the country have been obtained."

"Thanks to both of you for the update," Warren said. "Also scheduled for next week is the long-awaited Report on Corporate Welfare. Jeno, a few words please."

"Well, it is a sizable tome. The title is 'Corporate Welfare Kings: Rolling the Taxpayers in the Service of Greed.' Nothing like it has ever been assembled before, which is why it's late, though I'm amazed the compilers didn't take many more months to finish. It has something for every ideology, viewpoint, and gripe, and the writing pinpoints each of these nerve endings in a very adroit manner. It includes a ranking of the Top One Hundred Welfare Kings based on a sound methodology and some very well done internal government agency memoranda that we obtained, on who gets the subsidies. For the press, the report will have long legs because it names thousands of companies in thousands of communities, including some of my own companies—sometimes I simply had to do what my competitors were doing. Country club talk next week will get a lot less routine, I'll bet. The takers and the givers are going to know who they are in no uncertain terms, and the givers are not going to like it one bit. The report concludes with sensible recommendations about what needs to be done so that the people can find out about these giveaways, challenge them, and end them, or at least channel them toward broader public interest objectives. Of course Promotions has been well-briefed for action. I think the Clean Elections Party candidates should run with this issue too, because dirty money in campaigns is what greases the skids in Washington for all these massive detours of taxpayer money and corporate tax dodges."

"Thanks, Jeno. Does anyone have anything to add? What about you, Sol? You've been unusually quiet."

"Does a starving man have the strength to speak?"

"Apparently so," Warren rejoined. "All right, time for dinner, then our silence period—you know the drill—but let's depart from our meeting format in the morning. We've all got a lot of personal catching up to do since Maui Four, and I also think we need some time for informal discussion. Anything we've overlooked is more likely to come up that way."

By noon the next day, Maui Six was history, and the Meliorists returned to the mainland, but not before Warren reminded them to collect on their IOUs from the billionaires they'd cultivated. "We won't have much time to dun them after the Fourth," he cautioned.

The Sunday of Maui Six found Lobo—that was what he liked to be called, just Lobo—racking his brains in the solitude of his office high above Manhattan. Lobo liked to rack his brains. It gave him an adrenaline rush, fueled his imagination, and drove him to push the envelope further than any of his competitors. That was why he was the preeminent corporate raider.

His new job gave him plenty to rack his brains over. He'd read thousands of clippings, seen hundreds of video clips on the SROs' individual causes and confrontations. He'd consulted with the American Enterprise Institute and the other conservative think tanks. He'd met with trade association executives who should have been alarmed by the unprecedented eruptions all over the country.

He'd devoured books and Harvard Business School case studies on how corporations and industries had counterattacked their adversaries in the past. He'd studied the way commercial interests had beat down reformist third parties. He'd debriefed his CEO bosses about their meetings with the SROs. He'd even tried to contact Dick Goodwin for a friendly tête-à-tête, but he was told this venerable man in the know and speechwriter to presidents was in London completing a stage play. It was all a quest through Preposterous Land—but wasn't everything about the SROs preposterous until you looked around and saw that more and more, every hour of every day, they were rousing the country from its subservient slumber?

After all his exertions, Lobo came up empty. He had no real leads, no feet in the door, nothing. He'd been a chain smoker and stopped, replacing his cigarillos with raw carrots. Since accepting the CEOs' assignment, he'd devoured so many carrots that his skin was turning orange. Had he taken on more than he could deliver? If he failed, that would be big news, and his reputation as a world-beater would collapse. For years reporters had wanted nothing more than to see his arrogant pride pricked. They would be waiting and watching ravenously. Naturally he kept all these twinges of self-doubt to himself—Lobo never confided, never!—and consoled himself with the thought that he was still in the conceptual stage and had been instructed not to commence operations until the CEOs gave him the go-ahead.

Lobo's unwonted introspection didn't prevent him from moving quickly to prepare his capabilities for surveillance, infiltration, attrition, and the all-important assault on motives and integrity to sow fear of the SROs among the people and manufacture a mass sense of insecurity about the future. For these tasks, he called on the smartest dirty-tricks PR firm in Washington and hired hard-bitten experts in penetration tactics—boy, did those guys look hungry! The more delicate job of marshaling the corporate world's "deadwood muck-a-mucks," as he called them, he would do himself, working intuitively on his assessment of which of them could be roused through his calculated provocations.

Of all the people Lobo had spoken to, only one really impressed: Brovar Dortwist. He had fire in his belly, a high sense of alarm, mental acuity, street smarts, and phenomenal Washington contacts. Lobo picked up the phone.

"Hello, Brovar, Lobo here. You remember our recent conversation?"

"Yes, of course, how are you?"

"Fine enough to invite you for dinner tomorrow evening at my office to talk about the SROs." Lobo explained the acronym, and the two men shared a laugh at CEO Bump's expense.

"Okay, I'll be there," Brovar said.

"Excelente. Adios."

The next evening, the dapper Dortwist arrived five minutes early and was admitted by a butler who seated him at a beautifully set table. A few minutes later, Lobo strode in and greeted him with an abrazo. Then he broke out a bottle of Dalmore 62 that he'd purchased in London last year for $22,000, and they proceeded to down three straight shots each in preparation for a bare-fisted strategy session.

Lobo looked his guest in the eye. "Brovar, in all my years of going after corporations, I never dreamed a fraction of what the SROs have been doing to them since early this year. It's an ingenious, deep, broad, diverse, clever, tough, motivating, empowering awakening of the masses. Social scientists might call it a breakthrough movement. And it appears that it's just getting started and there's a lot more on the way. The SROs are recruiting what the Marxists call 'a revolutionary cadre' from all ages and backgrounds. I must say, speaking as my old self, pre-conversion, it's almost inspirational when you think of the huge problems the country is experiencing. What do you say?"

The butler served the salad course. Brovar took a bite and chewed thoughtfully. "I too find some of what they're doing not unacceptable. They're telling capitalists to act like capitalists and stop freeloading on huge deficits in Washington. But overall they're threatening the whole power system that assures stability and continuity, and that I cannot abide. Forces will be unleashed that they will not be able to control, even if they want to. When the people get a taste of power, they develop a thirst for more and more. The result is invariably tumult, chaos, anarchy, and collapse. We are the two people in the country who want to and can set forces in motion to counter this looming threat."

"I couldn't agree more. After all, I've made a pretty good living feeding off the overreaching greed of that 'whole power system,' as you called it. Let me bounce some thoughts off you. The usual corporate response to a serious challenge is to wear down the citizen groups or reformist politicians by confronting them at every point of potential victory. Remember when the environmental groups went to federal court to block the construction of the Alaska Pipeline and won their case? That big oil consortium simply went to Congress and passed legislation that reversed the court decision and then some. The enviros, while capable in court, had no second-strike capability in Congress, where money talks. All company strategists operate this way. If they lose in court, they go to the legislature, and if they lose in the legislature, they tie up the regulatory agency implementing the bill. If they finally lose at the regulatory level, they go back to court or to the Congress to overrule the rule. And all along the way they use the business media at full throttle to advance their mission. Meanwhile, the briefly aroused public loses interest and subsides.

"Question to you, Brovar. Is that how we confront the SROs, by pushing back at every point or intersection where they're pushing forward—lobbying, litigation, media, Astroturfing, front groups, chambers of commerce, PACs, dealers and agents back in the communities, the whole ball of wax? You know what the complacent trade association world in Washington thinks. They declare that nothing has actually changed. Except for a few victories in small claims court, it's all been publicity, petitions, mobilization, and some new organizations that don't have anything concrete to show for themselves. There have been no new laws or regulations, they say, no official decisions, no company surrenders, nothing that's diminished the power of the corporate world in the slightest, blah blah blah."

The butler came in with the main course, Wagyu strip steaks with black truffle vinaigrette. Brovar waited for him to serve the food and clear the salad plates before he replied. "I'm not sure we have time to do all you've suggested before the SRO initiatives morph into real political, economic, and spiritual power on Capitol Hill and on Election Day, but what other choice do we have? None that's legal, as far as I can see."

"So," Lobo replied, "what you're saying is that we pursue a conventional all-fronts confrontation strategy, because we certainly don't want to do anything illegal. But just hypothetically, suppose the strategy fails and our clients are on the brink. Shouldn't we consider all our options under the rubric of skirting legality? There's not much risk if we're caught. We'll make sure our people are willing to take the modest punishment provided for by the modest sanctions of corporate criminal law, or else we'll have fall guys take the rap. I'm not talking about anything raw, just things like money flows, defamation, the usual dirty tricks. When time is short and billions of dollars are at stake, when power, position, status, and whole companies are at stake—well, what is it the Boy Scouts advise? 'Be prepared.' Just hypothetically, of course, Brovar."

"Just hypothetically, Lobo, an old Chinese proverb says, 'He who plays with fire is likely to be burned.' Tidal waves are heading to Washington. Nothing like this has ever happened in any country— the super-organized revolt of the older super-rich against the entrenched super-rich! It's the stuff of Hollywood, for heaven's sake. Automatic mass media. We usually crush our opposition because they have trouble getting any media. Now the media itself is being told to pay the rent, and the print press is having a field day reporting it. As for the members of Congress, they're quietly having nervous breakdowns from all the populist pressure building on them from back home. They can feel what's coming in an election year when their most senior legislators are being challenged by candidates from a well-funded Clean Elections Party. Sure, Lobo, unleash the conventional sallies against the SROs, but don't bet too heavily on our success in the time frame we're talking about. It's only five months to Election Day. Our side may have dawdled too long."

"You're provocative in the best sense, Brovar. So where does that leave us?"

"Well, that depends. How much money are your CEOs willing to spend once they give you the go-ahead? And do they have it in hand, or are they talking vague pledges?"

"I'm waiting on them for the answer. They've given me my office and staff budget, but they won't be ready to tell me how much they're raising and committing personally until late June. Usually in a fight between populism and oligarchy, oligarchy has to spend ten times more to have a chance to prevail. I mean, look at those solar festivals that people are flocking to every weekend now. They have credibility. We can't exactly match them with coal-burning festivals, can we? On the other hand, our side already has a multibillion-dollar infrastructure in place—organizations, communications, media, transportation, captive legislators, a corporate White House, all kinds of networks around the country, an aura of invincibility. But does that infrastructure have the heart and the stomach for the fast-approaching battle? As of now I doubt it seriously. The big boys are too fat, dumb, and happy, too smug, too used to an unbroken string of victories. They may have to lose a few times before they'll wake up. I know none of this is news to you, Brovar."

"My rough guess is that just this year you're going to need five billion dollars. If the conventional counteroffensive doesn't work, you may be forced to fall back on those hypothetical tactics that we never discussed. If push comes to shove, you'll have nothing to rely on when the barbarians are storming the gates but fear, smear, and the Khyber Pass."

"The Khyber Pass?"

"Exactly. It's the mountain pass through which waves of invaders rode into the Indus Valley to conquer the Indian subcontinent. If they weren't stopped there, then India lay before them, essentially defenseless. A nice metaphor for our intensifying predicament. Let's assume the SROs mobilize so much popular force that they have the votes in Congress to pass a whole backlog of legislation that the liberals and progressives, so called, have been salivating for these last twenty-five years. Your last stand is the procedural power of the committee chairs and our seasoned friends in the leadership to block the legislation at every turn. They are the Khyber Pass where we can choke off the invaders, at least for this year. All bets are off after the election."

"Well, your sources must be telling you the same thing mine are—that the SROs' legislative allies on the Hill are indeed preparing to introduce a wide brace of legislation, the whole liberal agenda on health insurance, a living wage, labor rights, investor rights, tax equity, pension preservation, consumer protection, energy and the environment—the usual list. Our corporate clients have been discrediting, delaying, and blocking these measures for years. Those guys have the propaganda and the television dramatizations down pat. It's the new rising power behind these bills that changes the entire equation for us."

"Lobo, you have to tread very carefully here. Start the usual campaigns to discredit the bills as economically unworkable, too costly, too radical, too likely to undermine the precious free market and our global competitiveness. Trot them all out, brush them off, give them a new gleam, a fresh focus. But you may have to use smear tactics to save the ship when and if the time comes. If you deploy them too early, when you don't yet know whether the conventional campaigns are going to fail, they may backfire on you. The press will see them as acts of desperation by corporatists on the brink of defeat. Our friends in Congress will disassociate themselves from such tactics. I repeat, you have to be ready, you have to get those ducks in order on the QT, but you only want to use them at the eleventh hour, when you have everything to lose if you don't. It's a tightrope act of the first order."

"Excellent advice. Are you with me, Brovar?"

"Of course, Lobo."

"Dessert and brandy, Brovar?"

"Of course, Lobo."

CHAPTER 12

The report on Corporate Welfare Kings hit the streets on the first Monday of June. Literally. That day's *Bugle* was devoted entirely to the report, and the "Read all about it!" kids peeled off one copy after another, sometimes right in front of a Welfare King's headquarters building. The mainstream newspapers picked up on a remarkable finding: although individual companies that received government largesse might still pay net federal taxes, corporate welfare handouts as a whole cancelled out corporate tax liability as a whole and then some. In short, as a practical matter, corporate America was tax-exempt. The tabloids in New York, Boston, Los Angeles, and other cities went all the way with page-one headlines like "Business Behemoths on Welfare Escape Taxes," or "Big-Shot Welfare Kings Exposed," in huge type over unflattering blowups of scowling CEOs. One cartoon showed the corporations as pigs feeding at the public trough, with the caption "Only the Little People Pay Taxes," a reference to New York real estate baroness Leona Helmsley's outburst after she was caught cheating on her taxes. Even the Style pages got into the act. One enterprising columnist, Rally Zwinn of the *Washington Post*, did some follow-up and found that many of the Top Hundred Welfare Kings named in the report had cancelled all their social engagements and golf outings until further notice. Quite a scoop for Rally, who'd gone a while since her last one.

More important was the follow-up commentary and the steady spread of the subject into ordinary conversation. There were also signs that academia was becoming more interested in corporate welfare research. A *USA Today* survey of economics majors in their junior year revealed that some 15 percent of them were planning to write their senior thesis on some aspect of corporate welfare. Clean Elections candidates held news conferences about the report and showcased local people vainly trying to get public funds for clinics or school repairs. Nothing like the crisp, vivid politics of juxtaposition to get the citizenry aroused. "That ain't right," said a cabbie to Phil Donahue about a case in which City Hall, acting on behalf of a large company, used its power of eminent domain to condemn dozens of homes and small businesses, as well as two churches, and then gave the land to the company for free. The list went on and on. Drug companies ripping patients off at the pharmacy while getting all kinds of free research and development from the government. Gambling casinos, billionaire owners of sports teams, the tobacco industry, agribusiness, banks, insurance companies, and even foreign companies, all on the dole in one clever way after another.

The Clean Elections Party had a field day connecting corporate giveaways with campaign contributions targeted to senators and representatives on the pertinent committees, or to otherwise well-positioned legislators responsive to cash register politics. Completely on the defensive, the lawmakers fell back on lame excuses about jobs and meeting the global competition—until the CEP produced a list of European and Asian companies on the US welfare rolls. With American workers being laid off in droves from their manufacturing jobs, with household income stagnant or falling, with consumers shackled by enormous debt, with pensions being raided or drained or dumped on Uncle Sam, the usual sheen and shine of the incumbent politicians, the supreme complacency they drew from their unchallenged reign in their one-party districts or states, started to crumble.

Of all the sticky issues beginning to stick on the Capitol Dome, none was more adhesive than the "Pay the Rent!" eruption. For politicians, the TV and radio stations in their home regions were untouchable. Look at them critically or challenge them to "pay the rent" and they could turn you to stone. They were the latter-day Gorgons of congressional folklore. So when the demonstrations in the fifty largest broadcast markets went live, Congress collectively braced itself.

A full two-thirds of the stations ignored the protests. Through quick coordination with the National Association of Broadcasters, their similarly besieged trade association, they issued curt press releases that were all very similar: "Channel 3 does not consider matters relating to this station, pursued by a special interest, to be of interest to our viewing audience. It would be self-indulgent to burden viewers with internal administrative matters having nothing to do with the gathering of the day's news. Clearly, these demonstrations were orchestrated to force us into covering them, an unconscionable assault on the freedom of the press. Our station creates jobs, pays taxes, and serves our community, and no outside intimidation will ever keep us from performing our responsibilities day after day to the best of our ability."

The print media begged to differ about the stations' self-serving definition of newsworthiness. The story made the front pages all over the country, and a chorus of editorialists called for congressional action. Luckily the protests had occurred on a weekend, so the solons had time to sort out the marbles in their mouths. Come Monday morning, however, they had to respond to the newspapers in their communities. There was no way out, no way to dodge the simple question "Should the people's airwaves be rented at market rates by the broadcaster tenants who are profiting hand over fist and can't threaten to go to China? Yes or no?"

Temporizing became the order of the day. The usually languid Monday floor session was suddenly filled to the gills with legislative business requiring the lawmakers' constant attendance. "We'll get back to you," they said. Or, "We haven't seen an actual legislative proposal and cannot comment until we do." Or, "Well, it would depend on the amount of rent, wouldn't it?"

But not all 535 members wanted to duck for cover. More than fifty of them said that of course the people should get a return on their property and that the money could be used to fund better programs. Some two dozen true mossbacks were vocal in their opposition. "Hell, no! We oppose all tax increases," thundered Senator Thinkalot defiantly. Tax increases? It was a transparent semantic sleight, but the broadcasters and the Republican National Committee and the usual suspects bought into it. "No more taxes, no more taxes!" was the rant from the raucous realms. The late-night comics loved it, gleefully shredding this bad joke with satirical comparisons. Would the yahoos like to tell the private owners of buildings that house government agencies to stop charging the government rent?

Nothing worked for the congressional minions of Big Media. They didn't pass the laugh test. There were deficits to reduce. The people's commonwealth extended to public lands rich in timber and minerals, lands that should be leased or sold at market value instead of being given away free or at bargain-basement prices. The controversy began to expand to include these and other giveaway resources owned by the people but in the hands of the corporations. "Things are getting out of hand," grumbled the mossbacks. "It's just wonderful," exhaled the progressives.

It was a tribute to the skill of the "Pay the rent!" campaign, and the degree to which it scared the trousers off the broadcast moguls, that the Redirections news began to crowd out some of the sensational, violent, celebrity-and-sex-ridden material that passed for news on network and cable television. "If it bleeds, it leads" was becoming "If it seethes, it leads" in more and more newsrooms. Charges that TV was a round-the-clock wasteland of tawdry trivia and saturation advertising sent producers into overdrive generating more serious content and what they called "public service programming." Even silly, sadistic, screaming afternoon shows like Jerry Springer's began to find room to showcase heroic civic action groups in communities around the nation, going so far as to put their e-mail addresses on the screen for interested viewers.

In mid-June, Congress opened hearings on two of the Meliorists' most volcanic decoys: the bills to change the wording of the Pledge of Allegiance and replace "The Star-Spangled Banner" with "America the Beautiful."

People started lining up before 5:00 a.m. to get into the House and Senate hearing rooms. By 7:00 a.m. the lines, three deep, stretched from the doorways of the Rayburn Office Building and the

Hart Senate Office Building far down the sidewalks outside. The people appeared to come from all walks of life and to have little in common except a fierce and determined look. Bleary-eyed reporters were already interviewing them. James Drew of the *Washington Post* leaned over to Rick Dawn of the Associated Press and said, "I'll bet they're the evangelicals and the old veterans, with a few Daughters of the American Revolution sprinkled in. Rick Dawn agreed, scarcely suppressing a yawn. Ten minutes later, most of the crowd began humming "America the Beautiful." What gives? Drew wondered as he took down one pro-change comment after another.

What gave was that one of Cecil Zeftel's retired staffers, Walter Waitland, had tipped Bernard off about how to stack the hearing rooms and change the whole atmosphere for the committee members as well as the press. When he was working on the Hill, he used to rail against corporate lobbyists who took up all the seats by hiring college students to stand in for them beginning at 6:00 a.m. Three hours or so later, the lobbyists would saunter in and take their places. Meanwhile, unsuspecting citizens would arrive and find themselves shut out. Waitland never forgot his outrage over committee chairs allowing the corporations to take over the seats this way, just as they had tried to do when Peter Lewis testified about the insurance industry. Now the tables were turned. The difference was that nobody here had been paid. They were all volunteers from the PCC and the CUBs and the lunchtime rallies, or simply from the ranks of the millions whose lives had been touched by one or more of the Redirections and who jumped at the chance to come.

At 9:00 a.m. Chairman Michael Meany of the House Committee on Administration brought his gavel down hard. A burly Republican from Pecos County, Texas, he couldn't have been a worse choice from the pro-change viewpoint. He was known to have a hot temper and to brook no disruption of his hearing room. The Republican leadership wanted to downplay the importance of the two bills, so they had assigned them to Meany's committee.

The chairman opened with a brief statement. "Today we convene to hear testimony on HR 215 and HR 300, relating respectively to changing the National Anthem to 'America the Beautiful' and changing the Pledge of Allegiance to read 'with liberty and justice for some.' I oppose both bills, but I will chair a fair and open hearing and will not try to keep them from being voted out of committee should my position only command a minority. I oppose HR 215 because I believe a national anthem should convey strength before spirit, which is not what 'America the Beautiful' conveys. Besides, there's nothing very beautiful about West Texas flatlands other than their people. I oppose HR 300 because a pledge of allegiance should embrace the ideal over the real. People everywhere know there is liberty and justice only for a few. They need to be inspired by the ideal—liberty and justice for all.

"Now I call on the ranking member of the other party for an opening statement before we go to the witnesses. Representative Randy Realismo from the great state of Iowa, which has plenty of amber waves of grain."

"Thank you, Mr. Chairman. I favor these two bills for reasons exactly the opposite of yours. I believe America's spirit is the source of all its strength, its can-do attitude, its pioneering ways, and its military effectiveness. I favor the Pledge the Truth bill because our youngsters should not be fed illusions; they should be toughened by reality so they can seek to change it for the better. And for adults, the present ending, 'with liberty and justice for all,' amounts to knowingly mouthing a lie. Our allegiance should be based on truth, not lies."

"Thank you for matching my brevity," said the chairman. "Now we go to the first panel, composed of four witnesses supporting this legislation. You each have three minutes, and your complete statements will be placed in the printed hearing record. You may begin, Mr. Vision."

"Thank you, Mr. Chairman and members of the House Committee on Administration. My name is Vincent Vision, and I am a professor of anthropology at Indiana University. Rituals in any society are a composite of myth and motivation. The Anthem and the Pledge are no exception. They are sung and uttered millions of times daily in our land, and they leave a deep imprint. Their routine repetition plants them in the subconscious, where they are never subjected to scrutiny or criticism. They are meant to be revered to a point where they lose much of their conscious meaning. The fervor for the Pledge of Allegiance, it is commonly understood, comes mainly from the right of our political spectrum, yet the struggle for liberty and justice for all has come mainly from the left, which finds the Pledge to be an instrument of conformity and obedience to the ruling classes. And as an historic aside, may I point out that the Pledge of Allegiance was written by a socialist? The irony persists unabated. As for 'The Star-Spangled Banner,' it is much easier to control people with a sacred symbol like the flag than with a reality like the landscape of our country. An anthem replete with descriptions of America's natural splendors will encourage us to preserve those splendors. When it comes to symbol versus reality, we should take the latter every time if we are to view ourselves as thinking, inquiring people. Besides, raising children to sing about 'bombs bursting in air' cannot compare with lyrics about our country's skies and mountains and plains. Give them their childhood. They'll have time enough to worry about bombs later in life, unless peace bursts out all over. Thank you."

"And thank you, Professor. The next witness is Dr. Cynthia Chord, who has a PhD in music and sings professionally at the Toledo Opera House."

"Mr. Chairman and committee members, I would like to simply sing both 'The Star-Spangled Banner' and 'America the Beautiful,' in that order." Whereupon Dr. Chord thrilled the hearing room with her renditions and sat down to loud applause.

The gavel slammed down three times for silence. It was clear to the astonished chairman that most of the applause was for "America the Beautiful." He hastened onward. "The next witness is Frederick Ferrett, dean of the Yale Law School and a leading historian of jurisprudence. Proceed, Dean Ferret."

"Mr. Chairman and committee members, I shall restrict my oral testimony to the results of a lie detector test given to six professors from six different law schools. All of them specialize in the study of justice, its primordial relation to liberty, and the distribution of both in our country. They were asked to say the Pledge of Allegiance while wired to a lie detector. All six flunked the test. Thank you."

"Dean Ferret, do you have a more detailed treatment of these tests and their methodology in the testimony you submitted for the record?"

"Yes, I do, Mr. Chairman."

"Very well. The next witness is the aptly named Peter Poll, president of a major polling organization in St. Louis."

"Thank you, Chairman Meany and distinguished legislators. We polled a representative sample of three thousand two hundred Americans on three questions. When asked, Do you want to see the National Anthem and the Pledge of Allegiance changed in any way? eighty percent said no, fifteen percent said yes, and the rest had no opinion. To the question, Which would you choose for our National Anthem, 'The Star-Spangled Banner' or 'America the Beautiful'? the response was about fifty-fifty. When asked, Which do you prefer at the end of the Pledge of Allegiance, the present 'with liberty and justice for all,' or 'with liberty and justice for some'? sixty-four percent liked 'for some,' thirty percent wanted the Pledge to remain the same, and the rest were undecided. Our analysis is that, as many previous polls have shown, the American people know that established power and wealth control the many for the benefit of the few in this country, because they feel the effects or read about the effects or see the effects every day. Therefore, we were not surprised by the large majority favoring the change in the Pledge to conform to reality. Thank you, Mr. Chairman."

Chairman Meany was looking a little red in the face. "I have no questions. Are there questions from the members of the committee?"

"Yes, I have a question for Dean Ferrett," said Congressman Pierre Prober. "Dean, were you saying that when the six professors came to the last few words of the Pledge of Allegiance, they felt they were lying?"

"Yes, Congressman, that is exactly what I was saying, and exactly what registered on the lie detector."

"My question is directed to Professor Vision," said Congress-woman Elaine Suspicio. "Is it not true, Professor, that national anthems under dictatorships are almost always militaristic and boast of victories and triumphs in warfare?"

"That is generally quite correct. And when democratic countries are taken over by dictators and the anthem is changed, it goes the route you have described, yes."

Congressman Dick Direct glowered at the panel. "My question is to any of you who choose to respond. Why in the name of all that's holy are you wasting your time and ours with this left-wing tripe? Look at the huge press turnout, the sixteen television cameras, the mass of radio microphones in front of your table. Is this what we should be concentrating on while the world is exploding with terrorists and their extremist supporters?"

"With respect, Congressman Direct," said Professor Vision, "in the past year your Administration Committee has had sessions and hearings on the following topics: use of House credit cards by members and staff; whether the House cafeteria should serve more vegetarian meals and organic food; whether the visitors' center, under construction with massive cost overruns, should be managed by a new general contractor and a new auditing firm; whether the House Barber Shop and Beauty Salon should increase its prices; and so on. All this, Congressman, while the world is exploding with violence of all kinds and imploding from neglect. The National Anthem and the Pledge of Allegiance are not trivial matters, and public opinion is deeply divided on the two bills before you, as this hearing will surely demonstrate."

"Amen, amen," warbled Cynthia Chord.

"I second Professor Vision," Peter Poll chimed in. "As a specialist in measuring public opinion, I have found again and again that traditions and symbols like the Pledge and the National Anthem are very important to people's sense of solidarity, their sense of collective identity, and their need to allay their anxieties by clinging to something that endures from the past into the present and sanctifies the future."

Chairman Meany was about to dismiss the panel and move on when a committee clerk scuttled across the dais and whispered in his ear, "The hearing is going out live on C-SPAN, public radio, and CNN. Thousands of e-mails and phone calls are pouring into the committee, your congressional office, and your district office in Pecos County. We haven't had time to determine whether the reaction is breaking pro or con. All we know is that the congressional switchboard is overwhelmed with callers. Obviously this is touching nerves. I thought you'd want to know." The chairman nodded thoughtfully and turned back to face the audience. "If there are no further questions, I thank the panel for coming here this morning to present their views. Now we will hear some opposing views. Mr. Ultimata, where are the other three witnesses on your panel?"

"Mr. Chairman, my three colleagues have agreed to cede their time to me. Unless you object, I am authorized to speak on their behalf, and I trust my cumulative time is now twelve minutes."

"A little unconventional, but why not? Please proceed."

"Thank you, Mr. Chairman and members of the committee. I am Ulysses Ultimata, former CEO of Gigante Corporation, with operations in fifty-two countries. Gigante is the world's leading manufacturer of pile drivers. I represent the Coalition of True Patriots, formed recently after provocations that were orchestrated by two very rich men and have ended up as H.R. 215 and H.R. 300. The coalition is composed of nearly one hundred stalwart Americans of achievement who have in common their unalterable opposition to these two subversive bills. We agree with your opening statement, Mr. Chairman, but we wish to go beyond it. Let me be blunt. These bills are treasonous. Their intent is to destroy venerable American traditions in the name of anemic pacifism and radical egalitarianism."

Loud murmurs of disapproval rose from the audience. Ulysses Ultimata was not deterred.

"American soldiers died singing 'The Star Spangled Banner.' This Anthem is our blood, guts, and pride. Our Pledge of Allegiance has come from the mouth of every soldier, sailor, and airman who has worn the uniform of the US Armed Forces since the Spanish-American War. It is their sacred oath. Here and now we take our stand for these great traditions. We will fight in the hearing rooms, in the halls of Congress, in the town halls of America, on the village greens—and if necessary in the streets—to protect and defend our Anthem and our Pledge from dilution, contamination, and manipulation by the wimps who are behind all this."

Now the audience was shouting, booing, calling for rebuttal. "We weren't wimps at Guadalcanal and Anzio," a veteran yelled. "We weren't wimps on D-Day. What did you do in the war, Ultimata?" A short olive-skinned man with a crew cut jumped up from his seat. "He called us traitors! I've worked hard for America, and I have two sons in the Marines. How dare he?"

Chairman Meany, who had been pleased by the civil tone of the hearing thus far, was banging his gavel furiously. "Sit down, sir! I will call the sergeant at arms to escort you or anyone else from this hearing room if you do not settle down. Please continue, Mr. Ultimata."

"Let me be more specific about the consequences if these bills pass into law. Our multinational companies will be the laughingstock of the world, as will our country. What nation would ever degrade itself by conceding in its Pledge of Allegiance that there is liberty and justice only for some? We call ourselves the greatest democracy on Earth every day. How could we continue to do that in our worldwide information programs? And while I concede that 'America the Beautiful' might bring in more foreign tourists to see our fields and forests, let's face it, other countries do not respect America for its beauty, for its laws, for its economy, for its freedoms. They respect us because of our military power, because we win wars as long as we can get the wimps and the bleeding hearts out of our way." Ultimata was fairly shouting now, in part for emphasis and in part to be heard over the rising crescendo of outrage from the audience.

"The poor people fight your wars, big shot!" roared a deep-throated guy in a "Union, Yes!" sweatshirt. TV cameramen were elbowing each other for the best shots—this was going to make some juicy television. The members of the committee were clearly agitated, envisioning a maelstrom of angry messages from their constituents.

Already their assistants were passing them notes saying that their office phones were ringing off the hook. The callers wanted to know where their lawmakers stood. One member got a note from his wife complaining that their home phone wouldn't let up.

"Order, order! I will not have a witness before my committee shouted down. I will clear the hearing room before it comes to that. Finish your testimony, sir."

"Thank you, Mr. Chairman. As I was saying, if you look weak, you're asking for trouble. Pacifists look weak, talk weak, are weak. America got to where it is by slamming its way to the West Coast and the Rio Grande, by calling out the cavalry, by rejecting gun control. If we hadn't taken charge in 1775, Bostonians would still be slurping their tea out of Chippendale cups. Our country would still be a narrow strip of land up and down the Atlantic coast. I end with a warning. Debate these bills all you want, but there are those of us who will never allow our sacred traditions to be sullied. God bless America, and cursed be the meek, because they will forfeit the Earth."

Some of the pastors in the audience found the twisted biblical reference sacrilegious and made their protest clear by silently but strenuously wagging their fingers at Ulysses Ultimata. Leaving the witness chair, he responded with a laugh and a curled lip. Boos and hisses erupted in spontaneous condemnation.

In the back of the room, Bill Gates Sr. turned to Joe Jamail and said, "If a congressional hearing is this unruly, just imagine what's going on in the rest of the country. And the focus is just where we want it to be, on the Congress. Operation Distraction just hit pay dirt, Joe."

Chairman Meany, gaveling down the uproar, adjourned the hearing until further notice and ordered the sergeant at arms to clear the room, which was presently populated by people singing "America the Beautiful" or bellowing "With liberty and justice for some!" Moderate pandemonium ensued as the crowd departed, reporters and photographers at their heels, still puzzled by the overwhelming audience support for the bills.

Predictably, the evening news was dominated by the hearings and the public reaction in Everywhere, USA. Barry even had to suspend

his provocative and increasingly popular Injustice of the Day segment to make time for full coverage. The waves after waves
unleashed by the Meliorists were provoking just about everyone to
drop the small talk and express their opinions on the way to work,
in car pools, at shopping malls, in waiting rooms, around the water
cooler, you name it. More and more youngsters were getting into
the act as their schools debated whether to pick up the Pledge revision. The more thoughtful teachers used the occasion to delve
deeper into the arguments pro and con and learned that they could
teach American history in a way that genuinely caught the attention
of their overwired students.

So successful were the Pledge and the Anthem, both as decoys
and in advancing the national discussion of substantive issues, that
it wasn't long before Joe and Bill began planning a new drive, this
time to replace the bald eagle with the white dove. Joe drafted a
memo to Promotions describing the eagle as a glorified vulture, a
flesh-rending predator that would even feed on carrion, its powerful
beak and talons exuding violence, aggression, and imperial designs.
Should this be the symbol of the United States of America, already
regarded by much of the world as an imperial predator? The dove,
on the other hand, was the universal symbol of peace, representing
the highest aspirations of humankind. To wage peace was to
renounce waging war. To wage peace was to give justice a chance to
spread its wings. Some of the bird watchers probably wouldn't be
too happy about the Doves, Not Vultures campaign, but it was
another feint sure to send Bush Bimbaugh and company up the
wall. Joe and Bill would keep it in reserve for stage two of the
Agenda drive, after the August recess.

With an eye to the future need for decoys and distractions, Promotions was also working up an action plan for Yoko's idea that the
quickest way to stop pollution was to pass a law requiring polluters to
inject a nontoxic red dye into their emissions. Once support for the
Agenda builds in Congress, it wouldn't be difficult to find sponsors
to introduce the legislation with fanfare and a video simulation that
would drive the polluters into a costly and time-consuming counter-

offensive frenzy. When the proposal was sent to the Secretariat, Barry received an uncharacteristically scathing memo from Patrick Drummond. "This is exuberance run amok, a heaven-sent instrument that the plutocrats and corporatists will use to organize the people and distract *them*. Nobody wants to go around with red stains on their person, their home, their car, and just about everything else. The bill will be stopped in its tracks on Capitol Hill, but meanwhile it will be seized upon to tarnish and discredit anybody and everybody associated with it. Enthusiasm untempered by common sense can lead to disaster. Recommend internal review to determine how this one got past you and how to tighten up quality control immediately. Will bill you later for saving your ass." Barry was startled by the language but had to agree with the message, though he wasn't looking forward to breaking the news to Yoko.

June was crunch month for Wal-Mart. The giant company was being squeezed from all sides. One editorial cartoonist depicted it as Gulliver tied down by the Lilliputians with ropes labeled "Union." Except for the mom-and-pop fire sales, the models and tactics Sol had deployed against the first five stores and the additional two hundred were spreading spontaneously throughout the Wal-Mart world. The Wal-SWATs were working triple shifts without making a dent. The company hired four more top executives in crisis management, and it was a drop in the bucket. Ted's billionaires had turned their assignment into a hobby and were arousing institutional investors, whose calls of protest rose as their shares declined. They were demanding one-on-one meetings with officers and members of the board. They were threatening shareholder lawsuits. They were demanding a stronger say in company policies and compensation packages.

The Wal-Mart brand was turning into a popular epithet. "To Wal-Mart" meant to chisel workers or to union-bust or to freeload on the taxpayers or to squeeze people beyond endurance or to send US jobs on a fast boat to China. The company's trademark name, valued at an estimated $12 billion dollars under "good will" in its assets column, was moving into the debits column, though the accounting profession had yet to quantify the loss on the other side of the ledger. Sales were suffering. Morale was plummeting. Recruitment of young middle managers and MBAs was becoming much more difficult. The steady decline of Wal-Mart shares was most worrisome to Bentonville—why, their stock options were in jeopardy! The board of directors felt increasingly under harassment in their own communities as they were pestered for interviews, chided, or shunned, even by some of their business peers.

Everything Wal-Mart put into play by way of improving its image and countering Sol's assault on the citadel either fizzled or backfired. Its public condemnation of the unionization drive just drew more attention to the rebels. The toughest argument to rebut was the now widely publicized treatment of Wal-Mart employees in Western Europe, where the company was legally obliged to provide benefits beyond the dreams of its US workers and to recognize real unions. There *was* no rebuttal, really, other than to intimate higher prices for shoppers, which only provoked critics to raise the executive pay issue again. Even the announcement that Wal-Mart was opening stores in inner-city areas didn't wash. It was interpreted as an admission of guilt or a move to exploit low-wage labor.

In mid-June, the top officers in Bentonville arranged an emergency conference call with the board of directors. All the participants were well aware of the relentless news reports and the rapidly deteriorating situation.

"Ladies and gentlemen," CEO Clott began, "at our February meeting, some of you asked for more data, and what we've painstakingly assembled since then has led us to call this emergency session of the board. We're losing ground by the day. Our adversaries are multiplying like rabbits, and carrots are of no use with this species. There is no wearing them out or wearing them down. Their frontal assault is taking up so much time in our managerial ranks, down to the Superstores, that we can't attend to our business. Decisions are being postponed. Just yesterday we lost out on purchasing the third-largest retail chain in Argentina—as you know, this is how we establish a strong market position in other countries. One of our US competitors picked it up simply because we didn't get around to making a bid.

"The costs of maintaining our traditional business model are rising faster than the benefits. What we see on the horizon is not just more stormy weather but unintended consequences—those who have been cowed by our supremacy are suddenly becoming emboldened. There are moves against us that even Sol Price doesn't even know about, such are the forces he has unleashed. After careful reflection, we therefore propose to act on Gerald Taft's earlier suggestion that one of us have a face-to-face meeting with him to find out more about what he wants and how much he has behind him. We believe that our fellow board member Sam Sale, a high school friend of Sol's back in New York City, is the best qualified among us for this highly sensitive and confidential task. Of course Price will have to assure us of complete secrecy, or there's no point. But if he does give his word—and he's nothing if not a man of his word, which is why Sam Walton liked him—is it the sense of the board that such a meeting be arranged?"

A wave of fatigued ayes floated into the CEO's office.

"Any objections?"

"Nay," replied three tight-lipped, clenched-jawed directors. "Sam may have liked Sol Price then, but now he would be calling out the Marines," one of them growled.

CEO Clott ignored the remark. "The ayes have it. Can you come down to Bentonville tomorrow for an intensive briefing, Sam?"

"I'll clear my schedule right away."

Sam Sale arrived in Bentonville at noon the next day, by limo from the airport. The retired CEO of the largest sporting goods chain in the country, he was in his eighties now, but his physical and mental fitness was remarkable. He'd been two years behind Sol in high school, but they became friends because of their ardent support of the Brooklyn Dodgers.

Leighton Clott met Sam at the headquarters entrance and personally escorted him to a small secured conference room where lunch was waiting. He handed Sam a sheaf of succinct briefing papers and asked him to spend the afternoon reviewing them so that his meeting with Sol would be more likely to achieve results on the spot, without further back-and-forth.

After lunch, Sam settled in with the briefing papers and learned just about all there was to know about Sol—his background, his health, his family, his business activities, his hobbies—except for one missing detail. He buzzed CEO Clott. "When is Sol most upbeat and fresh during any given week?" the Dodger fan wanted to know. Clott put him on hold and came back with the answer in a matter of minutes. The CEO wasn't kidding the board when he'd told them earlier that the company had full intelligence.

"Sol is at his most receptive in the early evening, especially on Sunday evening, when he's looking forward to his weekly brisket dinner."

"Then that's when I'll ask to meet with him, at his home, where his guard will be down and he won't be afraid of bugs. Thanks, Leighton." Sam hung up and took the elevator down to the lavish company fitness center and spa. As was his habit, he went for a swim and got a vigorous rubdown. Then he repaired to his hotel, ordered in a working dinner, and retired early to start the next day ready for a call to Sol.

Sunday afternoon found Sam Sale being chauffeured up to Sol's home in a hilly and very upscale San Diego suburb with a beautiful view of the Pacific. His driver was a recent Filipino immigrant fluent in Tagalog but very sparse in English. He'd been deliberately chosen so that he wouldn't have a clue as to whom he was taking where.

Sol greeted his old friend at the door with grace and warmth. "Sam, it's been decades! You know, I used to consider expanding my discount stores into sporting goods, but I always thought better of it because of my respect for your tenacious competitiveness."

"Needless to say, Sol, I've watched you go from success to success for years with no little envy. Oh, I've done all right for myself, but a man always tries to outrich the richest of his high school friends." Sam clapped Sol on the back with a laugh.

Sol was laughing too. He returned the clap, just a bit harder. "Well, I've never had that feeling, you know, because I've always been the richest. You're my Avis, Sam. But come in, come in. Come sit with me in my study. Can I pour you a drink?"

"Sure, I'll have a spicy tomato juice, if you've got it, no ice, lemon on the side."

"I'll stay with my dry martini," Sol said as he went to a drinks cart in the corner of the study and returned with the juice. "Here you are, Sam. Now, why did Wal-Mart send you here?"

Prepared for Sol's bluntness, Sam responded in kind. "Quite simply, to see if we could cut a deal. If we do, I know you're a man of your word. This meeting has to go no further on your side. You're your own boss. On my side, I have to report to the CEO only. We know, of course, that you want unionization. You haven't said much about what else you want, if anything, regarding other criticisms of Wal-Mart that both preceded you and were escalated by your campaign. And there are many layers involved in discussing unionization. So my question is this. What exactly are your conditions for settling this growing conflict, which entails such resources and energy on both sides?"

"Are you trying to test my stamina and my resources, Sam? If you are, you can forget about any negotiations. You must know that kind of tactic only makes me dig my heels in. We discuss the merits or nothing!"

"Fine, then let's start by asking what you mean by unionization."

"Here's what I don't mean. I don't mean unionization meat department by meat department. I don't mean unionization Superstore by Superstore or warehouse by warehouse, or only blue-collar or only white-collar. I mean company-wide unionization—one prime labor-management contract covering wages, benefits, work rules, grievance procedures, and civil rights and liberties in the workplace, as negotiated by your workers and your management under the fair labor practice rules of the NLRB. Obviously, prior to the negotiations, management must observe strict noninterference in the freedom to organize for collective bargaining and company-wide union certification. And that means an immediate union card-check, to reduce the prospect of subtle interference."

"That's a pretty hard line, Sol."

"No, it's not a hard line, because Wal-Mart is a contagious disease driving down wages and benefits throughout the economy. Remember the supermarket chains in Los Angeles that broke their union contracts in anticipation of Wal-Mart's entry into that large market? What about the China price pressure on your suppliers, who also supply other retailers? Do I need to give you more examples of the vast downward sweep of your colossus?"

"All right, you've put your unionization cards on the table. What about other aspects of Wal-Mart's operations? What do you want in those areas?"

"Nothing, Sam, not a thing. But I do have one additional demand outside that box. My colleagues and I have taken a substantial stock position in Wal-Mart. We're going to make three nominations to the board of directors, and we want you to accept them, of course after the customary due diligence as to ethical probity and competence."

"I can't decide whether I'm more relieved or surprised. Three directors? And that's your only condition apart from your union stipulations?"

Sol nodded and sipped his martini.

"Well, that only leaves one question. Are your demands non-negotiable?"

"It's the wrong question at the wrong time, Sam. Take this back to your CEO and tell him two things. One, that I'm a hard-bitten son of a bitch, and two, that I'm having the time of my life. More spicy tomato juice?"

"Well, why not? It'll give us time to remember when baseball players were baseball players, when pitchers pitched nine innings, when catchers caught doubleheaders, when they didn't come any tougher than Pistol Pete Reiser, until he cracked his unprotected skull on the center field wall."

"And made the play anyway," Sol said with a smile, rising to refresh Sam's drink.

"Those were the days, my friend. If only we could go back to the time when we were dreamers, the time when we thought we could do anything because we hadn't done anything yet. Hell, make it a double shot of Jim Beam, Sol."

Back in Bentonville on Tuesday morning, Sam went straight to Leighton Clott's office.

"Come in, Sam, sit down. I can't wait to hear what happened with that crusty old bastard."

"Believe me, they don't make them that crusty anymore," Sam said, and went on to relate his conversation with Sol in detail. "When I asked if his two demands were nonnegotiable, he told me to tell you that he's a hard-bitten son of a bitch and that he's never had more fun in his life. I have to say that his concern for Wal-Mart employees and other workers in similar situations seemed genuine. He's a man with nothing to lose, and he knows it. There you have it."

Clott stroked his chin. "Hmm. Sam, did Sol mention any timetable or deadline for recognizing the union and entering into collective bargaining?"

"He said he wanted the cardcheck immediately, which would be a massive job, though I gather he could easily hire the necessary crews. But he said nothing about how soon he expects a union-management contract. He's dealt his cards as if he could care less how we play our hand."

"So you're telling me that if we don't accept his demands, his tightening vise, his SWAT swarms, his collateral allies initiating anti-Wal-Mart moves in their own right, his stirring up the regulatory agencies and fomenting community rebellions against us"—the CEO's voice was rising steadily—"you're telling me that all these will continue to intensify, continue to demonstrate our defenselessness, continue to drive down our share price and our sales, continue to drive us to distraction so we can't conduct our daily business?"

"I couldn't have put it more succinctly myself," Sam said. "You must have given our tribulations much thought."

"Indeed I have, and I've come to some conclusions that I'll share with the board shortly. Sol is a shrewd man, and it's time to make some hard decisions."

"I don't envy you, Leighton. Just remember that corporations have a secret weapon. They don't lose face, because everyone expects them to behave expediently in keeping with their capitalist ideology. They don't fall on their swords out of principle."

"Sam, your wisdom is penetrating if not clairvoyant. Thank you for performing your mission so well."

When Sam had departed, CEO Clott moved to his favorite deep leather chair and resumed his chin stroking, something he always did before a major decision that only he could make because the buck stopped with him. Weighing the Sol attack variables against the Wal-Mart counterattack variables, he mulled and mulled and mulled. Every time he searched for an exit strategy, he hit a wall. Slowly he came to accept what he had to do. For him the evidence had reached a critical mass that was daily becoming more critical. But what about his board of directors, especially the hardliners and traditionalists? Would they brush off the incontrovertible trends in sales, profits, share price, regulatory activity, and so forth? Could he persuade them that this was one mother of a crisis that was not going to blow over?

Sinking deeper into his chair, he stopped stroking his chin and brought his thumbs and fingertips together into a triangle of authority, a gesture that meant he was gaining confidence in his forthcoming decision and his ability to sell it to the board. First Wal-Mart would have to take an even bigger battering, but time would take care of that. Clott buzzed his secretary and told her to postpone the next board meeting until after the Fourth of July weekend. With a weary sigh, he flicked on his plasma TV just in time to see footage of hundreds of kids at busy intersections belting out, "Extra, extra! Read all about it! Wal-Mart CEO makes more than ten grand an hour while workers make under nine bucks." Shaking his head in disgust, he flipped to a rerun of *Who Wants to Be a Millionaire?*

If June was crunch month for Wal-Mart, it was breakout month for the Clean Elections Party. The candidates had met or were about to meet the various state deadlines, and they were in high gear, capitalizing on the raised expectations of the voting public and drawing the kind of crowds that only the many grassroots and media mobilizations of the Meliorists in previous months could have stimulated, albeit indirectly. The press was more than intrigued by the head-on challenge to the forty-seven most powerful members of the House and the ten most influential senators up for reelection. Talk about a David and Goliath scenario all over the country. But this one had a single intense focus—getting dirty money out of politics and replacing it with public money and electoral reform. The result would liberate our society, the candidates argued, and turn it toward a just pursuit of happiness. Some things in a democracy should never be for sale, and elections were among them. That really hit home with people. Not for Sale buttons started popping up everywhere. Not for Sale speeches were delivered before packed audiences. Not for Sale T-shirts, posters, puppets, and playing cards were in great demand. At every opportunity, the CEP candidates described in eloquent detail what happened to the folks back home when politicians were for sale. People began to expand on the theme. Our children are not for sale. Our environment is not for sale. Our religion is not for sale. Our schools and universities are not for sale. The discussion broadened into a systematic critique of corporate domination over a society in which everything was for sale, including our genes, our privacy, our foreign policy, our public land and airwaves.

Back in Congress, the legislators were inundated with demands that they declare themselves Not for Sale. The sheer variety and distribution of the calls for reform left their heads spinning. There were so many bandwagons that they couldn't figure out which ones to jump on. There were so many pressures coming from so many new sources that they couldn't keep track. More and more people in more and more cities were attending the lectures and lunchtime rallies and leaving with a glint in their eyes. The Congress Watchdogs were demanding accountability sessions in every state and congressional district during the August recess. The tell-all valedictories at the National Press Club were reverberating back home and turning the heat up on local companies; a speech last week involving occupational diseases among foundry workers made waves wherever there were foundries. And the counter-pressures from the big business boys were at full throttle too.

It was all too much, but it would have to be digested and made sense of, because the lawmakers knew that their positions on pending legislation would be under intense scrutiny during their upcoming campaigns. Not to mention the new bills they were expecting from the progressive hard core that had suddenly come alive. They could feel the foundations of incumbency shaking, beyond their powers of control or even discernment, given the pace of events.

Most alarming was their growing uncertainty about the objectives of the swelling stream of business lobbyists coming up to the Hill. A new breed was knocking on their doors, shorn of the customary garb of greed. They came from the ranks of the newly formed People's Chamber of Commerce, and their legislative priorities were almost invariably the opposite of what the usual K Street cohort and the trade associations urged. The lawmakers were caught in the crossfire, with campaign money and potential scandals on one side, and conscience and no campaign money on the other. Ordinarily they would have sided with the power and money without a second thought, but the PCC people got a lot of media attention and seemed to have connections with some of the upstart agitators back home.

A possibly momentous phenomenon was in the offing. The senior Bulls who controlled the committees were getting demoralized while the younger progressives were soaring in morale and purpose. One veteran senator was heard to say to another, "It's no fun anymore. I'm thinking of retiring. Why do I need these daily tornados?" What made the progressives' current agenda different from previous false starts was that they had big-time backing from an infrastructure they had never expected to materialize. They had a full-court press from the Meliorists—at this point, as far as they knew, just a bunch of savvy billionaires each shepherding his own chunk of justice through Congress. Even so, they felt they were being drawn together for more than passing a bill here and there, as if by some unseen hand. The stirrings all around the country, together with the regular calls and visits they were receiving from prominent retired legislators and staffers—people whose reputations preceded them—were disciplining them to a new intensity of endeavor. Rumor had it that something big was going to break on the Fourth of July, and they wanted to be ready.

Thousands of business lobbyists and their corporate attorneys had heard the same rumors and were filled with apprehension. They couldn't keep up with what was already happening week after week, much less contemplate something larger on the horizon. In their nightmares they recalled the prophetic warnings of Brovar Dortwist, but in their waking hours they were still telling themselves that nothing had actually changed in the power game they had dominated for so long. They had only to turn to their favorite radio, TV, and newspaper commentators to hear a reassuring blast at this eccentric business rebellion against established business, the very pillar of our economic prosperity. They took refuge in inertia, a force very difficult to reverse, even in the face of the turning tides. It would take an extraordinary mind to break through it, and for all his gifts, that wasn't Brovar Dortwist. He was too right too soon.

The rumors, of course, were true. The Meliorists' preparations for the Fourth of July blastoff were proceeding apace and then some. The Mass Demonstrations project was getting parade permits for two thousand small and midsize towns whose parades had been discontinued because the towns were consolidated with larger towns or because too many residents and band members were away on vacation. Leonard's organizers tracked down the people who used to put on the parades, and they were delighted to have support in resurrecting this grand tradition. They immediately began dusting off their fifes and drums.

A chief problem concerned the vitally important graphics for the Meliorist branding. They had to encapsulate the Agenda's deep and broad reach, all its arguments and evidence, in a way that was crisp, upbeat, and indelible—no mean feat. Yoko asked the Secretariat to reserve an entire closed-circuit briefing for her unveiling of the Meliorist insignia, which she displayed on a large posterboard propped on an easel. It was a wreath of greens, signifying spring-time and rebirth, with a backdrop of yellow symbolizing the sun. In an arc over the top, in elegant lettering, was "The Golden Rule," and at the bottom, "Equal Justice Under Law." In the center was an abstract red, white, and blue image suggesting the Stars and Stripes unfurled in a bracing wind.

Paul whistled. "Wow. I love the way the design and colors tap into so many different associations and emotions. My only suggestion is that you incorporate 'The Meliorists' into the flaglike image in the center so there's no doubt about who and what is being branded."

"For purposes of comparison, can you show us some alternative designs?" Joe asked.

"No, because they were all so awful that I tossed them."

"For my money, I don't think we could ask for anything better than this one," Warren said, "but what about the Seventh-Generation Eye? It's already got high recognition. Shouldn't we capitalize on that?"

"Shall we quickly test both images in focus groups?" Yoko suggested.

Warren nodded. "I think that's the way to go. I suspect there will be groups and occasions for which one or the other image is more appropriate. Send them both over to Promotions, Yoko, but for secu-rity purposes, don't add 'The Meliorists' to the insignia yet. When we get the focus group results, we'll have the Secretariat cost out buttons, posters, banners, bumper stickers, and T-shirts in batches of five million and see how quickly they can be manufactured. I'm sure we'll need at least that many of each for the Fourth and our debut the day after."

"Which reminds me that Dick Goodwin's Paine pamphlet is finished," Bernard said. "As expected, it's a smashing weapon of mass education—beautifully done, respectful of its readers, rooted in historical high points, and foreshadowing a purposeful and fundamental redirection of our country. It needs a cover design ASAP so we can roll the presses."

Yoko nodded. "Send it over and I'll have something for you in a couple of days."

"If that's all on the art front, Leonard has an update from Joan Claybrook on the Blockbuster Challenge," Warren said.

"Yes, and it's an encouraging one. Joan thinks she's solved the problem of how to give incumbents large sums of money without violating the five-thousand-dollar limit on PAC contributions to each candidate. Working with the two-billion-dollar budget we allocated to wean Congress from the special interests, she recommends that the money be spent to raise an equivalent or larger amount in small contributions from millions of voters. In other words, campaign money for each incumbent who accepts the buyback will come from mass mailings, Internet outreach, fundraising dinners, and so on. Under FEC rules, these small contributions can't be solicited directly for the candidates by name, but the donors will understand what's expected of them.

"Joan argues that this roundabout approach has many benefits. It will bring millions more ordinary citizens on board for the Agenda. It will strengthen our network of contacts in each community by bringing out local fundraising talent, activists, artists, supportive columnists, and editorial writers, all the natural leaders and 'influentials,' as the pollsters say. It will turn the billions of the few into millions from the many, with an enormous ripple effect."

"What if the incumbent refuses the buyback offer?" Peter asked.

"Then," replied Leonard, "all these fundraising efforts go to the incumbent's challengers. A no buys a boomerang. Granted, it's difficult to see how all this will work in practice since everything in this project is de novo and there's very little time for pilot projects. But we must have pilot projects in order to get the bugs ironed out. Joan is setting them up to be done in full in July in about six districts, and in a couple of states on a smaller scale. She's in constant consultation with counsel steeped in the FEC regulations and is confident that both the larger and the subsidiary questions will be resolved in our favor. By the way, she told me that working on this project has been exhausting, exhilarating, and the highlight of her career. She predicts historic reverberations."

"Let's hope her prediction is on the way to becoming a reality," Warren said.

"Let's hope lunch is on the way to becoming a reality," said Sol.

On Friday, June 16, at exactly twelve noon, Lobo got the call he'd been expecting from CEO Jasper Cumbersome. The conversation was brief.

"Lobo, we are ready to receive you on Monday, June twenty-sixth, at nine a.m. sharp. Bring with you all your intellect and all your savvy. Leave the pit bull in his doghouse. By the twenty-first we expect a detailed memorandum on everything you have learned thus far. What are the strengths and vulnerabilities of the SROs as a group, individually, and operationally? What potential allies have you considered? Where is 'the core battlefield,' as you put it? What is your estimate of cost, month by month? We also want a general idea of the momentum your plans will generate, a review of the quality of the talent you're assembling, and whatever else you deem important for us to digest before our meeting. Any reactions or questions?"

"Reactions? I like your energy and sense of immediacy. Questions? How much money are you coughing up? I can tell you right now that you're going to need mucho dinero—no, make that muy mucho dinero. This is going to be a galactic battle. The tsunami that's heading your way is going to sweep the high ground right out from under you. And the low ground, for that matter."

"Come now, Lobo. The situation is undoubtedly serious, but don't get carried away with yourself.

"The 'situation,' as you call it, is beyond serious, Jasper. Fortunately, it is not beyond my powers to master."

"That's the spirit, Lobo. Very well, we'll read you on the twenty-first and see you on the twenty-sixth. Good day."

Lobo's parting words to the CEO belied his feelings. He was about to enter the phase of the mission where success depended not just on himself but on his operatives. No more lone wolf. He called the little pit bull, who jumped into his lap and started licking his lips madly. Lobo licked back. This ritual, known only to himself and the canine, calmed him down during moments of high tension, though the same could not be said of the canine.

The lone wolf did have one last task to complete on his own, the June 21 memorandum. Thinking and reading and refining his findings and educated guesses late into the night, night after night, he finally honed his memo, or dispatch, as he preferred to call it, into a précis of some seven hundred words. He started with his most important discovery. "The core battlefield will be the Congress," he wrote, "which is a relief. It is terra cognita, happy hunting grounds for you CEOs and your thousands of lobbyists. To date, a place well in hand." His fingers hovered over his laptop for a moment, then began flying over the keyboard.

> But there are troublesome stirrings in Congress. The progressives, usually placid except for their rhetoric, have become unusually active, urging more and more of their colleagues to support a raft of bills that will apparently be introduced shortly. They are also, with some diplomatic finesse, starting to request that hearings be held on these bills, hearings chaired by their adversaries in the Republican Party. Some liberal Republicans, from New England mostly, are being courted to make the first representations to the chairs. I'm told the exchanges are very civil. For the first time in years, the chairs are feeling the heat from back home, and they want to be seen as 'fair and understanding.'

Our sources see this as an early sign of weakness. But remember, Congress hasn't heard from our side—yet.

Every one of the SROs has vulnerabilities, but how consequential and useful are they? We all have past troubles, professional and personal, we've all made dubious statements and associated with dubious people. The question is what our media specialists can do with the SROs' liabilities. I'll tell you one thing they can do. They can outsmart themselves and generate sympathy for our opponents, who have the money and media capability to fight back. Barring some really hot stuff, the SROs can turn the tables and do to you what we're doing to them. Therefore, we should put this approach on the back burner.

As for their operational vulnerabilities, they seem to be meticulous about compliance with the law. Their attorneys are experienced and well regarded. That we know. We will know much more when our people start reporting from inside their operations. Call them spies, call them infiltrators, call them what you will, but they are vital to our endeavor. I call them patriots. I've assigned a special team of them to find the club, lodge, or hotel where the SROs must be meeting, and to apply for any open staff position, however lowly. These are elderly people, and they are not always going to meet electronically if they can avoid it.

Most of the personnel I need are now on board. For obvious reasons, I'm going to leave you in the dark about the specifics. Suffice it to say that they are all characterized by loyalty, a proven commitment to business values, experience, good judgment, a critical ability to reassess and revise, and zero tendency to procrastinate. They are mostly in their thirties and forties, physically and mentally fit, and daring without being reckless. My own executive corps consists of a dozen people of the highest caliber.

Who are our allies? Big business in its entirety, along with its dealers, agents, and franchisees. The question is how much we can expect of them beyond lip service. They're a fairly independent crowd at the trade association and CEO level. Imagine whipping such august groups as the Business Roundtable, the Greenbrier Club, the National Association of Manufacturers, and the self-styled US Chamber of Commerce into the fast lane They have always marched to their own drumbeat, and they won't want to change drummers. They'll want to go their own conventional way of fighting back and lobbying. And while that's not worthless, it's also sufficiently unfocused to increase the risk of mixups, screw-ups, and dust-ups. There simply is no time for pratfalls. You'll have to marshal your collective prestige and address this problem directly with your peers. There's nothing worse for momentum than bumps in the road and sinkholes.

As for costs, it will be mostly media, organizers, handout money to community groups, and campaign contributions. Our allies already have their infrastructures in place, of course, and that will save money. Still, I think we're talking about a ballpark figure of $5 billion over the next five months. Precisely what resources you're putting behind this operation needs careful discussion on 6/26.

Finally, momentum means recovering the offensive. Repeat: the offensive. When you're behind, you don't catch up by playing defense. Period. End.

Lobo hit Save and e-mailed the memo to the CEOs, along with a not too burdensome attachment of cogent articles and historical materials for them to read before the meeting. He added a postscript telling them that it was of utmost importance that they also read John Gardner's *On Leadership* "from cover to cover." Then he sat back in his desk chair and sighed. Writing the dispatch had fatigued him. He was glad it was over with and didn't much care what the CEOs thought as long as they came through with the money. He preferred to rely on his forceful persona, his oral presentations, and his quick wits to carry the day. That day was the twenty-sixth of June. Then came the showdown, the contact sport that would release new creative energies fortified by inside information. A man could only hypothesize so much. Lobo couldn't wait to get into the sweaty public ring with biceps bulging.

For all the people power that was building both as a direct result of the Meliorists and from the indirect stimulation of organized energies, the real proof of the pudding would be getting the Agenda through Congress. Throughout June, the Redirectional projects responsible for various parts of the legislation—the PCC, the CUBs, the Congress Watchdogs, the Zabouresk-Zeftel group, which had taken to calling itself Double Z—were working with their congressional allies in an intensive collaboration that went on below the media's radar. These shapers, movers, and shakers did not want publicity. They just wanted to work at their highest level of professionalism so as to meet their critical deadlines. Everything had to be ready by the Fourth of July. The bills had to be introduced in the right sequence, with impregnable backup material for the rebuttal battles that lay ahead. And everything had to mesh smoothly—the publicity, the political muscle to support the legislators who were up front on the bills, the back-home pressure on all members (especially the committee chairs and the leadership) the discrediting of the business lobbies as chronic negativists, the responses to their think-tank cronies, the mass media ripostes to the inevitable corporate campaign of fear and threat, and the splitting of the opposition. The lights never went out in the offices and dens of these Agenda champions.

In the midst of all this meticulous preparation, the sub-economy was materializing rapidly along the complementary lines laid down by Jeno, who envisioned it as a Trojan horse within the established economy, and by Jerome Kohlberg, who emphasized its role in promoting sustainable economic practices and applied ethics. Jeno's acquisition specialists had gone down the Department of Commerce list of business categories and purchased hundreds of retail businesses around the country—medical practices, beauty salons, lawn-care companies, pharmacies, oil dealerships, auto dealerships, real estate firms, machine shops, grocery stores, clothing stores, restaurants, bars, pest exterminators, tax preparers, accountants and financial planners, plumbers, electricians, carpenters—along with a small foundry, a handful of other small manufacturing facilities, a few wholesale firms, and a dozen or so midsize agribusinesses, mines, banks, and insurance companies. The owners of these businesses were now streaming a steady flow of internal information about their industries and trades to the Sustainable Sub-economy headquarters, which was run by some of the smartest ex-merger-and-acquisition whizzes around, some of the best ex-managers, ex-efficiency experts, ex-marketeers, ex-recruiters, ex-PR chiefs, and ex–brilliant-but-disgruntled corporate advocates of a green economy. All these exes were thrilled to be free at last to bring their consciences and brains to work every day.

Always looking ahead, Jeno wanted to know whether the Trojan horses had heard of any lobbyists or trade association executives or CEOs who were canceling their customary August vacations—a good gauge of rising anxiety and consternation over the recent wave of attacks on them. If the business establishment were the Navy, Jeno thought, this would surely be an all-leaves-canceled, all-hands-on-deck situation. According to the feedback from the sub-economy, all vacations were on. Complacency persisted among the top brass. They were either clueless as to what was coming in September or too attached to their luxuries. The Congress was on vacation in August and so were they. That had always been the routine in past years, and it would be the routine this year.

Jeno promptly notified the Secretariat of this neat bit of intelligence, just the tip of the iceberg of inside information that would flow from the sub-economy. Not only that, but early sales figures across the range of sub-economy businesses showed no decline since purchase, and in some cases even a rise as the fresh images of these energetically managed companies took hold.

The CUBs were on the march too. An unchallenged backlog of overcharges, ripoffs, cover-ups, and commercial shenanigans awaited them on every corner. It was like fishing off the banks of Newfoundland in 1800. George's purchase and conversion of the hotel had been a stroke of motivating genius. The building surged with excitement and productivity, as a dozen or more federal regulatory agencies were finding out. The CUBs coordinated their activities, cross-fertilizing ideas, tactics, and strategies. The tone, tempo, and quality of the whole project were due in no small part to John Richard and Robert Fellmeth, who maintained close contact with the project manager and the CUB directors.

A spate of CUB reports justifying regulatory action or investigation made news around the country. People were paying ever-higher prices for gasoline, home heating oil, utilities, insurance, and banking transactions. Hospital bills were indecipherable and out of sight. One mom brought her eight-year-old daughter to a California hospital for a cut finger, and by the time the separate bills were totaled up, the tab was $2,100. Agencies accustomed to auctioning off or giving away the communications and broadcast spectrums found petitioners and public interest groups arrayed against the grasping companies. Demands for the reinstatement of cable regulation met with widespread community and customer approval.

The Cable CUB went to town pillorying the dreary cable channels saturated with infomercials, with hucksters peddling tacky jewelry and miracle diets and reruns of low-grade dramas and sitcoms, the cheap way out for steadily rising monthly charges. There was even a channel for chimpanzees dressed up as humans, but none for all the good things citizens were fighting for in one community after another. Using incisive visuals, satire, and withering criticism, the Cable CUB called for a student channel, a labor channel, a consumer channel, and a round-the-clock citizen action channel, for starters. "Yeah," people began saying, "that all makes sense. We don't have to be pandered to day after day. Why didn't we think of this ourselves? We just took what they gave us."

The Investor CUB was plowing new ground with gusto. Branding high-level CEOs "anti-capitalists" who set their own pay, rubber-stamped by their handpicked board of directors, the CUB was all over the Securities and Exchange Commission to require large companies to put top executive pay to a proxy vote. With a membership of 400,000, and growing by the week, the Investor CUB was a new power player in Washington and on Wall Street, where it had another bustling office. Its advisory committee included former SEC commissioners and chief accountants, former stock exchange executives, prominent mutual fund founders turned reformers, an ex-governor, two ex-CEOs, several retired state regulatory officials, and most recently, Robert Monks. Some of these distinguished people had not previously distinguished themselves by putting steel behind their long-held conviction that something should be done about the farce the corporate chieftains unblushingly called "people's capitalism." Now they were turning their guilt complexes into action.

As the Investor CUB vigorously pursued a comprehensive corporate reform program in Congress or the SEC, as appropriate, stockholder approval of executive pay became the most urgent and distracting matter on the minds of CEOs and top executives. Stock-optioned to their gills, these big fish were having nightmares about the conflict inherent in opposing measures that were very bad for them but very good for the shareholders with whom they had a fiduciary relationship. The flight began. As the weeks produced more headlines, more CEOs cashed out their stock options, stashed their fat retirement packages under their arms, and headed for the door. "I'm Outta Here!" was the *New York Post*'s front-page headline over a photo of corpulent CEO Dirk Desmond of Amalgamated Health-care plunging through his office door. The photographer caught just the appropriate expression on his face, a mixture of fright and greed with a touch of leer.

In Omaha, scanning the major papers as he did every day,

Warren came to Dirk Desmond and smiled. He grabbed a pair of scissors, cut the photograph out, stuck it in a frame, and hung it on the wall in his den, deciding that it would not contribute to the pictorial decorum of his business office. No sooner had he finished admiring his mischief than the phone rang.

"Warren, you won't believe who just called me!" Ted exclaimed without preamble. "It was one of my Billionaires Against Bullshit, not a particularly active one—too busy working on his third billion—until he started following the Health CUB's exposés of phony overbilling. For years he's been doing a slow boil about the coded bills he gets, can't understand them or double-check them or even get through to someone on the phone for an explanation. Now he wants to put twenty-five million behind a group that will do nothing but collect, expose, and prosecute computerized billing fraud, whether against Medicare, Medicaid, insurance companies, unions, or individuals. And if they do a good job, he says, there's another fifty million for an endowment. He expects that success will bring in more fee-generating cases under the False Claims Act, so that the group can expand its staff. He wants to call it Battle Bogus Bills, with a triple-B insignia. So how's that for another example of our serendipitous impact, Warren?"

"Perfect, Ted, just perfect. Have him call Promotions right away. We want an announcement sooner rather than later, because this is a blockbuster issue that everyone's angry and frustrated about."

Warren replaced the receiver and looked over at the wall. "It would appear that you resigned just in the nick of time, Dirk," he said, reflecting that once the rage for justice was widely seeded, once the capability to advance justice in one area of society after another was demonstrated, more and more people of means would come forward to expand the mission. That had been the Meliorists' premise all along. Goodwill, strategic smarts, and precise organization were preconditions, to be sure, but with these at the ready, it came down to money. Even the noblest impulses needed the engine of money to have a practical impact in today's dollar-driven culture. The dollar was the dynamo. Take that away from the Meliorist arsenal, all other variables in place, and they would still be a utopian discussion club perched high above the island of Maui.

Of all the CUBs, the one composed of 550,000 taxpayers and counting probably had the broadest ideological support. Who wanted to see their taxes wasted? Who didn't believe they *were* wasted? The network news programs had been hammering this point futilely but persistently for years in running segments like "It's *Your* Money." Exposé after exposé, and the corporate cheaters and bureaucratic bunglers just laughed at them, because nothing happened. Because the only ones who could make something happen were the people footing the bill, and they weren't organized. Until the Taxpayer CUB. Talented auditors, accountants, economists, organizers, and investigators flocked to the new group, some from inside government, corporations, and accounting firms, others who had retired early in disgust over what they had observed or were compelled to do. The Taxpayer CUB occupied an entire floor of the hotel.

Heading the group was Robert MacIntyre, a widely respected tax reformer who had crunched numbers for the media for more than three decades. He hadn't burned out, but he knew that accurate information and crisp disclosure were not enough to effect change. If anything, the tax code was now more unfair, more inscrutable, and more wasteful than when he started in the seventies. When the Taxpayer CUB came along, MacIntyre came alive. He arrived at his new job loaded with data about how the big companies and the wealthy get away with underpaying their taxes. He surveyed his members with a set of questions designed to get them thinking fundamentally about what kind of tax code they wanted. Would they favor a 0.5 percent tax on all stock, bond, and derivatives transactions if their income tax rate could be cut by 50 percent? Would they favor restoring the corporate income tax to its level in the prosperous sixties if the revenues would eliminate the current federal deficit each year? Would they favor a tax on pollution, gambling, and addictive products that would pay for a tax reduction of a third or more on incomes below $100,000? Would they prohibit govern-

ment contracts, subsidies, and giveaways to any corporation domi-
ciled in a foreign tax haven to avoid federal taxes? These questions
and others like them gave the membership a framework for taking
an informed position on how taxes should be distributed in a complex society so as to suppress certain less desirable activities while
freeing positive activities from current tax burdens. For example, a
tax on pollution would foster the use of cleaner fuel, solar energy,
and fewer toxic chemicals and pesticides. Higher taxes on tobacco
and alcohol would discourage consumption and benefit users'
health, as had already been shown in the case of existing tobacco
taxes and rates of cigarette smoking among youth.

MacIntyre also zeroed in on the IRS budget, which allocated far
too little to the corporate and partnership auditing sections, costing
the Treasury Department tens of billions of dollars annually in
uncollected tax revenues. Similarly, the IRS skimped on fair enforcement designs to recapture some $300 billion annually in
unreported individual income. Imagine the prudent use of such
monies for critical public works, or to repair schools and clinics,
clean up the environment, protect people's health and pocketbooks,
and establish educational trust funds for every young American.
Imagine the concomitant creation of well-paying, useful jobs that
could not be exported.

MacIntyre had a broad practical vision, but he knew broad public
education was needed to overcome deep vested interests in the current tax laws. What better place to start than House and Senate
hearings on a comprehensive overhaul of the tax code? It took a few
calls from the Meliorist powerhouse to the reluctant chairs and
ranking members of the House Ways and Means Committee and
the Senate Finance Committee, along with some timely help from
the Double Z, before Congress finally agreed to hold hearings in
July. The Taxpayer CUB was now deep in preparation, marshaling
issues and witnesses never entertained on Capitol Hill before.

The Consumer CUB found its field of dreams in the slumbering
federal regulatory agencies, which had forsaken their enforcement
role to become patsies for the businesses and industries under their

jurisdiction. In the seventies and eighties a hysterical propaganda barrage from the corporatists about the horrors of deregulation had rendered these agencies toothless. Lost in this farrago of deception were the men, women, and children left defenseless against dangerous products, toxic workplace chemicals, pollution, contaminated food, unprosecuted corporate fraud, and pension looting. Lost were the workers trapped in frozen-minimum-wage jobs and sub-minimum-wage sweatshops. Lost were the patients who died or suffered grievous harm in the absence of effective medical malpractice regulation. Lost were the hundreds of thousands of innocent victims of this vast federal indifference. Who wept for these Americans?

The wave of formal petitions that had so alarmed the editors of *Regulation* magazine was now a torrent thanks to the Consumer CUB. Promotions set up a special team to publicize its work beyond the regular media attention it was receiving. The goal was to establish this CUB as a group that genuinely cared for the people, stood with them, and would not leave them defenseless at their hour of need. It was Promotions at its best, tapping into the emotional memory and intelligence of the populace. Everyone knew from their own experience of life that there were forces on their side and forces most definitely not. Skillfully, Promotions used human interest stories tailored to a variety of media to associate "They're on your side" and "They care for you" with the Consumer CUB in the public mind. Broadcasting and webcasting this message was a high priority for the months leading up to Election Day.

All told, the full-time staff of the CUBs now exceeded one thousand, almost doubling the entire full-time corps of citizen advocates in Washington. And probably, George thought to himself as he reviewed the figures, more than quadrupling energy levels, hours worked, and results achieved.

On Wednesday, June 21, Washington, DC, was host to its largest lunchtime rally yet, fifteen thousand strong, with a parade permit to march down Constitution Avenue all the way to the barricades before the Congress. Carried live by C-SPAN, the rally began in front of the new Department of Labor building, with a range of speakers including representatives of organized labor and unorganized labor, ordinary workers, clergy, social workers, academics, and four members of Congress. Among the no-shows, who had been invited a month ago, were the secretary of labor and five assistant secretaries, the head of the US Chamber of Commerce, the chairs of the House and Senate Labor Committees, and the president of the United States. The speakers invited them again, to another rally two weeks hence, when fifty thousand were expected to attend.

Today's event was the rally of the overworked and underpaid. Its pivotal demand was for legislation taking the minimum wage to $10 an hour gross. According to estimates by First-Stage Improvements, that would put about $350 billion a year more in the pockets of workers and give the consumer demand side of the economy a big boost. The posters held up by the crowd told the story: "Work to Live, Not to Borrow!" "American Wages, American Dignity!" "Try Living Without a Living Wage!" "No Living Wage, No More Congressional Pay Grabs!" "Workers Fight Your Wars, You Reap the Profits!" "Workers' Needs vs. Corporate Profiteers!"

When the march was over, some of the ralliers went to visit their members of Congress. As Leonard's organizers well knew, most protest rallies in Washington took place on weekends, for obvious reasons of maximizing turnout. But on weekends the politicos left town and could easily shrug off the protests. Weekday rallies might be smaller, but they often had a greater impact because Congress and the press were at work.

A delegation from the Tennessee Congress Watchdogs, mostly textile workers, had wrangled a meeting with their senior senator, Majority Leader Tillman Frisk, who was making noises about running for president. He was an MD, and a millionaire many times over from his family business, which owned a chain of hospitals. When the workers were ushered into his office, he rose from his desk and greeted them warmly, asking them where they hailed from and managing a homey sentence or two about Johnson City,

Nashville, Oak Ridge, Knoxville, Memphis, and so on. Pleasantries completed, the head of the delegation, Alvin York, got down to business.

"Senator, why haven't you introduced a living wage bill? I understand you always support an annual pay hike for yourself and the rest of Congress, but the minimum wage of five-fifteen an hour has only been raised once in the last eighteen years. According to the Department of Labor, it has less purchasing power than the minimum wage in 1949."

The senator was nodding deeply. "I understand, and I sympathize with your concerns."

"Then why are you opposed to a living wage, say, a ten-dollar minimum wage, which only adjusts for inflation since 1968?"

"Well, I'm no economist, but my top economic advisers and many other economists say that raising the minimum wage to anywhere near that level will cost jobs. The poor and the teenagers will suffer."

"By that logic, why not reduce the minimum wage to create more jobs? Do you see where you're going here—the road to serfdom, meeting the Chinese competition? Senator, will you or will you not support a living wage? Your position will sway the entire Congress. Your support will uplift tens of millions of hardworking people who can't meet their family's needs. Health bills are shooting up, gas prices too, home heating oil, food, rent—"

The senator held up his hand. "You make some good points. Let me rethink the issue."

"You've had years to rethink it," said Bettie Page, a copyeditor at the *Nashville Tennessean*. "Are you trying to get us out of here without answering one simple question? Will you support *any* raise in the minimum wage?"

"I can't answer that question until I balance the job loss figures against the benefits of increased pay. What good is a living wage if you don't have any job at all, my dear?"

"We're going around in circles here, Senator," said Casey Jones. "How much do you make an hour? How much will you get in pension payments?"

Senator Frisk ahemmed. "Well, I've never figured it down to the hour. Good heavens, I must work eighty hours a week around here."

"Well, let me figure it out for you," Casey said. "Counting your perks, benefits, and allowances, you make over a thousand dollars a day, five days a week."

"My good friend, I'm not in this for the money. Do you know what I used to make for an open-heart surgery?"

"Our taxes give all of you up here a very good salary, life insurance, full health insurance, excellent retirement security, and on and on," said Flora Hamilton. "What makes you think you have the moral authority to govern when you deny forty-seven million full-time American workers a subsistence living wage? Haven't companies raised their prices big-time over the past two decades, Senator? Hasn't management's compensation gone up over the past two decades? I'm really getting tired of your evasions."

Senator Frisk sensed that the meeting was getting out of hand. "My dear, I'm not being evasive. This is a very difficult issue. We've had many small businesses tell us that raising the minimum wage will shut them down, and many larger ones claim that it will make them go abroad. I have a responsibility to address their concerns as well."

Alvin jumped back in. "Senator Frisk, you represent people, not corporations, unless I'm mistaken. People are hurting. Their children are hurting. America is being Wal-Marted to death. Your first responsibility is to the people. You're making some of the same arguments used against the abolition of child labor, but the Congress went ahead and abolished child labor, and the children went to school instead, and the factories had to hire their parents. Did our nation collapse?"

"Senator Frisk, remember Henry Ford I?" asked Archie Campbell, a firebrand from Chattanooga. "In January 1914, he announced to the world that he was going to double his workers' wages from $2.50 to $5.00 a day. When his fellow auto executives angrily demanded why he was destabilizing wages in the industry, he replied that he wanted workers to be able to afford his cars. Wages up, consumer demand up—that was the American way until the eighties, when the reverse race to the bottom began. Lately I've been reading a lot about the history of wages in our country, and your response just doesn't wash."

A loud buzz pierced the room. Senator Frisk looked gratefully at his intercom and pushed the button. "You're wanted on the floor, Senator," his secretary announced. "Thank you, Dixie," he said, standing and smiling at the delegation. "Well, you heard the boss. It's been a delight to get your views, which I am sure are sincerely and deeply held. Don't forget to sign the guest book on your way out so we all can stay in touch."

Alvin stood too. "Senator Frisk, they say you're going to run for president. We've been trying to get an answer from you about a living wage for tens of millions of voters whose support you'll need. We've come all the way from our home state, your home state. We are entitled to a direct answer. Fifteen thousand people just rallied here in Washington to demand a ten-dollar minimum wage. We ask you again, do you support a living wage in this country? If not $10.00 an hour, would you back any raise at all, or do you support the current freeze at $5.15? Tell us now, one way or the other."

Senator Frisk walked briskly toward his office door. "My apologies, friends, but I have to rush to the Senate floor for a vote. Good day. God bless."

"Well, we'll still be here when you come back, Senator," Alvin said.

Archie got to his feet and gestured around the office. "And we're not leaving until we get an answer. There's plenty of rug room and sofas for a good night's sleep," he said with a friendly smile.

Senator Frisk blanched and stormed out of the office. Carefully closing the door, he turned to his secretary and said, "Call the sergeant at arms and have them escorted from the premises. Call me on the floor when they're gone."

Seven minutes later, four Capitol Hill police officers arrived at the senator's office and asked the workers to leave.

"Officers, we haven't finished our meeting with the senator," Alvin said. "We'll wait for him to get back from the floor."

"I'm afraid you'll all have to leave, at the senator's request," said the captain.

"Probably best if we do," Bettie said, walking to the door. No one followed her. Outside, in the hallway, she slipped into a restroom and called Congress Watchdog headquarters on her cell phone so they could alert the media that a confrontation was brewing in Senator Frisk's office. "It looks like things are heading for a sit-in," she said. "We'll wait as long as we can before we drop to the floor so the press will have time to get up here."

"Hang on," said the assistant who'd answered the phone. "I'll put you through to the project manager."

"What?" the manager said after Bettie explained the situation. "Are you crazy? If you get arrested, they'll book you at the police station and ask you all kinds of questions that we may not want you to answer. Not yet, anyhow. Look, all of you are workers, but we know and you know that you have skills and experience that go beyond your jobs. You've all participated in citizen action and taken civil disobedience training. You've all been vocal in your communities on a wide variety of matters. That's why you were drawn to the Watchdog groups. That's why you were chosen to go up to Capitol Hill. A sit-in at Frisk's office would throw us on the defensive, and that violates our cardinal rule: Never volunteer yourself into a defensive position."

"Well, what do you want us to do?"

"Above all, stay calm. Say that you're waiting for the senator to return so that he can decide. Just keep repeating, 'Let the senator decide.'"

"He already has, and we already said we're not leaving."

"'We' who? Who said that?"

"Archie. He mentioned the comfortable couches and all the rug space."

"Only Alvin has the authority to make such a drastic decision. Did he try to override Archie?"

"He didn't have a chance, because Senator Frisk left. He seemed a little upset."

"Do you remember the code phrase for backing off from a confrontation, Bettie?"

"Sure."

"Well, get back there and use it before all hell breaks loose!"

Bettie rushed down the hallway to the senator's office to find the workers remonstrating with the increasingly impatient officers. The police had already decided that the workers would have to be dragged out, but they were waiting for reinforcements to be on the safe side.

"Why can't we all be civil with one another?" Bettie shouted over the hubbub.

Everyone froze, the police startled by her return, the workers catching the code that meant they should leave peacefully just before they were arrested and make the most out of the press coverage that was on the way.

"Aw, hell, she's right," Alvin said in his best down-home drawl. "Us Volunteer Staters tend to get ourselves a little too worked up sometimes. Say, any of y'all from Tennessee?" Whereupon the police and the workers fell into friendly small talk—one of the officers had attended Middle Tennessee State, and another was born in Nashville—which served both sides, since the police were waiting for reinforcements and the workers were waiting for the press.

As it happened, the reinforcements and the press arrived at the same time. The senator's secretary asked the press to stay in the hallway and ushered the police into the office, where the two sides faced off.

Alvin broke the tense silence. "We aim to wait for the senator to return. It's the natural thing for constituents to want to do. We'd like to bring our discussion of the living wage to closure. I mean, what do you expect us to say to the reporters outside if we don't see him again?"

"Senator Frisk will be on the floor for several hours for a lengthy debate on an appropriations bill," the captain said. "You'll have to leave now."

"You're sure that's what Senator Frisk wants? Okay, we're going. Nice to meet you, Captain, you're a gentleman."

Out in the hall, the workers were besieged by reporters. Alvin gave a mini press conference facing six cameras: "Senator Frisk, majority leader of the Senate and a prospective presidential candidate, refused to answer the simple question vitally important to forty-seven million full-time American workers: Will you support legislation for a living wage and lead it through the Senate?" The other workers got their say in with their own variations and some great sound bites, and then strode down the hallway together, with cameramen trailing them for the usual cutaways. As the elevator doors closed, Alvin, Archie, and Bettie raised their fists.

Watching the news that evening at home in Waco, Bernard turned to his wife, Audre, and said, "The pitchfork people have breached the gates of the cowardarians. The Rubicon has been crossed."

June 26 arrived. When Lobo was ushered into the Leviathan penthouse boardroom, the first thing he noticed was that the number of CEOs had more than doubled, to nearly thirty. What massive industrial, commercial, and financial power was represented around this burnished mahogany conference table! Lobo was impressed but didn't show it. He had to assume a commanding presence at the outset.

CEO Cumbersome made the necessary introductions crisply. "You may commence, Lobo," he then intoned. "The floor is yours."

Lobo stood at the end of the table facing them all. "Gentlemen, if there is one reality I have grasped in my work since our last meeting, it is this. Nothing that I convey to you as to how, when, and where to mobilize will be as important as the intensity and depth of your individual and collective determination. Why? Because that is how the SROs have brought us to this pass of erupting crisis. Permit me to ask how many of you have read John Gardner's *On Leadership*, a hundred and ninety-nine pages of paperback dynamite."

Three of the original eleven business tycoons raised their hands. One who did not, William Worldweight, CEO of the largest machine tool and robotics manufacturer in the world, grumbled, "Lobo, we are already leaders by definition. You're treating us like students."

"Sir, this book presents a treatment of leadership far beyond what it takes to rise to the top in a large corporation, although there is some overlap. It's a historical overview of the leadership traits pervasive throughout the ages and cultures. Just scan the table of contents and you'll see what I mean. You'll never view yourself in the same way again. If you dive into what Gardner has to say, you'll come up far more ready to defeat this current assault on the American business way of life."

Newcomer Norman Noondark lifted his heavy lids and asked, "Why didn't you provide us with an executive summary Lobo? We're busy people."

"Mr. Noondark, the entire book *is* a summary, and a very concise one, of twenty-five years of thinking, reading, and writing about the subject of leadership. Surely Gardner is worth a few hours of your time. I won't belabor the subject, other than to repeat that for the task at hand, the bottom line is *all of you*."

"I found Gardner's book to be philosophically and operationally motivating," said Wardman Wise, trying to get the meeting back on track. "I'm sure my colleagues will turn to it as soon as possible. Please continue."

"Thank you. You have before you my dispatch of June twenty-first. Before we discuss it, a caveat: in everything we undertake, there must be no false starts, no worthless detours, no dead-ends, no matter how plausible they may appear. There is no time for such diversions. Now, the core battlefield, as I said, is the Congress. Our friends on the Hill tell us there is furious activity up there. The raft of bills we expect soon are of the kind we are accustomed to opposing. But first things first. We must launch a national media attack on the SROs by tapping into people's fear of instability, of the unknown, of losing whatever little they now have economically. We raise the specter of soaring taxes, corporate flight, spreading unemployment and impoverishment, and then we say something along the lines of, 'But the SROs don't care, do they? They're old, they're super-rich, they don't have to worry about the future.' We'll use Sol Price's attack on Wal-Mart to drive this theme home with dramatizations featuring everyday folks—remember Harry and Louise and what they did to healthcare reform? The fear campaign must embrace the business community as well. If stock markets falter, if economic indicators become shaky, if business and consumer confidence begins to decline, so much the better in the short run. In the seventies, the popular Labor prime minister of Australia was literally fired by the Queen of England's representative—a reserve power never used before—because the business bloc saturated the country with scare stories about economic instability. A few well-timed announcements from foreign companies that they were pulling back investments Down Under, and the rest was history. The same tactic has worked in many less developed countries, but its success in Australia shows how feasible it is here. Already we've seen stories about European and Japanese CEOs wondering what's happening to the business climate in the world's largest economy. A rebellion of the super-rich against big business is beyond their comprehension. Some commentators in the foreign press have suggested that their governments shift away from the dollar and look at other countries' bonds instead of pouring so much into US Treasuries. Just imagine what would happen if the Japanese and Chinese started selling their Treasuries. It's been giving Wall Street and the Chamber of Commerce nightmares. Instability? Uncertainty? Unpredictability? These are poison darts into the heart of their dominance. It's our job to make them see that we can catch the darts in midair and throw them back."

CEO Justin Jeremiad frowned. "You are aware, of course, Mr. Lobo, of the detailed alert sent out by our friends at the American Enterprise Institute regarding the sudden surge of regulatory petitions. If we are to launch any public relations drive, I should think it would be on the subject of overregulation stifling innovation and breeding more paperwork, more big government. That's what the SROs want—the iron yoke of Big Government on our back."

"Exactly, Mr. Jeremiad, exactly the way to go. Yes, I'm very well aware of the AEI alert, and it's wonderful grist for our fear mill. At this point, we needn't go into detail about the content of the first-stage media buys to delegitimize those obsolete businessmen. Suffice it to say that my teams are ready and raring to go. My dispatch outlines the parallel paths that must be pursued on a strict timetable. My structure of action allows for adaptation and expansion as we detect and foil SRO initiatives. And as my people move into their groups at various levels, we'll be finding out more and more earlier and earlier. But the central question remains, gentlemen. What resources, material and human, are you yourselves prepared to commit?"

CEO Cumbersome looked around the table. "We have collectively committed to giving and raising two billion dollars for the immediate revving up of the engines—an unprecedented sum from us, unencumbered by corporate governance and SEC rules. Obviously, this is not a blank check. We will assign three of our best staff to work with you on a daily basis to assure the efficient flow of money to your operation and then out of your operation into the fields of action. More money will flow when the attacks by the SROs present a clear and present danger to specific industries. Then we will be able to tap into corporate funds, but to what extent I can't say. Remember, the trade associations will be issuing a barrage of frantic alerts and dunning their member companies, as is their wont.

"Now, as for our personal involvement, that's a tricky proposition. You are looking for a dramatic mano-a-mano confrontation on the media front lines. You want us to pair off against men like Joe Jamail and Warren Buffet and Bernard Rapoport and Peter Lewis and George Soros. Fine, but any one of us who goes up against them will have to clear some hurdles. First, he will have to be a publicly visible executive, or at least well known to the business press. Second, his debate skills must be up to his opponent's. Third, he will have to take an indefinite leave of absence. Fourth, he will need a gut sense of the mortal danger to the unfettered marketplace and our economic way of life. Tell me, Lobo, how many CEOs will make it to the finish line?"

"You tell me, Jasper."

"From the top rank, I can think of three, possibly four. We've had some volunteers from start-up companies, Silicon Valley types, youngish, angry, brash, supremely self-confident. We're not sure they're sufficiently well known or sufficiently seasoned, and we worry about the image factor—young brutes beating up on distinguished old retirees who are already folk heroes. You know the media, Lobo."

"Well, it's a problem only you can solve, I'm afraid. Perhaps more calls, interviews, and personal contacts will bring some leaders forward. Try to raise their sights. Give them a sense of their historical significance if they enlist in . . . We need a brand name here—in what?"

"Yes," said CEO Edward Edifice, "our cause needs a memorable name that goes beyond the usual Chamber of Commerce clichés about free enterprise, beyond the usual tired slogans like 'Defense of the American Worker' or 'Defense of the American Way of Life.' How about 'Enlist in the Defense of the Greatest Economy in the History of the World'? That's general enough, and at the same time hits lots of specific buttons for lots of people."

"I like it, I like it very much," said CEO Roland Revelie.

Lobo did his best to assume an appreciative look. If this was their idea of a motivational catchphrase, things were worse than he thought. "I like it too, but on a matter of such import, perhaps we should retain a good PR firm to give us a few more options?"

"Let's do that," CEO Martin Mazurowski said gruffly, "and let's get back to brass tacks. A mentor of mine, at the time CEO of Coca-Cola, once told me that big business appears invincible but is in reality very fragile and can easily shatter under certain pressures. We have to be very careful here. How are we going to feint destabilizing the economy and then accuse the SROs of doing just that? You suggest we bring down the stock market a bit, as if we could control whether it goes out of control in a panic. I find some of the tactics you've proposed highly dangerous in execution, Lobo, and possibly illegal. I was trained as an engineer, and a basic principle of engineering is to keep it simple. Let's have some plain talk. Let's declare straight out why we don't think this is good for the country, folks, and don't you agree? Two billion dollars can do a lot or do us in. Let's be sure we don't have more money than brains."

"I agree only to the extent that we're mostly flying blind right now," Lobo said. "The prizefighters are circling each other and haven't yet clinched. But our opponent has been in training for months now, whereas we're surrounded by all these powerful trade associations, business groups, dealer organizations, big banks, big insurance companies, big HMOs, big this and big that, and for this big battle, they're flabby, out of shape, complacent, unready, not thinking outside the proverbial box, and not even aware of how off balance they are. By contrast, those of us in this room feel the danger keenly. We know a great deal about the SROs and will know more every day. We have a vastly greater sense of personal commitment and urgency, and we must turn everything we have into a crowbar to pry the sleeping giants into action.

"Look," Lobo went on, his voice rising, "it's true that we can't be reckless and precipitous, but it's finito if we're too cautious. America is the land of the bold and the brave. That's what has marked the breakthroughs and victories in our pioneering country and its expanding free market economy. Our nation has the great eagle as its symbol, not the pigeon or the robin. The great eagle kills its prey and eats it. It takes no prisoners. Haven't we all sung 'The Battle Hymn of the Republic'? Don't we need a 'terrible swift sword'? When we first met, I began by asking you what you don't want me to do. It's time for an answer. I have to know how far I can go to win, to defeat these superannuated troublemakers who should be playing checkers or shuffling on the golf course."

CEO Cumbersome responded without hesitation. "Take it to the outer edges of the legal limits, but stay within those limits. Stay in close consultation with your legal counsel. Anything further?"

"I think more talk at this point will only confuse us," said Wardman Wise. "In Lobo, we have an offensive weapon with sonar and heat-seeking capabilities, and soon we'll discover where and when and how to zero in on the forces of disruption. Lobo, we must have good internal communications. You'll need to create a closed-circuit system so that we can safely contact each other and you. You'll keep us regularly informed about what you're doing, and we'll do the same as we work on lining our peers up to contribute their money, influence, and time. And I don't know about the rest of you, but I'm ready for some dinner now. The hotel dining room is superb."

"Hear, hear!" swept around the table. Lobo was hungry too, but how could they be thinking about their stomachs at a time like this, especially after his impassioned peroration?

Just as Cumbersome was about to adjourn the meeting, Sal Belligerante spoke up. "A passage in John Gardner's book is appropriate here, in case we're ever tempted to exchange the mantle of leadership for the shroud of despair. I quote: 'Leaders cannot hope to have that kind of impact unless they themselves have a high level of morale. There is a famous story about a general on George C. Marshall's staff who reported to Marshall that some of the officers had morale problems. Marshall said, "Officers don't have morale problems. Officers cure morale problems in others. No one is looking after my morale." It is a sound principle. Low morale is unbecoming to a leader.'" Belligerante looked up and smiled as he finished reading.

Lobo smiled back. Perhaps there was hope after all.

CHAPTER 13

On the Friday preceding the Fourth of July, the Meliorists gathered at Warren's home in Omaha instead of going to Maui. There was too much to do before the Great Launch to waste time on extended air travel. The Fourth fell on a Tuesday this year, which meant that many people would be taking long weekends. Perfect. The corporatists would be luxuriating at their watering holes and vacation spas while the Meliorists massed their forces at the gates of Congress. It was Samarkand and Bukhara before the Mongol horsemen swept down from the steppes.

When everyone was settled comfortably in Warren's living room, he opened with a welcome and a brief rundown of plans for the public unveiling of the Meliorist Society on July 5th. "We are in good shape, my friends," he said. "The ballroom of the National Press Club has been reserved. Appropriate security and crowd control measures are in place. Each of you has your own role to play and your own statement to make before what will undoubtedly be a phalanx of reporters. Phil will be our emcee because of his experience in tight interview situations and because of his disarming style and quick humor. He'll put the audience at ease, and he's less likely than most of us to be seen as a threat by the powers that be."

"Right, we don't want to unduly alarm the business bosses," Barry mocked. "We just want to duly jolt the jagers off them."

Bill Joy reported that he had a mole in Lobo's rapidly expanding war suites. "He's their all-purpose gofer, the guy who deliverers lunch, snacks, mail, packages, whatever—a humble job, but a perfect interface with everything that goes on there. Last week he overheard Lobo's media people discussing a national media buy slamming the SROs for sabotaging the country. He says they were looking over mockups of a TV ad and chuckling. I suppose he could be a double agent, but I doubt it. He knows who I am and was eager to talk to me because of our shared interest in futuristic science. I think he regards me as a kind of mentor, and I'm almost certain he has no idea that I'm connected to any of you. That makes him all the more valuable to us, since there's no more perfect mole than a mole who doesn't know he's a mole. For reasons you'll understand, I'm not at liberty to tell you exactly how I found him, but it's obvious that I can't appear with you at the National Press Club, even in the audience, since I might be recognized. As of this moment, consider me undercover," he finished with a smile.

"Well, if that isn't the icing on the cake," Warren said.

"Move to applaud," Paul said.

Once the clapping died down, the next order of business was to review the DVD prepared by Promotions for the branding of the Meliorists. Bill Cosby slid the disc into the machine and asked his colleagues not to comment until they'd seen the entire thirty-five-minute presentation. When it was over, everyone was temporarily speechless. It was so sophisticated, so steeped in idealism and at the same time rooted in practicality. It profiled each of the Meliorists individually, highlighting their achievements against the odds of life, their own experiences of intolerance and injustice, their business successes, and their military service where applicable. It presented them as exemplars of a patriotism of care, of promise, of love. It drew on the best of the past and showed how community spirit and civic action could make this best of the past blossom into a glorious future. It showered the viewer with solutions readily available in a country as wealthy as the United States, concrete ways to redress the systemic inequities that made life so materially and spiritually impoverished for so many millions of Americans. With Yoko's wreath symbol prominent throughout, it portrayed the Meliorists as the great rescuers, selfless leaders without guile, willing to take the heat for people they would never meet, and more than capable of besting the big boys on their own turf. It ended with a collage of clips of the Meliorists' activities since January—Patriotic Polly, Yoko's light bulbs and the Seventh-Generation Eye, the Pledge the Truth drive, Peter's testimony on the insurance industry, George's speeches, the People's Court Society, the People's Chamber of Commerce, the CUBs, the Sun God festivals, the corporation jamborees, the Beatty campaign, and on and on—all meant to show that change was already happening, that it wasn't pie in the sky, that the train had left the station but would stop for all Americans who wanted to turn their country toward real liberty and justice for all and the real pursuit of happiness.

Bill Gates was the first to break the silence. "All along, our hardest decision has been how to step out and speak out, how to put ourselves personally on the line without losing control of the Agenda and inadvertently making ourselves into distractions for a media obsessed with personalities and peccadillos. Since we're about to cross that bridge at our press conference, I can't imagine a better backup than this magnificent DVD. Kudos to you, Barry, and to your whole team."

"Thanks, Bill, labor of love," Barry said. "The plan is to distribute it to everyone at the press conference and go national with it at the same time. By evening, it will be all over the place—TV, radio, Internet, you name it."

"Terrific, Barry," Warren said, adding his thanks. "Now for the two big questions. Who says what at the news conference regarding the Agenda? And how much do we say about our core group and what we've already accomplished?"

"Hell, let's let it all hang out," Ted said. "What our opponents gain in knowledge of our collaboration will be more than offset by the people's excitement over having a team of billionaires batting for them. The drama becomes part of the mobilizing message. Sure, it may frighten the other side into firing up the counteroffensive, but the building pressure on Congress to enact the Agenda is going to scare the daylights out of them anyway, so what's the difference? We've got—"

"Hold on," Ross interrupted. "Just wait a minute. Let Maui out? Tell the world how much we've raised and are prepared to spend?"

Ted hesitated. "Well, I guess not. There's no tactical reason to expose those facts. I meant everything about our collaboration that will further our mission."

"Seems to me," Joe said, "that we ought to open with a brief statement about our collective identity and then go right to our personal statements. We start by describing what propelled us to do what we're doing—our children, our country, our respect for our fellow human beings, our self-respect, the Golden Rule, it's just that simple, folks. We suggest that the real question is why thousands of very wealthy people aren't doing the same thing. Then we talk about what we've already done, and that's it. Keep it factual, keep it personal, keep it down to earth."

"I agree," Warren said. "The more substance we give them to fill their column inches and TV segments, the less likely they are to speculate and the less off base the columnists and commentators are likely to be, though the market fundamentalists will still bray their catechism."

George was nodding. "Warren is quite right, from my dolorous experience with these experientially starved ideologues. We should stress that the giant corporations and their apologists—i.e., said ideologues masquerading as conservative capitalists—are supplanting authentic capitalism with state-sponsored corporate capitalism. That will put them into an amusing bind and get them going on theory, practice, and contradictions while we're on the ground changing the direction of Congress. It's a good fit with our distraction strategy, at least for the short term, but it will be a critical short term for us."

"George's point about 'capitalism' is right on target," Max said. "We are entering a period where the word/deed perversity will be manifest in all its bizarre cultural inversion. If I've learned anything from my experiments, it's that we must always, always take this bull by the horns. I view this as an essential part of our educational mission to prevail with a new set of deeds over the old set of controlling words. Just watch the opposition's ads, watch how they revert instinctively to word over deed. They'll try to ignore or obfuscate the destructive deeds afflicting our people and country by throwing everything they have into winning the war of words."

"Well put, Max," Barry said. "And I would add that body language also counts as 'words' for purposes of our press conference. We've all got to be alert to how we come across to the media. Except for C-SPAN and radio stations that carry us live, we're going to be giving them so much that they'll have to pick and choose. If there are any stumbles, any displays of anger, a lip curled at the Chamber of Commerce, a laugh at the expense of some high-profile CEO, that's what will make the evening news or page one. We don't want that first impression. We want to project a cool, determined demeanor, a calm conviction that what we're doing is the simple and right thing to do. If there are any digs, they should be at our peers, along the lines 'Just because we're billionaires, that doesn't mean we have to be greedy, insensitive, lazy, uncaring, and golfing in our retirement.' Say we reject that stereotype and we reject it decisively in the name of the human spirit. If any of you want to say that you're inspired by a religious calling, by all means do. Try to head off the obvious question, which is essentially, 'What makes you tick?' Maybe we should list the likely questions right now? Suggestions?"

"So it's true that you're one big conspiracy. How often do you meet and where?" Yoko offered.

"Do you really expect to beat the big business lobbies?" This from Peter.

From Phil, "Are you on some revenge trip for old wounds you suffered in your past battles with certain companies?"

From George, "Do any of you have short positions in the various companies you're going to be regulating, lambasting, or exposing? Are you going to release your personal financial statements?"

From Bill Gates, "Given government deficits and the precarious position of the dollar, are you worried that the changes you're pressing for may tip the stock and credit markets and lead to a recession or worse?"

From Sol, "How are you going to pay for all of your changes and regulations? Are you out to soak the rich?"

From Leonard, "Who have you been in touch with on Capitol Hill and in the upper ranks of academia, business, labor, and religious institutions? How much are you planning to spend to get this Agenda through Congress and the White House?"

"Time out, time out," said Bill Cosby. "Obviously, we need to put a time limit on the press conference. There are seventeen of us. Two minutes each plus a few minutes to sit down and get up and you're at maybe forty minutes. Say forty-five for slippage, right, Ted? So what about another forty-five for questions, and then Phil cuts it off. Fair enough, don't you think?"

"I'll buy that," Phil said. "If we take questions for forty-five minutes, no one in the media can accuse us of running for cover. But our answers will have to be relatively brief, or else the prima donnas of the networks and the major newspapers and weeklies won't have their day in the sun. They'll have to content themselves with our press packet—and the rest, as they say, is commentary. By the way, another question that's likely to be asked is whether we intend to testify at the congressional hearings."

"You know, I'm fascinated by this Lobo fellow and his aggressive personality," Yoko interjected. "Why not out him at the press conference? That will steer the reporters away from us to the secret CEO cabal."

"It's not exactly a secret," Peter said. "After all, they did take out a full-page ad in the *Journal*."

"Yes, but the press doesn't know the identities of the CEOs or of the man they chose to lead the attack against us," Bernard pointed out. "Or if they do, they haven't reported it."

"I like Yoko's idea," Jeno said. "It will certainly juice up the drama Ted spoke of earlier. It may even throw Lobo off his rhythm a bit."

"Yes," Warren agreed. "In my experience with Lobo, the more pressure he's under, the weaker his judgment and the greater the chance of his taking a risky gamble. As I keep saying, we must always be on the offensive, never on the defensive, and outing Lobo and his CEO cohort is nothing if not offensive. It will send them reeling because it will come as a complete surprise."

"On the other hand," Jeno said, "if we blow their cover, it may speed up their timetable and increase their support from the business community. It may work to our disadvantage."

"True," Warren said, "but they're going to get plenty of accelerated motivation and support when they watch the media coverage on the fifth and see the full breadth of our Agenda. And the reporters will be demanding answers not just of Lobo, a control freak extraordinaire, but of those sheltered CEOs. That will diminish the impact of their early advertising campaign, because people will know where to look when some patriotic-sounding 'Save America' front group comes along."

"But what would outing them do to our mole?" Sol asked.

"Probably not much," Bill Joy said. "He's too far below the radar. And besides, they won't suspect him because he doesn't suspect himself. Even if they make everyone take a lie detector test, he ought to pass because he doesn't think he gave any secrets away to anyone."

"I think it's a go," Jeno said.

"Well, if there's no objection, will you do the honors, Yoko?" Warren asked.

"With pleasure."

"Now, do we need to go through the questions you predicted a few minutes ago? I can tell you what I'm planning to say. If they ask how much we're going to spend, I'll tell them the truth: 'Whatever it takes—and you know we *have* whatever it takes.' If you wish to release your financial statements, that's up to you, but I won't be releasing mine. Remember that we're private citizens, not public officials, and this isn't a grand jury proceeding. By maintaining our privacy we set an example for all citizens who suddenly become fair game because they gain some prominence. If I'm asked about our meetings, I'll say that we're in touch regularly and get together in person whenever we can, but I won't mention Maui. No need for them to know, as Ross says. As for congressional hearings, I'll testify if I'm asked, and I may even *ask* to be asked. Whatever they throw at us, I suggest as a general rule that we recall the master of the shrug and smile, that escape artist Ronald Reagan—and he made them like it. That's my two cents' worth."

Bernard tossed two pennies on the coffee table. "Here's mine. I think we're all old enough, rich enough, smart enough, and honest enough to handle anything they throw at us. Besides, it will all be over in the blink of an eye. We just have to try not to let them spend too much time on us and too little on the Agenda for the Common Good."

"Which is what we must spend the rest of our own time on this weekend," Warren said, "but I can tell Sol's ready for his dinner."

While the views in Omaha weren't quite as spectacular as the vistas at Maui, the deficit was filled by Warren's warm hospitality. During the fruit cocktail around a candlelit oak table, there was a palpable sense of relief that the months of furtive deliberation were at an end and the frontal confrontation was at hand. Regardless of the outcome, the Meliorists and the country would never be the same again. All the spectacular activity of the last six months would now be connected—heaven forbid!—to a single organized source. No more idiosyncratic billionaires. They were a team, a conspiracy, a brigade assaulting the citadels of power, privilege, and presumption head on, no holds barred. That was how the press would read it, no matter how often the Meliorists referred them to the infrastructure they had built since January—the PCS, the PCC, the CUBs, the Congress Watchdogs, and all the rest—but still they would continue to hand off the reins of the new democratic society they were striving to achieve. As Max put it, "We're the shoehorn, they're the shoes. We're the bloodstream, they're the heartbeat. We're the head-knockers, they're the brains." This cascade of metaphors put the diners in a jovial mood, and for once their talk was entirely small—family matters, aches and pains, recent graduations of grandchildren, dreams of going fishing, or even golfing.

In the morning, refreshed and relaxed, the Meliorists descended to Warren's basement conference room for Patrick Drummond's report on the status of the Agenda legislation, which the First-Stage Improvements eggheads had honed into what had to be called perfection in the sloppy congressional world. They had broken the Agenda down into seven comprehensive bills dealing with a living wage, health insurance, tax reform, sustainable energy, more equitable distribution of wealth, electoral reform, and the seeding of deeper forms of democracy. The intense and nuanced exchange among the Meliorists following Patrick's presentation matched the scholarship and practical experience that had gone into both the drafting of the legislation and the accompanying section-by-section explanations and substantiations. Their discussion continued unabated all day Saturday and into Sunday morning as they decided which of them would take primary responsibility for which bills.

Just before noon, a tired but happy Warren declared their work finished. "My friends," he said, "we have done all we humanly can to ensure the passage of the Agenda. Before you head home, I hope you'll join me for sandwiches and a fruit salad as close to Ailani's as my chef could make it."

In the dining room, there was a contented buzz around the oak table as the Meliorists ate and chatted. Suddenly Bill Cosby clapped his hand to his forehead. "'Wisdom hath builded her house, she hath hewn out her seven pillars,'" he said loudly.

Everyone stared at him, forks in midair.

"Proverbs 9:1. It's as though it was written especially for us. Don't you see? Those bills we've been parsing down to the last comma—they're the Seven Pillars of the Agenda for the Common Good."

There was a sharp collective intake of breath. "That's beautiful, Bill, just beautiful," Warren said. "I guess we weren't quite finished after all."

As the Meliorists were dispersing Sunday afternoon, a brief notice from the Secretariat went out on the AP wire.

> Several elderly individuals of means who have been publicly espousing measures to better our society since

the beginning of the year will hold a joint news conference in the ballroom of the National Press Club in
Washington, DC, on Wednesday, July 5, 2006, at 10:30
a.m. Accredited news reporters and columnists are
advised to arrive early to find seats in their demarcated
section. Twenty seats are reserved for freelance
reporters. Representatives of civic groups are encouraged to attend. Members of Congress and White House
officials should call for reservations.

That evening the announcement led all the network news shows,
the anchors vying with one another to pull down clips of Jeno and
the PCC, George before the editors' convention, Joe throwing down
the small claims gauntlet, Warren tearing into runaway executive
pay, Peter's devastating testimony before Congress . . .

It was the perfect free media buildup to zero hour.

If they could have seen their about-to-be-outed opponents that
weekend, the Meliorists would have been happier still. True to form,
the CEOs were vacationing all over, from the isles of the Caribbean
to the Canadian Rockies, from the Hamptons to Jackson Hole. That
was what they always did to celebrate the Fourth of July. Sure, they
had some concerns this year, but what could they do over a long
weekend? Besides, that was why they'd hired Lobo.

Lobo did not disappoint. To some grumbling from his associates,
he cancelled all leaves. He delighted in doing this. It pumped his
adrenaline. Lobo was a workaholic and had no time for a social life.
Under other circumstances, he might have gone the way of a male
Mother Teresa instead of becoming his own version of Gordon Gekko.

Lobo's core teams were in *Battlestar Galactica* mode. They were
readying a spate of media attack ads to be unleashed the moment
the sponsors of the anticipated SRO legislation dropped it into the
congressional hopper. Some of the ads were targeted at the members of Congress allied with the SROs, others reflected the theme

that the SROs were destabilizing the economy and the Republic. Even without the precise details of the bills, Lobo knew enough to pull the traditional strings of fear and political bigotry. There were plenty of historical precedents to learn from. Lobo's favorite was the 1934 California gubernatorial race between Upton Sinclair, the great progressive reformer and author of *The Jungle*, and Frank Merriam, the Republican incumbent. Running as a Democrat, Sinclair started the campaign as the easy favorite in depression-torn California. After a nonstop personal and red-baiting assault orchestrated by the public relations firm of Whitaker and Baxter, fearful Californians gave the Republicans a narrow majority. The election was a turning point in American politics, as the Whitaker techniques were copied in whole or in part in many subsequent elections around the country. To beat an Upton Sinclair in a state wracked by poverty, a state where wealthy growers cruelly exploited hundreds of thousands of farmworkers through all the abuses depicted so powerfully by John Steinbeck in *The Grapes of Wrath*, emboldened the ruling oligarchies throughout the United States.

Lobo chose his media carefully. He had good intelligence on Barry Diller, what stations he owned, what stations he effectively controlled, and he avoided those. One series of ads for the afternoon TV talk shows was designed to appeal to women and turn their everyday anxieties into "garrulously driven fears," as he put it. He went to the evening cable shows for "the redneck males," and to the cable business shows for "the stock market crowd." And of course there was always all-right-wing-all-the-time talk radio. Lobo put in a call to Bush Bimbaugh to give him a heads-up.

"Hey, Bush, got a minute? I'm going to blow your socks off with a scoop that will make your blood boil."

"Make it fast, Lobo. I'm right in the middle of working on a show that will annihilate those stupidos pushing for a change in our National Anthem."

"Bush, you've got bigger fish to fry. Try this out. The rich old guys you've been denouncing in your surgical on-air manner are about to show their hand in Congress. They've lined up your favorite libs, and body-snatched some conservs too, behind a Commie-pinko, bleeding-heart, blame-America, destroy-capitalism agenda that's about to roll out. And they're not ignoring you, Bush. They're ready to proclaim you the Corporate Welfare King of Kings."

"What? Are they nuts? I earn my money the hard-assed way every day, pounding feminazis, queers, peaceniks, consumer fascists, and all those enviros squawking hot air about the planet melting down. What are you talking about, Lobo?"

"Get ready for it, Bush. You're going to be crowned Corporate Welfare King because your boss corporation and all the radio stations that carry you use the public airwaves free and pass part of the windfall on to you. Get the picture? You must've heard about all those 'Pay the rent' demos."

"Preposterous! Possession is ninety percent of the law, Lobo, that's basic conservative doctrine. That's how we took away the Injuns' land and built this country. The treaties were just an afterthought cover story. No one in my hordes of dittoheads is going to believe any corporate welfare bullshit about me. In fact, they'll call in and yell, 'Go, man, get all you can get from the feds!'"

"Don't say I didn't warn you, Bush. I'm going to take a big media buy on your show, so if you have any ideas about how to sharpen our attack on the old guys, let me know. We still haven't come up with the right catchphrase. Oh, and one last bit of advice. If I were you, I'd be looking over my shoulder. You've never experienced anything like what's coming. You've had it pretty easy so far in your choice of enemies."

Bimbaugh bridled but held his temper. He could smell the ad dollars. "Thanks, Lobo, sorry if I was short with you before. I hear you, friend, and I'm on full alert. Ten-*shun*! Stay in touch and watch me soar!"

Shutting his cell phone, Lobo shook his head. "Once they're on top, these big shots never think they can fall," he muttered to himself. "Well, I did what I had to do with the King of Shout Radio."

Lobo turned back to reviewing his three-pronged strike strategy— fear, smear, and the Khyber Pass. Fear was well in hand with the first wave of attack ads. The smear campaign was in the works, with inbuilt safeguards to assure the CEOs complete deniability, but it would have to wait until the other side fully revealed its intentions and the conventional counterattack played out. The Khyber Pass was a last resort, but the troops had to be up to strength, and Lobo was already assembling a crack team of veteran lobbyists. As he made clear every time he interviewed one of them for the patriotic opportunity of joining him, his main requirement was that they be able to move on Lobo time at Lobo speed with no learning curve, which immediately eliminated most of these five-day-a-week corporate warriors, who'd had a soft time of it flacking for big business in cushy jobs. He told those who passed muster that they'd have to take a four-month leave of absence but would be well paid and would not be bored. They would be in the eye of the biggest political hurricane in the country, dealing with challenges that would draw on all their experience and talent. "You'll be facing the most cunning, determined, ingenious, well-financed, and organized foe of your lives," he said, adding with arched eyebrow, "And you'll be working for the most cunning, determined, ingenious, well-financed, and relentless taskmaster of your lives." Whereupon more dropped out, until fifteen men and five women finally grabbed the "cast-iron ring," as one of them put it, and signed on to start immediately.

As Lobo saw the upcoming strife, his side already occupied the Khyber Pass. The immense burden of dislodging the defenders of the corporate society was on the backs of the SROs, who had a vertical climb over jagged rocks, some of which could easily start rolling down on them. But occupying a position of logistical superiority and coming out on top were two different matters, as waves of invaders had proved more than once. Just remember the Mongols who thundered through the Pass hugely outnumbered and conquered much of India.

Lobo's main problem was that most of the troops on his side were also in his way. More than a hundred trade associations, and many more corporate law firms and public relations firms and lobbying entities, would want to start riding hard once the bills moved onto the floor of House and Senate and into the media spotlight, but they would be brandishing the old weapons, rusty from disuse because a prostrate Congress had given them nothing much to oppose. Their whole professional culture was geared toward buttonholing congressional committees for favors, privileges, deregulation, subsidies, and government contracts. Few forces were arrayed against their incessant demands. Most of their work consisted of making sure the demands were clothed in complexity and symbolism—like the tax code with its Swiss cheese loopholes—and providing tender loving care for the lawmakers, with a stick waiting in the wings as needed. With a judicious mix of perks and pressure, they maneuvered legislation through the labyrinthine maze of committees and subcommittees to the floor of the Senate and House and then through the Joint Conference Committees. There were always little differences here and there to be ironed out, always lawmakers with outstretched hands who would concede for the price of an earmark project in their districts or states. It was all very time-consuming, but these silver-tongued corporate demanders had ample time to give.

Lobo had three objectives. First and most difficult, he had to change their orientation from pushing their own interests to stopping a wave of bills that addressed heart-rending conditions in the country, represented voices of conscience begging for reform, and beat the drum for a fair society affording its citizens material sustenance and a life of dignity. Second, he had to make sure that these inconstant allies were a net plus to the forces that he would unleash, that they didn't interfere with, embarrass, or obstruct the far smarter and more energetic drive of the CEOs. Third, they would have to share the information they had collected over the years on every member and legislative staffer on Capitol Hill.

Sitting in his corner office hour after hour, his staff working on overdrive around him, Lobo wondered from time to time why he was doing all this. It wasn't his convictions that led him to change his colors and join his former opponents. It wasn't that he wanted revenge on Jeno Paulucci and Warren Buffett—he did, but that wasn't enough. Finally he told himself that he wanted to be the biggest rainmaker of them all by taking control of Capitol Hill for the biggest showdown of his generation, then relax and bask in the eternal gratitude of the giant businesses that had hated him all these years. Still, beneath the hard exterior that was Lobo, there were yearnings that could not be explained even by this anticipated titanic victory. Softer yearnings.

Elsewhere in Washington, a different kind of unusually intense activity was afoot. On Capitol Hill more than a few offices were on the job day and night. The Capitol Police could not remember so many members of Congress and their staffers working on a long weekend, much less so late at night. There was a feeling of productive exhilaration in the air, absent the vacationing legislators and the legions of lobbyists, reporters, and tourists. Precision and resolve marked the collaboration between the congressional progressives, the Double Z, and the volunteer scholars and lawyers gathered for one final review of the Agenda legislation and the sponsors who would guide it through Congress. These lead legislators, chosen after taking into account a veritable library of political and personal intelligence and strength of character—no wobbly knees invited— were masters of the arcane parliamentary procedures of the House and Senate, and were ready, willing, and able to clear the congressional decks at every stage. Close coordination with the Congress Watchdogs was also a high priority for the congressional Agenda allies, since the Watchdogs in each district were the conduit for the local segment of the Meliorist epicenters, which were all in a state of advanced readiness and focus regarding public funding of public campaigns.

The much-touted Blockbuster Challenge, hatched in Maui and developed by Joan Claybrook, was slated for an extravagant unveiling right after the Fourth of July, but after much back-and-forth between Joan, Theresa Tieknots, the Secretariat, and some of the Meliorists, it was decided to suspend the effort, primarily because of FEC regulations restricting individual contributions to a candidate to $4,200 and PAC contributions to $5,000. A party's national and state committees could receive additional donations, but those were limited too, and could not be part of a member-by-member quid pro quo. Under the provision for "independent expenditures," there was no limit to how much an individual or a PAC or a single-issue group could spend, but then there could be no contact whatsoever between these individuals or groups and the candidates and parties. There just was no wiggle room, other than to use the $2 billion Blockbuster budget for cold mailings that urged small donations within the legal limits but could not solicit these donations on behalf of a particular candidate. Even if the mailing lists were composed of declared sympathizers with the Redirections projects, the logistical problems would be formidable, and there wasn't time to get an advisory opinion from the FEC on the various unique options conceived by the lawyers. The Meliorists learned the hard way that not every honest and lean political idea was legally permissible.

The fallback position for the coming weeks was to raise individual contributions for the "good guys" up to the legal limit, and use separate independent expenditures to oppose the "bad guys." Joan would remain in charge and allocate money based on the incumbents' and challengers' records, behavior, and capabilities. The Meliorists pledged a sizable budget to be disbursed candidate by candidate as needed, with an iron wall separating independent expenditures from direct donations. Joan's legal advisers would issue guidelines for setting up the relevant entities so that they were in complete compliance with FEC regulations. Naturally she was disappointed, as were her patrons, over having to abandon the aptly named Blockbuster Challenge, but it was clear that much more planning would be required to execute such a path-blazing overthrow of the established ways of dirty politics. Moreover, the Clean Elections Party and its candidates needed direct contributions, and for those purposes traditional political fundraising infused with reformist energy would do the job.

Meanwhile, in those pre–Fourth of July days, the Secretariat was wrestling with a troubling problem. They had names and contact information for millions of volunteers and supporters of the various Redirections, but they were trying to assess intensity and stamina. Large turnouts for rallies and lectures and festivals were important in both reality and perception, but when the Agenda battle began in earnest, the Secretariat had to have some sense of how many people would dig in their heels, weather storm after storm, and fight back with even greater fervor, determination, and ingenuity.

Their deliberations produced what Patrick Drummond's chief of staff, a retired master sergeant, called "the lesson plan." The idea was to have the seasoned field organizers of all the Redirections assemble as many of their supporters and volunteers as possible for a thirty-minute presentation generally outlining the coming drive in Congress, its historic urgency, the expected vicious counterattack, and the rough timetable for four months of maximum effort culminating on Election Day. After an hour of discussion, the field organizers would circulate among the attendees at an informal reception and ask each of them how much time they were willing to commit to a range of activities, from stuffing envelopes to attending rallies to doing the nuts-and-bolts work of the Redirection in question. The organizers would mark the responses down, as thoroughly as possible including data on age, gender, occupation, background, and recent civic action, and then tabulate the results in three columns: passive sympathizers, modest volunteers, and self-energized enthusiasts.

This gauging of intensity was critical. The corporatist opposition could energize its base with clear monetary incentives and appeals to economic self-interest. The civic world had to rely on less material and less immediate gratifications, such as those to be found in Dick Goodwin's eagerly anticipated pamphlet, which the Secretariat sent to the field organizers in quantity along with their instructions. It was beautifully designed, down to the feel of the paper, with the Seventh-Generation Eye under the title: "You, Your Children, and America's

Future." Goodwin started from the universal instinct of humankind to protect and nurture its progeny and worked outward to connect that instinct with the building of a just society where no one went without the basic necessities of life, a national community embracing all its members in the pursuit of happiness—in short, an America true to the best of its past and worthy of its ideals. The pamphlet provided eloquent inspiration and warmly insisted on perspiration. "We have the means," Goodwin wrote, "and we have democratic and sustainable solutions within our grasp. All we need is the will to turn the visionary ideas of our Founders into everyday realities for our children." Bernard was overjoyed by the pamphlet. He had grown up on the classics of the genre, starting with Paine, and had immense faith in the power of the written word to provoke action.

The Fourth of July arrived with a bang that had nothing to do with fireworks. All over the country and at the main event in Washington, DC, the Redirections were out in full force. The week before, Patriotic Polly had returned to the airwaves proclaiming "Independence Day for the Sovereignty of the People" and telling the public to watch for a facsimile of the Declaration of Independence in the mail. The lecturers, the Congress Watchdogs, the CUB and PCC chapters, the lunchtime ralliers, the *Daily Bugle* youngsters, and assorted groups from the rest of the Redirections had contingents marching in all the official parades of the larger cities. The "people's parades" organized with Meliorist help in two thousand smaller cities and towns drew wildly enthusiastic crowds.

Large or small, this year's parades were like none in living memory. Everywhere in the crowds, people were sporting Seventh-Generation buttons and T-shirts, holding up their copies of the Declaration, and thrusting Dick Goodwin's pamphlet on their friends and neighbors. These were parades for a new America. Alongside the usual military and martial displays were huge banners emblazoned with phrases from the Gettysburg Address and the nation's founding documents: "Toward a New Birth of Freedom," "Toward a

More Perfect Union," "With Liberty and Justice for All." Other banners and floats addressed what those words meant in concrete terms: "Freedom from Poverty," "Fair Taxation," "Workers' Unions Of, By, and For Workers," "Health and Health Insurance for All," "Safety in the Workplace, Marketplace, and Environment," "Freedom Is Participation in Power," "Education to Think, Not Memorize," "Modernize Crumbling Public Services," "Fund the Arts," "Shareholders Are the Owners, Not CEOs," "Corporations Are Our Servants, Not Our Masters," "Save Our Children from Mammon," "Take Over Congress, Take Over Washington," "Clean Elections, No More Dirty Money," "Citizen Action Is Patriotic Action," "Dissent Is the Mother of Assent." The parades represented a substantial investment for the Meliorists, but the returns more than justified it. They had arranged to have the floats mass-produced to save money for the individual parades and send a message to the entire country that the marchers were part of a unified movement for change. That alone assured national media coverage, and the parades themselves assured local coverage. The parade organizers and the spokespeople for the various floats and contingents had been well briefed for the press and were prepared to drive their own passionate arguments home with local illustrations.

An unexpected dividend was the army of people who spontaneously recruited themselves for this great cause of a more just society. They turned out by the thousands. They'd have to have been living on Mars not to know of the ferment of the past six months, but they'd been observers, not participants. Now the parades had come to them where they lived, worked, and raised their children. That was what brought them out to rub shoulders with their fellow citizens and some of the elected officials who had been invited to take seats of honor on the floats. Normally parades were dream events for politicians—they were far less likely to be booed than in more contained forums, and they could leave without interrupting the proceedings—but not this time. When the parade organizers drew up the invitation lists, they had a great time matching the pols with the float slogans and waiting to see who would accept.

One impression all the politicians took away that day was that the parades were not just local events but part of a vibrant new movement. A shiver of apprehension traveled up more than one officeholder's spine. They couldn't just wave and smile their way through this Fourth of July revelation. These parades, with their constant background drummers, put meat on the banners, gave substance to the traditional American symbols. Bands played "America the Beautiful" over and over again, along with "This Land Is Your Land." Patriotic Polly toys were hot sellers. People on the bandstand spoke from their hearts about what was on their minds. Onlookers used their cell phones to send digital images of the parades to friends and relatives around the country. Promotions was on the scene in all two thousand smaller communities to videotape the entire parade festivities for future replay on local cable access channels and elsewhere. Their teams collected sample comments from the crowds and transmitted them to National Parade Headquarters in Kansas City.

> "I just never knew there were so many people in my town who feel the same way I do about big business controlling our lives and our country. I signed some petitions and made some new acquaintances."
>
> "I didn't stay very long. Fourth of July Parades shouldn't be political. They should be all about fun and loyalty to America. But the free food was yummy."
>
> "This is one parade that will stay with me. I'm going to one of the marchers' homes next week for an action meeting."
>
> "I'm a World War II veteran. Finally I've seen a Fourth of July Parade that talks real patriotism—caring about one another. I belong to the VFW, and I'm going to find out why they weren't there."
>
> "Our American Legion post in Lubbock organized its own parade to protest the so-called people's parade. A bunch of marchers from Veterans for Peace split off and

came over to talk to us, and pretty soon some Legion-
naires were shaking hands with them. Not me. A tough
world needs tough guys."

"It was a blast watching the politicians caught
between the military style of the old parades and the
spirit of people power in this one. A lot of them were
squirming because they knew that if they let themselves
get swept up in the moment, their financiers would
make them pay for it later. Serves them right for
wanting to have things both ways."

Over the following week, the analysts at headquarters studied
the parade footage, tabulated the comments, and reviewed the
media coverage and commentary. Among the most insightful
observations were those of syndicated columnist A. J. Eon. "Many
reports seem to have missed the wider significance of these new-
style Fourth of July parades. They represent a well-organized effort
to reclaim the nation's public symbols from the commercial, conservative, and martial groups that have dominated such public
traditions as the Fourth, Memorial Day, and Veterans Day. In the
past, too many liberal-leaning people have looked down on the celebration of these 'holidays' as vacuous and jingoistic. It appears
that their condescension has been transformed into a drive to take
control of our traditions and infuse them with an agenda that puts
the people's plight and the people's needs up front on the bandstand. There can be no more portentous struggle than one over the
nation's most hallowed symbols and traditions. To the victor goes
the enormous power of legitimacy and communication. This past
Fourth was a display of drum-major sophistication that will be hard
to reverse, for if there is anything more powerful than symbols, try
symbols with substance, symbols that communicate our highest
hopes for the future of America—the ultimate symbol."

Eon's words flew across the airwaves, the blogosphere, and the
media machine of Promotions. To his astonishment, he was flooded
with interview requests. Many of his fellow columnists took envious

note of his sudden prominence and turned their attention to this unique populist resurgence and the forces behind it.

On the morning of July 5th, there were monumental traffic jams all around the National Press Club by 7:30 a.m. In front of the building, dozens of camera crews were unloading their gear. People who worked at the Press Club found the entrance blocked by Japanese reporters finishing their dispatches on Japanese time and readying themselves for the big event. By 9:00 a.m. the ballroom was full. The Secretariat quickly rented two spillover rooms with closed-circuit TVs, and by 10:00 a.m. they were full too.

The news conference was to be televised live, not only by C-SPAN, CNN, and PBS, but by the three major networks, which were breaking all precedent for this group of private citizens without portfolio. Bill Joy had hired cameramen to videotape the whole session in case of future attempts at distortion, along with a photographer to take pictures of everyone in attendance. He suspected that the audience would include corporate lobbyists and the usual grim gumshoe types who just couldn't learn how to dress. Luke Skyhi and some associates from the PCC were there to take notes so they could go to the media fast with the progressive business reaction.

At 10:15 a.m., the Meliorists walked briskly to the dais at the front of the ballroom. The cameras went wild in a frenzy of metallic clicking that sent images of the core group, publicly together for the first time, all over the country and the world. In the back row, Lobo sat erect and alert, scanning the SROs one by one—until his eyes alighted upon Yoko. It was as if a silent lightning bolt had struck. Her eyes, her facial features, the way she held her dainty hands, the angle of her chin, her beautifully styled hair, her confident posture— he was a man consumed. His long-repressed libido erupted into a series of escalating fantasies, culminating in the recognition that she was quite a bit older than he was. She also despised everything he stood for, but didn't James Carville, arch liberal Democrat, share a matrimonial bed with Mary Matalin, arch conservative Republican? Wild thoughts careened through his brain and sent his pulse rate soaring. He tried to compose himself, for the news conference was about to start, but his superego was wrestling mightily with his id in the classic Freudian tussle.

Phil stepped up to the lectern, which looked like it might topple over from the weight of the twenty or so microphones attached precariously to the front edge.

"Good morning, folks, thanks for coming. I'm Phil Donahue, and we"—he paused as his arm swept the group sitting behind him on the platform—"are the Meliorist Society. Since January, we've been working together for the betterment of our country, which is what our name means, no more, no less. We hear that the corporatists who oppose the changes we've initiated refer to us as the SROs, for Super-Rich Oldsters. Apparently they forgot that the initials also stand for something else, which I leave to your quick wits. We've got an acronym for ourselves too. It stands for Prodigiously Rich Oldsters, so feel free to call us the PROs. Each of us will make a brief statement, and then we'll take questions for forty-five minutes. There will be no one-on-ones afterward, but we'll make ourselves available in due time. My colleague Warren Buffett will begin."

"Thanks, Phil. I've spent my whole adult life investing my own and other people's money with some success. I had intended to leave my estate in its entirety to a charitable family foundation, but I've changed my mind. Our country is sinking deeper and deeper into troubles that are sapping its collective spirit and blinding it to the solutions that are ready at hand. From my observations of the rarefied world of business leaders, I've concluded that the vast majority are not leaders except for themselves. A society rots like a fish—from the head down. I want no part of that lucrative narcissism, that abdication from the realities that are blighting our country and the world. I am here to do my part, my duty, in persuading some of my very wealthy peers to live by the words of Alfred North Whitehead: 'A great society is a society in which its men of business think greatly of their functions.' The Agenda for the

Common Good that you will find in your press packets is only a down payment on a great and caring society."

Warren sat down, and the rest of the Meliorists rose to make their statements one by one.

"I am George Soros. I was born in Hungary, but I came here as an immigrant in the aftermath of World War II. The United States is my country by choice, my home. My personal experience of both fascism and communism has attuned me to the urgent need to reinvigorate and expand democratic institutions constantly, for the concentration of power also goes on constantly, left to its own many devices. The concentrated power of the few over the many is the antithesis of democracy. It breeds injustice and chronic suffering. In recent months I have joined with my colleagues to help launch many new democratic institutions with millions of dues-paying members. These are growing every day, helping to shift power from the blinkered few to the informed many, helping to build democracy. They have reached critical mass and are close to self-sufficiency. If they remain steadfast in purpose and diligence, their impact in creating a fair and equitable economy will be formidable and will portend well for the future of our country."

"I'm Ted Turner. You all know me. The world is going to hell in a handbasket. We've got to do something about energy and the environment. We've got to enlist the services of the Sun God. Those festivals are just the beginning. We're going to make the twenty-first century the Sun Century, and not a century too soon. The big fossil energy companies have had us looking under the ground for our hydrocarbon BTUs. We're going to look up toward the sun and toward a carbohydrate economy. No more obstructionism from the fossil and uranium companies. Either they convert to solar or they'll be fossils themselves. From now on Congress stops being their feed trough and patsy. When we stop to think about conditions in our country, the good ones were most likely brought to us by the organized demands of the people throughout our history. Time for an encore. This is the twenty-first century, when democracy becomes an adult."

"You may remember me, I'm Ross Perot. I'm here today for many of the same reasons I ran for president in 1992. I love my country, but my country is not in the hands of people who love her or her children and grandchildren. Piling debt on our descendants is what the power boys love to do. Mortgaging our country's future to the hilt is what they love to do. Well, they're not going to get away with it anymore. From now on, they'll be paying their fair share of taxes individually, and so will their corporations. They'll be getting off the corporate welfare gravy train. They'll be standing on their own feet and taking the verdict of the marketplace. They say they're capitalists? Okay, they're gonna act like capitalists. No more Uncle Sam to bail them out while small businesses go under. The *Business Week* poll was right—most Americans believe big business has too much control over their lives and their government. The *Business Week* editorial in the same issue was also right—corporations should get out of politics."

"I am Bernard Rapoport, from Waco, Texas. Too much is wrong in our country. There's too much greed, and too much power attached to the greed. Too much poverty, illiteracy, hunger, and homelessness. Too much despair and too pervasive a sense of powerlessness. Too many good people doing nothing about all this and making too many excuses for themselves. Too much graft and too much waste. Too much lying and too much sighing. Too much speculation and too much sprawl. I've spent a lifetime in the business of insuring risks, but all the things I've mentioned are things no one can insure, even though they are huge risks for our society. So we're going to get control of these risks—we, millions of aroused Americans—in the streets, in the voting booth, in the hearing rooms and courtrooms and boardrooms. The people are already on the march, and they are unstoppable. This news conference is only an anticlimax to the work that has been done already, and a prelude to the work to come."

"My name is Max Palevsky, and I am proud to be a Meliorist. As one of the pioneers of the computer business, I used to believe that this new technology would work to the vast betterment of our society. That hasn't happened. Why? Because promising technologies that are under the sway of concentrated economic powers and their political agenda never come close to fulfilling their promise. Until we break the grip of big money on our public elections at all levels of government, fundamental democratic values and critical economic priorities will not be translated into political policy and implementation. It was Thomas Jefferson who described representative government as a counter to 'the excesses of the monied interests.' His hope must become our reality. The electoral reform platform of the Agenda for the Common Good will clear the way with its call for public money for public elections, full ballot access for voters and candidates of all parties, and open competitive contests to produce the best results on Election Day, with *all* the votes counted, including those for binding None of the Above. No more one-party districts, and no more two-party elected dictatorship. We're ready to take on the merchants of politics once and for all."

"I'm Joe Jamail, and I sue big corporations hard. I want everyone who's wrongfully harmed or defrauded to have full access to our courts of law so as to secure justice and deter the greedy miscreants by proving them culpable before judge and jury. The courts are the last resort of American democracy when the other two branches fail us. For too many years, regular folks have had the courthouse doors slammed in their faces by legislative fiat greased with corporate money. Faith that justice can be achieved is crucial to our social solidarity. For us Meliorists, open access to the courts, without political interference, is bedrock constitutionalism. The same goes for the exercise of defendants' rights in criminal trials. We are a nation of checks and balances. The checks have been out of balance for too long. That will change."

"I'm Paul Newman, and I'm here to say that the people believe our country is on the wrong track. They want to see America move in a direction that spells a better life for themselves and their children, and this is not a partisan sentiment. Check out the veterans' groups, the NASCAR crowds, the senior centers, the voluntary associations and clubs down at the community level, and you'll see how disdain for those who rule us is growing. For a long time the people have wanted change, but they've felt trapped, powerless, helpless to make it happen. Now those feelings are giving way to a sense of empowerment and hope. You've all reported on this rising tide over the last six months. The Congress is starting to feel the heat and the light from the aroused citizenry, and that's just the beginning. Congress itself will be redirected. Votes will start to nullify money instead of the other way around. The Corporate Congress will become the People's Congress. Once Americans taste popular sovereignty and its benefits, they'll want it on the menu daily. They'll tell their senators and representatives, 'Stand with the people or stand down.'"

"I'm Bill Cosby. Look, folks, you know something has to be done when there's no correlation between hard work and having the necessities of life. The bottom half of America is working harder all the time and falling farther and farther behind. The rich are getting richer beyond their wildest dreams. Those of us here on this stage represent the older rich, and we are doing our best to multiply our numbers and help more billionaires find a purposeful life. As far as I know, our coming battle with the entrenched super-rich on behalf of the people is unique in recorded history, and as a sometime actor, I find it a prospect filled with drama and suspense. How, where, and when are the corporate supremacists going to respond? Stay tuned."

"My name is Peter Lewis. This ballroom is already historic for all the valedictory speeches that have been delivered here in recent weeks. There will be many more, synchronized with the introduction of the seven bills comprising the Agenda for the Common Good. Imagine the high-level whistle-blowers who'll come forth once Congress starts debating universal quality-controlled health insurance. They'll be lined up from pillar to post. You know of my views regarding my industry's abdication of its responsibility for loss prevention. Today's insurers operate on the principle that making money from waste, inefficiency, and damage is part and parcel of doing business. As Meliorists, we intend to redefine what productivity, efficiency, and superior management really mean in this twenty-first century. Our yardstick will be the well-being of the people, and you know the axiom—whoever controls the yardstick controls the agenda. So to big business I say, we're taking the yardstick out of your hands, and with it your control over public expectations, not to mention your wholesale stifling of invention and innovation."

"My name is Sol Price, and I'm a consultant to Wal-Mart." Ripples of laughter coursed through the ballroom, which had been preternaturally quiet till now. "I came of age in the 1930s, a time of economic depression, but also a time of forceful response from FDR's Washington, a time of deliberate, thoughtful striving to jump-start the economy, diminish the armies of the unemployed through useful public works projects, and bring Americans together in a common cause. Today we have immensely more wealth, more ways to communicate and mobilize, more of everything except heart, will, and leadership. At my age I don't want to leave my country in decline, dominated by greed and gluttony, in a downward spiral of lower wages and a lower standard of living for the majority. I don't want to leave our children and grandchildren a country where 'only the little people pay taxes' while millionaires become billionaires and billionaires become trillionaires, a country where millions can't pay their fuel bills while oil chieftains running sure-bet companies subsidized by the taxpayers make more than a hundred thousand dollars a day. That's why I've joined hands with some of my peers in age and wealth to give back to our beloved land, not a little charity masquerading as justice, but the real thing—systematic justice safeguarded by a permanently organized populace."

"Phil Donahue again. Our culture is in decay. Our media is a relentless merchandising machine. It has insinuated itself into the minds of our children, turning them into feverish Pavlovian bundles of conditioned craving, and undermining parental authority. Corporate commercialism, in alliance with the forces of repression around the world, is ruthlessly trampling down budding civic efforts to alleviate agonizing destitution and redress staggering inequality. Four hundred of the world's richest hold wealth equivalent to the assets of the bottom three billion humans sharing that same world. What in hell are we, the super-rich, doing with our days in our later years, wallowing in a leisurely drudgery when we could be changing the world? Ours is not a messianic mission. It is a dutiful, deliberate quest to achieve today what should have been achieved years ago in a society with pretensions to 'liberty and justice for all.' We intend to make good on 'for *all*.'"

"I am Yoko Ono. Our society is dying of spiritual starvation. Everywhere the human spirit labors under the yoke of materialism, the dull and the bland usurp aesthetics, the myopia of instant gratification keeps us from looking toward the horizon for our posterity. A society that genuinely cares for its offspring and future generations is a society that cares for its adults today. That wreath"—she gestured gracefully to the Meliorists' banner—"symbolizes an embrace, a caring and reaching out and ministering to our collective anguish and our collective needs. We on this platform strive to become worthy ancestors for our descendants, for if we do not, they will surely curse us."

Lobo sat transfixed as Yoko left the lectern. He was losing control of his bodily fluids. Blood rushed to his head and extremities, his stomach gurgled, sweat poured from his armpits and dampened his palms. It was all he could do to keep from trembling.

"I am William Gates Sr., and I heartily second Yoko's emphasis on posterity. That is our proper measure. Wisdom, judgment, and knowledge—in that order—must be our bequests. Only real people—not artificial persons, not corporations, those mere legal fictions—can leave behind such a legacy. Real people must be supreme over corporations in our constitution, in our laws, and in our regulations. There can be no equal justice under law, no equal access to the law, under the present empire of corporate supremacy. Global corporations bestride the planet, commandeering governments and writing their own laws and rules of adjudication. They are becoming the government de facto, they are corporatizing governmental functions de jure, and through their amassed control of capital, technology, and labor, they are creating a new serfdom. Artificial intelligence, genetic engineering, nanotechnology, communications technology—all are in their grip. Distributive justice is deteriorating from an already low base. In past years, some of the super-rich have organized to preserve the estate tax. Now some of us are engaged in a broader revolt against the enveloping matrix of plutocratic privilege and power. Rest assured that if the corporatists refuse to bend before the oncoming pressure, they will break."

"I'm Jeno Paulucci, and I'm a veteran of many clashes with business competitors and predators. Like my fellow Meliorists, I know how the business barons think, how they react, and how artfully cunning they can be. I know how practical, expedient, and opportunistic they are, I know when they are likely to cut the deck and make a deal. I also know how they swing from fury to fragility, how they save their own skins or line their own pockets at the expense of the very companies they run. To them I say, take heed of the rapid growth of the People's Chamber of Commerce, take heed of the hundreds of thousands of smaller and midsize businesses for whom you do not speak through your sprawling trade associations in Washington, DC. The coercive harmony of the business world is no more. 'Stand up and speak out' is replacing 'Sit down and keep quiet.' More and more flowers are blooming. There is more than one way, one path, one ideology to animate economies and sub-economies. Note that word, sub-economies. Note it well, for the sub-economies will turn the stubborn and stagnant status quo upside down."

"They call me Leonard Riggio. Half of democracy is just showing up. Today, people all over the country are showing up at marches, rallies, hearing rooms, courts, city council meetings, and the fountainhead—their neighbors' living rooms. The lunchtime rallies are growing and spreading all the time. Leaders and orators are emerging from their midst. These rallies are showcasing new directions, nurturing determination and stamina, producing mass resolve for a basic shift of power in our society. As a child growing up in New York City, I could never stand bullies. The downtown skyscrapers are full of bullies of a different kind, bullies in three-piece suits, and they're at work all the time. What's different these days is that when they look out their windows, they see the ranks of those who will send them home sniveling in the very near future. And it's worth noting the rendezvous points for some of the ralliers: fraternal organizations like the Elks, Kiwanis, and Knights of Columbus, women's clubs, senior centers, farm associations, union halls and churches, even the VFW and the American Legion. Sure, not all of them or even most of them, but who would have thought that thousands of members of such groups are joining the ralliers? The rebellion is swelling—just what Thomas Jefferson called for in our country from time to time."

"I'm Barry Diller, and you're wondering what I'm doing on this side of the bench. Hey, media moguls are people too. Broadcasters can be broad-minded citizens too. I've chosen to use whatever influence and knowledge I have in the cause of my county and its aborted promise. The big media outlets are straitjacketed by their clients' advertising dollars. They ignore the voices of conscience and the cries of affliction among our people. I want to see the public airwaves reverberate with these voices and cries. The people own the airwaves that we in the industry use so freely and so lucratively. The people must reclaim their property in the public interest and use it to air suppressed or unpopular views, calls for change, demands for responsible government and accountable corporations. The first test will come in Congress, that stained and monetized arena, when the Agenda for the Common Good is introduced. We ask viewers and listeners to join with us in support by e-mailing us at info@RedirectAmerica.org or logging onto our website, RedirectAmerica.org. The power of good people pulling together for the good life can overcome all opposition, no matter how wealthy, greedy, and powerful. Organized power can only prevail over unorganized people. Join together, throw off that subservience, speak your minds, and power shifts in your favor. Take it from someone who knows a little about corporate power and who has *been* corporate power until recently."

"Well, that's it folks," Phil said, returning to the podium. "I want to second Barry's invitation to the viewers at home to extend their talents and time to the Agenda for the Common Good. The forthcoming action in Congress demands action back where you live and work—in your cities, towns, villages, farms, and neighborhoods. What you do there will feed the thunder rolling over your senators and representatives. The Agenda consists of seven bills—we call them the Seven Pillars of the Common Good—so simply select the one best suited to your interests and talents and put whatever time you can afford behind it. Be part of this rising citizen movement to shape the future for the benefit of all Americans now and to come. The RedirectAmerica.org website is packed with information and ways to participate at all levels, and it will guide you to others in your community working along the same paths. We need you, folks, and thanks. Now we'll take questions for forty-five minutes. Out of consideration for your fellow members of the fourth estate, please be brief, and please identify yourself and indicate which of us your question is addressed to."

Hands shot up by the dozens. Phil called on Basil Brubaker of the *New York Times*.

"My question is for Mr. Buffett. What if any legal entities are you all working through, how much money have you spent, and how much have you budgeted?"

"We are working through a number of nonprofit corporations, 501(c)(3)s and 501(c)(4)s, and several PACs. Each of us is also spending our own money, directly as individuals, on various improvement projects that have been reported in the press over the past half year. As for amounts, what the law requires to be reported is on the public record. What the law does not require will remain confidential, for reasons obvious to those of us in the business community—you don't show your hand in a struggle where resources signal levels of capability and persistence."

Yoko popped up beside Warren at the podium. "You wouldn't expect Mr. Lobo and his clients to reveal their war chest, would you?"

"Lancelot Lobo, the corporate raider?" said Brubaker. "What's he got to do with it?"

"Surely you saw the full-page ad that an anonymous group of CEOs took out in the *Wall Street Journal* some weeks ago?" Yoko replied. "Well, Lobo is the spearhead they hired to lead the charge against the Agenda."

In the back of the room, a reporter recognized Lobo—his picture was often in the papers—and shouted, "Hey, he's right here!" For a few seconds Lobo was oblivious, utterly enthralled that Yoko knew his name and what he was doing, and those few seconds cost him his exit. In no time he was surrounded by reporters bombarding him with the basics of their profession: Who? What? Where? When? Why?

Phil rapped the lectern with his pen. "Can we please have order? Mr. Lobo, will you kindly go outside to answer their questions so we can finish up here?"

Lobo did not oblige. He did go outside, but he didn't stop to answer questions. Pursued by a dozen scribes, he no-commented his way to the elevator and down thirteen flights to the front door of the National Press Club, and thence into a fortuitously waiting taxicab that sped him away. Half of him was outraged by his outing, the other half was still in libido land. Fortunately, the taxi driver was talking on his cell phone in Urdu and did not try to converse with him. Unfortunately, the photographers got what they wanted, and their pictures would speak a thousand words in the next day's newspapers.

Back in the ballroom, the press conference resumed.

"James Drew, *Washington Post*. My question is directed to Leonard Riggio. Sir, there is an old saying that 'when you're everywhere, you're nowhere.' There are so many proposals in this Agenda and so many causes you've been espousing individually in the past six months that it seems to me you're spreading yourselves too thin and have no focus. Are you going to winnow your proposals down when Congress returns from its Fourth of July break?"

"We are working to build a deliberative democracy with a broad embrace. The more issues we take on, within limits, the more people will organize and swell their own leadership ranks. Down at the street and neighborhood level, they'll select the causes currently most pressing to them and take advantage of the winds of democratic possibility sweeping across our country. People are motivated by what Saul Alinsky, the legendary Chicago organizer, called 'perceived injustices.' And if you study the Agenda more closely, you'll see that it is in fact a very careful and detailed winnowing down of urgent and long-unaddressed needs and reforms into seven precisely drafted bills. Taken together, they represent a great advance in two respects: the substantive improvement of the material conditions of life in our country, and the expansion and safeguarding of our democratic institutions."

"Mark Melville of CBS. Mr. Diller, are your television and radio networks going to support the Clean Elections Party and its candidates, and if so, just how do you intend to do that without violating FCC and FEC rules?"

"Simple, Mr. Melville. We'll report all the news on all the candidates who have something to say or have done something of note. We'll do features and interviews and sponsor open debates for all ballot-qualified candidates of all parties, large and small. The Clean Elections Party is running exclusively on the single most important issue of electoral reform—money in politics. It has pledged to disband once it secures public financing of public elections in law and in fact. It has over fifty candidates on the ballot, among them challengers to the most senior incumbents in the House and ten of the most powerful senators. Finally, what I do to support candidates as a private citizen is between me and the Federal Elections Commission, as it is for everybody."

"Laurie Newsome, ABC, question for anyone. I've been covering Capitol Hill for years, and I can tell you that Congress and its committees have a whole arsenal of tactics for delaying, hamstringing, and hogtying legislation. What makes you think you can steer your Agenda quickly through the congressional maze of arcane rules and procedures?"

"I'll take the question," Bernard said. "First of all, our deep awareness of the workings of Congress as you describe them underlies all our efforts in this regard. You will see that our relative inexperience on Capitol Hill, though some of us have lobbied it often, does not translate into naiveté about what it's going to take. I might add that the members of Congress have no experience whatsoever with what's coming at them from the folks back home. What's more, among our allies in this fight is a group of seasoned former legislators and staffers who know the rules inside and out. Some of them helped write the rules. They know the escape hatches, the dodges, the moods that can sweep Congress into action. Corporations push their special bills through Congress all the time. We'll just be doing it on a grander and more public stage."

"Rita Dawn, Associated Press. Ted, what can you tell us about your Billionaires Against Bullshit? Will you release their names? What they are working on? How much they are donating?"

"Well, you know some of them already. Jerome Kohlberg on campaign finance reform, the ones who are after Wal-Mart, the ones interviewed in *Billionaires on Bullshit*. I'll ask those who haven't gone public yet whether they're open to interviews. There's a lot of autonomy among these billionaires, as you might expect."

"Alberto Adelante, Univision. Speaking of Wal-Mart, are you trying to destroy it, Mr. Price?"

"As I've said on previous occasions, what we're trying to do is give workers an opportunity to form a union, if they so choose, without intimidation and Wal-Mart SWAT teams descending on them. The overall objective is to turn Wal-Mart into a pull-up giant instead of a pull-down behemoth outsourcing its suppliers to China, hollowing out communities, offloading its responsibilities to its workers onto the American taxpayer, and driving its competitors to break their labor agreements and downgrade wages and benefits. Otherwise the vast Wal-Mart sub-economy will keep metastasizing and depress the standard of living for millions of American workers. This is not the way our economy grew in the past."

"Charlene Jepson of the *Liberator*, question for Bill Cosby. How do you feel in this sea of white men?"

"Andy, the Meliorists are all about justice. Justice is color-blind.

We speak of the people, not blacks or Latinos or Asians or Anglos. Segregating our attention to injustice peels off those not in the circle of concern. Look at the white working-class males who've been turned off by identity politics and whose alienated votes have helped make corporatist right-wing government possible."

"Archibald Aldrich, *National Review*. You are aware, I presume, of the recent torrent of petitions to the federal regulatory agencies, seeking to regulate to death just about everything that moves in the business community. You come from business. Are you responsible for these petitions, directly or indirectly, and how do you justify them without calling yourselves socialists or worse? And what *do* you call yourselves, other than Meliorists. Are you a collective, a collaborative, a cooperative, a joint partnership, an association, what?"

"They're a conspiracy," yelled Fred Froth of Fox News, "and they've finally admitted it!"

"A bunch of billionaire codgers getting together over their Postum to improve the country?" Sol said. "You want to call that a conspiracy, be our guest."

"I'll take Mr. Aldrich's question," Max said over a wave of laughter. "The names of the authors of those public petitions are on the petitions. They hail from consumer organizations that want your car to be safer and your food healthier, from environmental groups that want your air and water to be cleaner, from taxpayer associations that want your public property to be rented and not given away to private companies, from a whole array of groups that want your procurement dollar to be efficient and free from graft, your aircraft to be equipped with the latest safety features, your highways to have fewer potholes, your medicines to be thoroughly tested, your hospitals to be more competent and less infectious, your antimonopoly and corporate crime laws to be enforced, and—of particular interest to those in your economic class, Mr. Aldrich—your investments to be free of fraud, deception, and conflicts of interests Without endorsing every iota of the petitions, the Meliorists supported these groups in going before the agencies and demanding a hearing at long last, after being shut out for decades by both parties in power.

Meliorists are for betterment, remember. As for your second question, no, we are not incorporated or in a partnership. We are a voluntary association of individuals coordinating, collaborating, and cooperating with one another in what we believe to be the national interest."

"Stan Rustin of the *Dallas Morning News*. Who are your allies in the Senate and House? Surely you know their names."

"They're the ones who are sponsoring and signing on to the various bills about to be introduced," Bernard said, "so you'll know when we know."

"Tom Tempestiano, *Newsweek*, three-part question for all of you. Are you willing to testify before congressional committees, are you willing to debate your opposite corporate numbers, and are you predicting victory for your Agenda before Election Day?"

"Yes and yes to your first two questions," Warren said. "As for the third, we are not predicting victory for the Agenda, but we believe the people of this country will be victorious before Election Day. We believe their organized mobilization will affect the congressional elections and will make the Clean Elections Party a force to reckon with if the clean elections plank of the Agenda doesn't pass this time around."

"Danielle Demure of Spectrum News. I'm a reporter for your syndicate of stations in Washington, DC, Mr. Diller, and I fear that in the coming days my colleagues will view me as compromised because of your open involvement with the Meliorists. They'll say I'm not objective, and there will be rumors of your heavy hand. I'll deny any pressure to slant or hold back, since there's been none, but I need to know the nature of your Chinese Wall. And I have a follow-up."

"Ms. Demure, my policy is that reporters should be diligent and inquiring and call things as they see them. My partisanship will be channeled into paid television and radio ads at market rates, on stations where I have no equity interest and my company has no ownership share. My philosophy of news is to report on all subjects of importance, not just on the doings of the political and economic establishment. It's news if voters are viewing or listening to more voices and choices. It's news if new information is coming forth, regardless of how powerful or lowly the messenger. That is standard ideal journalism. Both the overdogs and underdogs in our society deserve coverage."

"My follow-up is on your drive to get the electronic media to pay rent for the use of the public airwaves. I know that Channel 7 and other stations rejected your ads. What's the latest?"

"Well, as you know, our ads urged rental payments to the Federal Communications Commission. We suggested recycling these pay-ments back into cable access stations and other media access programs for improved content on behalf of the audience. The cur-rent plan is to have the stations within our own networks announce that in lieu of paying the FCC rent for their licenses, they'll pay into a nonprofit fund to do what I've just described. Through our publi-cized example, we expect Congress and the FCC to come around and end this eighty-year-old giveaway of public property. We hope the communities we serve will be so pleased with our financial donation to their own participation in their own programming that they'll spread the word around the country and to Washington, DC."

"Paul Profitikoff of the website Business Hourly. Mr. Paulucci, how do you think big business is going to react to your Agenda? Please give us a detailed response."

"Well, some of my colleagues will probably want to respond to your astute question too, but for my part, here's what you can expect. The entire corporate community will gear up and do its thing, steering more campaign money to its indentured servants on the Hill, whipping up its dealers and agents and franchisees, beefing up its full-time lobbying staff, plastering TV screens with lurid ads predicting the destruction of the free enterprise system— to the detriment, of course, of working families everywhere. They'll have their allies on key committees try to stymie or stall the legisla-tion through procedural maneuvering. Nothing surprising here. They'll try every destructive tactic at their disposal to keep our country from moving forward."

"If they're really stupid, they'll try to smear us," Bill Cosby said. "Not directly, of course, but through surrogates. Just look what happened to John McCain during the Republican primary in South Carolina in 2000. We have investigators of our own, and we're prepared to respond."

"Did you see Mr. Lobo a few minutes ago?" Yoko chimed in. "The CEOs who hired him did so because they don't believe the traditional business response to perceived threats is enough. I respectfully urge all of you to find out more about Lobo's operation and his backers. Perhaps they can be persuaded to have a news conference such as this one."

"Lady Lake of the *Arkansas Baptist News.* There's a big dose of the holier-than-thou in what you all say, yet none of you seem to be religiously inspired in any way. Can it be reported that you believe yourselves to be in possession of the truth, the whole truth, and nothing but the truth? And aren't you more than a bit arrogant if you are your own highest authority?"

"I'm delighted to answer your question, Ms. Lake," George said. "We believe in the open society, where minds are persuaded through reason and fact, through genuine concern and earned trust. One of my university professors, Karl Popper, convinced me long ago that we must always revisit and revise what we think and do, because we can never know all the complexities of human behavior and the forces of nature. That means that all voices must have the right of expression and access to the means of expression, especially when communications technology uses the public's property. All of us have obviously been around, and have accumulated a fund of experience from which we've developed a sense of the fundamentals of the good society, the good life. We've decided to engage our beliefs in a fight for these goals, a clean fight, honestly undertaken. We haven't discussed among ourselves what our religious or antireligious beliefs may or may not be, but we all believe very much in the wisdom of the Golden Rule, as you see from our insignia. And we don't mean that they who have the gold rule. It's just the opposite: those who must rule will likely have very little gold, for they are the people."

"Michele Mirables of *USA Today*. I've repeatedly heard you refer to 'the people' as the force that will turn the situation around in our country. What exactly do you mean by 'the people'?"

"For six months the media has been covering what we mean by 'the people,'" Max said. "We mean 'the people' who have stepped forward on so many fronts in so many ways, we mean the millions who've indicated by their actions a readiness to exert themselves individually and in an organized civic manner, to recruit others to the cause, and to accept the assistance we've offered. Like a venture capital firm jump-starting small innovative companies, we and an ever-enlarging base of the super-rich have fostered these efforts and will continue to do so. We are coining a saying, Ms. Mirables: 'It takes organized money to take on organized money.'"

"That doesn't sound very American."

"Oh, but it is, Ms. Mirables, it is. Read your Tocqueville. 'Americans when confronted with a need quickly form an association to treat it,' he wrote some hundred and seventy years ago. We're just upping the ante and quickening the pace. Some commentators have described what we're doing as the revolt of the older super-rich against the entrenched super-rich. A little oversimplified, of course, but essentially accurate for a culture with a boxing match mentality. Sparks will surely fly, and you in the media will decidedly be yawning less."

"David Roader, *Washington Post* syndicated columnist. I'd like to inquire where you're heading with your high-voltage movement. With apologies, none of you are spring chickens. There must be limits even to your energy. My guess is that you've spent and are spending billions of your own dollars, and as impressive as that is, your opponents can far outspend you in all categories. Would any of you like to comment?"

"Mr. Roader," said William Gates Sr., "there is a consensus among us that is best summed up by that grand citizen of a united Europe, Jean Monnet, who knew without people, nothing is possible and without institutions, nothing is lasting. That is precisely what the Meliorists are about. That is why some of you may be surprised by the strong popular support for the Agenda for the Common Good. We're not talking about a flurry of e-mails or phone calls to Congress. You, sir, are about to see a civic outpouring such as you have never seen in all your years of distinguished reporting. I was informed a few seconds ago that even as we conduct this live news conference, five hundred thousand Americans have already e-mailed us or visited our website to express their eagerness to participate on the ground. That alone will not provide the necessary cutting edge, but with the requisite resources, many of these motivated citizens will become community leaders in neighborhood after neighborhood. Many of them will join the new democratic institutions that have been established in recent months, like the Congress Watchdogs, the People's Chamber of Commerce, and the consumer, taxpayer, and labor CUBs. They will find themselves sustained, advised, and defended by a well-appointed infrastructure of resolve, experience, and stamina. We have observed that these institutions and the people involved at all stages are multiplying themselves without any central direction. The one cohesive element here is the determination to forge a better country, an exemplary economy, a caring society—all the goals of the Agenda. People are beginning to believe in themselves and their vaunted sovereignty in our republic. Remember, the preamble to our Constitution starts with 'We the People.' Those whom FDR once scorned as 'economic royalists' are about to be dethroned. We expect that small numbers of these latter-day royalists will abdicate voluntarily and join us in becoming responsible elders for our posterity."

"Tamika Slater of the *Nation*. Let's be candid. Big business is like a giant accordion: it can expand its war chest to meet the occasion. It has so much in reserve, so many ultimatums it can issue to make opponents in Congress and elsewhere cave. The business response Bill Cosby and Jeno Paulucci predicted doesn't begin to take the measure of their means. What makes you so confident?"

"I'll tell you what," Joe said. "Many of my colleagues are too modest to say so, but they've been spectacular successes in the world of big business. They know how it operates, what moves it, how it bluffs, and when it's likely to buckle under pressure and make mistakes. They have the feel, like people say I have the feel of the courtroom. They know many of these CEOs and bosses personally, some from when they were in middle management years ago. They've played golf with them, gone to their children's weddings, and negotiated deals with them. So I have to disagree with my colleague Leonard Riggio. Whatever you may predict about the pending battle in Congress, you can't accuse the corporations, their trade associations, and Mr. Lancelot Lobo of being bullies. This time around, they're up against guys their own size. We know the business lobbies are in charge of the economy. We know they can destabilize the economy, start making noise about shipping more plants and offices abroad because of 'overregulation' and the rest of their bullhorns of alarm. But they're not going to get away with it. Our Agenda is in tune with the needs and aspirations of the people, and the people are the ones who vote. And Patriotic Polly will have a thing or two to say about the Agenda too."

Scattered applause floated through the ballroom.

"Reginald Sesko of *Business Week*. Are you implying that the business lobbies would actually stoop to deliberately damaging the economy they're profiting from? Isn't that a little conspiratorial, Mr. Jamail?"

"Not at all, in the sense you mean the word, and their strategy will not be so crude. But of course they're going to conspire in the original dictionary meaning—they're going to work together intensively—and of course they won't be doing it in the mall. When Congress starts to light up for the Agenda, when the lawsuits, regulatory petitions, and rallies are placed in the context of what's happening here in Washington, the stock markets may go down a little, and then the corporate flacks and pundits will start talking about 'the deteriorating business climate.' Comparisons will be drawn with the more favorable and often tropical climate in other countries that beckon US companies to flee their native land and bring their jobs and capital with them. 'Business confidence is battered,' we'll be told. Well, it's a gigantic bluff. As long as this is the most lucrative market in the world, as long as foreign companies are still beating down the door to get into the US marketplace, we'll be able to call that bluff in front of the American people. You see, we've got the resources."

Warren consulted his Timex. The forty-five minutes were up. Some of the reporters had already left to file their stories. The cameramen were packing up since there would be no one-on-ones afterward. He stepped to the lectern.

"Ladies and gentlemen, the time allotted for questions is exhausted. You'll have further opportunities to question any or all of us should you wish to take them. Please note that we're each handling our own media requests. I'm sure that I speak for all of us in thanking you for attending. Be sure to sign the clipboard if you didn't on the way in. You all have copies of the Agenda and further information in your press kits. And once more, to the live audience, please get in touch with us so we can get in touch with you and join together to lift our society to the highest levels of human possibility. Again, the website is RedirectAmerica.org and the e-mail address is info@RedirectAmerica.org. And now, good day from the Meliorist Society."

With Warren in the lead, the seventeen stalwarts strode out of the ballroom as briskly as they had entered, heaved a collective sigh of relief, and repaired to a popular new restaurant at V and Fourteenth Street NW, an area that was developing quickly. They had reserved a large private room for an afternoon of repast, relaxation, and reflection before going their separate ways. Earlier Bill Joy had made sure the room was secure.

Once the door closed, they broke into animated conversation about how well the news conference had gone overall and about the extraordinary Internet response that had registered right on the spot. Recruitment, they agreed, would be deliriously happy. "And beyond overworked. We ought to let them hire a couple dozen more people," Ted said. "Of course," came the unanimous response. With the tension diminishing, food had never tasted better, even though the menu was a little too heavy on the vegetables to suit Sol. The diners took their time with each course and filled the intervals between with their hopes for the critical month of July, when the Agenda and the hearings would tell their stories.

Meanwhile, somewhere in Maryland, Lobo was hitting bottom. After hurling himself headfirst into the cab, hurting his elbow in the process, he'd ask the taxi driver to head due north up Connecticut Avenue. At the District line, he told Urduman to keep going, straight to New York City. When he demurred, Lobo whipped out twelve crisp one-hundred-dollar bills and spread them out like a Japanese fan across the front seat. Urduman took one glance to his right, swooped the C-notes into his jacket pocket, and drove on. The cab's air conditioner was struggling on this warm summer day, and Lobo was sweating profusely, but not because of the heat. Pushing away thoughts of the fallout from the press conference, he took out his laptop and googled Yoko. There she was in all her pallid beauty, there were all the laudatory and envious and scurrilous articles written about her, there were her shoulder-shrugging dismissals and concise epigrams. He could barely contain himself.

But he had to. Though he knew he should be googling all the news stories about himself that must flying around the country and the world, he couldn't bring himself to do it. He had to clear his head, assume the worst in print and photos, and prepare his recovery with his staff, his CEO superiors, and the media, which was no doubt mocking him at this very moment. Lobo had been down before, if not so personally. But his inner core of steel didn't distinguish between different kinds of down. He just had to connect his steel with his mind, his brain, his cunning, his resourcefulness, his imagination, his gift of jab. He had four hours in the cab, his cell phone off, his whereabouts unknown. He had to fight back his Yoko fantasies and concentrate, concentrate, concentrate.

His preliminary assessment of his predicament was that he had clearly been ambushed. Just as clearly, there was a leak or a mole or a bug in his suite of offices. Not likely the latter, because he debugged daily, but whatever the source—which had to be found—the damage was done. He and his clients had been put on the defensive, revealed publicly before they had chosen to reveal themselves. The CEOs were probably stunned. They would expect a call from him explaining what had happened. Worse, explaining himself. CEOs, at least publicly, were all about dignity. They had learned from their predecessors that lying, cheating, and stealing proceeded more smoothly on an appearance of dignity, a well-dressed style of prudent solidity and gravity. They expected these qualities not just in their corporate attorneys but in all their retainers. At all costs, preserve your public bearing and dignity, no matter what your mistresses might titter about privately or your wives might be thinking about your double personality.

Lobo decided to tackle the problem head-on and turn a swine's ear into a silk purse. He would go to his CEOs and admit that this was an ambush he hadn't foreseen. He would accept the temporary embarrassment and take the fall, but he would take the hard fall and use it to bounce back more formidably than ever. That was the way he was built. "You have a fighting mad Lobo now," he would tell the CEOs, they of the pursed lips and folded arms, "and you know what a wolf aroused to fury can do to its enemies." Besides, with the gloves off and the spotlight on, he could marshal his forces without inhibition and roll out his attack ads earlier than planned. His growing band of bulldogs could leap into the fray because the war had been declared before the entire nation.

But Lobo wasn't sure his legendary tongue could carry the day. He knew he had to give his CEOs some insightful substance about the news conference and his evaluation of the Meliorists. He also knew that his usual keen powers of observation and analysis had been blunted by the heavenly Yoko, who had recognized him, anointed his name with her pretty lips, and obliterated his storied self-control. He reopened his laptop and began to read the transcript of the news conference, already online, to refresh his memory and fill in the gaps created by his lustful fantasies. He began to apply his fabled powers of concentration, absorbing and memorizing whole sequences, analyzing, synthesizing, and digesting them for the make-or-break meeting with the CEOs, who would no doubt summon him tomorrow morning on the double.

Passing Newark on the Jersey Turnpike, Urduman asked for directions. "Just follow the signs for the Holland Tunnel and I'll tell you what to do from there. I'm on the corner of Fifty-third and Madison." When they arrived, Lobo tossed another hundred to the smiling driver, shook his hand, wrote down his license plate number, company name, and cab number, and went into the building in a hat and sunglasses. It was 5:45 p.m. He used a private door to enter his expansive suite, which now covered an entire floor. His secretary had left for the day. Still sweating and fantasizing, Lobo peeled off his clothes, took an ice-cold shower, toweled down, and prepared to do battle. It was going to be a long night. There was an emergency message on his desk phone and another on his computer: "CEO Jasper Cumbersome summons you to an executive session at 9:00 a.m. tomorrow morning, no ifs, ands, or buts." Leaning back in his leather chair, he thought, "Well, I guess I'm lucky they didn't fire me on the spot. It's their curiosity that saved me. Besides, I know too much." He felt his confidence and composure swelling.

The night wore on and Lobo wore well. He was at the height of his powers and combativeness. He would turn adversity into an aggressive asset. He would show the Meliorists that you could humiliate Lobo once but you'd pay for it in multiples. He prepared his presentation for the next morning step-by-step. His plan of attack would soar far above his casual but respectful explanation of what happened at the news conference. At 3:20 a.m. he went home to catch a few hours' sleep, just enough to give him the edge he wanted. At 8:56 a.m., he checked in with Cumbersome's secretary.

In the penthouse boardroom, the CEOs were not in a good mood. They were shaken by the Meliorists' cool determination and extensive groundwork, and appalled by the front-page photographs of Lobo that had people lining up at the newsstands. Spread out on the conference table before them were shots of Lobo looking like a deer in the headlights when Yoko first mentioned his name, Lobo in his flight out the ballroom door, Lobo streaking toward the elevator, Lobo *in* the elevator surrounded by the press, looking like a snarling canine half-crazed with fright, and finally a posterior view of Lobo diving into the cab. The CEOs couldn't help laughing, furious though they were. It was bad enough that Lobo had suffered deep public humiliation, but what concerned them most was whether it would rub off on them. Thank God none of their names had been mentioned.

Enter Lobo, looking confident, with a calculated touch of contrition. "Good morning. What happened yesterday was caused by a mole somewhere in my office or a careless leak to a third party inimical to our interests. I deeply regret it and have already taken steps to insure that nothing like it will happen again. Its intent was to derail us. It will not," he said firmly, and proceeded to deliver his plan of attack before any of the bosses could break in. "A huge multimedia buy that will completely drown out the so-called Agenda for the Common Good is on for next week. Obviously, should there be another September-eleventh-type sabotage, it would melt the Meliorists down indefinitely, but God forbid. So our campaign to unmask these pseudo-capitalists starts by declaring a fact: Bernard Rapoport's late father was an immigrant from the Soviet Union and a confessed Communist who made no apologies. This first wave of ads will leave the impression that more shockers are on the way for the Meliorists at the personal level. In tandem with this campaign is another wave of ads that uncannily anticipate exactly what the Meliorists told the press we would do—an endorsement, as I see it, of how effective our message will be. The themes here are that the Meliorists are ruinous to our nation's business climate and our economy's ability to meet the global competition, that they're destabilizing the workforce, that they're bent on costly overregulation that stifles innovation and productivity—and all this because they're palpably in the grips of a late-life psychiatric crisis."

Lobo paused and swept the CEOs with his steely gaze as he walked to the boardroom's TV and slid a DVD into the player. The ads rolled forth, exquisitely produced and highly emotive, with a small line of type at the bottom identifying their sponsor as a group called For the USA.

For a long moment no one spoke. Lobo was beginning to wonder whether he'd misjudged the quality of the ads when Sal Belligerante said, "They're knockouts. Actually made my all-American blood boil. They catch your attention and keep it. No one will be hitting the remote during these commercial breaks."

"That's just a sampling," Lobo said. "We've got more ads covering every possible variation on the theme of SRO sabotage, tailored to our target states and congressional districts, and we've got them in print, radio, and Internet versions too."

"All well and good as far as it goes," said Justin Jeremiad, "but if your strategy is to slam them personally and at the same time meet their Agenda head on, it's not going to be enough, given what we saw on C-SPAN yesterday. You need a third wave. What is it? With all the money you're spending, you better know by now. We have a lot less time to lose than we thought."

"The third wave? What is it?" Lobo asked, ever more confident that he was off the griddle and turning the tide. "The answer is *you* and *you* and *you*," he said, pointing his finger at the CEOs in turn.

"Just what do you mean by that?" asked CEO Celeste Thackery, in attendance for the first time.

"The third wave is for each of you to take responsibility for threatening to shut down a major US plant or operation and transfer it abroad if these regulations and bills go into effect. You can do it directly or via your extended network of CEO friends. It can't be a bluff, although you can, of course, announce plans already formulated months ago in private to take the plant abroad. That's probably the easiest way to go for the immediate future. Be sure that whatever countries are named aren't all in one region—for example, China, China, China would create too many problems. It's hard to go after Bernard Rapoport's Communist father while announcing that you're going to lay off workers here and ship whole factories to a giant Communist dictatorship."

Wardman Wise was nodding in approval. "Yes, Lobo, I think what you seek can be arranged on an expeditious schedule. Plants are going overseas every day, to Bangladesh, Indonesia, Vietnam, and our friends at the Department of Commerce will give us their daily listings, which they used to make public but now do not, for obvious political reasons."

"Excellent, Mr. Wise. To continue. Now that their cat is out of the bag and we've seen their Agenda, we can push the steak-and-potatoes lobbying drive by the Washington corporate establishment. We've already touched base with eighty-two trade associations, fifteen public relations firms, twenty-seven boutique lobbying groups with a heavy presence of former members of Congress and former top congressional staffers, and twenty-six of the most powerful corporate law firms. We put some noses a little out of joint on first contact—'Who the hell are you, newcomer?'—but we quickly mollified them by mentioning our principals and our superior information about the SROs. In Washington power circles, inside information is mother's milk, the currency they trade in, and they realized that by comparison with your humble retainer's knowledge, they were in the dark.

"In two days we're meeting with the directors of three hundred and eighty-two corporate political action committees (PACs) at a private and suitably secured hotel ten miles outside Washington. These PACs are personally well-connected with members of Congress who can be expected to be on our side. Because several dozen of these incumbents are being challenged by the Clean Elections Party, the PAC men will be unusually attentive. I welcome your observations and advice on this meeting, but first a word about yesterday's news conference. I'm sure you all have your own impressions, and I'd like to hear them. For my part, having sat in that room and felt the atmosphere, I can only repeat that these are not dilettantes arrayed against us. We're up against seventeen tough hombres who are supremely confident as a team and individually."

"You forgot the lady, Mr. Lobo!" interjected Celeste Thackery.

"Yes . . . yes, of course, the lady . . . Yo . . . Ms. Ono." Lobo bit back the dreamy smile his lips were trying to form. "As I was saying, the so-called Meliorists did not seem rehearsed. There was nothing slick or scripted in their presentations and answers, and that made the reporters less aggressive than I thought they'd be, even though we know many of them are liberals, unlike their CEOs. The press didn't dwell on the public mobilizations of the last six months—didn't even ask about the lunchtime rallies, for God's sake—but it's clear that the SROs are behind all this activism, which is increasingly taking on a life of its own, though most of the money still comes from them and their billionaire friends. Throughout the press conference, there was a disarming quality to the SROs' demeanor and an authentic ring to their words, and I emphasize this point because, as you know, they expressed an eagerness to debate you or any CEO of your choice. The media won't ignore that challenge and will soon be asking who's going to step forward from your ranks, so you've got to make it a priority to find seventeen CEOs who are capable of taking them on in public."

There was an awkward silence around the conference table, until Ichiro Matsuda finally said, "Mr. Lobo, we are active, full-time, busy executives. They are retired and have nothing but time on their hands for their hobbyhorses. Let's have our own retired CEOs debate them."

"I don't think that will go over very well with the press," Lobo said. "And given the wave of valedictories from their retired CEOs, our retired CEOs are going to be less inclined than ever to get into this hornet's nest. Besides, they won't be up to snuff on current controversies and accusations.

"But to return to the press conference, you may have noticed that numerous persons in the audience were not reporters. Nothing unusual about that, except maybe the three gentlemen from reputable private detective firms who were there on our nickel to get a feel for their subjects of interest. There is obviously more to learn about the SROs and their force fields, much more indeed. I'll call the PIs tomorrow with further instructions, the details of which would only bore you. I've also got some sartorial and behavioral advice for them. It's amazing how even the most seasoned private dicks haven't figured out that they have to dress casually, loosen up, and smile once in a while. They're worse than ever now that their profession is so automated."

"Automated, Mr. Lobo?" asked CEO Lester Manchester III.

"Just a way of saying they use more gadgets these days to ply their trade. Now, to continue, I didn't detect any body language indicating envy, disagreement, or dismay in the rest of the SRO lineup when one of them was speaking. Given their legendary egos, I can only presume that their leader, probably Warren Buffett, carefully selected them so that they wouldn't work at cross-purposes and would each have their own unique missions along with the common cause. As for their clutch of legislation, as I've said before, it consists primarily of proposals the corporate world has defeated in the past, so there's no wheel to be invented here. However, what we don't know is what furies may be released in the form of riders and other bills if the revolt of the SROs and their masses gets out of hand. If you know what I mean."

"What *do* you mean, Lobo?" said Wardman Wise a little impatiently.

"I mean that the revolt may catch on to such a degree that both we and they lose control over it as it moves for a peaceful but for us decidedly uncomfortable rearrangement of the power grid—and I'm not talking about electricity. I mean that the revolt may become a genuine popular revolution."

CEO Wise shuddered visibly. "I see," he said.

Lobo tried to resist the feeling that he now had the CEOs in the palm of his hand, but he didn't try hard. "In a few days we should know which of the bills will be introduced when. I'll brief you in detail then, but we can't wait. My first two waves and your third wave have to roll out now if we are to take the offensive and not be caught napping."

"The way you were yesterday," said CEO K. Everett Dickerson pointedly. "Quite candidly, Lobo, I still can't get over the collapse of your composure. You were hired in part because you're so quick on your feet. I myself have seen you in far more dire circumstances, when your corporate raids hung by a thread in a courtroom or when a reporter blindsided you at a news conference—and wham! You always fired back with high-velocity effectiveness. Did something or someone distract you?"

Lobo froze, coughed three times to gain three seconds, took a drink of water to gain two seconds, excused himself to gain two more, and then manfully decided to tell the partial truth and nothing but the partial truth.

"Mr. Dickerson, I can only say that I was concentrating so hard on weaving together everything I was seeing and hearing that I was caught completely off guard. I certainly did not expect to be named. We all have a bad day now and then. It won't happen again, I assure you. You'll get more than your dollar's worth."

This last twist generated a few chuckles among the CEOs, along with a good deal of quiet admiration for the agility of Lobo's answer. Jasper Cumbersome looked around the table at his colleagues and summed up the sense of the meeting.

"Well, Lobo, you've reassured us once again, but you must realize that your margin of error is narrowing. Let's conclude and reconvene in a few days to hear your update. You have your work cut out for you, judging by the media's treatment of the Meliorists. Pretty respectful overall, and some editorials were actually laudatory. Your flight made them look better than they would have, unfortunately."

Lobo could not let this remark pass. He had to leave the meeting on his terms. "Unfortunately and temporarily, Jasper. The psychological makeup of Americans is such that they often favor people who stumble, who show some human frailty. Consider the election campaigns of our recent presidents, who actually surged with the voters when the media hound dogs were trumpeting a weakness, a deficiency, a faux pas. Shrewdness can often turn a setback into a gain. And before we leave here today, I want to add one more observation from the news conference. I didn't notice even a whiff of reluctance in any of the SROs, no voluntary or involuntary indication that they were being led faster than they wanted to go or pushed along by peer pressure. Can you all say the same? Do you all without exception feel the same dynamic harmony and symmetry of energy? It does make a difference when the rubber hits the road, you know."

"Lobo," declared Samuel Slick, "this is as smooth an operation as any collection of prominent, successful, rich CEOs can be. Not even a conspiracy of price-fixers fearful of discovery would operate with such perfectly meshing gears. Fear makes for a powerful glue."

"Well, on that reassuringly sticky note, I bid you a brief farewell and plunge back into my twenty-hour days," Lobo said, and turned to stride out of the boardroom, confident that he had commanded the high ground.

After the door closed, the CEOs shook their heads in amazement at Lobo's suave performance. "Could any of us have pulled the rabbit out of the hat like that in a similarly intimidating environment?" asked Roland Revelie unnecessarily as the meeting broke up.

Lobo got back to his office at 12:25 p.m. and went in by the side door to skim the newspapers laid out on his desk and review some television news tapes. At 1:00 p.m. he went on the office intercom to summon his chief aide de camp and field captains to a meeting in the conference room in an hour. Then he conducted a rigorous review of all the operational mandates and sub-mandates, with their precision timetables and repeated checks before launch.

At 2:00 p.m. sharp, Lobo stood before his dozen captains at the end of a long, narrow mahogany table. A student of history, he had studied photographs of dictators with their subordinates and noticed that the conference table was always long, narrow, and rectangular, with the dictator dominating at the head. No round tables for him. His was a premeditated table.

"O captains, my captains!" he began, knowing that most of them wouldn't catch the reference. Still, it pleased him to invoke Lincoln at this grave hour. "The war is at hand, and we shall strike the first blow. You all have your missions, and I trust you have studied them down to the last detail. Remember, they must fit together as tightly as the stones of the ancient Egyptian pyramids."

"Boss," said Brad Bashem, a seasoned gut-fighter in the political trenches of the past four decades, and an admirer of Senator Joseph McCarthy. Bashem was in charge of Wave One. It was his job to choreograph the business about Bernard Rapoport's father. "Boss, that Commie ad is just too soft. It needs some scarier footage—Soviet tanks rolling into Budapest, the Rosenbergs, Stalin blockading Berlin—"

"Stalin who?" asked one of the younger captains.

"Oh, Christ," growled Bashem.

With any doubts about the Lincoln reference dispelled, Lobo proceeded to explain to the young man as patiently as possible who Joseph Stalin was and what his regime had done after Lenin's death, and then he explained who Vladimir Lenin was. "All right, enough history lessons," he said. "What do the rest of you think about the ad?"

"I think Brad's right," said Captain Brig Bigelow, who was responsible for Wave Two, the series of print and television ads straight from the old business playbook, with their dire warnings about the catastrophic consequences of passing legislation designed to improve people's lives: THE SKY IS FALLING, AND IT WILL LAND ON THE WORKERS AND THEIR FAMILIES!

Lobo frowned. "Well, maybe you're right. I'll call the Beef Busters and ask them to work something up fast," he said, referring to a Madison Avenue ad agency renowned for thirty-second and one-minute masterpieces that had crushed advocates of even the most appealing and necessary substantive reforms. One of their more recent victories was over bereaved mothers seeking safer crib designs. The Beef Busters left the fluff fights to their lesser colleagues on the Avenue. In the office, they routinely used language like "masticate them," "show the fangs," "send the bleeding hearts to solitary," and "drain the blood from their veins." The office walls were covered with bloodcurdling stills from just about every vampire movie ever made. The war room where they devised their frightful mind-lasers was called Transylvania. The name of their numero uno was Horatio Hadestar, and the firm's business card featured its motto in ghoulish calligraphy: "We push the envelope."

"Are you sure about that, sir?" asked Lobo's aide de camp, Lawrence Nightingale, in a tone of prudent alarm. "Don't the attributes that make the Beef Busters so compelling to us also increase the risk of their going too far? Of course we'll have final review, but we're on an extremely tight schedule, and we may not have time to send them back to the drawing board. And those are very forceful personalities over there."

"Here too," Lobo snapped, "but I applaud your sensitivity to our time constraints, Larry. There can be no slippage. We're not at the nanosecond point yet, but we're getting closer. Equally important is the targeting of our gamma rays, what marketers call positioning but I prefer to call beaming." Lobo paused and gripped the edge of the table. The moment he'd uttered the word "positioning," Yoko flashed into his brain. With a heroic effort, he shoved her back out, but not before some odd facial twitching that did not go unnoticed. Recovering, he proceeded to bark commands regarding the placement strategy for the ads, which he had formulated after much careful mining of data. He assigned one captain the task of tracking the ads in the chosen congressional districts and states so that the immediate fallout could be gauged and the campaign adjusted as necessary. He ordered another to follow the news closely and see what free publicity was provoked by the ads themselves so that such opportunities could be maximized over the coming weeks. The remaining eight captains he divided between Bashem and Bigelow for the urgent work of contacting the media and making the actual buys.

"Exactly how long do we have, boss?" Bashem asked. "When do we declare war? Have you finalized the date yet?"

Lobo gave his captains an ironic smile. "Fourteen July." Bastille Day, another reference that would go right past them. "Next Friday. One week and one day from today."

Groans followed—that meant another weekend in the office—but soon yielded to whistles and cheers. Lobo's troops were ready to see some action.

The Meliorists were not idle on that key weekend before the launch of the Agenda. Boisterous rallies filled one city square after another all over the country. Mass Demonstrations made note of one of the better banners, held high by a Congress Watchdog contingent in the Pittsburgh march: "What's the Big Deal About the Agenda's Fair Deals? We Earned Them!"

These were no ordinary marches and rallies. They were professional to the last detail. Experience was adding up. The press could see the cool determination on the faces of the speakers, organizers, and participants. Buckets were passed through the packed crowds for contributions, giving the people a stake in the whole funding effort. Dick Goodwin's pamphlet was passed out by the thousands to eager hands—the demonstrators were people who read. Some reporters tried random interviews in hopes of showing that these masses were of the great unwashed variety and were being used by the SROs, but their hopes were dashed by the sophistication and plain eloquence of the interviewees. Clearly, months of work had paid off for the Meliorists, who among them managed surprise appearances at twenty-two of the rallies, to the delight of the crowds. The erudite Bernard got a huge ovation at Cowboy Stadium in Dallas, of all places, when he hollered over the public address system, "You know why there are so many Texas rednecks? Because they're red-hot mad about injustice, and they're not going to take it anymore. When they pledge allegiance to the flag and say those last words, 'with liberty and justice for all,' they're going for it big-time— Texas big-time, and you know it doesn't get any bigger here in the USA." The crowd went wild with laughter and applause, "rednecks" and progressives alike.

The rallies and marches weren't the end of it. By the thousands the participants walked to the local offices of their representatives and senators and formed human chains around the buildings, even the larger federal buildings. No one was inside on a weekend, of course. The purpose of the encirclement was to take photographs, e-mail them to the legislators, and leave huge blowups at the entrances next to big signs that read, "The First of Many Bear Hugs. We'll be back. Love, The People." Other ralliers headed to any number of storefronts that the Redirections projects and their off-shoots had rented in low-income neighborhoods. These storefronts were rapidly coming to be viewed as backbones of the community, places staffed with knowledgeable advisers who could tell people where to get help, how to qualify for public services, how to find work or get refunds. Many of the local residents came out to join the marchers in going from tenement to tenement to enlist support for the Agenda.

All the Sunday news shows featured segments on the rallies, their commentators remarking on both the level of organization and the destinations of the marchers right after the rallies broke up. These were no ephemeral events that left behind nothing but bottles and cans, cigarette butts, and paper cups. They left some of that behind too, of course, but the debris was quickly collected, sorted for recycling, and taken away.

On Monday, July 10th, the first pillar of the Agenda for the Common Good was introduced in Congress: the $10.00 minimum wage, with exhaustive backup documentation on the human needs that would be addressed by it and the beneficial consequences that would flow from it.

Tuesday witnessed the introduction of comprehensive health insurance coverage for all citizens, taking off from Medicare but with many refinements in the areas of quality control, cost control, and organized patient participation in the oversight of this nationwide public payment program for the private delivery of healthcare. There would be no more corporate HMOs and many more health cooperatives, no more tens of thousands of deaths and hundreds of thousands of undiagnosed injuries and illnesses every year. The backup documentation showed that the entire overhaul, preserving choice of doctors and hospitals, was less expensive than the present $6,500 per capita expenditure on healthcare. The statistics were all clearly explained, and the press ate them up, especially the estimated $200 billion annual savings from eliminating computerized billing fraud and abuse because there was only a single payer.

Wednesday was the day for comprehensive tax reform. This bill blew away all other topics on the cable and network news shows. It called for a 0.5 percent sales tax on all stock, bond, and derivatives transactions, higher taxes on pollution, gambling, manufactures of addictive products, and commercial entertainment, restoring tax rates for capital gains, lower taxes on the necessities of life, and a corporate tax neutralizing corporate welfare disbursements. Most dramatically, it abolished the federal tax on incomes below $100,000 per year, reduced or eliminated the blizzard of federal fees for public parks and museums and other public services, and projected a significant surplus. That evening the Meliorists consented to dozens of TV and radio interviews, chatting easily but with authority about the tax bill and the Agenda as a whole, studding their remarks with down-to-earth examples, and generally making viewers and listeners feel like their friendly neighborhood billionaire grandparent had dropped in for a visit.

Lobo watched it all with mounting concern, pushing his captains mercilessly day and night. His kiss fests with the young pit bull became more frequent. He swapped the carrot sticks for celery sticks because the orange tinge to his skin was heading toward pumpkin. He was munching on a celery stick when Horatio Hadestar arrived at noon on Wednesday with a DVD of the Rapoport ad that made Lobo blanch. Over footage of goose-stepping Red Army soldiers, mass starvation in the countryside in the wake of forced collectivization, and heavy iron doors clanging on emaciated prisoners, a stern voice intoned, "Communist dictator Joseph Stalin was one of the biggest mass murderers in history. So-called Meliorist Bernard Rapoport was sired by a Communist who was proud of it, both before he left the Soviet Union and after he immigrated to the United States. The deadly legacy of Communism runs through the Meliorists' so-called Agenda for the Common Good, their Red Plan for America. Guilt by association? Hardly. Bernard Rapoport rarely misses an opportunity to quote Papa. Tell your members of Congress to send the Meliorist Agenda back to Russia, where it came from. Call them at 202-224-3121 or log onto their websites and e-mail them today!"

"Hadestar, you've pushed the envelope right over the cliff," Lobo said when the ominous background music died down.

"Do you want to win or not, Lobo? The public is so saturated with advertising that you've got to hit 'em right between the eyes and sock 'em in the solar plexus. Deep down in your marauding soul you love it, Lobo. Admit it."

"I'm seeing beyond that, Hadestar, way beyond. I'm seeing your ad come back and kick us in the cojones—not that you'd have much to worry about. I'll call you tomorrow."

As an indignant Horatio Hadestar stormed out of the office without a word, Lobo was already deep in reflection. Should he even bother sending the ad to Cumbersome and company? His reflections turned to reverie. He was back in Little League, pitching in the state championship game, his team ahead five to four in the final inning on his opponents' home field. He had just walked three straight batters, and the bases were loaded, with two outs and a three-two count. The coach gave his catcher the fastball sign, but Lobo threw the lanky batter a slider and struck him out to win the game. A slider in a situation like that was unheard of. Despite the win, the coach was furious, because he knew Lobo's insubordinate impetuousness would come back to haunt him on and off the ballfield.

The coach was right. Snapping himself back to reality, Lobo copied the DVD onto his computer and transmitted the ad to Cumbersome. Two hours later the CEO consensus came back: "So long as all the facts are exactly true, there is no reason to withhold it."

Lobo summoned Bashem and thrust the DVD at him. "Get this to all the media outlets on the A-list right away and report back first thing tomorrow," he commanded, already knowing what Bashem would tell him. There would be no static from the major networks and their particularly finicky morning talk shows, for the simple reason that the Meliorists wanted the broadcast industry to pay rent for the public airwaves. Presto, out went the standards-and-practices malarkey, in came pure self-interest. Open sesame! The Commie ad would be a go.

On Thursday morning, as Captain Bashem was delivering the report Lobo expected, the Solar-Carbohydrate Energy Efficiency Conversion Bill was introduced in Congress, with a dozen senators and a dozen representatives—a mix of Democrats and Republicans—as sponsors. They jointly declared America's energy needs a national emergency and urged passage of the bill as a blueprint for the future.

Ted Turner was the proud author of the bill's preamble, titled "The Ecology of Justice." With none of the joshing and sparring that usually marked his style, he portrayed America's dependence on fossil and nuclear fuel as a grave threat to national security, and the resultant pollution as a silent and expanding form of violence against the health and well-being of the citizenry. He described specific measures like closed-loop systems of pollution control, precycling, and recycling, in close coordination with relevant reforms of the tax system; he charted the course for an expeditious displacement of fossil and nuclear fuel through several innovative strategies to be laid out in the bill itself; and he persuasively connected it all with a soaring vision of the goals that could be achieved by enactment: clean air and water, a diminishment of environmentally caused disease, an expansion of affordable housing, and even an end to hunger.

The bill's first section dealt with new efficiencies for fossil fuel that would increase BTU productivity greatly over the next dozen years—more output from less energy—and reduce pollution as a result of the more efficient conversions. Backing up this feasible projection were written statements from the well-known experts Art Rosenfeld, Amory Lovins, and Paul Hawken. Section Two laid out an accelerated national solar energy mission—passive solar architecture and active solar thermal, photovoltaic, biomass, wind, and some tidal. Section Three was devoted to fiscal conversions. It stripped the fossil and nuclear companies of all the tax breaks, subsidies, and rapid depreciations that kept the playing field so uneven, and allocated these benefits to startup renewables at more modest levels. Federal procurement of products and buildings was to be guided by the massive solar conversion called for in Section Two, as was federal research and development. Reductions in government contracting waste would fund a program offering financial assistance to consumers who wanted to go green with their purchases and their homes. The final section dealt with citizen empowerment, asserting an affirmative government responsibility to facilitate the formation of advocacy, oversight, and cooperative associations dealing with energy matters. The idea was to aggregate the power of consumers—economic and political—at the consumption end of the energy production stream.

One new feature of the legislation's background documentation—perhaps attributable in part to the Sun God festivals and sustainable economy shows—was supportive testimony from a few representatives of coal, gas, oil, and nuclear power companies speaking the same language: "If the sun is profitable, we'll go sun. It's safer, it's cleaner, it's abundant, it's everywhere, no one can deplete it, expropriate it, or tax it, and it'll be around for another four billion years. Just make it profitable and we'll never look back." The documentation also included a predictable condemnation of the bill from the US Chamber of Commerce and a rousing endorsement from the PCC.

In his office in Manhattan, Lobo was receiving reports on the reaction to the energy legislation from his people on the Hill—they were alarmed because there were more Republican defections to this bill than any of the others—but he scarcely gave them a glance. He'd had a tip about a big announcement coming any minute from Wal-Mart headquarters in Bentonville, and he was glued to C-SPAN. Sure enough, shortly before 11:00 a.m., CEO Leighton Clott strode to a phalanx of microphones in front of the headquarters building, flanked by his board of directors.

"Ladies and gentlemen, a brief statement. Throughout its history, Wal-Mart has succeeded because it has responded to reality. The past weeks have presented us with a new reality—a drive of unprecedented organization, spearheaded from without, to make us abandon the business model that has worked so well for Wal-Mart customers and Wal-Mart shareholders for nearly half a century. Our new business model will require us to adjust prices to respond to higher wages and benefits. Henceforth Wal-Mart will offer no opposition, philosophical or operational, to unionization. If Wal-Mart associates want to establish themselves through union structures, store by store or nationwide, the board of directors and management will accept the collective bargaining choice and work through those frameworks for the benefit of our associates and our company. One last personal word, to Sol Price. Congratulations, Sol. You began your career as the pioneer of the modern discount chain, and you end it as the pioneer of the price hike movement. Thank you, and good day."

Lobo grabbed a handful of celery sticks. Oh, brother, talk about watching Goliath come crashing down. The Wal-Mart capitulation was really going to gum up the works. The story was huge, with way more than a day's worth of legs. It was a defeat by proxy of Lobo's CEOs. It was demoralizing. It would be seen as a people's victory, since the weeks and weeks of news coverage had focused not on Sol Price and his billionaires but on the workers, picketers, and small businesses—the people, dammit! What would Lobo say to the CEOs? They'd want to know why he didn't see this coming, what he was going to do about the week's launch. What *was* he going to do? Should he delay the Commie ad or pull it altogether? Should he push back the rollout date for Wave Two?

Lobo sat at his desk wolfing celery sticks. He invited no counsel from his associates. He had to think this through alone. He went into the private suite adjoining his office, shut the door, and whistled for the pit bull. Then, feeling a little more relaxed, he turned off the lights, lay down on the couch, and allowed his 100 billion neurons, give or take, to whir.

Ten minutes of whirring later, he decided to let the Commie ad run the next evening as scheduled. For one thing, it would show weakness on the part of the CEOs to concede another setback and display hesitation in the midst of the first week's pitched battle. Besides, regardless of its reception, the ad would distract the Meliorists and the public, and cast the CEO front group as the aggressive, daring protagonist. It was time for action, not reaction. He would have no surprises for the CEOs. He would stay the course with his three waves. The Meliorists were the talk of the country, the talk of the talk shows, the talk of the news and the late-night comedy shows. There was no public patience for a detailed rebuttal of the Agenda legislation. The Meliorists had generated such a pervasive public mood in their favor that the need to reverse it with a negative campaign was greater than ever.

Lobo summoned his captains to his office over the intercom and gave them the final go-ahead for Operation Rapoport. He told them to anticipate every conceivable backlash to the Commie ad so they would have an instant response capability, with no loss of initiative for Wave Two next week. Then he called Hadestar and ordered an immediate modification of the ad. It had to end with a question, not a condemnation. Instead of a blunderbuss approach that might just blunder, it had to plant corrosive seeds of doubt.

The Wal-Mart news hit like a rocket. "Capitulation!" the late-edition headlines screamed. "Wal-Mart to Be Unionized!" "Stock Analysts Fear Inflation!" "PROs Bring Wal-Mart to Its Knees!" Reporters flooded Sol with requests for interviews. He decided to accommodate them with a brief press conference at a rented hotel ballroom in San Diego at 6:00 p.m. By 5:30 p.m., the place was packed to the rafters—SRO, Sol noticed with a wry smile as he strolled in half an hour later and sat down at the front table. He had no statement other than, "I'll take your questions now."

"What led mighty Wal-Mart to capitulate so suddenly, given its longstanding take-no-prisoners reputation?" shouted Roger Diamond of the *LA Times*.

"Not so suddenly. Two factors. Management was beginning to lose some control to outsiders, and sales were down in a couple hundred stores. They saw these two trends continuing to intensify and decided like the smart company they are to cut their losses."

Fran Jordan of CNN managed to get herself recognized amidst the clamor. "You say loss of control to outsiders. Were you the chief outsider, Mr. Price, and who are the rest?"

"A number of my fellow Meliorists and others known to you in a general sense—some Wal-Mart workers, some ex-Wal-Mart workers, some competing small businesses, many peaceful picketers, and all mom-and-pop stores on the deserted Main Streets all over America. Oh, and several vocal billionaires who got their calls returned," Sol added, calling on a *San Diego Union* reporter he'd known for years.

"Wal-Mart says in effect that they're going to have to raise prices and you're to blame, Sol. Do you agree?"

"Would they have to raise prices if they lowered the price they pay in salaries, bonuses, stock options, and perks for their top executives and upper management? Wal-Mart has realized enormous savings from constant advances in labor productivity, through automation and the like. Would they have to raise prices if they passed those savings on to consumers? Just give me a look at their books and I'm sure I can help them find plenty of other ways to avoid raising their prices. In the meantime, their workers will have more money to spend on goods and services. Isn't that the way Costco operates? Isn't that good for the economy? Wasn't that always the way in our economy before Wal-Mart? Of course. And now just one more question, as I'm pressed for time this evening."

Abe Simon of the *San Francisco Chronicle* elbowed his way out of the pack. "Mr. Price, you took on the biggest corporation in the world and beat it. Are you proud of what you did? And what's your encore?"

"I think a better word is 'pleased.' I'm immensely pleased that billions of dollars a year will be going to underpaid, overworked Wal-Mart employees and their families. As for encores, you all saw the Meliorist news conference on the fifth, I'm sure. The victory over Wal-Mart will energize millions of low-paid workers to roll up their sleeves and rally behind our Agenda for the Common Good, now pending before Congress. It may also energize the CEOs amassed against us behind their chosen warrior, Mr. Lobo. That remains to be seen. Thank you for coming on such short notice."

Sol wasn't trying to dodge the media when he said he was pressed for time. He was not about to rest on his laurels regarding Wal-Mart. He foresaw a rush of existing unions moving in on the Wal-Mart scene to organize this large population of downtrodden workers one store at a time or one supply depot at a time. Sol had his sights set on one national Wal-Mart union, independent of other unions and setting high standards for union democracy and membership participation.

He went straight home from the press conference and got on the phone with his field organizers and SWAT teams. He told them to stay in place on the ground, keep working with the support constituencies of existing and former Wal-Mart employees, and let the small businesses in the five communities sell off their inventory. His plan was to use his great prestige with the Wal-Mart workers to call a national organizing convention in Chicago in early August. His teams were to find two representatives from each Wal-Mart Superstore and associated installations to send to Chicago. Sol continued to work the phones for the next two hours, until he had lined up all the necessary legal, negotiating, and logistical personnel, including three respected veteran labor negotiators who agreed to chair the proceedings. At the closed-circuit briefings that night— the Secretariat had added an end-of-day wrap-up because of the pace of events—the Meliorists agreed to pay travel and hotel expenses for the nearly ten thousand Wal-Mart workers to the convention.

In his heyday as king of the major discount chains, Sol had chosen his management staff with care, interviewing them personally and peppering them with questions and hypotheticals before taking them on board. He was a master at delegating responsibility, so much so that his family jokingly accused him of abdication. But it had worked then, and it would work now, in this final chapter of the Wal-Mart revolution.

Friday was drop-in-the-hopper day for the Equity in the Distribution of Wealth bill, which was far more nuanced than its title suggested. The preamble narrated the grim facts about the widening gap in returns on capital as compared with labor. It took crisp note of the winner-take-all nature of the contemporary economy, which rewarded the concentration of power, not merit or hard work or even, in most instances, innovation. It outlined four causes of the concentration of power in corporations and in the wealthiest classes: first, the maldistribution of the tax burden through loopholes and the diversion of taxpayer dollars into corporate welfare giveaways that swelled the coffers of big companies whose stock was held largely by upper-income investors; second, the maldistribution of law enforcement, not just in underenforcement against corporate crime and fraud, but also in negotiating paltry cash settlements of the few corporate prosecutions that were undertaken, without any admission of wrongdoing or any sanction against the corporations; third, the government-corporate contracting complex, in which companies were allowed to keep patent rights to taxpayer-funded innovations and receive the unearned increment of government contracts—from surges in the value of land or licenses, for example—for other commercial and proprietary uses; and finally, the stupendous imbalance of political power, which was effectively in the hands of the giant corporations and gave them incalculable policy leverage on issues affecting their vested interests, such as the minimum wage and universal health insurance.

Following the bill's preamble were four sections paralleling these four causes with corrective legislation. What the Republican cosponsors liked about the legislation as a whole was that it would reduce the size of government, respect the use of tax dollars, crack down on corporate outlaws, and protect the public's property from being given away or sold for a fraction of its marketplace worth. They also liked the provision giving small business and regular people the same access to government as the big boys. They did not particularly care for Section Four, which provided for full public financing of federal elections, but they tolerated it because it was probably unconstitutional under the existing doctrine of "money is speech," and besides, they could probably lop it off during the give-and-take over the legislation should it move toward enactment. What they did not yet know but would shortly find out was that the progressives had put the public financing provision in several other bills in a form that would pass constitutional muster. Section Four was clever negotiating bait to give up in return for broader support from legislators. The bill's chief sponsor was not named Terrence Tradeoff for nothing.

Friday afternoon, as the corporate media was readying an all-out assault on the bill as "the mother of all class warfare legislation," the Meliorists blanketed the airwaves with the first of the series of ads they had prepared in anticipation of a Chicken Little scare campaign from their opponents. Lobo couldn't believe his eyes. He'd been scooped. He taped the Meliorist ads and watched them again and again, grudgingly admitting to himself that they were masterful—ingenious, penetrating, and insightful. Thank God he hadn't decided to pull the Commie ad, which would air in just a few hours on the local evening news nationwide. Once again his native combativeness would prevail. Lobo didn't need Max Palevsky to tell him what words-over-deeds travesty was about to unfold. He knew in his bones which story was going to lead the nightly television network news, and it wasn't going to be a bill proposing the most radical redistribution of wealth in the nation's history. It wasn't even going to be the Wal-Mart debacle. No, the slider was going in again, and the game was his.

In Waco, Texas, Bernard was at home with his wife watching the CBS Evening News when lo and behold, onto the screen came a picture of Papa wearing his trademark 1930s fedora, then a contemporary head shot of Bernard, and then a sequence of historical footage narrated in a menacing baritone with even more menacing background music. Then Bernard's picture filled the screen again, and the voice asked, "Would you entrust your future, your children's future, to this man?"

Bernard sat stunned on the couch as anchorman Rob Shiffer, having played free of charge most of the ad that had run commercially an hour ago, proceeded to provide the context—Bernard's appearance on *Oprah* back in January to promote his Egalitarian Clubs, the more recent activities of the Meliorists, the introduction of the Agenda—and then brought on the usual pro and con pundits. "It's about time to call a spade a spade. Billionaires in their dotage can afford to be communists as long as they get theirs before the vast wasteland comes to America," said Ima Wright of the Joseph McCarthy Memorial Institute. Hugh R. Knott of the Nelson Proxmire Center shook his finger at her. "When shady groups like the one behind this ad don't have the facts, they resort to smears. Bernard Rapoport is the capitalists' capitalist. He just wants to reduce the greed. He loved his father, who left this earth sixty-six years ago and was a peaceful man who abhorred violence."

"Yes!" exclaimed Bernard, jumping up and spilling a cup of tea on the rug.

"Yes!" echoed Audre.

The phone started to ring—the house phone, the cell phone, the private phone. Bernard picked up the private phone. It was a conference call from Luke Skyhi and Evan Evervescent, Barry's right-hand man at Promotions.

"You've seen the ad, Bernard?" Luke asked. "Unbelievable."

"Yes, I've seen it. Factually it's all accurate, except that Papa left Russia before the Soviet Union came into existence. If he was still around, he'd be having a ball answering these creeps. He had a lot of practice in the twenties and thirties when the Commie scare was growing."

"It's obviously too early to assess how damaging or distracting the ad will be in terms of the Agenda," Evan said, "but evening and late-night cable and radio are dominated by the right, so you can be sure they're going to run the string out on this. And you know they preach to the converted, so the call-ins will be even more vicious. Two questions: Do you want to respond to interview requests tonight and tomorrow? And should we put together a quick counter-ad? We just spoke to Hillsman a minute ago, and he's licking his chops."

"Well, you fellows are a lot younger and far more proficient in public relations than I am, but my instinct is just to make fun of . . . Who took credit for the ad anyway? That type at the bottom was too small for an old man to read."

Luke laughed. "Too small for anyone. It's some bullshit front group called For the USA, but we know from Bill Joy that Lance Lobo is behind it."

"Perfect," Bernard said. "Sure I'll do interviews, and I'll slam the ad for what it is: Wolfshit. How's that? Smother them with ridicule, laugh them out of the ballpark. Hell, even 'rednecks' aren't afraid of communists anymore—if they can find any. The scare word today is 'terrorists.' I don't think you should spend a dime on Hillsman. It'll blow over because I'll blow it through the roof. I've always wished more Americans could know about Papa, since he loved our country so much, even with all the warts he complained about daily. This is my chance, thanks to Wolfshit. Go ahead and set me up with the media. Let's do telephone interviews on radio for tonight and concentrate on television for tomorrow. Meanwhile, I'll send you a short statement for the morning papers so Lobo's handiwork doesn't get all the ink."

"Bernard, you are one cool dude," Luke said. "Okay, Evan and I will line up the interviews, and I'll put out a paragraph from the PCC mentioning, among other points, that you're a capitalist who makes a big deal of saying that capitalism doesn't have *enough* capitalists and that greedy giant business isn't good for any economy, any democracy, any society."

"Go to, Luke, put out whatever you want. All to the good. But this one is basically mine. Can you get Lobo to debate me?"

"Evan, what do you think?" Luke asked.

"I'll put out a challenge in your name right away, Bernard, and you can challenge him directly when you're on the air. I'm sure he won't welcome another outing. These guys thrive in the shadows, in the dark recesses of their executive suites."

"Oh, I'll challenge him all right. How's this? 'I hereby challenge Lancelot Lobo, the creator of this hilariously dirty ad campaign, to a debate. If he accepts, I'll unmask him as a corporate wolf in sheep's clothing. If he declines, I'll treat him to dinner: braised mutton with a side of fried timberwolf tongue.' Or will that get me in trouble with the animal rights folks?"

An image of a supercilious waiter setting a steaming plate in front of Lobo arose simultaneously in the three callers' minds, and they plunged into an involuntary laughing jag that lasted a good two minutes. Finally, Bernard managed to choke out, "This is better than exercise, boys. I feel so refreshed. I can actually feel my blood circulating."

"According to the latest medical findings, hard laughter is equiv-alent to vigorous exercise like running and swimming," said Luke, drawing on his immense knowledge of factoids, and going off into another aerobic peal.

"Get a grip, Luke," Evan said, but he was laughing too. He pulled himself together. "How long do you want to go this evening, Bernard? I want you to do the big stations for sure, but I don't want to ignore some of the smaller ones. We'll keep them all short."

"Hell, I could go all night, but let's say three hours with ten one-minute breaks interspersed through each hour so I can rest my voice and drink some water. Start in thirty minutes. I'll have a few words up to you by then. Hasta la vista."

Bernard hung up and went to his study, laughing all the way. He poured himself a glass of wine, sat down at his computer, and began typing.

> The claws of Lancelot Lobo ripped through national tele-vision screens a short while ago. Greased by fat-cat money, Lobo's jaws came down hard on truth and decency. Leave my beloved, long-departed father out of this fight for America's future, Lobo. Papa was a humble peddler who went door to door to support Mama and us three children. Yes, he was a communist, if a communist is someone who believes that working people and the downtrodden deserve the necessities of life, but he also thought that anything beyond that basic level of economic security was fair game for initiative and competition. He abhorred dictatorships and violence. He left Russia before it became the Soviet Union and turned communist theory into brutal totalitarianism. Call him a biblical Jewish com-

munist, because all his life he believed in the equality of mankind, equal justice, and an equal chance for everyone. Lobo, emerge from your den. I'm your full moon, and I challenge you to bay at me in a televised debate on the conditions so many Americans have to suffer and endure because of corporate domination of a puppet government. Debate me or go down in history as a corporate wolf in coward's clothing.

Bernard sat back and reviewed his statement. Satisfied, he e-mailed it to Luke and Evan, with a copy to his son Ronald, a professor of political science in Virginia. Then he took another sip of wine to fortify himself and spent the next three hours talking to three dozen interviewers, from Hawaii to Maine, from Alaska to Puerto Rico, who all wanted to find out whether he had any Commie DNA. He did the big right-wing shows, calmly answering questions from a lot of snarling callers and a few sympathetic ones, among them some of the "rednecks" from the Dallas rally. He lost no opportunity to regale his listeners with stories about Papa, his faith in hard work, his favorite proverbs and nuggets of wisdom, his *real* family values, his compassion for the down-and-out, his skepticism about party politicians, his belief in the creative spirit of rebels, whether political rebels or ordinary people who know that a lot of what they're supposed to believe just ain't so, and above all, his passion for justice. Whenever Bernard felt himself flagging, he thought about how much Papa loved a good argument and how proud he would have been of his son.

By the end of the night, even some of the most savage talk show hosts in the country had nothing but praise for Bernard. After all, he was a super-successful capitalist and philanthropist, a man who made his fortune by wit and work and knew the language of the people because he came from them. After a warm glass of milk with honey, Bernard crawled into bed and fell contentedly asleep beside Audre, ready for the next day's media hoedown.

In the morning, he rose at the crack of dawn to be ready for a live

TV special hosted from New York by Tatie Youric, queen of the weekday a.m. airwaves, soon-to-be network news anchor. Sitting comfortably in his study with the CBS cameras trained on him, Bernard spoke eloquently about Papa while Tatie nodded and waited for an opening to ask one of her hard-hitting questions. When Bernard paused to clear his throat, she said, "Your father sounds like a lovely man, Mr. Rapoport, but can you tell us about your own economic philosophy? Does it go beyond making billions by selling insurance?"

Bernard gave her a warm smile. "That's a good question, Tatie, and I'll answer it the way Papa would have, with a story. About a year ago I was having lunch with a top executive of Bank of America, and I was giving him an earful about the badness of bigness in business—nice phrase, with all that alliteration and sibilance, don't you think, Tatie? Feel free to use it. Anyway, he wasn't buying it, of course, so I said to him, 'Dexter'—let's call him Dexter, Tatie—I said to him, 'Dexter, if your bank gets into serious trouble, the federal government will bail you out with taxpayer money. You're so huge that you're on the Federal Reserve's too-big-to-fail list.' Now, Tatie, if instead of one giant dominant bank, there were twelve smaller banks and one of them was going down, the taxpayers wouldn't be required to save it because the other banks would pick up the business. And it isn't just about the taxpayers. If you want to put your money in a bank, or if a business does, it's natural to prefer the extra safety of Bank of America, which is backstopped by the US Treasury. The very size of an institution like that gives it an unfair competitive advantage over smaller banks, which have to sink or swim with nothing but FDIC insurance behind them. Does that philosophy sound 'Commie' to you, Tatie? The Bank of America is redder than Papa ever was, with Uncle Sam as its silent partner."

"Well," Tatie said briskly, "you make a point, Mr. Rapoport, but I'm afraid our time is up. Thank you. After the break, we'll be back with Sly Psikick, who has just broken the world record for eating the most sardines in fifteen minutes."

By midday on Sunday, after Bernard had made the rounds of all the press shows, there was nothing left of Lobo's seedy salvo except egg on his face. The CEOs had summoned him to a command performance first thing in the morning, and the media was besieging his office with calls about responding to Bernard's debate challenge. "Ignore them," he told Lawrence Nightingale. "It will only add fuel to the fire. It should be obvious even to a first-year PR major at Podunk U that I am not the issue."

Lobo was very much the issue around the conference table in the penthouse boardroom as the CEOs waited for him to arrive on Monday morning. When he did, they greeted him with a stony silence.

"Sit down, Lobo," CEO Cumbersome said curtly. "It appears that you started too late and are reaping the bitter fruits of the SROs' advance preparation and media savvy. The collapse of the Commie ad is most distressing. Our opponents beat us to the punch, perhaps in possession of some of your internal tactical memos. And the collapse of Wal-Mart, while in no way attributable to you, has added immeasurably to their momentum and to the morale of the masses. There are grounds for dismay around this table. What do you have to say for yourself?"

Lobo rose and squared his shoulders. If there was ever a time for inner steel, this was it. "May I remind you, Jasper, that you signed off on the ad. Clever as Rapoport's response was, the seeds of doubt have been sown, and will flourish with the rollout of Wave Two later today. Our congressional allies are about to meet with the president to synchronize our opposition to the SRO avalanche of legislation and regulatory petitions. I've whipped the laggard trade and professional groups into a semblance of shape behind us. But the bottom line, as I've said time and again, is all of you. You're the only ones who can galvanize your immensely powerful but complacent corporate brethren. I've just recently crossed the aisle. They don't know me well, and they don't trust me. I'm your facilitator, your adviser, your agitator, and your cover for derring-do, but you're the armored division, the heavy lifters in Washington, the know-how. You're going to have to go all out with your power and prestige, and in the final analysis you're going to have to put yourselves on the front lines mano-a-mano with the Meliorists.

"It takes two hands to clap. Your hand is invisible, and while that may be fine in the world of Adam Smith, it's phantom suicide for your declared mandate to me. Even if you raise five times the two billion you've pledged, you won't be able to buy your way out of the SRO vortex. For the first time in your lucrative lives, your money will not be enough. If Bernard Rapoport hadn't gone out head and heart first, our Commie ad wouldn't have been shredded in twenty-four hours. Do I make myself clear?" Lobo asked with a withering look, then sat down and folded his arms across his chest.

An uncomfortably long silence ensued. The CEOs fidgeted. They had expected contrition from Lobo, not aggression. Their expressions reflected embarrassment, indignation, discomfort, resentment, and wariness, with an occasional flash of grudging recognition. Finally Hubert Bump, who hadn't said a word all month, rose slowly from his chair.

"My fellow CEOs, Lobo speaks the truth, disagreeable as he may be. In the face of an external threat like communism, we all know what it takes to get the masses and the politicians behind us, but this is a seismic revolt from within, a revolt from the very top by business peers who have seized our controlling ideology and turned it against us. We're done for if we think we can prevail merely by beefing up the old war chest and redoubling the old battle plans. To effect the counterrevolution, we must revolutionize ourselves. We must go where no business leaders have gone before, do what no business leaders have done before, and above all think like no business leaders have thought before. The debacle of the past weekend that has catapulted Bernard Rapoport to fame and made him a national hero illustrates perfectly the old way of thinking. We set out to red-bait a billionaire who made it the hard way, by his bootstraps, more Horatio Alger than Horatio himself. Who were we kidding?

"Soon the second wave will be underway—scare 'em out of their wits. It may slow the speeding train a little—to our financial disadvantage, incidentally, and not only in the stock markets—but what if it doesn't stop the train? Then we're left with the desperation stand at the Khyber Pass, and even if we win on the Hill, we're assured of losing, both on Election Day and in terms of the SRO Agenda next year. And then where are we? Where is Lobo? What's left of our dominion, our reputation among our peers and countrymen? With or without our consent, our identities will be made public shortly. First impressions are critical. Do we hide and confirm the public's worst suspicions about how we use our formidable powers, or do we step forth with strength of purpose, real concern for the issues, and a healthy dose of humility?

"All my life people have made fun of my name, and I can't blame them. Who would name a child Hubert Bump? But the teasing hurt, almost destroyed me—you know how cruel kids can be—so when I was twelve, I told my parents that I wanted to change my name. It was then that they showed me their greatness. Mom and Dad sat me on the couch between them, put their arms around me, dried my tears, and told me about my ancestors on my mother's Hubert side and my father's Bump side, a long line of people who fought for our country, founded great enterprises, created jobs, became explorers and inventors. Did my valorous forebears allow their names to hinder them? What would they say from the heavens if they could see me now? 'Hubert,' my dad told me that day on the couch, 'always remember what Great-grandfather Silas Bump used to say. "The great ones turn adversity into success." Adversity into success, Hubert. Being teased about your name doesn't even come close to adversity. You're not sick, you're not bleeding, you're not dim, you're not poor, cold, hungry, and homeless. You're Hubert Bump, and you will rise to unprecedented heights on the shoulders of all the Huberts and Bumps before you.'

"Those words changed my life. As you know, I kept my name and went on to some success in the scientific, academic, and business worlds. What my parents did for me we must now do for ourselves. Facing demoralization and disaster, we must turn ourselves around and ask this question: What is the purpose of big business if it is not to deliver an economy that provides sufficient livelihoods, a safe environment, and yes, even 'liberty and justice for all'? You may say that these objectives are not our responsibility, that our only responsibility is to run productive businesses and make a profit for our investors. That is a myth of a bygone age. Let us not deceive ourselves. We run this country. We own this government. We control capital, labor, technology, we shape expectations, and we can pick up our marbles and go overseas if any force defies us here. That is, until now. We must live in the present, not in our nearly omnipotent past. And living in the present, seeing what's coming over the ramparts right now, can we not think more grandly of our functions?

"Since January I have been closely studying and analyzing the activities and groundbreaking challenges of the SROs, the resources they have committed both in money and personal capital. If the rest of you have to hit your heads against this advancing wall in the next few weeks to learn the lesson I've learned, go right ahead. You're certainly on track to do just that. But I repeat: first impressions are lasting impressions, and first losses tend to multiply themselves. Consider these words well at this juncture when our saturation scare campaign is about to flow into millions of living rooms."

There was another long silence. CEO Roland Revelie broke it. "Hubert, thank you for your deeply felt and eloquently conveyed expressions. I'm sure all of us can read between your lines. I have always respected your intellect and your ability to connect theory with practice, but there are times when profound insight breeds pessimism and pessimism breeds unintended folly. As I listened to you, I couldn't help wondering why you didn't make this presentation at one of our earlier meetings. You speak flatteringly of our power, but whose power is it? Even conceding a new direction, we are merely a self-selected ad hoc group of concerned executives."

"If I catch the drift of the exchange between our two distinguished colleagues," said Wardman Wise, "the current situation presents us with a constructive hiatus to observe and deliberate, as long as the spotlight for the second wave and the media reaction to it shines on the Washington lobbies, PR firms, and law firms. That will give us a respite during which to make a considered evaluation from the sidelines. I don't think the Washington lobbies will mind in the least taking credit for the second wave. What say you, Lobo?"

After the pummeling he'd taken in recent weeks, Lobo was ready for a hiatus. "I believe that can be arranged, and I think it's warranted, because it gives us two bites of the apple if we're really going to consider revising our strategy along the revolutionary lines suggested by Mr. Bump. I believe that's the subtext to what I heard just now, but you may not want to get into it with me presently. That is at your discretion, and I am at your service."

"Thank you, Lobo," CEO Cumbersome said. "We are all absorbing the subtext right now, but I don't think any of us wants to open that door at this time. Do I reflect the sense of the meeting?"

Most of the CEOs were too perplexed and alarmed by the unexpected turn of the discussion to do anything but murmur their concurrence.

"Very well, we are adjourned," Cumbersome said.

"By the way, Lobo was right about *On Leadership*. Read it," Norman Noondark added as Lobo was making his exit.

Back at his office, Lobo heaved a sigh of relief. He knew it was a gamble to come on so strong with the CEOs, but it had paid off and won him an unlikely ally in the person of Hubert Bump. Now all he had to do was steer the Washington lobbyists as per his instructions. He'd already worked with them extensively to get them on board, but to finish the job he'd need a Washington insider. He called Brovar Dortwist.

"I've just come from headquarters, Brovar, and I need you to head up our Washington office to strengthen and accelerate the Washington lobbies' opposition to the SROs. You won't believe the budget and staff you'll have."

"What took you so long, Lobo? The money may be in New York City, but the political power is here in DC. Why don't you come down pronto so we can discuss design and implementation?"

"Fine, how about Wednesday?" Lobo said.

"How about tomorrow?" said Brovar.

Meanwhile, as if Lobo and Wal-Mart and the subtext weren't enough to contend with, the CEOs learned upon returning to their offices that the greatest proposed shift of power since the Constitution and the Bill of Rights was heading toward public hearings in the House and Senate Judiciary Committees in the form of the last two bills of the Meliorist Agenda.

The first of them, the Electoral Reform Bill, was essentially the longstanding menu of reforms advocated by citizen groups for years but never passed. The bill called for public financing of campaigns, uniform and less restrictive ballot access rules, publicly sponsored debates, broadcast licensing adjustments to give all ballot-qualified candidates free airtime for six weeks before Election Day, elimination of the Electoral College, binding none-of-the-above for each ballot line, and a voting age of sixteen. Standing-to-sue rights for all citizens seeking to enforce the bill's provisions on a fast track because of election deadlines were also mandated.

The second bill, grandly called the Expansion of Dynamic Democracy Act, lived up to its name with its detailed provisions for an across-the-board shift of power from the few to the many. It interpreted the Constitution as authorizing an affirmative governmental duty to cultivate the political and civic energies of the people. The constitutional theory came from a little book crisply titled *"Here, the People Rule,"* by distinguished Harvard law professor Richard Parker, and the preamble to the legislation, written by Dick Goodwin, would have made Thomas Jefferson proud. It explained clearly the functional relationship between democracy and what people want out of life. It detailed all the various levels of democracy from national elections right down to community spirit and individual aspiration. It distinguished between rights and duties, freedom and power, civic motivation and personal indulgence. It argued for the claims that true democracies have to make on the time and talents of their citizens if government is to work for their well-being. Finally, it spoke of civic personality—that crucial trait that moves the aware mind to determined action.

The preamble was followed by the text of the actual legislation, which ran to several pages in the *Congressional Record*.

SECTION ONE: Every citizen of the United States, of any age, shall have legal standing to pursue claims in courts of federal jurisdiction without limit or exemption, whether private or public in nature, whether filed against the government or private persons.

SECTION TWO: Corporations, partnerships, and legal associations of any kind shall not be deemed "persons" for purposes of applying or interpreting the US Constitution. "Person" is hereby defined by law as "human being."

SECTION THREE: The government of the United States, through its departments, agencies, and federally delegated authorities and incorporations such as the US Postal Service, shall facilitate affirmatively, and with all deliberate speed, opportunities for the citizenry to organize themselves vis-à-vis the mandates, activities, and pursuits of such departments, agencies, and delegated authorities. These civic associations shall be independent of government and open to all, with reasonable annual dues not to exceed $50. Their boards of directors shall be duly elected in accordance with bylaws promulgated by the Federal Trade Commission within six months of the enactment of this legislation. The Congress shall revisit this mandate each year through public hearings and reports in both the House of Representatives and the Senate.

SECTION FOUR: All public corporations and their associated entities with revenues exceeding $1 billion a year shall provide well-promoted checkoffs so that their shareholders, customers, and workers can form voluntary associations to represent their collective interests in all public arenas where policy, grievances, and suggestions are considered. "Public arenas" are defined as the courts, the legislatures, the executive branch agencies, and all forums for mediation, voluntary arbitration, and the settling of disputes, be they governmental or corporate.

SECTION FIVE: Intermediary institutions shall be established to facilitate the organization of workers vis-à-vis their pension fund managers, and of viewers and listeners vis-à-vis their television and radio stations. There shall be similar facilitation of organized popular access to and participation in the control of commonwealth assets owned by the people, including the natural resources on public lands and the government's intellectual property.

SECTION SIX: The federal government shall require the public elementary and secondary schools receiving federal funds to introduce civic curriculums that engage students in the public life of their communities and their nation, and shall provide funding for such curriculums. The objective of this section is to graduate students with a broad array of civic skills and knowledge to match the demands and opportunities of a deliberative democratic society in the 21st century.

Unlike the reaction to previous Agenda bills, the media response to the electoral reform and democracy legislation was "Dullsville." Replacing the two-party elected dictatorship, abolishing the farce of an Electoral College that allowed a presidential candidate to lose the popular vote and win the election, giving the vote to young people who could legally work and drive a car, empowering the people to take control of every aspect of their government and their public life—nope, just not sexy enough. But Promotions had anticipated the media's big ho-hum, and when viewers all over the country turned on their TVs on Monday evening, there was Patriotic Polly. Over a running caption with capsule highlights of the two bills and lists of federal phone numbers, the famous parrot squawked, "Build democracy! It's only your life!" Polls commissioned by the Meliorists a few days later found that "Dullsville" had a higher public awareness level than all the other bills except for health insurance and a living wage.

Tuesday morning, the president of the United States left the Oval Office unobtrusively and went over to the old Indian Treaty Room, where so many promises had been made to Native American tribes and subsequently broken. Sitting around the large table were his key allies in the House and Senate, the core congressional enforcers of the corporate government, so trusted by the plutocracy that there was no need for any direct corporate presence.

Everyone rose as the president entered the room. "Sit yourselves down, boys," he said with an impatient wave. "Listen, the White House switchboard is flooded. All the operators are hearing is Agenda, Agenda, Agenda—support the Agenda, pass the Agenda. The country's going bananas. Are you getting the same heat on the Hill?"

"We are, Mr. President," said Senator Frisk. "Same thing with the congressional switchboard, same with our office phones and e-mail traffic. People are even flooding us with letters because they can't get through electronically. Quaint. But remember, we're still in control. Sure, we're conceding hearings to our pro-Agenda colleagues all this month, but they and we know the parliamentary rules. The issue is whether we want to win by impasse or by counterattack. The difference is highly consequential for the near and foreseeable future, as I think you'll agree."

"What makes you think we have the luxury of that choice, Senator?" asked Congressman Bullion. "Sure, in your body you have the filibuster and other forms of delay foreign to our procedures in the House, but read your history. Populist revolts have swept over Washington with far less organization, money, and high-powered backing than what's looming over us presently. The country has been on fire for some months now, and the flames are leaping higher and higher. You saw the response to the events of the Fourth and the Meliorists' news conference and the Rapoport ad. You saw the Wal-Mart announcement. You saw—"

"Enough, Bullion," snapped Senator Tweedy. "Why prejudge the fire this time either way? Why not develop ways to test it? No point running scared. Our CEO friends have just unleashed their media counterattack, and those ads are doozies. There's plenty of money and corporate clout behind them, both directly and from the whole K Street crowd here. The corporate fellows have had it pretty easy for so long that they may be surprised at their own power when they're up against the wall."

"Well put, Senator," said Congressman Beauchamp. "Let's see how the hearings play out but remain on full alert and stay close to the lobbies, without whom—let's be frank—we wouldn't be here right now. We owe it to them to give them a chance with their own counterattack before we say anything about an impasse strategy."

"Billy's right," said the president, "and time is on our side. There aren't too many legislative days left in the session, and the upcoming elections are starting to absorb everyone. And who knows, a hurricane here, a flood there, and before you can say 'adjourned,' the year is up."

"And what then, Mr. President?" asked Senator Thinkalot. "It could get worse next year, much worse, because the public will be angry over an impasse and there may be quite a different Congress."

"Well, you know my motto for political success: Take one year at a time. Foresight is great, but without myopia, you can't get across a busy street."

All joined in hearty laughter, the members from Texas slapping their thighs as if they'd come straight from Central Casting.

"I reckon you're right, Mr. President," said Congressman Bullion, "but if you ask me, we still can't go wrong with the old Boy Scout motto: Be prepared."

"I guess that pretty much sums it up, Bullion," the president said. "Let's adjourn to the dining room."

CHAPTER 14

The battle of July was well and truly joined both in Washington and throughout the country. Congressional hearings on the Agenda legislation were underway in the House and Senate, with witnesses ranging from academic experts to think-tank apologists to business lobbyists. Each hearing gave prime time to testimony from affected Americans. The progressives demanded and received an end to the predawn practice of lobbyists hiring stand-ins to save seats for them. Seating was now reserved for ordinary citizens, families of those testifying, and of course the media, which packed the tables along the sides of the room. The denizens of the Hill were always exceptionally quickened by what they perceived to be "new energy" from the hustings. It had happened when the evangelicals mobilized in 1980, and it was happening now with the SROs and the immensely layered activity of the folks back home in support of the Agenda. The solons had never seen so many varied eruptions among their constituents, not to mention the phone calls from very rich people singing the songs of the SROs. Members of Congress were used to dealing with one-issue groups, and their usual responses weren't adaptable to wave upon wave of informed and motivated human energy. No pundits or professors or anyone else, including the pompous pollsters, had come close to predicting what was now transpiring, not even the acclaimed Zogby outfit, which went where other polling companies feared to tread.

At the same time, the salvos and the pressure from the business side were going through the Capitol Dome. In the normal course of congressional legislation, controversy was more or less confined to the specific interest groups with the most at stake, but this Agenda tumult had all the corporate lobbies fully staffed and media-budgeted, and all the PACs writing checks to legislators right and left. No Washington summer doldrums this year. The taxi and limousine business had never been so good. The trendy restaurants and bars were brimming with customers. Hotels were overbooked. Flights to National Airport and Dulles were full day after day. The media hired new hands and forked out overtime as they battled one another for scoops, leaks, and gossip. The lights in the K Street buildings and congressional offices stayed on late into the night.

Out in Omaha, the Secretariat was putting the finishing touches on a Geographic Information System (GIS) for the Meliorists, under the brilliant tutelage of GIS pioneer Jack Mangermond. Software layer after software layer provided minute-to-minute visual locations on the rallies, marches, lectures, CUB events, and Congressional Watchdog activities. The system was a kind of master matrix created from ingenious data patterns that allowed the Meliorists and their project managers to absorb at a glance what was happening when and where. For example, there were maps of each state and congressional district showing the number of legislators for, against, or neutral on each bill of the Agenda. Another map broke down PAC contributions to members of Congress by geographical region. An enormously useful tool and time-saver, GIS was a hit with Promotions, Analysis, Recruitment, Mass Demonstrations, and all the rest of the Meliorists' far-flung projects, which each turned it to their own distinct purposes. The managers fed the system additional information to be geographically modeled, and got GIS patterns on their adversaries wherever the data permitted. All in all, they were light-years ahead of the corporatists in spotting trends, causes and effects, weak spots, gaps and imbalances that required corrective action.

At the end of the first week of Agenda hearings, Warren suggested that the Meliorists pay courtesy visits to selected members of Congress, one on one, without publicity if possible. His colleagues seconded the idea and began dropping in at the House and

Senate in the evening to confer individually with two or three members. These visits gave the Meliorists an opportunity for personal contact and direct appraisal that they couldn't get through intermediaries or from the public record. The arrangement suited the legislators too. They didn't want the distractions or burdens that an impulsive press might generate, and they were flattered by the attention, especially from Paul, Phil, Bill Cosby, Warren, Yoko, and the other more famous Meliorists. The visits served to strengthen backbones on the Hill and were generally so successful that the Meliorists decided to meet with the legislators back home in more leisurely settings during the August recess. Meanwhile, Zabouresk and Zeftel, the Double Z team, was all over Capitol Hill, assessing, assessing, assessing, breaking the legislators down into categories of yes, no, and leaning one way or the other, feeding back in microdetail which members needed what kind of carrot or stick, what kinds of people were calling on them, what kind of press needed to be nudged.

Donald Ross and his Congress Watchdogs were in overdrive too. Always looking over the next hill and anticipating what would be needed at crunch time, Ross was zeroing in on the reelection campaigns of the entrenched incumbents most likely to block the Agenda legislation. In the coming months, these Bulls were sure to hunker down in their home districts and states and cater to their voter base to firm it up. They would expect to lose the liberals and the left, but they couldn't afford to lose their traditional constituency, which included the Reagan Democrats, white working-class males who had made the difference in one presidential and senatorial race after another. Knowing that one defecting voter had more impact on an incumbent than four who voted against the incumbent, Ross developed a sophisticated software program to screen out those voters most likely to defect. Then the local Watchdog groups would go to work on them person to person, at living room meetings and potluck suppers, in beer halls and bowling alleys, during softball games and Saturday morning hikes. The goal was to develop a corps of voters who could go to their particular Bull and say, "We've been your supporters for years, but it's time for a change. Make it happen and you'll be our hero." Careful advance work would be required—for instance, making sure the press got wind of a potentially disastrous margin of defections and conducted the appropriate interviews—but the most important predicate was already in place: new energy. Nothing startled and spooked an entrenched politician more than new sources of civic energy or old civic energy turning a new corner.

The congressional hearings continued throughout the month, with all the attendant publicity and lobbying. There were some lively TV and radio debates, and even midnight vigils in honor or in criticism of specific members of the Senate or the House. Millions of people started to give this historic confrontation the attention usually reserved for major sporting events. Millions of others were contributing in their own ways to this movement for an unprecedented shift of power behind the needs of the American people. Mass attention bred more mass attention. As ever more members of Congress registered their support for the various Agenda bills, the Watchdogs organized large rallies to praise them so loudly and publicly that it would be political suicide for them to change their minds.

By the beginning of the third week of July, the corporate scare campaign was reaching just about everyone who turned on the television or radio. With the Agenda legislation under close public scrutiny day after day, Lobo's Wave Two became more targeted, with a barrage of thirty- and sixty-second spots attacking specific proposals in the various bills. The bond market began to get the jitters, and the stock market went into a very gradual but noticeable slide. The business press, which was not all on the same page, reported first the possible impact on "business confidence," then the likely impact on "the business climate," then actual announcements by CEOs that their companies were rethinking their investments in the United States.

Well before the emotional meeting with Lobo that led to Bump's excursus, the CEOs had been busy lining up companies that would announce, whether it was true or not, that they were moving plants or facilities overseas because of the "instability" allegedly caused by the revolt of the SROs. It was an old ploy, based on the theory that fear repeated over and over again creates its own facts and breeds its own rationalizations. Not to be outdone, Bill Hillsman floated over the airwaves short messages featuring similar scare-mongering claims that had been made by the business barons of the nineteenth and twentieth centuries about the abolition of slavery and child labor, the doubling of Ford workers' pay to $5 a day, the creation of Medicare and Social Security, and the issuance of auto safety regulations. The coarseness of the business alarms before each of these steps forward for America stunned television and radio audiences. Hillsman dramatized just how fraudulent, mean, and wrong the claims were at the time, and all the more so when viewed from the vantage point of the present. Each ad ended with a rhetorical question and answer: "Have you been watching similar scare tactics on your television set lately? Let's repeat history and toss the lies away."

Out on the hustings, the candidates of the Clean Elections Party were starting to turn the screws on the incumbent Bulls, who were having trouble adjusting to another kind of "instability"—the possibility of their defeat at the polls. For years they had walked effortlessly to reelection in their one-party districts and states, the other major party having long ago decided that it was a waste of money to field a candidate against a certain landslide. Running unopposed had become run-of-the-mill for the Bulls. Now the CEP was moving into the vacuum and becoming the number two party in these districts gerrymandered to the advantage of either the Republicans or the Democrats.

Well-funded, well-advised, and well-organized, the hyper-motivated CEP candidates found receptive audiences everywhere for their message about the abuses and lost opportunities stemming from public elections funded privately, by greed, as compared with the virtues of public elections funded publicly, by principle. Although the party strictly observed an organizational separation from the Meliorists, there was a policy-by-policy, solution-by-solution parallelism between its campaigning and the Redirections projects, a mutually reinforcing relationship that worked to the benefit of both sides. The CEP web-site was getting more and more hits, which produced more and more donations. Its candidates were moving up in the polls and getting more press, which brought them to the attention of more voters, which further upped the polls. Soon they were sufficiently visible in neighborhood after neighborhood to issue credible debate challenges to the incumbents.

The candidates were by far the CEP's most valuable asset. They were congenial, knowledgeable, caring, and creative. They were people like Willy Champ. They were people like Rachel Simmons, a fifty-two-year-old accountant for a large food distribution charity in Orlando, Florida. She was unusually gregarious for a bean counter and had run successfully for three terms on the local board of edu-cation. She wanted to aim higher but recoiled at the shredding of conscience and candor required by campaign fundraising. She kept up to date on the political scene, paid her annual dues to a half dozen reform organizations, and waited for an opportunity that she doubted would ever come. One day she got a call from a CEP organ-izer asking her to come to a small exploratory meeting, but only if she was truly interested in becoming a candidate. One thing led to another, and soon she found herself running against Congressman Charles Carefree, an incumbent Bull who had held his seat since 1968. Years of frustration erupted into waves of energy as Rachel vowed to meet every adult in the district.

The Bulls were at first slow to react to the CEP challenge, but during July some of them started running ads on local television extolling their irreplaceable pork-laden incumbency—a highway here, a public building there, a clinic here, a dam repair there. They began going home on weekends to slap backs and pick up babies for the photographers. To their chagrin, people would come up to them and say things like, "Hi, Earl, haven't seen you around here in ages." The Bulls were alarmed by such remarks, a sign of sinister trends in the making, and resented the time they had to spend on unaccustomed travel. It was hot and sweaty out there on the cam-paign trail, and they still had to deliver for their patrons back in

Washington. They began to wonder if they were up to the double duty. If one duty had to go, the path of least resistance told them to stay in Washington, where they had their comfortable homes, all the privileges of office, and social circles happy to defer to them. Meanwhile, the CEP candidates, hungry and full of zeal, kept coming and coming up the long, steep hill.

As a matter of mutual defense, the Bulls formed an alliance across party lines. They called it the Maginot Club, and they met in one of the many secluded, unmarked offices deep in the Capitol building, a nicely appointed room where the chairs were comfortable and drinks from the well-stocked bar were readily at hand. There, every other day at 7:00 p.m., they assembled to assess the situation vis-à-vis the Meliorists and recalibrate themselves for the next day. One of their first acts was to call their favorite lobbyist, Brovar Dortwist, who had quickly assumed leadership of all the Washington lobbies whether the lobbies liked it or not.

"Brovar," said Senator Thinkalot, "we're on a short time leash, so we have to get right down to business. We're pretty well up on what the lobbies are doing and how they're doing it, but what we need is a daily gauge of the effect they're having on our colleagues, on the media, and on the people back home. Are they getting the Rotary Club and Kiwanis types? Are they waking Main Street up to the SRO peril, and if so, in what specific ways beyond the usual rumbles? Let's face it, Brovar. For all their sound and fury, for all their daily talking points, the lobbies are basically lazy, egotistical bureaucracies. They've had it too easy for too many years—just like us, I suppose."

"Couldn't have given myself better marching orders, Senator. We're right on course, and we're going seven days a week. I've got a big Rolodex full of influential people all over the country, not just inside the Beltway, and it's getting the exercise of its inanimate life, you can rest assured. But on your end, Senator, you need to line up some witnesses besides the usual think-tank and trade group types. I'm sure you've seen the CEOs' scare ads about the 'business climate' and companies pulling up stakes, and that's fine as far as it goes, but you need some real workers up there testifying about losing their jobs, you need some ordinary Americans who'll have to pay more taxes or higher prices or whatever because of the Agenda. It shouldn't be too hard to find them and get them up to snuff and up on the Hill for the hearings."

"Just what I was thinking, Brovar," said Congressman Carefree. "The SROs have witnesses like that telling their sob stories every day, and it's working. We need their counterparts. Get a hold of the Falwell folks and have them canvass their huge Sunday morning flocks."

"I'll do that, Congressman," Brovar said, and for another thirty minutes he and the Bulls exchanged information and talked about how best to fortify the Maginot Line against the populist Leviathan.

When he got off the phone, Brovar felt elated and increasingly in charge. He loved a good fight, especially one he'd been warning about before anyone else in his camp. He recalled how the trade association flacks scoffed at him at that meeting back in March and carried the day with their "We're still completely in charge, no losses in sight" mantra. Now, with the capitulation of Wal-Mart, they were changing their tune. They were feeling the tremors, and they were far more receptive to Brovar, even humble.

Like the Meliorists, Brovar was always thinking ahead. He was known to have prepared and distributed a thirty-year plan to shrink government to the point that it could be "flushed down the toilet." Consistency wasn't his strong suit—he favored a large, powerful military, for example, which couldn't exactly be funded by passing the hat—but he fancied himself a seer. Whenever he had to take his mind "further down the pike," as he put it, he would go for an evening stroll by the Tidal Basin with his Doberman, Get'em, no matter what the season. Tonight was one of those times.

As he walked along with Get'em alert at his side, sniffing the air for muggers or possibly squirrels, Brovar posed himself a question out loud. "What if the Bulls were facing certain defeat in November unless they relented and dropped their blockade of the Agenda?"

"Ruff," said Get'em.

Brovar gave him a pat on the head. "Rough is right, boy, but you know what I'd do?"

Get'em cocked his head and pricked up his ears.

"I'd ask my business pals to offer them lucrative jobs in their forced retirement, with plenty of free time for family and recreation. That way they could block and go down as martyrs for free enterprise."

Brovar doubted it would come to such a drastic crossroads, but he had to start preparing for it now, for two reasons. First, the offers had to be made well in advance so that no one could say they were quid pro quos—deniability, with the calendar dates to prove it. Second, Lobo had floated some on-the-edge battlefield ideas during their New York meeting, and Brovar didn't want to be implicated in any such extremism. A jobs program for the Bulls would protect him and keep Lobo from going over the legal line when Capitol Hill went white-hot in the final days, or so Brovar hoped.

There was one more contemplation that occupied him that evening along the Tidal Basin. Not all of the Meliorists' bills were objectionable to him. In particular, the elimination of corporate welfare appealed to a deep feeling he had always harbored about the hypocrisy of big business spouting free enterprise and pocketing tax dollars on the dole. While it was usually easier to hold a diverse coalition together by opposing everything slam-bang, these were not usual times, so why not win one for the Brovar? He was more consistent than most about his economic ideology in a town full of forked-tongued corporatists who wanted to milk big government for the goodies instead of cutting it down to size. In the give-and-take over the various bills, conceding a significant plank in the Agenda might help to defeat many of the others.

Get'em was straining at his leash. "Okay, boy, let's go home. Halima has a delicious Arabic dinner waiting for us. She knows how much you like raw kibbee with pine nuts."

While Brovar was strategizing about the nation's future with Get'em, Phil Donahue was at Promotions headquarters doing his daily scan of the GIS maps and marveling at the multiplying energy levels portrayed so vividly. Behind the dots and patterns were human beings. More and more of them were getting on radio and TV and having their say in the newspapers and weekly magazines. Some were even being profiled in the style pages.

One of those dots was Arlene Jones, the Pennsylvania truck-stop waitress who'd been following the activities of the billionaire rebels ever since she saw Phil on the news back in January. Like millions of Americans, she'd been captivated by Patriotic Polly and intrigued by some of the other early initiatives of the core group, but at first she thought it was all just a gag, a kind of ongoing senior reality show. Into April and May, she realized these billionaires meant it. They weren't fooling around. Week by week, she noticed the usually profane small talk at the Treezewood turning into conversations about where the country was heading and the ruckus those "super-rich old guys" were creating. Never had she expected the truckers to talk about anything serious, other than their own personal or business woes.

Arlene began discussing the old guys and their ideas with her customers, friends, and neighbors. She collected clippings and reports. She logged onto some of the Redirectional websites. She soon found out who her congressman and two senators were, and began writing them letters. She went to a couple of rallies in Pittsburgh and Philadelphia on weekends. Her address book filled up, and at age forty-four, unmarried, she found her formerly humdrum life transformed.

In mid-June, Mason Fluery, reputed to be one of the best of the crop of lecturers drawing crowds around the country, came to a town near Arlene's home. She went to hear him with some likeminded friends. His energy was infectious, his words full of practicality. He argued that the people had the power against big business, but only if they organized and moved. Moved! Economic justice in this country was long overdue and was no more than what was owed to the people for all their hard work. After the lecture, Mason invited the audience to a get-together at a local restaurant. He knew it would be a smaller crowd—parents had to get home to their children—but that would help create a more intimate bond with the movement he was speaking for day after day. Mason urged them to join a CUB or a Congress Watchdog Group, if they hadn't already. "The whole country is waking up," he said. "Be part of its history."

On the drive home, Arlene's old Chevy was filled with excitement and energy as she and her friends discussed the lecture and the points Mason had made. "Hey," she said suddenly, "I've got an idea for a slogan." Less than a month later, that slogan was rippling on parade banners across the nation: "What's the Big Deal About the Agenda's Fair Deals? We Earned Them!"

Among the GIS dots on the other side of the country were Arnie Johnson and Alfonso Garcia, the McMansion day workers who'd watched Warren Beatty's bus caravan of billionaires with such skepticism back in February. As the weeks passed, they saw that Beatty was serious about taking on the Governator, and that a bunch of other super-rich guys were serious about taking on the whole system. Soon Arnie and Alf were talking more politics than sports, with their greatest scorn reserved for black and Hispanic politicians spouting off about the poor, and especially the black and Hispanic members of Congress.

"Look at those cats," Arnie said to Alf one afternoon in April. "They got it made. They raise their own pay, give themselves great benefits. Health insurance, life insurance, pensions—you name it, they got it. Safe districts, no worries about anything except getting away with fooling the folks in the hood. Same with your people, sucking up to the big boys, letting some business bucks to the charities shut them up. Man, after all the struggle over the years to get the vote, what do we have to show but a bunch of silk-talking, kowtowing Uncle Toms and Tio Tacos?"

"You said it, amigo. Those pendejos got it so made they do nothing about conditions in their own barrios, nothing about all the slumlords, loan sharks, crappy storefronts, cruddy food, dirty streets, violent crime—ah, where do you start and where do you end? But now, with the super-rich hombres, there is esperanza.

There's a big huelga on the way for justicia por el pueblo. Si se puede! Those viejos are driving los ricos loco. It's getting so I can't wait for the news every night. Hey, want the rest of my second burrito? Do I have to ask? They don't call you Arnie the Appetite for nothing."

By May, Arnie and Alf were veterans of the lunchtime rallies, leading the chants and yelling out their reactions to the speakers. It made them feel part of something powerful and exciting, and they didn't mind the free lunch either. With all the uncertainty of working from job to job, you forgot that you had a voice, you counted, you could be part of a movement for justice. These mansion jobs weren't unionized, and the construction boss could toss you aside if he didn't like the color of your shoes. So you learned the right tone of voice and the right demeanor—just short of "Yes, massa"—you learned to swallow any complaint or injury, you learned to keep your mouth shut about shoddy materials and sloppy workmanship.

What Arnie and Alf heard at the rallies stayed with them. They hadn't known that the multimillionaires who contracted for these mega-mansions paid a smaller percentage in taxes on their stock and dividend income than the two friends paid on their construction wages. As one impassioned speaker had said, "You sweat and pay more. They sit and pay less. All they do is make money from money, and that doesn't help working folks. It doesn't help the sick and the poor. It doesn't help anyone but those who don't need any help." Over the weeks, Alf and Arnie widened their circle of friends. They joined up when the Congress Watchdog organizers came around. They went to a training meeting with lecturer Carlos Cruz, learned how to sharpen their arguments, and picked up literature in English and Spanish. They talked up the Agenda in their neighborhoods and asked for meetings with their members of Congress and the State Assembly. They sought out blue-collar stiffs who'd voted for politicians who turned around and voted with the corporate boys once they were in Washington or Sacramento. If reason and facts didn't work, Alf and Arnie weren't above resorting to shame. "You've been rolled, guys," they'd say. "Are you just going to stand there and take it?" It turned out that a lot of them weren't.

Mason Fluery and Carlos Cruz and the other lecturers were responsible for connecting a lot of those dots on the GIS map. There were now 1,400 full-time lecturers, backed by an organizing staff of 650. The Meliorists weren't about to make the same mistake Clinton had back in 1993-94, when fewer than fifty people were going around the country trying to organize voters behind his misbegotten health insurance legislation. With the organizers scheduling the lecturers at one venue after another, and with the lecturers becoming media-famous in their own right, each of them spoke to an average of a thousand people a day, all kinds of people, across the whole American spectrum, at high school and college auditoriums, at Elks, Knights of Columbus, Grange, and union halls, at VFW and American Legion posts, at every conceivable gathering place. Daily, more than a million people were listening to the lecturers talk about how to lift up America, participating in discussions afterward, and going home with armfuls of handouts and DVDs. The lecturers and organizers learned as they went along, getting better and better, exchanging experiences and tips, like checking the local Ramada or Holiday Inn for conventions or business luncheons where they could say a few words. With the DVDs, the extent and quality of what Promotions called the "reach" was indeterminate, but there were encouraging anecdotal reports of people watching them and signing up with the CEP or the Congress Watchdogs or the CUBs.

For all its sweep and sophistication, GIS didn't begin to capture just how taken the country was with the Meliorists and their directions for their country. Scarcely a community was untouched by some form of activism, and it wasn't just about the Agenda for the Common Good. Long-suppressed civic energies burst forth like crocuses in springtime. Groups surfaced to demand the regulation of tanning salons to prevent skin cancer, and of beauty salons to protect workers from chemicals and particulates. The stalled movement to reform the corporate student loan racket, with its government guarantees and high interest rates, erupted on campuses and inside Congress. Progressive legislators found renewed vigor as they went after the authoritarian rules and procedures that gave the majority party a virtual stranglehold on congressional legislation. The dormant advocates of recreational sports came alive to challenge the dominance of commercialized sports, demanding that the newspapers call their sports pages the Spectator Sports section unless they started covering participatory amateur sports in their communities and nationwide. Whether it was the hospital infection epidemic, Channel One and commercialism in the schools, crumbling subway systems, decaying housing projects, municipalities using eminent domain to take over private homes for the use of corporations, or the endless robotic menus that cost customers hours on the phone with airlines, utilities, banks, and so many other big companies, citizens were up in arms! From petty peeves to the big issues of economic and political justice, the people were arising!

A few days after the last of the Seven Pillars was introduced in Congress, with all the paid and free media coverage pro and con still in full swing, the Meliorists commissioned polls on each of the bills and found to their delight that approval ratings ranged from 72 percent to 85 percent. Soon thereafter, the big polling companies registered about the same range of approval, except on the healthcare bill, which hit almost 90 percent. Lobo and the CEOs brought up the rear with polls whose questions were so obviously slanted that when the results came in at about 47 percent approval and 50 percent disapproval, the media declared them a victory for the Meliorists. Once again, the CEOs were on the defensive.

Even so, the Washington lobbies found themselves gravitating to the superior organizational efforts of Lobo/Dortwist, if only to escape complete despair. On a fraction of a fraction of their budgets, Luke Skyhi was showing them what it was like when the opposition batters came from the Major Leagues. No more pounding on pitiful protestors, semi-starved consumer and environmental groups, or demoralized unions operating on default. The US Cavalry had come to town.

The faceless lobbyists were especially infuriated by one of Luke's more inspired strokes: a rogue's gallery of mug shots of the Capitol's hundred most ruthless corporate pitchmen and greasers, captioned with lists of their sins. Luke printed the photos up on high-quality poster paper and distributed them by the tens of thousands. Half the members of Congress hung them in their reception rooms, declaring the miscreants persona non grata. Hand-wringing indignation ensued among the pitchmen and greasers. During lunch one day at the lavishly carpeted and chandeliered Metropolitan Club, a senior corporate lawyer said to the head of the National Coal Industry Association, a longtime friend, "Dammit, Buford, this is the last goddamn straw. The nerve of that guy, putting 'Wanted' over our pictures like we were common criminals." Buford sighed and downed a double shot of Jack Daniel's. "And I thought this was going to be a nice, quiet summer, at least as long as there were no hurricanes or terrorist attacks," he said. "Wake up, Buford," said the lawyer. "We've got a different kind of hurricane and a different kind of terrorist attack, and frankly, I'd prefer the real thing."

All through July, interview requests and invitations to speak poured into the offices of the PROs, as the press was routinely calling the Meliorists now. *Time, Newsweek, People, Business Week, Fortune, Vanity Fair, O,* and a host of other national magazines wanted them for cover stories. They became household names, folk heroes, if they weren't already. Then there were the Billionaires Against Bullshit. Reporters fell all over them and their social circles. Before they finished their interviews or got off the air, the Meliorists and their allies always tried to focus attention on the Congress and the Agenda.

Meanwhile, the right-wing media was tying itself into knots. Even Bush Bimbaugh, the hitherto undisputed king of talk radio, couldn't seem to make his hysterical rants stick anymore. His dittoheads just weren't calling in like they used to, jamming the switchboard and drowning out the voices of the treasonous libs. He was so down he started taking uppers again. The Bimbaugh star was being eclipsed, and he knew it. The more he attacked, the more strident and repetitive he became. Finally he decided that there was only one thing to do: beard the lion in his den. Courage wasn't his strong suit—he was big on soliloquies and screened callers—but he knew an approaching freight train when he saw one. Well, okay, so he'd give one of the SROs thirty minutes. The only one he could barely stomach was Ted Turner. Bush popped another pill, placed the call, and extended the invitation. Ted accepted with ill-concealed relish.

On the appointed day, Ted showed up a few minutes early at Bush's elaborate studio. Bush greeted him cordially, although Ted couldn't help noticing his sweaty handshake. They went into the sound booth and began.

"Good day, red-blooded Americans, you're listening to the Truth, and if you abide by it you will be enlightened to the shining heavens. My special guest is Ted Turner, of cable TV, Atlanta Braves, and latifundia notoriety—hey, look it up, unilinguals. Welcome, Ted, to a Bimbaugh first—a one-on-one with one of you billionaire subverters of America."

"Well, Bush, that's a nice, impartial, lying piece of cowshit. You know, I've always wanted to be on your show so I could ask you how it feels to be a corporate welfare king, you bulbous freeloader, you! Folks, he's using your property—the public airwaves—free of charge to make his twenty million bucks a year."

Bush went ballistic. Reflexively he pushed the Silent button on his aggressive guest so he couldn't be interrupted as he delivered his stinging rebuttal.

"Why, you slimy cur, you wife-swapper, you . . . you . . . you sucker for the feminazis, the commies, the queers, and the left-wing wackos! How do *you* feel having your brain so far up your anal cavity?"

Ted grabbed his mike to reply, discovered it was dead, and did what came naturally. He jumped up, grabbed Bush's wheeled chair, spun him into the far corner, and took over his mike, which was very much alive.

"Hey, dittoheads. Bush Bimbaugh is getting rich off you by shilling for the big business tycoons and peddling all kinds of bigotry. Have you ever heard him take on a big company? Have you ever heard him go after big oil, big drug, big auto, big insurance, big bank? Of course not. They own him because they sponser him. He's a coward, can't take any criticism, though he sure dishes it out. But what do you expect from a draft dodger who thinks it's great to send other people's sons and daughters to fabricated wars? What do you expect from a sponger who insists that five-fifteen an hour is plenty as a minimum wage while he's pulling down a hundred grand a day, or thirty-three thousand three hundred and thirty-three bucks an hour, for slinging his manure? Want more? Just log onto RedirectAmerica.org."

By now, Bush had recovered and was about to assault Ted from behind when he spotted a producer frantically holding up a sign behind the glass partition: "Don't, he'll sue you! Tort!" Bush froze, seething with rage, and swiped his finger across his throat to signal the producer, who pulled the plug just as Ted was saying, "Take it from a recovered redneck—" The telephone lines were lit up like Times Square on New Year's Eve.

"Get the hell out of here, Turner," Bush shouted. "By the time I'm done with you in the next forty minutes, they'll think you escaped from the nuthouse. I am going to pulverize you. You're no redneck, you're just plain red."

"Don't worry, jocko, I wouldn't want to pollute my lungs in here any further. But ask your legally inspired producer over there about the Sullivan case. Ask him about intentional and false defamation of a public figure. You might want to look before you leap into a court-room for an eight-figure verdict. So long, chowderhead."

As Bush well knew without any help from his producer, *New York Times v. Sullivan* set an extremely high standard for defamation suits, making it difficult for public figures to prevail unless they could prove malice and intent. It was a landmark in Supreme Court decisions supporting freedom of the press, and had greatly eased the flow of sharp and critical free speech in the decades since it was handed down. Normally it was a mainstay of Bush's show, but today it tamed his tongue, because he was full of malice and intent.

Returning to the air after a very long commercial break, he recovered his composure and reverted to form: ignore the previous dustup and go back on the offensive against some easy target. "Listen up, people. Our National Anthem is under attack again, this time from a bunch of Hispanos out in LA. Get this, they want to sing 'The Star-Spangled Banner' in their so-called native language. Well, El Rushbo's got some news for them. No way, Jose!"

On Capitol Hill, the hearings ground on day after day, with an army of stenographers taking down every word for the public record. That was fine with the Bulls—so long as the hearings were underway, the hard decisions could be deferred. Every afternoon, in a suite near the Rayburn Office Building, the Double Z met with the congressional progressives to advise on the testimony and how to keep the media focused on it. Now and then, they'd ask the valedictory speakers to stay over a day after their Press Club tell-alls and testify at the relevant hearings.

For the time being, the progressives were keeping a low profile. Staying out of the media limelight helped them in their negotiations with the Bulls and gave them the leverage of going to the press as a last resort if the Bulls didn't cooperate. But their names did not escape Brovar Dortwist, who began compiling information on these "ringleaders," as he called them, and arranging for companies in their districts or states to announce that they were taking their plants or white-collar operations abroad, with a scarcely veiled reference to the inhospitable views of the incumbent progressive. The Meliorist response teams did their best to put out a statement the next day exposing the move abroad as something that had been planned long ago and would have happened anyway, but sometimes it was hard to get accurate information promptly enough. The Dortwist tactic was having some effect, meshing as it did with the CEO's daily saturation scare campaign on TV and radio.

Wherever it was determined that public opinion was starting to trend against the progressive incumbent, the lecturers were rerouted to provide the bigger picture and respond to local fears.

"Corporate flight is part of business as usual for the big companies," they told their audiences at community meetings and press conferences. "They've been going abroad for years, and the government gives them incentives to do it. Representatives of the Department of Commerce attend business conferences to expound on all the ways Washington encourages companies to expand their foreign investments, including outsourcing and moving US facilities overseas, often to dictatorships all too willing to supply them with serf workers. Meanwhile, these same companies are collecting federal and state contracts and subsidies and tax breaks right and left. They're having it both ways—serf labor abroad and freebies at home—and we need legislation to stop them. Their flight isn't just an abandonment of your districts and states, it's a flight from loyalty and allegiance to the country where they were born and prospered. Tell that to the corporate patriots!"

Max Palevsky came up with another wrinkle. He asked Analysis to tally the announcements of flight abroad in the progressives' districts and those in the Bulls' backyards. The results were dramatic: 80 percent to 20 percent. Analysis also concluded from previous trends that companies in the Bulls' districts were holding back announcements they would otherwise have made over the past few weeks. Promotions went public with the data in a big way and kept the Meliorists on the offensive, notwithstanding the energetic efforts of Dortwist and Lobo, who were now realizing just how deep and powerful the Meliorists' strike-back capabilities were.

The Washington lobbies weren't used to contending with such a formidable opposition phalanx. They were used to fielding a media blast, pumping money into campaign coffers, expanding their lobbying intensity on the Hill and back in the districts, and uncorking the champagne. For at least three decades, Congress had reliably yielded to the demands of one business sector after another, including the oil, drug, chemical, auto, real estate, mining, banking, insurance, agribusiness, genetic engineering, defense, fast-food, and brokerage industries. Now there was not only resistance, but resistance with muscle behind it. The lobbyists' local dealers and agents were feeding back their impressions, almost unanimously reporting that folks were aroused and determined and angry, as if they'd had quite enough of all the greed, all the propaganda, and all the lies. "No more 'crush the local reformers and be done with it,'" as one insurance agent put it. "These reformers can call on outside agitators who are very, very adept and motivated. I don't even trust my own employees anymore. They're always whispering on their cell phones and disappearing on their lunch hour." A distressed realtor e-mailed his trade association pleading for guidance. "It's just a whole new scene, not one we have any experience in handling. What do we do? Help!" In every region of the country, in every arena, new civic energies were putting the Meliorists ahead of the curve and drawing their adversaries into unknown territory.

Toward the end of July, the National Association of Health Maintenance Organizations—health insurers that amassed large numbers of customers mostly by merging themselves into ever fewer giant companies—decided to take the bull by the horns and do something about the Agenda's universal healthcare bill. They invited representatives of some allied trade organizations, including the fast-food and big-box discount chains, to their swank new offices for a no-holds-barred strategy session. The discussion began with the tried and true buzzwords "socialized medicine," which had worked so well ever since President Harry Truman first proposed a national healthcare system back in 1945. Then the participants moved boldly on to the tried and true charges about big government rationing healthcare and tying doctors and hospitals up in interminable red tape.

"Well, it's worked before," said the CEO of Monument Insurance, one of the biggest HMOs, "but let's not forget that this is the most popular bill on the Agenda, with approval ratings pushing ninety percent. We've got to match them and go them one better. I say we bring back Harry and Louise, who performed so brilliantly on television to deep-six Clinton's plan in 1993. Our surveys back then showed that Harry and Louise had a ninety-percent recognition factor by the time we vanquished the reds. Why not a return engagement? I'm sure our intrepid couple haven't aged a bit."

"I'll tell you why," said his media adviser. "Because guess who the SROs will trot out to go up against H and L."

"Hillary Clinton?" asked the CEO of McBurger's. "Just kidding. Go ahead, who? An ex-surgeon general? A famous physician?"

"No, a famous parrot."

Groans filled the room.

"Calm down, gentlemen," said the director of the Everyware discount stores. "Nobody's invincible, not even Patriotic Polly. If we put Harry and Louise in a series of different ads with different attack themes, the bird will never be able to keep up. She'll be squawking some tired one-note refrain that will make her an object of mockery. She can't possibly learn enough new words and phrases fast enough to respond to the devastating specifics of our ads." He paused. "Can she? Smithers," he barked at his young assistant, who was sitting behind him taking notes, "get me the top avian consulting firm in the country to advise on the mental capacity of a parrot."

"Perhaps an ornithologist, sir?" Smithers ventured timidly.

"Whatever it takes, Smithers, just do it!" The director turned back to his colleagues. "We'll wait for the report to be on the safe side, but I've got a powerful hunch that Patriotic Polly has finally met her match in Harry and Louise."

"I've got a powerful hunch you're right," said the Monument CEO. "Okay, we'll get the text of the SROs' budget-busting legislation over to the ad agency right away so they can start breaking it down into sound bites. Assuming confirmation that Polly's a birdbrain, Harry and Louise will hit the airwaves in a couple of days."

The meeting adjourned on a note of enthusiastic self-congratulation. It didn't matter to these barons of the business world that the Meliorists' bill provided for public payment but competitive private delivery of health services under careful quality and cost controls. It didn't matter to the HMO chiefs that unlike the health plans they offered, the bill mandated free choice of doctors and hospitals and equal access to health services for all. It didn't matter that the bill would dramatically reduce red tape, the collection bureaucracy, the one-secretary/one-doctor paperwork ratio, the huge administrative expenses accounting for more than 25 percent of all healthcare expenditures, and the enormous computerized billing fraud of the current system. It didn't matter that the resultant savings would be enough to cover all Americans with less per capita spending than was exacted by the soaring prices and waste of the status quo. All that mattered was propaganda, the charming evasions and prevarications of a fictional celebrity couple named Harry and Louise.

As the HMO bigwigs and their friends were repairing to their favorite watering holes, the Agenda division of Promotions was poring over the daily transcripts of the public hearings on the Seven Pillars. "Too voluminous, too overwhelming," declared Pauline Precis, the division's top editor. "We must find the compelling, persuasive, vibrant details, the nuggets that will become national currency, part of daily parlance, part of the daily understanding of the damage done to basic principles of fairness and justice. Get to work, people."

They did. Three hours later, Pauline's staff presented her with a potent sampling of the testimony.

> A single mother in Appalachia: "I'm working to live and support my children, but my boss made sure I couldn't make a living from my work."

> A hotel maid from Queens: "My son got lead poisoning from the paint in our apartment. I couldn't afford the treatment. He died. When I buried him in a pauper's grave, the gravedigger looked up at me and said, 'Sorry for your loss, ma'am. Stinks that this is a pay-or-die country.'"

> A community organizer in Boston: "Every day I walk through crumbling neighborhoods and breathe dirty air. In the distance I can see the skyscrapers of the rich, who work in comfort and go home to well-kept neigh-

borhoods. I've studied the tax code, and I know that work is taxed way more than capital. In the good old USA, we tax food, furniture, and clothing instead of stocks, bonds, and options. That's crazy. Let's tax what we don't need, not what we need."

❯ An Oglala chief from the Great Sioux Nation: "The power of the Sun created the Earth. After many generations, let the Sun do the work for the Earth before the Earth returns to dust."

❯ A labor organizer in Peoria: "When the few rule the many, when their greed overruns our need, they seed rebellious deeds. So it has been forever, and so it will forever be."

❯ A political economist at Harvard: "The new slavery of the corporations, by the corporations, and for the corporations requires a new abolitionist movement—no less moral, no less legal, no less constitutional, no less fundamental than the old abolitionist movement against the enslavement of African Americans. The new slavery is not just one of daily life indentured to the power and whims of giant global corporations; it is an enslavement of our genes, of our commodified children, of our environment, of our intelligence, of our inalienable right to a decent livelihood under a government of the people, by the people, and for the people. The reigning dogmas of authoritarian corporatism must be overthrown before it's too late, before our nation and mankind as a whole become one immense Brave New World."

❯ An auto worker from Detroit: "I lost my arm and my job in a plant accident. I'm a mom, but my kids were all grown and out of the house. I had plenty of time on my hand, so I decided to start a group home for street kids. I want to improve my country. I want all Americans to improve our country. That's our God-given right, but we can't exercise it because our country isn't a true democracy. It's a country where the rich dictate power to truth. We are the unseen, the shadow people who do their work or have to pick up after their devastations. We are expendable. This must stop. This must stop everywhere."

"That's more like it, people," Pauline said. "Now get me the visuals, get me the witnesses at the table in a packed hearing room, get me their back stories—where they came from, what they've been up against in their daily lives. This is a media gold mine for news, features, ads, DVDs, whatever we want to make of it. Get me reaction shots from the committee, get me interviews with the witnesses' families, get me—"

A tinny rendition of the William Tell Overture interrupted her. She unholstered her cell phone and snapped it open. "Um-hmm, I see. . . . Yes, Barry, of course, I'll be right there." Snap, reholster. "Gotta run, people, back in ten, get on it."

Arriving in Barry's office, Pauline flung herself into a chair. "So the rumors are true. The HMOs are dusting Harry and Louise off for a national media duet against universal healthcare."

"Yup," Barry said. "I just got confirmation from the Secretariat. They're moving fast, and we've got to be ready to come back at them. Any ideas?"

"Patriotic Polly, of course. She can say something simple but powerful, like 'Your health—not for sale to the HMOs!'"

"I like it," Barry said. "I'll call Clifton Chirp right away and get him on the job. But we need something less generic too, something that addresses the specifics of the Agenda bill and the mud they're going to sling at it. Bill Hillsman would be perfect, but he's already up to his eyeballs with the energy legislation and the Dynamic Democracy Act."

Barry and Pauline sat thinking for a minute, then grinned at each other across Barry's desk. "Blister!" they said simultaneously.

Blister Blurr was a counter-advertising specialist who had come on board with Promotions just after the Fourth. He'd been waiting for an opportunity to show his stuff, and was delighted to get the call from Pauline. Working at breakneck speed, he pulled up all the 1993 Harry and Louise skits for close scrutiny and then fashioned his antidote, heavy on satire. His first script had a couple named Lou and Harriet chatting in their kitchen about Harry and Louise.

"They sure must've got themselves tuckered out back in '93, popping up all over the TV day after day the way they did," Lou said. "And here they are, thirteen years later, doing it again. Don't they get tired of spouting the same old falsehoods?"

"No," Harriet said, "because they're actors. In real life, they've got full health insurance, and their parents are on Medicare. Gracious, what people won't say on television just for money. Are you an actor, Lou?"

"Honey, we've been married for going on twenty years. You know I'm not an actor. You know I work at Wal-Mart, just like you."

"Yes, and we both have second jobs, but we don't have health insurance. We just can't afford it with two teenagers in the house."

"Say, Harriet, do Harry and Louise have any kids? Let's invite those actors over and ask them. Let's sit them down right here at this table and see what they have to say to two real Americans."

Blister reviewed the sixty-second script and pounded out another one on the cries of "Red tape!" and "Socialized medicine!" that were sure to come from Harry and Louise. Then he sat back and admired his handiwork. The ads would prompt viewers to skepticism or outright laughter when the HMO thespian duo came on the screen. There would be a backlash against the fakery, and the press would want to interview the actors about their own health coverage. Reporters might even start hounding their poor parents. Lou and Harriet would get the water-cooler chatter going and deal a body blow to a multimillion-dollar brand name that was still remembered by a substantial portion of the adult population. There was just one problem. Blister called Pauline.

"I need you to find me a couple of down-to-earth working folks for my ads," he said.

"No problem," said Pauline. "There are scores of them up here testifying on the Hill."

"They have to be married, uninsured, and preferably Wal-Mart employees with two kids."

"Well . . . well, okay, there must be hundreds of couples like that, maybe thousands."

"And they have to be named Lou and Harriet."

"What?" said Pauline, and then the light dawned. "Oh, Blister, that's brilliant! Okay, it won't be easy, but I'll see what I can do."

Blister went home to grab a bite and walk his basset hound— everyone worth knowing in Washington had a dog—and returned to the office a few hours later. He was working on a third ad, a thirty-second spot featuring Lou and Harriet with Patriotic Polly, when the phone rang.

"Long story short," said Pauline. "I called Barry, Barry called Sol, Sol called his lead SWAT team in Bentonville, they called their people at the two hundred stores, and Mrs. Harriet Robinson is on her way up here from Atlanta with her husband, Henry. Everyone calls him Hank, but his middle name is Louis."

"Close enough!" Blister said. "Thanks a million."

Now the only remaining question was whether to wait until Harry and Louise debuted again or to run Lou and Harriet preemptively. Blister consulted Barry, Phil, and Bill Cosby, and they all agreed that it was best to wait until the first Harry and Louise ad hit and imme-diately slap the Lou and Harriet nullification on the air with the same media buy. Going out first with Lou and Harriet might force the HMOs to cancel Harry and Louise, and then the ads wouldn't make much sense. Far better to confront the HMOs with the choice of persisting with a fatally weakened Harry and Louise or suffering the humiliation of withdrawing them.

The resurrected duo premiered on a Thursday, their brows fur-rowed with concern over the horrors of the Agenda's healthcare bill. Hot on their heels came Lou and Harriet, calmly skewering the fabrications of their HMO counterparts, with an assist from the hugely popular Patriotic Polly. By Monday, Harry and Louise had been yanked off the air to a chorus of mocking catcalls from the late-night comedians and millions of Americans who would not be fooled and cheated a second time.

As Harry and Louise were retiring their act in disgrace, three unlikely middle-aged men of ramrod bearing were registering as guests at the mountaintop hotel in Maui. A day later, an athletic-looking woman in her thirties joined them. They did their best to fit the customary guest profile, chatting casually with the other guests and the hotel staff about how exhausted they were from their jobs as drug company "detail" salespeople constantly on the road, going from one physician's office to the next. They spoke loudly of shucking their cell phones and Blackberries and telling the front desk to hold all calls. They were here to relax their brains out as far away as possible from work. They just wanted sun, mountain breezes, walks through the lush Hawaiian landscape, and rest. During the day, they napped ostentatiously on chaises by the pool or in armchairs in the common rooms. Late at night, on the pretext of being restless, they strolled through the grounds and bugged the place silly with parabolic microphones and miniature cameras.

Lobo's detectives had hit pay dirt. They'd followed a trail with many detours that finally led them to the Maui hotel where the SRO movement was spawned. The first clue came when Ted and Peter were overheard at one of the Sun God festivals talking about a forth-coming trip to Maui. Then Sol and Jeno, in Washington for a CUB event, mentioned Maui during a phone conversation at their hotel near the National Press Club. It happened that the DEA was tap-ping all the hotel phones for a drug sting, and that the tapper was an old friend of Lobo's. Over an informal lunch at a restaurant near the White House, the tapper told Lobo what his eavesdropping had inadvertently swept up. From there it was relatively easy. Paul Newman and Bill Cosby had been sighted at the Maui Airport in

February and mentioned in a *Hollywood Reporter* gossip column that came up on a Google search. After a couple of weeks of sleuthing, the detectives closed in on the hotel.

It was a high-stakes game Lobo was playing, but it was a measure of his determination to salvage all he could for his side. He had weighed the odds, realized how far behind the CEOs were, and knew by now that total victory was out of the question. It was a matter of how much they were going to lose. In his war room he had his own GIS electronic wall, cruder than the Meliorists' system, but sophisticated enough to show all the alarming activities taking place across the country day by day. Every time he looked at it, he prayed that the CEOs were looking at it too. He was not at all sanguine that they had what it took in terms of direct involvement, passion, and willingness to back the effort with sufficient funds. The day he'd dressed them down, exhorting them to step up to the plate personally in this World Series of power struggles, he was floored by Hubert Bump's stunning gauntlet, so much so that he remembered every word: "We're done for if we think we can prevail merely by beefing up the old war chest and redoubling the old battle plans. To effect the counterrevolution, we must revolutionize ourselves. We must go where no business leaders have gone before, do what no business leaders have done before, and above all think like no business leaders have thought before."

There was thus far no indication that the CEOs were going to take Bump's challenge to heart. True, everyone had agreed at the last meeting to let the Washington lobbies do their thing at least for the month of July, but in August the Bulls and their backbenchers were going to be facing the most organized and inescapable accountability recess in congressional history. Lobo and Dortwist were busy scheduling their own local business accountability events and counter-demonstrations extolling deregulation and free enterprise, and pointing ominously to closing factories and withdrawn investments, but Lobo knew it was an uphill battle. And the Harry and Louise debacle had confirmed his worst fears, revealing the pettiness, the shallowness of the tactical thinking of the fully insured lobbyists.

That was what was giving Lobo nightmares about never getting ahead of the curve, just stumbling from one giant pothole to another and falling further and further behind as the minutes ticked away into hours into the preciously few days left for any recovery.

Over at AFL-CIO headquarters, on the other side of Lafayette Park across from the White House, the mood was very different as the labor chiefs of the member unions assembled in sublime elation, the kind of joy that follows receipt of a wondrous and unexpected gift. Tommy Tawny, head of the AFL-CIO, gaveled the meeting to order and summarized the sunny scene. Labor's long-stalled and quite modest legislative menu was suddenly the cat's meow. Sympathizers of the past had become out-and-out supporters of the present. Loudmouth opponents of the past were behaving like mice these days. Notably, the Bulls went out of their way to be polite when labor sent witnesses up to testify on the Meliorists' Agenda.

"The Hill is in a revolutionary state of tumult," Tommy declared. "Throw away the conventional wisdom, to use Ken Galbraith's phrase. It's a whole new ball game. We at the AFL-CIO are even planning to picket our notorious next-door neighbor, the Chamber of Commerce. No matter how often they crushed us in Congress, we've never done that before, and it'll be good for our members to hoof it a bit." He paused and walked over to the long side of the conference room, where labor's GIS map was blinking. "Look at all our locals. They're no longer rusting and creaking. They've come alive! They're flexing their muscles as part of the aroused masses, all those people out in the streets and at the rallies and picketing Wal-Mart. Their leaders are even organizing discussion circles with the rank and file about the Agenda for the Common Good and its historical background. Man, it's lucky the old-timers insisted on building or buying their own union halls. It was a sign of permanence, they always said."

"Do the PROs want to meet with us?" asked Sparky Lightman, president of the International Brotherhood of Electrical Workers.

"No," Tommy said, "they want to keep their distance from all the liberal Washington lobbies. So do we, for that matter. The more each lobby pursues members of Congress on its own, the less likely it is that our opponents can tar us with some damaging stereotype, and the more flexibility we have. Lobbies can do things individually and do them faster than they could as a coalition."

"Besides, we have to focus on labor law reform, and no coalition is going to do that for us," added Ned Navastar of the Long-shoremen. "We have to clear the deck so that workers can form unions without having to jump through a hundred hoops thrown at them by union-busting law firms or consultants. And we have to quadruple our AFL-CIO lobbyists too, Tommy. When the Hill door was closed, you didn't need too many people up there. Now that the door's wide open, there's a lot more ground to cover."

"You're reading my mind, Ned," Tommy said. "Yes, this has to be done. Is there any objection?"

Ann Moro of the California Nurses Association spoke up. "There sure is. It's way too vague. We need to know exactly how many lob-byists we can deploy on the Hill immediately. We've got to seize this rare moment in history. There's no time for recruitment and training, so let's have a show of hands around the table. I'll start. The CNA is small, but we'll volunteer fourteen of our lobbyists, beginning right now with myself and my deputy for the remainder of the congressional term. Who's next?"

"You're a pistol, Ann," Tommy said. "Fair enough. I'll reassign a hundred of our headquarters staff to the Hill, including me and my vice-president. Let's see what the rest of you can field."

Within thirty minutes, the union chiefs had pledged a total of 865 lobbyists to work full-time on the Hill. Ann clapped her hands. "Well, that's not quite twice as many as the drug industry sics on Congress—just one industry—but it's a start. Now, how are we going to make this coming Labor Day like no other Labor Day before it?"

"You tell us, Ann," yelled Larry Strong of the United Auto Workers.

"All right, I will. As the newest member of the AFL-CIO, may I say how appallingly pathetic Labor Day has become over the decades? To most Americans, it's nothing but one giant sale. As leaders of your unions, why are you hiding your light under a barrel? Tommy, why aren't you on *Meet the Press*? Larry, why aren't you on *Face the Nation*? And what about the Labor Day parades? They used to be demonstrations of worker power, but now attendance is so low that the marchers look like stragglers. Well, here's what I suggest we all do, and what we're definitely going to do in California. We're going to do whatever it takes to bring out the rank and file, tear them away from their backyard grills for a few hours. Our union leaders are going to make appointments with our senators and representatives and notify them in advance that our membership will be encircling their local offices in a silent vigil, waiting to see if the leaders emerge from their meetings with these lawmakers with a clear declaration of support for the Agenda—not just the labor part, but the entire Agenda for the Common Good. If the lawmakers say yes to the Agenda, cheers will go up and they'll be asked to say a few words to the packed crowd of workers and their families. If they say no—well, there are going to be a lot of people talking to a lot more people in a very personal way about how the representative or senator took them away from their barbecue festivities in vain. The visuals will be perfect for the evening news, and the vigils will present a fine opportunity to collect the names of the really committed for further pressure on Congress in September and October. You'll all get to know more of your members too. So many of them see you as all rank and no file."

"Boy, Ann," said Buster Boyd of the Boilermakers, "you sure know how to present a great idea and then sour it at the end by sticking it to us. I came up from the ranks, spent many a year in nearly unbearable heat in the plant. Were you ever a nurse, Ann?"

"Touché, Buster. I take your point, so let's get back to planning a super Labor Day that will make our opponents sweat."

"I think we all agree that Ann's idea is a winner," said Tommy, "but how do we implement it? We're not used to showing labor's muscle on Labor Day, at least not in recent years. Ann, will you head a task force to plan for maximum turnout and report back by the end of July so that we'll have five weeks or so to actually get it down?"

Ann nodded.

"I assume all you presidents around the table will cooperate," Tommy went on, "and some of you may want to join the task force. You've all read the Agenda, and there's nothing objectionable to us in any of its sections. Okay, next on our own agenda is the sticky matter of union jurisdictional conflicts, so let's get to it before we break for lunch."

Ann could barely conceal a smile of pity, but it was quickly extinguished by an idea that popped into her head. She would get in touch with the managers of the "Read all about it!" newspaper kids. She was determined to include all workers, not just union workers, in the Labor Day parades and Agenda vigils, and the kids could blare out announcements of both in cities all over the country in the days leading up to Labor Day. Perfect, she thought. And with Warren Beatty handily winning his primary, California labor ought to be more upbeat by the day. Ann could hardly wait to get to work.

As July headed toward August, the public hearings in both houses of Congress continued to build an extraordinarily detailed record of contemporary, historical, and forward-thinking testimony and accompanying documentation. The quality of the questioning was impressive both from the progressives and the Bulls—an example of how solid public procedures elevated content and behavior.

Over at Analysis the staff was working two shifts processing the daily transcripts and summarizing their contents for distribution to all relevant destination points throughout the expanding network, including websites and blogs where they were devoured and covered with commentary and debate. Since the hearings featured pro and con testimony at each session—the Bulls had insisted on this to get their rebuttals and their side of the story in the press every day—the subsequent public discussion was nourished in the same way. All over the country and on the Internet, a thousand town meetings bloomed.

Analysis then broke the transcripts down for selected audiences interested in this topic or that. Labor material went to the unions; consumer and investor material to those groups; material on health, the environment, and democracy to lists of credibility groups and specialized action organizations. All dispatches were set in a crisp typeface and beautifully designed. The Analysis breakdowns also yielded a trove of material for the *Daily Bugle* youngsters: "Lawmakers asked to get tough on crime in the suites! Read all about it!" "Topple corporate welfare kings, demands ex-CEO welfare king! Read all about it!" "Clash over corporate greed on Capitol Hill! Read all about it!"

Analysis was full of former academics and citizen researchers used to grinding out material and wondering if anyone was reading or listening, so they were astounded at the interest in what they were disseminating from their current shop. "The difference is obvious," said super-wonk Mark Green during a coffee break. "Remember all those polls showing heavy majorities in favor of much of the Agenda long before there was an Agenda? Well, the soil was fertile, but there was no rain, just year after year of drought. Now the glorious spring rains have come, and the seeds have burst forth, first the sprouts, then the flowers, and then the pollination. The Earth is green again, sustaining all kinds of vibrant and constantly reproducing life. The dust storms are no more, and all because of drops of rain, millions of consistent drops of rain. Long-repressed hopes have grown into change, into compassionate, creative realities rooted in the moist, firm, life-giving soil."

Back in their respective headquarters in New York City and Washington, DC, Lobo and Brovar were pondering escalation options against the Meliorists. On their short list—their very short list—were two items: destabilizing the economy, and offering lucrative positions to any Bull who wanted to go out batting a home run for the status quo. They would have to be very careful. The first option was intrinsically risky and was bound to incur more charges from the SROs that business was behaving unpatriotically. The second could be seen by prosecutors as a bribe. It would be best not to have to resort to either tactic, but there was nothing else in the Lobo/Dortwist bag of tricks, as even Brovar had to admit. The media scare buys were in full swing, and the Washington lobbies were going all out within their limitations, but the results weren't encouraging. The pressure at the community level was already getting to more than a few dealers and agencies long accustomed to having their way with a malleable public. Now they were noticing that the more aggressive, overt anti-Meliorists among them actually lost business. People just weren't going to bestow their buying dollars on vendors who fought against the common good, and they told them so.

Brovar called his potential partner in crime. "Can't we find out more about the SROs' forthcoming moves, Lobo?" he asked. "That might be of some help. By the way, have you found your mole yet?"

"I've given all my people lie detector tests, and they all passed. I've had my captains interview all of them, and nothing came up, except one guy blurted out that he was having an extramarital affair. As for finding out more about the SROs' plans, I've got some things in the works, and I'll keep you posted. For now, though, we're slipping further and further behind, and our base in Congress is showing fissures everywhere. It's like we're facing some giant crusher machine that expands its grip in a thousand new ways every day. You've got to hand it to the old guys. If they've lost a little bounce in their step, they're still way ahead of us."

"Much as I don't want to, I have to agree. But in a situation like this, Lobo, it's the better part of valor to stay calm and keep thinking. In any battle there are always two general ways to win. Either you defeat the enemy, or the enemy defeats itself. We haven't tried the latter approach yet. How can we provoke the SROs to defeat themselves, since they seem incapable of doing it all by their lonesome?"

"Beats me. Got any ideas?"

"Not yet, not yet, but there's always a way. The problem with the

SROs is that the usual dirty tricks just don't work. Say we show that they cheated on their wives years ago, defrauded someone years ago, abandoned their children years ago, watched porn flicks years ago—it's all 'years ago.' People want fresh prey. The public says 'So what?' to exposures that might bring down someone in their forties or fifties. Even assuming we can connect the proposals in the Agenda to the SROs' stock portfolios or other investments, people will say they're so rich they couldn't possibly be in it for the money. And the media will say what the SROs always say—that they're capitalists, of course, only they're doing on behalf of the people what the current capitalist bosses are doing against the people. Face it, Lobo, these guys are knights in shining armor, invulnerable to conventional smears. Besides, since people are now mobilizing on their own, it's almost too late for any discrediting of the SROs to matter. Except maybe for the money flow."

"And except for the Bulls. As you know better than anyone, Brovar, the SROs have to win in Congress by veto-proof margins, or else our lame-duck president can turn back the tide with the stroke of seven pens. It's time to move to the third wave—the last stand at the Khyber Pass—but we can't convey our sense of grim reality to anyone, including the CEOs, who must be challenged anew to come out swinging one on one with the SROs."

Lobo needn't have bothered to contemplate this series of square-offs. He needn't have worried about the ticklish matter of going back to the CEOs and telling them even more forcefully that they had to take the SROs on personally. Once again the Meliorists were ahead of the curve and sprang their challenge the next day. Mercifully, their news release did not mention the CEOs by name or refer to them as a cabal. With the Seventh-Generation Eye at the top of the release, the message was brief and direct: "The Meliorists hereby invite any CEO of any corporation with annual sales of $25 billion or more to debate us individually on national television, before an impartial moderator, under rules of engagement acceptable to both parties. Our purpose in making this offer is to elevate our deliberative democracy to new heights of discourse and civility at a time of intense congressional attention to the Agenda for the Common Good. All inquiries from CEOs will be treated confidentially until they agree to a public debate. We do not wish to inhibit inquiries by premature publicity."

That afternoon the *New York Post* gave the release a front-page, full-page banner headline: "TITANIC SHOWDOWN: PROS VS. CEOS." The accompanying article on the jump page reported that the paper had called dozens of CEOs to elicit their reaction, with no success. Two days later, after more deafening silence from the CEOs, the *Post*'s full-page headline read, "CEOS: MUM'S THE WORD. CHICKENS??"

Unbeknownst to Lobo, there was another option on Brovar's short list, the one he had begun to formulate during his walk with Get'em. He summarily convened the Washington lobbies and their think-tank apologists for a meeting of a kind they could never have imagined in their wealthy complacency only a few months ago. He had tried to warn them, only to be met by their dismissive scoffing. Now, as at his Wednesday morning gatherings of the greed and power brigades, he sat at the end of the long conference table and took charge, opening the meeting without preliminaries.

"I'm not going to belabor all the ways that things are not going well for us, to put it mildly. We are on a downhill course to defeat. Sure, you'll all have your jobs, and your organizations may even grow in staff and budget. Isn't it the nature of corporate power that it's always able to take care of its core defenders? That's why left-wing dictators can't do anything but shut it down. If they don't, the corporatists keep coming back again and again, like bamboo trees.

"Here in America, the power situation is far more complex when it involves an intense disturbance of business as usual. The SROs aren't pushing to shut us down—that would be an easy fight for us to win. Instead, they're holding us to our own bullshit standards and principles, which we've used for so long to control the population to suit our purposes. No, the SROs aren't trying to shut us down—though the HMOs may not be negotiating long-term leases—they're just telling us to share a little more of our wealth with the workers, to stop mistreating consumers and blocking investor control and ignoring known solutions, to start meeting some of the long-neglected needs of millions of our fellow Americans. And they've set in motion such a fundamental shift of power to those millions of Americans that there's no going back to the status quo ante. Cleverly, and as you might expect from their past successes in the business world, they are persuading many more members of Congress than we would like, and more and more of the press, that their Redirections are more economically efficient and productive than the current system of corporate dominance. All in all, a neat package, isn't it?"

Low grumbling rumbled around the massive conference table.

"So I ask you," Brovar went on, "why not recognize their Agenda and go along with it in such a way that we can sow the seeds of gradual repeal and the future restoration of our control? That's what the docs did when they dropped their longstanding opposition to Medicare in 1965. It's turned out pretty well for them, no?"

There was a loud creaking and scraping of chairs as all the attendees sat bolt upright and leaned forward on the table.

"What in the world are you suggesting, Brovar?" shouted Edgar Exerson, head of the Hospital Chains of America. "Did I hear you right? Did you all hear him right? Are you leading us down the road of surrender? Is this the Wal-Mart capitulation on steroids? Explain yourself!"

"Don't get so steamed, Edgar, it clouds your analytic mind. Remember the old saying 'Refusing to bend, they broke'? You know what's going on around the country. And if you don't, just look out your office window. Haven't all of you seen the demonstrators and pickets and newspaper kids in front of your shiny office buildings? The steadily expanding breadth and depth of this movement—rural, urban, and suburban—has no precedent in American history. The great populist revolt of the 1880s and on was born and stayed mostly in the countryside. The teeming cities just teemed. This movement is not going to run out of money, talent, and media—again, it has no precedent in American history. You, Lanky Lightshaft, you and your broadcast industry powerhouses, tell 'em, Lanky, do you think you can do the usual, put out the word and black out the coverage on your stations? You couldn't even black out coverage of the SROs' demand that your industry finally start paying rent for your broadcast licenses. Would you care to rebut me, Lanky?"

Lightshaft clenched his jaw and shook his head.

"Would anyone care to rebut me? No takers?" Brovar stared slowly down the table at each one of them. "All right, to continue, July is coming to an end soon. The hearings will be over, though by no means the fallout. Then there's the month-long August recess, when all hell is going to break loose on our Hill buddies back home. Okay, all you tough guys, you fight-to-the-finish guys, how many of you have canceled your usual August vacations?" Again Brovar eyeballed each of them, down one side of the table and up the other. Finally, a hand went up.

"And who are you, madam?" Brovar asked.

"The name is Fiona Future, executive director of the National Association of Renewable Energy Industries. I canceled my four-week cruise in the Greek islands."

"There you have it. One person out of the forty-seven of us here, and not exactly in the most vulnerable of industries, is staying in the summer heat of Washington, DC, because of the crisis situation. In addition to me, of course. So I can only surmise that the rest of you don't like what I've been saying. Okay, let's hear from you dissenters. Tell us what we should do, what we can do, what we must do. Take the gloves off. Earn your pay."

Arnold Adverse cleared his throat in the tortured silence. "Speaking for the pharmaceutical industry, I would launch a campaign of delay to give us time to regroup for next year's session. If congressional history teaches us anything, it's to avoid panic legislation. Major bills require careful deliberation and should not be rushed through Congress. Pell-mell lawmaking can have many unintended consequences, many side effects that we, the American people, will rue. In a period of big deficits and a shaky dollar, let us not rock the boat just because some old billionaires took it into their heads to throw their weight around."

"Fine speech, Arnold, but I've got news for you. The SROs have anticipated you. For weeks, through their lecturers and the media, they've been trumpeting how long overdue the changes proposed in the Agenda are, how many times in the past half century similar proposals have been considered and rejected because of corporate lobbying. Haven't you seen their latest national TV ads, which make this point in brilliant, memorable, personal fashion, by showcasing ordinary Americans whose lives will be dramatically improved by this or that Agenda provision? They've also got a series of ads giving examples of corporations ramming through gross special interest legislation via paragraphs stashed away in bills running to hundreds and hundreds of pages, with no public hearings, no public notice, no declared sponsor, no nothing—sneaky little paragraphs with big results, like big tax breaks, scuttling safety budgets, and so forth. What's the matter with you, Arnold? Are you under the influence of one of your clients' medications? Not only will it not work, it'll backfire. Next proposal?"

"Here's one for you, Dortwist," barked Jim Mobilaski of the Defense Industries Association. "We take all the things we're doing now, which individually aren't enough, increase the intensity, and deploy them all at the same critical time. I call it the Blitzkrieg Strategy. We expand our media buys, step up the announcements of plant shutdowns and capital flight, triple our operations on Capitol Hill, stir up opposition to the progressives in their home districts through our own demonstrations and marches, and top it all off with a press conference at which we declare in grave tones that we are compelled as sellers of goods and services in America to make known our fear of a total economic collapse should the Agenda pass into law. We call a general strike—one full twenty-four-hour day when we will shut down all operations, except for emergency services. No gasoline, food, medication, clothing, transportation, banking, insurance, repairs—no nothing for a solid day. The first general strike by vendors in our history ought to get their attention."

George Watson of the Bankers Association paled visibly. "Even if you manage to pull all that off, how can you guarantee that it won't ignite more anger against us? There comes a point when more is less, and we may have reached that point. Already, our moves to rattle the economy have scared our side more than the Meliorists and their supporters. Stock markets continue to slide, companies that planned to go overseas in phases are now uprooting their entire operations because they believe they've got cover. What makes us think more of the same won't produce an even sharper blowback?"

"I agree," said Warly Wynnit, president of the Association of Gaming Companies. "Why not a Hail Mary with our first-string team, the Bulls? Let's stick to the Khyber Pass and make the most of it. As long as the Bulls control the congressional red and green lights, nothing can pass to the floor without their approval, right?"

"Wrong," Brovar said. "There is such a thing as a discharge petition, which a majority of members of the House can sign to get bills to the floor. The progressives may just have enough votes to carry it off, and it's such a humiliation to the leadership that some of the Bulls, especially given the pressure back home, may quit on us. It's not likely, but it's possible, and at the worst possible time.

"As for Jim's Blitzkrieg Strategy—a term with most unfortunate associations—it ranges from the redundant to the preposterous. A general strike of vendors is a kamikaze dive with no enemy ships below. We're talking super blowback here. Remember when Gingrich caused the temporary shutdown of the US government? That marked the decline of Gingrich—he turned lots of people off, including some of his supporters. Americans view such tactics as blackmail, dirty pool. Gingrich was smart, though. He quit and changed his name to Getrich, which is more than we'll be able to do after the so-called blitzkrieg turns around and flattens us. Anyone else?"

"Why the hell don't we bite the bullet and take the SROs up on their challenge?" asked Paul Pain, president of the Nanotechnology Industries Association. "Why don't we put our most articulate CEOs in the ring with them, one on one, to unmask these aging egoma-

ONLY THE SUPER-RICH CAN SAVE US!" 533

niacs once and for all as senile saboteurs whose Agenda will wreck our great economy?"

Brovar folded his arms across his chest and leaned back in his chair. "It's been three days since the challenge, Paul. Have any of our valiant CEOs stepped forward? Is there an intrepid soul among them? Can anyone here name a CEO who's likely to put on the gloves? It's hard to understand, really, when you consider the patsies they'd be up against: the Wal-Mart slayer Sol Price, the firebrand Jeno Paulucci, the street fighter Leonard Riggio, the cunning trial lawyer Joe Jamail, the beloved Bill Cosby, the awesome Warren Buffett, or maybe Bernard Rapoport, aching for a second victory, or the demure Ted Turner, or what about the tongue-tied Phil Donahue or that introvert George Soros? Hey, come on, let's stop kidding ourselves. They're beating us. All we can do is go through the aggressive motions and hope for a miracle. Think about what I said at the outset. I haven't made up my mind yet, and I don't know about the CEOs, but just think about how bad a smaller, compromised SRO victory would really be compared to the wholesale popular revolt that might follow if we manage to drag things out into next year. Meanwhile, I'll keep in touch if there are any new developments, and I trust you'll do the same. By the way, before we break up, have any of you reconsidered canceling your vacations? No? No one? All right, then, see you in September."

Also unbeknownst to Lobo, Jasper Cumbersome summoned the CEOs to the penthouse boardroom for a quo vadis meeting in response to a stinging editorial in the previous day's *Wall Street Journal*. Titled "Whither the Withering CEOs?" the editorial recounted the weakening position of big business vis-à-vis the Meliorists and slammed the "inactivity, inattention, and insipidness" of the CEOs. "And this was supposed to be the supercharged vanguard army for free enterprise capitalism?" the writer asked mockingly. "About the only elbow grease we've seen from them has been their flat-out opposition to their investors voting on the fat pay packages they give themselves. Bring back the tough John D. Rock-efeller and the wily J. P. Morgan." The newspaper did not know that the CEOs' temporary withdrawal was a deliberate strategy on their part, designed to give them greater "flexibility," and that much was being done by Lobo's sizable operation without their being up front. But a month had passed, a month filled with congressional hearings and rising public tumult and demands. It was time for an evaluation.

CEO Cumbersome brought the meeting to order and reported that the money was flowing in nicely. The war chest was now up to $3 billion after some large contributions from a few hedge fund billionaires. "But I'm afraid we've got more money than strategy," he lamented, throwing the meeting open for suggestions.

"As a lifelong sailor," said William Worldweight, "I know what a good trim tab can do to the ship's direction. Our power has always been our trim tab. So long as we kept piling it up, we never had to think about what to do if we ever started losing it from within. We were ready for the Communist threat because we could fire up the hot rhetoric and call out the Marines, the Army, the Navy, the Air Force. I don't think the 101st Airborne will be of much use to us now against their own families and friends. Sure, we still have the power to bring down the economy and blame the SROs, but it will be on our own heads, and our heads will roll. We'd be betting the house, and we'd lose."

"If I may interject on that point," said Wardman Wise, "Lobo has sent us an intercept of what appears to be an authentic communication between some of the SROs, and that's exactly what they want us to do. They want us to be in fight-to-the-finish mode. They directly challenged us to those public debates to polarize us further. They don't want us to be flexible and position ourselves so we can cut the deck on Capitol Hill. They smell total victory for their Agenda. But please continue, William."

"I don't have much more to say, except to ask my friends around the table to give their interpretation of what seems to be the most popular poster in the daily demonstrations and marches. I'm sure you've all seen it many times on television and in the newspapers: 'What's the Big Deal? We Earned It.' I am eager to hear your views."

Samuel Slick slapped the table impatiently. "Just listen to yourself, William. Where have you been? Our wealthy classes have had a great run, longer than could ever have been imagined. As we grasped for more, we got more. As we acquired more power, the people contented themselves with less power. It's astonishing in the light of history, really. Arthur Schlesinger postulated that reform movements arise every thirty years or so in the United States, but after the tumult of the 1960s, the 1990s came and went with barely a whimper. I'd have thought that the multitudes had more fight in them. More recently, I'd have thought that the Internet would give them the tools to connect, to find each other, to organize. Instead they've been playing computer games, gossiping, and exhibiting themselves and their pathetic lives on their websites, blogs, and Facebook. Marx would have had to revise his definition of the opiate of the people from religion to the Internet.

"But those days are gone now. It's taken more like forty years, but the masses are on the move. What does that poster mean, William? Obviously, it's about the Meliorists' Agenda. And how can I say that the people carrying the poster are inaccurate or greedy or misled? They work their fingers to the bone, holding down one, two, three jobs, and still their bills pile up and they go without. They work for us while we make ten or twenty thousand dollars an hour. I know I'm supposed to be a hardliner here, especially coming from the oil industry, but hell, I grew up with people who could carry that sign. I was born into a poor family. I saw my aunt die at forty-six because she didn't have the money for surgery. My dad came home once with his hand crushed from a power press accident in the shop. My mother made a few bucks as a seamstress while raising five children in what you'd have to call a glorified shack. Some of you have similar stories of hardship and deprivation. Some of you tell me you teach Sunday school. What the hell for, given what we all do during the week? What a farce we play, Lucifer. Do we believe in the Bible? Do we believe in the Golden Rule? Sure, who doesn't until Monday morning, when the gold rules. How much money do we need to provide for seven generations of progeny? I'll bet when you were in your twenties, if someone asked you how much you expected to make by the time you were sixty, your answer wouldn't even be a hundredth of what you're making now. Adjusted for inflation.

"Maybe we should start saying what we think instead of thinking about what we should say. The Meliorists represent the mildest rebellion we're ever going to see. What do you think is likely to come later, not only for us but for our children and grandchildren? You know how Americans are. They take it and take it and take it, and then they explode and tear it all down if their rulers cling rigidly to greed as their sole creed. The Meliorists? Just think about the soft meaning of the name they've chosen for themselves. Is it ever going to get better for us than that? Workers, after decades of loyal labor, are losing their jobs to China as corporations blend criminal communism with criminal capitalism. Their sons are sent overseas to fight, kill and die for crooked politicians and their corporate paymasters. Pensions are disappearing. Those lucky enough to have jobs watch their benefits and pay shrinking while we accumulate more pay, more bonuses, more stock options, more golden parachutes. Millions of American children go to sleep hungry, with diseases of hunger. The masses aren't going to stay dumb forever just because they're the masses. Every empire in the world has fallen apart or decayed because the people who ran the show believed it could never happen there. Have we got some drug that immunizes us from this historical fact?"

Slick paused and looked directly across the table at Hubert Bump. "Maybe you think I've disqualified myself from this august group of CEOs. If you think I should quit, just tell me and I'll go quietly, keeping your confidences. But first I want to hear what's really on your minds and in your hearts now that Hubert and I have broken the ice of self-censorship and double-talk. I guess I'm too old for that endless bullshit." He sighed, took a long drink of water, and waited.

The silence in the boardroom was total. It went on for one minute, two minutes, three. Many faces around the table were red. A few were ashen.

Finally Cumbersome spoke. "Well, who's next on the block? If we're ever going to let it all hang out, now is the time and place, I suppose."

"Can we have a little consideration of context and consequence at this point, if Mr. Slick doesn't mind?" said Justin Jeremiad facetiously. "Does anybody know whether any of the Washington lobbies are indulging in this kind of introspection? And suppose we were to commence negotiations with the SROs and their forces on Capitol Hill. How would our Washington allies react? And what would Lobo do now that we've unleashed him? It's getting complicated."

"Our information," said Wardman Wise, "is that the lobbies are proceeding as expected with the straight-arm approach to their opponents. We can't be seen as saboteurs or weaklings by our peers, not to mention our growing number of donors who think that we too are proceeding resolutely and effectively with our own straight-arm, not to overuse the football metaphor. It looks to me like we may have gotten ourselves into a box we can't get out of, not even to get into a different box. Some important thoughts have been expressed by our two colleagues, unwelcome as those thoughts may be. Perhaps that's why the unadulterated pursuit of profit is so enjoyable—it spells unity, solidarity, with no broader concerns intruding. It's almost martial in its discipline. Greed has few doubts at its extreme. I don't believe any of us is anywhere near that extreme, but we know there are those in the world of commerce who do fit that description."

"Without impeaching anything that's been said, aren't we getting a bit airy?" asked Edward Edifice. "I mean, we do have an elaborate Agenda to cope with. Why don't we meet in a couple of days and go through the Agenda item by item to see what we'd like to modify, within the reality that after August we're likely to get our asses hosed. I don't see Lobo as having any special August strategy. This is going to be the hottest peacetime summer in American history, and I'm not talking Fahrenheit. There's just no escaping the Meliorists and their throngs of supporters. Everywhere I go, everywhere I look and listen and read, they're there. The people are a-coming, and not just in a song. The level of organization, the speed of response, the discipline, preparation, and depth, the quality of their bench, their seemingly inexhaustible resources—their presence extends so far and wide that they've obliterated the Red State/Blue State boundaries. You can even feel it on the golf links, in the clubs, in our children's private academies, at the symphony and the theater during intermission.

"I know what some of you are thinking, even now. Sure, we're still in charge, nothing has happened yet, our temples aren't crumbling. It reminds me of the optimistic man who fell out of a skyscraper. As he passed the fifty-fourth floor, a secretary looked out the window. 'How are you doing?' she asked. 'So far so good,' he replied."

"I endorse Ed's excellent suggestion," said Roland Revelie. "May I urge the chair to schedule another meeting after we've all conducted a section-by-section analysis of the so-called Seven Pillars of the Agenda? I think it will take about ten days, which will put us into the August recess, when the Congress is out of town."

"Is that the sense of the meeting?" asked Cumbersome. "All in favor say aye. . . . Fine, the ayes have it, but you'll have to let me know how to reach you, since we'll all be out of town too, taking our well-earned vacations. Before we leave, does anybody here want to take up the SROs' debate challenge? I know I don't. I can't see anything but downside to that trap."

"But if Lobo can come up with someone who can really put on a show of strength," said Ichiro Matsuda, "then why not? We may learn something from new minds who see things in a more combative way than we do."

"Fair enough," said Cumbersome. "We'll ask him. Meanwhile, until further notice, we're adjourned."

A few days before Maui Eight, Bill Joy arrived at the mountaintop hotel to conduct his usual sweep of the premises, with more than the usual reasons to suspect an intrusion, because of some tidbits he'd picked up from his unsuspecting and still undetected mole.

Amazing how the powerful could turn a blind eye to the so-called lowly who served them.

That evening, Bill was sitting out on the deck sipping pineapple juice when the effusive Ailani brought him his freshly cooked dinner of mahimahi with papaya salsa. "I think we've just had some guests who may interest you," she said. "They asked lots of questions and seemed to be working hard to act like vacationers. Anyhow, I was cleaning the atrium one morning when I saw one of them dart away, but not before he dropped something. I picked it up, but I couldn't figure out what it was." She fished around in her apron pocket. "Here it is. Maybe you'd like to have it?"

"I would, Ailani, thanks. And how are your children?"

"They're fine, just fine, full of energy. In fact, I can't wait for the summer to end so they can get back to school," she laughed, continuing on her rounds.

Bill studied what Ailani had given him. It was the lens of a tiny camera. He finished his dinner, went to his room, and unpacked his detection equipment. Several hours later, he had located twenty-eight microphones and seven micro-cameras in the hotel and on the grounds, but he didn't disturb any of them. At breakfast the next morning, he spent a long time chewing his food and reflecting. Then he rose slowly from the table, retrieved his rental car, and drove six miles to a bluff designated by the Maui Tourist Office as a scenic overlook. He stepped out of the car, walked fifty yards or so, just in case whoever bugged the hotel had got to him too, and turned toward the ocean to put in a call to Omaha.

"Hi, Warren, Bill Joy here. Well, it's finally happened. The place is wired to the rafters with all the latest in cameras and mikes. The way I see it, I can either do a full sweep and hope I get them all, or I can leave them there so we can give our spies a weekend of disinformation. That could be fun, but it'll take a Newman-caliber performance from of all of us. Besides, we'd have to find some other secure place to meet and plan our scenes. What do you think?"

"Well, I need a little time to switch gears here, since I've been absorbed in our CEO distraction legislation on executive compensation and investor control. It's really sapping the CEOs' attention, especially because they can't go public with it. Instead, they have to make dozens of lengthy 'educational' calls to their brethren to get them contacting their members of Congress. This major tilt in their lobbying is costing them on the Agenda legislation because they're spending their political capital on their own greed and perks. I'm feeding the story to some major media friends so that the publicity will erode their position further. Call me back in half an hour, will you, and I'll refocus on Maui. In the meantime enjoy the vistas."

Thirty minutes later, Bill called back.

"This is a tough one," Warren said. "I'm going back and forth. On the one hand, the easy way out is not to go to the hotel at all and rent another place instead, maybe on another island. Whoever did this would only know one thing—that we're on to them, assuming their bugging hasn't spread to our other networks. But you've been checking those, right?"

"All clear, as far as I can tell, which is plenty."

"The harder path is to go there and do as you suggest—lead them down the road of false leads. But what might those be? We won't know until we meet somewhere else to thrash them out. And do we want to take the risk when we're winning? What risk? Well, suppose we all put on an Academy Award performance with a great disinformation script. Still, given what modern technology can do, they could splice the pictures in such a way as to show me on your lap in an amorous pose, Bill. You really can't win when you give them the raw digital material in a private location where there are no reporters or third-party observers, as there are at a congressional hearing or a news conference. And they could use their audio and visual recordings to clothe our meeting in an aura of conspiracy at odds with our championing of an open society. In other words, they can create their own disinformation if we let them.

"But we do have to meet. We have important matters to discuss. We can't postpone for another month, because in August we'll be gearing up for the home stretch on the Agenda drive, starting with Labor Day. So how about this? We go to Hawaii, but to a different hotel on a neighboring island. We'll have to find a small one with no guests because of a cancellation, or else just buy the place out and let the owners cancel on whatever guests are there, with more than adequate compensation. Over at our old hotel—damn, I hate to be driven out of there—we'll play a practical joke on our bugging pals. We'll find some raucous rock band, or a gathering of antique car buffs or realtors or salespeople, or—wait a minute, I've got it! Alpha Sig!"

"Pardon me?" Bill said.

"Alpha Sigma Phi. It's the fraternity I joined when I was at Penn. It happens that the graduating seniors are getting together in Philly this weekend to talk about what they can do on behalf of the Agenda for the rest of the summer, and to have a last fling before they start work. I know because they invited me to come speak to them. I had to decline because I'd be in Maui, but now *they're* going to be in Maui, because I'm going to give them an all-expense-paid trip to our hotel. I'll tell them it's just something I want to do for them as a fraternal gesture, to make up for my absence. They're good kids, but with everything on the house, I'm sure we can count on them for some good old-fashioned wild behavior that will give our buggers an eyeful and an earful. It will all have to be done lickety-split, of course, but it's manageable when the money is there. What say you?"

"I say they don't call you the Oracle of Omaha just for your wealth, Warren. But let me make sure I've got it right. I go back to the hotel and say we unexpectedly have to cancel for the weekend but we're still paying the full tab and sending a replacement party. You contact your boys and fly them out here for their free stay in paradise, with one stipulation. I think you should tell them that a crew from an ad agency will be filming on the premises all weekend for a series of spots showcasing the hotel, if they don't mind. That way they'll have indirectly waived any right of privacy they may later claim was violated by the hotel or anyone else. I'm sure it won't come to that, but it's still a wise precaution. Then we search the other islands for an exclusive hotel or club to host our meeting under the usual anonymous cover. Can we get all that done in time to notify the rest of the core group of the new location?"

"Patrick and I will begin making the arrangements right away. Since you're already there, stay put, and as soon as we find a new hotel, you can hop over and spread around whatever gratuities are necessary to empty the place out. Once you've done that, our trap will be fully laid. In the immortal motto of Alpha Sigma Phi, 'The cause is hidden, the results well known.'"

"Alpha Sig forever!" Bill said.

CHAPTER 15

On the last Friday of July, the Meliorists began arriving at the oldest of the Hawaiian islands, Kauai. Patrick Drummond had persuaded the owners of a small hotel under renovation to reopen a week early to accommodate some elderly people who had always wanted to see Waimea Canyon, a natural wonder that was smaller than the Grand Canyon but no less spectacular. The hotel's principal claim to fame was that it was perched on a knoll high above the canyon. Certainly it wasn't known for its cuisine or its roughhewn rooms. "It reminds me of my old summer camp in New Hampshire back in the thirties, except it's got running water and toilets," Max said. Bill Joy had swept the place the day before just in case. Now he smiled to himself as he thought about the frat party that was getting underway over in Maui.

The Meliorists had been in constant contact all through July, so there was no need for an update. They were all looking ahead to what Bill Cosby called the "August Ascension" and the "September Showdown."

"Welcome one and all to this place of the primitive gorge and stunning scenery," Warren said that afternoon when they were all gathered. "Let's get some housekeeping items over with first. You are fundraising Einsteins. More than I could ever have imagined, you've broken through the parsimony of the plutocrats. You've created the buddy system of all buddy systems for raising money. You've pitted them in a race against each other, a kind of modern mega-potlatch competition. Which is a long way of saying our receipts have hit fourteen billion dollars, with pledges—get this—of eight billion more by Labor Day. Apparently the amount of money

543

being made from money is going off the charts. America is Hedge Fund Heaven, and you've struck celestial gold. To all of you, congratulations, but frugality and efficiency still rule this golden roost, I assure you.

"As for expenditures, we are up to six and a quarter billion in paid expenses and two hundred fifty-five million in incurred expenses. Some of these payouts were in advance—such as those for the CUBs, to keep them in robust revolving funds for their mass mailings, or to get discounts for our media buys through August—but just look what we've done with a sum less than two months' profit for ExxonMobil. Political scientists will not only study this performance for years to come, but they'll revise their judgment about what it takes to make social change. Mind you, I'm not counting my chickens just yet. The scene looks pretty good, but our watchword remains 'Take absolutely nothing for granted.'

"I have a request from Promotions about reaching the many people whose awareness of what we're doing is still largely confined to TV sound bites and doesn't go much beyond 'Oh, those rich old guys are giving the big boys fits.' Promotions wants to produce millions of DVDs focused on the Agenda topics and geared to various constituencies, along with a composite DVD to give people the whole story. They plan to get celebrity endorsements to help our networks move the DVDs into millions of living rooms, clubs, and eateries. They point out that further motivation, contemplation, and discussion will follow, so that it will be easier for all our outreach programs and budding organizations to bring more and more people into the movement. It's hard to argue with their logic, and their fifty-million-dollar budget seems more than reasonable. Do I hear any objections?"

"Do we object to the sun coming up or to the rains coming down on parched earth?" Yoko asked.

Warren smiled. "I suppose it's unanimous, then. Patrick Drummond of our Secretariat will now present several items for our attention."

"Thanks, Warren. I'll begin by noting an interesting aspect to our opposition. There is no fascistic element arising because the business community believes that the CEOs and the Washington lobbies have the situation about as well in hand as can be. They are impressed by the mass media buys, by the past invincibility of their side, and by the continued dominance of the Bulls in Congress, with their corporate president in the White House. Thus, we do not have to deal with the rogue element that would have made it more difficult to combat or control the CEOs' counteroffensive. Our avoidance of foreign and military affairs has also helped to preempt these extremists. But more hecklers are showing up at some of our events.

"We've succeeded in distracting many CEOs through the proposal in Congress to give investor-owners authority over executive compensation. They're all over it, like bees to flowers, and it's diluting their overall effort. They know it, too, so they're not ballyhooing their work on their pay, but the *Wall Street Journal* certainly picked up on it. On another front, our counter-ads seem to have shown up their scare campaign as a case of crying wolf. The satiric touch has made them look even more foolish than their predecessors over the past hundred years who did the same thing with Social Security, Medicare, tobacco, labor laws, and so on. The most effective ad was the one about dire business warnings against abolishing child labor.

"We're now coming down to the vote-counting stage on the Hill. We need enough votes to override White House vetoes—two-thirds or more. We know we have a third of the Congress, because they've already declared themselves. About fifteen percent have expressed solid opposition, though for some it may be an act to help them keep raising money. The rest of the members are playing things close to the vest, reading the tea leaves, waiting for shoes to drop, and barring the lobbying locusts from their offices. Their refrain is 'Let's keep an open mind and let all sides have their say. This is a time to listen to all concerned.' Convenient, isn't it?

"Our sources are conveying a puzzling situation with regard to the CEOs. They just seem to be raising money and letting Lobo, and now Brovar Dortwist, do the work. Lobo can't seem to get them directly involved. They're hunkering down for some reason. They've turned down media interviews, held no news conferences, ignored your debate challenge, and generally put themselves on hold while the Washington lobbies go through their humdrum motions, goaded by Lobo and Dortwist. Question: Is it time for you to seek them out for individual meetings the way they sought you out earlier? We don't seem to have any other way of getting more information about this puzzle."

"I don't see why not," George said. "What can we lose? We'll get more out of them this time around because they're up against the wall."

"I agree," said Sol.

"Same here," said Jeno.

"Of course," said Yoko.

"Sure," said Bill Gates, "but we need to pair ourselves off carefully to maximize the value of these get-togethers."

"And we need to do it in a way that doesn't start counterproductive rumors that we're cutting some kind of deal," added Joe. "The CEOs will insist that the meetings be private, so let's have evidence for the files ahead of time about the purpose of these meetings, in case of leaks."

"One of our chief purposes," said Paul, "should be to see if there's any budding statesmanship among them that we can nourish. We shouldn't assume we're dealing with one-hundred-percent intransigence. After all, the pressure bearing in on them may be having some meditative impact. They're so used to winning that this must seem like a trauma to them, and we should probe for any such psychological vulnerabilities. They may be entering a phase of face-saving and what they view as flexibility."

"Right," Ted said. "And we'll be busy as all get-out in August, but we still have to take all these meetings before the end of the month."

There were nods of strenuous agreement around the table.

"Okay," Patrick said, "I'll pass out the CEOs' names and addresses and you can check off your preferences, but remember that you probably won't find them at home. The oligarchs just will not sacrifice their August vacations even to save themselves from the Agenda. They'll be heading for Jackson Hole, Sun Valley, the Hamptons, the Maine coast, Nantucket, Bohemian Grove, the Canadian Rockies, the French Riviera, Switzerland, and the other haunts of the rich and famous."

Ted grinned. "Well, we'll just have to make the best of it."

"You know, we're becoming action heroes whether we like it or not," Warren said, "so are we on the same page when I suggest that we spend much of the month energizing and inspiring the various mobilizations and events? Ten or twelve appearances each where we're most needed shouldn't be too exhausting. Short notice is probably best so our opponents don't have time to shift their resources to our venues. I think the crowds will really appreciate our grasp of the details of the Agenda legislation and how it will improve their lives."

Joe jumped in. "And that's exactly what people individually have got to feel. The cleaning woman should be figuring out what kind of life she can now afford at ten dollars an hour with health insurance. Workers should begin to dream of how their family situation will improve once they have a union bargaining for them to protect their workplace, their safety, and their health. Workers, down at the basic level of daily life, deserve having a say."

"I have a general question for Patrick," said Bill Gates. "As the Secretariat marshals the daily input from all our networks and from Analysis, Promotions, Mass Demonstrations, and Recruitment, have you been able to identify any soft spots?"

"Well, as of now, there's always a potential soft spot regarding the level of intensity among the millions of people standing for our Agenda. You all know about my chief of staff's 'lesson plan,' and our organizers have been using it with mixed results. When all is said and done, intensity is hard to measure, and our people haven't really been tested yet as they will be at crunch time. It's easy to roar approval, much harder to be speedily resilient when many things have to be done without delay and done well to get the Agenda through Congress. At the same time, it's worth mentioning that we are neither fully knowledgeable about nor in control of what will be happening on our side, and that's a measure of our success. People aren't waiting on us, although our resources continue to be crucial.

"As for other soft spots, the big one, or at least the big unknown, is Congress. The sooner we get more members committed publicly, the more difficult it will be for the CEOs when the arm-twisting really begins in earnest after Labor Day. Our side is flooding the members with messages and requests for meetings. The press is on the Agenda story locally and nationally every day. But until we get better signals from the Double Z about each of the Bulls, we can't tailor our next moves as precisely as we'd like."

"Still," said Peter, "there's good reason to believe that the mood in Congress is shifting powerfully to our side, so I think we should be looking ahead to what collateral amendments and legislation we can get through in the wake of the Agenda bills. I'm especially interested in finding out what we might be able to repeal of all the bad legislation that was passed when the business lobbies were in the ascendant for so long. Can you send us a memo on repeal possibilities?"

"We certainly can," Patrick said, "and we'll survey the conventional citizen organizations in Washington to see what they may have in mind. But we have to make sure that any repeals don't get caught up in the congressional tradeoff game on the Agenda. We need to move them through quietly in the midst of the chaotic final days."

"What I want to know," said Yoko, "is how all of you are feeling. How are your spirits, your energy? Are you getting enough rest? How are your families and friends holding up?"

Phil snorted. "What are you, our shrink, Yoko? Though I guess you've got a point. If any one of us has any serious problems, it's only fair to the rest of us to tell us now. We can't have any unexpected dropouts due to shattered nerves, medical problems, or marital splits. Anyone in any of those categories?" He paused and looked around the table. "No one? Okay, does that satisfy you, Yoko?"

"Testiness is often a sign of nervous exhaustion," Yoko replied tartly. "I rest my case for rest."

"This appears to be an excellent time to break for a relaxing dinner," Warren said diplomatically. "Afterward, we'll have an hour of silence and then retire to follow Yoko's wise advice."

Whereupon the Meliorists repaired to a plain but delicious meal in the rustic dining room, took in the sunset over the canyon, and returned to the conference room for the hour of silence. When Warren had first introduced this elbow-to-elbow solitude—"time for myself among ourselves," as he put it once—many of the core group found it weirdly countercultural. No longer. Now they marveled at how productive and concentrating and stimulating these hours of silence were—even Ted, for whom they were at first challenging and then transformative. "Silence disciplines," he often said, to the mild surprise of his colleagues.

In the morning, Paul opened the discussion. "We've been developing wonderful distractions for the right-wing media, for the CEOs, and for certain members of Congress, but let's talk about our lame-duck president. He's distracted himself with his endless costly military quagmires in Asia. His polls have dropped to a new low, but he seems determined to persist in his rock-headed stubbornness. We know that he'll want to veto most of the Agenda, but can he? Even if we don't have two-thirds or more of the Congress to override his veto, his party still wants to get reelected. His vetoes will hang Republican incumbents out to dry, exposing them to an even greater risk of defeat than they're already facing. He may not care personally because he's in his final term, but does he want to go down in infamy and take his party with him? Even if we have the votes to override his vetoes, they still taint the Republicans as standing in defiance of the large majority of the American people in their pursuit of a caring and competent government.

"The president's wars and military budgets are draining the country's resources and generating massive annual deficits. Ordinarily he could claim that there's no money for our Agenda. Unfortunately for him, the Seven Pillars either cost the government very little, or pay for themselves by cutting waste, or can be funded by the tax reform bill, which shifts the tax burden from ordinary people and raises revenues by closing loopholes and shelters. I think we need to keep his overseas distractions and his limited options as an unpopular president on the front burner as we move the legislation through Congress. We have to be prepared for how fast the president's role will come up the moment Congress finishes its job. Which is another way of saying we have to win the Congress and the White House as if they were one. We win the White House through the way we win in the Congress."

"But in this complicated chess game," said Phil, "the president, to the extent that he's not too distracted by his foreign adventures, will try to reverse the sequence. He'll try to win as president by winning in Congress. That means we have to find ways to soften him up and keep him on the defensive as well. Warren, I think the Secretariat should transmit our discussion, everyone willing, to Analysis, Promotions, the Congress Project, and Electoral Reform, to make sure their forward strategy absorbs this White House dimension sooner rather than later."

"Unless there's any objection," Warren said, "so done. Leonard, did you have something to add?"

"We've spoken often of a layered capacity for prevailing in Congress and against the CEOs through second- and third-strike capabilities that reformers rarely possess. It's this relentless reserve power that takes the opposition by surprise and breaks their will. As I see it, given our growing preparations at the community level, and given the CEOs' and the lobbies' late start and their continuing complacency, we should be going for knockout blows, faits accompli, rather than squeaker victories diluted by compromise. The Congress Watchdogs, with their two thousand core people in each congressional district, need to be alert to every opportunity for keeping the pressure on. For example, they should be working on the legislators' staffers, not just on the legislators, finding the budding dynamos among the congressional aides and policy analysts. Or they should be thinking ahead to a late wave of organized relatives, children, and friends of any vacillating members of Congress. These people usually bring up the rear, for obvious reasons, but when they do step forward, as we saw often during the Vietnam War years, their impact on the legislators can be decisive.

"Yesterday Patrick mentioned the intensity of our supporters as one of the unknowns, but as I see it, when you have the structures in place that we have right now, building intensity is a ready process of feasibilities. With the Congress Watchdogs, it's a matter of continually assessing the emotional and intellectual preparedness of the core two thousand, and of having our organizers go all out to step it up during August. Sure, the two thousand are on board, and they've accomplished a lot and learned a lot beyond what they brought to the project, but I'm speaking of taking them to another level in preparation for the grueling months of September and October."

"I find it encouraging," Yoko said, "that the Seventh-Generation Eye and the Meliorist wreath are seen everywhere these days, on millions of T-shirts, buttons, hats, even lawn signs for the CEP candidates. Promotions has discouraged tattoos, but all kinds of promoters and copycats are getting into this lucrative act, and no way can we control them. Still, there's no substitute for real dissemination, so that's fine by me. We want people giving these items out personally, or even selling them, with all the face-to-face conversation that entails. Art in the service of humanity, conveying the pathways to a decent society—with a little commerce thrown in."

"By the by," Sol said, "your new design for the Eye with the Seven Pillars is great, Yoko. It's being posted prominently in the stores and offices of the sub-economy, and many of these businesses are reporting increased patronage as a result. That's terrific. Every day it gets better and better, which is what momentum and replication are all about."

"Are the lawmakers being sent invitations to the Sun God festivals and other events in their states?" Ross asked. "Can you give us an update on the invitational tactic, Patrick?"

"Gladly. There are so many personal invitations going out to each member of Congress for the August recess—parades, rallies, meetings, fairs, festivals, reunions, debates, accountability sessions, teach-ins, church suppers, service club anniversaries, and so forth—

that if the members accept just ten percent of them, we'll be very pleased. But the fact is that they'll have to say no to a lot of them, just because of the sheer volume, and since that will upset the groups they turn down, they're likely to send assistants in their place, and then the assistants will report back the energy and substance they'll have witnessed firsthand. At every event, the legislators or their assistants will be asked to speak about one or more of the Pillars, which gives us another squirm factor for the members who haven't yet declared themselves on the Agenda. For all suitable venues, the media will be invited as well. Personally, I must say that at first I was skeptical about this tactic. Now I see it as smart and nearly costless since all the events will be going on anyhow."

Warren arched an eyebrow. "All of you may take that as an exceedingly rare compliment from the estimable Patrick Drummond, who is now passing out a suggested schedule of appearances for each of you at major events in August, as we discussed yesterday. Our field staff will handle all the logistics. I hope that in addition to speaking to these large audiences, you'll find time either before or after to meet briefly with some of the lecturers and organizers and members of the Congress Watchdogs for some personal time and mutual encouragement.

"And now I suggest we break for lunch and spend the afternoon strategizing about our meetings with the CEOs. Patrick will supply us with a list of them so we can make our choices and avoid duplication. I think it best if we all make our own arrangements directly with our selected CEOs—once we track them down at their resorts and vacation homes. After the meetings, we'll feed the relevant intelligence back to the Secretariat. Let's reconvene in the dining room at seven for dinner, and then an hour of productive silence before we retire to be fresh for tomorrow's half-day wrap-up and the long trip back to the mainland. A word of advice. Beautiful as our surroundings are, don't go walking around the premises. The terrain is too rugged and in some places treacherous, even for young people."

That night, as the Meliorists went to their modest rooms, the ever cautious Bill Joy walked the rugged and treacherous terrain with his trusty Husky flashlight and his state-of-the-art detection equipment. Although he would never say so to Warren, it wasn't all that rugged. Finding nothing, he earned the special peace of mind that made for a good long slumber.

Seven a.m. found Leonard in the breakfast room sipping a large glass of fresh pineapple juice while reading fact sheets about the members of Congress whose districts and states he was scheduled to visit. These printouts on the members and their circles, originally prepared for the Congress Watchdogs, were remarkably distilled and focused. For example, they listed the top ten most influential friends and associates of each lawmaker back home—business people, attorneys, educators, local politicians, judges, and even personal physicians and accountants—along with rankings of these people's support for the Agenda insofar as it could be determined. These influence circles would be crucial in swaying the members one way or the other.

Soon the other Meliorists sauntered into the breakfast room to partake of a dazzling variety of fruits and grains and egg dishes laid out by the proud waiters and the even prouder hotel manager. They spent a relaxed hour selecting, ingesting, and going back for more, chewing slowly and thoughtfully, as if observing some Buddhist ritual prior to meditation.

At 8:30 a.m., Warren called them into the conference room to put a question on the table. "At an earlier Maui meeting, we discussed at length the probable reactions of the corporations and lobbies once the struggle began. They've pretty much met our expectations so far—but I stress *so far*. At this point, from now until Congress adjourns in late October, what do you think might go wrong for us operationally? What's left for us to anticipate and forestall?"

"Well," said Bernard, "the other side of our blitz on Congress is a reverse blitz of inaction. The CEOs will pull out all the stops to get the Bulls to delay until the end of the session. That's their master play—blocking any action at all through manipulation of the rules and procedures by the key committee chairs. I know we're concentrating on this eventuality and pouring our troops into the states and districts where the Bulls preside, and I know that if they can't be persuaded, they can be overridden by discharge petitions. But what's to prevent them from buying time by deceptively assuring the progressives that the bills will be reported out once a fellow Bull's committee exercises its jurisdictional right to look them over, and so on ad infinitum? From my years of observing Congress, its genius is procrastination, stretching matters out to the point of no return. Some of the Bulls may even have been offered cushy jobs so they don't care if they lose in November. The stakes are so high for the corporatists that golden parachutes are chicken feed."

"So what that means," said Jeno, "is that we have to get commitments from as many Bulls as possible in August. That is the great challenge. Among us, we've met with most of them on Capitol Hill over the past few weeks, but meeting with them back in their districts and states is different. They may open up more on their home turf so that we can appeal to their better natures. There are no more than twenty-four real delay Bulls, and we should be able to get this done, since our speaking events have been deliberately situated in their jurisdictions. I'm a great believer in eyeball-to-eyeball. I've always done it in my businesses, I've done it with tough labor bosses and stubborn suppliers and regulators, and there's no substitute. After face-to-face meetings, the Bulls just won't be able to demonize us as our opponents are trying to get them to do."

"It doesn't hurt that the Double Z is all over this matter of the delay syndrome," Warren added. "They've already reported some breakthroughs and are coordinating with our activities back home. We expect most of the Bulls to fall in line if only because they fear being humiliated when the discharge petitions get going after Labor Day."

"I hope you're right," said Bill Gates, "but let's remember that the ranking members of the committees and subcommittees have leverage either way they go. We expect that they'll largely be with us, especially after their August experience with the people, but if they're not, there's an option we haven't yet discussed. Among the masses of information flowing from our operations in the field, I've begun to notice a pattern that comes as a very pleasant surprise, and one that should shake the CEOs, Brovar, and the Bulls to their shoe tops. Self-styled conservatives and libertarians are joining our efforts to limit corporate welfare, renegotiate global trade agreements, cut government waste, make corporate freeloaders pay marketplace rents for the use of public assets, step up law and order for corporate crime, protect investors, strengthen civil liberties and the right to privacy in the marketplace, and reform ballot access for third parties. It's possible that our adversaries may discern this pattern in the polls, but not unless they think of looking for it. We have it through direct reports from the field, names of people and organizations who have actively collaborated with our projects. Up to now they've come to us, drawn by the media coverage, but from now on we should reach out to them and tighten the alliance through all our forces on the ground, though without formalizing it. When the final crunch comes in Congress, this alliance will be the coup de grâce. No one in Congress can stand up to such combined pressure—it's the Bulls' ultimate nightmare. I can only imagine the expression on the faces of Lobo and Dortwist should it be necessary to unleash what we might call the right-left nuclear option. So, to the Secretariat, please pay special attention to this emerging unity during August."

"By all means," Warren said. "Patrick will ask Analysis to isolate the relevant data and feed it into the GIS. It will indeed give us a formidable weapon in the fall." He looked at his watch. "We have a little time left. Does anyone have anything to add?"

For the next hour, until they boarded their business jets for Honolulu Airport, the Meliorists discussed what could go wrong, the early signs of something going wrong, the ways they might have to respond personally, and the need to stay loose and light. "And to rest," Yoko added.

Meanwhile, across a few hundred leagues of ocean, the boisterous fraternity party was coming to an end as the participants dispersed for home. Sunday evening, the snooping quartet reappeared at the hotel as if to have a nice dinner, which they did, but of course they were really there to collect all their surveillance toys. Once they were back in their Mercedes, their leader, Sergei, called Lobo and excitedly told him that they had the entire meeting of the Meliorists in their hands, audio and video. Lobo ordered them not to dare listen or look, but to head for the Maui airport and ship the tapes immediately to his office in New York.

The package arrived early on Monday afternoon. Triumphantly Lobo received it and summoned his captains to the conference room for a viewing. He popped the first videotape into the player and sat back to enjoy the show.

Onto the screen of the big plasma TV came a group of clean-cut but obviously tipsy young men in Hawaiian shirts and leis. "Man, can you believe this is all on the house, guys? It's almost too good to be true," one of them shouted, throwing his arm around the young man next to him. "'Now everyone knows Alpha Sigma Phi,'" he sang, "'that they are the best just cannot be denied,'" whereupon the others joined in for a bibulous rendition of the fraternity song.

At first Lobo couldn't believe his eyes. There must be some mistake. Packages got mixed up. No, that was the hotel. Had the SROs discovered Sergei's handiwork and fabricated the hoax of hoaxes? Damn, but it was a good thing he hadn't called Jasper Cumbersome about what he believed was on its way from Maui. That would have been the end, the living end. Suddenly he was possessed by a consuming need for a quick tryst with his young pit bull, but not in front of his trusted associates, whose facial expressions betrayed deep concern, disbelief, and suppressed smiles that finally gave way to uncontrollable laughter as it dawned on them what had happened.

Soon Lobo joined them. They called for cases of cold beer, which were brought in one after the other by the unsuspecting mole. Uncontrollable laughter veered into slapping the table and leaning back in their chairs, some of them falling over in outbursts of mirth. Fueled by alcohol, they proceeded to watch all the tapes for the next three hours, drinking steadily and reacting with hilarity to the antics of America's future leaders. Ordered to stand by the entire time to fetch snacks and whatever else the revelers demanded, the mole, keen observer though he was, was utterly bewildered, but dutifully did as he was told.

The zenith of the evening was a conference call from Lobo to Sergei and his associates, who by then were celebrating in a Honolulu bistro. The fifteen-minute exchange between New York City and Hawaii burned up the wires and left the foursome floored, not to mention unemployed. When it was over and all his captains had gone home, Lobo's pit bull got a workout. Lobo slept on the floor that night, in his clothes, dead drunk, with his shirt half open. Even Lobo had his limits.

On the first day of the August recess, Congressman Billy Beauchamp once again boarded the Viscous Petroleum corporate jet and flew home to southwest Oklahoma. All through July, Willy Champ had regularly extended his polite invitation that Billy join him for a discussion of the issues, and by now Billy was in no mood to say no. For weeks his local and Washington offices had been overwhelmed by the escalating activities of the Meliorists' supporters. Rallies, marches, parades, lectures, meetings of Congress Watchdogs and local CUBs and chapters of the PCC—they were all over the Fourth Congressional District. Astonished and alarmed, Billy knew he had to step up to the plate in front of the citizenry he had served so faithfully—tracking down pension and Social Security and veterans' checks and so forth—for so many years.

He agreed to debate Willy Champ on Friday, August 22nd. That would give him a few weeks to make his usual rounds of the county courthouses, rodeos, and luncheon gatherings at the service clubs, the Legion, and the VFW. There were no union halls. There were no unions to speak of, despite labor's resurgence in other parts of the country. Billy's website neatly listed his entire schedule of appearances and addresses. He knew the Agenda people were ready and planning to be out in force with questions and proposals the likes of which he did not care to imagine.

Billy called up his old friends in hopes that they could help him get his bearings. They met for breakfast at Fran and Freddy's Feed, where pro-Meliorist buttons and T-shirts were more disturbingly in evidence than before, among the customers as well as the staff. Billy looked at the menu, saw that the breakfast specials were listed under the heading "Fair Deals," and lost his appetite.

"Okay, boys," he said, "let's not beat around the bush. How do you like my chances in the fall? Give it to me straight."

"Billy, you know we're all with you," said Hal Horsefeathers. "We're a longtime mutual admiration society. You've always been there for me and the other ranchers when we needed your intervention. But the district has changed dramatically in the past few months. For your own sake and for your upcoming tour, you need to get a handle on all the new developments."

"He's right, Billy," said Ernest Jones. "Even my employees at the bank are getting themselves stirred up. The way I see it, you have two choices: you can be briefed about the agitations, or you can experience them for yourself. There are events happening almost every day. Why not come with us to one of them and be an eyewitness, without us or your advisers filtering things for you? You can wear a disguise so no one recognizes you. What do you say?"

"I say it's a good thing I'm only seventy. Just listening to you fellows might send someone older into early retirement. Okay, I'm going to feel like a fool, but I'll take the disguise option. I like to see things for myself and assess them firsthand. When do we go?"

"Well," said John Henry, "the Clean Elections Party is holding these staggered 'Brain Fests'—that's what they call 'em—in halls and auditoriums around the district. There are introductory Brain Fests and advanced ones. Admission's free but by invitation. The CEP organizers have scoured the district to find the best combination of people from different occupations and ethnic backgrounds, young and old, a mix of politically seasoned Sooners and folks who don't have a clue about mobilizing themselves or influencing Congress. When the people arrive, they're greeted cordially by name and escorted to their seats. There's good food and drink available, and some great country music. Thursday there's an introductory meeting here in Lawton, and then an all-day advanced gathering in Oklahoma City on Saturday."

"Okay, I'm game, but how do we get invitations?"

"We haven't been twiddling our thumbs all these weeks, Billy," said Gil Groundwork. "We've already got invitations for ourselves, and we'll just say you're our guest, George Whitman, retired farmer. In case anyone sees through your disguise and raises a ruckus, we'll make a joke out of it—you were just trying to avoid distracting the audience and the speakers, didn't want to grandstand and crash the party, y'all understand."

Two days later, a minivan carrying Billy and his band of four pulled into the parking lot behind the five-hundred-seat Lawton High School auditorium. As he'd expected, Billy felt ridiculous in overalls, beard, and straw hat, but Gil assured him the getup was very convincing.

The place was throbbing with activity. People seemed upbeat, curious, and expectant. Every seat was taken, and the standing room was filled to the limit set by the town's fire marshal. The stage was attractively decorated, with Old Glory on one side and the Oklahoma state flag on the other. Doug Dauntless, a Will Rogers impersonator, opened the proceedings by asking the audience to sing "America the Beautiful," and then delivered a stingingly funny down-home critique of the powerful and greedy interests that thrived on making America the Ugly. Will Rogers would have been proud of the way Dauntless pushed many in his audience to the limit and then brought them back to shaking their heads in agreement. He was giving the assemblage a tough-love mental workout, drawing on the wrongs he knew they had endured for so long in one way or another. He had words for the younger Oklahomans and for the older people and for just about everyone in between. He ended with some of Will Rogers' choice descriptions of Congress. The applause and the approving shouts were so loud that he knew he'd reached his audience, even the novices among them.

Billy leaned over and whispered to Hal, "I know quite a few of these folks. What are they doing here? They've been my supporters for years. What on earth is old Alma Gannon doing in a Patriotic Polly T-shirt?"

"What's that Dylan song from the sixties?" Hal whispered back. "'The Times, They Are A-Changin'?' It's just taken forty years, that's all. And the food's better now."

Before the next presentation came the first of a series of one-minute intervals designed to give members of the audience a chance to say a few words. A burly man in farmer overalls just like Billy's jumped up on the stage. He looked to be in his mid-forties, and had a broad red neck and a mess for a haircut. "You know what I think we're about here, pardners? It's time to apply the Golden Rule, Do unto others what ye want to be done unto you so we can get rid of the bosses and their big companies and their Rule of Gold, which is, Do us in and make sure we can't do back unto them." The speech took thirty seconds—farmers tend to be sparing with their words—and the crowd loved it, corny though it was. The man returned to his seat beaming.

Then onto the stage bounded Frosty Cloy, the lone populist publisher in the state of Oklahoma. For decades, his twice-monthly newspaper had been living up to its motto, "To comfort the afflicted and afflict the comfortable," borrowed from the inimitable Mr. Dooley, a.k.a. Finley Peter Dunne. Frosty occasionally displayed some contrary political prejudices that made him a little unpredictable, but he was a dynamic public speaker.

"Hello, neighbors, I think you all know me. I've been around so long one of my friends says I'm like barnyard manure—it just keeps coming day after day."

Groans rose from the audience, along with a few guffaws.

"You think that's a bad joke?" Frosty boomed. "Well, here's another one for you. We have a government of the people, by the people, and for the people."

His listeners sat up in their chairs, startled.

"Who's the joke on?" he roared.

Back came a scattered chorus of voices: "It's on us."

"And that ain't funny, is it?" Frosty rejoined.

"No," muttered the crowd.

"Now, who's the joker?" Frosty asked.

Amidst a mélange of answers, the red-necked farmer shouted out, "The big companies!" Many nodded in agreement. Then, as the audience quieted down, Alma Gannon stood up and said, "We're the jokers, for letting them control us."

"Aha!" said Frosty. "Now we're getting somewhere. The lady is correct. Why? Because if we only exercise it, *the people have the power*." Whereupon the lights dimmed and Patti Smith appeared on a big overhead screen with her band, singing her famous song "The People Have the Power." Many in the audience joined in. When the song ended and the lights came back up, the crowd was buzzing.

"Do you remember your state's history?" Frosty went on. "About a hundred and twenty years ago, the dirt farmers of Oklahoma were getting their heads pushed in the dirt by the interest-gouging banks and the price-gouging railroads. Then, with help from the surging farmers of East Texas, they started lifting their heads up, higher and higher. They started acting like the people have the power. It wasn't long before they took over the statehouse and the legislature as the vanguard of an American populism that was bent on putting the people before the robber baron corporations. The government and the politicians started listening to them and accomplished some good things, but after World War I the companies began reasserting their control. Over the past four decades they've turned our state into a corporate plantation with almost no opposition. The people do not have the power in Oklahoma. You do not have the power to achieve a living wage and insurance coverage for your families, to raise your children in a clean environment, to get full service or value for your tax dollars, to make the tax-dodging corporations pay their fair share so your load is lighter. Big business is always blocking Oklahomans from improving Oklahoma in all kinds of practical ways. Big companies are our masters, which is not what Thomas Jefferson, Abraham Lincoln, and Franklin Delano Roosevelt wanted for our country.

"So here's my question: There's a time for work and a time for play, a time for family and a time for community, a time to joke and a time to be serious. This is a time to be serious in concert with our community of neighbors, friends, relatives, and coworkers. How many of you are prepared to do that? How many of you want the power?"

Hands shot up all over the auditorium.

"And how many of you will put in the time to organize your power, to make things right in America and shape the future for your children so they can realize those last words of the Pledge of Allegiance, 'with liberty and justice for all'?"

By this time people were standing and raising both hands.

"All right! But now I'm going into risky territory. I'm going to make you indignant, uncomfortable, and embarrassed with a series of simple questions that you can answer silently to yourselves. But first, how many of you know the name of your congressman?"

Almost three-quarters of the audience raised their hands.

"Very good," said Frosty. "That's way above the average for the country, but then your congressman, the one and only Billy Beauchamp, has been in office for thirty-eight years doing the bidding of the business lobbies. Yet every two years people like you send him back to Washington with large majorities. He's flattered, fooled, and flummoxed too many people in this district, partly because he's had no opponent to expose him, or only a nominal opponent who might as well have waved the white flag from the get-go. That is not a democratic election. Democratic elections must give you a choice between at least two significant candidates, and better yet, lots of other candidates from smaller parties with big ideas, just like back in the farmer-populist days. Our state is a one-party state now, a Republican kingdom backed to the hilt by a giant media baron. While they're robbing us down to our skivvies, we're arguing about the fine points of Sooner football. And while they've got us tied up in their cash register politics from Oklahoma City to Washington, DC, we're paying the price and wondering about our bills, our financial security, our schools, and just plain getting through the day. Honest candidates—independents and folks from third parties—can't get on the ballot without a bathtub of money, and even then they have to cross their fingers and hope that their political opponents in charge of the state election machinery don't disqualify their petition signatures. Did you know that Oklahoma, on a per capita basis, is the state that makes it toughest for challengers to get on the ballot to give you a real choice and give the entrenched politicians a real run for their dirty money?

"Okay, let's play make-believe for a few minutes. Suppose you think of Billy Beauchamp and your two senators, Alvin Crabgrass and Fred Flagrant, as neighbors of yours whose salaries and benefits are paid for by your tax dollars, and who happen to have the power to spend twenty-two percent of your income every year, to raise your taxes so that the big boys pay less, to send your children off to reckless wars, and to funnel much of your tax money to the greedy few who fund their campaigns. How much time on average would you spend each month keeping an eye on these neighbors and trying to control them?"

Frosty paused and looked out over the sea of faces for a full minute. Billy Beauchamp shifted uneasily on his overall-clad derriere. Finally a few people raised their hands. Frosty called on them one after the other.

"Whatever it takes?"

"Maybe twenty hours a month. Depends on whether it can make a difference up there."

"How much time for what, with who? I need to know more."

"None. I don't even have time for my kids, with two jobs and a house to run."

"Me, I'd spend a hundred hours a month with all the other neighbors I could sign up to get the job done now so I could relax more in the future."

"Do it for us, Frosty. We trust you, and we'll raise the money."

"Isn't that what the Clean Elections Party is promising to do for us? Clean things up in Washington?"

"I'd have some tough meetings with these so-called neighbors at a backyard cookout where I'd grill them along with the burgers.

Nothing like sizing them up directly. But the thing is, they're *not* our neighbors. They're too far away, and not just geographically."

"Whoa!" barked Frosty. "Most of you are just making excuses for yourselves. They're different excuses, but they boil down to the same thing: it's too difficult to find the time, or if you have the time, you've got too many preconditions. Instead, your bottom line should be to make it happen *period*, just as you would if these Washington pols were sticking it to you as your next-door neighbors. Let's back up a bit. How many of you are spending a hundred hours a year—less than two hours a week—on watchdogging your members of Congress? And I'm not talking about asking them for favors or pork."

Out of more than five hundred people, two hands went up.

"How about fifty hours a year?"

No hands went up.

"Ten hours a year?"

Four hands went up.

"Well, how about no hours a year? Come on, come clean."

The vast majority raised their hands.

"My friends, you've just given yourselves the most important civics lesson of them all. Without you, how can the people be sovereign, how can they rule, how can they make government represent them instead of turn against them to serve the money boys while they pay for it twice, first for the government and then for what it does to them at the behest of big business? *You* are the people. The people are *you*. All over the country, folks have given up on themselves as founts of power. They don't think they count. They really believe they can't fight city hall or Washington or Exxon or Bank of America or DuPont. So what it comes down to is that you yourselves have done the job for the privileged, powerful few who control us. You've made it very easy for them. We're patsies, all of us. Okay, not quite all of us. We all know a few people who don't take it without a fight, and these people have done a lot for us over the decades, but there are nowhere near enough of them.

"Remember that movie *Network*? How bad do things have to get to make us madder than hell so we won't take it anymore? Our country is going downhill for everyone except those on top. I'm not going to go through the whole slide show of injustice. You can click through it just from your own daily experience, your daily pain, frustration, and anxiety. And what do you think is in store for your children? They're never going to know what a fixed pension is, what a small farm or ranch is, what an inexpensive public university education is, what privacy from the snoopers and hucksters is, what a jury trial for personal injuries is, what clean water is, what a clean election really means, what a good-paying job with full benefits and the right to strike is.

"Those of you who voted for Billy Beauchamp in the last election, raise your hands." Frosty surveyed the audience. "Looks like slightly over half of you did. And how many of you voted against him? . . . Okay, less than a fourth. How many didn't vote at all? . . . Looks like another fourth or so. All right, now I'm going to show you how important it is to do your congressional homework. Will the Lawton High volunteer seniors please pass out the cards?"

Two dozen seniors in "Sooners Rather Than Later" T-shirts quickly circulated through the crowd with printed cards listing fourteen questions to be answered yes or no.

1. Should all Americans have full Medicare coverage?

2. Should Social Security remain a public institution, or should it be partially or entirely privatized?

3. Should more resources be allocated to federal law enforcement against corporate crime, fraud, and abuse, and should penalties for the guilty be stiffened?

4. Are corporations paying their fair share of taxes, or should they receive more tax breaks than they have now?

5. Should public elections be funded publicly by a larger voluntary checkoff on the 1040 tax return, or should we retain the present system relying on private donations?

6. Should tax dollars go to subsidizing big companies through bailouts, handouts, and giveaways that tilt the playing field against companies that don't ask for or receive them?

7. Should the minimum wage be set at $10.00 per hour, which represents the same purchasing power the minimum wage had in 1968, adjusted for inflation?

8. Should Congress oppose White House budgets that come in year after year with large deficits, now totaling $9 trillion, with interest that will have to be paid by your children and grandchildren?

9. Should shareholders who legally own their companies have the power to approve or disapprove the salaries and bonuses of top executives?

10. Should the broadcast media have to pay rent to the Federal Communications Commission for use of the public airwaves that belong to all Americans?

11. The last time fuel efficiency standards were issued by the US Department of Transportation was thirty years ago; should updated standards go into effect to raise fuel efficiency by at least one mile per gallon per year?

12. Should Congress revise agribusiness support programs so that smaller farmers receive the bulk of the benefits instead of the factory farms receiving the lion's share?

13. Should Congress establish a nonregulatory federal consumer protection agency to oversee the health, safety, and economic interests of consumers, on a budget that amounts to 1 percent of the money the Department of Commerce currently spends to promote business interests?

14. Should taxpayers have the right to sue the government when they see waste and corruption affecting its programs, or should they be barred from the courtroom entirely without a chance to make their case, as they are now?

While the audience was checking off their answers, the high school band was providing the visceral rhythm of the Roman Army drumbeat in the background. Billy knew what was coming and was inclined to head for the exit, but his pride and his fear of being recognized, or accosted by a sharp reporter asking why he was leaving, kept him frozen in his seat.

When Frosty saw that the audience had finished with the cards, he gave the volunteers a signal to lower the screen again. The fourteen questions began scrolling down, with Billy Beauchamp's votes or his expressed positions noted alongside each of them. The scroll kept repeating against the low backdrop of the drumbeats as people compared their answers with Billy's record. Seconds turned into minutes, and the sound of agitated whispering grew throughout the auditorium. This was a Billy Beauchamp his constituents never knew. It wasn't so much anger they were expressing as a feeling that they'd been taken, just as Frosty had said—flattered, fooled, and flummoxed. Some recalled receiving a letter of congratulations from Billy when they graduated from high school or turned twenty-one or celebrated a twenty-fifth wedding anniversary. Such a nice, considerate man, they'd thought. Some simply refused to come to the natural conclusion, for to do so would be to admit how gullible they'd been, and that was too hard a pill to swallow.

Frosty called the session to order. The whispering stopped, and all eyes turned to him. "Now, don't be too hard on yourselves. What you've just discovered is being discovered in congressional districts all over the country where the Clean Elections Party is fielding candidates. So tell me, how many of you disagree with Billy Beauchamp on at least eleven of the fourteen issues?"

Almost 90 percent of the hands went up.

"How about all fourteen issues?"

About four out of five hands went up.

"If you'd known during the past several congressional elections what you know now, how many of you would have voted against Billy, either by voting for another candidate or staying home?"

Again, close to 90 percent of the hands went up, which meant that most of those who'd voted for Billy were now wishing they hadn't.

"Okay, how many of you will still stick with Billy even though you disagree with him on eleven or more of the fourteen issues?"

A dozen hands rose weakly into the air, but in back an arm shot adamantly straight up. It belonged to a muscular man in a tight T-shirt, perhaps in his early thirties.

"Friend, can you stand up and give your reasons?" Frosty said.

"Sure can," boomed the man. "Billy Beauchamp brings the bacon to his district—repaved roads, drought relief, programs to assist small business, a new courthouse, a hospital, and a federal prison. I know because I worked as a bricklayer on two of those projects. See this tattoo on my arm? It's the BBB brand, stands for Beauchamp Brings the Bacon. The best I can expect from politicians is them doing what's good for me and my family. I got good-paying jobs with benefits because of him. That's why I'm sticking with Billy in November, even though I disagree with him on other things, because those other things aren't that personal to my livelihood."

For the first time, a smile came over Billy's face. Hal gave him a friendly jab with his elbow and grinned at him. It wasn't just what the young man had said that gratified Billy and his little entourage. It was the million-dollar slogan he'd just given the campaign—in ranch country, no less—the triple-B brand. Beauchamp Brings the Bacon. Manna from heaven! What a combination—Billy's huge war chest and a great slogan!

"Folks," Frosty said, "our neighbor has done us a favor, taking our discussion to another level. If we can assume that most people wouldn't vote for a legislator who votes against their many legiti-mate interests and in favor of the lobbies that fund his campaign, what about the factor of bringing home the bacon, the pork? How should you weigh pork-barrel projects in your calculations? For starters, apart from the fact that you're paying for the pork, it's clear that you're also paying a big, big personal price in many directions and far into the future. Just look at those fourteen issues—and many more could have been added—that are driving our country downward, and most Americans along with it. Second, if the people ran their government, many of the projects our neighbor mentioned would be built anyhow, and probably more efficiently—a hospital, a courthouse, and so on. Maybe the prison would have gone else-where in any rational decision by Congress or the Department of Justice but, keeping the honest use of your tax dollars and your well-being in mind first and foremost, who needs a job from a prison? Likely there would be far fewer prisoners if we reformed our drug policy. I say let the prison go elsewhere, and let it have a special wing for crooked politicians."

A roar of approval erupted.

"And the problem isn't just Washington, DC. I've spent forty years covering the rot and ruin coming out of the state legislature and the governor's office. Let me run by you just a few examples of the cor-ruption that's brought so much suffering and so many plain raw deals to so many Oklahomans, and not only the poor ones." Frosty pointed to the screen, which was now showing one headline of out-rage after another from his award-winning newspaper: coverups of toxic drinking water, brutal treatment of institutionalized children, corporate ripoffs of school districts and local taxpayers, and on and on. After a while, it was enough to make some people gasp and hold their hands to their astonished open mouths.

"I bet you didn't read much about these displays of greed and raw power in the other Oklahoma papers. Our media baron, Flaylord, who controls what much of the Oklahoma press tells you—or refuses to tell you—is too busy looking out for his advertisers and his investments. But enough of him. So far we've been talking facts, opinions, issues. Now it's time for the agony of innocent human beings to be seen firsthand."

Frosty gestured to the front row, and onto the stage came twelve Oklahomans who one by one told their stories of abuse at the hands of the powers that be. The authenticity of their accounts had been thoroughly checked beforehand by Clean Elections Party researchers.

Up first was Helen Bradford, who in late middle age was diagnosed with ovarian cancer and lost her $19,000-a-year job along with her co-payment health insurance. Her cancer was advanced, but her physician told her she might have a chance with the drug Taxol. She asked how much would it cost. He said $14,000 for six treatments. She poked around to find out how the drug company could charge so much and learned that Taxol was discovered and tested by the National Cancer Institute with $31 million of taxpayer money. It was then given gratis, with a monopoly marketing agreement, to Bristol-Myers Squibb, which was free to charge whatever it wanted. As it certainly did. Helen couldn't go on Medicaid because she owned a six-room house and a six-year-old car. She had no relatives or friends to give her the money. "I just hope I live long enough to vote against Billy Beauchamp," she said.

Next was Gary Gomez, who suffered from a maddening body rash and respiratory ailments coming off a job involving prolonged application of pesticides and herbicides to dozens of acres of farmland, with no protective gear. When he applied for Workers' Compensation, the company that owned the sprawling agribusiness challenged his case, saying there was no evidence of causation between the chemicals and his disease. The case was now on appeal. He had no health insurance. He couldn't work. He had a wife, three children, and no income.

Mariah Grayson, a single mother from a poor neighborhood in Oklahoma City, bought some major household appliances on an installment loan, fell behind on the payments, and then found out that the fine print allowed the retailer to take her house as collateral. She held a foreclosure notice in her trembling hand. "How can this happen in America?" she wailed. "Where can I go for help?"

Sarah and Frank Harris told of an eminent domain order issued by their city government for their house and a dozen neighboring houses. The city's redevelopment agency intended to seize the homes, compensating the owners very modestly, and turn the land over to a shopping mall for expansion. "It's awful hard to get an attorney, even if you can pay, which we can't," Sarah said. "The mall guys have all the high-powered lawyers, and they've sure greased the city council. What happens to private property rights when the government can take your home and give it to a greedy corporation? I wrote to Billy Beauchamp, and a staffer replied that the congressman couldn't do anything to help us save our neighborhood because it's a local matter. I thought he had a lot of influence around here to help little people like us."

Following the Harrises was Jenny Tutt, who described the "overwhelming sense of disaster" she felt when local authorities told her that the entire housing development where she lived had been using drinking water with very high levels of lead for the past ten years. The problem stemmed from a combination of underinvestment in a new municipal water facility and the city's negligence in testing the water in the antiquated pipes. "My children, my three little children—they're four, six, and eight—have been drinking this poisoned water since they were born, and so was I when I was pregnant with them. It's harmed their bodies and their brains. My family will never recover from this. The politicians are quick to pay for more and more overpriced ships, bombs, and bombers, but they aren't interested in building modern purification plants for the American people, like me, who trusted them to do the right thing. Trusted them." She wept.

And so it went, one sad story after another, from the heart. The audience sat in silence, deeply affected. A few people were shedding tears along with Jenny because the stories seemed so hopeless, the words trailing off into futility, the speakers trapped, with no way out.

Then a tall, weatherbeaten man strode to the microphone. "My name is Jack Soaring Eagle, and I'm part Cherokee. Until last year I was earning fourteen dollars and twenty-six cents an hour as a foreman in a factory that made simple kitchen appliances. One day, the owners' representative called us together and told us the plant was closing down in four weeks and moving to China. We could stay on another month with double pay if we agreed to train our Chinese replacements, who would be flown over here for that purpose. The guy said the owners were sorry but they couldn't pass up sixty cents an hour. I had no choice, needed the money for my family. It was one of the worst feelings of my life. I started at that factory right after my stint in the army, and I worked for them for eighteen years. Plenty of the assembly line employees—none were in unions—had worked there their whole lives, given the place their all, and what did they get for their loyalty? Unemployment. There were no other jobs in our small rural town, and we had no other skills. We don't matter, have no say either with the owners or with the politicians who keep voting to export our jobs under these crazy trade agreements full of broken promises to the workers. Who's protecting us? The politicians want to make desecration of the flag a crime. Hell, they're desecrating our flag without touching it day after day. Well, it's time to do something about it. It's time to get a strong grip on our government and take control of our lives, for the sake of our families and our descendants for seven generations to come."

Frosty returned to the mike. "Amen to that," he said. "Look, folks, we're going to pass the hat a little later to see what we can do for our neighbors whose stories you've just heard, but that's not a real solution. We need fundamental, systemic change that offers long-term solutions to the heartbreaking problems they've described. Anyone care to come up here and give us a minute's worth of ideas?"

A woman in a flowered housedress made her way to the stage. "My name is Clarissa Clements, and here's what I want to say to Billy Beauchamp, wherever he is. You are not representing us. Your place of employment should be called the US House of Big Business Representatives. You've been deceiving us all these years, patting us on the head like we're children waiting for a little candy. Well, with meetings like these all over, you better believe your political days are numbered. It doesn't matter how much money you spend on TV or how many sugary slogans you come up with. So why not call it a day and just plain quit?"

All over the auditorium, people jumped to their feet. Some shook their fists. Others started a chant: "Quit, quit! Quit, Billy, quit!" The cadence happened to match the Roman Army drumbeat exactly, which was not lost on the band's drummers, who quickly joined in. "Quit, quit! Quit, Billy, quit!" Boom, boom! Boom-boom-boom-boom! As for the subject of the chant, so many of the people around Billy and his friends were standing that Gil and Hal jumped up too, to avoid being conspicuous. Billy couldn't bring himself to move. He'd broken out in a cold sweat, a sensation he hadn't felt since the newspapers reported twenty years ago that the Justice Department had caught him in a sting operation. Turned out not to be true, but it had given him the scare of his life. Until now. Still, he was determined to stay till the end so he could hear his opponent, Willy Champ, who was the evening's featured attraction.

Frosty called for quiet. "Thank you, Clarissa Clements. You just gave us a great idea. Why don't ten more of you take a minute each to tell us what you want to say to Billy Beauchamp? To speed things up, just line up at the microphone down there in the aisle and go at it."

A file of more than ten quickly formed. Not all of them tore into Billy. Three men praised him for helping them personally: he'd written a recommendation letter to West Point for one of them, had another moved to a better VA hospital, and steered a small business loan to the third. The others criticized his positions in principle or spoke of stands he'd taken that affected them adversely. One bespectacled young man commended Frosty for picking up on an idea from someone in the audience and changing the format a little: "Nice bit of open source thinking, pal. My thanks from a self-described geek."

Frosty took the compliment with a broad smile and announced that it was time for "a deee-licious, nuuu-tritious break. Help yourselves, folks. There are tables of food and drink out in the lobby, it's all free, and the volunteers will be around with the hat and to collect the containers and bottles for recycling. When you finish, we'll bring on Willy Champ, the next congressman from the Fourth District if people like you want him and real change bad enough!"

At the improvised but well-stocked snack counters, Billy and company filled their plates and went outside to eat, something his four pals did with gusto despite all the horseshit they'd been swallowing in the auditorium. Much as they agreed with a lot of what had been said, they didn't take kindly to the attacks on their old friend. John Henry took a big bite of his turkey sandwich, chewed thoughtfully, and poked Gil. "Look at our Billy boy, pretending to be munching nonchalantly while he moseys through the crowd listening to the small talk."

On the campaign trail, Billy was always a good listener. He said he wanted the feedback, but it also saved him from having to make commitments pro or con. But this time there wasn't any small talk, no discussions about sports or the weather, no gossiping. Clusters of people were talking about dirty politics and clean politics, about him and Willy, about what they'd heard and said during the preceding hour and a half, about what they expected of themselves and the Clean Elections Party. Amazing, Billy thought. Knowing that quite a few such meetings of all sizes had been held in his district, and that and many more were going to be held, he decided for the first time in twenty-five years to commission a poll. He wondered how the CEP could afford such sumptuous feasts for its guests. Hal had told him that the CEP had money to spare because it didn't plan to spend anything on television advertising. That was some small comfort, at least, since Billy believed that no one could win elections nowadays without TV ads, especially a new party.

The assemblage of satisfied diners returned to their seats for the climax of the evening's program. Twelve more Oklahomans—five men, five women, and two children—had been asked ahead of time to introduce Willy Champ with one sentence each. They all came on stage, and an older woman began.

"I like Willy Champ because he's worked his farm for years and won't forget where he came from when he goes to Washington, DC."

"I've always voted for Billy Beauchamp," said a middle-aged

National Guard reservist, "but I'm switching to Willy Champ because he's an ex-Marine who has been to war and now fights for peace and an end to war."

"Willy Champ is my choice," said a young mother cradling her baby, "because he's courageous to the core, risking his life and suffering burns to save that little girl while everyone else just stood there paralyzed or terrified."

"Willy Champ is the man," said another young woman, "because he selflessly goes out of his way to help all kinds of people in distress, out of a sense of moral duty to humanity."

A girl in pigtails stepped up and stood on tiptoes to reach the mike. "I love Willy Champ because he reads lots of history books and thinks I should too."

"Willy Champ wants us to have the power," said an old man with a cane, "he wants regular people all over America to have the power so that he and new lawmakers like himself can make the necessary changes for our lives and for our children and grandchildren."

"Willy Champ can win because he's a good, no-nonsense Oklahoma farmer," said a man in a feed-store cap, "and he has the full backing of the Clean Elections Party and its hardworking, honest organizers."

A middle-aged couple approached the mike holding hands. "Willy Champ has a strong marriage and three studious, well-behaved children who respect their parents and are leaders among their friends," the wife said, "which tells you a lot about their mother and father."

"Right," said her husband, "and Willy subscribed to the agenda of the Clean Elections Party and the Agenda for the Common Good long before he ever heard of either one."

Vigorous applause greeted this declaration as a boy in a baseball uniform stepped forward.

"Willy Champ is my hero because I heard him say, 'If everything we do is for the good of the children, it will be good for the adults too, and for our country and the world around us.'"

A woman in a beautifully tailored suit took her turn. "We need a candidate who can bring people together for basic fairness from the force of his arguments, his knowledge, his commanding presence, and his strong voice—and that's Willy Champ."

"I've had my eyes and my mind opened," said a man in a Kiwanis T-shirt, "and I'm switching my vote from the Republicans to Willy Champ, who's *for* the people because he's *from* the people and believes that *in* the people resides the active power of the Republic, which means me and you and you and you!"

Then all twelve turned toward the side of the stage with their hands outstretched and said in unison, "Ladies and gentlemen, doers and shakers, mobilizers and voters, here is our future champion public servant who we're going to send to Washington, DC—WILLY CHAMP!"

To a prolonged standing ovation and a brisk drumroll from the band, the lanky, dignified, smiling Willy Champ walked on stage. He embraced each of his introducers and, linking arms with the two in the middle, faced the audience and applauded them. He had no prepared speech, holding that if you know and believe what you're going to say, you don't have to read it, but that didn't mean he was winging it. He knew what had to be said without trespassing on eternity.

"A hearty good evening to all of you friends and neighbors in attendance at this refreshing and serious gathering. After what has preceded me tonight—Doug Dauntless, Frosty, your own participation both out there where you're sitting and up here—there's less for me to say, so you'll have a shorter stay.

"As you know, I'm running on the Clean Elections Party ballot line to replace Billy Beauchamp as your congressional representative for the Fourth District. The CEP has surmounted the high hurdles our state imposes on third parties, and has gathered three times the required signatures on the ballot access petitions. There's no Democratic Party candidate opposing Congressman Beauchamp this time around, so we're the main challengers.

"The political potentates in this country are experts in sugarcoating and flattery, coverups and class warfare conducted from the top against the majority of the people. That's why the Seven Pillars of the Agenda for the Common Good—publicized for weeks now and given to you in handouts as you entered this auditorium—seem so long overdue, so reasonable, so clearly earned by working people and those who are desperately looking for work but can't find it. And yet it's fitting that the Agenda is subtitled 'First-Stage Improvements for America,' because there's still much work to be done to make a great democratic society apply known solutions to everyday problems and future needs. Who's going to do this work, I ask you?"

"We are," yelled the audience. "WE ARE!"

"Are you sure? Are you sure you're not going to drift away after this exciting, promising meeting and leave it up to me and my associates? Because if you drift away today, we'll be sure to drift away afterwards. You are our collective mother. More than a hundred years ago, Oklahoma farmers and ranchers helped give birth to probably the most sweeping populist movement in American history. Their leaders were anonymous like them. They did not select themselves. They were pressed forward by the passion and drive of their neighbors, passion and drive for a decent livelihood from the land and from their labors, with no banks and railroads and politicians squeezing them and driving them and their families to the brink of poverty. They refused to be broken. They had nothing to work with except their heads, their hearts, and their hands. No motor vehicles, no telephones, sometimes no passable roads, and no electricity. Today we have instant communication, plenty of technology that connects us to each other. But the best connector is each of us ourselves. When we don't believe in ourselves, we weaken our cooperative effort for a new age, a new country, a new community. When you believe in yourself and become a stronger and stronger public citizen, you strengthen our prospects for victory.

"To seek justice and peace and a better life for all, we need to keep acquiring knowledge, which in turn informs judgment, which in turn produces wisdom. To the question 'What is justice?' I have a simple reply. Did you see those anguished people relating their personal stories of injustice here tonight? When you're on the receiving end of injustice, you have a pretty good idea of what justice is. If you're making ten thousand dollars an hour as a big-shot CEO, you're not likely to be sensitive to workers in your own company trying to support their families on eight dollars an hour. But the closer you get to where the pain and strain are, the more you're likely to know what justice looks like.

"As for peace—well, I've experienced the horrors of war as a soldier. Forget about the glory. It's all about bloodshed, death, dismemberment, torture, rape, destruction, and the grisly aftermath. There is nothing glorious about war. It is a failure on the part of the people who were in a position to head it off before the violence began. Politics should be about waging peace and avoiding war so that people can live to realize their dreams. With periodic wars and the despicable manipulations of high-profile warmongers who profit from armed conflict either commercially or politically, people never get a chance to build the good life and keep refining what the good life means for themselves, their children, grandchildren, and great-grandchildren.

"Here at home, I know Oklahoma and the Fourth District very well. I know its farms and villages and towns, its grasslands and hills. I know its history and the outside pressures that face it. I count hundreds of its families as my good friends. I've worked and done business with many of its small businesses and some large ones too. I've volunteered for many boards, councils, clubs, and community projects. What I've observed all too often in all too many areas is that we're slipping backward or just barely hanging on to survive. There's a numbing poverty of spirit among us, as well as a poverty of income. Our tax dollars have been so mismanaged or wasted, if not stolen outright, that few believe in the noble cooperative effort called self-government anymore. There's also a poverty of leadership, which is a major reason why we're here.

"Let me tell you how I'm running my campaign. First of all, I'm running with the people, their local concerns, their needs and rights. That means I don't want spectators. I want participants, collaborators, and leaders to campaign with me. The more people I have on board, the more ideas and activities will flower in all directions to advance our common cause. Remember the young man who thanked Frosty earlier for his 'open source thinking' when he took an idea from Clarissa Clements that led to a dozen or so people speaking their piece to Billy Beauchamp? I want more open source thinking in this campaign. Not all ideas click, of course, but nobody is smarter than everybody.

"As for campaign funds, I'm raising money in small contributions from many citizens. That's the way the Clean Elections Party works, and they really know their business. No PAC money, no money spent on outside consultants or television advertising. Word of mouth, the good old grapevine, is still the fastest, most credible form of communication. There are a little more than five hundred and fifty thousand people in the Fourth District. There are maybe three hundred and fifty thousand eligible voters, half of whom don't vote. This campaign is winnable because we've got the future we desire in our hands and we've got a fast-growing corps of motivated campaigners who are spreading the word with the example of their deeds. We'll be outspent but not outhoofed. We'll be outsloganized but not outthought. We'll be outdelegated because we won't delegate to proxies and advertising firms. We'll do it ourselves, person to person, farm to farm and ranch to ranch, neighborhood by neighborhood, community by community. We'll start getting out the vote now, in August, not a week before Election Day. We know how to get out the vote, and the voters know how to get Billy Beauchamp out of office."

Another roar of approval went up from the crowd.

"Permit me a few words about Congressman Beauchamp. He's been in Washington for a long, long time—thirty-eight years. Have things gotten better for workers and small farmers? Are we shrinking the national deficit that our descendants will have to pay for? Is there respect in Washington for our tax dollars, sensitivity to the health and safety and educational needs of our children, concern for our water, air, soil, and parklands? Has this powerful lawmaker stood with us on any of these matters? To ask these questions is to answer them.

"Billy Beauchamp is said to be a proud man. Evidently he's not proud enough to put his voting record on his congressional website so all of us can check it whenever we want to and checkmate it whenever we need to.

"Billy Beauchamp has plenty of money to spend, but money doesn't vote. It only buys votes if we let ourselves be fooled. Voters vote, and they can nullify money if they act on knowledge informed by their own abiding values. If you get yourselves up to speed on the issues, then you will not—I repeat, *will not*—vote for legislators who repeatedly vote against the interests of your family, your community, your country, and what's best for this world of ours.

"Billy Beauchamp has rarely been challenged in his career, but he won't be overconfident in this race. There's been too much political agitation in our district these past weeks for him not to have noticed, too many meetings and rallies and workshops, too much canvassing and organizing. It may well be that his people are here tonight taking in the scene and dining on our good food. So in his own way, he'll be ready for us"—here Willy's voice rose uncharacteristically—"only his way isn't our way of electing our representatives, because we're here, we're there, we're everywhere, and we're not staying home anymore!"

Whoops, whistles, and boisterous applause filled the auditorium.

"Now for the moment of truth. The objective is clear, and the vision lies before us and our children. If we are truly serious, we will now commit Time, Talent, and Tenacity to our campaign. That's the fuel without which the campaign is just an armchair conversation. Please make the triple-T commitment. There are pledge cards at three tables in the back staffed by our volunteers. Each table represents a different time commitment spread over the ten weeks until Election Day: fifty hours, a hundred hours, or two hundred hours. Take your choice, make your solemn pledge, and pick up your mission manual, which has the name of one of our full-time precinct dynamos who will be working with you street by street, neighborhood by neighborhood, to produce a huge turnout for the Champ campaign. Pick up a batch of Agendas for the Common Good on your way out, and go home and use your living rooms for action meetings with your friends, neighbors, and coworkers. Find public halls in your community if you need more space. Call these events Jamborees for Joy and Justice or whatever, but if it's important, it's gotta be interesting too. Go with any idea that motivates, maybe a contest for the biggest time commitment—hour-raisers instead of fundraisers. The manual is just a starter. If you put your heads together, you'll come up with more ideas than can fit between covers. Remember, this is a political movement of thinkers.

"Now, I know the usual way of ending a political speech is not with a to-do list. A political speech is supposed to be a fiery stemwinder that demonizes the bad guys and the terrible conditions they're responsible for perpetrating. Then the orator moves to flattery, and the massed partisans eat it up, yelping and hooting and stomping their feet. They may even be inspired to cough up some money in response to the candidate's urgent requests. When it's over, they all go home while the candidate and his or her entourage head for a rented TV studio to cut the next sixty-second campaign ad, which conveys nothing of authentic substance except authentic deception."

A wave of knowing laughter swept through the crowd.

"But this isn't politics as usual. We're different, because we're hungrier, angrier, livelier, funnier, gutsier, and brainier, and that will make all the difference on Election Day. Know that I draw my strength from your aspirations for the good life and your determination to make them a reality, and thank you all for coming here tonight to defend yourselves and your families."

The audience rose as one, clapping thunderously, but with an almost palpable sense of thoughtfulness and communion. The man with the triple-B tattoo turned to the friend he'd come with. "I guess Willy really is one of us," he said. "Maybe the best of us," came the reply.

As the crowd broke up, Ernest Jones leaned across Hal and whispered to Billy, "Now let's see how many head for the exit and how many sign up for the hours." In a few minutes, the banker got his answer as long lines formed at the three tables. Some people had gone to the restroom and were already coming back to pledge their time.

"Are you sure these folks aren't trained cadres?" Billy asked. "They sure don't behave like all those constituents who show up at my district meetings clamoring for earmarks."

"Naw, Billy," John Henry said, "I reckon they're just ordinary people who've been exposed to all the fuss you've witnessed from Capitol Hill and have got themselves up in arms about it. Like Willy said, they're here, they're there, they're everywhere."

"You kinda gotta hand it to Willy," Gil said. "He knows who he is, all right. You've sure got your work cut out for you, Congressman."

Billy grimaced and let the comment pass. "If that was an introductory session," he said, "I'd hate to see an advanced one." He removed his straw hat and mopped his brow.

"Yeah, but you're gonna," said Gil.

Two days later, four thousand people from all over the state gathered at the Parmalee Convention Hall in Oklahoma City for an advanced training session that was a marvel of political sophistication. Almost all of those in attendance had participated in introductory sessions back in their districts, and most had already started on their missions, talking up the Clean Elections candidates and the Agenda, holding meetings and hour-raisers and justice jamborees.

Out in the lobby and in the back of the hall, people were talking excitedly and picking up free materials from the numerous tables—DVDs, leaflets, Dick Goodwin's pamphlet, buttons, banners, bumper stickers, T-shirts—while they waited for the program to start. One pile of T-shirts was stenciled with a drawing of a lithe young man and woman rope-climbing up a sheer perpendicular cliff, with the woman saying to her partner, "This is okay for beginners, but when are we going to get a real challenge?"

This time Patti Smith and her band appeared in person to kick things off with "The People Have the Power," and nearly everyone joined in. Then the master of ceremonies, Darrell Dispatch, took the mike. He'd been a Meliorist recruiter earlier in the year, but since he displayed a gregarious talent with crowds, he was asked to become a roving emcee for CEP events.

"Ladies and gentlemen and infiltrators, may I have your attention?" he began.

Farmer Billy Beauchamp and his friends exchanged glances and shifted in their chairs.

"During the introductory sessions you've attended, there was plenty of inspiration. Now you're advancing to the state of perspiration. That means the workshops in the breakout rooms off the sides of this fine hall and in the mezzanine. There are fifteen of them—you all received a list at the door—and they'll each last about half an hour. Participate in as many as you can, and sign up to receive DVDs or online videos of the ones you couldn't attend.

"But first, as you know, the Clean Elections Party is fielding candidates against Senators Alvin Crabgrass and Fred Flagrant, along with several other House incumbents. Since Oklahoma is such an entrenched one-party state, its legislators in Washington have chalked up a great deal of seniority, but today you'll have the pleasure of hearing from each of the candidates now speeding toward those hoary seats in Congress. They'll be introduced by their campaign managers, so here we go. Please welcome Grace Grenadier to introduce Senator-to-be Alicia Runrun Randolph."

"Thank you, Darrell. Friends, Senator Crabgrass is ripe for mowing."

The crowd groaned good-naturedly.

"He sits in the Senate like a Sphinx, does little more than say 'yes, sir' to his party leaders and their financiers. He looks like a senator—erect, white-maned, deep-voiced, and sartorially encased in expensive suits. Over the years he has anesthetized a majority of the voters in our state with his three-part formula for reelection, in his very words, 'God, Gays, and Guns.' Those disrespectful, demeaning days are *over*. It gives me enormous pleasure to introduce Alicia Runrun Randolph, who is already redecorating the sure-to-be-ex-Senator Crabgrass's office suite with handmade furniture and folk art, Oklahoma style."

Bursting with energy, Alicia Runrun Randolph waited for the ovation to subside and then belted out her message. "We know why we're here—to establish clean politics for people who have been bearing all the burdens of dirty politics while the good-ol'-boy network gets richer and more oppressive. We're here to show ourselves and the world a revolutionary way of winning elections of, by, and for the people, even though the people are outfunded and outresourced in every traditional manner by the powers that be. People power, as you will make sure, is not just a terrific song by Patti Smith. Except for quantity, and except for the populist campaigns, elections today run in the same primitive ruts they did a century ago. Field the candidate who is obedient, fund the candidate who will take orders, and elect the candidate on slogans and imagery, with the votes of hereditary Republicans or Democrats who choose from choiceless ballot lines. Add one century-long trend: there are so many candidates running unopposed, and so many one-party-dominated districts and states, that more and more elections are foregone conclusions, mockeries of what a free, honest, competitive democratic process should be like. What's more, here in Oklahoma, the two-party cabal has made it almost impossible for independent or third-party candidates to get on the ballot, and has made it illegal, I kid you not, to count—yes, even to count— your write-in votes.

"From the gas lantern and the horse and buggy to the present day of jet planes, computers, and cell phones, our campaign practices have remained inert, insipid, and inane. Go to your workshops and participate in inventing the future, a future where clean elections chase out rigged elections. Get ready for a giant leap toward liberty and justice for all."

The audience loved the freshness of the message and its delivery, so different from the customary bull and blarney they heard on the

Oklahoma political hustings. The clapping was prolonged, as it was for the other managers and candidates, who presented equally fresh approaches in equally rousing language.

"Okay, people," Doug Dispatch said, "an army marches on its stomach. At the tables in the lobby, a terrific lunch awaits you. Fortify yourselves and come back at two for the workshop workout of your lives."

As the participants tucked into their food, standing in animated groups outside the hall, reporters mingled with them and plied them with questions. Billy Beauchamp, who was once again floating through the crowd to listen to the conversations and take in the mood, saw a feature writer for the *Oklahoma Constitution* accost a woman wearing one of the rock-climbing T-shirts. "Why aren't these workshops confidential?" he asked. "Aren't you afraid your opponents will use your political trade secrets against you if you give them away? I mean, businesses don't divulge their marketing plans in advance, do they?" The woman, who was a physical therapist from Ada, wagged her fork at him. "Just let them try," she said. "You think they can use our techniques to sell their latest outrageous tax shelter or tax haven for the wealthy? Our techniques are tied to the just stands we take. They can't be adapted to the greed of the secrecy-obsessed rulers and bosses."

Billy got an overdose of focus that afternoon. Almost everyone was talking about which workshop they had opted for and why, or about what meetings they were organizing or planning to attend in the coming week. To Billy's ears, their conversations had the air of competitive sports—it was them against him, and they were going to win, and win big. A sudden feeling of weariness overtook him even as he downed his excellent lunch. He just wasn't used to a contest. He'd been thinking of retiring before long anyway, but he'd never run away from a fight.

The familiar Roman Army drumbeat announced that it was workshop time, and the breakout rooms started to fill. There were workshops on raising issues and raising money, on avoiding burnout, on learning from Abraham Lincoln's classic little manual on getting out the vote, on changing minds, on motivating people to show up, on getting them to identify themselves with victory, on campaign techniques, on flushing out the various layers of the opposition, and on applying open source techniques to maximize the talent pool way beyond the staff.

The Open Source Workshop was among the most popular. Directing it was Drill Daylor, a principal proponent of this fast-spreading business phenomenon, and the author of a bestseller on using and rewarding open source competitors who want to go up against the cream of the crop and learn from them anywhere in the world. Drill was a nonpartisan enthusiast for breaking down bureaucratic, commercial, and ego barriers to get the job done with the best and the brightest. He'd written extensively about the business world in this respect, but he'd always wanted to see if open source could succeed in the civic and political arenas. As his presentation went on, he found himself struggling to make the case to his audience of activists, until a mechanic in the room taught Drill the lesson he was trying to teach them.

"Mr. Daylor, if I get what you're saying, would you mind if I jump in and save your ass?"

"Go for it," replied a relieved, slightly perspiring Drill.

"Okay, let's say the problem is how to get people off their asses and motivate them to join the Clean Elections movement right away. You put out the call on the Internet that you're offering three cash grand prizes for the three best motivational suggestions, but the condition for all submissions is that the submitter has to get off his or her ass first. To qualify for the prizes, the submitters have to actually attend—guess what—a gathering of Alicia Runrun Randolph supporters or a Willy Champ rally or some other CEP event. How's that for working off what you were trying to teach us?"

"Not bad," Drill said, "not bad at all. Unfortunately, our time is almost up. If any of you are interested in follow-up, meet me this evening at six at the information table, and we'll develop the contest idea and post it online for immediate testing, together with a schedule of the coming month's CEP events."

The Fundraising Workshop was considerably more tumultuous, because the leader, Larry Lucre, was deliberately provocative. "Okay, people," he began, "there is nothing harder, more uncomfortable, and more tiring than asking people for money for political campaigns, right?"

Just about everybody nodded.

"Wrong!" he shouted. "Wrong! There is nothing more rewarding, fun, and easy than asking people for money. Let's start with all of you. How many of you earn more than twenty-five thousand dollars a year and spend at least a thousand dollars a year on coffee, soft drinks, candy, alcohol, tobacco, and so on? How many of you leave lights on wastefully and don't review your savings accounts to make sure you're getting the highest interest available?"

Three out of four people raised their hands.

"Fine, since you're in an advanced training workshop for the most motivated supporters of the Clean Elections Party, my volunteers will now ask each of you for a two-hundred-dollar donation to the party—cash or check or credit card—or else you can sign a pledge for that sum collectible within the next forty-eight hours. It's an investment in your future! You also have to fill out a simple form to satisfy the Federal Elections Commission's reporting requirement. Volunteers, please proceed."

"Isn't this kind of coercive?" asked one of the participants.

"Only if you're blistered by moonbeams," Larry replied.

"What's wrong with spending a little money on ourselves?" asked another. "Are you trying to lay a guilt trip on us?"

"If you need a guilt trip, I don't see anything wrong with laying one on you, but you don't have to feel guilty, you just have to reflect on your priorities. Look, people, the super-rich and the corporatists are buying Congress and the White House for about two billion dollars every four years, give or take, and less than that for midterm elections. Obscure dot-com startups have gone for more than that. Imagine the bargain! In a presidential year, two billion bucks buys the most powerful, well-funded institutions in the entire world. Who gets the shaft? The more than two hundred and twenty million

American adults who are able to vote—and of course their children. Now, suppose these Americans contributed an average of only five dollars a year to buy back the US government. That's more than a billion dollars every year, and close to four and a half billion every four years. No sweat. Twenty dollars every four years—a sum that would barely buy dinner for one, with tax and tip, in a family restaurant. Best investment based on returns in human history. The sweat is all in the organizational appeal to collect the money efficiently.

"Now, you don't have to deal with such large numbers and so much territory. Oklahoma is a small state, and it's been getting educated fast over the past half year. The CEP has thousands of volunteers already, and their numbers are growing by the day. This allows for lots of personal one-on-one conversations, or one on two or three or four or five. And you can bring those conversations down to money easily, with a script that might go something like this.

"'Howdy, Jim or Jane, we've been first cousins forever, and they can't take that away from us, but they sure can take away our democracy, our rights, our elections, our livelihood, our pensions, our peace, our safety and health. That's why I've become active in the Clean Elections Party, as an investment in my family's future and in improving things for working people as soon as possible. I've donated two hundred dollars to the cause of getting rid of dirty money in elections and sending good people to Congress. You're better off than I am, but I'll go easy on you and just ask you to match my contribution. And it would be great to see more of you, have you put in some fun time with me and some of our friends when the campaigns really go into high gear after Labor Day.'

"You're all smart people, and you can add, subtract, and embellish as you please. Share memories, joke, get serious, whatever, but do it in your own words, tailored to your relationship with the person you're talking to—kin, friend, coworker, neighbor, bowling buddy, bridge partner, what have you. You've got it all over those distant, impersonal mass mailings, e-mailings, and telephone solicitations, because you've got a longstanding relationship with your prospects, you've demonstrated the moral authority of example, you're credible and don't raise suspicions, and you see them frequently for feedback, approbation, or reminders. Who can beat those advantages? The fancy word we use for your personal circle of family, friends, and acquaintances is 'epicenter.' Work your epicenters as far out as you can. Most of us have epicenters of about a hundred people with whom we talk or interact at varying levels of intensity.

"It's all about pulling together, people. Farm folks used to do it at barn raisings after a fire or to give a new family a start. Americans have always done it in time of war and emergency—floods, tornados, fires, earthquakes. We have to do it again now, because we've got the Seven Pillars of the Agenda for the Common Good to raise, along with the legislators who will pass it. What I've given you this afternoon is just the bare-bones approach. Imagine what you could accomplish by giving a potluck supper or brunch at your home or organizing a race or a bicycle marathon. Give your people a competitive sense and a goal you've imposed on yourself to focus their interest. And if you're still feeling squeamish, still letting yourself off the hook with that 'I just hate to ask anyone for money' excuse, get over it. No one is going to bite you. Consider your squeamishness something to grow out of, an indulgence to be vaporized for the sake of what's at stake for Oklahoma and the nation. Rise above it and *will* it away."

Over on the other side of the hall, at the Changing Minds Workshop, most of the participants were already active in the Congress Watchdogs or local CUBs and had been trying to change minds for the past several weeks, so the topic particularly grabbed them. The leader was a former psychiatrist who had rejected the excessive psychoanalyzing of human behavior and the dead-end, reality-starved theories of his profession. His name was Buff Brainey.

"Greetings, men and women. We only have half an hour, so let's get down to it. Changing minds is very difficult. You know because you've tried it. People put labels on themselves that freeze their minds—Republican, Democrat, liberal, conservative, a Beauchamp voter or a Crabgrass voter. Frozen minds freeze out contrary facts and arguments. Frozen minds breed immovable egos that merge with their labels.

"How do you change a frozen mind? Through a form of jujitsu—use what's there to change what's there. Start with a question. 'Why do you support Crabgrass?' The customary answers are usually very abstract, except maybe on the abortion issue. People mouth what's been drilled into them by the propaganda apparatus: strong defense, lower taxes, less government—the Republicans' first-string trilogy. Never mind the contradictions between them. Slogans do not flow from critical minds. They are simply extruded. But consider the following simple dialogue.

"'Do you support Senator Crabgrass because you agree with him?' 'Yep!' 'On what?' 'Strong defense. Lower taxes. Less government.' 'Well, what if I could show you that he voted again and again for a wasteful defense budget, and for weapons systems that are strategically obsolete in the post-Soviet era, because the big defense corporations are funding his campaign and want the multibillion-dollar contracts you pay for? And what if I could show you that his votes on taxes gave most of the breaks to the already rich and to the big companies, not to tens of millions of working Americans, and that his other votes helped pass red-ink government spending that increased the deficit by hundreds of billions of dollars because of waste and the revenue declines from these big tax cuts for the rich? I'm talking about huge deficits that your children will have to pay for—Crabgrass's children's tax. And what if I could show you that Crabgrass votes for bills that lead to Washington snooping on you and leave your government unable to enforce the laws against business ripoffs by the banks, insurance companies, oil companies, credit card companies, and many other enterprises? What if I could show you that you're defenseless and unable to have your full day in court thanks to the Crabgrasses in Congress? To top it off, what if I could show you that on a dozen matters of importance to you, his votes were exactly opposite to where you stand? Would Senator Crabgrass still have your vote?' 'Hell no, assuming what you say is true.'

"Naturally, you'll want to use your own language to frame the argument, but you get the point. You turn Crabgrass's record against the beliefs and the awakened, informed, unfrozen minds of his voters so that they start thinking, 'Hey, Crabgrass opposes my positions over and over again.'

"One last point. The more significant issues you put before the people whose minds you're trying to change, the less likely it is that they'll give Crabgrass a pass. More important, the less likely it is that Crabgrass will be able to hoodwink his constituents, and the more power these constituents will have over Crabgrass. You see, keeping the number of issues small works to the advantage of incumbents, because they go for the poll-tested hot-button issues that satisfy their one- or two-issue supporters. Okay, any questions?"

"I'm a hairdresser," said a young woman, "and I chat with lots of people in my line of work. I find that they either absolutely support a given politician or they have nothing to do with politics. Has the approach you outlined actually been shown to work?"

"Yes, that's the obvious next question, isn't it?" Buff said. "Our research shows that it's worked in the past in some local races here and there, but the Clean Elections Party is the first movement to start using the approach in a big way. It's too early to know. People may tell you that the information you've given them, pitting their interests against the record of their favorite politician, will change their minds, but then there are two additional steps before we can determine whether it works. The first step is convincing them that what you've told them is more than a 'what if,' that it's accurate and verifiable. The second, of course, is whether they actually switch their votes to the source of their enlightenment—in this case, the Clean Elections Party."

"Maybe the best way to put it isn't that we're changing people's minds," said an older man in a Home Depot vest. "It's really about people changing their own minds once they find out the truth."

"Exactly," said Buff.

Up in the mezzanine, the Get Out the Vote Workshop was standing room only. The preceptor—a term he preferred to "leader"—was Dan Deliverman, an army veteran and a veteran community organizer for poor people's rights. He was new to GOTV, however, beyond knowing only too well that poor people have the lowest voting turnout of all income classes.

Dan opened with a summary of Lincoln's manual on getting out the vote, written for the elections of 1840. Honest Abe was practical. He recommended dividing the voters in each precinct into three categories: those who are with you from the get-go, those who are susceptible to persuasion, and those who are against you from the get-go. Then he guided his readers meticulously through the step-by-step process—or more accurately, the doorstep-by-doorstep process—of meeting with every voter except the opposition hard-liners. There was nothing derivative or remote about Lincoln's advice, in part because there was no technology of remoteness, no telephones, television, or e-mail, nothing but the US mails, which were not used for political campaigns at the time. In those days, getting out the vote had to be personal and conversational, and advertising meant posters and handbills.

"In the 1840s and 1850s," Dan said, "people knew their neighbors and their communities and had to communicate directly. Today, if we're smart, we'll follow their example. Starting right after Labor Day, we'll attend and participate in the meetings of all the various community organizations in our districts so that when doorstep time comes, we'll be on a first-name basis with our neighbors and be able to draw on shared remembrances and experiences from past gatherings. The idea is to create a chain of core voters who will each be responsible for getting twelve other voters to go to the polls as a group and then maybe go out for lunch or supper or a drink. If you think of these core voters as 'twelvers' and start doing the math, you'll see that the effect is exponential."

And so went the workshops, throughout the afternoon into the evening, each in its own way taking the participants one or two or three steps beyond the amateurish, stagnant state of political campaigning in which the country was stuck. When the last workshop had concluded, everyone returned to the auditorium for a spirited sendoff from Darrell Dispatch, some people stopping by the lobby to pick up a drink or a snack.

"Stalwarts of Oklahoma, shapers of the future," Darrell said in ringing tones, "do not leave this building thinking in any way that you are determined but lonely pioneers. Mobilizations and training operations similar to and sometimes well beyond what's occurring in our state are taking place all over our country. We are in the stage of natural transition from all the wonderful agitations and heightened expectations that the Meliorists have inspired since early this year. Will those of you who have been regularly messaging your activist counterparts around the country please raise your hands?"

Billy Beauchamp swiveled in his seat to check the reaction as a sea of hands went up. He sighed and faced forward again, not a little dejected.

"See what I mean?" Darrell said. "Take great heart from our growing network, and surpass your friends in other states by learning from them. Nothing like some competitive spirit to spur us on to greater heights. For those of you who have fought the good fight for years, this time you are not alone, decidedly not alone.

"The materials from all the workshops, whether you attended them or not, can be picked up on your way out. Digest them and make them part of your hearts, minds, and souls. Since the first of June, when our slate of candidates was announced, we've held dozens of local meetings, fourteen district-level assemblies, and one other statewide gathering besides this one. There will be many more such events, at all levels. Check our website, www.oklahomadynamos.org, and let your friends know what they've been missing. Tell them they need to come join us to defend themselves, their families, and their country. And until next time, fare thee well."

A huge culminating roar reverberated through the convention hall as Billy Beauchamp and his friends rose and walked briskly to their minivan without saying a word. Once they were on the road, John Henry broke the silence. "Two years ago, you were elected with eighty-one percent of the vote, Billy, and your approval level was about there too. Your coming poll will tell you what toll the past three months of CEP perpetual motion have taken, but if you ask me, I wouldn't wait for the poll. Assume it's down and contact the

RNC for advice and assistance. I know it'll be the first time for you, but this is the first time you've had any real opposition. And check out what the business trade groups are ready to do to help you like you've helped them so much over the years. I'm not talking about campaign donations—you're already up to your ears in those—I'm talking about getting people to help you on the ground and kick some butt for you with the local business community."

Billy sighed again. "Guess I don't much feel like talking right now, too much to take in and chew on, but I owe you all for bringing me to these two events, troubling as they were. Being briefed could never have conveyed what I saw and heard with my own eyes and ears. Thanks, gents. Will you all come over tomorrow for brunch so we can take a dig at all this from scratch?"

"Sure, Billy," Gil said, "sure we will."

Sunday morning, at his rambling Victorian-style home, Billy greeted his friends. "Come on in, fellows. The family and grandkids are all at church, and then they're going to a church picnic, so we've got the place to ourselves. The girls have laid out a breakfast buffet in the den, so let's go on in there and dig in."

When everyone was settled with heaping plates of sausage and eggs and biscuits and gravy, Billy said, "Listen, boys, when I got home from the Parmalee rodeo last night, I found confidential briefings from Brovar Dortwist and Lance Lobo waiting for me. Holy hell is all I can say after reading about the latest doings of the Meliorists and the Clean Elections Party. You know, our side of the political tract is used to short-term surges by progressives on some dustup or another, but the spark-and-sputter crowd has never had much staying power. This time, what Dortwist calls 'the quantitative difference of scale and resources' and 'the qualitative nature of their business backing' render history meaningless. There's just a staggering number of activities and events going on everywhere—did you know there was a Sun God festival yesterday in Woodstock, right on the same grounds where all those hippies did their thing in the sixties?—and new groups keep popping up to petition regulatory agencies, lobby legislators, file lawsuits, and on and on. I know firsthand from all the flow into my Rules Committee, which gives me a panoramic view of what's looming over the horizon because it isn't specialized like the other House committees.

"But what I didn't realize until the last few days is how far down into the communities the Meliorists and the CEP have penetrated. And just about everything they do gets on the mass media—not to mention the blogs and websites and DVDs and whatever else—to the point where they're squeezing out the police blotter and the weather on the local TV news. The business community, which pays the freight for the mass media, is obviously off its game here. They're not making sure they get something for their advertising dollars besides sales, if you know what I mean."

Listening to Billy, Gil was struck by how alive, how sharp, how on top of the situation the old warhorse seemed. Too bad he hadn't listened to Gil and the others months ago when they told him the same thing. Must sound more believable when it came from Washington.

"So what are your plans?" asked Hal, sinking his teeth into a gravy-sopped biscuit.

"Well, in a nutshell, I can keep doing what I've always done and try to straight-arm Willy Champ, or else I can try to blur his message by coming out for some of the reforms he's pushing. That might raise charges of expediency because it smacks of an election-year conversion, but on the other hand, it might flatter voters into thinking they'd changed the mind of an old man with no further ambitions for higher office. Who knows? Not much to do until we get that poll data except eat up and relax and watch the Cowboys exhibition game."

It took Jasper Cumbersome's secretary nearly the whole ten days the CEOs had allotted for their study of the Agenda to set up a conference call among them at their various resorts, spas, mansions, and villas, on islands, oceanfronts, and mountaintops all over the world.

"Well," Cumbersome began, "we knew August was going to be a hot one for us, but not this hot. Every major national news magazine has a cover story on one or more of the Meliorists. *People* has Yoko Ono on the cover. *Business Week* has pictures of all of them in the shape of a flame. *Time*'s cover line is 'Old Age Pushes New Age.' The TV and radio coverage has been so intense that they hardly have time for the five-day forecast. I don't think the Meliorists have much control anymore over what they've unleashed, except for the Agenda legislation. Wardman, will you do the honors and walk us through each of these bills?"

"Certainly, Jasper. I'll read out each proposal and assume that all of you are willing to accede to it, or at least negotiate on it, unless you speak up to the contrary. First is universal health insurance—public payment for private healthcare services."

"I absolutely oppose it," said Edgar Exerson of Hospital Chains of America, who had begun attending the meetings of Lobo's CEOs after the Harry and Louise debacle. "It will inevitably lead to price controls and restrictions that will put us out of business as insurers."

"Anyone else in opposition?" Wardman Wise asked.

There was silence over the phone lines. The other CEOs were relieved at being relieved of the spiraling expense of this worker benefit. Though employers would still be assessed something under the Agenda bill, Medicare for everyone would shift the burden away from them and onto the government, thereby making US companies more competitive with foreign businesses whose governments provided healthcare.

"Okay, so far, so good," Wise said. "That was the easy one, with apologies to brother Exerson. Next is electoral reform, which includes public funding of federal campaigns for ballot-qualified candidates through a well-promoted checkoff of up to three hundred dollars on 1040 tax returns, limited free access to radio and television time for these candidates, the prohibition of corporate-sponsored PACs, federal election standards to replace restrictive state voter registration and ballot-access laws, plus instant runoff voting and binding none-of-the-above on all ballot lines."

"This is a radical change from business as usual, and if we don't fight it, we'll regret it," said K. Everett Dickerson, head of the nation's largest media conglomerate, but once again there was silence from the rest of the CEOs, who were tired of being endlessly shaken down for political contributions and often berated for donating to candidates of both parties. It was a perennial irritation, and they would be glad to be rid of it, even at the expense of buying what they wanted from the government, as long as every one else was also prohibited from such payola. Dickerson accused them of putting their personal unease ahead of their business responsibilities to "purchase access," as he delicately put it, but no one came around to his view.

"All right," Wise said, "let's move on to labor law reforms making it easier to organize unions, lifting the minimum wage to ten dollars an hour, and strengthening the occupational safety and health laws."

More silence over the phone lines.

"No objections?" Wise asked. "None? I must say I'm surprised at how agreeable we all seem to be today, but I guess we're just following my late mother's advice. 'Wardy,' she used to tell me, 'you'd better take your cod liver oil now.'"

"Look," said Hubert Bump, "I know we're supposed to react to the Agenda as if we were under ultimate duress on Capitol Hill—which isn't all that hypothetical by my reading—but I wouldn't have much trouble with labor reform in any case. My industry is mostly unionized, and we pay well above ten dollars an hour. Our sense of productivity and our institutional compassion already make for high job safety. So what's the big deal—to borrow a phrase?"

"The big deal," said Sal Belligerante, "is that there are many employers who are not in your circle, Hubert. They're afraid unions will put them out of business. On the other hand, unions are not known to commit suicide, and the growing ability of companies to outsource provides a strong incentive for union restraint in bargaining. In the white-collar area, the employees themselves don't like the idea of unionization and are sensitive to employer downsizing and outsourcing. So that basically leaves the retail chains—fast food, Wal-Mart, and so on. And of course ideology."

The remainder of the Agenda for the Common Good did not fare anywhere near as well. The CEOs came down decisively against the sections on consumer empowerment (the CUBs, etc.), investor control (especially over executive pay), taxation, access to the courts, corporate governance, and issues of corporate "personhood."

"Well, we've all spoken," Wise said, "and we know where we stand on the Agenda, but where does that leave us in these dog days of August?"

"I think it leaves us in a state of suspended reaction," said Bradford Knowles. "We have to wait for the adversary's specific moves and for the evaluations of our congressional friends before we know how to respond. Presumably, the trade lobbies will keep charging along and risk breaking their straight arms, and the Lobo/Dortwist battalion has yet to come up with whatever miracles might arise from their groundwork. By the way, did we ever find any challengers to debate the SROs?"

"Lobo got back to me on that," Jasper Cumbersome said. "He told me the only volunteers were some no-names and clenched-jawed business professors who would embarrass us. He offered to debate them himself, in his frustration, but I replied with a sympathetic no. By the way, I see the SROs are returning our compliment by asking for one-on-one meetings with us." Indistinct muttering was heard. "Well, I assume we all know how to get more out of them than they get out of us. Now go back to your golf games and martinis, gentlemen. We are adjourned until our next meeting with Lobo right before the Labor Day weekend."

At the beginning of the second week of the "vacation" month of August, the Meliorists sallied forth on their grueling schedule of appearances and meetings with the CEOs and the Bulls. Warren had been asked to speak at a major rally in Oklahoma City, so he'd put in a call to Billy Beauchamp requesting a meeting afterward in Billy's district office. He knew that the Rules Committee might be the opposition's last stand, and he also believed that neutralizing

Beauchamp was the strongest message that could be sent to the other Bulls, short of the prospect of defeat in November.

Billy received word of Warren's request while lunching at a VFW hall. He was flattered that the world's second-richest man wanted to come to southwestern Oklahoma to see him, but the politician in him quickly shifted from warm self-congratulation to cunning calculation. Buffett was coming to feel him out about the Agenda, but what else? Would he be offering anything by way of a legislative deal, or maybe something more personal like a post-retirement position? There was only one way to find out. Billy told his campaign manager to call Buffett's office and arrange the meeting.

At the appointed time, Warren arrived at Billy's modest suite in the Lawton post office building. They exchanged pleasantries and chatted about mutual acquaintances. Warren thanked Billy for supporting the repeal of the Public Utility Holding Company Act nestled into a larger energy bill that was quite controversial. The repeal of this legendary and highly effective Depression-era law made it easier for Warren to expand his growing electric company empire by acquisition and merger, and Billy didn't like the consumer groups that vigorously opposed the repeal, so they hit common ground.

"May I take you to lunch, Congressman?" Warren asked. He'd always believed that breaking bread together enhanced the possibilities of breaking through, and a little wine wouldn't hurt either.

"That's very kind of you, sir. I know a nice little café that's quiet and private at this time of day."

When they were seated, Warren ordered a cherry Coke for himself and a bottle of Chardonnay for Billy and started right in. "Mr. Chairman, let's talk about the Agenda for the Common Good and the awakening of the American people. I won't repeat our justifications for these reforms and redistributions of power, because you've heard them many times, from many mouths and pens. I wanted this meeting so I could talk to you as a peer—we're about the same age—from my experience as a businessman and a patient observer of history and societal convulsions. The ties that bind us as a society are fraying badly. Traditions that work are being tossed aside as so much flotsam and jetsam by a rampant commercialism, by the notion that everything is for sale. But you and I know that if everything is for sale we can't retain our basic values, which by definition can never be for sale. As one who has bought and sold all kinds of products, securities, and companies, I'm not exactly coming from the priesthood, but I do know the importance of drawing that bright line.

"One of our basic values is justice. Granted, justice is in the eye of the beholder, but millions of beholders are starting to see it the same way. The raw injustice that afflicts Americans is reported and exhibited everywhere, all the time—and while the GDP keeps growing, no less. The evidence is irrefutable. Just start with the poverty and pain and insecurity of working families in the millions. When everything is for sale—say, in a commercial healthcare industry that tells people to pay or die—that means life-preserving justice is for sale. And not everyone can afford it. If members of Congress have been astounded at the reaction to and the spread of our activities since early this year, so have we, but it's obvious we've struck a deep chord of decency in the American people. Optimism and a new public spirit have been liberated because more and more Americans believe critical changes can be made, and soon. Elders like us now have to guide those changes along beneficial paths. Long-suppressed expectations have been awakened. You may have heard of the waitress at a truck stop in Pennsylvania who thought up the slogan 'What's the Big Deal? We Earned It!' That about sums it up. Lots of back pay there. Lots, and I'm not just talking about money."

As he spoke, Warren was watching Billy's face carefully. He was something of an expert in the discernment of voluntary and involuntary responses, having negotiated so many acquisitions and recruited so many executives and met with so many boards of directors. He noticed that Billy's eyes welled up slightly twice, once when he said that basic values couldn't be for sale, and once when he used the phrase "elders like us."

"I see two possible scenarios when Congress returns," he went on. "One, that what the lawmakers experienced back home in August brings out their better natures, as contrasted with their politically calculating natures, and they sit down to make American history, which will resound far beyond our borders as an authentic example to the world of a functioning democracy taking itself to new levels of human dignity. In a darker scenario, the senior incumbents and chairs dig in their heels and hunker down with the business lobbies to block a Meliorist-sparked movement that has now taken on a life of its own. If that darker scenario prevails before November, none of us knows what will follow, but you can bet that the people who emerge to lead the ongoing struggle will not be calling themselves Meliorists. That's the lesson history teaches us when the powers that be don't relent and respond to popular demands for a fairer deal."

While Warren was speaking, Billy Beauchamp was listening and wondering. What in the world was motivating this man who had it all—riches, friends in high places, the respect of the business community, the adoration of his tens of thousands of shareholders who came from miles around to attend his annual meeting? Why was he subjecting himself to conflict, stress, and slanderous attacks? Why was he spending August traveling around the country making speeches and talking to the likes of Billy Beauchamp? Certainly there was nothing in it for him financially. If anything, he was putting some of his business undertakings at risk by alienating partners who didn't want these kinds of fights and distractions from their boss. Could it be something as simple as trying to be a good Christian and a good human being?

Warren was finishing up and putting his cards on the table. He didn't believe in loose ends. "Mr. Chairman, I'm here to ask with the utmost respect that you move the Agenda to the floor rather than bury the bills in the Rules Committee as the business lobbies are expecting you to do. Beyond that, I dare to hope that you'll become a leader for the Agenda and write this chapter of the American story in your image. Our history shows again and again that every social justice movement that caught hold has expanded our economy, our freedom, and our legacy to our descendants. That's what the Homestead Act under President Lincoln did, what the abolition of slavery did, what women's suffrage did, what the elevation of worker dignity did, what the breakup of the giant monopolies did. When everybody wins, everybody wins."

Warren stopped and took a sip of his cherry Coke while Billy took a gulp of wine and blew his nose. The waiter came to the table for their orders. "Have you decided, gentlemen?" he asked. They gave him their selections and their menus. Warren waited.

"Well, sir," Billy said finally, "you surely know how to bring out at least one incumbent's better nature, as you put it. I'm at that stage in my life where I do think about how history will view my years in the House. Call it my Rubicon, my crossing over from a time for deals to a time for ideals. I'm being very frank with you, and I expect what's said to stay between us."

"Absolutely," Warren assured him.

"Many years ago," Billy continued, "my grandfather took us grandkids on vacation at Big Sur in California. The surf was majestic, and the surfers were spectacular. 'See those waves, children?' Grandpa said. 'When you encounter giant waves like that in your grown-up lives, don't fight them, because you'll just plain lose. Instead, ride them.' Well, from what I know is going on around the country and from what I've experienced in my own district in the past week, I'd say the Big Sur surf has arrived at Everytown, USA, and I'm about ready to decide to ride it. I won't make a public announcement, but I'll do it through my public actions as chair of the Rules Committee."

"You mean you don't intend to signal the other chairs in advance so as to influence them, or at least not to anger them by catching them off guard?" asked a pleasantly startled Warren.

Billy stiffened. "I'll do it my way," he replied tersely.

"Of course," Warren said, saved from an uncomfortable moment by the arrival of the salad. "Well, don't these tomatoes look great! Waiter, may I have another cherry Coke?"

Back in Omaha, Warren quickly sent a message to the other Meliorists, saying that if they hadn't yet met with the Bulls, he recommended three approaches that had worked well with Billy Beauchamp: the appeal to their better natures, the point that advances in justice lift everyone's prospects and expand economic activity, and the subtle warning that what would follow if the Agenda failed to pass would not be described as Meliorist. At the Bulls' age, he added, they might wish to undertake their own Redirection of how history would judge them. He again emphasized how critical these meetings were to turn the Bulls around or at least persuade them to let the legislation go to the floor.

Meanwhile, the Meliorists were also arranging their meetings with the CEOs. Jeno had selected Sal Belligerante because of their shared Italian roots and his love of a good fight. Sal was a synergy genius, holding together firms in the entertainment, financial, real estate, and shipping industries, plus a blue-chip mutual fund operating globally. In the sixties and seventies, his massive conglomerate had somehow avoided the fate of its counterparts, which were forced to sell off their corporate subsidiaries. Jeno had received a briefing paper filling him in on all of Sal's business dealings and indicating that he was one of the group's hardliners.

They met in Florida at a penthouse Sal owned, with a gorgeous view of Biscayne Bay. Sal greeted his guest in a white silk three-piece suit and invited him to take a seat in the lavishly furnished living room.

Jeno settled into a white leather armchair. "Sal, good to see you again. It's been a while since we shared a table at the annual Italian-American dinner in Washington. How you doing, paisan?"

"Well, you're probably doing a lot better than I am, Jeno. You guys are turning our world upside down."

"Or right side up," Jeno said with a smile. "Sal, I'm going to make you an offer you can't refuse, one that may initially seem so outlandish as to cast doubt on the sanity of the paisan who proposed it."

"What's with all this 'paisan' stuff? Are you playing the ethnic card with me?"

"Of course! After all, we have a common heritage, even though your forebears sailed from Sicily while mine came from Naples. Ask most Americans what they associate with Sicilian Americans and they'll say—"

"The Mafia," Sal broke in bitterly.

"Right, and it's very unfair, but there's a dash of truth in their impressions. Young Italian Americans today need role models for endeavors other than crime, sports, and Hollywood. They need Italian stallions who exceed the notable achievements of our compatriots in those three areas of American society. The vast majority of them have never heard of Garibaldi, Mazzini, and Croce, much less Marcus Cicero of Rome."

"Cicero is my hero," Sal said. "I took Latin for three years in high school, and he was that language's finest orator and scholar. I can't tell you how much of him I read into the wee hours. Anyway, I'm still waiting for the connection."

"In all your reading of Cicero, Sal, did you ever come across his definition of freedom?"

"No, can't say I have."

"Well, here it is—the best definition I've ever heard. 'Freedom,' he said, 'is participation in power.' How much freedom do you think ninety-nine percent of the American people have in the good old USA by that venerable definition?"

"Hell, if they're in the military, they've got plenty of freedom, what with all those weapons systems on land, sea, and air."

"Sal, I'm serious."

"Are you? Okay, I get where you're going. You want me to be a twenty-first-century Garibaldi running around spouting Cicero to liberate the country my father and mother came to—land of the free, home of the brave—in order to escape Benito Mussolini. Get the irony, you thick-headed Napolitano?"

"But look what it took to get our parents here, Sal—a Fascist dictator for yours, poverty and strife and suppressed dreams for mine. It shouldn't have to come to that. That's part of what the Meliorists are about—jolting the established business community into a risk assessment of its own self-interest. We've got greed spreading like a cancer through our society, so many families losing ground. We've got a visible global warming meltdown way up north and way down south, and these fossil-fuel fossilheads are turning up the acetylene torch. And those are just two of hundreds of examples. Look, you're rich and smart and successful, and I think you're sincere, but the business jungle out there has hardened a shell over your best instincts. At seventy-three, what have you got to look forward to? A gold watch? I've been successful in business too, as have many of my Meliorist colleagues. The difference is that we started asking some fundamental questions about what kind of elders we want to be, what kind of trustees for the vulnerable generations that will follow our descent into the mists of history. What are you and your fellow CEOs safeguarding that can compare with the gravity, the majesty of that question? Especially in a country that has the wealth and capability to pull off what no other nation in history could do."

"And how, might I inquire, was all that wealth created?"

"Through a combination of great natural resources, freedom of capital formation, federal laws restraining the excessive concentration of power, a brain drain of the rest of the world, and the assumption by the taxpayers of the costs of public infrastructures, public education, Social Security, R and D, and enforceability of contracts. But in the past twenty-five years, too much corporate power over government policies has thrown our political economy out of balance and reduced government to a short-term handout operation for big business. In a word, I describe the corporate state."

"Like Mussolini in his *Stato Corporativo*?"

"Not bad, Sal, not bad. Keep surprising me."

"Stop patronizing me. You're lucky you and I never met head-on when you were competing big-time, because you'd have lost."

At that moment, Jeno sensed that he was starting to break through Sal's shell. "Too bad we never had the pleasure. You wouldn't have had to wait until now to see how straightforward I am. Here's that offer you can't refuse, Sal. On behalf of the Meliorists, I invite you to become a full member of our core group and undertake a sublime, truly historic commitment to advance the Agenda for the Common Good through Congress by the end of the year. We'll of course have to interview you first, for reasons you'll understand. While you're thinking about it, can you point me to the bathroom?"

Sal looked directly at Jeno, scowled, and without a word jerked his head toward a hallway off the living room. Jeno rose and found the bathroom, where he spent five minutes leafing through a yachting magazine to give Sal some time to digest what he must have seen as either a stunning act of statesmanship or a cunning trap.

"What kind of game are you playing, Jeno?" Sal said when his guest returned. "You know that what you've offered me is a 'heads you win, tails I lose' proposition. If I say yes, then one Sal Belligerante instantly forfeits his role among the CEOs. If I say no, then you can leak it to the media—you're all so moderate and open that you offered a chief adversary equal membership inside your strategic sanctuary, with full access to your everyday maneuvers, and he refused. Jeno, you truly should have been a son of Sicily. So let the record state, 'He said nothing, smoothed his tie, and requested that his visitor depart.' Ciao, paisan."

"As you wish, but before you graciously agreed to meet with me, I read everything I could get my hands on about you, and I still believe in you, Sal, in spite of yourself."

Back in his limo on the way to Miami, where he was scheduled to speak at a sub-economy shindig the next day, Jeno leaned back in his seat and smiled reflectively. He hadn't expected to get a clear yes or no, not because Sal was so tactically smart—though in fact he'd turned out to be—but because Jeno believed he was genuinely floored and flattered by the invitation. Nor had Jeno expected the abrupt termination of the meeting, but even so, his Neopolitan intuition told him that the mental yeast had been planted and Sal's better nature would rise in the coming days.

August 22nd arrived, and with it the highly anticipated public discussion between Billy Beauchamp and Willy Champ at

Southwestern Oklahoma Community College. Before a large audience, with no moderator, the two men opened with several sharp but civil exchanges. Their tone was deliberate and responsible. Neither man overtalked or interrupted. Each seemed to know when the other had finished making his points, and listened attentively before replying.

Billy Beauchamp stressed his knowledge of public affairs, his wisdom as an elder, his public works projects in the Fourth District over the decades, and his experience in Washington, which meant seniority and control of the gateway House Rules Committee. There was no bombast in his voice or demeanor; he didn't patronize the younger man. For his part, Willy Champ spoke of his travels to every corner of the district and vividly described all the injustices he had encountered, citing them not as isolated examples, after the practice of Ronald Reagan, but as representative of the plight of many. Without slamming his opponent directly, he decried the chronic corruption in Congress and the great Washington stall that had left a country of tremendous resources and talents paralyzed. He gave illustration after illustration of the practical solutions that were available if politicians represented real people instead of greedy corporations and their vastly overpaid bosses. Thanks to all the publicity about the activities of the CEP and the Congress Watchdogs, his examples were fresh in the minds of his audience, and people were nodding in agreement as Willy told them what he hoped to accomplish with their votes and their participation. The implicit message was clear. For all his experience, Congressman Beauchamp had produced few real benefits for the people and a lot of policies that stood in their way. It was time for a progressive change, time for new energy and new blood.

During the question period, the audience responded magnificently. Their questions weren't the expected and easily evaded ones based on headlines and sound bites. They were fundamental and informed inquiries that demanded concrete answers. How would the candidates handle the corporate donors and lobbyists? How, specifically, would they address the various problems of the district?

The audience wasn't interested in abstractions and empty reassurances. They were conducting a genuine dialogue with the candidates, testing each man's character and personality.

One of the first questions, from a middle-aged man in a cowboy shirt, had to do with health insurance. "Medicare is working pretty well, though there could be more prosecutions of vendor fraud," he said. "Both of you have supported Medicare for the older folks, but why not full Medicare for all Americans, no matter what their age, as proposed in the Agenda's healthcare bill? Medicare's administrative expenses are a fraction of the expenses of the HMOs, and unlike those giant companies, Medicare gives folks free choice of physicians and hospitals. What's your specific position here?"

"I'm all for the Agenda bill," Willy Champ declared without hesitation. "It spells out a universal healthcare plan in a form structured for quality and cost controls, and with provision for constant feedback and organized patient-consumer watchdogs."

"I support healthcare coverage for everyone too," said Billy Beauchamp, "but Oklahomans don't want more big government, more bureaucracy, more politics between you and your doctor. I believe competition in healthcare is better, and I have a six-point plan that will cover just about everyone by 2014." As he finished his answer, Billy saw many in the crowd rolling their eyes, as if to say, "Here he goes again," but he couldn't help himself. He'd been so programmed for so many years that he couldn't make the adjustments he knew he needed to make after attending those two boisterous CEP training sessions.

Near the end of the evening, a distinguished-looking woman rose and asked, "Will both of you gentlemen agree now to no less than half a dozen such discussions around the district after Labor Day?"

Billy looked at Willy. Willy looked at Billy and then at the audience. "Fine with me," he said. In the front row, Gil, Hal, Ernest, and John Henry swallowed hard.

"Fine with me too," Billy finally said.

The next day, the top headline in the Lawton newspaper was "It's the Triple-B vs. Triple-T Road Show—Six of Them!"

All through August, the Meliorist pressure cooker built up steam by the day in every precinct and congressional district in the country. One commentator on *Meet the Press* called the unprecedented activism "a raging prairie fire incinerating the conventional political wisdom in Washington, DC. The people are hungry for fairness and justice. They can feel a new day coming because they're making it happen, with some crucial help from the PROs."

Some state attorneys general chose what would normally have been the slow news month of August to release their State of Justice reports, which were real eye-openers, with their groundbreaking efforts to jettison myths and actually measure the prevalence of justice or the lack thereof. Then there was Jerome Kohlberg, that tireless offshoot of the Maui core group. He and his crew were organizing meetings in every community with a population of more than ten thousand on the theme of money in politics. "Come see how dirty money makes so many of you so miserable," ran the invitation, "and start feeling less miserable on the spot when you become part of getting the dirty money out of politics. Supper on the house." Jerome was spending some of his fortune fast, but not as fast as he was making it.

At Radio City Music Hall in New York, a show featuring both the corporations that were running as candidates (reduced to write-ins by adverse court decisions) and the people who had declared themselves corporations was playing to packed houses night after night. The highlight was an animated short produced by one of Yoko's art teams that rang all the comic changes on these dual themes. In Virginia, Max made a big splash after a senator cruising to reelection with a record of voting for big business roughly 100 percent of the time used a pejorative ethnic term about an Asian American staffer of his opponent's. Never mind the senator's deeds, his votes against lifesaving worker, consumer, and environmental programs—what got him in trouble was a word. He'd never apologized for leaving Americans defenseless against corporate depredations, but he was apologizing all over the state for this verbal campaign crisis, and Max called him out on it in a withering series of ads.

It was against this disheartening backdrop that the CEOs convened for their meeting with Lobo on the Friday before Labor Day, grumbling about having to cut their vacations short. They were in no mood to listen. They were in a mood to cross-examine, as Lobo knew when he entered the penthouse boardroom with sweaty palms.

"Lobo, you've been working double overtime," CEO Cumbersome began, "and we are all eager to know how the five-point plan you outlined months ago is working out. Not to restrict you to these forays, mind you, since your dynamic intellect has probably come up with many more ways to stop the SROs in their autumn tracks. Proceed, please."

"Gentlemen, a giant hurricane is best understood by entering its eye, the calm within the vast turbulence surrounding it. Let's enter the eye of the SRO hurricane for clarity of purpose and action. All the forces on our side are in retreat. As with any army in stages of retreat, the general keeps looking for more defendable positions as his troops grow weaker from their losses. Outwardly, we're all blazing away and keeping our spirits high. Inwardly, the reality is retreat. But retreat does not mean defeat. It means fighting on terrain that gives us an advantage. And unlike a retreating army, we're not losing strength. Just the opposite. The resources—human, technological, and monetary—are growing every day as the business community absorbs the urgency of the moment."

"Excuse me," interrupted Norman Noondark, "but I've never heard such a load of double-talk in my life. Enough with the meteorological and military metaphors. Just tell us about your five-point strategy and give us your analysis of how you've done."

Lobo took a deep breath. "Very well, gentlemen. The first and second fronts were to penetrate the enemy's communication systems and then their face-to-face meetings and their staff. We've got informants here and there, but by and large we haven't had much success thus far. Their electronic defenses and their recruitment systems are extremely tight." Lobo conveniently omitted any mention of the Maui surveillance tapes. "However, the SROs themselves have provided us and the nation with most of the information we thought we'd need infiltration to obtain. They're working together, they have an endless amount of money to spend—far more than we do—and they're at least indirectly responsible for the surge in regulatory petitions and probably for Beatty's gubernatorial campaign. They're keeping a scrupulous distance from the Clean Elections Party, on the insistent advice of their counsel, Theresa Tieknots, but otherwise they wear so much on their sleeves that we don't see much point in infiltrating them anymore, even if we could."

"I'd have to agree," said Sal Belligerante, recalling his meeting with Jeno.

"To continue, the third front was to tie them up, obstruct them, and draw them into a war of attrition, and that's still our best option. Trouble is, at this point it relies on the Bulls in Congress, and our tracking polls on their standing in their districts and states are not encouraging. Many have dropped from approval levels in the high seventies and low eighties down to the fifties or high forties—and this before voters start concentrating on the fall elections and before the CEP candidates really bear down on the Bulls by name, record, and attitude. We're finding that longtime one-party-district incumbents can be quite vulnerable. I've just received the results of a poll by Billy Beauchamp, our friendly House Rules Committee chairman, whose approval ratings have dropped from the low eighties to just under fifty percent. Now, that is very worrisome.

"As for the fourth front, attacking the SROs' legitimacy, their motives, and their credibility, I have these words for you: Bernard Rapoport, Harry and Louise. True, we've had some success with our scare ads about America's global competitiveness and the business climate, but by and large we've hit a stone wall here. Which brings us to the fifth front. All the corporate and trade lobbies, the corporate law firms, the public relations firms—all the combined muscle

of corporate America, except for the PCC navel-gazers and their academic and think-tank cohorts—are now geared up to the nines for
the titanic battle ahead. They've aroused their constituencies, and
they're keeping in close touch with one another, or at least that's
what they tell Brovar Dortwist. I have to confess, however, that a lot
of this has been on paper, because just about all their executive
directors and staff have taken this month off."

"Has our opponents' side done likewise?" asked Sam Slick.

"Just the opposite. They're in overdrive, probably working harder
in August than they did in July. The curve is arching upward on all
indicators of their activities, so far as we can determine."

"Maybe I'm just a grumpy old man, Lobo," said Justin Jeremiad,
"but it seems to me that much of what has or has not happened
would have happened or not even if you and your operation weren't
around. Am I right?"

"With respect, Mr. Jeremiad, if I may continue, I think I can
address your concerns. Our resources on all fronts are increasing—
our capability, that is—but toward what tactics, what strategies? We
don't have time to experiment. Ironically, history must be our guide,
even as the SROs are writing new history. In my judgment, after
canvassing all ideas and probing all weaknesses in our opposition,
I've come to the conclusion that barring some bolt from the blue,
our best hope lies in the private investment sector and the delay-
and-block strategy in Congress. We've discussed both before, but
now it's a matter of intensification and escalation.

"By the private investment strategy, I mean an organized investment strike by the industrial and commercial corporations and the
banking community. Coming off our saturation fear campaign, this
move is credible, however unpleasant. All pending factory construction is put on hold. Companies significantly step up their
announcements that they're moving their facilities overseas,
blaming the disastrous investment climate created by fear of the
Agenda's passage. Credit begins to tighten up even before Congress
makes its decision, and that will get the millions of small businesses
activated. None of this should be couched in threatening or personal

language—it's just sound business decision-making by free market companies. The stock market won't like it, except for the short sellers, but we shouldn't have to keep it up for more than a few months to succeed.

"As for the Khyber Pass strategy in Congress, we've been counting all along on the powerful committee chairs, but for the first time in many a year, they're beginning to run scared. They'll respond to their reelection fear in one of two ways. Either they'll turn into born-again populists to fend off their CEP challengers, or they'll get their dander up and become more intransigent than ever. Which way they go will depend in part on their opponents. If the CEP and the SROs resort to personal attacks or dirty campaign tactics, that helps us; if they're diplomatic and civil and focus on what they call the Bulls' 'better natures,' that does not help us. On our shoulders lies the responsibility to support the Bulls generously and treat them with kid gloves both in terms of their committee responsibilities and in their campaigns back home. It has also been suggested to them delicately, by sources distant from us, that a wonderful career and an easy life await them if they stand firm against the Agenda and lose their elections.

"If you'll recall, gentlemen, I made a sixth point in my initial presentation to you, about what I called the great unknown—all of you. As I've said time and again, your personal involvement is crucial. I'm now going to make a recommendation that may not sit well with you. Your opponents are a whirl of activity, though most of them have fifteen years or more on you. As you know, they've been speaking at rallies and meeting with the Bulls and with some of you over these past few weeks. It's imperative that you respond in kind, that you become directly and openly engaged with them and against their Agenda. There's an entire floor of suites available at a good hotel in Washington, not far from Congress, that could house you securely, privately, and very comfortably if you take up residence there for the remainder of this congressional session. I urge you in the strongest possible terms to do so. You have to be on location, on tap for the media, for members of Congress, for White House appointments, and for each other, in person. Brovar Dortwist agrees. There's no substitute for being where the action is unfolding."

"Let me stop you right there, Lobo," said William Worldweight. "As we have told *you* time and again, we don't have the temperament for daily verbal slugfests. We have our noses to the grindstone running businesses that keep us up at night worrying. The SROs are retired, with no daily business responsibilities. How many of you around this table agree?"

Somewhat sheepishly, all the CEOs followed Worldweight down the path of least resistance and raised their hands—all except for Wardman Wise, Hubert Bump, Sam Slick, and Sal Belligerante.

Lobo curbed a sneer. "In my experience, money and personality will beat money without personality in most public struggles, but I guess we'll just have to hope that Congress is the exception. Still, I beseech you to ponder my urgent recommendation and reconsider it in a few days. Meanwhile, do I have your full support to do what has to be done on the private investment side and on the Bulls' side—the upper and lower jaws that will crush our opposition?"

Belligerante opened his mouth to speak, but Cumbersome cut him off. "You do," he said.

"Look, Lobo," said Wardman Wise, "I think we recognize the need to get closer to the senior members of Congress and some of the younger sparkplugs as well, and we'll do that, but not in the high-profile way you'd like. As I've noted before, it's up to you to find CEOs or company presidents who have what it takes to go one on one with the SROs."

"As I've noted before," Lobo said acidly, "I've been trying to find such people, with no success. There just isn't anyone out there who comes close to having the power, the connections, the knowledge, and the judgment all of you have. That said, I'll keep trying."

Ichiro Matsuda sighed. "Let's face it, Lobo, what you see around this table is dejection and a very low expectation that you can turn things around, no matter what the size of your budget. The forecast is that Labor Day this year is going to be very different from past Labor Days in turnout, energy, and agenda. I'm told that major labor

leaders are going to be on all four Sunday morning network interview shows, and that's certainly a first. I assume you'll have spotters
at all the big parades?"

"Yes," Lobo said, ignoring Matsuda's pessimistic assessment of
his efforts. "The SROs are determined to make Labor Day a big
momentum builder for the Agenda drive. By the way, it would be
helpful if those of you who've met with them would pull together
your impressions and get them over to me right away."

"And with that," said Cumbersome, "I believe we are adjourned."

Only too glad to take his leave of the pusillanimous CEOs, Lobo
returned to his office, grabbed a fistful of celery sticks, and put in a
call to Brovar.

"I've never been so low in my adult life," he said, chewing fiercely.
"Sometimes I feel like everything we do gets turned into smoke and
mirrors by the SROs' brilliantly designed, timed, and executed battle
plan. We're hitting a brick wall. Our efforts just aren't resonating."

"I'm afraid I'm feeling the same way these days. We've got thousands on the job, but no imagination, no passion. Everyone's on
automatic pilot, spending money, grinding out promos, ads, place-
ments, fact sheets, more ads. We can't seem to find a handle. It's
tough fighting people who just a few years ago were at the top of the
same kinds of businesses we're supposed to be representing. And
have they ever got the public's eyes, ears, hearts, minds, and feet."

"While we've got a bunch of lazy assholes."

Brovar heard a loud crunch at the other end of the line.

"Let the jury disregard that remark," Lobo said. "But imagine,
they're in the fight of their lives and they voted down my advice to
relocate to Washington for a couple of months."

Lobo described his meeting with the CEOs, and Brovar promised
to use his Rolodex to help locate a CEO B-team that could take on the
SROs. "Meanwhile, tell all your people to spend a long, relaxed Labor
Day weekend and think creative thoughts for dynamic action. That's
what I'm doing with my team. We can't let the SROs get us down,
Lobo. We've got to clear our heads for the confrontation of our lives."

CHAPTER 16

L
abor Day USA was one for the books. Record crowds came
out in city after city, but it wasn't just the turnout that made
the day so memorable, it was the quality and substance of
what was conveyed across the land.

In St. Louis, Missouri, a quarter of a million people lined the
streets to watch the floats, the pageantry, the fife and drum corps,
the flags and banners. Beyond the superficial sights and sounds—
sidewalk vendors selling snacks and balloons, activists handing out
buttons and bumper stickers—the deeper message was clear. In the
union contingents, the labor rank and file marched proudly, surrounding their leaders, not following them. Along the parade route,
other union members in the work clothes of their various trades
held up giant murals of men and women working in the steel, auto,
coal, textile, and construction industries. These full-color, historically precise murals had been loaned to the specially constituted
Missouri Mulers for Labor Justice by the Wall of America, a nonprofit collaborative that was portraying the entire history of
American labor in what would eventually be combined into one
massive painting, 120 feet long and four stories high, to be housed
in a nineteenth-century Connecticut textile factory that was being
converted into a permanent museum. The visual power of the ren-
derings awed the densely packed crowd and drew attention to big
placards mounted behind them, featuring each of the Seven Pillars
of the Agenda for the Common Good, with a website address for
those wanting further information. News photographers and television cameramen bounded back and forth recording the
extraordinary display while the spectators used their cell phones to

transmit these images of beauty and truth to friends and relatives across the country and around the world.

The members of Congress from Missouri and southern Illinois had been invited to be present on the parade platform. Like all the politicians and "dignitaries" who'd been asked to attend the Labor Day parades around the country, they were given to understand that they were there to look, listen, and absorb—with one exception. If they'd already endorsed the Agenda or were now willing to do so, they'd have two minutes to speak about their support and the reasons for it. Under no circumstances were they to march in the parades. They could only be there on the platform, either coming out for the Agenda or standing out like silent sore thumbs. This was a new Labor Day, a Labor Day of, by, and for the people, and the workers wanted action, not cheap posturing. If the politicians weren't going to march for the Agenda in Congress, why should they be invited to strut their hypocrisy on the avenues of St. Louis or any other city? As for the politicians, the opportunity to make a statement before such huge crowds was either a public relations dream or a nightmare, depending on where they stood on the Agenda.

The climax of the Labor Day parades across America was the reiteration of support for the Agenda from already committed legislators, along with new declarations of support from the hitherto uncommitted. It would have been a brave soul from Capitol Hill who showed up, sat down, and remained silent. Naturally, no one in that camp was stupid enough to appear, but the names of the absentees were read aloud over the public address system. In Missouri and Illinois, the number of committed legislators rose from 20 percent to 45 percent, and in other states the percentages varied widely. The results were a little disappointing to the parade organizers, but they realized that some lawmakers probably thought they were being hustled into an intimidating situation and didn't want to be show horses. Others may not have been willing to commit to the whole Agenda because they had reservations about some of the bills or wanted to fine-tune others.

Nonetheless, the wide coverage of the parades and the labor leaders' clear-eyed responses to questioning on the Sunday morning talk shows were an impressive tribute to the organizers, and especially to the indefatigable Ann Moro of the California Nurses Association. With half a dozen nurse colleagues, she had journeyed to each of the fifty states, using shame, guilt, and pride to blast the unions out of their defeatist mind-set, as she'd done earlier at the AFL-CIO. All over the country, the unions contributed millions of dollars, much of the money raised at potluck suppers as urged by Ann, to make Labor Day a raging success, with a long arm reaching to Washington, DC. More than 10 million Americans marched in the parades, not all of them in the big cities by any means, and millions more men, women, and children crowded the sidewalks and eagerly took the posters, bumper stickers, Seventh-Generation Eye buttons, and DVDs handed out by the junior parade marshals drawn from the "Read all about it!" brigades. Other young women and men circulated with clipboards for anyone wishing to sign up and join the movement or receive timely information about what they could do in the fall. The marchers had already registered their names and addresses with Parade Central and had been well briefed, showing in their demeanor and inter-actions with reporters and neighbors that they knew exactly why they were marching. Ann herself spoke at the New York City parade, 1 million strong.

The Labor Day events this year went far beyond the parades and platforms. There were concerts featuring the great classic protest songs from the historic struggle for unionization, going back to the days when it was defined as a struggle against "wage slavery" and the plutocracy's definition of labor as a "commodity." Many young people learned of these songs and the dramatic efforts they described for the first time in their lives, since in the past half century "organized labor" had been all but moribund and anything but organized.

In general, one of the delights of this Labor Day for its vigorous, visionary organizers was the youth turnout. Young people in their teens and twenties packed movie theaters to see a wide selection of the best films on labor battles with management, such as *Norma Rae,* and came away discussing what they had seen. Productions of plays like Odets' *Waiting for Lefty* also enlivened the weekend's festivities. There were special events for preteens where workers demonstrated skills that had long preceded the mesmerizing Internet. Sailors in the merchant marine showed them how to tie all kinds of knots. Carpenters showed them how to fashion simple tables and chairs, while metalworkers dazzled them with welding displays and glassblowers entranced them with their ancient art. Surgeons held them in fascination with a mockup of a broken hip and how they went about repairing it. Cooks and chefs concocted appetizers, main courses, and desserts that were enthusiastically sampled. The world of work came alive in all its dailiness and necessity as the youngsters watched wide-eyed. They saw how seeds were planted and how crops were harvested to make the packaged food they took for granted in the grocery store. They saw how paper was made and turned into magazines, newspapers, and books. They were shocked by movies showing the sweatshop working conditions in China and Indonesia and Vietnam where their iPods and cell phones and shoes were manufactured, and the poverty of the workers and children who hand-made the baseballs and soccer balls they played with. On television news, the world of work was largely reduced to statistics about unemployment or layoffs, but these young people got a bracing dose of reality that they wouldn't soon forget.

All in all, it was a Labor Day that shook America. Commentators marveled not only at the turnouts but at the variety and vitality of the speakers and the power of their arguments for a new economic order where the people would be supreme over the corporations and sovereign over their government. It was a day when working-class dignity took a stand and left the country feeling that this stand would not be denied in the coming weeks and months.

High above Manhattan, in a private dining room on the 103rd floor of the Bank of the Globe building, fifteen Goliaths, as they were known in the slang of the business world, gathered for an emergency dinner meeting on Labor Day evening. These powers behind the throne of international business operated at a rarefied level far above that of Lobo's CEOs. They were new to the agitations of the Meliorists because of their global preoccupations and a knowledge base about what was going on in the world that relied on unexamined assumptions rather than empirical observation. Now they were trying to appear in casual self-control as they watched a bank of live screens showing the culminating Labor Day events around the country, but they were visibly rattled. Long ago, the Goliaths had written the United States off as a large but steady-state economy. What you saw was what you were going to get. The big money was to be made in the Third World and in parts of the former Soviet Union. The Bank of the Globe was already reporting that 70 percent of its profits came from outside the United States even though it was the second-largest bank in the country. Why? Wild profit margins overseas. Fractional costs. Little countervailing power either in government or civil society, if the latter existed at all.

The Goliaths talked while they dined.

"When you boil the whole day down," said Hugh Mongous, "it seems to me that the message is 'Workers of America, unite, you have nothing to lose but your chains!' Sound familiar, my brethren?"

"Are you joking, Hugh?" said Stan Selitoff. "It seems to me that they just want a piece of what we owe them. If you think a Marxist-type revolution is what they're pushing, revolution must be going down deep into the minor leagues. They're not trying to replace us or seize the reins we hold."

"Unless they're taking it in stages. Do they have a theorist?" asked Manny Tentacles.

"Not as far as our staff can tell," said George Gargantua. "Unless you think these Meliorists are doubling as theorists or economic philosophers. The problem I see is the spillover effect into the Third World. I'm not worried about Canada or Western Europe. They'll just look at what's happening as the US playing catch-up with them after years of neglecting labor, health insurance, electoral reform, and so on."

"No theorist, no beliefs. No beliefs, not to worry," Manny remarked.

"That gives me an idea! Damn, this avocado salad is good!" said Sy Clopean. "Why not launch a global ad campaign that paints the Common Good Agenda as just what George called it—a modest catch-up, no big deal after thirty years of no gains for those who will benefit if these bills get through Congress. We can also inform the countries of South America, Asia, and Africa that the Agenda will increase US labor costs and put their economies in an even more competitive position."

"Hold on!" expostulated Cole Ossal. "As an American, you're talking economic treason. And you're running an American company to boot!"

"Who says I'm running an American company?" Sy retorted. "When it comes to big multinationals like the ones we all run, there *is* no nationality. Call us global straddlers or anational corporations."

"I like Sy's idea," Stan said. "It will pretty much take care of our concerns and responsibilities. The Washington trade groups have been asking us for big bucks to fight the Meliorists, and we keep telling them that it's their fight, not ours. Now we have an initiative to back us up here, a very credible argument that we should all take care of our own business priorities first."

"You mean, essentially, domestic takes care of domestic and international takes care of international, right?" asked Hugh.

"Exactly," Stan said, "though I don't suppose it will hurt to throw our domestic brethren a bone by getting some big foreign companies to announce that they're suspending planned investment projects in the US indefinitely, until they get a better read of the business climate after this congressional term. Do we have a consensus, gentlemen, for our new global economic order?" He laughed as his colleagues around the dinner table nodded their vigorous assent, some with their mouths full.

"Then I guess that does it," Hugh said. "We've had a distasteful day watching the masses, so let's continue with our dinner. I think we've earned a little epicurean relief."

The Tuesday after Labor Day marked the return of the 535 denizens of Congress and their thousands of staffers from an August recess that was either bruising or energizing, depending on their views. An army of freshly tanned and rested lobbyists was waiting for them with their checklists and political cash registers, but the lobbyists knew the ring of the cash registers was beginning to sound a little tinny. *Congressional Quarterly* reported that 54 percent of the House and 55 percent of the Senate were already committed to the Agenda for the Common Good in writing and that the Bulls' approval ratings were continuing to decline.

Attendance at the pro-Agenda public events of August had reached magnitudes that could only be accommodated by the largest indoor arenas in the country—the Target Center in Minneapolis, the Boston Garden, Madison Square Garden in New York. Each time one of the Meliorists made a surprise appearance, the audience went wild, as if Shakira or the Rolling Stones were performing. Clearly, the Meliorists had become the justice equivalent of rock stars.

When Yoko stepped onto the stage at the Oakland Coliseum, there was a near riot of acclaim. Had any of the CEOs been scanning the crowd in front, they would have spotted the enthralled, catatonic face of Lancelot Lobo, who had come out on an afternoon flight from JFK and returned on the redeye to be back at the office bright and early so as to avoid arousing suspicion. The obsession lived on.

The Meliorists' increasingly confident and savvy allies in Congress had worked with the Bulls to complete the extensive hearings on the various parts of the Agenda by the end of July. During August, sufficient staff had remained on the job to complete the committee reports with majority and minority views. That meant the committees could now schedule the first meetings to mark up the legislation and vote on sending it to the House or Senate floor. The Double Z resumed their tireless daily trek to congressional offices so that they could provide steady feedback to Promotions, Analysis, and the Meliorists themselves.

Just as Congress was settling back into its routine, Lobo blanketed the airwaves with the opening salvo of his investment strike strategy. It was Lobo at his ferocious best. The ads were verbal velvet gloves conveying iron-fist determination. Using data from the Commerce Department, and an advertising firm with a far subtler touch than Horatio Hadestar's, he analyzed proposed or tentative investments geographically and then saturated the local media with suspension announcements from one company after another in region after region. Naturally, local television, radio, and newspapers gave the announcements top billing. In a reversal of his previous strategy, Lobo made sure that as many of the companies as possible were situated in localities represented by the Bulls, on the theory that the Bulls would be so furious at the Meliorists that they'd dig their heels in on the Agenda.

For example, Zintel Corporation suspended negotiations for locating a billion-dollar computer chip factory on the outskirts of Dallas, Texas, in the district represented by Sid Swanson, longtime chairman of the House Labor Committee. The suspension of a large hotel, condo, and retail store development near Atlanta would surely get the attention of Senator Duncan Dredge, chairman of the Finance Committee, which handled all matters involving tax legislation, public investment, and business subsidies. Senator Dredge, up for reelection, had already touted his role in bringing these jobs to Georgia in his campaign literature. Back in August, the seventy-six-year-old senator had met with William Gates Sr. and told friends he was charmed, but he probably wasn't charmed any longer.

In addition to the suspension announcements, Lobo launched some national media displaying silver-haired, avuncular spokesmen—actually paid actors—delivering a somber message about dislocating our great economy through risky social engineering promoted by disgruntled has-beens from the business world. Three labor unions broke ranks and supported the campaign of fear, with actors playing workers who declared in one-minute spots that they didn't want anyone experimenting with their livelihoods either. The tag line was the demand that Congress "stop the Meliorist Mania."

A day or two after Lobo's first ads broke, the syndicated cable and radio hosts picked up on them and began devoting the entirety of their allotted time to another round of guests and talk denouncing "the bleeding heart Common Goodism that would wreck our free enterprise system," in the hyperbolic words of Bush Bimbaugh. Not to be outdone, Pawn Vanity trumpeted in hysterical tones the probable job losses in every locality struck by a suspension announcement. He called for congressional investigations. Immediately! The *Wall Street Journal* put out a special edition with maps of the localities and profiles of the communities and profuse statistics on how the suspended investments would have alleviated unemployment and other local problems.

Lobo's last-gasp smear campaign was fully underway, flooding the airwaves and the right-wing blogs with ruthlessly false and lurid accusations against the Meliorists by name and against anyone associated with them, including their congressional allies and the "subversive" new CUB and Congress Watchdog organizations. The lecturers were compared to the Wobblies—members of the Industrial Workers of the World, so many of whom were maliciously prosecuted as Communists after World War I. It was a mass media convulsion, a final desperate lunge of the deluders, distracters, deriders, defamers, and would-be destroyers of the social justice movement.

A puzzled, uncertain stock market steepened its slide by the day. The baying pack kept up its jeremiads against the Meliorists and darkly wondered whether "these ex-business tycoons" were making big money by selling short. Bush Bimbaugh and imitators evinced a sudden touching concern for the trillions of dollars in worker pensions invested in stocks and how the retirement of "millions of hardworking patriotic Americans" was in jeopardy.

It was a full week before Promotions started a comparable media counterattack, though it put out short rebuttal press releases right away. Barry's top lieutenant, Evan Evervescent, came up with a sharp idea. The Double Z had been working closely with the progressive members and staff on each of the pertinent committees, helping them to write their sections of the committee reports on two levels: the quantitative data and evidence supporting passage of the bills, and the human abuse, fraud, and devastation resulting from the conditions the bills were designed to reform. Citing House and Senate committee reports had an authoritative ring in the public mind, so Evan saw a chance for a double whammy here: he could rebut the yahoos with "official and verified heartrending material" and at the same time focus the public on the congressional process regarding passage of the Agenda.

Evan called on Bill Hillsman, who produced a series of ads that were funny, acidic, and so creatively specific that they made news themselves and got another play in the media that way—his trademark. People everywhere were talking about them because they zeroed in on the injustices of their daily lives—indecipherable over-billings, medical or hospital malpractice, depressed wages that forced them to work second and third jobs, price gouging by the oil companies, waste of their taxpayer dollars, unaffordable housing and healthcare, loss of their pensions, layoffs due to corporate flight, long waits on buses and trains to get to work, daycare that was too expensive if it was available at all, while the rich had daycare and chauffeurs for their dogs! What a stinking way to have to live! In particular, the ads directed at Bush Bimbaugh became instant website classics and the rage of college campuses. Up against the Minnesota maverick, Lobo and his propaganda were laughed out of town. It didn't help when two whistle-blowers revealed that their own companies had faked investment plans in order to suspend them.

The attack and counterattack between the CEOs and the PROs lasted for two weeks and cost both sides a bundle, but when the dust settled, the center had held. Horatio was still at the bridge, and the polls were still trending steadily in favor of the Agenda. All Lobo had accomplished was to exhaust his arsenal of fear-mongering.

Lobo knew that he and his team were just about cornered. The options were quickly being reduced to one—the Khyber Pass. The CEOs had once again rejected his recommendation that they take up residence near Congress for September and October, so he reluctantly set about finding some worthy, aggressive surrogate CEOs or entrepreneurs, as his bosses had directed. He and his captains interviewed dozens of preselected candidates and winnowed them down to seven who accepted: Dexter D. Delete, scion of the nation's largest private detective firm, well versed in winning through silent intimidation by dossier; Sally Savvy, CEO of a trendy lingerie company whose customers included Hollywood's most glamorous female stars; Elvis Inskull, founder and jovial CEO of a chain of lucrative psychiatric hospitals; Adam Agricoloff, the self-styled third-generation Asparagus King, who owned half a million acres in California's Imperial Valley and employed thousands of migrant workers; Steve Shredd, principal designer and manufacturer of cluster munitions and late-release napalm bombs; Gilbert Grande, CEO of the venerable Arthur D. Small consulting firm, whose clients included more than seven hundred New York Stock Exchange companies; and Delbert D. Decisioner, chief executive of Conflict Resolution, Inc., a chain of arbitration centers specializing in business-to-business disputes.

Though their business specialties differed, they had many traits in common. They were right-wing, presentable, energetic, gregarious, and congenial. They wore their ideology proudly and articulately, and were able to convey a convincing apprehension about the threat posed by the Agenda. They all liked Lobo and were prepared to work closely with the strong-willed Brovar Dortwist. Lobo cleared them with the CEOs and installed them on the second floor of the hotel, which he'd already reserved in hopes that the CEOs would change their minds. He nicknamed them the Solvents—the force that would dissolve the opposition. In mid-September they began attending intensive briefings by Dortwist's specialists on all matters and locales relevant to their assignment. They were grilled in mock interviews, press conferences, and meetings with friendly and hostile legislators. Theirs was a tough challenge—to be the

human and authoritative face of the business community, spontaneously volunteering for duty, in contrast to the trade group execs
who were viewed on Capitol Hill by friend and foe alike as yesterday's
soup.

When Luke Skyhi heard of the arrival of these new kids on the
block, he turned to his chief of staff and said, "This is good news.
Lobo has planted the seeds of dissension between the CEOs in New
York City and the hard-charging new dynamos down in DC. They're
bound to disagree, and that will take up valuable time, blur their
focus, and breed internecine disputes that will reduce their flexibility
on the Hill. A Hydra is born, but it only has two heads, and they'll
be paralyzing each other instead of striking out at us. Be careful what
you wish for, big boys." He laughed into his omnipresent mug of
root beer. "This is Lobo's biggest mistake, just watch."

Committee markup time for contested legislation on Capitol Hill is
normally a work in regress. Formerly these markups were conducted in private among the legislators and their staffs only, but
after the sunshine reforms of the seventies, the markups became
public, like the hearings that preceded them. Not surprisingly, the
real markup work retreated to the back rooms, where tradeoffs,
deals, and legislative language were bargained over and decided.
Lobbyists swarmed over these supposedly secret markup sessions,
rushed to the lawmakers' offices afterwards, huddled in the congressional cafeterias, and ingratiated themselves with reporters by
giving them "inside tips." Or such, at least, was the prevailing style
of influence peddling before the Age of the Meliorists.

This September things were decidedly different. The corporate bat-
tlements were crumbling, and the lobbyists were scrambling to see
how much they could salvage instead of how much they could get.
They were also adding to their ranks as fast as they could. The drug
industry, which already had the largest lobbying corps, with some 450
full-timers, was adding another hundred extracted from the state cap-
itals. The already bursting Washington hotels were turning away

guests. Suites in new condo buildings were being taken sight unseen. The demand for apartments spilled across the Potomac River into the busy Virginia suburbs. Every day there were industry-specific meetings, trans-industry meetings, meetings of manufacturing trade groups, financial trade groups, organizations of utilities, raw materials producers, food processors, real estate investment companies, communications and broadcasting companies. Lights burned even later into the night than in August, even at the AFL-CIO headquarters, where ordinarily anyone standing near the entrance around 5:00 p.m. would have been in mortal danger from the employee exit stampede.

For decades the corporate supremacists had been in charge almost to the point of boredom. They'd plundered tax dollars and pillaged the government. They'd brazenly tried to take over Social Security, Medicare, and Medicaid. They'd demanded and won outsourcing of the most established governmental functions, such as some of those involving military services, national security recruitment, data management, and space exploration. Their domination was so complete that earlier in the year a satiric street-theater troupe had conducted tours of the US government without visiting a single government building. Instead they drove the tourists past the Chamber of Commerce building, the American Forest and Paper Association headquarters, the modernistic home of the National Association of Broadcasters, the inverted architectural specimen housing the National Association of Realtors, and the American Bankers Association edifice. But those days were over. The corporatists were now in a state of near panic.

In a state of total panic were the Bulls, who knew with greater and greater certainty that they were facing the prospect of unemployment come January. The various committees and subcommittees had reserved the usual dozens of amendments, tax loopholes, and appropriations riders that had been carefully nourished by campaign money and junkets from the merchants of greed. "Get rid of them!" the Bulls bellowed to their chiefs of staff. "We don't need these lightning rods to complicate our situation."

Meanwhile, the Meliorists' congressional allies, still trying to remain under the media radar, were methodically working the Agenda bills through markup. Before the August recess, they had succeeded in persuading the Bulls to produce majority committee reports on the legislation in neutral, analytic terms. That wasn't hard to do, given the storm the Bulls knew they were facing on their return home that month. Neutrality helped them avoid controversy. Neutrality made them appear above the fray, statesmen conveying considered assessments for the deliberation of their colleagues. In their dealings with the minority, they had reached a state of unexpressed awe, realizing that these Meliorist allies were the hands and hearts of the American people. Still, it was all upside down to them. The majority in Congress represented a shrinking minority of citizens, while the minority in Congress was speaking and acting for the majority in the country.

That said, the Bulls were no fools. Given their tenure, they had steadying reserves to draw on, and none of them more than Raymond E. Tweedy III, the prestigious chairman of the Senate Judiciary Committee and a former chief justice of the Supreme Court of Alabama. Justice Tweedy, as he was known to one and all, surveyed the realm and decided it was his duty to call for a weekend retreat of all the Republican Bulls in Congress. He quickly secured the assent of his counterpart in the House, Chairman Sebastian Sorrentino of New Hampshire.

By Friday noon, three dozen Bulls had arrived at the palatial Bunkers Hotel in Virginia's fox country, a favorite gathering place for congressional leaders over the years. It was secluded, confidential by strict management decree, and oh so inviting in decor, luxury, and cuisine. But this weekend's running of the Bulls was all business. No golf. No tennis. No entertainment. Nothing but serious talk about what to do in the face of the tidal wave of popular power and the relentless internal and external pressure for complete floor votes on the Agenda before the session ended.

Justice Tweedy opened the meeting. "Ladies and gentlemen, perhaps for the first time in our long careers of public service, we don't know what to do. We are facing a barrage of what can only be called ultimatums. To be sure, they are not delivered bluntly or coarsely. They are delivered by inference, by expectation, by a gentle suggestion to look out the window and see what's coming in a daily drumbeat from all points.

"The Meliorist Agenda has been distilled into the most professional legislative presentation in my memory, together with meticulous section-by-section analysis and constitutional backup. As a longtime baleful eye on sloppy, ambiguous language in bill after bill, I quietly admire their competence. You surely noticed that the preparation of the minority during your committee hearings in June and July was most thorough and most impressively backed up by their staff, by the finest if not largest law firms, by the so-called progressive think tanks, and by the thoughtful, learned cream of the nation's law, business, and graduate schools. That is the first of their concentric circles of support.

"The next and wider circle is comprised of the institutions and grassroots organizations established by the Meliorists, with paid membership rising into the millions. The third concentric circle embraces the currents unleashed by the Clean Elections Party and its candidates. The fourth is the daily mass media and Internet attention to every thrust, every move, every advance, every everything. If we put our collective finger to the wind, can any of us doubt that this is the most powerful and encompassing gale we have yet encountered? It's like a category five hurricane, like Katrina—you can be told it's coming, you can watch it coming on television from afar, but you have no idea what it's really like until it hits.

"For what it's worth, here's my political assessment. The Meliorists have a majority of the Congress already, but not a veto-proof majority. Unless our corporate friends engineer an unlikely rollback, that means the spotlight moves to the White House. The next month will tell if the president will have the votes to sustain his vetoes, but it's not that simple. If the momentum continues from week to week back in the districts, what's at stake is not whether we can defeat a veto override in one or both houses but whether we're willing to pay the price of a landslide that throws our party out of power, throws some of us out of Congress, and bids fair to take over the White House in two years. That is the unpleasant macro scenario. There are, however, many micro scenarios that may present opportunities more within our jurisdictional and procedural control. At this point, I seek your views at any level."

Benjamin C. Bullion, chairman of the House Appropriations Committee, adjusted his spectacles on his nose. "The Seven Pillars are conceived in a way that for the most part nullifies my major institutional objection. As far as I can tell, they do not cost the Treasury. Am I right, Paul?" he asked, deferring to the chair of the Joint Budget Committee.

"Right you are, Ben," said Senator Paul Pessimismo. "We're almost done with costing out all the bills, and our findings support your seat-of-the-pants assessment. The provisions having to do with what the other side calls 'shifts of power' don't draw on the Treasury at all, nor does the living wage. The CUBs and Congress Watchdogs are funded by member dues and Meliorist cash. The electoral reforms are either taxless or rely on voluntary contributions on the 1040 forms and on free television and radio time. Payments from companies for the use of public assets actually contribute to the Treasury. The main drain—and it's a big one—would be universal health insurance, but the opposition will counter by saying that public opinion decided in favor of Medicare for everyone long ago. They'll say that a single payer means huge savings from greater efficiencies and an end to widespread billing fraud. Federal, state, and local government already pays half of the two-trillion-dollar annual bill anyway, and big business would love to have an anticompetitive financial burden lifted from its shoulders. Finally, new taxes imposed on financial transactions in the options markets will bring a torrent of revenue into Treasury, even with the abolition of federal income tax on people earning less than a hundred thousand dollars a year. I wouldn't say this publicly, but the whole package is brilliantly choreographed for defense as well as offense."

"I wonder whether we should find this news so grim," Bullion remarked.

"Perhaps Ben has a point," said Harry Horizon, chair of the House Transportation Committee. "Our friends on the outside have a generous expectation of our ability to delay all the way and close the Agenda down before the election. Everybody else is expecting the same thing, including the media. All this makes me uncomfortable. They expect us to sit on top of a volcano that's ready to erupt. No way. Power is perceived to be unchallengeable until it's challenged. Not that our power is going to cave in like papier-mâché, but we around this table know its limits better than anyone. It does, after all, come down to the votes we have in our committees, and bottling things up isn't really going to work this year. The Seven Pillars have been skillfully positioned as ideas whose time has come. I'm losing members to the Meliorist side every week."

Martin Merchant, chairman of the Senate Commerce and Industry Committee, was nodding. "The Meliorists' allies have been taking regular internal polls of Congress, showing a steady increase in their votes, and they're doing another one next week. I suggest we take our own poll of ourselves. How many among us are hard-liners? How many are still prepared to say with Calvin Coolidge that 'the business of America is business' and that the Meliorists are cooking the golden goose?" He looked around the table slowly. Many of his fellow solons were smiling nervously or shaking their heads wistfully or sighing. A few were gritting their teeth.

Billy Beauchamp spoke up. "Last month all of us met with one of the Meliorists. Did they pound their fists and threaten us, shout us down, display quiet cunning and shiftiness? From my experience and what I've heard from the rest of you, the answer is no. Whatever they may have been thinking, they respected our intelligence, laid their wishes out calmly, and listened to us. If they had an attitude, it was 'What's the Big Deal? We've Earned It!' and their fervent belief that the Agenda is great for the USA. Listen, I'm from one of the most conservative districts in the country, and I've slipped below fifty percent. My opponent is a newcomer to electoral politics, nominated by a brand-new party nobody had heard of a few months ago. They're tapping into a deep vein of resentment among voters against the rich and powerful. Obviously, more than a few are our voters—or were.

"In my judgment, the struggle this fall comes down to one question: Are we prepared to go all out, pull out all the stops with our frantic business partners, to deny the American people a decent livelihood, a rightful voice in government, and a political and economic system that will no longer betray them and abandon them? If we are, we may destroy our party's control over the three branches of government for a generation, if not longer. And that's assuming we can beat the Meliorists. We may very well end up losing to them and losing our seats in one heave-ho."

"You've all made it easier for me to speak my mind," said Francine Freshet, chair of the House Environment Committee. "As I read the tea leaves, we have two choices left: either we surrender with slow-motion grace, or we take the Bulls by the horns, as it were, and ride the Agenda wave to victory, getting some get credit for it and saving our party in the process. I don't happen to think the Meliorists are revolutionists."

Duke Sabernickle, chair of the House Commerce Committee, slammed his fist down on the table. "I've heard enough! What disgraceful defeatism, and well before any defeat can be considered imminent. Look around. We're the leadership. We're still in charge. And we still have the nuclear option."

"And what, may I ask, is that, Duke?" inquired Daniel Dostart, the energetic speaker of the House.

"The nuclear option is to choose the right time and announce adjournment. Under the Constitution, the president can order us back, but not this president!"

"Adjournment?" exclaimed several Bulls at the same time.

"Exactly. Close up shop, take off, go on some European parliamentary junket," Duke said, almost spitting the words.

"We can't do that," objected Elaine Whitehat, chair of the House Education Committee. "Aside from the Agenda, there are vital defense and health-education appropriations bills that make up about three-quarters of the government's operating budget and that still need to be reported out of committee, debated, passed, and reconciled with the other body."

"So?" replied Sabernickle with curled lip. "We'll pass 'em and then vamoose."

"It won't work," Whitehat said levelly. "The other side has anticipated you by not allowing much distance between these must bills and the Seven Pillars. Besides, anyone who votes for adjournment would be best advised to flee the country. It would be political suicide."

"What an opportune moment to pause and reflect!" interjected Justice Tweedy. "Let's break for dinner and resume on a full stomach."

Everybody nodded to that except for the furious Sabernickle, who swore under his breath, "Goddamn jellyfish!"

In the large dining room, a mustached pianist with a permanent smile and practiced fingers was playing the old standards in subdued octaves so as not to intrude on the diners' conversations. There wasn't much to intrude on. A weariness had settled over the Bulls, perhaps because each of them had hoped to hear more fire and brimstone and defiance from the others than they were feeling themselves. Some made desultory small talk about their "quality time" with their grandchildren or a recent spectacular performance at the US Open or Yankee Stadium. After dessert and brandy, they reconvened in the conference room.

"What an excellent meal!" said Justice Tweedy, trying to start things off on a positive note, "Shall we continue our exchange of views?"

"Well," said Senate Majority Leader Tillman Frisk, "since our room for maneuver is contracting, the ball is more in the Senate court than over at the other body. As my distinguished colleagues in the House know full well, Senate rules allow for unlimited debate, the filibuster, the endless offering of nongermane amendments, and an armload of parliamentary obstructions that our full-time parliamentarian spends years trying to figure out and interpret from one vague precedent after another. However, given the weekly attrition of our numbers, one rule becomes paramount, in that it can dissolve all these obstructions. I refer to the discharge petition to move bills out of committee. If more than sixty percent of the vote is there, down go our historic tactics of delay and blockage."

"In the House," said Speaker Dostart, "these same discharge petitions can overcome the temporal prerogatives, shall we call them, of the committee chairs. And don't you think the other side isn't planning for that eventuality even as we sit here?"

"Of course," said Senator Frisk. "Once an idea whose time has come comes—and this one is coming on eighteen wheels—all bets, all old ways and means, go by the board, I hazard."

"Defeatism, defeatism, and more defeatism!" thundered Duke Sabernickle, pounding the table again. "Maybe I've had one too many dinners with our business friends, maybe it's because I'm younger than most of you and because I want to and can stay in the House longer than most of you, but aren't we the last stand of the free enterprise system, as many of you have repeatedly stated in the past? Aren't we the last stand for economic freedom against social engineering and the leftist plan for America's decline? The Seven Pillars? Hah! They're Seven Slides down the slipperiest slope in American political and economic history. I know whereof I speak in these matters. The Meliorists are always talking about 'Redirections.' What's our direction? Where is our courage? Or are we now no more than lily-livered, Janus-faced opportunists?"

A protracted silence followed Sabernickle's tirade. Then, slowly pushing back his chair and standing ramrod tall, Armand Armsbuckle, former air force captain, veteran decorated in two wars, and immemorial chairman of the Senate Armed Services Committee, commenced a reply to this junior Bull's unusual dressing-down of his seniors.

"As someone who has faced enemy fire and paid the price in combat, I should take umbrage at your taunts, Mr. Sabernickle, but that would only dignify them with an attention they do not deserve.

Instead, I wish to make a personal statement before my colleagues. Brave as I was in war, I became a coward in politics. I didn't start out that way. I entered politics with a patriotic fervor to keep our country strong, honest, and prosperous, and a determination to respond to my constituents. As the years passed and my reelection became just about automatic, I slowly but surely came to see my constituency as the defense manufacturers who treated me so well, the helpful majors and colonels assigned to my office as Pentagon lobbyists, the corporate PACs and their handlers who made sure my campaign coffers were overflowing, the business associates who golfed with me, wined and dined me, and enjoyed my company and my family's at many social occasions."

By now the other Bulls were hanging on every word of this extraordinary confession from the normally reserved, proud chairman who commanded the disposition of half the federal operating budget.

"It was a comfortable life, full of accolades, flattery, and deference—just so long as I was following orders from the military-industrial complex, as Ike put it so well. I learned to say yes to every weapons system, every inflated military contract, every foreign adventure, every episode of 'so sorry' collateral damage costing the lives of so many innocent dark-skinned civilians in those God-forsaken countries abroad, every fabrication by my presidents, secretaries of defense, and secretaries of state, every drain on our national budget to appease the defense budget Moloch. I learned to say yes to it all, and I did it at the behest of those desperately looking for enemies overseas both before and after the Soviet Union collapsed, and at the expense of needy people and their children, public services, and the preservation of our precious natural resources here at home.

"Like you, I have watched the awakening of our fellow citizens of all backgrounds and opinions. It made me start thinking about myself, ourselves. When I saw on one television program after another the salt of the Earth, our American people, taking stands, attending rallies, challenging the greed, power, arrogance, and imperiousness of their masters, even while knowing it could mean their jobs, their livelihoods, and their modest ambitions for their children, shame overcame me. I asked myself, What have I ever done for these people, other than giving some of them jobs manufacturing cluster bombs, napalm, missiles, artillery shells, bombers, aircraft carriers, submarines with multiple nuclear warheads, chemical and biological lethalities? Talk about weapons of mass destruction. My answer embarrassed and humiliated me.

"Like many of you, I enjoy spending time with my little grandchildren. I praise them, admonish them, play with them. They know of my position, of course. What can I say to them when, at a young age of curiosity about the world and its injustices, they sit on my knee and ask, 'Granddaddy, what have you done to help?' Do I keep quiet? Do I lie to them? Or do I tell them I did nothing because I was too busy making sure our country acquired enough weapons to blow up their entire world three hundred times over and send the rubble into outer space?

"The Meliorists were wise to avoid completely matters of military and foreign policy, including the gigantic waste and theft in military budgets. You may be thinking, since their Agenda for the Common Good excludes these areas under my jurisdiction, that this battle is none of my business. You're the ones dodging the brickbats. Things are relatively quiet over at the Armed Services Committees. But I am a United States senator, not just the senator from Lockheed-Martin, as one poster put it cruelly. I am a veteran, a lawmaker, a husband, father, and grandfather, and I am determined in this final stage of my public career to be faithful to the responsibilities inherent in those fundamental roles.

"During the recess, Paul Newman called and asked to meet with me, and I agreed. We've all enjoyed his movies over the years and marveled at his continuing skills as a professional racer at age eighty. What I did not know was that he fought in World War II, and that many of the other Meliorists did too. He is a thoughtful gentleman. We had a thoughtful meeting. No bluster, no posturing, no dissembling on his part. He met me elder to elder, as part of a generation whose wisdom has for too long been neither offered nor requested. He used a wonderful phrase about his children and grandchildren. For them and for their generation, he said, he wanted to be a *good ancestor*. He was so different from the legions of high-powered lobbyists and CEOs who come to me for their special procurements and favors. He didn't even ask me to support the Seven Pillars. He just wanted to explain personally who the Meliorists were, where they were coming from, and what they hoped to leave behind for our beloved country during their remaining years. He spoke about their past achievements and described their decision to move from success to significance, to work for a country where the rights of power are replaced by the power of rights. I never felt better than when I let him take me to dinner.

"Lest you think I'm going soft"—the senator looked straight at Sabernickle—"let me define what being tough means. Asserting moral courage is being tough. Waging peace is being tough. Standing up to arrogant power is being tough. And until we have the deeply just society our people deserve, doing the right thing even if it costs us in the short run is being tough. What's being soft? Not thinking through why we are in Congress is being soft. Kowtowing to the interests that fund our campaigns and our appetite for power is being soft. Rallying behind every warmongering political charlatan who sends others off to kill and die is being soft. How do I know? Because up until now I've been soft in all those cowardly ways. But no more. On Monday morning, I will hold a news conference applauding the Seven Pillars and announcing my support. I would welcome it beyond gratitude if any of you were to join with me. Thank you for hearing me out." Armand Armsbuckle slowly sat down.

In the hushed room, four chairmen looked down at the table and blew a ripple of air through their lips. Another muttered, "I'll be a buzzard's uncle." Two others leaned back and looked up at the ceiling with their hands clasped. Several kept their eyes on Armsbuckle with expressions of serenity. Harry Horizon and Francine Freshet clapped twice and broke off. Billy Beauchamp nodded with understanding. Benjamin Bullion furrowed his brow and put his fingertips to the bridge of his nose.

"Oh, for God's sake. This is too much. Iron man turns bleeding heart. Give me a damn break," Duke Sabernickle said disgustedly.

Several chairmen who had been trying to remain neutral shot him a dirty look, and one said, "Duke, you're out of order." Senate Majority Leader Frisk said quietly, "Thank you, Armand, for your service to your country," while Speaker Dostart added, "Ditto, Armand, and don't be so hard on yourself." Half a dozen chairmen who silently agreed with Sabernickle's views if not his tone instantly began thinking about how to marginalize Armsbuckle after the news conference, assuming he couldn't be dissuaded from that point of no return. Finally the chairman of the House Labor Committee, Walter Workman, who had been silent until now, said in a loud voice, "Bravo, Senator Armsbuckle, bravo!"

Justice Tweedy sensed that matters were getting out of hand. The strategic analysis and consensus he had hoped would come out of the retreat had been extinguished by Armsbuckle's announcement. And he was going public on Monday, no less. Justice Tweedy stood up gravely.

"Armand, who among us does not respect your experience and your views? Who among us has not entertained doubts over the years about the declining state of our country in the midst of growing capabilities? As events move faster and faster, I myself feel that things are spinning out of control—just look at public and private debt levels, for example. But we came here to see if we could forge a common understanding regarding what we need to do vis-à-vis the Meliorists' drive through Congress. Not perfect agreement. Not an iron-clad united front, desirable as that would be. But common ground that permits us to move to the next level in handling this challenge. Now you tell us that on Monday the nation will watch you supporting the Agenda for the Common Good. If you go forward with your plan, you will have aborted the whole purpose of our being here this weekend. We need time to get our bearings, to determine our current power, our bargaining possibilities, the state of our allies, our options for revision. We've just returned from the hottest August of our lifetimes, and we need some time to digest that roiling month. The press, the lobbies, and our worthy opponents in Congress are all knocking on our doors for interviews, meetings, statements, committee schedules. As you noted, because the Seven Pillars do not cover the defense budget and military policies, you are not on the receiving end of these insistent entreaties. If you tie your immense prestige and credibility to the Agenda, that becomes the story of the week, followed by who knows what consequences. Can you give us another week, Armand? Let me ask all of us, how many would urge our distinguished colleague to defer his news conference by just another week?"

All raised their hands except Duke Sabernickle, who sat silent and grim-faced with his arms crossed.

"Armand?" asked Justice Tweedy.

"Your words and our long friendship touch me. I'll relent for another week, but we'll have to meet again next weekend to digest what has transpired in the intervening days. Agreed?"

Justice Tweedy scanned the faces around the table. "Does anyone disagree? . . . Very well, it's unanimous. At this point, I think it best to adjourn, get some sleep, and get back to Washington tomorrow. I'll be in the breakfast room in the morning if any of you wish to exchange additional thoughts. It's been an arduous day for all of us, so thank you and good night."

As September wore on, the hordes of business lobbies found themselves in growing disarray. Most of them were not yet at the point of every lobby for itself, but they were thinking more and more along those desperate lines. The urgent need to hold together a united business front fully backing the united front of the Bulls was at the top of the pile of worries afflicting Brovar and Lobo. Brovar had intercepted an internal PCC communiqué revealing that Luke Skyhi had formed a task force of progressive business owners devoted to just this divide-and-conquer strategy. Already the thriving businesses of the sub-economy were in close coordination, urging from the inside that each lobby look out for its own interests on

Capitol Hill before it was too late. Brovar called Lobo and told him to come down to Washington for the duration. He said that if the Meliorists succeeded in splitting the offense, it could spell disaster for the entire mission. This was no time for corporate narcissism. It was bad enough that the CEOs were obsessed with beating back shareholder approval of their enormous compensation packages. Lobo knew that Washington was now ground zero and agreed to spend most of his time there with a small, elite staff.

Meanwhile, the anonymously passionate progressives in Congress were shaping, moving, and troubleshooting both bills and Bulls with the crucial assistance of the Double Z. The task was enormously complex, but the Agenda allies were at the top of their spirit and expertise. They did not disdain diplomacy. On the contrary, getting things done in the hidebound Congress required hand-holding, face-saving, the generous allocation of credit, and the avoidance of public posturing and criticism. Fortunately, these were not needed to motivate the public, for in this epic struggle, the shift had begun: the followers were now leading, and the leaders were following. It helped mightily that the Meliorists, directly and by stimulating private donations large and small, were making sure the invoices were paid on time. Besides, the allies had had a taste of the public mood and civic activity in their districts in August, and they were still savoring it, especially those who had committed themselves to the Agenda from the start. On their return home for the congressional recess, their constituents had hailed them as heroes, and there wasn't any better adrenaline than that.

Every evening the allies met in their own boiler room, a block from the Rayburn Office Building, to assess the day's progress and make assignments for the next day. They took turns chairing the meetings, without regard to seniority or congressional protocol. It was all about getting the job done—check your ego at the door. They had been famished and ridiculed for so long that a massive reservoir of human energy awaited release. They felt no weariness, no exhaustion. Why would they? They were making history.

On the second Tuesday of September, they devoted their meeting to the matter of distracting and splitting the business offense. They'd invited Luke Skyhi to present the latest intelligence from the sub-economy.

"It always amazes me how bad habits breed more bad habits," Luke began. "We've become accustomed to management spear-heading leveraged buyouts of shareholders at undervalued prices so they can turn around and make a killing by selling the company off at its true asset value. They get away with it because present law doesn't prohibit this secretive breach of fiduciary duty or address the conflict of interest between management's responsibility to represent the best interests of their shareholders and management's greed fed by inside information. The noted financial writer Ben Stein says such management buyouts should be criminalized and banned. Distraction number one.

"Then there are the efforts of the individual trade groups—the timber and mining industries, the credit card companies, the oil and gas moguls, the insurance and banking companies, the retail chains, and so on—to carve out some immunity, some exception, some privilege. They're not looking at the big picture. They're just fending for themselves, which will shortly mean fending against each other. Corporate cannibalism is in their nature once they're cornered, and they do believe they're cornered. If you think the Bulls got heat in August, our reports reveal that the pressure on the companies was immense from every direction and every point of contact, right down to the surge of whistle-blowers inspired in part by the regular valedictories at the National Press Club.

"Some of our sub-economy merchants have turned out to be very gregarious and energetic, volunteering for task forces that get them included in high-level strategy sessions of their various trade associations. You'll be interested in what they tell us. The meetings—and there are plenty of them—often end inconclusively, which is a departure from the past. The participants are expressing doubt, anxiety, anger, indecisiveness. They're torn between charging ahead ideologically in total opposition or bending pragmatically to look out for themselves. The Lobo/Dortwist axis is furious, fearing that any possibility of a united coalition is swirling down the drain. Increasingly, the two men are going it alone with their own huge budget and their new public spokespersons, a bunch of parvenu CEOs they call 'the Solvents,' who are about to debut."

The progressives listened intently and asked pertinent questions about the coordination between the business groups and the Bulls. "No one on the other side is happy with that situation," Luke replied. "The plugs aren't connecting with the sockets." The conversation continued into the wee hours, until the allies finally called it a night and went home to sleep for a few hours and resume their anonymous legislative labors the next day.

If anybody was more upset these days than the corporate lobbyists, it was the congressional press corps. Used to grandstanding from publicity-hungry lawmakers, the media found it difficult to get interviews, a quote or two, or even background remarks from the progressives. David Roget of the *Wall Street Journal*, widely considered the most perceptive of the reporters on the Hill, wrote that the progressives were "like modern-day Buddhas, quiet, meditative, self-disciplined, friendly to their adversaries, focused, and almost scholarly in their attention to detail. To many observers, that makes them dull, but this is a luxury they can well afford."

When the opinion polls started to register not only victories for the Clean Elections Party in one district after another, but some landslides, the Oval Office took notice. The president summoned his top advisers to a meeting in the Indian Treaty Room, whose fraught history was the farthest thing from the minds of those assembled.

"Well, friends and seers," said the president genially, "it looks as if we don't have much choice but to go down to defeat or bet the store— our party, our White House, and our Congress—against the Seven Pillars. They're sure worth a lot to the people, but are they worth that much to us? Would any of you geniuses care to comment?"

"Yes, sir," said Chris Topper, his chief of staff, "From our recent rapid-fire meetings with a wide range of our core constituencies, two contradictory impulses emerge. First, they are defiant and expect us to issue a magisterial call to battle, but when we probe deeper, they seem weary, exhausted from being pounded and pulled asunder week after week by the Meliorist swarm—their favorite word for the popular agitations of recent months. They seem rootless, as if their predicates, frameworks, ideologies, and energies have vanished into the ether. Remember, they're not used to sacrifice, discomfort, or challenges equal to their own resources. Only in this room would I say that they're behaving like bullies finally being called to account."

"But is there any doubt that we can stop all this nonsense in its tracks by summary adjournment?" the president asked.

"There is grave doubt," said Lester Linx, his congressional liaison. "The defense and health-education appropriations bills have to be passed. The Allies can block adjournment as long as these bills are still pending. They've got or will have the veto-proof votes to arrange for simultaneous passage of these bills and the Seven Pillars, just as in a delicate exchange of hostages."

"What if we adjourn, block the Pillars, and take up the key appropriations in a lame-duck session, which I can unilaterally call after the election?" asked the president.

"That won't work because we don't have the votes for adjournment," Linx said. "Can't we get used to our minority status?"

A minute of anxious silence elapsed before Linx spoke again. "We just aren't holding the cards anymore," he said firmly.

"Well, there's always a putsch," said one of the president's special assistants, trying to break the tension. "Remember the Reichstag?"

Nobody laughed. The president shot him a look of irritation. "Let's turn the subject around for a seditious moment," he said. "Would the country be stronger and better with or without the Seven Pillars? Let's start with a clean slate and be completely candid. What do you say, Hal?"

Harold Featherstone III, a rising star among the special assistants, looked his boss directly in the eye. "I say, is this why I joined the *Dartmouth Review*, then went to work for *Forbes*, wrote for the *Wall Street Journal*, and edited the *National Review*? If this is the beginning of a new course you're charting for us, Mr. President, you have my resignation."

The president reddened. "Your mind is more than closed, Hal, it's foreclosed. You're so blinkered you can't even contemplate hypotheticals in the privacy of this room."

"As long as they remain hypotheticals, I can play the game, sir," Featherstone said, "but once you start down this perilous hypothetical path, where do you stop? You're not positing a steady-state hypothetical. I posit that there can be no steady-state hypothetical with hypothetical limits, boundaries, and ambitions. That's my historical, realistic, and experience-based hypothetical, sir."

Shelburne Sherwood IV, Featherstone's chief rival among the assistants, rolled his eyes. "Whatever that may mean, I say our choice is either to fight the war and lose it, or to fight the battle and lose it but remain in position to fight the war again. I have a distinct preference for the latter. Instead of betting the farm, why not give in, stress the conservative dimensions of the Pillars, ride the wave as if the victory were ours, and survive for the presidential race two years hence?"

"You're sliding into tactics here," the president said. "Stick with the hypothetical question I asked."

"As your adviser on community and ethnic relations," said Clarence Fairchild, "I've come to the conclusion that the country would be much stronger standing on the Seven Pillars. Let's not kid ourselves, Harold. This is all about the redistribution of power, wealth, and income in accordance with the people's just desserts and their long-ignored constitutional rights. I think you're confusing your pretensions with intellect."

Featherstone's eyes fairly bulged out of their sockets. "And I think you're displaying your true pink and yellow colors. You're jumping off our party's platform and besmirching it with mud. You're tearing up our president's speeches and replacing them with idiot Agenda babble. How revealing to see what passes for your inner thought process finally oozing out of your duplicitous mind."

"In the interests of time, and out of respect for you, Mr. President, I'll refrain from commenting on Featherstone's vapid bilge," Fairchild said.

"Enough," snapped the president. "This is getting us nowhere. Here's how I see it. Our base economically consists of the rich and powerful who respond to our deeds—like the Houston Petroleum Club boys, for instance, just to pull an example out of the hat. Our base politically consists of the tens of millions of people who respond to our words. I act as a business booster, but I speak as a politician. When our economic base becomes dangerously weak, as it has for the critical time being, we're left with our political base, who are abandoning us in droves week by week. We have fewer and fewer people who can speak persuasively to their skeptical ears. All of us in this room would describe ourselves as conservatives, but let's admit it—we've allowed the corporations to maul and usurp our conservative beliefs and have become their tribunes. So what do we find ourselves defending, promoting, and falling on the sword for? Global corporations that have no allegiance to the country that nurtures them and sends its soldiers abroad to protect their interests. Is that true conservatism, Hal?"

Featherstone sat in stony silence, looking in the direction of his feet.

"Come on, Hal, speak up. How do you feel about the loss of our sovereignty to a World Trade Organization that circumvents our courts and moves disputes with other countries to private tribunals in Geneva, Switzerland, where secret judicial proceedings force us to obey their dictates and repeal our own laws and regulations?"

Featherstone looked up. "Sir, I—"

"Do you support all those subsidies and giveaways to business, paid for by the taxpayers, who are then prohibited by our own judges from challenging these handouts in federal court?"

Slowly, Featherstone shook his head no.

"All right," said the president. "Now, you and I do not like regulations on business, but do you approve of businesses lobbying to keep our courts fully open for companies and restrict access for wronged individuals?"

"No," Featherstone mumbled.

"As a devout Christian, do you approve of corporations riding roughshod over any moral or religious constraints and making tens of billions of dollars from gambling, pornography, and other sin industries?"

"No."

"Would you applaud a neighbor who put some capital into an enterprise while you put in the hard work, and who left you with so little pay at the end of his super-profitable day that you couldn't begin to support your family or pay for healthcare?"

"No."

"Should companies be allowed to pollute our God-given air, water, and soil just to make more profits when the result is sickness, private property damage, and medical expenses?"

"No."

"Should companies escape prosecution if they sell you a product or expose you to a chemical whose dangers are known to them but hidden from the public?"

"No."

"Well, there are plenty of other questions where those came from, but I think you're probably getting my point by now. Those questions are also answered in the negative by the Seven Pillars you've been fulminating about. If, over the years, the big corporations have appropriated our conservative power for their own objectives—recall Mammon from your Bible—and left us with our conservative rhetoric to fool our faithful followers while we advanced ourselves, why should we object if the Meliorists and their supporters are pushing us closer to some of our conservative beliefs? Like privacy, sovereignty, civil liberties. Like real freedom of contract, not the one-sided, fine-print contracts we all have to sign. Like clean elections, and control of our borders, which so exercises the cheap-labor interests puffed by the *Wall Street Journal*. Sure, the Meliorists stand for things we will never abide, but you and your charming wife probably don't agree all the time either, do you, Hal? It's not a matter of black and white. It's how the Seven Pillars add up, and I can see them adding up to a stronger USA. I can certainly see plenty of people being happier, healthier, freer, and able to pay their bills and spend more time with their children. The Institute of Medicine reported recently that eighteen thousand Americans die every year because they can't afford medical care. I'm sure my well-bred, well-paid, well-covered staff doesn't know any of these fellow Americans. But think about it. What *is* the big deal? I'm tired of mouthing the corporate catechism and suppressing my resentment over it. Maybe the Meliorists have made it possible for us to free the conservative movement from its commercial shackles. What do you say, Chris?"

His chief of staff was staring at him. "What do I say? I say I'm speechless. It's going to take me a while to digest your words. Unless they were just a Socratic exercise," Topper ventured hopefully, but the president made no response.

"What about all those suspended investments and dire warnings about a declining business climate if the Pillars are enacted?" asked Shelburne Sherwood.

"Chicken Little," the president said. "Just tactical bluffing. They're also trying to get me to threaten vetoes so as to shore up the Bulls. Check out the Budget Committee's report next week."

"What about your veto thinking, sir?" asked Lester Linx.

"It's not relevant to the present escalating situation. As Shel said, it would be betting the farm, even if the vote is decisive—or should I say, especially if the vote is decisive." The president paused and looked at his advisers one by one, knowing that many of them were shaken or dispirited. "Cheer up, fellas. We don't have time for gloom and doom. Just go back to your offices and consider what I've said. We'll meet again in a few days, and meanwhile, no leaks. Repeat, no leaks. Keep your eyes, ears, and antennae on full alert, and as Abe Lincoln said, keep thinking anew. Chris, get me the latest read on the CEOs in New York, and be sure to ask them for their views on the Solvents. I suppose it's just barely possible that some new blood may be able to put a new spin on things."

For a solid week, virtually around the clock, the Solvents had been preparing for their debut at the National Press Club, scene of so many stirring speeches and valedictories in the past months. They'd been briefed to the gills on the Agenda and the Meliorists. They'd crafted their statements with the utmost care, reviewed them as a group for overlap and consistency, and committed them to memory so they could deliver them flawlessly. They'd studied profiles of the reporters who were likely to show up, and drilled each other with the questions that were likely to be asked. Lobo and Brovar had made sure the event was massively publicized and that the Solvents had all the resources of the CEOs and the hardline trade groups behind them.

As they strode to the dais and sat down to arrange their papers, they sensed an unusual atmosphere in the Press Club ballroom, not the usual kidding among the camera crews and scribes, but a kind of disdainful amusement. Well, thought Dexter Delete, he and his colleagues would soon wipe those smiles off their faces. They were there to communicate unyielding resolve in opposing the Meliorists and everything they stood for and intended to do to the country. Their concise and focused presentations would lay out the battle lines for the autumn showdown in Washington, DC. They had to avoid bluff and bravado and show the nation exactly what was at stake. They knew that because of the intense media interest their words would reach some hundred million people or more, and that they were already "personalities," which was fine by them if that was what it took to awaken the masses to the Meliorist peril.

Dexter Delete led off. He vividly portrayed the shakiness of the investment community and the stock market, and the devastating imminent effect on jobs, exports, and small businesses on Main Street. As a corporate private investigator, he had cause to know from the inside of his clients' premonitions and fears. "Our economy is formidable, our companies energetic," he declared, "but taken as a whole they are vulnerable precisely because their very energy overextends them in the credit and other markets. This overextension is vital to our continued economic growth, but it carries within itself the seeds of a sudden contraction in the face of trauma, as is well known to economic historians. The Meliorists are that trauma."

Next up was Gilbert Grande, the business consultant chieftain. "The pace of globalization these days means an enhanced inclination for capital flight under adverse pressures. The rapidly expanding economies of Asia, in particular, are happy to accommodate these shifts in plant, equipment, and startup industries that will become the big factor in coming years. Wherever these companies go, momentum, worker training, infrastructure, and R and D will follow. The Meliorists understand this very well. They cloak it in their continuing outcry that transnational corporations have no national loyalties, but in fact they are abetting it. The convulsions they've caused in our society since early this year are distracting my clients from the business of America, which is business. Their employees are either attending the lunchtime rallies or following the action on their computers and ignoring their work. Then they go home and are bombarded by media reports, excited neighbors, evening meetings, and the like. Productivity is declining as a result. Motivation is plummeting. Economics starts with psychology, contrary to the dogmas of the dismal science, and this Meliorist-inspired mass psychology is a catastrophe for our nation."

Elvis Inskull took the podium. "The Meliorists present a fascinating psychiatric profile. They're successful business people nearing the end of their active lives and searching for meaning, for their place in history, no matter what the cost to others of a more tender age. What do they have to lose if their gamble boomerangs on our country? Nothing, because they can blame it on the opposition's intransigence—not to mention that they're all billionaires. This is the hallmark of the dogmatic mind, a messianic belief in the

rightness of its cause, which can only be derailed by the machina-
tions of evil foes. The media persistently describes the Meliorists as
rational, cool, gradualist reformers. That is completely at odds with
my assessment based on long experience in treating psychiatric
patients and establishing healing residences for their cure. It is vital
to go behind the PR dazzle and plumb the psychological depths. The
Meliorists clearly have no economic motivations or political aspirations. Logic points to residual psychiatric disorders as a probative
explanation of their behavior and the lengths to which they are prepared to go to satisfy their unacknowledged psychological cravings."

Some of the reporters were nudging each other and snickering
as Steve Shredd rose to speak. "I come from a hardheaded business
too often misunderstood, so I know it won't surprise you when I say
that the task at hand is immediate, all-out opposition to the so-called
Agenda for the Common Good. This battle with the Meliorists and
their many tentacles here in Washington and throughout the
country will be the most ferocious, well-financed struggle in the history of the American corporation. Simply put, it is a battle over who
will lead this country—the invisible hands of bustling, innovative
corporations or the palsied hands of frustrated corporate retirees? I
am authorized to inform you that three billion dollars and thirty
thousand full-time lobbyists will be deployed on Capitol Hill not
only to block this Agenda but to preclude its return forever. A cluster
of advocates representing many categories of economic activity will
be assigned to each member of Congress, both here and in their
states and districts. Back home, these advocates will torpedo the
Clean Elections Party wherever it is fielding candidates against
incumbents who are committed to the defense of our great nation.
The overall command will be in the hands of Lancelot Lobo and
Brovar Dortwist."

Delbert Decisioner stepped up to play good cop to Shredd's bad
cop. "Resolving conflicts has been my business for thirty-five years,"
he said in honeyed tones. "Short of warring spouses or outright war,
there's scarcely a conflict I haven't produced arbitrators to resolve.
However," he said with a rueful smile, "I regret to inform you that

this conflict with the Meliorists is not resolvable by any other means than their total defeat. They won't give an inch. They maintain that the Agenda's very modesty and the careful drafting of all its interconnected parts precludes compromise. To which I say, balderdash! I personally am mobilizing the enormous world of conflict resolution firms to demonstrate that even those most skilled in settling disputes believe there is no chance of making so much as a dent in the Meliorists' authoritarian stubbornness. That will send a very clear message to the American people."

As Decisioner sat down, *Washington Post* columnist David Roader leaned over to Zack Lermond of the *Baltimore Sun*, his longtime competitor, and whispered, "I can't figure out their game, can you? Isn't this just recycled claptrap, or am I missing something?" Lermond shrugged his shoulders as Sally Savvy, the Lingerie Queen, took the mike. The press corps perked up perceptibly while the cameramen refocused and clicked away.

"You may wonder what I'm doing here. Well, I've had fantastic success in clothing my customers transparently, and I can clothe these Meliorist emperors the same way. I represent the textile industry, where the labor reforms of the Agenda spell extinction. There aren't many domestic clothing operations left, and we're hanging by a thong. The minute the Agenda passes, we're all outta here for Bangladesh or Vietnam."

"All of which," said Adam Agricoloff, the Asparagus King, stepping forward and gesturing to his colleagues, "is why we're sponsoring an open source competition for the seven best detailed proposals for stopping each of the Seven Pillars in its tracks. The prize for each winning idea is a million dollars, along with a budget of another million to publicize it and expose the fatal flaws in the corresponding Meliorist idea. Full information about the contest is available on our website, www.crisiscountdown.com. We cordially invite the millions of you watching on television or listening on your radios, both here and abroad, to participate. And now we'll take questions from the press."

As dozens of reporters rushed from the room to file their stories about the three-billion-dollar war chest and the thirty thousand lobbyists, David Roader stood and asked pointedly, "Just what are you trying to convey to the American people with this mishmash of declarations and accusations?"

"The grim reality of the political equivalent of war, Mr. Roader," said Steve Shredd, "and the urgent necessity for every American to enlist in this struggle against the Meliorists and for the twenty-first century."

"If things are so grim and so urgent, why aren't the CEOs here instead of you, their eleventh-hour substitutes?" Zack Lermond asked.

"Just my point," said Elvis Inskull. "The role of psychology is decisive. The CEOs are upstanding, successful, and very generous with their contributions, but they're all introverts. They're not publicity hounds like the Meliorists."

"I find it hard to discern anything new here other than yourselves and the three billion dollars. We already know what the business community has been doing. Just what are we supposed to find newsworthy in your statements?" asked Basil Brubaker of the *New York Times*.

"Intensity, all-out defiance, no compromises, a fight to the finish," said the Asparagus King. "In my business of growing fruits and vegetables by the zillions, we are in a seasonal fight to the finish against pests, fungi, rats, and drought. Only those growers with a focused intensity and a take-no-prisoners drive prevail. Those are the qualities we have conveyed this morning to a television audience of millions. What you write for tomorrow's newspapers will be your own take, through your own filters, and we can't do anything about that. Our side has had the upper hand in resources, manpower, and superior congressional contacts. What it lacked was what sportscasters encapsulate in the phrase 'the will to win.' That is what it has now, in us, and that is why we are here today."

"What are you going to do about the divisions and conflicts among the various business lobbies?" asked Linda Lancet of the *Wall Street Journal*. "Some would say that a lot of them are looking out for themselves at the expense of the overall opposition."

"That's a good probe," said Delbert Decisioner. "We know our opposition would like nothing better than to split our offense, and we're in the process of gathering detailed intelligence on the nature and depth of these divisions, with the goal of resolving them as quickly as possible. One of the reasons Lobo, Dortwist, and the CEOs brought us Solvents together was so that we could use our outsider status in the service of healing these potentially mortal clashes. We have no axes to grind."

"Pat Boylan of *Newsday*," said a craggy-faced man chewing on an unlit cigar. "The Las Vegas oddsmakers are putting your chances of stopping the Meliorist juggernaut at one in six. They have a good track record for being on the money. What do you say to those odds? And how much of the three billion is going into the campaign coffers of Republican senators and representatives?"

"We can't answer that last question," said Gilbert Grande. "Ask the Republican National Committee for their estimates. As for Las Vegas, let them stick to blackjack and roulette, and we'll stick to saving the Republic and the free enterprise system for which it stands."

"And would you add 'with liberty and justice for all'?"

"You're a smart aleck, Mr. Boylan," said Steve Shredd.

"It's a simple question. Please answer it."

"It's heckling. Next question, please."

Back at headquarters, Lobo and Brovar winced. All it took was one nasty remark to give the press their lead. They held their breath and waited for the other shoe to drop. Boylan was a war correspondent and Pulitzer Prize winner. He wasn't going to be dismissed by the likes of Steve Shredd.

"Wait a minute, I want an answer," Boylan shouted. "Mr. Grande just used a Pledge of Allegiance metaphor in describing your group's ideology. I want to know if the metaphor embraces the entire Pledge, including the last words. If you want to dodge the question, that's your prerogative, but don't call it heckling."

Delbert Decisioner saw the press conference starting to unravel. He moved in, nudging Shredd to one side. "Of course, Mr. Boylan. We all believe in every word of the Pledge of Allegiance."

"So we can write that your opposition to the Agenda for the Common Good is in furtherance of liberty and justice for all, correct?" Boylan said.

Laughter erupted in the ballroom.

Decisioner calmly waited for it to subside. "Naturally, you can write whatever you like, Mr. Boylan. Just let your journalistic conscience be your guide."

Lobo and Brovar breathed a cautious sigh of relief but were soon wincing again as a number of reporters asked questions about the group's contacts with the Bulls, the CEOs, the White House, the PCC, and the trade associations. It became apparent that the Solvents' vaunted networking operation had yet to leave the gate, and the remainder of the press conference did nothing to dispel the media's general impression that they were greenhorns.

David Roader returned to his office at the *Washington Post* in a reflective frame of mind. He sat at his desk deep in thought for a good thirty minutes, and then he began to write.

> In my fifty-one years of journalism, I have never witnessed anything like what is now almost certain to occur in our nation's capital—a bloodless popular revolution against the bastions of corporate power. Nor have I ever witnessed the retired super-rich taking on the entrenched super-rich. I have never witnessed the mobilization of the populace behind such a comprehensive leap forward for our country as the Agenda for the Common Good. I have never witnessed what increasingly looks like the wilting of the corporate supremacists under pressure coming from all directions in all dimensions.
>
> Perhaps Thomas Jefferson would not have been completely surprised by these developments. As you may recall from American history class, Jefferson foresaw that when the 'monied interests' grew extreme in the pursuit of their goals, the political sphere—the voters— would arise to counteract them. What neither he nor

any of our political ancestors foresaw was that the voters would arise with the help of other 'monied interests,' selfless and patriotic billionaires with a conscience and a passion for justice. No one foresaw it as recently as a few months ago, for that matter.

The popular movement set in motion by the Meliorists is spreading on its own, contagiously, even as it continues to receive guidance, publicity, and funds from these remarkably astute elders. We in the press can't begin to keep track of all the activity on Capitol Hill, much less around the nation. In the absence of some deus ex machina on the corporate side—and the Solvents clearly don't fit the bill—the Meliorists may be on the brink of total victory. Certainly that is what the polls are registering in an upward curve for the Agenda and the Clean Elections Party week by week, and a corresponding downward curve for the incumbents, especially those of the majority party in Congress. Local newspapers are reporting on the electric atmosphere back in the districts, the spreading sense that it's time for a real change, a mood that is very difficult to counter, even with the saturation media scare we've been treated to of late. Normally, clever political advertising can work to undermine its targets because there is no one on the ground in the communities to cry out, "Nonsense, we know better!" Now, however, there is a growing rampart of civic knowledge. Harry and Louise never had a chance for an encore this year for that very reason, though it didn't hurt that Patriotic Polly was waiting in the wings, as it were.

My congressional sources tell me of infighting and depression among the leadership and the committee chairs. "They seem unable to get it together," said one high-placed source who asked not to be identified. "The disarray on the Hill reflects a similar disarray among the

K Street lobbies, and there are no corporate lawyers of towering stature whose strategic experience and wisdom could begin to unite them. Part of the problem is that there has been nary a sign that any part of the Agenda deck can be cut. There are no deals on offer." And indeed, part of the genius of the Agenda's congressional backers has been their consistent message that they will not allow the Seven Pillars to be watered down or traded off against one another. The Pillars have been very effectively presented as an interlocking legislative package that will shift the power in our political economy away from the corporations and toward the citizenry. The architectural metaphor is apt. The pillars of a building are integral to its structure. None are expendable.

More and more, it appears that the Bulls and their 'bears' are left with one option, short of unconditional surrender: to jump on the Agenda bandwagon and try to avert a public relations and electoral disaster. They can try to adjust to the new balance of power, regroup, and hope that reformist fatigue sets in so they can reassert their power in coming years, just as their predecessors did after the populist-progressive wave petered out before World War I. The corporations roared back with a vengeance in the 1920s, with the Depression and FDR only briefly slowing their inexorable march toward a corporate state in the decades since. As the Meliorists said only a few remarkable months ago, stay tuned.

Roader's column was not well received on K Street, nor on Wall Street, State Street, LaSalle Street, nor Wilshire Boulevard. The unease in the corporate suites proceeded not only from the substance of his piece but from the fact that he had made public in the 380 newspapers that carried his biweekly column what they privately knew to be the case. Other commentators and editorial writers were sure to pick up Roader's prediction. Most had already weighed in with similarly dismissive appraisals of the Solvents. High in their stories was the Boylan exchange with Shredd, whose business was described by one of them as "the manufacture of advanced cluster bombs widely condemned by human rights groups."

"We'll have to lower our expectations of the Solvents," Lobo said to Brovar a couple of days after the news conference. "They're not the heavyweights we'd hoped they'd be, and the press has no use for them. Damn, but I hope that open source contest brings in some new ideas."

On the weekend before Armsbuckle Monday, the Bulls reconvened at the Bunkers Hotel. Justice Tweedy called them to order with a sobering introductory statement.

"Friends and colleagues, our backs are to the wall. We interpret the wall in various ways, I know, but my own evaluation of the situation since we last met is that the Meliorists are gaining at an accelerating rate and the people out there know it. Editorial cartoonists are cruelly caricaturing us as relics heading for 'the dustbin of history.' The late-night comics have millions of viewers laughing at our expense. The Agenda allies are breathing down our necks to give them the schedule for final committee votes. They're being very cagy about not letting the defense and health-education appropriations bills get out in front of the Seven Pillars. Our retired colleagues in the Zabouresk-Zeftel group are proving invaluable to them in this regard. Personally, I'd like to see us come to a unanimous decision this weekend, rather than each of us going our own way or trying our own blocking maneuvers."

"You mean we should all go down with the ship together," said Duke Sabernickle sarcastically.

"Or maybe save ourselves together," said Elaine Whitehat.

For the next three hours, the committee chairs went over the same old ground and came to the same conclusion: their only options were to accept the Agenda and "heed the loudly declared will of the people," as Harry Horizon put it, or to cling to the slim possibility of defiance to the end, with the attendant likelihood of a double defeat on the Seven Pillars and on Election Day.

Dinner came and dessert went. At the evening session, they once again discussed the possibility of cutting deals on the Agenda, but they came to a dead end simply because they didn't have the votes. Adjournment was not a possibility for the reasons given at the earlier meeting. They shifted their attention to the White House. If the president dramatically vetoed all the bills, he would doom his party, and he would be easily overridden by lawmakers looking to save their own necks on Election Day. Another dead end. Even if the Bulls didn't care about being reelected—and they were already getting subtle offers of lucrative positions, which disturbed them because they knew why—their own junior followers would rebel if they tried to block the Agenda. They ended their meeting and went to sleep knowing that the inconclusiveness of the day's deliberations could not be repeated on the morrow.

After breakfast, an unusually silent repast, they reassembled in the conference room. The meeting was mercifully short. Within an hour, they had agreed to ride the Agenda wave and make the best of it. Armsbuckle would drop his plans for a press conference, and the group would prepare a statement for a joint press conference next week. The decision was unanimous. It was obvious, even to Sabernickle, that it had to be. Self-preservation is the cardinal instinct of legislators.

Once the decision was made, there were certain courtesies to be arranged. The Bulls would have to ask the president for a personal meeting, with no aides present on either side. Lobo and Brovar were next in line to be notified, but the Bulls knew Lobo would insist that the CEOs be included, at least via a closed circuit teleconference, to protect his hide and forestall any rumors that he was two-timing his reclusive bosses. A suitable representation of other corporate leaders would have to be notified personally as well. The problem here was an almost certain leak to the press, whether directly or indirectly, so the meeting would have to be held on the eve of the announcement, with apologies for the short notice. Major contributors and political friends and backers would only be informed on the morning of the news conference that an announcement was forthcoming, which would put their noses out of joint, but that couldn't be helped. The Bulls felt they had to keep things under wraps as long as possible to derive the maximum public relations benefit from their startling decision to come out in support of the Agenda.

Some of the Bulls were deeply upset by that decision but felt they had to go along. The majority knew they had done the right thing to avoid a nightmare of conflict and threatened retribution, but no one felt good about it except for Armsbuckle and a few others. Certainly, their former hardcore ideological backers would accuse them of cowardly treason—or worse, cut them off entirely. There would be a terrible backlash from those quarters. Fortunately, the deadlines for qualifying a right-wing party or candidate had passed in every state. And none of the Bulls could deny the one indisputable advantage to riding the wave. There would be no discharge petitions to overturn their authority in their committees, the ultimate humiliation. If chairing a committee meant anything, it meant remaining in charge.

Before returning to Washington, they had what Justice Tweedy called their last lunch. It was polite enough and not entirely humorless, even displaying some grace, for they all knew that this would be the last time they assembled as the unchallenged masters of Congress in the old political style of a bygone era. As they said their goodbyes in the hotel lobby, it was probably a coincidence that the piped-in background music was Frank Sinatra singing "September Song."

Three days later, the omnipresent White House press corps sighted a stream of congressional committee chairs alighting at the White House one after another. To reduce their visibility, the Bulls arrived in ordinary cars, not limos, but that only served to arouse the reporters' suspicions. Something was up. White House Press Secretary Teddy Dodgem issued a one-paragraph statement saying that the president was meeting with his party's congressional leadership for a normal post-Labor Day review of pending legislation.

In the Indian Treaty room, the president greeted each of the Bulls personally. When they were all seated around the conference table, Justice Tweedy delivered the news, and was surprised at how calmly the president absorbed it. "It is most fortunate," Tweedy went on, "that none of us chairs has yet taken a stand on the Agenda. Our majority reports were scrupulously analytical and neutral, in contrast to the vigorous endorsement by the minority Agenda allies. Our circumspection will pay off during tomorrow's difficult news conference."

The president listened patiently until Justice Tweedy finished. Then he said, "Friends, you have made the politically expedient decision, and for once, paradoxically enough, that happens to be the best decision for the American people."

All around the table, jaws dropped. Evidently the president had been even more circumspect than the Bulls over the past months.

"Now that you've made your courageous decision, and I know it couldn't have been easy"—here the president shot Duke Sabernickle a look—"your challenge, I think, is to make your announcement and your subsequent engagements with the allies authentic not only in appearance but in reality. Some advice along these lines. Examine the Seven Pillars carefully for the provisions that are foursquare with conservative philosophy. Think about it. You don't oppose all government regulation. You decry corporate crime just as you decry street crime. While you may disagree with the environmentalists on the details, you too want to conserve our God-given Earth. You oppose corporate welfare and waste in government contracting because you believe the taxpayers' money should be wisely and efficiently used. You approve of the voluntary nature of membership and dues in these CUB groups. And why shouldn't the government behave like a business and get a fair market return for the use of public assets instead of giving them away? The Agenda also demands shareholder control over executive pay and company policies. Well, isn't it a basic tenet of capitalism that owners should control what they own? As for the raising of the minimum wage, isn't it just a first step toward fair pay for an honest day's work? What Christian, or for that matter what Jew or Muslim, could object to that? I could go on, but you get the drift. The Agenda for the Common Good may be the best thing that's happened to conservatism since Edmund Burke."

Just then, waiters arrived with coffee and cookies. The president took an Oreo and munched for a moment. "Your announcement will have to be carefully prepared with the help of your top staff and advisers. The press will be incredulous and therefore aggressive. They'll probe for cracks, for a hidden agenda. They'll remind you of some alleged inconsistency in your past remarks and hope for a slip of the tongue. They'll push you on the parts of the Agenda you abhor. You'll have to be on full alert for this major first impression. Damn, but I'd like to see the expressions on the faces of the Meliorists and their allies when they watch your press conference. The thing I love best in politics is turning the tables on my adversaries, surprising them, blasting their stereotypes of what they can expect from me."

"I'm not so eager to see the expressions on the faces of the CEOs and the Solvents when they find out," said Benjamin Bullion.

The president took another Oreo and dipped it in his coffee. "The Solvents are inconsequential, and the CEOs have made themselves irrelevant. Sure, it's not going to be all roses, Ben, but which side would you rather be on? And where are the CEOs and their cohorts going to go anyway? Off to start a new corporate party? They already have one or two now. Besides, the history of reform demonstrates that once the line is drawn in the political sand, the corporations will adjust and go happily on their profitable way. They're amazingly opportunistic and expedient institutions, in the best sense of those much-abused words. Take some of the major restraints aimed at corporations—the ban on child labor, breakups under the antitrust laws, and mandatory safety standards, to name just a few. In every case the corporations adjusted and grew and became more profitable by the year. I see little in the Seven Pillars, despite some pretty fundamental shifts of power and wealth, that uproots the basic system of private property and market enterprise. The only exception is full Medicare, which will put an end to the insurance HMOs, but they asked for it with their profiteering, bureaucratic, wasteful ways, and in any case it's not irreversible.

"We conservatives like to say we favor clean, honest elections, but many of us don't welcome the public financing approach in the Agenda. To that I can only note that the financing is voluntary on the 1040, with a ceiling of three hundred dollars per taxpayer, so I can't see any real conservative downside here. Who among you likes to raise money? Most of us in this room don't have to because the money boys come to us, but for our more junior colleagues, fundraising is distasteful, forcing them to grovel and walk that fine line between bribery and extortion. Wouldn't it be refreshing if all the companies and lobbyists knocking on our doors had to make their arguments on the merits, not on the money?

"The Meliorists are pay-as-you-go types, except for emergencies. They don't want Social Security surpluses hiding the government's true annual operating deficit. Our nation is heading for a big debt-deficit-entitlement crash if we don't turn things around, and the Meliorists are giving us that opportunity. Ending the bulk of corporate welfare reduces spending. Taxing securities transactions, pollution, and the addiction industries brings in revenue while cutting individual income taxes. There are many parts of the Agenda that you've resolutely opposed, but by and large it sure beats the French Revolution. Instead of going to the guillotine, you can share in the credit.

"History will beam down upon us in the wake of the Agenda, and in that light I've been coming around to your position on my own in the past weeks. Nothing like watching an irresistible force overtake an immovable object to help your common sense along and flush out your better instincts. I think we needed a cold shower to jolt us out of our knee-jerk complacency. And if you don't make it in November, it's not the end of the world. In two years, I'll see you in the private sector."

"Mr. President, what a breath of fresh air!" exclaimed Francine

Freshet. "You've always been able to express what some of us feel but weren't ready to say out loud. Thank you."

"Sometimes the hardest decisions, the most agonizing decisions, turn out to be the greatest decisions," said Billy Beauchamp. "I'm immensely relieved that we are all on the same page. How do you plan to make your announcement, Mr. President? I presume you wish to follow ours, or am I mistaken?"

"Well, Billy, political ego tells me to go first and show that I'm leading the Congress, but institutionally it's better if you take the lead, resolve the present deadlock, and pass the legislation for my signature. That's the sequence laid out in our Constitution, of course, and I'll follow it. As for exactly how and where to respond to your enactment, I want to consult with my advisers."

"Mr. President," said Duke Sabernickle, "you've allayed some of my short-run concerns about the Agenda, but none of my long-term worries that they represent the first steps toward totalitarian socialism. Once the masses organize, once they taste victory, what's to stop them from going all the way?"

"You mean all the way with the backing of the Meliorist capitalists?" asked the president.

"Before long, they won't need the Meliorists," Sabernickle replied. "The Agenda essentially gives them all the gold on public lands, and that's just one example of the wealth that will be theirs under its provisions."

"It already belongs to them, Duke," said Billy Beauchamp. "They are the people, after all."

"To respond to your long-range worries," the president said, "I'm not clairvoyant, but I do have enough confidence in the American people and their institutions to believe that totalitarian socialism isn't in the cards. And now you'll have to excuse me. I have a meeting with the prime minister of Chad, where the situation is heating up. Stay in touch and keep me posted. You know any of you can always reach me by secured phone. Good day."

"Good day, Mr. President," chorused the Bulls.

As they left the White House one by one by a back exit and walked to their cars, the Bulls were again accosted by the press corps. "What's up, Congressman Meany?" a fresh-faced young reporter asked the chairman of the House Administration Committee.

"Just preelection politics, sonny, have a nice day."

That evening, Lobo and Brovar met in their office suite and ordered in dinner from Luigi's, a gourmet Italian restaurant on Pennsylvania Avenue. They had expected to review the Solvents' semi-debacle and the responses to the open source contest, but on the agenda prepared by Lobo's chief of staff, Lawrence Nightingale, a new item caught their attention: Rumors of Collapse. Lobo called Nightingale in and asked him to explain before they started on their appetizers. Nightingale was anything but an alarmist, but he'd received a call from a staffer friend over at the Senate Armed Services Committee that he thought Lobo and Brovar would want to know about. The friend had overheard Chairman Armsbuckle speaking with his wife. The gist of the conversation was that Armsbuckle was canceling a press conference at which he'd planned to make an important announcement, and would appear instead at a joint press conference with the other committee chairs, who had "come around on the Agenda."

"Thanks, Larry," Lobo said. "We'll call you if we need anything else."

Brovar picked up a jumbo shrimp and studied it as Nightingale exited. "Something's up for sure when you add that to the other tips we've gotten," he said. "I don't know about you, but my appetite's dwindling. We've racked our brains, but nothing's working. The open source ideas are ludicrous or worse. There were several suggestions about inducing a terrorist attack against some major public target in such a way that it couldn't be traced back to our side. 'This is a tough choice,' one guy wrote, 'a choice only for patriots brave enough to see that such an attack is the only way to save our free enterprise system from these insidious capitalist turncoats.' He didn't say whether any of his 'patriots' would be willing to go down in the attack as the ultimate test of their sincerity. Can you believe such evil rot? These people float wild schemes like that because they're not close enough to the scene to come up with any remotely applicable strategy or tactic."

Lobo nodded. "I'm not impressed with open source problem solving either. It never seems to produce a formula that addresses people's lives and failures where it counts. It's good for solving some slice of a software program or easing some marketing delivery problem, but it's not ready for prime time on the important struggles."

Brovar poured them both a large glass of Chianti. "Here's to us and our faltering counterattack, Lobo. May the end be swift and merciful."

"Do you know more than you're telling me?"

"No, it's just the feeling I have more and more. And what are the Bulls up to with this press conference? It can't be anything good."

Lobo drained his glass of wine and poured himself another. "I knew we were in trouble when the CEOs wouldn't put themselves on the line like the SROs do. Conflicts have to be personalized. People want to see passion, fireworks. Instead I end up with a bunch of shrinking violets who want to stay in the back room when backroom business as usual is exactly the issue. You'd think they were monks instead of some of the most powerful men in the country. No wonder my poor dog gets such a workout."

"I know what you mean," Brovar said. "When I'm stuck with something, I take my dog for long walks too." He sipped his wine. "You know, one of our main problems has been the lack of vivid imagery that grabs people and makes them remember something and talk it up with their friends. Take the Beatty campaign steamrolling over Schwarzenegger out in California. Ask any ordinary Californian about that race and you'll get, 'I was bowled over by Warren Beatty and his buses of billionaires going around the state demanding that they be taxed more to eliminate the state deficit and make life better for people like me.' That's enough right there to beat the muscleman, even with all his flexing. Now, there's much more to Beatty's platform, plenty of proposals that mean something to voters, but just ask them to remember anything else. It's the imagery and what it conveys day after day. With all our media saturation and lobbying campaigns, we've never come anywhere near the equivalent of those billionaire buses. And we never could have, no matter how hard we tried. You know why? Because we're not perceived to be on the side of the people. We can tell them we are until we're blue in the face, but they aren't buying. They simply know more now."

Lobo took a big gulp of Chianti. "I guess I have to agree, but that doesn't change the fact that I haven't fulfilled my contract with the CEOs."

"No, Lobo, the CEOs are the ones who haven't fulfilled the contract. They never went as far as they led you to believe they would—not that it would have helped, more than likely. You know, what's amazed me throughout this entire battle is that we tried all the boilerplate tactics that have worked so well in so many other showdowns over the decades and none of them came through for us. Some, like the attempt to delegitimize our adversaries, actually backfired. Right now my imagination—supposedly the envy of my peers—is shooting blanks. I'm tapped out."

"Well, there's only one solution," Lobo said, hiccuping. "More wine. We have to keep our spirits up. Let's change the subject and enjoy this fine meal. How's life with your new bride?"

As September drew to a close, the Meliorists intensified their focus on the Congress. Without being overbearing, they personally called the members and some of their staff people, and made it clear to the Bulls that they were available to meet with them at any time. They knew they already had a majority. Now they were going for a veto-proof Congress. Nor did they ignore the president, whom many of them had met at public occasions in the past six years. Warren Buffett made sure that word was very politely conveyed to the White House that the Meliorists were prepared to speak with the president at his convenience, should he so wish.

Meanwhile, if Brovar and Lobo were exhibiting signs of despair, the trade associations were in free fall, frantically fighting each other for preferred positions, grasping at straws to pacify their anxious memberships around the country, and trying to keep track of their newly expanded corps of lobbyists, many untutored in the ways of Congress and the capital. Luke Skyhi's early-alert system in the sub-economy kept him fully informed on the flailing of these elephantine organizations, and he made sure that the PCC exacerbated the strains among them. Perhaps too eagerly, he sensed the collapse, not just the defeat, of the K Street crowd.

Two days after their meeting with the president, the Bulls scheduled a news conference in the main hall of the Cannon Office Building to announce their support of the Seven Pillars as a unitary package. They took pains to point out that they had never really opposed it. After all, hadn't they held prolonged public hearings of impeccable impartiality? Didn't their majority reports hew to an analytic, informative standard for committee and congressional deliberations? Hadn't they eschewed delaying tactics, of which they had plenty in their quivers? They knew the room would be packed and tried to anticipate as many questions as possible in their statement so the event wouldn't drag on too long. Politicians tended to lose in the course of an extended Q and A. Fortunately, their announcement was so astonishing that many reporters rushed off to file their stories before any questions were asked.

Those who remained were largely from the regional papers and television stations. Their questions were routine: When did you all decide to do this? Were there any dissenters? Did you discuss this with the president, and what did he say? Do you think this will work decisively in your favor in November against the Clean Elections Party? What's the reaction from K Street? Do you expect that your support of the Agenda will cost you in campaign contributions? Do you intend to urge the president to sign these bills?

As he listened to the questions and the responses from Justice Tweedy and others, Billy Beauchamp thought to himself how easy it was to answer when you'd done the right thing. He and the Bulls were wearing their hearts on their sleeves.

Just then, Reginald Sesko of *Business Week* stepped forward and asked sharply, "How do you propose to stop the downward drift of the stock markets and the decline in business confidence in the United States both at home and abroad?"

Billy jumped on that one. "I'd say that a living wage and universal health insurance are very good for the economy's prospects because they'll enhance consumer demand. Many European nations have some version of these same provisions, and their economies are prospering. Sometimes I think this 'business confidence' stuff is nothing but economic saber rattling so that the big companies can get what they want from Congress and the White House. It's far more important that the people have confidence in business, and the Agenda will advance that confidence."

The veteran reporter for the *Oklahoma Constitution* could hardly believe this was the Billy Beauchamp she knew. She was about to ask how he reconciled his newfound support for the Agenda with his past positions when Sam Sniffen of the *Atlanta Journal-Constitution* said, "How are you going to pay for all this?"

Senator Pessimismo, chair of the Joint Budget Committee, took the question. "Our staff has conservatively concluded that the savings under the Agenda exceed the added expenses of new programs, mainly universal healthcare. Please note that the Agenda shifts healthcare costs from the business and nonprofit sectors to the government. They are still assessed, but minimally compared to what they're currently paying. Note too that although the government is absorbing more health costs, it will realize large savings in lives, paperwork, fraud collection, and so on. Moreover, the estimates of revenues from the new tax on securities transactions, replacing some individual income taxes, are also very conservative."

"This Agenda has legs," said Zack Lermond of the *Baltimore Sun*. "Once you pass it, those legs may march most of you out of office in a few weeks. How would you assess the impact of enactment on Congress in the coming months and years? Does it spell the end of the old ways of doing business on Capitol Hill?"

"Well, Zack," said Senate Majority Leader Frisk, "we're not

prophets, and we'll certainly know more after the elections, but I think it's safe to say that a shift of priorities and orientations is probably in the cards for the next couple of years at least. It can't but be, it seems to me. Still, I wouldn't count the traditional lobbies out. It may take some time, but they'll regroup. Too many goodies up here for them not to."

There were a few more questions, and then, just like that, the press conference was over. A strange mixture of relief and foreboding seemed to settle over the Bulls as they dispersed quietly and walked back to their offices with their aides.

Over on K Street, twenty-five grim-looking trade association heads were already gathered at the law offices of Crusher, Vine and Clamber for an emergency meeting of the Temporary American Coalition for Economic Freedom (TACEF). The venerable senior partner and victorious veteran of many battles against "the rabble," as Chives Crusher privately called the American people, sat down at the head of an enormous mahogany conference table and began the meeting.

"Friends, we are defeated, notwithstanding our extreme exertions for weeks now. There is no hope on the Hill. Even Sabernickle has thrown in the towel. Constitutionally all that's left is the president, and even if he had the votes to sustain his veto, he may not use it for fear of destroying his party. All this you know. So what else do I have to say? Nothing. For the first time in my sixty-year legal career, I have no strategy, no tactics, no glimmer of a second-strike capability. We can always fight the appropriations process, the proposed regulations, the enforcement, and we will, but the sperm of the renegade oligarchs has germinated, and the hungry child of the rabble is about to be born. I just got off the phone with Dortwist, Lobo, and Jasper Cumbersome, and they are as speechless as your humble counselor. I invite your reactions."

"Brother Chives," boomed Horace Heath, the grand chief lobbyist of the rapidly consolidating HMO giants, "where the hell are the drinks?"

"Hear, hear," shouted the dispirited group in unison.

With a barely concealed smile, Crusher pushed a button under the table, and in came two valets with two large carts stocked with expensive whiskeys, bourbons, gins, and vodkas, along with a variety of enticing canapés. "I couldn't foresee the depredations of the barbarians even when they were at the gates, Horace, but I did foresee your thirst. Let's drink to our doom with the finest liquor this—what does the press call us?—this 'powerful and prestigious law firm' could sequester."

Whereupon the lobbyists began drinking with the zeal they usually reserved for their labors in the congressional fields. As evening darkened to night, their cheeks grew rosier, their ties looser, and their trips to the john more frequent. Mordant words and snide remarks directed toward their adversaries in the early hours of imbibing began to turn against their comrades-in-lucre: the CEOs, the Bulls, Lobo and Dortwist, the business media, the president. As the hours wore on and more refreshments were ordered in, they began to light into each other for perceived lassitude, narcissism, miscalculation, and utter stupidity. Then a forearm knocked into a shoulder, a hip into a torso, and the fracas commenced. Glasses clattered to the floor and shattered. Brother Chives got in a few good licks and then called security. It all ended with a clutch of limousines in long and loyal service to the powerful and prestigious law firm of Crusher, Vine and Clamber taking the soused and battered defenders of the plutocracy home to their respective mansions.

The scene in the penthouse boardroom the next morning was more sedate but no more upbeat. The CEOs had watched the press conference live on their plasma TVs, and the near life-size images had unnerved them, as if the Bulls were right there next to them. Now, as they waited for Lobo, they were angry and demoralized. They'd been checking their stock portfolios, which were dropping every day. The last-ditch effort to block shareholder authority over their compensation packages had collapsed, though they'd escaped a legislated maximum cap. Their multibillion-dollar drive to stop the SROs was in tatters.

A somber Lobo arrived at 8:45 a.m. and sipped some fresh orange juice while waiting to be summoned. He had one more idea in his arsenal. It had come to him during an intense "Bésame Mucho" exchange with his pit bull. He saw the boardroom door open and heard CEO Cumbersome call, "Come in, Lobo." Entering, he noticed that the eyelids were heavier and the jowls weightier around the familiar table.

"We have three questions for you, Lobo," Wardman Wise began without preliminaries. "What went wrong? What did you do wrong? And what's next?"

"Are you firing me?" Lobo asked. "I haven't earned my dollar yet."

"Just answer the questions one at a time," said Wise.

"What went wrong? In a nutshell, the business community wasn't hungry enough, smart enough, or fast enough. No one took Dortwist's early premonitions seriously. In fact, he was ridiculed.

"What did I do wrong? Ultimately, nothing, because by the time we started, there was no way to win. Dortwist and I gave it all we had and more, but we were up against an irresistible force. In hindsight, even if you'd paired off against the SROs in early April, it probably would have been too late, but as you'll recall, we didn't get going until late June. After all these decades, the Agenda's time has come. Even the seemingly bottomless well of popular apathy has run dry.

"As for what's next, you have more than a billion dollars left. You can give it back to the donors through some prorated formula, or you can use it for independent expenditures to help save the Bulls in November. That's our last clear chance. Barring a White House miracle, the Agenda will be enacted, but we can prevent or delay or blunt implementation next year and the year after. To repeat, there will be enactment, but there doesn't have to be implementation. Riders to appropriations bills have stopped implementation of enacted legislation cold in the past, and they can do it again. The downside, of course, is the aroused fury of the citizenry and an encore confrontation with the Meliorists."

"That downside is decisive, Lobo," said Sal Belligerante. "I, for one, am not interested in another groveling defeat involving a struggle that might further radicalize the people."

"Nor am I," said Norman Noondark.

"The time has come to let matters cool down, Lobo," said William Worldweight. "It's over as far as I'm concerned."

Murmurs of agreement followed.

"By the way," asked Wardman Wise, "is there any indication as to whether the president, futilely or not, is going to veto the Pillars?"

"The indication is that he's going to sign them, and do so in a mass media event at some undisclosed but highly symbolic location. The politics of it is that the majority party wants to 'ride the wave' and steal the credit from the progressives, who have gone out of their way to avoid publicity. They may pay for their modesty by being coopted."

CEO Cumbersome looked around the table. "Lobo, the consensus here is that your services are no longer required. We thank you for your selflessness, your peerless dedication, and the candid honesty you brought to this most arduous mission. Will you join us for lunch at the Four Hundred Club?"

"Forgive me, gentlemen, but I have to take my pit bull to the vet. It's something of an emergency. My staff will be in touch with yours about an orderly windup of operations. Good day." And with that, shorn of his trademark swagger, Lobo got up and left the room, closing the door quietly.

The president was thinking grandly. Having sunk in the polls because of his perceived disinterest in the needs of ordinary people, his extravagant White House lifestyle, and his foreign misadventures, he wanted to give the historians a contrasting display of political courage. A very big contrasting display. He had decided that the signing ceremony would take place at Mount Rushmore, beneath the imposingly sculpted faces of four great presidents. The television networks would go wild over the spectacular visuals, but there was more. Prominently seated at the ceremony would be the Bulls on one side and the Meliorists on the other—yes, the Meliorists themselves. Such, at least, was the president's plan. He called his advisers together to get their reaction over dinner.

"Welcome, gentlemen, take your seats," he said with a flourish as they filed into the residence dining room. "My chef has prepared a meal worthy of our lofty deliberations. The entree is Chilean sea bass."

Harold Featherstone III remained standing. "With all respect, Mr. President, I feel compelled to say at the outset that swallowing one bitter pill is difficult enough but swallowing seven of them is taking the Kool-Aid. The Agenda is so utterly and entirely at odds with everything we've fought for, campaigned for, and stood tall for during the last six years that it sears my soul to contemplate your signing it into law."

"Sit down and listen up, Hal," the president ordered sternly. "We're not in slumberland anymore. The alarm clock has gone off, and the people are awake. They're done with eating deception for breakfast, distraction for lunch, and rah-rah for dinner. So if you don't mind, let's talk about the signing ceremony."

"The Dakotas gave you your highest statewide percentages in the last two elections," said Chris Topper, the chief of staff. "They won't be pleased that you're signing off on the Agenda beneath Mount Rushmore. These people are not the type to demonstrate or march in protest, but they do have newspapers, broadcast stations, and blogs. Is there a public works project in the pipeline that you can preannounce? And the day before the signing, why not set up an exclusive teleconference with the major editors and television anchors, at least in South Dakota? The local media always appreciates these courtesies."

"Excellent ideas, Chris," said the president. "Put them in motion. We only have a few days."

"Why do you want the Meliorists there?" press secretary Dodgem asked. "Isn't that rubbing the noses of the Bulls and the party in the dirt?"

"Better they play second fiddle to our party's triumphant demonstration of compassion and action out at Mount Rushmore than that they have their own extravaganza in Washington and take full credit for what they forced us to do. It's possible that they'll have their own event anyway, but it will have to come after the signing, and it will be a distinct anticlimax."

"What if the Meliorists decline your invitation, Mr. President?" Shelburne Sherwood asked.

"They can't afford to decline. We'll be the big story dominating the media for days, and they'll want to be there to try to dilute our impact. No, they won't decline. They'll be confident that they can squeeze something out of their participation, but we'll get more out of them than they'll get out of us. I can see the headlines and leads now: 'Statesmanship of the highest order,' or 'The president displayed extraordinary grace with his erstwhile adversaries, rising above the partisan fray as our great presidents have done throughout our history,' or 'It's been a long time since the nation has seen such an extraordinary display of political unity in the interests of the American people,' or 'On this glorious morning in South Dakota, our president has demonstrated his generosity of mind by putting his John Hancock to the first steps toward a functioning democracy that will benefit millions of American families,' or 'The effects of the president's farsighted act on this historic day will be felt far from Mount Rushmore. Bravo, Mr. President!'"

Featherstone, who had been picking at his escargot appetizer, mustered himself. "Excuse me, sir, but I can see those leads and headlines too: 'No president in American history has so cruelly betrayed his political base as our current president did yesterday at Mount Rushmore,' or 'This day of infamy will be known as the Mount Rushmore Massacre, with untold consequences for the future of the president's party,' or 'Six leaders of the party's right wing e-mailed hundreds of thousands of their supporters today, inviting comments about the advisability of forming a new party dedicated to the principles just abandoned by a cowardly president,' or 'The Business Roundtable issued a rare warning to the president today of severe volatility in the securities markets in the wake of his signing the Agenda into law.'"

"You've always been a contrarian, Hal, and I appreciate that, but now you're bordering on gibberish. Where are these right-wingers and the business community going to go, especially after Rushmore broadens our base? Besides, you're looking at things from a narrow political viewpoint that simply doesn't recognize what's happened this year. Didn't you write an article for the *National Review* called 'The Challenge of Change,' on the ossification of the political world?"

Lester Linx, the congressional liaison, looked up from his cell phone. "Mr. President, I've just received a text message saying that Speaker Dostart and Majority Leader Frisk have a new vote count and that the Agenda is now veto-proof. They'll put in a call to you once we've finished our meeting."

The president nodded. "Well, we were expecting it, weren't we? It makes Rushmore all the more important."

"Indeed it does," said Chris Topper, "and I have a few thoughts on your remarks, sir. Besides describing how the Pillars address real needs and injustices, it might be wise defensively to say a few words about past reforms that were initially opposed by business but were later seen to enhance profitability. You'll need a similar nod to your right wing about all the conservative principles adopted by the Agenda. You should also recognize the younger generation of Americans with a spirited appeal to their idealism and optimism. Finally, Mount Rushmore faces southeast and has good exposure to the sun. If you mention this in connection with the solar energy conversion envisioned by the Agenda, it will not go unnoticed either by the locals or by the growing number of sun fans, though of course you'll need a contingency plan in case of rain."

"Again, those are excellent ideas, Chris," the president said. "Thank you."

Clarence Fairchild, the community affairs adviser, cleared his throat. "If I may raise a rather sensitive historical point, sir, the US Army took the Black Hills from the Lakota tribe by force in 1876-77.

Feelings on the subject run high among Native Americans, who regard the hills as sacred ground. Recognizing this in your remarks will go a long way toward salving old wounds."

"And you should bear in mind, Mr. President," said Lester Linx, "that many members of Congress besides the Bulls will want to attend. Ordinarily the number of congressional VIPs is limited by the number of seats on Air Force One, but you can bet that for this occasion plenty of representatives and senators will get there on their own. My advice is to take the usual VIPs along according to the usual criteria but announce that seats will be reserved for members of Congress near the visitor center. Courtesy also requires seating for the governor of South Dakota and other state dignitaries. Invariably there will be ruffled feathers, but as long as we have clear explanations of space constraints and guest protocol, we should be all right. It won't be easy to accommodate everyone who wants to attend, even in the great outdoors, but I guess we can always move the Meliorists and the progressives to folding chairs along the Presidential Trail, which is out of sight."

The president chuckled. "Very amusing, Les. I leave the logistics to you. Is there anything else?" he asked, looking around the table. "All right, let's proceed to the sea bass."

"Excuse me, sir, but I have a prior engagement with my conscience," said Harold Featherstone III, rising and walking stiffly out of the dining room to write his letter of resignation.

The last Friday of September was a crystalline fall day. Half a dozen eagles soared high above Mount Rushmore in a symbolic aerial spectacular as the president prepared to make his counterintuitive debut as a progressive political progenitor. With his first lady, he bounded up the stairs to the long rectangular outdoor stage and greeted the Bulls one by one, and then the Meliorists. Even in the outdoors, the media crush was apparent. TV news helicopters circled overhead. The wildlife on the ground didn't know what to make of it and scrammed. With his back to Mount Rushmore, at just the place where a fifth presidential head might be carved one day, the president, just three days after Congress passed the Seven Pillars, began his address to the nation.

"My fellow Americans, here at home and all over the world, what you see before you is the grandeur of our nation—the rugged mountains and majestic forests, the eagles that represent our freedom and our strength flying across the wide blue skies, and these magnificent sculptures fashioned from solid granite to memorialize George Washington, Thomas Jefferson, Abraham Lincoln, and Theodore Roosevelt, four of our greatest presidents.

"It is a historic day. Our country is about to take a great step forward and upward. This did not come about by chance. It was inspired, and continues to be inspired, by certain leaders of our business community, now mostly retired. They call themselves the Meliorists, a modest name for a truly revolutionary movement that has remained true to its high ideals and has liberated the people to take their lives and their future into their own hands, which is the finest expression of freedom. By their force of example, dedication, brilliance, and perseverance, the Meliorists brought the country to the Congress. It was there that an unprecedented bipartisan effort unfolded. It was there that the exhausting, meticulous work of the public hearings, the committee reports, the markups, and finally the televised floor debates and votes transpired. It was there that the veteran committee chairs of my party cleared the way and actively supported the Seven Pillars of the Agenda for the Common Good. Let us have a round of applause for the Meliorists and the committee chairs." The president gestured toward both groups as the audience of invited guests clapped and cheered enthusiastically.

"Those great presidents," he went on, pointing to the sculpted faces, "came to their high office with many signal accomplishments of intellect and deed, but they also grew as they served. They grew not just through their own reflections and observations but because they had sufficiently open minds to listen to their countrymen and countrywomen, to heed their demands and their hopes and their impatience with inaction and misfeasance. Over the past nine months, I too have had the opportunity to grow, whether I liked it or not. Day after day, you the people made me take notice of your discontent with politics as usual, favoritism for the privileged few, the misuse of taxpayer dollars, and the abuse of your trust. With your minds and hearts, with your marches and rallies and new organizations, you demanded change after decades of unacknowledged patience. That demand made me realize that vested ideas are more impervious to change than vested economic interests or even vested bureaucratic interests.

"When I took the oath of office, my mind was closed. I was certain what I wanted to do and what I wanted to prevent. Too certain. Then came the fresh breeze of the Meliorists. At first I scoffed, then seethed, then resisted. Then I reflected, revised, and opened my arms to their good works and their vision for our country—a catchup vision, an accountability vision, a democracy vision, a civic vision with staying power into the distant future. They grounded this vision in fertile soil and watched the seeds grow into a bountiful harvest of populist power, and they did it all in record time and with their own fortunes. Not a cent of tax money was involved. These are Americans who believe that from those who have acquired much, much is expected. Well, they have delivered and then some, and so will I."

The president paused and swept his arm toward a stack of documents on a table beside the podium. "There are the Seven Pillars, which I will now sign with presidential pens made entirely of industrial hemp, in soy ink, on paper also made from hemp—the same kind of paper on which our Declaration of Independence was written in 1776."

As cameras clicked furiously, the president sat down at the table with the Meliorists and the Bulls on either side, methodically signed each of the bills numerous times, and gave the pens to those assembled around him. When the last bill was signed and the last pen handed out, there was a momentous silence, and then the audience burst into applause, joined by some 150 million viewers nationwide.

The president returned to the podium and spent the next fifteen minutes concisely reviewing the benefits and conservatism flowing from each of the Seven Pillars, with the aim of laying the public groundwork for implementation over the next two years, when the furious interest groups would reconnect with their congressional collaborators to set up treacherous hurdles to derail the reforms. He made it clear that he expected Congress to heed both the content and the determined tone of his words, which he had written himself, and to implement the bills without delay. He would be president for another twenty-seven months, and he wasn't interested in a Pyrrhic victory. During this oratorical performance, those who knew him best found themselves wondering if they'd ever known him at all, including the dumbfounded first lady, who managed to keep a smile frozen on her face even though she'd assumed, like almost everyone else on her husband's team, that his endorsement of the Agenda was a ploy.

When he concluded his tour de force, the president engaged in some hearty backslapping with the Bulls and mingled with the Meliorists. He shook hands with Warren, who said, "I'm curious, Mr. President, about why you chose not to meet with any of us. Was it because you didn't want to be accused of coming under the influence of us 'subversives'?"

The president smiled. "You're not only a shrewd investor, Mr. Buffett, you're a shrewd political analyst as well. But I kept myself informed about your activities, and today you see the result. I'm grateful to you and your colleagues for being here, by the way. Your presence made my themes of unity and implementation more credible. I'll catch hell from my longtime supporters when I get back to the White House, but those are the lumps of the job."

Bill Gates Sr. and Joe Jamail urged the president to appoint a special White House Task Force on Implementation, with regular reports to the public. They noted the almost total absence of federal reporting on industry compliance with health and safety laws, for example. The president reacted favorably and said that he'd keep the task force on its toes by locating it in the White House, as part of the Office of Management and Budget complex.

Bernard told the president that he could use some help with his after-school Egalitarian Clubs. "They're going well where they've been set up, but in too many places the initiative is flagging. You've said that no child should be left behind in the schools, Mr. President. These clubs address the needs of youngsters left behind in the afternoons, when they often get into real trouble, especially in the cities. You could help give the effort a high profile."

"Your clubs sound like a perfect complement to my school program, which is also flagging a bit if the truth be told," the president said. "Let me know when you're free and I'll set up a meeting at the White House with my secretary of education, the PTA, the League of Women Voters, and the Urban League."

The other Meliorists all had words of praise and advice for the chief, who listened attentively. For his part, he cautioned them against continuing to support the ouster of the Bulls, who could be very useful during the implementation phase as known quantities who endorsed the Agenda. Phil Donahue immediately jumped in. "Sir, I think you have the wrong impression. We have no connection with the Clean Elections Party, whether operational or monetary, as required by federal law." The president winked. "Well, you know what I mean—you all have moral suasion."

As the crowd at Mount Rushmore was dispersing, people all over the country were gathering joyously in parks and public squares, carrying posters of the Meliorist emblem and the Seventh-Generation Eye. For so long their marches and rallies had centered around the public demand for the adoption of the Agenda for the Common Good. Now, at last, they were celebrating, not demanding. Bars offered free champagne. Toy and novelty stores handed out free gifts and ice cream to children. From the village greens of New England to the sunny plazas of California, the people hailed their representatives in Washington with a roar of recognition and gratitude.

And they had reason to be grateful. Out in Tucson, Eugenia Lopez was thinking about how she would be able to reduce her debts and buy her three children the things they needed now that she'd be earning $4 more an hour. In Seattle, Tim Fullwell felt a crushing anxiety lift from his shoulders as he realized that he wouldn't have to go without food or fuel anymore to pay for his prescription drugs. In St. Louis, Martha and Albert Slayton breathed a sigh of relief. They'd moved to a more expensive suburb to avail their two children of better public schools and were feeling the pinch, but now they'd be able to keep up their mortgage payments with $20,000 in tax savings on their combined annual income of $100,000. In Philadelphia, Chesty Fuller, a full-time baker and part-time super-activist, was thinking about the millions of people who'd cut their civic teeth with the Meliorists and had their appetites whetted for more victories. He'd received dozens of e-mails from similarly energized friends in other states noting that all the new groups inspired by the Meliorists would be welcome and powerful allies in their many worthy but previously losing causes.

For Tony Lazzari, a World War II vet and union organizer of legendary fame, the Agenda was a dream come true. After many organizing successes in the fifties and early sixties, Tony had hit a wall. Taft-Hartley, the notorious antiunion law, was kicking in, and soon became the attack vehicle of choice for the union-busting industry of consultants, law firms, and their executive clients. Now, in his mid-eighties, he would live to see a resurgence of unionism in the fast-food industry, many other retail chains, and the vast pool of Fortune 500 office workers.

In a Georgia mill town, Morgan Moses, known as the resident curmudgeon, wasn't scowling today. For years he had been the scourge of the wasters in local government, and once in a while he'd give the hotfoot to the state's congressional delegation about reckless spending in Washington. Now, finally, he could go to court with his Northeast Georgia Taxpayers Association and tackle these federal boondoggles. "No standing to sue," the despicable phrase that had been hurled at him for so long, was now consigned to the dust heap of legal history. His phone and e-mail traffic with taxpayer groups all over the country reached record levels as he threw himself into the fray with renewed intensity,

along with countless other long-thwarted activists who saw the
new day dawning at last.

There were scowls aplenty at Republican Party headquarters the next
morning when the newspapers hit the stands. "President Signs on
to Meliorist Revolution!" the *Washington Post* trumpeted. "Seven Pillars Signed by President! Meliorists Can Claim Victory!" blared the
New York Times, while the tabloid *Post* screamed, "President Kow-
tows Seven Times!!!" The visuals on the television news were good
to both the president and the Meliorists, who had diplomatically
declined all press interviews, saying through Jeno that this was the
president's day and that they would hold a news conference of their
own next week in Washington.

Despite their displeasure, the Republican operatives were in the
business of winning elections. Their jobs and their reputations were
at stake. For now, ideology would have to take a back seat, and so
would placating the fat cats. All that mattered was the winning political move, and they smelled a big turnaround in the forthcoming
polls. They didn't care where the dramatic presidential makeover
came from as long as it reversed what looked like a landslide for
their opponents. Ideological concerns could reassert themselves
once the Republicans maintained their majority. As for the Agenda,
they were convinced that what the president had said about implementation at Mount Rushmore was a fine example of his political
cunning. Surely there would be many a slip between the cup and
the lip in the implementation stage. Apparently they hadn't bothered to examine the legislation, which was tightly crafted to
anticipate any betrayals or delays after passage. Except for universal
healthcare, the bills required little in the way of appropriations and
imposed deadlines and penalties on the officials charged with their
execution.

On the Monday after Mount Rushmore, ahead of the release of
the major polls, the political pundits rushed into print with their
predictions as to how the president's surprise signing of the Agenda

would affect the midterm elections. Their observations and their hasty "man in the street" interviews were good news for the president, but his party didn't share in the glow. The Clean Elections Party candidates were quick to claim a major victory even before their predicted Election Day triumph. With help from Dick Goodwin, they took credit in their campaign material for pushing the Bulls in the right direction, and then they focused on the all-important implementation stage, declaring that CEP electoral victories were indispensable to insure against backsliding, and that none of the incumbent corporatists could be trusted if they were returned to office. They also reminded the opposition that their party's pledge to go out of existence depended not just on the enactment but on the full implementation of the Agenda's electoral reforms.

Most of the business columnists took the signing of the Agenda hard. They foresaw business volatility, the resurgence of union bosses, overregulation, and trouble of all kinds from the newly organized groups of workers, consumers, and taxpayers. A prominent exception was Patrick Paydown, a persistent critic of the huge public, corporate, and consumer debt spirals, which he believed were unsustainable. To him, the Meliorists' main virtue was their fiscal restraint, their aversion to postponing hard decisions by laying on more and more credit, deficits, and debt. He favored their emphasis on true efficiencies and their tax on speculation in the securities markets, especially the $500 trillion a year in computer-driven derivatives trading, and said so in his widely syndicated column. But the bulk of the business press, led by the *Wall Street Journal*, kept attacking the Meliorists, and the more they did, the more the voters saw the necessity of electing the CEP candidates. There were so many fulminations and alarms coming from the upper classes and their mouthpieces that they were losing their propaganda value. This time the folks back home had the shield of knowledge and of their own mobilization, and now they had the president too.

Meanwhile, the business lobbies were huddling and wondering

how to assuage their enraged members, who were demanding to know why all their dues, all their PACs, and all their macho lobbyists had gone down to ignominious defeat. The solution the influence peddlers came up with was to storm back to Capitol Hill and play the victim. They would strongly imply that the Bulls had let them down and therefore owed them this tax break and that pending subsidy, this proposed weapons system and that opening of federal lands to logging or mining, this escape from an industry's further pension obligations and that waiver of law enforcement.

The Bulls took umbrage. They knew a shakedown when they saw one. They had just done what nearly the entire country believed was the right thing to do, and now the corporate boys wanted to reinstate the old way of doing business and exact their payback. Duke Sabernickle, of all people, sadly explained that he'd had to go along on the Agenda even though he didn't want to, but that he'd be happy to put some of these bills, amendments, and riders into play. However, they would never make it through the Rules Committee, and did the business groups want to taint the bills as losers in case they wanted to start fresh next year? The stunned lobbyists took Sabernickle's advice and dropped their demands.

The congressional progressives were not so restrained. Seeing the seismic move in their direction, they seized every opportunity to offer the amendments that had been solicited from the traditional citizen groups at the behest of the Meliorists weeks ago. In went the reinstatement of the seventy-year-old, very successful, recently repealed Public Utility Holding Company Act, which blocked future pyramid mergers and the kind of holding companies that collapsed in the 1930s. In went a ban on all leveraged buyouts by management of publicly traded companies, as being so riddled with conflicts of interest and insider shareholder sabotage as to be illegal per se. In went a requirement that the entire texts of all government procurement contracts, leaseholds, and grants above $250,000 be posted online, together with a list of recipients, so that competitors, citizen associations, the media, and scholars could review and monitor them at their leisure. These and a host of other provisions, like tougher government purchasing standards for software, food, and fuel, found their way into the giant appropriations bills or were introduced and passed easily on the floor.

All in all, as September gave way to October, the business opposition was not only defeated, not only distracted by their sudden vulnerability in the November elections, not only facing the aroused critical energies of the people—they were plumb exhausted. Political scientists took note of the new phenomenon of the rich but powerless and slated it for intensive research in the near future.

As Mount Rushmore was the president's day, the following Wednesday was the Meliorists' day. The Press Club ballroom was packed with an avalanche of reporters, editors, columnists, foreign correspondents, producers, camera people, sound people, and bloggers, along with some invited guests from the Hill, the White House, and various citizen groups. Warren opened the proceedings.

"Welcome, one and all, and thank you for coming. The Agenda for the Common Good is now law, and our nation is the stronger for it. I think you've heard enough from all of us in the past nine months, so let's get right to your questions."

For the next half hour, the Meliorists responded to the press graciously and succinctly. Several reporters asked questions designed to elicit signs of boasting, gloating, contempt for their adversaries, lust for power, premature declarations of victory in November, and the like, but none of the core group took the bait. They were asked in a variety of ways how they had accomplished such a fundamental redirection of the country, to which their replies were variations on the theme that what they had done was provide critical material resources, well-calibrated, timely strategies, and solid infrastructures to engage the passion, intelligence, time, and talent of the American people in a broad-based movement for change, as was the proper way for a democratic society to conduct itself. A few reporters were still harping on the claim that the Agenda reforms would create a tumult in the economy, but the Meliorists were old hands at fielding such questions and dispensed with them handily, with wit, wisdom, and a little barnyard humor from Ted.

More difficult were the questions about their future plans, because they hadn't yet discussed them. That was at the top of the agenda for their next Maui meeting, which they'd postponed until the coming weekend because of the Rushmore event. The press wanted to know how much money they had left and what they were going to do with it, whether they were going to continue funding the infrastructure, what role they intended to play as a group, and whether they would continue their involvement with their pet projects, like the Posterity Trust, people as corporations and vice versa, the People's Court Society, dead and live money, the Sun God festivals, and so on. The Meliorists replied frankly that they were undecided about their collective role but would continue to pursue their individual projects.

The room grew quiet as the doyenne of the White House press corps, Helen Promise, stood to ask her question. "Tell us candidly why you think the Bulls and the president—not exactly beloved in the country—changed their minds so dramatically and so quickly?"

"Ms. Promise," said Bill Gates Sr., "I respectfully submit that no one is better qualified to answer that question than you and your colleagues. You saw how the American people joined their hands and hearts and started to take control of the country over which they were supposed to be sovereign. All we did was give them a programmatic lift, a head start, a shoehorn, a bullhorn, a sense that we would be with them all the way with all the means at our disposal. The people did the heavy lifting, turning easy hope into hard reality against all the odds, and despite the message they and we have absorbed since elementary school that those odds are unconquerable. Let this be a lesson to all those who believe that apathy is immutable. Once the people found their cadence, they found their confidence, and there was no stopping them. The Bulls and the president saw this overwhelming force coming and decided to represent it instead of resenting it."

Yoko rose and held out her hands to indicate that the question period was at a close. "But we do have another response to your question, Ms. Promise," she said, "a musical one," and before the startled eyes of the audience and millions of television viewers, Patti Smith and her entire band came on stage and invited everyone to join in on "The People Have the Power." Perched on Patti's outstretched arm was Patriotic Polly, who had been taught the inspirational refrain and more or less blended right in. The press corps had never seen Patriotic Polly in the flesh, and they were transfixed. Some of them even abandoned their professional objectivity and started singing.

"It's truly a Hollywood ending," Paul said to Phil, "except that it's real."

CHAPTER 17

At the mountaintop hotel, high above the Alenuihaha Channel, the Meliorists greeted each other with smiles, handshakes, and hugs. They were thrilled to be back at their old haunt, with its breathtaking views and celestial cuisine. The hotel staff, who by now knew who their generous monthly guests were and what they were up to, were more than their usual gracious, beaming selves. Warren led the core group, as they still liked to call themselves in private, to the familiar conference table of silences and conspiracies, where they sat down to commence Maui Ten, but not before helping themselves to some luscious Hawaiian fruit grown on the island's organic farms.

"Welcome to the contemplation of the fruits of our labors since January," Warren said. "It's all so spectacular that it's sobering. With victory come many new opportunities and challenges, and the first order of business is to make sure that all across the country all hands remain on deck and on full alert, and that our institutions continue to build, digging deeper roots and growing stronger branches. The moment the oligarchs sense any slacking off, any sign of reformist fatigue, they'll recover from their intransigence fatigue and go on the counterattack. Besides, there are elections to win. Our mantra remains 'Take absolutely nothing for granted.'

"At our earlier meetings, we've spoken often of serendipity, and it just keeps coming and coming. I'm pleased to relate that Andre Engaget, who passed away last month in Santa Fe at the age of eighty-eight, has made me the trustee of a bequest of $2.8 billion for what he calls 'a Meliorist Project in Perpetuity.' The funds are to be utilized 'for the widespread and deep advancement of civic skills and civic practice, both in the nation's public and private elementary and secondary schools, and through a network of franchised adult education storefronts in all communities whose population exceeds three thousand. I realize how easily such a bequest can be frittered away on soft civics. That is not my testamentary intent,' Mr. Engaget writes in his will, and goes on to spell out clearly that he intends his grant to be used 'to foment a high-energy democracy.' He wants classroom learning connected to experiential learning in the community. He does not want rote courses in civics. He cites reports by citizen action groups as models for classroom materials. He provides prize money for students who perform best in various categories. He provides special funds for summer classes that will train teachers to teach these courses. He establishes auditing groups to keep standards high. He endows studies of outcomes, real societal improvements flowing from a civically skilled citizenry. He declares that if the schools reject his curriculum grant for whatever reasons, the money will still be available for extracurricular programs after class. There you are, B."

"I should say so," Bernard replied with deep emotion.

"There are many more specifics, including a fundraising corps to amplify his bequest so as to cover more and more schools, but for now I'll just say that a billion dollars of the bequest goes to an endowment, and the remainder to establishing infrastructure and operations. As a delicious irony, Mr. Engaget's fortune is much larger than this bequest, but he wryly notes that the $2.8 billion came from his early investments in various IPOs that skyrocketed in value. 'Wall Street and the stock exchanges will be funding this civic resurgence,' he writes with evident satisfaction."

"My kind of guy," Ted exclaimed with delight.

"And now," said Warren, "our Secretariat director par excellence has a few points for your consideration. Patrick?"

"Thank you, Warren. As you all know, after passing the Seven Pillars and the overdue appropriations bills for education, defense, health, and so forth, Congress suddenly adjourned yesterday. The Bulls ran out of patience with all the repeal amendments, figuratively threw down their gavels, and went home. Most members welcomed the adjournment because they wanted time to campaign.

"Now that the Agenda has passed and the focus is on the November elections, some of you have inquired as to whether it might be advisable for you to undertake direct campaigning on behalf of the Clean Elections candidates. As you'll recall, on the advice of Theresa Tieknots and our other experts in federal elections and campaign finance laws, we decided early on that the Meliorists would maintain a scrupulous distance from the Clean Elections Party. As a matter of policy, the Secretariat recommends a continuing avoidance of any electioneering. What we propose instead is what we're calling 'the Plunge'—a ten-day tour of the deprived, ignored 'Other America,' in Michael Harrington's phrase. You would meet the people behind the statistics. You would see poverty, pollution, waste, price gouging, public facilities in disrepair, overcrowded prisons and juvenile institutions, concrete manifestations of greed and injustice—the conditions that authentic politics should be confronting. With your high media profiles, you can generate a coast-to-coast atmosphere of concern for those of our fellow Americans who are suffering the most. Otherwise, the media this fall will be nothing but nonstop attack ads from opposing candidates—utterly the wrong tone for this great year of change."

The Meliorists looked at each other around the table, as if wondering why they hadn't thought of this before. For a moment no one spoke. Then Phil raised his glass of mango juice.

"That's one hell of an idea, Patrick. There's a great deal to be said for coming to grips with the grim reality from time to time. As sensitive and empathetic as we try to be, there's no substitute for seeing crack babies in inner-city hospitals, or undernourished, asthmatic children playing near waste dumps."

"Or the destruction of streams and hollows from the coal barons' mountaintop blasting," Peter said.

"Or a hundred other outrages we could name," said Sol. "We should never forget the constructive uses of anger."

"Boy, do I ever have some destinations to propose!" Leonard said.

"Are you envisioning us all going out together?" Ross asked Patrick.

"I think you can cover more ground if you split up in twos and threes, maybe fours."

"What shall we call our tour? I'm not sure 'Plunge' conveys the right impression. How about 'Faces of Injustice'?" Yoko suggested.

"Or we could take a leaf from Chris Rock and call it the 'That Ain't Right' Journey," Bill Cosby said.

Jeno was nodding enthusiastically. "I like that a lot. It's not hackneyed, not pompous, not abstract. It has just the right vernacular touch."

"So we say that the Meliorists are going to tour conditions in America that would make most people cry out, 'That ain't right!' Does that work for a press release?" Patrick asked.

"I'm afraid it may carry a whiff of condescension," Bill Gates said. "What about 'Faces and Places of Injustice' as an official name, with 'That ain't right!' as a colloquial slogan that emerges in the course of the tour?"

"Sounds good to me," Max said.

"Any objections?" Warren asked, scanning the faces of his colleagues. "All right, Patrick, set the tour up for the last two weeks of October. And now Barry has an update for us on the Beatty campaign."

"It's more like a rout," Barry said. "Arnold is twenty-seven points behind in the polls. Like a bloodied prizefighter, he's clinching with Warren by adopting one plank after another of his platform at choreographed news conferences around the state. Nobody's buying it. In fact, it's boomeranged. Following the lead of a radio talk show host in Fresno, everyone is now calling the governor 'Beatty's dittohead,' and the surge behind Warren has indirectly helped the Clean Elections Party take the lead against the four Bulls from the Golden State. All in all, everything's coming up roses. Warren couldn't be happier, especially because the campaign money is coming in nicely, so he doesn't have to spend any of his own. Besides, with so much free publicity, he doesn't need much TV advertising."

"Is he running with the Agenda in substance if not in name?" Joe asked.

"He sure is, adapting the various proposals to state requirements and adding some of his own, though he doesn't mention us or the Common Good Agenda. He wants to be his own man, which is the right thing for him to do politically. It's good for us too, since we never wanted anyone to see us as a central directorate pulling the strings."

"On that encouraging note, let's break for dinner," Warren said. "Then we'll reconvene for an hour or so to discuss the exciting developments in the sub-economy."

Over dinner, the talk was almost all about the passage of the Seven Pillars and the president's performance at Mount Rushmore. The Meliorist victory, as the press called it, was so overwhelming, and the debates in the House and the Senate so quick and anticlimactic, that legal observers bewailed the lack of a legislative history to guide judges in any future cases. The heart of the exchanges between the Maui diners was how the lopsided vote would affect the upcoming elections. Had they succeeded too well and given incumbents who belatedly supported the Agenda an opportunity to win, or would the voters react like the Californians who saw through their governor's leap onto the bandwagon? The first state polls after passage of the Pillars should give a glimpse of any trends in either direction.

Back around the conference table after dinner, Warren asked Jeno to report on the sub-economy.

"With pleasure, Warren. My friends, this is a movement that could well grow to be as revolutionary in its way as the political movement we've launched. You're already well aware of the useful information Luke Skyhi has received from the sub-economy businesses that bored deep inside the Washington-based trade groups and proved invaluable to the PCC. What I want to convey this evening is a sense of what these Trojan horses are accomplishing to usher in a new age for business.

"First, and most pertinent to current events, they are galloping at breakneck speed to neutralize the knee-jerk injustices perpetrated by the trade groups cadres. Amazing what can be done from the inside by energetic business leaders possessed of a public philosophy for the marketplace. Amazing to me, at least. These sub-economy leaders—I'll call them SELs for short—are outworking the other members of the state and national boards, mobilizing their own epicenters to challenge their trade association bureaucracies, and demanding a reorientation of efforts away from scaring higher and higher dues out of the members and toward what they call foresight programs. For example, instead of obstructing seriously injured workers and consumers from suing over toxic industrial conditions or unsafe products, they want to go all out in the direction of enhancing safety and health to prevent such lawsuits in the first place. Pretty elementary, as Peter demonstrated in the spring, but sluggishness, obstinacy, and inertia require a push toward rational business policies directly from the inside. Since most business people active in trade association politics want to rise in the hierarchy, they curry favor with their superiors, but our SELs could care less about such 'standstill escalator promotions,' as they call them. They're getting their way more and more through hustle, argument, networking, and good press relations with the trade journals. Locally, they're filling the volunteer gap.

"Now project these currents of progressive business attitudes and actions through a steadily enlarging sub-economy over the next few years, and you can get really excited. The SELs are showing that honesty is the best policy in business and challenging the 'mum's the word' stance of the trade groups on members who engage in corporate crimes and abuses. They're redefining innovation not as the intricate trivia that make up much of what is called competition—software modifications, advertising, minute but expensive product differentiations—but rather as fundamental marketplace services that meet real needs and enhance consumer well-being.

"And how are these SELs doing in the marketplace, apart from their trade association maneuvering? Well, they're practicing what they preach. Live operators answer the phones. The workers are happy, the products and services honest, and the contracts readable, with no fine print about binding arbitration and no boldface caveats about the vendor reserving the unilateral right to change the provisions. These big-print, clear-language contracts have already become the talk of business sectors from insurance, banking, and brokerage to hospitals, car dealerships, and mortgage companies—you name it. Uproar and outrage galore. All this comes to the attention of more and more customers, who learn just which vendors are on their side and reward them accordingly.

"The SELs are in close touch with one another and with the PCC, and are moving toward a rapid adoption of each other's best practices. Compared to the businesses as they operated before the SELs purchased them, sales, profits, worker satisfaction, and community support are on a steady upswing. The business pages are starting to do features. The business schools are initiating case studies and inviting the SELs to lecture to their students, which the SELs are only too happy to do. They're recruiting more and more graduates of these schools and sending them to a kind of reeducational halfway house where they unlearn much of what they've been taught and prepare themselves for maverick business entrepreneurship.

"The speedy results we're seeing are in no small part due to the fact that the SELs took over existing businesses rather than starting new ones. Many of these were Main Street retailers, and we know a lot about their performance because their operations don't require long lead times. Soon we'll start hearing from the wholesalers, the shippers, the agriculturalists, and the manufacturers. I'm particularly intrigued to see how honest middlemen, brokers, and procurement firms are faring.

"A word about financing. You'll recall that the preferred method was credit, using the acquired business as collateral. Then there was the loan pool you established. The growth in the demand for credit has been so rapid that capacity is oversubscribed. Predictably, the new SELs are being received with hostility by the finance industry, which increasingly does not want to deal with them. My project staff recommends that we consider both an enlargement of the credit pool with a revolving fund feature and a regional banking structure that would place this source of capital formation and business growth on a more permanent footing. Cooperative ownership of these banks by the SELs is another possibility.

"As for the numbers, the projection for next year is that collectively the SELs will account for one tenth of one percent of GDP, which means that only a fraction of the economy is now facing SEL competition. So, as they say, the growth opportunities are immense. I welcome your comments."

"Fascinating, Jeno," George said. "Obviously you can only scratch the surface of what's happening, but is it too early to tell whether there's any organized retaliation underway from the business establishment? For every action there will be a reaction, and not just in physics."

"So far, just bewilderment, consternation, some sporadic rebuttals. By and large, the establishment was caught off guard, and then surprised by the tumult in the conventional world of the trade associations. That's what big money on our side can do—lightning moves on a breakthrough scale. It helps that the SELs are level-headed and polite and work silently wherever they can. They don't come on like gangbusters. Again, a great tribute to Recruitment. No doubt the time will come when half the *Wall Street Journal* is devoted to the interactions and frictions between these two ecospheres and the changes that are bursting out all over. No doubt the counter-attack will come too, and we can't discount the possibility that the big boys, especially the chains, will go to the government for help. As we know, there's ample precedent for that in our country's history. Look at how the banks have tried to hamstring credit union cooperatives through legislative action. Let us hope, should they try this avenue, that they'll find a different kind of government awaiting them."

"What preliminary indications are there for minority ownership, employment, and service to minority markets within the budding SEL world?" Bill Cosby asked.

"I'll take that one," Sol said. "I've had some involvement with these kinds of initiatives in San Diego, and it's a wide-open field for venturesome SELs. For instance, one of our acquisitions in Detroit was of a predatory lending operation that was immediately fumigated by the new owner, who replaced its avaricious routines with microlending for small business formation in the ravaged inner sectors of Motor City. Three hundred loans have been made, mostly to women, and there is every expectation, from the history of microlending abroad, of high rates of business success and repayment. Minority markets are beset by predators, often bankrolled by Wall Street money that doesn't want to get its hands dirty directly. These street-level predators control the neighborhoods while their bought political allies and police look the other way, so the SELs have to expect trouble. Already, one microlending storefront in Cleveland was torched during the wee hours of the night. It will take thought, planning, and coordination to anticipate and forestall similar sabotage. We have to make it clear to the people in the communities themselves why there are so few developmental credit unions serving them when thousands are needed. And minority employment goes hand in hand with these inner-city SELs, Bill, but I know from experience that training programs have to be set up first to create a pool of qualified entry-level applicants.

"I should add that it's not just credit that begs for an influx of SELs, it's health, affordable insurance, consumer products like furniture and appliances, home repairs, food outlets, and on and on. We're dealing with massively devastated neighborhoods, streets owned by drug dealers and pimps, millions of children, women, and men in dire need—just what we're going to see on our tour. It's true that the Pillars will be making their beneficial impact felt in a major way soon, but meanwhile we should try to expand the sub-economy in the communities most in need of help."

"Before closing on this invigorating subject," Jeno said, "I want to leave you with one further example to illustrate just how revolutionary the SEL model can be. One of our SELs in Kansas City, Missouri, took over a healthcare billing design firm whose clients range far and wide, including hospital chains and large medical practices. The billing design industry is part of one of the largest overbilling frauds in American history. Malcolm Sparrow, a professor of applied mathematics at Harvard, is an authority in this arcane field. He estimates that anywhere from two hundred billion dollars to four hundred billion dollars a year in healthcare billings goes down the drain due significantly to the overbilling that's built into these computerized coded designs. So here comes our SEL into this snake pit, and soon he uncovers enough to say whoa to the entire operation. He revamps the firm, hires new employees, and is now using his unique insider vantage point to track down who's perpetrating what in his industry all over the country. He tells us that within five months he'll have enough on the tentacles of this institutionalized fraud, which Sparrow calls 'a license to steal,' that it will take *60 Minutes* a hundred and eighty minutes to do the story. As we made clear in the Agenda, honest, accurate billing in the healthcare industry will save enough money to cover almost every uninsured American."

"Behold what we have unleashed," Warren said with a big smile. "We're reversing Gresham's Law. Honest money is driving out dishonest money, and good business is driving out bad. Now, it's getting late, so just two more matters on a lighter note before we call it a night. First, as some of you have mentioned to me, it's not too early to plan a mass celebration after the election, no matter its outcome. Millions of people have worked their hearts out on the Agenda and all our other projects—the staff, the organizers, the lecturers, the CUBs and PCC chapters and Congress Watchdogs, and countless others. Do I have your approval to retain a trusted events firm in Omaha to give us a plan on how best to convey our everlasting thanks in a multidimensional and multilocational manner?"

The proposal was adopted by acclamation, with Yoko offering to advise on aesthetics.

"Fine," Warren said. "Next is something that's been on all our minds. What can we do for Maui? This beautiful island has provided a hospitable refuge for our deliberations in a setting of unsurpassed natural splendor. May I suggest that we spend Sunday morning touring some of the island and thinking about how to show our gratitude for the benefit of the local residents? We can drive up the coast, stopping at towns and hamlets on our way to the airport."

On a further note of acclamation, Warren adjourned the meeting, and the Meliorists retired to their rooms under a full moon that shone down upon the little hotel and gardens like a giant spotlight. Bill Joy strolled along with his colleagues, having completed his customary sweep of the premises—as if it really mattered anymore. His task now was more to insure privacy than security, since there was nothing much left to be revealed.

On Saturday, the group breakfasted on the patio under a dew-smitten canopy of leaves and got underway in the conference room at nine sharp. The task at hand was a review of precisely prepared written reports from the managers of each project and initiative. The core group had let it be known from the outset that they had no use for power-point presentations. First up was Donald Ross's report on the Congress Watchdogs, which they had read before but were now paging through to refresh their memories.

1. CWs are operating in 60 percent of the congressional districts. All but thirty of them have at least one full-time staff member and a rented office. These thirty are new and will soon have office space and staff too.

2. CWs have been helped greatly by the activities of the lecturers and the continuing efforts of the organizers. The CUBs mesh well on certain advocacy policies as well. (There are now 7.8 million dues-paying members in seventeen sectoral CUBs—banking, insurance, etc.—and all have growing state chapters.)

3. CWs have focused almost entirely on passage of the Seven Pillars, but along the way have begun to develop a youth auxiliary, regular cable programs, and a post-Agenda agenda. The young people are being trained in door-to-door canvassing, community events, and congressional advocacy skills.

4. CWs are still within the budgets you allocated to them, but there is an ongoing drive for self-sufficiency of staff, facilities, and funds. Progress here is variable, depending on the location. Going very well in states like Minnesota, Wisconsin, Massachusetts, and California (where there are four offices). More difficult in the South and Southwest. Membership dues provide a solid minimal base, however.

5. CWs are learning from one another about what works and what doesn't work. Unified agendas are crucial. Otherwise efforts can dissolve into hundreds of legislative requests and everybody's pet reform or design. With the Pillars, unity has been easy. Afterward, it's anyone's guess, unless the CWs continue with an exclusive commitment to the implementation of the Pillars.

6. CW meetings are wonderfully rambunctious. The excitement reigns when the various means of influencing members of Congress are discussed. Here personal approaches and best practices from all the CWs are pivotal. Training sessions and concise manuals are proving their worth. The goal is to have the lawmakers view the CWs with a mix of respect, fear, and wonder. They have to believe the CWs are uncooptable, have deep reserve capabilities, and can continue to widen their base and diversify their tactics in surprising ways.

7. Remarkably, recruitment procedures for the CW core two thousand have produced a membership in which no social, economic, educational, or ethnic category predominates. The only trait they share is their commitment to no-nonsense work and a continuing education in the ways and means of the Congress so as to make it represent the best interests of the people.

8. One problem. When assignments are focused in their neighborhoods, there are few frictions among the members, but when they gather in larger groups, the traditional human frailties and personality differences emerge, even if there's no disagreement on substance or tactics. Some of them go after each other as if there weren't bigger adversaries out there. I don't want to make too much of this. I only mention it because democratic processes and solid consensus-building rarely take account of these personality conflicts, which can be trouble if not dealt with promptly.

9. Over the longer term, there are imponderables. It's difficult to predict how the CWs will do on their own, without the media saturation, the Agenda excitement, the upcoming elections, and the immense backup infrastructure and foreground assistance from the lecturers and organizers. But there's been a fast CW learning curve, and the future looks bright even if there's no Meliorist encore. This year, the CWs played a role in many turnarounds for the Seven Pillars, not a crucial role, but an important one. Up against the Bulls, they were bull terriers—"Here, there, everywhere," as their motto went—at every possible public occasion. Two thousand motivated people per district can make quite a difference.

"Perhaps the best way to proceed," Warren said when everyone had finished reviewing Ross's report, "is to have free-flowing responses around the table, followed by a more rigorous discussion of whether we wish to make an additional year's sendoff grant to each of our projects and continue the infrastructure support from Promotions, Recruitment, and so on. Naturally, some of our conclusions will be tentative, pending the outcome of the elections next month and the subsequent response of the American people."

And so it went with each of the reports that morning and through a working lunch. Toward the end of the day, Warren gave the budget report. "We have total expenditures to date of about eight billion dollars. Monies in hand since we started in January have reached sixteen billion, with five billion in serious pledges plus the $2.8 billion Engaget bequest. And who knows how much more is in the pipeline or will be in the pipeline after the election? This is a most pleasant fix to find ourselves in. It will require careful thought in the coming weeks to allocate thirteen billion dollars along sustainable, institution-building lines. There are certain fiduciary restraints, since some of the money was solicited with the Seven Pillars in mind, but that obviously includes implementation."

"You and the Secretariat run one tight ship, Warren," Max said. "If they didn't call us the Meliorists, they'd have to call us the Frugalists."

"You know, it's interesting," said Bill Gates, "that with all we've set in motion and all we've spent, my son's foundation has already spent more—fourteen billion in the past six years."

"That's very reassuring, Bill," Peter said. "I take it as a comment on our comparative paternal efficiencies."

Bill smiled. "You can take it that way, though the two money flows are really apples and oranges. It's a matter of different absorptive capacities and different opportunities for systemic initiatives. Third World diseases like AIDS, malaria, and tuberculosis are a different universe altogether. Anyway we're digressing, sorry."

"Let's digress to dinner," Warren said. "Ailani has prepared a feast of special Maui recipes tonight, and I'm having some old Hawaiian music piped in to set a relaxing mood."

When the Meliorists had reassembled in the conference room after their culinary and audio massage, Warren suggested that they skip the usual hour of silence. "We've really had a long day, and we have to get an early start tomorrow if we want to visit a number of towns and talk with the residents, so let's wrap up with whatever's on our minds and then turn in."

"At dinner, Sol and Bernard and I were exchanging concerns about whether we've peaked too soon as far as the elections go," Phil said. "After the great victories in Congress, there may be a public lull or a voter letdown—just think about athletic teams that beat their big competitor and then lose to a mediocre team the next week. With the CEOs putting up a billion dollars to fund an aggressive counterattack over the next month, the Lobo/Dortwist crowd may try to take advantage of a public attitude of 'Well, we got what we wanted in the Pillars, and this election isn't that important.' If there is such a mood, it could certainly be encouraged through clever political advertising, especially with the Bulls claiming credit for passage of the Agenda. So ponder this. When we were engaged in rapid response to Lobo's propaganda machine, we had a free hand because we were outside any electoral context. It was just plain, robust, old-fashioned free speech. Now the CEOs will presumably be using a good chunk of their billions to support the reelection of their congressional friends under the FEC rubric of 'independent expenditures.' When we reply with our own media blasts, are we under the FEC rubric or outside in the land of free speech?"

"Important question," said Bill Gates. "It's my understanding that we're still free and clear. The Lobo operation will be supporting or opposing various candidates by name in the local and national media markets. We don't want to do this, even under independent expenditure rules, because we want to preserve our separation from the Clean Elections Party and its candidates, as Patrick advised yesterday. Our approach should be to urge people to get out and vote for a society that is advancing through the Seven Pillars, and for a Congress that will brook no delay in their efficient and expeditious implementation, without mentioning specific candidates or specific parties. That will keep us out of the clutches of the FEC regulations, while also allowing Bill Hillsman to give full play to his imagination."

"Won't that put us at a disadvantage in terms of what the voters are being exposed to on television?" Sol asked. "Generalities from us, specifics and local interest from the opposition?"

"That depends almost entirely on how astutely the ads play off the CEOs' ads and rebut them," Bill Gates said. "That's why Hillsman is critical here. He'll know how to handle the situation."

"Well, we already know from experience that one Hillsman ad can have the impact of five or ten of the opposition's," George said. "I think we can count on him to head off the CEOs, but let's go on the offensive too. What about another wave of parades all over the country just before Election Day? Parades are great visible reminders of popular power. They'll energize the citizenry to get out the vote. Our parade teams from the Fourth and Labor Day are still in place and have even more experience now. Where I grew up, in Eastern Europe, the Soviets banned parades, except military ones, for fear of inciting the repressed masses to protest or riot or revolt. The Soviets knew the power of parades."

Bernard was nodding thoughtfully. "Papa always wondered why parades in his adopted country didn't look toward the future instead of just memorializing the past. I'd love to see us put together a nuts-and-bolts pamphlet titled 'How Local Parades Spark Change,' drawing on historical examples and our experience this year. What about it, Patrick?"

"I'll put Analysis on it tomorrow. They're already compiling reports on all the immense activity since January with an eye to what more can be done. This will fit right in."

"Okay," Warren said, "we have ads and parades on the table to counter a possible letdown. Any other suggestions?"

"What about personalizing the CEOs hiding behind the billion-dollar ad campaign?" Joe suggested. "You know, their pictures, their annual compensation, the average wage in their companies, the stands they've taken against social justice. Not all of them, since there were a few voices of conscience, just the hardliners, the greed-hounds. Is it worth suggesting this to Hillsman? Nothing like letting the people get to know some of their rulers, especially those with such dedication to their own anonymity."

Ted guffawed. "I wouldn't mind Jasper Cumbersome's mug becoming a household pinup."

"Well, let's let Hillsman decide," Warren said. "We certainly trust his taste, and we'll ask to see his drafts. We don't want to get into micromanaging here."

"We certainly don't," Sol said, suppressing a yawn.

Phil pushed back his chair. "I think our day is petering out. In the course of my sixty-five hundred TV shows, I developed a sense for when the audience was flagging. It's nine thirty, and we've been going hard since nine this morning. Let's hit the sack."

The next morning at 7:30 a.m., five town cars arrived for the east coast tour of Maui. The Meliorists split up into threes and fours, and each group went its own merry way, stopping in as many different towns as possible to talk with harvesters, strollers, people tending their gardens or sitting at outdoor cafés or on their way to church. At each stop they sought out old-timers and native Hawaiians to get a sense of what they felt they had lost or were losing and what they wanted as a community. Mauians were so used to tourists and visitors that they struck up conversations readily. The Meliorists rendezvoused for breakfast at Waianapanapa State Park, went on separately to Wailua, Keanae Point, Kailua, Pauwela, and a dozen other destinations, then met again for a late lunch at Hookipa Beach Park. All along the way, they gratefully took in the smells and sounds, the spectacular bird life, the ridges, valleys, and beaches, the play of sunlight on slopes, rivers, and trees. It was easy to believe the ancient Hawaiian myth that it was the demigod Maui who created the entire chain of the Hawaiian Islands from the deep sea.

Arriving at Kahului airport, the Meliorists exchanged notes on their day's journey while they waited to board their business jets. All told, they had spoken to hundreds of Maui residents and heard over and over again of their desire for local community centers. These congenial, gregarious people had no decent, attractive gathering places and made do with the outdoors or some school auditorium. They and their children would make good cultural, civic, recreational, and educational use of blended facilities that were both aesthetically pleasing and functional. Accordingly, as their gift to Maui, the Meliorists decided to fund six community centers and retain a green building firm in Honolulu to work with the local residents so that the siting and architecture flowed straight from their traditions, preferences, and needs.

When the planes were ready, the group said their farewells and climbed aboard to head for the mainland and the momentous stretch drive to the November elections. Halfway across the ocean, Warren turned to Patrick Drummond and said quietly, "You know, Pat, we've accomplished all this since January with an equivalent of a sixth of just my personal fortune. I'll be a long time wondering what took me so long. What in the world took me so long?"

In a converted high-ceilinged barn by a pretty canal in Minneapolis, Bill Hillsman sat deep in thought, turning his estimable media imagination to the task of making a national splash with the $150 million budget the Secretariat had assigned him to go up against the CEOs' billion-dollar ad campaign. Patrick Drummond had briefed him and told him there was another $100 million to add to his budget if the Meliorists liked what he came up with.

This was serious money for Hillsman. He wasn't one of the big boys in the advertising game, though he'd received more prizes for his news-making political ads than any single person in the country, as all the plaques and statuettes in his office attested. Still, each new challenge started with a blank page and a blank mind. He'd just come back from visiting his many sisters and brothers in Chicago, where he'd grown up. He often got ideas from thrashing things out in bull sessions with his siblings, but he'd come up empty this time. He liked to tell his associates how easy it was to think up great ads: "All you have to do is sit in front of your computer until beads of blood start dripping from your brow."

Today he was really straining. His desk was strewn with press clippings and profiles and pictures of the CEOs, but nothing leapt out. Sipping hot coffee, he started reading a wire service story that had just been filed and almost dropped his cup: "Attempted Kidnapping of Patriotic Polly Foiled." The copy went on to describe a break-in at the veterinary school in Delhi, New York, where Polly's trainer, Clifton Chirp, cared for her. At 1:00 a.m., two men in ski masks had crawled through an unlocked window, walked past a sleeping guard, and put a hood over Polly's cage, but not before the valiant bird cried out, "Wake up, wake up, wake up!" Apparently her trainer had anticipated that her guards might be prone to snoozing. The guard woke up, drew his weapon, and ordered the retreating men to put up their hands. The men unceremoniously dropped the cage and fled. After making sure that Polly was unhurt, the guard phoned the police and campus security to give chase to the intruders. A dragnet was underway around a large tract of woods where the kidnappers were believed to be hiding. There was no indication as to the motive behind their attempted seizure of the most famous bird in the world, "a parrot beloved by millions of Americans for her services to humanity and to justice for all."

"That's it!" Hillsman exclaimed.

That evening the network television news led with the Polly story. The anchors played tape and sound bites of the parrot's past exploits as the trumpeter of truth and the exposer of deceptive political ads. "Detectives on the case believe the botched kidnaping was a ransom attempt and was not politically driven. Although the suspects have not yet been caught, political operatives would have planned a smoother getaway," Tatie Youric surmised, evidently forgetting about the Watergate burglars. Bill Hillsman watched all the coverage in his wraparound television studio and knew that he had the star he needed for his constellation of ads. He put in a call to Clifton Chirp.

Lobo released the first wave of his media barrage a few days later. Hillsman replied immediately with one-minute spots that all began with Patriotic Polly crying, "Get up! Don't let the Agenda down!" He had easily anticipated what Lobo's themes would be—the same old alarmist claptrap decked out as sober concern for the country's future—and had crafted the body of each ad to rebut the claims factually and expose them as self-serving ploys to distract the populace and derail the Common Good.

With her reprise of a variation on the refrain that had first brought her to national attention, Patriotic Polly demolished the credibility of Lobo's billion-dollar extravaganza of falsehood and deception. Within seventy-two hours, his ads went the way of Harry and Louise.

The world of the Washington lobbyists had shut down. They'd lost big, and the object of their affections—the Congress—was in adjournment, so they headed back to their resorts and villas for another long vacation.

Brovar Dortwist had one last dinner with the Solvents, who were discouraged, disgruntled, and disgusted by the dismissive treatment they'd received at the hands of the media and the Congress. Always looking to the future, Brovar tried to turn their indignation into a resource for next year's counterattack. He shored up their morale, told them their job had been impossible before they even arrived on the scene, assured them that they had nothing to be ashamed of since they'd given it their best.

"If only we'd been unified from Wall Street to Washington," Delbert Decisioner muttered into his martini.

"We were divided, so those old farts conquered," said Sally Savvy, downing her white wine spritzer.

Brovar refrained from saying that there were far more elements at work than a divided business community and raised his glass for a toast. "To the corporate future and our victory over the radicals and the rabble."

"Hear, hear," mumbled his guests lugubriously.

As Brovar took leave of them, knowing that the Solvents had effectively dissolved themselves, Lobo was in his condo in Manhattan drowning his sorrows in scotch and his pit bull. With a few squawks, Patriotic Polly had obliterated his last-ditch ad campaign, and there was nothing left for him to do. His thoughts turned back to Yoko. He found himself dreaming about her every night—exotic, erotic dreams that sometimes left him waking up on the rug by his bed with the puzzled pit bull sniffing him and licking his face. What did he want from Yoko? Why did she provoke these intense feelings in him when she knew nothing about him except that he was the

CEOs' lead man? No drug, no psychiatry, no hypnosis could give him the answer. It was existential. He just had to be close to her, that was all, and it had to be soon.

The Faces and Places of Injustice Tour began the third week of October. The Meliorists broke up into five teams and covered twelve sites each. Promotions worked hard to publicize the tour and provide buses for all the reporters clamoring to be on board. Community residents were informed of the visits by the *Daily Bugle* kids, who were thrilled at the prospect of meeting their heroes in person. "Read all about it!" they cried. "The Meliorists are coming to town!"

As the teams soon discovered, "That ain't right!" was an understatement. With video streaming on their website every step of the way, they visited decrepit housing projects where children played on toxic brownfields, drug dealers brazenly plied their trade, and both streets and streetlights were in ruins. They went to a California prison and a juvenile detention camp, pointing out sharply that such institutions cost California taxpayers more than the state's entire higher education system, with over half of the inmates incarcerated for nonviolent offenses. They surveyed the terrible damage inflicted by the petrochemical companies on the ecosystem of the Louisiana Delta and its inhabitants. They walked through dilapidated inner-city schools in Cleveland and Baltimore—broken desks, filthy restrooms, pathetic libraries, junk food, and unruliness everywhere. They sampled the bumper-to-bumper daily highway congestion in Los Angeles and Dallas to get the feel of the commuting grind, compliments of GM's and the highway lobby's crushing of mass transit decades ago. They were shocked by the plight of migrant farm-workers exposed to a deadly stew of agricultural chemicals, and of their counterparts on the factory farms tending crammed chickens and pigs fed on grain doused with daily antibiotics.

In the Powder River Basin in Wyoming and Montana, reverberating around the clock with the screaming of gas compressors and the rumbling of water pumps, they saw what the coalbed methane companies were doing to thousands of helpless ranch families whose underground mineral assets had been leased to those companies by the federal government. In the coal country of Kentucky and West Virginia, they viewed strip-mined moonscapes and ravaged mountains, and met with the besieged inhabitants of the hollows who received no help from a government that had long ago surrendered this rich land to the rapacious coal barons. Outside Atlanta, they got a taste of ugly suburban and exurban sprawl, wasteful of time, fuel, land, and water, starved for efficient transportation, bereft of community.

Wherever possible, the teams highlighted contrasts, showing the faces of poverty—so much of it child poverty—in slums within sight of the gleaming tax-abated skyscrapers where the affluent made money from money and went home to mansions cleaned by the poor. Millions logging onto the Meliorists' website saw them standing before stadiums, arenas, and upscale gallerias built largely with taxpayer dollars, and then stopping in at run-down clinics, crumbling library branches with depleted collections, check-cashing stores, so-called food stores selling sugar, salt, and fat. The few derelict playgrounds in the slums just didn't have the lobbyists that the billionaire owners of sports franchises could retain, Leonard observed scathingly.

One team went to an inner-city school and then to a school in a nearby affluent neighborhood, both funded by the same property taxes under different allocation formulas. Another team went to the fields where workers harvested crops under dangerous, backbreaking, low-wage conditions, and then flew to the commodities markets in Chicago to show how big money was made by yelling bids in the pits. In one of the more dramatic comparisons, Bernard, Yoko, and Max visited a large hospital in Chicago and talked with the executive director, who complained about shortages of everything from flu vaccines to emergency room capacity. Then they were off to a nearby factory where workers were putting in three shifts daily making deadly cluster bombs for shipment overseas to whatever country had the money to pay for these destroyers of innocent men, women, and children. The manager proudly told Max that he always made sure to have a six-month supply on hand in case a sudden spate of hostilities spiked his orders.

In West Virginia, Barry, Joe, and Ross attended a Rotary Club luncheon for the executives and managers of a local cluster of chemical plants. In the large banquet room, they stood along with everyone else to pledge allegiance to the flag and sing "America the Beautiful." After lunch, they toured the plants, and then a neighborhood of workers' houses with tiny front yards where children played and frolicked, enveloped in a cloud of gases and particulates. Bordering the west side of the neighborhood was one of America the Beautiful's rivers, now a colorful sewer from the dumping of chemicals year after year. They completed their trip with a visit to a clinic where children with blotched complexions and bad asthma gasped for breath.

Each day the teams held news conferences that beamed live all over the country and on global cable networks. Against a backdrop of powerful visuals, the Meliorists made two points over and over again. First, it did not have to be this way. The nation had the values, knowledge, and resources to do the right thing by its people. The Agenda was a solid first step in that direction, and the Faces and Places of Injustice made clear the urgency of following through on implementation. Second, the sources of injustice were often out of sight and far removed from the scene of the damage, as with monopolistic pharmaceutical companies that hiked drug prices and made essential treatment unaffordable for millions of Americans. Gross negligence in the drug and hospital industries caused tens of thousands of deaths annually, and many more injuries and illnesses, but those were hard to "visit." Backroom decisions shaped by avarice and power could not be brought into the light of day by a tour, the Meliorists stressed, but only by the piercing vigilance of the citizenry.

Toward the end of the tour, Jeno, Paul, Phil, and Bill Cosby decided to go to the nation's capital to see firsthand what many writers had described as a race- and class-segregated tale of two cities: one the preserve of the oligarchs, largely in the northwest quadrant of the district, and then the desolate, rubble-swept "other Washington" where unemployment, infant mortality, and crime reigned within view of the White House, within minutes of K Street. Good schools versus atrocious schools, expensive bottled water versus tap water tainted with lead, country clubs, tennis courts and squash courts versus asphalt jungle playgrounds, overstocked super-markets versus no supermarkets at all, fancy private clinics versus overloaded Medicaid mills, stores catering to every want and whim versus pawnshops and liquor stores, late-model cars versus ram-shackle buses, police protection versus police sirens—the list went on and on. Only the main thoroughfares communicated a rough equality as shiny BMWs and clunker Chevrolets alike jarred through the potholes, a rare common experience for the impoverished and the affluent.

Washington, DC, had no excuses. With a huge and growing federal expenditure base, an army of corporate contractors, the vast influence-peddling industry, the unparalleled tourist attractions, the convention business, numerous public and private universities, and ever-rising real estate tax receipts, the city was Exhibit Number One of state capitalism accumulating and concentrating wealth amidst public squalor. It was America's litmus test, and America was flunking. It was proof positive that America did not take care of her own, and it didn't matter a whit that the Democrats were over-whelmingly dominant in city politics.

If the Meliorists' tour of the District of Columbia, the only national capital whose residents were denied voting representation in the national legislature, was big news at home, it was bigger news abroad, especially in countries that were adversaries of the United States. This unintended result discomfited the Secretariat and prompted a flurry of worried e-mails from the Redirectional net-works. Having assiduously maintained a domestically based reform drive, the Meliorists suddenly found themselves under attack from the cable and radio yahoos for "feeding the Hate America mob"—a public relations imbroglio they didn't need just a week before the election.

Fortunately, an energetic young reform candidate was in the process of sweeping his way to an easy victory in the DC mayoral race, despite the opposition of the local business establishment. During his lengthy campaign, Hadrian Plenty had literally walked the streets and knocked on the doors of half the households in the city. Bill Cosby, Phil Donahue, and Paul Newman were boyhood media heroes of his. He called them up and invited them to join him in a press conference at the Mayflower Hotel, two blocks from the White House. The trio were only too happy to accept. A joint appearance with Hadrian Plenty could only be a plus, they felt, and might keep matters from getting out of hand.

On the day of the news conference, the press turned out in force. The fourth estate had been waiting for months to see if the Meliorists would generate a crisis for themselves. Now the right wing had found its voice after a long period of frustration and was pouncing savagely. How would the Meliorists and their new ally cross this bed of hot coals?

Wise beyond his thirty-six years, Hadrian Plenty had the answer. Before an audience that included representatives of business, labor, tourism, the clergy, veterans' groups, civil rights organizations, and children's causes, he announced his theme: Facing Reality. Then he gestured to Bill, Paul, and Phil. "I want to begin by thanking the Meliorists for the invaluable service they've performed in publicizing the cruel inequalities in the District of Columbia. Facing reality is the first step toward a new reality. In the past ten days, the Meliorists have shown us harsh and heartrending realities not only here in Washington but across the nation. But in the past ten months, they have also shown us how people of goodwill and strong convictions can turn such realities around dramatically. It's not the Meliorists who've been running our metropolis down, it's the selfish power brokers in both the federal and local realms of the District. The Meliorists aren't running our city or our country down, they're lifting us up!"

When the enthusiastic applause died down, Plenty introduced the first of several invited speakers, a prominent businessman eager to ingratiate himself with the mayor-to-be. "When companies find themselves in trouble, the best way out is full candor," he declared. "Facing reality is just sound business practice, and isn't that what the Meliorists are doing in our city?" Then several labor representatives spoke of all the jobs that would be created by a revitalization of deteriorating neighborhoods and services, and thanked the Meliorists for spotlighting these more visibly than anyone had done before.

The clergy selected wonderfully apt quotations from the scriptures about not looking the other way when you know your neighbors are endangered, nurturing other people's children as if they were your own, and subordinating commercial interests to higher principles of morality and to God Almighty. Two veterans, one from the American Legion and one from the VFW, took out after the right-wing loudmouths who never served but never met a war they didn't want somebody else to fight. "The Meliorists, many of them veterans themselves, care deeply for their country," the Legion member said. "An active love of country is the true patriotism. A city that's falling apart disgraces our great monuments and war memorials."

A local NAACP leader spoke of the high promise of the civil rights marches and legislation, too often aborted by poverty and discrimination, and praised the Meliorists "for their valiant determination to confront the Other Washington. How dare these talk show hosts, from their gated communications pedestals, pour their bile on these great defenders of Americans most in need? A society can only be strong when it is critical, and it can only be critical when everyone has a voice, not just those who monopolize our public airwaves."

A children's advocate expressed the hope that the Meliorists' tour would prompt the city to address the plight of the thousands of children growing up poor in a wealthy city, the seat of government, where drugs, drive-by shootings, and vandalism formed the environment of their most impressionable years, where the infant mortality rate was among the highest in the nation and HIV rates were double the national average. A tourism promoter acknowledged that all the recent publicity might scare visitors off in the short term, but she was confident that in the long term more people would visit Washington with their children when a decent quality of life was the norm for everyone. "I'm tired of having to hide the Other Washington and warn people not to wander off the beaten tourists paths," she said.

Sitting on the platform, Paul noticed that the press was getting restless. The event was beginning to seem a little too staged. He leaned over and had a whispered conversation with Hadrian Plenty, then strode to the podium, blue eyes flashing with anger.

"Why are we all here? Because the radio and cable blowhards are trying to turn the Faces and Places of Injustice Tour into an act of disloyalty to America. I'm here to tell you that Bush Bimbaugh and Pawn Vanity are nothing but dyed-in-the-wool cowards, monopolizing their microphones, pulling the plug on any unwelcome views, and freeloading on the public airwaves all the way to the bank. They have empty minds and craven hearts. Only their tongues show any signs of life. You know what happened when Bimbaugh invited Ted Turner on his show in an attempt to pump up his audience. The man cannot stand to be challenged.

"Well, here and now, I challenge him. I challenge both of these bombastic bullies to invite all the representatives on this platform onto their programs right away for two hours of back-and-forth. I challenge them before tens of millions of Americans to put up or shut up. This is their career moment of truth."

As Paul sat down to loud cheers from most of the audience, the award-winning student choir from DC's Spingarn High School filed on stage and sang "America the Beautiful," with its stirring evocations of peace and prosperity. When the students were done and Hadrian Plenty had duly praised them, he asked if the press had any questions.

Pauline Quicksilver of the *Hartford Courant* was racing up the aisle from the back of the ballroom, waving her arms wildly. Plenty recognized her.

"I just called Bimbaugh and Vanity. Their spokesmen were watching the live feed. They put me on hold for thirty seconds or so and then came back. Both declined the challenge on behalf of their bosses. 'Tell Newman *nyet*,' Bimbaugh's guy said. 'He'll understand that better than no.' Any reaction, Mr. Newman?"

Paul flashed that knockout smile of his. "What more is there to say? These shining stars of talk radio have just said it all."

Sitting in the audience, Jeno and Luke Skyhi grinned at each other and traded high fives. They could scarcely believe their good fortune. Bimbaugh and Vanity had fallen into a trap the Meliorists hadn't even thought to spring. It was a perfect distraction, and just when it was most needed, right before the election, when the two gutless wonders were exhorting the faithful to go to the polls. Now they were on the defensive. Their credibility would be the issue in the coming days.

"I could be wrong," Luke said, "but I bet even the dittoheads are going to have trouble with this latest display of 'values' from their ringleaders."

"I'm not taking that bet," Jeno said.

As if nature were sending a message, the nation was bathed in sunshine on Election Day, except for a light drizzle in Seattle. For weeks, pollsters had been predicting a record turnout for a midterm election, and early signs suggested that they were right. In some communities, people had organized parades and were marching to their polling places together in sizable numbers. Exit polls clearly reflected the appeal of the Clean Elections Party and the effects of ten months of Meliorist dynamics. The voters' responses revealed that they were particularly taken with the Agenda's shift in taxation from work income to securities transactions, but at the top of the list, just edging out universal healthcare, was the Democracy Act, which had really struck home with its subordination of the corporations to the people and its eye-opening declaration that "'person' is hereby defined by law as 'human being.'"

In the early evening, instead of the usual hours of watchful waiting, celebrations and victory rallies broke out everywhere. Premature? Not to these Americans. While the candidates were suitably subdued, the voters were confident that victory was assured and that the only question was by what margin. The bloggers, of course, were all over the place, ranting and rumoring and sometimes beating the traditional media to definite tallies. By 10:00 p.m., most of the returns were in and the networks were making their calls, but election snafus and overloaded precincts delayed the final count in some districts and states. Both the Clean Elections Party and the Meliorists declined to issue statements or talk to reporters, preferring to wait until the counts were complete.

The morrow came. Forty-eight of the fifty-seven Bulls had been defeated, some by unexpected margins. Those who won were saved because the CEP candidates got a late start due to continuing court challenges to their candidacies based on arbitrary ballot access laws adjudicated by partisan judges, as in a notoriously anti-third-party jurisdiction of Pennsylvania where three Bulls survived. But with the passage of the Agenda and its single-ballot access standard for federal elections, these Pennsylvania pols and their counterparts across the nation would no longer be able to deny voters a choice by evicting independent candidates from the ballot.

The makeup of Congress the day after the elections set the political pundits scurrying to do the new math. The CEP now made up 17 percent of Congress and held the balance of power between the new Democratic plurality and the fallen Republicans. Since many of the CEP candidates had won what were long believed to be the most secure seats for incumbents in the nation, the two major parties were already sweating over the prospect of greater losses two years hence, when the CEP would have a lot more experience and a lot more lead time. The surviving Bulls pragmatically resolved to heed the will of the people and implement the Agenda. As Senator Paul Pessimismo observed, "If we don't, we're history."

To no one's surprise, none of the six write-in corporation candidates for state governorships won their elections, but to Bill Gates

Sr.'s immense delight, the Draft Corporations Yes Corporation won 9 percent of the Oregon vote.

In the Fourth Congressional District of Oklahoma, Billy Beauchamp breathed a sigh of relief. He'd lost to Willy Champ, but at least it was over—the dread of defeat, the ordeal of trying to salvage the unsalvageable—and he took comfort from the fact that the margin of victory was only eight points, 56 percent to 44. He was tired, but not perplexed. He knew why he'd lost. He put in a call to Willy.

"I want to congratulate you, not just on your win, but on the way you conducted yourself during the campaign. Together, I believe we may have set a new standard for enlightened discussion of the issues, without resort to invective or sound bites. But in the end, Triple T prevailed over Triple B."

"And I thank you for your graciousness and your willingness to contend with me on serious matters in open forums," Willy replied. "You made me a better candidate."

"Let's get together at Fran and Freddy's in a couple of weeks to discuss a move that will raise eyebrows. I'm going to recommend you for a seat on the Rules Committee, and if I succeed, that will truly be an unprecedented transition, and good for our district too. As my friend John Henry just told me, a man can go out with class or go out as an ass."

Out in California, there were no surprises. Warren Beatty swamped Arnold Schwarzenegger, who conceded right after the polls closed and went to the movies. Warren won 63 percent of the vote to Arnold's 33 percent, with the Green Party candidate, Peter Miguel Camejo, who had been shut out of the debates, taking 4 percent. The governor-elect eschewed the usual Los Angeles hotel celebration. Instead, he and his billionaire comrades piled into the now famous buses and went in a giant circle from downtown LA to Long Beach to Santa Monica. People lined the roads cheering and waving victory signs and throwing grape leaves before the path of the buses to symbolize the organic union of nature and politics.

Only in California, Warren thought to himself as he and Annette and their children beamed and waved to the festive crowds while the billionaires held large signs up to the side windows: "You did it! Stay tuned!"

By the middle of November, executives in droves were heading for business retreats at the better hotels and resorts to deliberate about "the New Politics" and "the New Congress." Since the Agenda was now federal law, it set the agenda for the retreaters. Should they adapt to it or continue to fight it? What were the cost-benefit consequences of either course of action? Where could they find new lobbyists with the experience and demeanor to connect with the practitioners of this New Politics, who were being driven, willingly or not, by the Meliorist Agenda. How could they build a new power base with new interfaces so they could prevail in the future? What could they do to take the steam out of the rebellion? What new language must they develop? Should they work directly with the Meliorists and bury the hatchet? One business commentator for Bloomberg News calculated that the sheer expenditures on these thousands of retreats, involving hundreds of different lines of industry, commerce, and the various professions, would give a measurable fillip to the gross national product.

Meanwhile, the Meliorists were heading for their own retreat, Maui Eleven. As they flew across the ocean to their beloved mountaintop hotel, their reflections were very different than they had been en route to prior Mauis. They felt elation, but also a kind of wistfulness, an incipient nostalgia. Many of them were thinking back to that first call from Warren and marveling over the stupendous breakthroughs since.

When they arrived, Bill Joy was already there, along with three of his most trusted and circumspect security men. He feared that after the Meliorist triumph, their adversaries, formerly bent on infiltration, might now be inclined to exact a measure of revenge. He wasn't about to let his guard down now, especially since Lobo knew about the hotel and had been so thoroughly humiliated by the Alpha Sig caper.

There was no taking away from the joyousness of the core group when they assembled around the conference table. They were too joyous for the discussion Warren wanted to have. "My dear colleagues," he said, looking at them fondly, "I hate to shift the mood, but with your indulgence, I have three questions for all of you. First, do you have any personal regrets arising from our work together? Second, what's the chief insight you've derived from this year's experiences? And finally, what do you think we should look out for in the coming year? Before you answer, may we have an hour of silence to focus our thoughts?"

"Of course, Warren," Sol said, sensing the importance of these questions to the man who had brought them all together.

The other Meliorists nodded, and the group fell into quiet meditation, elbow to elbow, occasionally jotting notes on their legal pads. The normally hyperkinetic Ted reflected to himself again that if he had learned nothing else all year, he had learned the value of silence.

"Thank you," Warren said when the hour was up. "And now for our regrets, insights, and premonitions. Max, will you start us off?"

"My greatest regret is that until this year I made my economic success a ceiling instead of a floor. Second, I learned from all of you that the real deed can in fact overcome the mythical word. Finally, we can't let our momentum slide in the face of what is sure to be a many-headed drive to roll back our Agenda. The strategy of fast-paced offense and surprise must remain standard operating procedure for our side."

"I regret all the time I devoted to leisure during the decade after the show closed down," Phil said. "What I learned is the stunning power that can come from unified, goal-driven, yet diverse minds like the ones around this table. What worries me is that our allies may become arrogant or messianic and overplay their hand."

"That for years I had neglected seeding democratic institutions and linking them with unquestionable corporate obligations such as loss prevention in the insurance industry," Peter said. "That plunging into the most abrasive controversies wasn't all that ostracizing, uncomfortable, or damaging. And I worry that a natural disaster or a terrorist strike, God forbid, will give the politicians an excuse to derail implementation of the Agenda. We haven't planned for this at all, though it's not clear to me that we could."

"I regret postponing my dream of a more just legal system for so long," Joe said. "I learned that the gap between people's need for justice and the supply of justice they have access to is far greater than even my cynical mind comprehended. Thirdly, I hope the president won't revert to form now that his party isn't facing elections. He and his bureaucracy have immense dilatory powers at their disposal. He may scuttle parts of the Agenda, stick his tongue out at Congress, and say, 'You don't like it? So impeach my ass and then try to convict me.'"

"I wish I'd thought of doing a movie where the rebellious rich take on the reigning rich," Paul said. "Second, I'm amazed at how relatively few organized resources and imaginations it took to awaken the latent humane instincts of the people and move them toward action. Democracy sure does bring out the best in people. Third, if there's an economic downturn, look out for resurgent yahooism stoking a virulent 'Who lost America?' backlash in cahoots with backroom business moguls writing the checks and pulling the strings."

"Given the way we mobilized ourselves," Bill Cosby said, "I regret that I never tried to mobilize rich black Americans in the same way—business professionals, artists, athletes—in order to continue and expand the economics of the civil rights movement. Next, I was astonished by the extent to which corporate power is unable to respond to quick, novel, and well-conceived challenges to its dominance. Last, watch out for ferocious opposition to the Agenda law requiring the media to pay for its licenses and give up some of its spectrum time to audience-controlled networks and programs."

"Obviously," Ted said, "I regret that I didn't put more energy behind organizing billionaires years ago, since they've been such a replicating bonanza for us. What I found out was that the super-rich—present company excepted—are the greatest conformists of all because they have the least reason to be, given their immense material independence. Third, look out for us and a possible second round, yeee-*hah*!"

"Throughout my legal career, I've tried to have as few regrets as possible," said Bill Gates, "but now I wish I'd raised the bar higher for myself so that I had more regrets. Second, extending Ted's point on conformity, I came to realize what a tremendously deep rut the super-rich have fallen into, an awareness sharpened by the heights that an aroused minority of our wealthy allies have achieved this year. Finally, look out for people of goodwill who may try to spend our surplus billions on something besides the implementation and the systematic building of democratic skills and power."

"In light of what live money can do," Yoko said, "I regret letting my wealth become dead money for so long. So many people wanted donations from me that I withdrew and just preserved John's estate. Second, I was confirmed in my conviction that facts are not enough, that there has to be a moral and aesthetic dimension to humanize intellect and analysis. Lastly, I hope the retired super-rich in East Asia and Europe will try to copy what we've done."

"I wish Papa had lived to see what us megacapitalists have done to his Marxist doctrines and to watch me defend him on television," Bernard said. "I learned the vital importance of a leader like Warren, who ever so subtly subdued our fractiousness and elevated our competitive compatibilities. And I think we should look out for ourselves, our health and well-being, in case of a second act of some kind. Together we're hard to beat."

"Your faithful curmudgeon and skeptic regrets waiting so long to harness those traits to a bold imagination and provocative initiatives like the ones that have emerged from this crowd," Sol said. "Second, I used to think that the rich donated either out of self-interest or guilt, but this year I saw the powerful results of our appeal to our wealthy peers' sense of civic duty and legacy. That was a big discovery for me, and maybe for you too. Lastly, we've got to hold the president to his vow to join with Bernard on the Egalitarian Clubs. That is our future, friends, and quite possibly the only good that will come from this White House."

"Given our three thousand large bookstores as locations, why didn't I think years ago of starting a chain of citizen skill workshops to train and empower millions of people?" Leonard said. "As we saw, in an age when everyone is glued to television and computer screens, getting people and youngsters out into the public squares and the streets is more effective than ever, since the media and the politicians don't expect mass rallies. What we have to keep in mind for the future is that people need to be continually mobilized to act, because when all is said and done, they are the backbone and the conscience that keep making it all happen."

"When I was the biggest stockholder in General Motors and was on the board of directors," Ross said, "I wish I had hustled together some large investors, taken over, and transformed the Big Guy through a leveraged buyout instead of being bought out myself. What amazed me this past year was that we achieved our objectives without any special breaks, no crises or disasters to take advantage of. That might have made our task easier, but doing what we did in 'regular times' made it all replicable. But if the big company executives we whipped aren't given broad public recognition for the changes they had to swallow, look out. They need positive reinforcement to do more, or else they'll sulk and plan to escape, or revert and counterattack."

"In my various philanthropies, with few exceptions, I've operated as a Lone Ranger to help build democracies in numerous countries," George said. "Now I regret my lack of collaboration here in the United States over the years, my not returning calls and rebuffing invitations from potential allies like all of you. But I'm not at all sure that a group of comparable wealth and determination could accomplish what we did outside the English-speaking countries, in case we're ever thinking of pushing such initiatives on the global stage. And we've got to make sure the implementation gets underway during the political honeymoon period, swiftly and openly and equitably, before inertia sets in."

"My regret is that I didn't meet up with all of you twenty years ago," Jeno said. "My insight, coming from the great success of the

PCC, is that beneath the surface there is a real yearning among business people for the union of profit with virtue and for the well-being of their fellow citizens. Finally, look out for Warren Beatty's behavior in office. Although he wasn't a CEP candidate, his progressive platform is very close to our Agenda, and we want to be sure he doesn't disappoint us. Right, Barry?"

"Right you are, Jeno. I'll keep an eye on him. As for my regrets, this year made me realize how often in the past the so-called notoriously outspoken Barry Diller went and censored himself on matters large and small. Never again. Insight? When there's a belief that the powers that be cannot be overcome, it's only because no one of power, gravity, and vision has tried to overcome them. And watch out for Barry Diller plunging back into his many businesses and getting totally absorbed in the world of the CEOs again. Don't let me do that."

"We won't, Barry, and I'm sure your television stations will report our denunciations on any occasion where you stray," Warren said owlishly. "My regret, it won't surprise you to know, is that I didn't put out the call to you some years ago. My insight—all other things being equal, including smart strategies and good fortune—is that this Meliorist endeavor of ours would never have made it through the spring if not for the way our characters, personalities, and temperaments synchronized. Bernard spoke of our 'competitive compatibilities'—an elegant phrase to remember. My thought for the coming year is that we keep our group together at a less intense level, at least through the disposition of the surplus funds and the early implementation stage, until we're sure that we can hand off to enduring new institutions. I believe the public and the media expect no less, and I believe that's the consensus among us."

Warren paused and looked at his colleagues, who were nodding their approval. "Fine, then. Before we move on, I want to thank you all for your remarks. No doubt we'll have occasion to refer to them more than a few times in future weeks. And since we're not bailing out, we'll obviously want to keep the Secretariat operating. On this point, I call on its incomparable director."

Patrick adjusted his bow tie with a smile. "I'm glad you all see the need to keep us bugging you, but since we won't have to bug you as much, we propose to reduce the staff by half. Our main tasks will be to follow up on the implementation of the Agenda and carry out your decisions regarding the effective disposition of up to thirteen billion dollars. Wow!" he said, permitting himself an uncharacteristic exclamation before he went on. "I'd like to take this opportunity to express my profound pleasure in serving you this year, and not only because of the inherent importance of your work. In my previous job, with a corporate board, I constantly found my energy drained by petty ego clashes, trivial detours, and randomly shifting priorities. Your competitive compatibilities, your vision, and your vitality, have made my position at the Secretariat an administrative Nirvana, and I'm deeply grateful."

Visibly moved, the Meliorists returned his thanks warmly. "We couldn't have done it without you, Patrick," Warren said, speaking for all of them. "And let's not forget Bill Joy, who I hope will agree to continue to play an active role in any ongoing activities of ours, since his perspective as a farseeing futurist is invaluable. Tomorrow we'll get down to the nuts and bolts of distributing our surplus, but for now let's see what delights Ailani has in store for us this evening."

After another fabulous dinner and brandies, the core group reassembled in the atrium for another hour of silence before turning in. While they were engaged in their meditations, Bill Joy had a cup of coffee with his three security men—Boris, Calvin, and Brad—to make sure they stayed sharp and alert. Then he did a final check of the grounds, found nothing, and went to bed, still vaguely uneasy.

In the morning, the Meliorists found a slim stack of papers waiting for them at their places around the table. "I hope you all had a good night's rest," Warren said, "because we've got our work cut out for us today. You'll note that there are several matrices on the pages before you. Patrick has prepared them as a framework for our deliberations. Please take a few minutes to review them, and then he'll elaborate."

"Okay," Patrick said when everyone had finished, "let's look at the first matrix, which focuses on the power nodes of the corporation as an institution. It shows their intersections with the three branches of government, the electoral process, the media, the market, labor, capital, shareholders, technology, communities, academic institutions, and mass entertainment. These are the points at which corporations assert their dominance. The countervailing and displacing institutions we have established, whether in research, advocacy, or delivery, must respond to all these corporate nodes if they are to be successful, replicable, and renewable.

"The second matrix maps the foci of these research, advocacy, and delivery organizations as regards procedural-content democracy, such as access to power centers both public and private, and substantive-content democracy, which delivers the goods, services, and more intangible qualities of a just society going into the future. This matrix should be considered alongside the third, which describes the universe of possibilities for externally and internally financing the daily operations of these organizations and endowing them securely.

"The final matrix plots our society's progress in terms of reasonably measurable criteria. As new data becomes available, we plug it in, so that the matrix serves as a constantly evolving real-time overview of where we stand on the implementation of the Agenda."

Patrick tapped his fingers on the pages in front of him. "So much for this high level of abstraction. Now it's time to get down to specific sums, proper names, and logistics. And remember that there are bound to be ad hoc organizations that don't fit into any of the matrices, maverick groups that shatter old paradigms with fresh eruptions of creativity, so you might want to consider using part of the surplus as a contingency fund."

For the rest of the day, breaking only for dinner, the Meliorists rose to formidable heights of concentration as they hammered out the details of their bequest to the future. Finally, just before midnight, they adjourned and went gratefully to their rooms to fall into bed, exhausted but satisfied with what they had accomplished.

They awoke refreshed to a glorious Sunday morning and gathered on the patio for breakfast. Yoko was admiring a stunning hibiscus in the garden when she thought she heard a distant din coming from way down the mountain road. At first she dismissed it, but a couple of minutes later the din was louder and the others had noticed it too. She rose, walked to the edge of the patio, and took out a small pair of binoculars that she'd begun carrying after Maui One to take in the flora and fauna.

What she saw startled her. A throng of men, women, and children, wearing leis and singing and banging on drums, was walking slowly up the winding road in the direction of the hotel. Yoko skipped over to Bill Joy, who was finishing a mushroom omelet, and dragged him to her observation post, handing him the binoculars. He scanned the approaching crowd and frowned. Maybe it was just some annual ritual, or maybe it was a celebratory march of some kind that would soon come to an end and return down the mountain, but maybe it was related to the presence of the Meliorists. In any event, he would take all precautions.

He ran into the hotel and down to the breakfast room, where Boris, Calvin, and Brad were ingesting enormous quantities of ham, eggs, pancakes, and fruit. "Showtime, boys," he said, and quickly filled them in. He sent Boris up to the roof of the hotel with a telephoto lens to get a better view of the apparent paraders. He stationed Calvin two hundred yards down the road with a barricade he'd had the hotel obtain months ago, just in case. He told Brad to park one of the limousines across the road a hundred yards down. The men sprang into action, and Bill went to find Ailani, who was cooking up a storm in the kitchen.

"Top of the morning to you, Ailani," he said.

"It's a beautiful one, isn't it, Mr. J? And what brings you here? Out of food? I have more for you."

"No, there's plenty of food, and it's all delicious, as usual. Listen, I need your help. There's something going on down the road, hundreds of people in flowers coming toward the hotel, maybe thousands. Is there some sort of local celebration every year around now?"

"Not that I know of, and I've worked here for twenty-two years. Anyway, don't worry, you've got the entire hotel exclusively until Monday."

"Listen, Ailani, don't you hear them?"

She went to an open window and cocked an ear. "Yes, it sounds like a pretty big crowd chanting and drumming."

"Can you stop what you're doing and run down there? I'd like you to join the marchers and find out who they are and what they want. They won't be suspicious of you. I'm sorry to trouble you this way, Ailani, but it's important."

"Sure, Mr. J, I'll change into something more festive and be on my way. I know a shortcut so I can casually join them from the side of the road. If I find anything out, I'll call you on my cell phone. Give me your number."

Bill returned to the patio, where the Meliorists were taking turns with Yoko's binoculars, intrigued and not at all suspicious. Okay, he thought, it was possible that the participants were completely innocent, but maybe the organizers were not so innocent and had invented some pretext for a parade as cover for nefarious deeds. After all, the narrow road only had one destination: the hotel.

On they came, singing, twirling, hoisting their children up on their shoulders, rhythmically beating their drums, many dressed in native Mauian costumes. Two acrobats were turning handsprings along the roadside, and several young women were passing around trays of sweets and drinks. As the marchers rounded a bend in the road, they came into clearer focus for Boris up on the roof. He called Bill on his cell and reported that there were three television camera crews in the crowd, and five or six reporters darting back and forth scribbling on their pads. At the head of the march were two Anglos who appeared to be advanced in years but lithe and agile. Next to them was a woman in a beautiful muumuu, smiling and waving. "She kind of looks like what's her name, the hotel cook," Calvin reported, adding that there were signs everywhere—"Lahaina Welcomes the Meliorists," "Wailea Thanks the Meliorists," and so on from Kookea, Pukatani, Makawao, Hana, all the different localities in Maui.

Bill still wasn't satisfied. He called Calvin—who was also equipped with a metal detector, another previous Bill Joy precaution—and told him to speak to the two men leading the parade, find out who they were, and put them on the phone with him. Calvin wondered whether Bill had seen one too many Bond movies, but he followed orders. When the marchers were fifty yards away, he put up his hand and halted them.

The two leaders came forward. "Sir, what is this roadblock all about?" one of them asked. "This is a public thoroughfare, and I don't see your police credentials. Who are you?"

"The question is, who are *you*?" Calvin said brusquely. "You'll have to speak to my boss and explain yourselves."

"Well, since you're the one blocking the road and we're simply on a pleasant Sunday stroll, I guess we better speak to your boss."

Calvin got Bill on the phone and handed it to the man.

"Hello, my name is Kenly Webster. With whom am I speaking? . . . Mm-hmm, I see. Well, my friend John Tucker and I are here to express our gratitude for what the Meliorists have done for their country. When we arrived yesterday, we learned that the people of Maui were organizing a parade for the same purpose, and they kindly invited us to join them as honored guests when they found out about our modest role in working for the Agenda. This may be an island of rich émigrés, but there are still plenty of regular folks who want to say thanks."

"Would you hang on for a minute?" Bill said.

"Certainly."

Bill turned to the Meliorists, who had crowded around him on the patio when his phone rang. He asked if any of them knew a Kenly Webster or a John Tucker. Joe broke out in a grin. "Hell, yes! Gates and I met them at our Pledge press conference back in February. They're retired lawyers, both Princeton grads of the firecracker class of '55, and they became overnight legends during our lobbying for the Agenda. Entirely behind the scenes, they put out one brush fire after another. They were selfless, anonymous, and savvy as hell. What in the world are they doing here? Give me the phone."

"Kenly, you old son of a gun!" Joe roared. "What gives?"

"Just a little gratitude for everything you and your co-conspirators have done. John and I came here to thank you. The people who live, work, play, and die on this island want to thank you too, exuberantly, Maui-style. Maui isn't a potted plant, you know."

Bill Joy took the phone back. "Listen, Mr. Webster, I know this may sound strange, but I have security concerns. Are there any troublemakers or worse in your parade? If there were, how would you know?"

"Well, we've got a pretty good sixth sense. Just ask the folks on Capitol Hill. All these people want to do is express their love and admiration."

Bill asked Kenly to hold on again and conferred with the core group. He said he was willing to let the marchers proceed to the hotel, but he wanted them to go through the metal detector first. Warren put his foot down. "We can't live in a bubble, Bill," he said. "Would you find Ailani and ask her to prepare food and drink for our visitors?"

"I have a feeling Ailani isn't here, but I'll talk to the hotel manager," Bill said, and went inside to phone his security detail. "Come down off the roof," he told Boris. "Remove the roadblock," he told Calvin. "Bring the limo back," he told Brad. But unable to help himself, he told all three to position themselves strategically and stay on their toes.

Within half an hour, the procession had filled the hotel courtyard, and the celebration began in earnest. After a haunting rendition of a traditional honorific chant adapted to the achievements of the Meliorists, seventeen children came forth and with a light kiss placed seventeen jasmine leis on seventeen Meliorist necks. Then the head ranger of Haleakala National Park presented the Meliorists with a magnificently carved sculpture of the great Haleakala Crater, "in eternal recognition of your noble labors on behalf of justice for the peoples of the United States of America."

By now, the usual reserve of the core group had melted away, and they joined in the festivities. Ted borrowed a drum and banged away with abandon. Yoko harmonized with a chorus from Hana on a traditional Hawaiian song. Sol attempted a hula to the fond amusement of one and all. And why not? The previous January seemed so long ago, and so much had happened since, and so much would continue to happen year by year. Maui's native peoples, so often abused by outsiders throughout its history, had been the cradle of a new birth of freedom.

The festivities were still going strong when the Meliorists departed for the airport. They were reluctant to leave, but they had prior obligations back on the mainland, mostly with their neglected families. As they were about to board their planes, Yoko mentioned that after two long, beseeching, and pitiful letters, she had reluctantly agreed to have dinner with Lobo next week at the Four Seasons.

"Dinner with Lobo?" Bernard said. "What does he want? Don't go looking at any etchings afterward!"

Yoko laughed and gave Bernard a confident hug. "It's time for a little pathos. I'll let you know what happens. Meanwhile, I'll just say that wonderful Hawaiian word that means both hello and goodbye, greeting and farewell, gratitude for the past and hope for the future. Aloha."

The *New York Times* has written, "What sets Ralph Nader apart is that he has moved beyond social criticism to effective political action." The author who knows the most about citizen action here returns us to the literature of American social movements—to Edward Bellamy, to Upton Sinclair, to John Steinbeck, to Stephen Crane—reminding us in the process that changing the body politic of America starts with imagination.

Named by *The Atlantic* as one of the 100 most influential figures in American history, and by *Time* and *Life* magazines as one of the 100 most influential Americans of the twentieth century, Ralph Nader and the dozens of citizen groups he has founded have helped us drive safer cars, eat healthier food, breathe better air, drink cleaner water, and work in safer environments for more than four decades.

The crusading attorney first made headlines in 1965 with his book *Unsafe at Any Speed*, a scathing indictment that lambasted the auto industry for producing unsafe vehicles. The book led to congressional hearings and automobile safety laws passed in 1966, including the National Traffic and Motor Vehicle Safety Act. He was instrumental in the creation of the Occupational Safety and Health Administration (OSHA), the Environmental Protection Agency (EPA), the Consumer Product Safety Commission (CSPC), and the National Highway Transportation Safety Administration (NHTSA). Many lives have been saved by Nader's involvement in the recall of millions of unsafe consumer products, including defective motor vehicles, and in the protection of laborers and the environment. By starting dozens of citizen groups, Ralph Nader has created a framework for corporate and governmental accountability.

Ralph Nader's most popular books include *Unsafe at Any Speed*, *Crashing the Party* and, from Seven Stories, *In Pursuit of Justice*, *The*

Ralph Nader Reader, Cutting Corporate Welfare, The WTO, and *No Debate.* His most recent bestselling books were *The Good Fight* (2004) and *The Seventeen Traditions* (2007). *"Only the Super-Rich Can Save Us!"* continues Ralph's Nader's spectacular publishing achievement and expands it in new and exciting ways.

ABOUT SEVEN STORIES PRESS

Seven Stories Press is an independent book publisher based in New York City, with distribution throughout the United States, Canada, England, and Australia. We publish works of the imagination by such writers as Nelson Algren, Russell Banks, Octavia E. Butler, Ani DiFranco, Assia Djebar, Ariel Dorfman, Coco Fusco, Barry Gifford, Hwang Sok-yong, Lee Stringer, and Kurt Vonnegut, to name a few, together with political titles by voices of conscience, including the Boston Women's Health Collective, Noam Chomsky, Angela Y. Davis, Human Rights Watch, Derrick Jensen, Ralph Nader, Gary Null, Project Censored, Barbara Seaman, Gary Webb, and Howard Zinn, among many others. Seven Stories Press believes publishers have a special responsibility to defend free speech and human rights, and to celebrate the gifts of the human imagination, wherever we can. For additional information, visit www.sevenstories.com.